D0991160

A
Winter's
Child

Also by Brenda Jagger

Verity

The Barforth Women

Days of Grace

A
Winter's
Child
Brenda
Jagger

William Morrow and Company, Inc.
New York

Copyright © 1984 by Brenda Jagger

First published in Great Britain in 1984 by William Collins Sons & Co. Ltd.

Permission to quote *The General* by Siegfried Sassoon
is gratefully received from George Sassoon.

All rights reserved. No part of this book may be reproduced or utilized in any form or by any
means, electronic or mechanical, including photocopying, recording or by any information storage
and retrieval system, without permission in writing from the Publisher. Inquiries should be
addressed to Permissions Department, William Morrow and Company, Inc., 105 Madison Ave.,
New York, N.Y. 10016.

Library of Congress Cataloging in Publication Data

Jagger, Brenda, 1936–
A winter's child

I. Title.
PR6060.A425W5   1985   823'.914   84-19089
ISBN: 0-688-04271-6

Printed in the United States of America

First U.S. Edition

1 2 3 4 5 6 7 8 9 10

BOOK DESIGN BY LINEY LI

To Phillip,

as always

1

MIRIAM Swanfield, believing herself to be lovable, had always felt entitled to the affection of others. Nor, believing herself to be generous had she ever felt the least hesitation in claiming her share of every good thing the world seemed perfectly pleased to offer.

She had been a pretty, pink and white girl with fluttering eyelids and a will of iron. As a pretty, pouting tea rose of a woman, she had made herself invincible. She had taken care, all her life, to appear guileless, helpless, terribly endearing and with these weapons had carved out a position which she did not intend — *ever* — to relinquish.

She had been born a Miss Miriam Harper, daughter of an undistinguished draper in a small industrial West Yorkshire town; and thoroughly disliking the drudgery of her father's shop counter she had taken, at eighteen, the traditional escape of marriage, not to a clerk or another small shopkeeper as might have been expected — thus exchanging drudgery for drudgery — but to a man of property. And while congratulations had been forthcoming in plenty, certain and very definite warnings had accompanied them, the gentleman in question, although indeed the master of a sizable fortune acquired in the textile trade, being also in possession of an arrogant disposition, a hasty temper and — himself approaching fifty — a five-year-old son.

A hard man, Aaron Swanfield, an ungenerous man, a lecherous man, a combination which had brought little joy to his first, late but evidently not-much-lamented lady. Poor Miriam. He had wedded her, the town of Faxby hinted darkly, because there had been no other way to get her, the price of a respectable girl, as everyone knew, being a wedding ring.

And once the price had been paid, the pleasure taken, she would be relegated to the scullery and laundry of her husband's affections, left alone night after night at his great, cheerless house at High Meadows, keeping her domestic account books in order, if she could, and bringing up the truculent, difficult child whose conception, after twenty sterile years, had greatly inconvenienced his father and proved fatal to his mother.

Faxby had seen it all happen before. A young girl in full bloom, an elderly, self-indulgent man desiring a change from the dubious enjoyments to be had, furtively but not cheaply, at Faxby's Crown Hotel. A month or two of passion, after which Faxby knew full well that the novelty, if not the bloom itself, would have faded sufficiently for the bridegroom to wonder if he would not have done better to take a woman in capable, grateful middle-age to keep his house and discipline his son. And for the bride to understand that money — since her husband would be unlikely to let her lay hands on very much of it — could never be quite enough.

Poor Miriam.

Yet, undaunted, she had tripped happily to church on her wedding morning, a vision of white lace and white roses and flushed, ready-to-be rumpled virginity, and had managed so strangely but surely to touch her husband's heart that for thirty years thereafter she had remained his spoiled darling, his "pretty Mimi." And now, seven years after his death, although her porcelain daintiness had puffed out to the stately, full-bosomed proportions of a dowager queen, she was, in spirit, his "pretty Mimi" still.

He had been a man dedicated to the making of money. With "Mimi's" guidance he had discovered how to spend it. He had been unsociable, treating his neighbors with contempt or, at best, ignoring them. But Miriam, who loved not only to sing and dance but to be heard and seen, had quickly converted High Meadows, the cold empty mansion bought as an investment with his first wife's dowry, into her own very warm and very personal stage. He had been a cynical, solitary man, expecting nothing from any woman beyond the satisfaction of his lusty appetites. But Miriam, with her chattering delight in flowers and parties and new silk dresses, her pretty little greeds for tinsel-wrapped Christmas parcels and chocolates in gold paper, her absolute determination to enjoy her life to the full, had charmed him and tamed him and made him quite foolishly content.

Dear Aaron. She well remembered how anxious he had been — so touching and quite unnecessary — when she had given birth, placidly, easily, to their first child a bare nine months after her wedding, a cir-

8

cumstance which had caused not a few of her dear friends and neighbors to do their sums. And then, some seven years later and again seven years after that, two more golden little darlings, her only son Jeremy and a second daughter, every bit as pretty, had declared Aaron — elderly by then of course and growing sentimental — as "Mimi" herself. Not quite, perhaps. But certainly with her three little angels clustered around her, all of them sheltered so firmly and so very luxuriously beneath Aaron Swanfield's wing, Miriam had been, for a while, hard-pressed to think of anything more to wish for.

She was fond of her daughters and adored her son. And there was Benedict, of course, her husband's son by his first marriage who, while he could not be said to adore anyone, was so very clever at taking care of things at the Mill, thus leaving his father free to take care of Miriam. She was the mistress of the finest house for many miles around, with a husband who worshiped her and had never once, in all their years to-gether, questioned the size of her bills. In the small tidal waters of Faxby's not particularly high but fiercely competitive society, no one swam more successfully or more gracefully than Miriam, her vibrant tropical colors making common haddock and herring of all the rest. She had everything she wanted. She did not expect either to lose it or to see it change.

"I believe I am getting old," Aaron said.

"Nonsense, dear." He had always seemed old to her. What he meant was that he might one day — well — pass on, she supposed. She decided not, for the moment, to believe it.

"Not yet, Aaron dear. I need you. Jeremy is only eighteen and Polly still quite a baby. How could I possibly manage them without you?"

"I'll see to it," he said.

"Of course, dear."

She had never doubted it.

And when, one shocking morning, barely three months later he had collapsed across the breakfast table with a dreadful oversetting of toast racks and marmalade pots and the silver coffee service, she had been heartbroken, of course, but — in everything concerning her own fu-ture — unafraid.

"Fetch Benedict," he'd gasped. And when this difficult, far-from-favorite eldest son of his had come up from the mill — his first wife's dark-eyed, dark-complexioned child with nothing of pink and white "Mimi" in him — he'd reached out a gnarled, already shaking hand, not in affection but the better to deliver a last command.

"Look after my wife," he'd growled, his fingers biting hard into Ben-edict Swanfield's perfectly steady arm. "I'm paying you well enough to do it. You've got control."

"Yes father." Benedict was a competent, cool-eyed man, bred deliberately to shrewdness and sharpness by Aaron who, with so much softness and prettiness around him, had needed somebody with a hard head on his shoulders. And there had never been much affection between them.

"So look after my wife and your brother and sisters. And make sure my 'Mimi' has everything she wants."

"I want nothing," murmured a sad, deeply veiled Miriam after the funeral. "Absolutely nothing. Except, of course, that everything should go on here at High Meadows just as it always has. We both know, Benedict dear, how much your father would have wanted that."

She had smiled up at him, candidly, confidingly, very much as she had smiled at his father on her wedding day, being in no doubt at all that the terms of her husband's will, which had amused Faxby and had been declared iniquitous by her eldest daughter, who was always in need of ready money, had been designed exclusively for her benefit.

Aaron had promised to take care of her and by bequeathing to Benedict his position as Chairman of Swanfield Mills he had simply wished to make certain that the Mills, under Benedict's efficient management, would continue to prosper and, therefore, to pay out the dividends upon which all Miriam's little luxuries depended. By giving Benedict control of all family finances and trusts, what had her husband done, in fact, but spare her a great deal of trouble since it would now be to Benedict, not to Miriam, that her own much-loved but rather expensive brood would be forced to apply for increased allowances, release of capital, new cars, new houses, seats on the Swanfield Board; practical matters which Miriam had never cared to understand. Let Benedict deal with them. Let *him* endure all the haggling and bickering which would certainly arise when it became clear to her younger son and daughter, as it had been immediately clear to their elder sister, that although they had inherited substantial sums of money they could not spend it, apart from fixed monthly allowances, without the permission of their never particularly approachable half-brother, Benedict.

Let *him* convince them of the good sense of this arrangement if he could, which she very much doubted, her own conclusion being simply this. Her husband had wished her to go on spending his money without taking responsibility for it, just as she had always done. And, in his tragically unavoidable absence, he had given her Benedict to be his deputy.

To Miriam it was as pleasantly straightforward as that.

One thing only had tended, for a while, to worry her. High Meadows, too, had been left to Benedict, not by his father on this occasion but by his long-dead mother, whose dowry had originally purchased it, Miriam retaining only a life tenancy. And Benedict had a wife who might have challenged Miriam's authority.

"Nola, dear," Miriam had murmured a month or two after the funeral, "should you care to be present in the mornings when cook brings in the menus? Eight o'clock?"

The younger Mrs. Swanfield, a woman of lethargic habits who rarely left her bed before noon, had looked amazed, a reaction Miriam had seized upon with satisfaction, proceeding, from that moment, to organize her domestic empire entirely to suit herself, to do things *as they had always been done*, just as Aaron — she insisted upon that — would have wanted. And so wrapped up did she become in her tea parties and tea dances, her tennis and croquet parties, her dinners and suppers, her "dear children" and her "dear friends" that even the outbreak of war in the summer of 1914 meant little more to her, to begin with, than the annoyance of parlor maids running off to the higher pay and shorter hours of the munitions factories in the middle of the garden party season. Such a nuisance. Until her son Jeremy had enlisted, long before the introduction of conscription would have made it necessary — and even then, surely, they could have got him an exemption? — and had been killed, with a quarter of a million others, in the three-day battle of Neuve Chapelle.

He had been twenty-one years old and her favorite child. Her elder daughter had always been too intense and rather too plain to please her. Her younger daughter was perhaps a shade too pretty. But Jeremy had been everything she believed a young man ought to be, brilliant enough to have taken a first at Oxford but not too academic to be amusing; gallant enough to have answered his country's call to arms without being in any way pompous about it; just old enough to have made a hasty, eve-of-the-battle marriage without her consent.

His wedding had seriously upset her. She had wanted a princess for Jeremy, if anyone at all, and certainly not the slip of a girl he had so astonishingly chosen, the stepdaughter of her own solicitor no less, perfectly respectable of course and *quite* suitable, as a wife, for the son of her bank manager or her doctor even: not her own. She had found it hard to forgive him and indeed had never really done so, his death, only three weeks later having made forgiveness irrelevant. But little by little — because, quite simply, one *does* — she had managed to submerge her loss beneath the minor wartime obsessions of food shortages, how to obtain enough coal and sugar; how to manage her large household when her butler, for reasons best known to himself — the mental processes of butlers being somewhat beyond her — had gone off and enlisted like her son, a gentleman, in 1914; when her chauffeur and all her gardeners had been "taken" at the start of forced conscription eighteen months later, and her last reliable parlor maid had become the conductress of a Faxby tram. She had sacrificed most of her back lawn to potatoes and cabbages, had tended her own flowers and learned to live without regular deliveries of groceries and the cheerful ring of the postman six times a day. She had given orders for her teatime scones to be spread with margarine and, when the German blockade began to bite, had spurned the back door offers of food profiteers and sent her cook to wait in the sugar queues and meat queues like everybody else.

She had chaired committees to find homes for Belgian refugees and raised funds for the relief of British soldiers' wives who could not really be expected to live on the governmental allowance of twelve shillings a week; her benevolence even extending to the "war babies," the inconvenient but altogether predictable results of the temporary posting to Faxby of a battalion of fusiliers. And by keeping herself thus occupied she had had no time to brood on the fate and fortunes of Jeremy's young widow, who, instead of mourning him in a properly sedate fashion, had rushed off at once to drive an ambulance in London and then to be a Red Cross nurse in France.

Restless creature. What *had* become of her? Naturally, her stepfather, Mr. Lyall, Miriam's solicitor, must know something about her. Just as naturally, and most conveniently, Miriam much preferred to forget. And she had, therefore, been considerably startled to learn, and more than a little offended by the offhand manner in which Benedict had imparted the information, that this girl, this stranger who by virtue of a ten-minute civil ceremony had supplanted Jeremy's mother — *herself* — as his next of kin would now, with the war six months over, be returning home.

Home? Whatever could he mean? She knew full well, of course, but just the same, she put the question to him, raising candid blue eyes to his dark and thoroughly disinterested face. Dear Benedict. So exceedingly efficient. Always so busy and brusque and *quite* forbidding. How easily he could intimidate almost anyone, she supposed, with those dark glances; certainly his sister Polly and his sister Eunice and Eunice's husband, certainly the departmental managers at the Mills. Anyone. Not Miriam, though. And it did no harm, now and again, to remind him of that.

"Oh dear I can hardly remember her," she said, remembering her exactly. "How am I to receive her? It has been four years, Benedict. And the tales one hears about those military hospitals. My goodness! And we must not forget that your sister Polly is still single."

She smiled at him quite sweetly, experiencing not the least difficulty with the double standard which decreed misbehavior between common soldiers and housemaids at an army camp on the outskirts of Faxby to be one thing; the perfect innocence of her unmarried daughter and the possible effect on her daughter-in-law of exposure to large numbers of wounded but no doubt attractive men, entirely another.

"Oh dear," she repeated, her eyes growing bright with speculation. What *had* the girl seen during her four years overseas? What unsuitable tales might she tell? And, rather more to the point, could she possibly settle down again in a world which must surely be returning to the state Miriam cherished as "normal"? Tea on the lawn. Strawberries with cream and sugar. Good manners. Long engagements. No more hasty, untidy passion but delicately prolonged romance. Young girls who wore gloves and corsets and who had but one safe and sensible ambition: to be the virgin brides of gentlemen. A regular and willing supply of nursemaids and nannies, cooks, butlers, parlor maids waiting discreetly in the wings; leafy, leisured days which now, in her memory of that prewar world, seemed always to be luminous, rainless, vibrant with birdsong and golden with pure sunlight.

Miriam had assumed, naïvely but very firmly, that on Armistice Day or, just possibly the day after, all shortages and austerities would automatically cease. The hero would return to his cottage or his castle, take off his uniform and begin his life all over again. The dead would be laid out neatly beneath rows of white headstones strikingly garlanded with poppies. The wounded — and Miriam's mind could not translate wounds beyond an empty sleeve, a limp, possibly an eyepatch — would take up quiet lives somewhere in becoming obscurity. Shopkeepers would be obsequious again, tradesmen efficient. Order, not only among nations which did not really concern Miriam, but among the social classes, would be instantly restored. And now, although sugar was still rationed, housemaids under the age of forty in short supply, and her butler having acquired a chestful of medals on the Somme and a commission after Passchendaele, had declined her offer of re-employment and gone off to manage a local hotel, Miriam felt that she had waited long enough.

She wished to entertain again this year, to celebrate her birthday in May with a garden party as she had always done, to give a few little dances and suppers with a view to finding some eligible young man who might take her daughter Polly off her hands. And in these days of increased opportunities for gentlewomen, which made it almost impossible to get anything approaching a decent secretary-companion, it had already occurred to her that "young Mrs. Jeremy" could be of great use.

"Really — one had only a glimpse of her. One scarcely remembers . . ." she murmured, closing her eyes the better to observe the perfectly retained image of the slender schoolgirl Jeremy had brought her, pretty enough if one cared for very dark brunettes, which Miriam did not, a quiet girl with serious, pansy-black eyes and a hesitant manner. Miriam, blond, curvacious, effervescent, had not cared for that either. "Mother, this is Claire." And he had had no need to say "I love her" with those rich vibrations in his voice, his young face aglow, *her* young face veiled in a radiant wonder which Miriam had recognized — oh yes, how could one fail to know it? — but had never actually felt since one needed youth to sustain such total enchantment, and Aaron — Ah well. Aaron had given her other things. And if it had troubled her that Jeremy had chosen a bride so unlike herself in every possible way she decided to ignore it now.

"Mother — isn't she wonderful?" No. Miriam had not thought her wonderful. But if the girl should possess a capacity for devotion, as Jeremy had seemed to think — "She adores me mother. Aren't I the luckiest chap on earth?" — then why should she not now devote herself, in Jeremy's absence, to his mother? What could be more fitting, or more natural? Indeed, what better compensation could the girl offer for her impertinence in insisting that that pathetic little wedding, over and done with in ten mumbled minutes, had made her Jeremy's next of kin so that his personal possessions, his kit bag, his letters, his diary, the very telegram announcing his death had been sent to this wife of three weeks, instead of to *her*, his mother?

Yes, compensation certainly was due. Miriam had always believed that. And, after all, if the girl could stitch wounds she could certainly address invitation cards. If she could drive ambulances it seemed reasonable to assume that she could collect one's shopping, meet the London train for one's parcels, take a firm line with inconvenient callers, turn her hand to any number of helpful, essential, *tedious* things. And Miriam — it went without saying — would be very kind to her. What a splendid idea. Not, of course, that she was ready, just yet, to own up to it and thus spoil her little game of power and pretense with Benedict.

He had been a silent, surly child just five years old when she had married his father, tall for his age and with good bones but alarmingly thin and pale, his dark eyes with their oddly disconcerting stare reminding her that his life's experiences, until then, had been made up of the death of one parent and the neglect of the other. Being only thirteen years his senior Miriam had decided to play the bountiful elder sister, envisaging a delightful relationship based on *her* generosity, *his* gratitude. She had wished only to charm and amuse him, and because, beneath the excellent manners, the unnaturally cool.exterior, he had remained uncharmed, unamused, had simply allowed her to be good to him — because his father would have thrashed him otherwise — she had felt disappointed to begin with, then hurt, then acutely resentful, accusing him in her heart of deliberately fastening upon her the role of "wicked stepmother," when she knew herself to be so suited in every way to play the "good fairy." But the birth of her own children, who had instantly and obligingly adored her, had absolved her from all blame. The fault, clearly, had been Benedict's and Benedict's alone. He was not shy after all, as she had charitably pretended, but unsociable; not ungrateful precisely, but simply unable to appreciate all the pleasant things she had been so ready to do for him. Breathing a sigh of relief she had confined her activities thereafter to his feeding and clothing and had otherwise left him alone.

But, now that he had become a man, now that her husband had bequeathed him to her as a rock to lean on, how reassuring, how very pleasant it often was to lean for the fun of leaning — just to see how far he would allow her to go.

"Oh Benedict, don't you see," she murmured, noticing with satisfaction that he had already glanced at the clock on her drawing room wall. No doubt he had pressing, profitable engagements that morning, men of substance with not much time to spare waiting for him in the oak-paneled office that had been her husband's. Good. Then she would detain him for ten minutes and — if she managed it — would consider that she had won.

"Forgive me, Benedict dear, but gentlemen do not always see the implications in these matters. The girl was a very prettily behaved little thing as I recall. But now . . . ! Heavens — we cannot even be sure that she has been nursing officers."

"I imagine," said Benedict curtly, dryly, his eyes straying once again to the parlor clock, "that the anatomy is much the same."

"Oh *that*," she said, not in the least dismayed, a gesture of her plump hand relegating the entire question of male anatomy to a proper insignificance. "Dear boy, I was referring to the language — the attitudes — the things that a common soldier might be likely to say — or even *do*. You must know what I mean."

He gave a brief smile, understanding her, she thought, perhaps all too well. Not that she minded that. Dear Aaron, who had loved her, had been so terribly easy to deceive. Whereas Benedict, who probably did not like her much at all, was far less inclined to be impressed by the mountains she so loved to construct from any little molehill which came her way. Such a provoking man, always so aloof and sometimes quite disdainful yet so much more of a *challenge*. She smiled at him, her eyelids gently fluttering.

"Dear boy — such a dilemma. I shall have to explain it so carefully to the others. At teatime perhaps?"

"An excellent idea." And noting the sarcasm in his voice, these teatime discussions being her favorite solution to every crisis, she smiled at him again. Dear Benedict. She was such a trouble to him. He bore it so very impatiently. She rather prided herself on that. Yet, nevertheless, being still in the mood to make a little mischief, she found occasion that afternoon at teatime, sitting with her married daughter Eunice among the comfortable paraphernalia of silver tea kettle and flowered china, to complain of Benedict to his wife.

"Nola, my dear, I don't wish to raise a storm in a teacup . . ."

"Of course not Miriam."

And looking at the blank, bored face of her daughter-in-law, Miriam knew that Mrs. Benedict Swanfield was barely listening and did not care.

That Benedict had married for money Miriam had never doubted and, indeed, could think of no other reason for choosing, some fifteen years ago, this particular bride, Miss Nola Crozier, a wool merchant's daughter from Bradford, whose family in addition to money had a great many foreign and vaguely artistic connections, cousins who played Beethoven sonatas or attended universities in such remote places as Leipzig and Budapest; possessing a general disposition to speak foreign languages and indulge in foreign travel which had somehow made Nola herself seem alien and therefore suspicious to Miriam, not *quite* to be trusted.

There had been no courtship. Nor had Miss Crozier of Manningham Lane in the wool metropolis of Bradford been brought up to expect it. Like Benedict Swanfield himself, the affair had been cool, dispassionate, successfully concluded. In the manner of industrial royalty — in exactly the way her father had married her mother — a wedding had been arranged, a diamond solitaire of appropriate value had been purchased, the size and terms of the settlement had been agreed, and Nola Crozier, educated at home by her mother to play the piano, to speak French and German and do very little else, had become Nola Swanfield, moving with her monogrammed luggage, her expensive *trousseau*, and — from the very first — her faintly scornful manner into High Meadows where she had lived ever since like an untidy, unpunctual, vaguely uncooperative guest.

She was not in any conventional sense a pretty woman, certainly not by Miriam's standards who, seeing beauty exclusively in tints of peaches and cream, ample curves, wide-set, startled blue eyes like her own and her daughters', had from the start, been dismayed by the lamentable flatness of Nola's bosom, the unfortunate hint of red in her hair, the sallowness — what kinder word could one find for it? — of her skin; and, perhaps most of all, by her odd partiality for plain, straight-skirted dresses in dull shades of mud and mustard and sage green. A strange girl who had become, at the age of thirty-five, whether Miriam cared to admit it or not, the exact type of woman referred to by every fashion magazine — now that the war had swept away the trailing draperies and tight corseting essential to the padded Edwardian silhouette — as "the very latest thing."

She was thin and brittle in her movements, her pale, pointed face and the auburn hair she wore low on her forehead giving the allure of a fastidiously groomed fox. She had narrow nervous hands, long, light green eyes, a straight flat-hipped, flat-chested boy's body adapted by its supple anonymity to the displaying of the new skimpy dresses, ending a shocking six inches from a lean, silk-clad ankle. She wore waist-length ropes of amber beads, a miscellany of gold chains and medallions, long earrings, an embroidered headband bearing astrological devices around her forehead. She painted her eyelids, smoked Turkish cigarettes through a gold-tipped ebony holder, kept her eyes half-shut, her manner languid and faintly weary, her voice extremely low, neither rising nor falling but remaining on a single note which — at least when speaking to Miriam — held nothing warmer than monotony.

"What has my husband done to upset you now?"

She was not even faintly interested to know, thereby increasing Miriam's pleasure in telling her, babbling on at some length, in fact, about the news she had had from Benedict that morning and the *frisson* she had experienced at the manner of its delivery.

"I know the dear boy means well," she said, managing in spite of her large soft bosom to look kittenish and frail, "and I do appreciate that he is *always* busy with very important matters, as gentlemen are. But just the same, Nola dear, I believe it was less than considerate of him to speak to me on such a delicate issue so abruptly . . ." And she made a pretty little gesture of her plump arms and shoulders, displaying her billowing lace sleeves, her bracelets, her short pink fingers sparkling and helpless with rings, presenting herself to Nola as the woman she had herself created for Aaron, "pretty Mimi" to be handled only with the utmost love and care.

"I dare say," said Nola, fitting a cigarette into her holder, her own fingers brown and brittle as twigs beneath the weight of emeralds and diamonds to which her status entitled her. "But then — I had forgotten Jeremy had a wife, Miriam. Does she matter?"

It was not true, of course, merely an opportunity to annoy Miriam; although indeed weddings, as such, did not appeal to Nola. Brought up herself — and very carefully — to be a wife and mother, she had fulfilled all her obligations as she understood them, had made an excellent match in the socially and financially impeccable Benedict and, in the first three years, had even produced two children of the right sex, healthy and — the nurse had said — handsome boys who had soon gone away to school. She did not miss them. Nor did the fact that she was bored — with Miriam, with High Meadows, with the man who had married her dowry — in any way surprise her. High Meadows, after all, was Miriam's house just as the somber and ornate villa in Bradford had been her mother's. And she had been bored there too. She was used to boredom and had developed her own methods of keeping it at bay. While under her mother's roof she had filled in the ocean of slow-moving time by reading French and German novels in yellow paper covers and, during the fifteen years of her marriage, had taken up — with sudden passion and just as suddenly abandoned — music, painting in oils and painting in watercolors, drama, philosophy, pottery, Greek dancing, hand-printed textiles, the painstaking art of applying oriental designs to fans and screens and ebony boxes; had developed intense if intermittent enthusiasms for the Hallé Orchestra, the Russian Ballet, landscape photography. And there were other games, more secret and sinister than all these, which she had learned to play.

Weddings were not among them.

"Nola," breathed Miriam, only pretending to be shocked, "you *must* remember."

Very little, in fact, of the young bride herself although rather more of the jealousy she had unwittingly aroused in Miriam, which Nola had observed with considerable amusement. "Your little boy has become a man," she had said wickedly, offering a deliberate taunt, replying with no more than a throaty chuckle when Miriam, moved to unusual honesty, had accused her of neglecting her own "little boys."

"There is a difference, Miriam dear, between mothering and smothering."

"Oh I see, dear. Is *that* why you go off to some music festival or other in Bayreuth or Vienna every time your boys are due home from school for the holidays?"

But Nola, too subtle for confrontation, had shrugged, blinked her long green eyes, smiled. And there had been no Bayreuth, no Vienna that year — the first of the war — in any case, with the prospect of her cousins from Leipzig and Hamburg facing her cousins from Bradford and Manchester across a No-Man's-Land of murder and barbed wire so real, so unthinkable, that she had decided to ignore it altogether. So that when somebody at Jeremy's wedding had mentioned it, asking her through too much champagne how the *Heinrich* Croziers and the *Henry* Croziers were getting along together now, she had employed, as so often, the weapon of her shrug and drawled that in her opinion — as in the opinion of a well known playwright — the best thing both sets of cousins could do would be to shoot their respective commanding officers and go home.

She remembered — *very* clearly — how shocked Miriam had been at that, how the young bridegroom had flushed and stiffened, how even Benedict her husband who rarely took much notice of her had raised an eyebrow in warning. But what of the bride? Inhaling her cigarette, Nola narrowed her long, light eyes in an effort of memory. Just a girl. And girls did not interest her, particularly when they were young and shy and proper. A boarding school miss clutching a wedding bouquet, she thought, mindful of her manners and her deportment, terrified of Miriam and so desperately in love with Jeremy that it had been — yes, what *had* it been? — comic, pathetic, *enviable*. Was that all there had been to her? Probably not. But Nola had had definite preoccupations of her own just then, with a certain technique for painting miniatures on ivory sticks and with a certain special friendship which had turned, during that wedding weekend, from riches to ashes. She was used to that too.

"Come, Nola," persisted Miriam. "You must remember Claire."

Nola smiled, blinked once again through the curling haze of nicotine in which she lived, one narrow hand toying with the carved amber beads and the Egyptian amulets around her neck.

"Why?" she said.

Why indeed? But it was not Miriam who answered but Miriam's daughter, Eunice Hartwell, who, being perhaps the only member of the family to believe in her mother's frailty, rushed quite unnecessarily to her defense.

"Nola, what a thing to say. And you don't even mean it."

"Don't I?"

Eunice shook an angry, flustered head.

"What *do* I mean, Eunice?"

She had not the least idea, nor — as she well knew — the faintest hope of extricating herself from any web into which Nola might choose to entangle her. Poor Eunice, thought Miriam, without precisely knowing why, except that one always thought of her thus. Poor Eunice, a somehow blurred and faded version of Miriam herself, pale yellow where Miriam was golden, plain light blue where she was sapphire, a woman of good intentions and abrupt rather startled manners, far too ready to rush to the defense of a husband who did not deserve it and most foolishly unwilling to hear a word of blame against the four unruly children she had borne him.

Poor Eunice: a plain, passionate girl who had grown into an emotional, inelegant woman, giving her affections clumsily, rashly and much too soon, having fallen in love at the first available moment with the first young man who had presented himself, a grand explosion of rapture, passion, adoration on her part — less, Miriam believed, on his — which had not only been ill-judged but final. She could love no one else. She had, from the beginning, insisted upon that. And being a woman who could refuse nothing to those she loved, she had remained fiercely loyal and almost slavishly devoted to her Toby through fifteen precarious years, a timid woman by nature who had, nevertheless, taken issue with both her father and her brother Benedict when, one after the other, Toby's business ventures had failed; and had finally obtained for him, by sheer and frequently hysterical persistence, a directorship of Swanfield Mills.

Poor Eunice; for Toby had not done well at the Mills, being a man of grasshopper inclinations who believed life should be lived pleasantly, easily, graciously, preferably over a fine old claret at the Great Northern Hotel or a champagne picnic at York Races, and had shown, from the start, a most aristocratic unconcern about the payment of bills. And, while Eunice herself remained not merely charmed but dazzled by all this well-bred, whimsical extravagance, her brother Benedict did not.

Poor Eunice. Had she come to High Meadows today, walking up the hill from her large, untidy house two miles away, full of noisy children and untrained dogs, where the maids never seemed to get the dusting done and dinner never came on time, to ask Benedict for money? Glancing at her tense hands and pale anxious eyes both Miriam and Nola thought it very likely.

While Eunice herself could think of nothing else.

Sufficient money, of course, had been set aside to give her a decent income — she could not deny that — but, like the rest of the family, she could not touch her capital without first convincing Benedict of the need. She had shares in Swanfield Mills, as they all had, which — as her husband's sporting friends had often pointed out to her — could be sold. Yes indeed. But only to Benedict, and only then if he wished to buy. Her father had left her a rich woman who frequently — far too frequently — could not find a penny in her pocket, who was hard-pressed, more often than not, to pay her servants' wages and settle her accounts with her grocer, whose only hope of stumbling from one financial crisis to the next was to beg, to plead, or to lie to her brother. And because Benedict was difficult to deceive and she was herself appalled by the emotional pressures which forced her, entirely against her nature, to be deceitful, there were times when she hated her brother Benedict with a violence that shocked and wounded her.

Eunice Hartwell, a loving woman, did not want to hate anyone. She wanted to be decent and generous and openhearted, to be absolved of the need to scheme and maneuver, for Toby, the things which should have been hers, surely, by right? Yet it was Toby himself who created that need, and she loved Toby. It was her father who had given Benedict control of her inheritance. And she had loved her father. Once, albeit at a distance, she had loved Benedict.

What a tangle. Just to think of it brought tears stinging behind her eyes. And because it would have been unwise to cry in front of Nola, she turned her mind quickly to the girl her brother Jeremy had so briefly married.

Yes, of course she remembered her. A tall, slim girl with a great deal of dark hair carefully arranged in heavy coils at the back of her head and with the kind of radiant quietness about her, the hush, which had fixed her for ever in Eunice's memory as a girl in love. She had looked both enchanting and enchanted as brides ought to be, even though she must have known that almost everybody had opposed her marriage, from Miriam herself to Edward Lyall, her stepfather and Miriam's solicitor, who had quite agreed with Miriam that Claire, his wife's daughter by a previous husband, was no fit match for a Swanfield. But Jeremy, in his charming, easy manner had insisted and Benedict, rather surprisingly, had agreed. Benedict! To her own considerable alarm Eunice Hartwell realized she was grinding her teeth with a tight and very painful fury. Benedict. Oh yes, he had agreed to that unnecessary wedding and all the implications and expenses it entailed. But nothing could persuade him — at least *she* could not — to pay Toby a salary in keeping with their requirements, so that she might be spared these dry-mouthed trips to High Meadows whenever she discovered a demand for payment, as she had done this morning, in Toby's pocket or stuffed into the copper vase on the hall table. School fees, this time and a particularly sharp-spoken letter from a wine merchant with the threat of legal action hovering behind every word. She had never realized wine could cost so much. Nor those "extras" for the boys at Porterhouse, which Toby in-sisted upon, the riding and fencing and shooting, the gentlemanly pur-suits by which he set such store. How was it they had mounted up? Where had the money gone? Benedict would certainly want to know. And wrenching her mind away from him she tried to fix it once again on her younger, sweeter-natured brother Jeremy and his young bride.

Yes, a pretty girl, a little overawed perhaps, even a little sad, yet, on the whole serene. Not at all like Eunice herself who had been pregnant on her own wedding day, having given herself hastily and absolutely to Toby the moment her father had threatened to withhold his consent. Not that anyone could really have kept her away from him for long. And thinking now of Jeremy's dark-haired, quiet bride and of what had separated them, she burst out, tears in her voice and nothing but pity and generosity in her heart, "We must make her as welcome as we can. Poor soul — how can she bear it?"

"What?" inquired Nola.

"Good Heavens — you know very well," said Eunice, astounded. "And apart from everything else, how sad — how dreadful — to be a widow at twenty-three."

Nola smiled, blinked her long eyes, inhaling tobacco in a languorous, lounging manner neither Eunice nor Miriam recognized as sensual although it made them both uncomfortable. "How sad," she murmured, "or — on the other hand — how merry."

"Nola!" Eunice, who could not even contemplate the loss of Toby without a shudder of cold fear and had pushed him into a reserved occupation at the first hint of military conscription in 1915, was badly shocked. "What a terrible thing to say."

But Nola, shrewd, unsentimental, merely raised her thin shoulders.

"Do you think so? What *I* think, Eunice dear, is that she has been a widow for some time — four years isn't it? — ministering to wounded soldiers, which may have aided her recovery. And one forgets."

"*I* do not forget," said Miriam.

"Of course not, mother." Eunice was all sympathy and contrition and, as so often, quite wrong for Miriam was not thinking of Jeremy as her daughter supposed but of Aaron, her husband. A thought, in fact, so tender that it took her completely unawares, filling her eyes most unusually with tears.

What *could* be the matter? She had married him for money, she had never lost sight of that. She remembered, very clearly, her jubilation at the prospect of being so rich, her lasting delight in its fulfillment. But what always escaped her memory was just when she had grown so fond of him. What precise event had given rise to it? Had it been a gradual, imperceptible conversion of gratitude into affection? And if she herself had only perceived the true extent of it now, so late in their day, had Aaron ever really been aware of it at all? Once again, for just a moment, the eyes of "pretty Mimi" filled with tears.

But she had always known how to shake off her sorrow. Like two of her children, her youngest daughter and her lovely, wasted Jeremy, she had been born in the month of May, the fragrant gentle blossom-time which, she believed, had given all three of them their easy sunny natures, their unquenchable optimism and good humor; just as the sultry, airless day in September when Eunice had come late and gasping into the world, accounted — her mother felt sure of it — for the fact that she had been flustered and clutching at straws ever since.

Miriam, like many leisured and by no means insensitive or unobservant women had her own view of life's mysteries, her personal conception of fate and fortune and destiny, and she had long been of the opinion that it was not so much the Zodiac as the weather which influenced the character of the newborn child.

Pleased with her own perceptiveness she glanced at Nola. March. A high wind, she supposed, a fierce day of sudden showers and bursts of sunshine which had made Nola a child who never knew what she wanted and a woman eternally dissatisfied. She could not remember the birthdate of Claire Lyall — Mrs. Jeremy Swanfield — but she rather hoped it might be June, easy indolent midsummer, warm days of plenty and increase, which made for a pleasant restful disposition; an obliging girl who would not bait her like Nola, nor harass her like Eunice, nor wear her out like her younger daughter Polly who was nineteen, pleasure-seeking, romantic, and therefore impossible. Yes. Miriam was in no doubt about it. A twenty-three year old widow with no home of her own and no income beyond anything Benedict might decide to give her would suit her needs exactly.

The door opened and, turning her head, her mind still drifting slightly toward summer meadows and that ever present sensation of Aaron hovering somewhere just beyond her vision, Miriam watched Aaron's likeness, or the closest she could come to it, walk into the room; although she could not remember that Aaron had ever been so separate, so critical, so permanently at a distance as his son Benedict.

He was a tall, intensely dark man approaching forty, a lean olive-skinned face in which the self-containment was immediately evident, eyes so deep-set as to appear coal black, a guarded mouth, an athletic build somewhat concealed by the dry authoritative manner of the businessman. And instantly, differently, they were all three aware of him.

"Oh Benedict — " said Eunice with a guilty and most unfortunate start, a sure indication, thought Miriam, that she was seriously in need of money.

Poor Eunice.

"Well, well," drawled Nola, "Benedict — at this time of day. How wonderful."

And stretching out her nervous, jeweled hand toward the overflowing ashtray she missed it by several deliberate inches and, gold chains and amber beads swinging, her long eyes narrowed but fixed speculatively upon her husband, she scattered cigarette ash lazily, provocatively, over the polished surface of the table and the deep pile of a Wilton carpet.

Poor Nola? Hardly that, concluded Miriam. Nola up to her tricks again, more likely, playing some devious game of her own. A game of power perhaps? Or a game, even, of sexuality? Catch me, chastise me,

23

overpower me. But Miriam neither knew nor cared anything for games like that.

"Benedict, I'd like a word with you," said Eunice almost shouting the words because her mouth had gone dry again.

"Yes?"

He was, unnervingly, at her disposal.

"Well — if you have time, that is — "

"Of course."

She swallowed hard. "Oh — there's no rush. I'll be here all afternoon."

What had he said to make her falter? Nothing. He had simply looked at her, knowing exactly what she wanted to say to him and how much of it was truth, how much a desperate and therefore clumsy invention; knowing exactly why she needed the money and how last month's allowance, which should have covered it, had been thrown away; knowing that she was a poor manager, an over-indulgent mother; knowing more about Toby, she supposed, his weakness, his incompetence, his easy, lovable, exploitable temperament than she knew herself. Things he would never tell her and which she would never believe in any case but which lay between them, heavy, bitter, without compassion. He would blame her, reprimand her, advise her, but he would not understand. She could not lean on him, could not turn to him for reassurance as badly — badly — she longed to do. Such a thing would have been unthinkable. She could never have survived the rebuff. *Almost* — and choking on her own injustice — she found herself hating her brother Benedict again.

Miriam, who had nothing to ask and therefore nothing to fear, smiled not fondly but perhaps appreciatively across the room at him. Naturally she had not been present at his birth but she knew that it had taken place in the middle of a frozen December, a black bitter night with snow drifting so high that the doctor's gig had foundered on the road to High Meadows, leaving Aaron Swanfield to deliver his own firstborn and not greatly welcome son, no doubt with clumsy hands and then to leave him unwrapped, almost forgotten in the cold room while he gave what comfort he could — and it would not have been much — to his dying wife.

Miriam — herself the child of a bright May morning — could perfectly understand that the world to Benedict must have seemed in those first moments to be a bleak and hostile place; the act of birth itself a conflict in which only he, not his adversary, had survived. Had life always appeared so to him? She shivered and then, with a quick return to her Maytime humor, gave him another quite playful smile.

"We were discussing the problem of our young widow, my dear."

"Is she really such a problem?"

"Ah well." And Miriam became arch in her manner, "pretty Mimi" at her sweetest and most caressing. "That depends on you, dear boy. You are the head of the family, after all, are you not?"

"I believe I am."

"Well then — I should not care to invite her to make her home with us, as seems only proper, and then find that I had acted against your wishes. Benedict dear — what would you like me to do?"

"Miriam," he said, his mouth faintly amused as it sometimes was with her, "I think you must do as you please."

Good. It had been, it must always be, her intention. But just the same, even Mimi with all her skill and charm and daring and the security of the promise Benedict had made his father, had so far never challenged her husband's eldest son directly without making sure, beforehand, that it was an issue about which he did not greatly care.

2

SITTING in the empty, suburban train, Claire Swanfield tried hard to remember the face of her young husband and failed utterly. He had been twenty-one when she had last seen him, a slender young man with a teasing smile, blue eyes, light brown hair, almost six feet in height with not enough weight to balance it, the loosely knit frame of youth all hollows and angles, waiting for maturity and good living to fill him out.

He had been twenty-one and highly pleased with himself. She had been nineteen and on her honeymoon, shy and adoring and still not entirely certain how it had been allowed to happen. He was not only a young warrior, a mischievous Sir Galahad indulging himself in a little honest enjoyment before setting off to find the Holy Grail, but he was also a Swanfield. She was Claire Lyall, no one in particular, who had caught his roving eye at a tennis party at High Meadows and held it because that high-charged atmosphere of patriotism and sacrifice and young heroic death had been so apt to generate romance.

Looking back down the far, thin distance separating her from that other dimension, that other reality of "just before the war," a hundred times four years ago, she could, if only very faintly, catch a glimmer of herself as she had then been, the well-mannered, impersonal product of boarding school and finishing school, recently returned to Faxby and ill at ease there, believing herself to be an intruder in the fastidious life her mother shared with her elderly second husband, Mr. Edward Lyall, legal adviser to the Swanfields. She had been serious, uncertain, conventional, intensely romantic, wonderfully naïve, seeing Jeremy Swanfield as he had seen himself, a hero setting off on a great and glorious adventure, who had chosen, by some miracle she did not dare to question, to lay his sword at her astonished and grateful feet.

Love, or a physical attraction sufficiently intense to pass for love had flared between them and burned long enough to overcome all opposition. He was going to the front and at least the men of his family understood that he did not wish to go virgin. Their marriage had been three days and nights in a London hotel, her body willingly given, avidly taken, a physical exploration beyond which there had been no time to progress. They had made love for three days and then he had gone to France. She had returned to the familiar tensions of her mother's house, to bicker mildly with her mother's husband. And three weeks later he was dead.

She remembered not grief, not tears but the precise physical effect of a hammer blow. She had gone upstairs to her room, sat on her bed and waited while, in Edward's study just below her, her mother, the Swanfields, and Edward Lyall himself had discussed what to do with her, where to send her, to what she was entitled, to whom she belonged. For three days she had belonged to Jeremy Swanfield. And if, already, those three fragile days had begun to blur around their edges at least they had freed her from the restrictions of girlhood. And rising to her feet, slightly dizzy and still vaguely aware of the voices of Swanfield and Lyall authority in the room below her, she had packed her suitcase and the next morning, still in that state of shock which had made it possible to ignore her mother's anguish as to what the Swanfields would say, Edward Lyall's barbed inquiries as to why his wife had so little control over her daughter, she had fled. Not far, perhaps, in actual distance, to the military hospitals, the casualty clearing stations, the waterlogged tents, the mud, the trench rats, the carnage of Jeremy's great adventure. But, in reality, a limitless, tortuous journey from which she would not return. She had left behind the child, the eager adolescent, the ecstatic young bride, all the many aspects of Claire Lyall with which she had been familiar. She had become "Swanfield" who dressed wounds, prepared gangrenous limbs for amputation, bathed eyes scorched and blinded by gas, mopped up the blood from severed arteries, spared a friendly gesture or a kind word, when she could dredge one up through the layers of bitter exhaustion, for men who were perishing from the inner cold of shell shock and the very many whose injuries were complicated by syphilis.

Her life as a young lady of Faxby had rapidly acquired the texture of a distant dream, her mother's preoccupation with food and dress, with pleasing her husband and "with what the Swanfields would say" sounding to Claire like the prattlings of infancy, so that her letters home became short and infrequent and, just occasionally, scornful. She had not openly rebelled. She had simply *grown*, moved on. And then there had been Paul.

She had been twenty-one herself by then, a woman in terms of experience and capability who still looked like an untouched girl, slender and straight, black velvet eyes set wide apart, short dark hair hanging in a heavy fringe above black, perfectly arched eyebrows, an oval face with humor in it and, at times, a deceptive, almost oriental repose. At first glance she appeared not only attractive but most pleasingly feminine, even gentle, a young lady still, as her mother had intended and of whom her governesses might be justly proud. But, in reality, although the war had not hardened her nature, it had sharpened it, tuned it to a high degree of self-containment, emptied out of it every particle of sentimentality, every vestige of illusion. She no longer asked why the massacre was taking place. She knew there was no reason. But since it had happened and she was caught up in it and could not stop it, she functioned, coped, narrowed her horizons to fit the limits between one convoy of wounded and the next, acquiring the wariness of a survivor so that she desired only superficial relationships without commitment. It seemed best to her — in fact it seemed essential — to sacrifice the possibility of joy in order not to run the risk of pain, until Paul. And even then she had fought very hard.

They had met on a Channel steamer, both of them coming on leave, she to visit acquaintances in Devon, he to sort out the complexities of a young wife who was expecting a child which could not possibly be his. They had stood on deck, a cold wind in their faces, and measured each other, both of them already seasoned pawns in the murderous war games of aging generals, both of them fully aware that their youth — whether or not their bodies survived — had already been sacrificed for nothing. He had been for eight continuous months in the trenches and his eyes were full of crucifixions by barbed wire and the swelling corpses which could not be recovered from No-Man's-Land, his nostrils plagued by the stench when they eventually blackened and burst open. She had been nursing gassed, burned, blinded men, and then either preparing them for burial or labeling them as "survivors" and shipping their choking, crippled remains back to England. A line of them had come aboard with her, shuffling up the gangplank in single file, each sightless man with a hand on the shoulder of the sightless man in front of him, a doctor to lead the way, Claire bringing up the rear. And whenever she closed her own clear eyes she could still see their macabre procession shuffling — eternally stumbling — engraved for ever, perhaps, on the inside of her eyelids. But if she and Paul had been spiritually crippled, mentally drained, or had passed far beyond mere disillusion to a blank acceptance of evil, their bodies, their senses, had refused to age accordingly.

Like Jeremy he had gone directly from university to the front, an officer immediately in charge of the lives of men whose only experience of command had been as captain of his school cricket eleven. He had learned rapidly about death and had so far managed to survive. She had gone straight from the schoolroom to her three-day bridal bed and then to those terrible encampments where she had seen death so often that she had started to hold herself aloof from life. They had spent a day together in London missing their respective trains, but when he had asked her to stay with him she had refused. On the platform, waiting for the Devon train, he had taken her in his arms as if she had always belonged there, kissed her with all the long-stored passion there would be no time to give, and she had scrambled into her compartment and closed the door, her head reeling, but glad — fiercely glad — to be making her escape from wanting him.

She would be safe now, or so she had imagined. But a few days later, having made financial provision for the girl he could barely remember that he had married, he had found the village and the inn where she was staying.

"Here I am. If you send me away I'm not sure I can go."

He had not said "I may be killed next week or the week after" since that was the first thing she had understood about him. But walking hand in hand down green English lanes which seemed less real to Claire in their quiet wholesomeness than the mudsoaked margins of battle, the moment came when refusing him appeared more painful, a degree more unthinkable than the desperate hazard she understood to be love.

For the two weeks of his leave they made love with the same sense of condensing weeks into moments, years into days, which she had known with Jeremy. And then, miraculously, as if they had both surrendered a second virginity, they had passed beyond urgency to a harmony of body and spirit which seemed to them to be timeless.

Her life became Paul, his letters, his leaves, the absolute joy of his presence, of eating with him in indifferent cafés, of sharing a narrow bed with him in French inns and cheap English seaside hotels, of strolling through nervous wartime streets or along empty sands vicious with barbed wire, talking to him and watching him answer, looking at him, touching him.

The war became Paul too, a terrifyingly simple matter of one man's survival. With each newly delivered letter in her hand she knew that he might already be dead. She was in a position to know, and to be reminded, every minute of every day, of the many obscene variations in which he could die. She was aware too, with atrocious clarity, of what shellfire, rifle fire, fire itself, mustard gas, a bowie knife, might — without killing him — do to him; of the crippled, castrated wreck she might discover one day, in a hospital bed which would be Paul. She got up every morning knowing it. She ate with it, worked with it, slept with it. Somehow — because what else was there to do? — she coped. She could have gone mad, of course. But to do so — or at least to admit to a higher degree of insanity than everybody else, since they were *all* mad by then, surely? — would not really have offered a lasting solution. And she did not consider it in any case.

They agreed to make no plans, yet, nevertheless, they made them. In order to avoid a scandal, with which his wife was too young and his mother too conventional to cope, he had acknowledged paternity of his wife's child, thus making divorce a chancy issue when the war should be over. Not that he would care to institute proceedings against "poor old Gwen" in any case, since he belonged to a world where such things were simply not done. If she would divorce him then he would be grateful and glad and would immediately marry Claire. If not, then they would just go ahead and make a life together, not in provincial, narrow-minded Faxby, of course, and certainly not in the even more strait-laced, ecclesiastical community where Paul's father was expected to become a bishop, but in some corner of the world where honest emotion might find a welcome. They were both of them too cautious, too wise, too superstitious to long for that golden future yet, nevertheless, they longed for it, believed in it, could accept no compromise.

It had taken her four anguished weeks to learn that he had died of wounds on a hot, dusty afternoon in September, 1918, since the friend he had asked to contact her in the event of his death had been killed an hour before him and, in the end, she had learned of her loss in a short, embarrassed letter from his wife. To Gwen Daneleigh that letter had been the repayment of a debt. By acknowledging her child, Paul had saved her from disgrace and she knew she had no right to begrudge him his love for Claire. She had even tried to be glad of it, for she was a well-meaning girl who meant no harm to anyone. But certainly — if he had lived — it would have caused her a great deal of pain. Definitely, most definitely, she had not wanted Paul to die. She desperately clung to that. But now, since he *had* died, she would no longer be obliged to go through the agonizing processes of divorce, would be safe both from scandal and from sympathy, from the constant anxiety that someone — her mother or Paul's mother — would find out that Paul was not the father of her child. Now no one would ever know. And when she finally came face to face with Claire across the chintz-covered table of a London teashop she had been appalled not only by the taut, controlled ferocity of Claire's grief but by the unnerving penetration of her dark eyes which saw all too clearly that Paul Daneleigh's official widow could not manage to grieve at all.

"Can I do anything?" she had said, flustered, intimidated. "Is there anything of his that I can give you?"

"Nothing," Claire had told her and getting up without another word had walked away.

The war ended a month later, on the 11th November, giving rise to an explosion of rejoicing on the home front and a great, puzzled silence which fell like a quick blanket of fog along the trenches. The war was over. There was dancing in the streets of London and Leeds, Manchester, Birmingham, Faxby, bonfires burning, jubilant, hysterical men and women hugging and kissing, singing themselves hoarse, drinking themselves ecstatic, amorous, senseless. While in France, not far away across the narrow stretch of water, two armies huddled in the November rain behind lines of barbed wire, facing each other across the obscene litter of No-Man's-Land as they had done for four years: except that now there was the silence. The war was over. It had killed nine million young men and crippled thirty-seven million others. But now it was over. Crabbed signatures on dry paper had ended it. What had begun it? Very few had retained even the inclination to wonder. But now the last shot had been fired, or so somebody had said. And we had won. Somebody had said that too. Slumping down into the familiar muck and muddle of the trenches there were men on both sides who no longer felt inclined to care.

Two men died that night in the ward where Claire still continued to cope. Three more, she thought, would hardly last until the following afternoon. There were still wounds to dress, last messages to be hastily scribbled down, lies to be told to the bereaved about the manner of a man's dying. It was quick. It was clean. It was merciful. Never — never — had it been any of those things. But the words came so automatically to her that she wrote them with her hands alone, entirely shutting off her mind. There was still work to do, hospital trains to empty and fill, those terrible telegrams to be sent. And already, invisible, insidious, more lethal in its way than mustard gas, there was the Spanish influenza which would consume, world-wide, more human life than the war itself had done. Someone had told her that in one particularly plague-ridden area the civilian dead were being packed in orange boxes for lack of sufficient coffins.

"Really?" she had said and continued with the compassionate falsehoods she had been writing to a dead boy's eighteen-year old wife.

31

She returned to London in December and, having sent no word to her mother of her arrival, spent Christmas alone in a London boarding-house, staring at a blank wall, greeting the New Year, the first year of peace, when it came, with hollow indifference. She had wandered for a bleak month or two thereafter, trailing herself on a frozen pilgrimage of the south coast hotels she had shared with Paul, losing him afresh at every trysting place, punishing herself until the urgency of her mother's letters and her own shortage of cash recalled her to Faxby.

It was the last place on earth she wished to be. But, as the train drew into the familiar station, she knew that her destination as such no longer mattered. She had told no one in Faxby of her relationship with Paul, knowing her mother would have been unable to see beyond the facts of a wife and child, fearing just a little, perhaps, in spite of herself, the combined authority of Edward Lyall and Benedict Swanfield, of whom she had been somewhat in awe on her wedding day.

Would either of them intimidate her now? She very much doubted it. But the fact remained that she was coming home under what she could only describe as false pretenses, the widow of a man whose family might not require her to be heartbroken after so long but would surely expect her to remember him. Poor Jeremy. She tried again to reconstruct his face, her mind filling instantly and distressfully with the quizzical gray eyes, the fine blond skin, the lean narrow head of Paul Daneleigh. No one else. Paul: and a blur of identical strangers. But with that too she could cope since not only the war but her training as a "lady" had taught her to pretend. She allowed the train to come to a decided halt, put on a new, Cossack style coat with its fur collar and hem which she had bought with the last of her money, knowing how much it mattered to her mother that she should look smart. She picked up her bag and gloves, adjusted her rather dashing little feathered hat, remembering as she did so the explanations she would be expected to make about her shorn hair and, realizing that she had grown unaccustomed to explaining herself to anyone, stepped out into a dull Faxby afternoon.

For the past four years she had traveled constantly in harsh and dangerous conditions and would have experienced not the slightest dif-ficulty now in organizing the conveying of herself and her various trunks and boxes to her mother's home in the quiet suburb of Upper Heaton. But Faxby did not like to see quite this kind of enterprise in its young ladies and, before her hand left the carriage door, she remembered that for her mother's sake she must leave such things to Edward Lyall.

"Claire?" Was it a question? She turned her head, smiled, held out her hand in a cool but pleasant fashion, a grown woman just faintly amused at the suddenly human size of a childhood ogre. But, in fact, her composure was less than it seemed, for if she had been unable to remember her own husband she had experienced no such difficulty with her mother's, who appeared to her now completely unchanged, the same taut, dark face and narrow scholarly shoulders, the same fastidious, slightly pained expression of a man constantly overburdened by some distasteful duty, his nerves permanently overwrought, his sensibilities overstrained.

"Good afternoon, Edward. How are you?"

"Oh — one mustn't complain, you know. And you? A good journey?"

"Passable. You are looking well, Edward."

"Ah yes — I dare say. But that has always been my problem, as you know. I look well, therefore everybody assumes I feel well, which is sadly very far from the case."

He was a hypochondriac still, she thought, at any rate, and smiling politely she stood aside, as Faxby believed a woman should, while he fussed and fretted and wore himself out over the disposition of her baggage, regarding its dilapidated condition with considerable alarm. All too clearly these bags and boxes had been stored in army huts, dragged about in the mud of field dressing-stations, transported on hospital trains which Edward Lyall did not even care to contemplate, much less transfer their possible contamination to the boot of his car, his spare bedroom and his attic.

"Good Heavens, Claire — one wonders why you thought it necessary to accumulate so much."

They had not met for almost four years. Both of them would have preferred never to meet again. But because of Dorothy Lyall who was Edward's wife, Claire's mother, they regarded each other as inevitable and, in their separate fashions, had long since decided to make the best of it.

"Come along then. Your mother will be waiting. I said we would be home by teatime."

And realizing that the daily ceremony of tea with hot buttered toast and raspberry jam was of far greater importance to Edward than any woman's return from France, she climbed into his elderly Talbot and briefly, with a spasm of distaste soon over, closed her eyes.

She had not been born in Faxby nor even educated there. Yet, when pressed to name the geographical location to which she accorded the status of "home," she could think of nowhere else. It was not the most thriving of Yorkshire's industrial towns nor the most impressive, its heavily populated acreage divided between the steep, cobbled alleyways of old Faxby, still bearing such names as Sheepgate and Millergate and Piece Hall Passage in tribute to the fleeces and the ancient water wheels upon which the town's prosperity had once depended; and the newer, bolder Faxby designed, in Queen Victoria's heyday, to suit the grand notions of her textile barons, a new élite created by the steam engines, the power looms, the automatic spinning frames of the Industrial Revolution.

These men had been concerned primarily with the construction of factories to house their machinery, competing with one another as to the height and elaborate stonework of their chimneystacks, the complicated scrollwork of their massive iron gates, surrounding these industrial palaces by countless, identical rows of low stone cottages with little concern for beauty and none for sanitation, each millmaster striving, in this instance, to squeeze in more human beings — more workers — per acre than his competitors. But, when the first feverish days of colossal fortunes riskily and ruthlessly amassed had settled into what seemed an eternity of steady profits, these manufacturers of fine worsted cloth had turned their attention to the improvement of their Metropolis, sweeping away a cobweb of old streets and derelict houses to form a square in which they sited their town hall — each one of them taking office as mayor in polite succession — with several broad thoroughfares leading from it, lined with offices, warehouses, banks, and named in accordance with the values of their occupants, Corporation Street, Providence Street, Perseverance Street, Temperance Road.

A concert hall and a general post office had been added to complete the splendors of Town Hall Square and two station hotels on opposite corners, appearing rather to ignore each other in the same way that the graceful, pale gray parish church with its high Anglican understanding of good living and good manners, managed not to notice the ring of squat, square Methodist chapels standing around the town like sentinels to guard the mercantile values of thrift, industry, teetotalism. All these establishments turning a faintly offended shoulder on the bustling Salvation Army citadel which had a cheerful nod and a wink for everyone.

From the window of Edward's car Claire noticed no outward changes although she knew that the war had been felt here, both in the profit it had brought to the factories and the appalling loss of its men. For this town, like so many others, had sent its street battalions to the front, its gallant company of "Faxby Pals" who, brought up together in the same neighborhood, had been slaughtered in the same trenches, on the same foggy morning, side by side. And to prevent her mind from connecting automatically, far too readily, with the agony in those streets on the day the telegrams came, when every house discovered it had lost at least one man, she turned brightly to Edward, thus considerably fraying his temper since he did not approve of — in fact could not manage — conversation while driving.

But Upper Heaton was only eight miles away, its old trees, its graceful Georgian squares, its quiet houses set within walled gardens appearing both untouched and unmoved by calamity, a little world apart where scholarly men like Edward Lyall sipped vintage port after dinner on fine, untroubled evenings and women like Dorothy — his wife, Claire's mother — still saw themselves as decorative, subordinate, naturally if pleasantly inferior.

"Here we are," said Edward.

"Yes."

Was she reluctant to go in? Was he reluctant to open the gate for her, to suffer once again the assault of her youth upon his solitude, the effect of her presence upon the total concentration he enjoyed from her mother? Very likely. A dozen years ago, a fastidious, highly conventional bachelor of fifty-three, he had succumbed most astonishingly to the charms of a fresh-complexioned, full-bosomed woman of thirty-two, a widow fallen on hard times who had taken employment as paid companion to one of his neighbors. He had wanted the mother, never the daughter. For the first eight years of his marriage, boarding school had taken care of that, then the war. What now? Claire swallowed hard, ran up the garden path, past the elderly stranger in starched cap and apron who opened the door, to the drawing room, where another woman, who should have been a stranger, awaited her.

"Mother."

"Claire."

They embraced self-consciously, finding it easier than talking to each other.

"You look well, mother."

"Darling — take off your gloves and your hat."

She did so, revealing her neat, gleaming, outrageously shorn head.

"Good Heavens," said Dorothy, biting her lip, her hand going automatically to the heavy coils of her own waist-length tresses. But she had expected this, had read of it in the newspapers, heard of it in other families, had warned Edward. They had discussed it at some length and he had agreed — or at least she hoped he had agreed — not to make a fuss. For as Edward had pointed out, with some wit she had thought, hair *grows*. But she was flustered, nevertheless, and quite shocked to find her daughter looking not in the least boyish as might have been expected but, on the contrary, so very female. Sophisticated. That was the only word she could apply and it would be too much to hope — far too much — that Edward would like it.

"Tea," she said, retreating to familiar ground. "Everything is ready. *Do* sit down."

And as she obediently took her place at the table Claire wondered how many times she had already witnessed this scene, how many times she would witness it again, her mother waiting with her tea kettle, biting her lip and frowning over the consistency of Edward's jam and — in this still meager postwar world — spreading on his toast her own share, and the maid's share, of the butter.

"Mother, how lovely to see you."

Yet there had never been any real closeness between them. Throughout the whole of Claire's life Dorothy had been too preoccupied for motherhood, first with the problem of Claire's feckless, spendthrift, gypsy-dark father: then with the hardships and humiliations of a debt-ridden widowhood: then with Edward. She had never regarded maternity as a joy in any case, only as a responsibility and she would have found difficulty in relating to Claire, who so very definitely had her father's eyes — and therefore might just possibly be tainted with his disposition — even if Edward himself had managed to care for her.

He had not.

Perhaps — and then only perhaps — had she resembled her mother, he may have found her more acceptable. But the sight of his golden haired, pink and white Dorothy beside her dark almost foreign looking daughter never failed to make him uneasy.

"Now, just who do you take after, little girl?" certain ladies of Upper Heaton had been fond of asking, their arch manner reminding Edward so forcefully that his Dorothy had once enjoyed intimate relations with another man that he began, without fully understanding the reason, to exclude Claire whenever possible from outings and invitations, discouraging her from attending the suburban church where — his health permitting — he often played the organ. Boarding schools, he sometimes felt, had been the salvation of his nervous system, his digestion and his marriage.

Whenever the school holidays permitted her return to Upper Heaton, Claire had moved carefully and quietly in the shadow of Edward's resentment, his strained nerves, his weak chest, his murmurs of the heart and congestion of the lungs, a hundred devices of the jealous lover, the hypochondriac, to divert attention from an intruder to himself. She had had no hope and, therefore, no thought of pleasing him and, despite the excellence of her school reports and her own naturally good manners, had never done so until, to everyone's surprise, she had married Jeremy Swanfield.

The Swanfields had always meant a great deal to Edward, not merely as his most important clients, but as a family worthy, in his view, of the highest esteem. Yet when Miriam, as a kind gesture, had invited Claire to a tennis party his first reaction had been to forbid her to go.

"I cannot take the risk," he had told Dorothy. "The girl will let me down."

But the even greater risk of offending Miriam by a refusal was more, in the end, than his nerves could bear and having reduced Claire to mulishness and then to tears by his warnings and his commands and the enormous fuss he had made about her hair and her shoes, he had taken her to the carefully manicured garden where she had met Jeremy.

She remembered it now: a drowsy summer afternoon which had barely warmed the chill of Edward's disapproval and then the miraculous excitement of a handsome young man staring at her, whispering "I must see you again," wanting her. But that young man whose Maytime gaiety had won her heart and to whom very probably she would have remained faithful had he lived, still had no face. She could neither see him nor hear him. He had gone.

"Tea without sugar, and no cake, you see," said Edward archly, "which goes to prove that we on the home front have suffered too. Although, in this case, it hardly matters since we are dining at High Meadows this evening."

"Are we really?"

Had she spoken sharply? Her mother raised a warning eyebrow conveying the old message "Don't upset Edward." But if she had been a little abrupt then Edward himself chose to ignore it, the prospect of High Meadows, of an afterdinner cigar with Benedict, a dimpling smile from Miriam, delighting him far beyond malice.

"They must naturally wish to see you," said Dorothy quietly; and Claire, giving in far more easily than she liked to her mother's unspoken plea of "You have only been in the house ten minutes. *Please* don't cause unnecessary fuss," obediently murmured, "Yes. So I imagine."

Neither one of them had referred directly to her service in France, to the war which had maimed a generation or to the uncertain peace in which Claire could see no guarantee for the future. Very abruptly, the room began to stifle her, the dark velvet curtains and the heavy oak paneling to close in, an air of distance to arise, not for the first time, between herself and these people — any people — who had not directly endured the constant likelihood of violent death.

"Do you realize," she had already been told several times, "that we almost starved in England in 1918."

Do you know, she might have answered, that in 1918 I died in France. There were times when she believed she had.

She knew, without needing to be told, that her mother had spent the war catering to Edward's fastidious stomach, going from shop to shop with her market basket to stand in patient line with Miriam Swanfield's cook whenever there was sugar or anything amounting to a delicacy to be had. Claire knew the miles her mother had been prepared to walk, the farm tracks upon which she had hazarded her reputation and her feet, the insults she had endured for Edward's fresh eggs and his illegal portion of extra cream, the coals she had carried to light his study fire when the sturdy young maid had gone off to make bullets and shells.

But Edward had always preferred Dorothy to prepare his meals herself, trusting her as he trusted no one else with the correct balance of his diet. And cheerfully, with no thought of praise, she had performed miracles of ingenuity, while the German blockade had lasted, to tempt his appetite. For he had needed a clear head and an untroubled constitution to cope with the work of Faxby's military tribunal which, from the start of conscription in 1916, had sat in judgement on those who wished to be excused from answering their country's call to arms.

An arduous task, he had made Dorothy well aware of it, and by no means a popular one. For these conscripts, after all, were not being sent out to die on the distant shores of our imperial territories in India and Africa, allowing the wounded — who would be professional soldiers in any case — plenty of time to heal on the long sea voyage home. *This* war was being fought next door, as it were, in France, a matter of a few hours away at most and the sight of those hospital ships constantly discharging recently and gruesomely maimed men into our ports had been intensely distressing to everyone.

"Yes," murmured Claire who, having loaded those ships, could think of nothing else she wished to say. Nor could she really be expected to appreciate the pain it had cost Edward to fetch her from Faxby Station that day since one of the porters, refused exemption by Edward's tribunal, had lost both legs somewhere near Béthune and was often to be found in the station yard propelling himself in a wooden box on wheels and begging. Edward could never look at him without a shudder.

"How terrible," said Claire.

"Dreadful," agreed Edward although they were very far from meaning the same thing.

But one point, at least, could brook no argument. The war was over. That much was quite certain and Edward, in common with many others who had lost nothing by it, believed it best forgotten.

"My dear, why speak of it? What can be gained by dwelling on what — thank God — is past? One must look forward, not back, and I cannot tell you how much it delights me to see butter again. Although when one might expect to lay hands on a decent *foie gras* or a ripe *Camembert* I dare not imagine."

Claire smiled and lowered her head.

"I will help you unpack," said Dorothy. And they went upstairs together to the rose pink bedroom Dorothy had decorated to suit the tastes of her own girlhood and in which Claire had never felt more than a guest.

"Heavens — what terrible luggage." But Dorothy was a practical woman who had never been able to afford the luxury of squeamishness and went down on her knees at once, undoing straps and buckles with large capable hands, perfectly at ease with Claire when their relationship remained at the level of undergarments, the stitching of frayed hems, train timetables, the roughness or smoothness of a Channel crossing. Slowly, deftly, she sorted her daughter's possessions into neat piles as she had always done on her return from school, one for the laundry maid, one for the sewing room, one for the local jumble sale. And if it shocked or surprised her that the starched cotton camisoles and petticoats with which she had sent Claire away had been discarded in favor of what could only be called by the new and decidedly wicked word *"lingerie,"* she gave no sign, simply whisking those flimsy garments of silk and lace and *crêpe de Chine* quickly away before — Claire supposed — the maids should see them.

For half an hour the two women worked side by side, Dorothy talking quietly and, she hoped, safely of the domestic and parochial issues which not only dominated her life but with which she was at ease, the delicate matter of who should present the prizes at Upper Heaton's Annual Flower Show, the eternal servant problem particularly now that the girls were returning from the munitions factories in such an awkward frame of mind, spending the colossal wages they had been earning on fur coats, of all things — would you believe it? — and strutting around the millinery department of Taylor & Timms as if they were as good as anybody.

"But at least," she concluded cheerfully, "now that the war is over there are no more bandages to roll and no more Balaclavas to knit. And no more queues."

"It must have been terrible," said Claire and with a brief very quiet smile she sat down in the armchair by the window, stretching herself full length against the deeply upholstered, gently sloping seat, and lit a cigarette which she smoked not with the brittle smartness of a Nola Swanfield but with the leisured satisfaction which Faxby was, as yet, accustomed to see only in its gentlemen.

"You smoke," said Dorothy, not accusingly but her head coming up with the alertness of a terrier on the scent of a rabbit. "I rather thought you would."

And closing her eyes, still lazily, luxuriously reclining, Claire inhaled once again, not with defiance but amusement and said almost dreamily, "I know mother. Not in front of Edward."

Still on her knees by the suitcases Dorothy shrugged her shoulders, a little heavier than they used to be but still white marble to Edward in the candlelight, her fair skin flushing with one of her quick bursts of indignation since she was mild with no one but her husband and always rushed to defend him.

"Well you may think him fussy. In fact I dare say you do. But he hates to be confronted with — well — things he doesn't expect. And it would simply never enter his head that you might smoke a cigarette."

"Then how do you know he would object?"

"*Claire!* Because I just do."

How many times had she heard that? Too many to count. Simply too many altogether. But, sitting in the deep, softly padded chair with the cool spring sun on her face, the thought of daffodils in the garden below her and old branches sprouting their tender new green, she was too comfortable for anger, still inclining to amusement and understanding rather than condemnation. Her mother, she knew, would wash those scandalous undergarments of black *crêpe de Chine* and peach-colored silk herself and dry them in secret so that the laundry maid should not gossip to the maid next door and give all Upper Heaton cause to wonder if all they had heard about women at war was true. What did it really matter? She had worn the garments to please Paul and was not ashamed of it. She simply regretted that she had been too young and shy and innocent to do the same for Jeremy. In an ideal world it would have been possible to tell her mother so, and to be understood. But Claire had schooled herself long ago to accept the limitations of the world in which she lived. She could not talk to her mother. But she understood her anxieties, her uncertainties, her needs. She knew why her mother behaved as she did and, therefore, allowed herself no right to be unkind.

"All right, mother. I won't smoke in front of Edward. And I won't let him catch me smoking elsewhere."

She had given in easily, without pain. But Dorothy, as always, could not feel she had won a victory until there had first been a battle.

"It may seem trivial to you Claire. But apart from everything else this *is* Edward's house."

"I know, mother."

"And he *does* have a bad chest."

40

"*Mother.*" Her voice had not hardened but cooled slightly. "He smokes a cigar himself occasionally, if there is someone like Benedict Swanfield to give him one."

The last phrase had been true but ungracious, possibly unnecessary. She waited for Dorothy to tell her so. But at the magic word of Swanfield, Dorothy's quite charming flush of anger faded and she at once became very serious and preoccupied, as one might expect a lady-in-waiting to look when talking of her queen.

"Such a clever man," she said abstractedly. "Edward has such a high opinion of him. You had better have a good rest this afternoon since he will want to talk to you tonight."

"Edward?"

"For goodness sake, no. Mr. Benedict Swanfield. Claire — you are not going to be silly are you? I had wondered."

"Silly about what, mother?"

"About your position with the Swanfields."

"What position is that?"

Dorothy Lyall rose to her feet slowly, quite heavily, and stood for a moment biting her lip, looking worried and puzzled as she had done at her tea table and then, shaking her head, heaved a great sigh.

"So you *are* going to be silly. I was afraid so." And she managed, but only just, to prevent herself from adding "Your father was just the same."

"What does Edward want me to do, mother?"

"Heavens — it is not a question of Edward . . ."

"*Mother.*" And although she was no longer amused or tolerant her voice was steady, unwilling to be maneuvered or emotionally pressured but perfectly ready to be rational. "To you mother it is always a question of Edward. So you had better tell me what he wants."

"And why should I not consider him? What you seem to forget Claire is that he and I . . ."

"I know. We are agreed on that. What does he want?"

"Only your good. And don't raise your eyebrows at me in that scornful manner because it is the perfect truth. The Swanfields are important people, the most important we know, and if Mrs. Miriam Swanfield is good enough to offer you a home at High Meadows then — Heavens — most girls in Faxby would give their eyeteeth for the chance."

"No, mother."

"What do you mean?"

But she had known, from the moment her husband had made his wishes clear to her, exactly what Claire would say. She had already rehearsed the dry-mouthed little speech with which she would convey to him her daughter's refusal. But what she could not convey was the calm yet troubling authority with which Claire had spoken, no act of defiance which could be browbeaten or otherwise overcome, but the reasoned decision of a woman who would only listen to reason. And how could she tell this rational, resourceful woman how Edward had actually rubbed his hands with glee, had even hummed tunelessly but recognizably with delight, when Benedict Swanfield had informed him of the family's plans for Claire? As Jeremy's wife there was a place for her at High Meadows where she might make herself useful to Jeremy's mother. She would have her own room, her personal maid, her monthly allowance, the glorious advantage of Swanfield credit in Faxby's better shops, the use of a Swanfield motor car. And even more important than all this, her residence at High Meadows must surely carry with it permission for her mother and her mother's husband to call as one would call on relatives and close friends, freely and without invitation. It would be a new lease of life for Edward. How could she tell her daughter that? And then, meeting Claire's eyes, she flushed a mottled, awkward red as she realized how easily and quickly her daughter had understood.

"I'm sorry, mother."

She was, in fact, very sorry indeed. But it would be Dorothy, not Claire, who would have to endure the reproaches of Edward who was often peevish in his disappointments, the barbed hints of ingratitude, the effect on his nervous indigestion which would require Dorothy's ministrations the whole of a sleepless night. How could she force Claire to change her mind? Edward would expect her to make the attempt. But she could no longer turn the key in the door, could not threaten this girl — this woman — with anything that would be likely to frighten her. Could she plead? Could she appeal to Claire's loyalty or her affection? Suddenly and very heavily as if some weight had struck the back of her neck, she hung her head, ashamed of the answer to her own question and of the tears in her eyes.

But what else could she have done? How else could either of them have survived without Edward?

"Claire — you seem to forget that Edward and I — that we are content together. You have never taken into account that I — that —"

Gasping most uncharacteristically for breath she could not finish, her cheeks and neck and even her ears flushed now by the stranglehold of embarrassment that had seized her tongue.

"You will not admit that I — "

And knowing exactly what it was her mother could not manage to say, Claire, with pity and kindness, quickly supplied a compromise.

"That you are fond of him."

"Well of course I am." Dorothy released from her perplexity, from the agony of wondering why, with her daughter's clear eyes upon her, she could not bring herself to say, "I love him," laughed suddenly, and found it expedient to glance at her watch. The first round of the battle had left her floundering in deep water but she had not entirely lost faith in her own tenacity, the dogged determination which had always allowed her to fight another day.

"Good Heavens, it is almost time to dress for dinner. And please be punctual Claire because it *is* the Swanfields and you know how Edward gets into a panic."

"Yes, mother."

Dorothy smiled, her cheeks turning to their natural rosy hue.

"Well then — we have had a nice little chat. Oh — and Claire?"

"Yes, mother."

"You do have an evening dress? I mean a proper one. The kind — "

"The kind Edward would approve of? Yes, I do."

"Oh good. Then if you could be downstairs by half past six, just in case the motor won't start and we have to send for Mr. Stevens from the garage. Rest a little now dear since it's a party night."

She closed the door carefully so as not to disturb Edward who would be taking his afternoon sleep in the study below. And, remembering first to slide off her shoes, Claire lay down on the bed, closed her eyes, and in perfect stillness and silence reconstructed with the entirety of her mind, her senses, her emotions, the image of Paul, filling the room with him until he was the reality and Edward had gone.

3

MIRIAM Swanfield greeted her rediscovered daughter-in-law with an emotion she considered essential to the situation and which Claire, sensing how much she was enjoying it, did not resist.

"Dear child, it seems like yesterday."

"Yes — yes of course it does."

But, in fact, she realized at once that her memory of Miriam had been quite inaccurate, the imposing, almost imperial dowager of four years ago having shrunk — in the same way that Edward had shrunk — to a self-centered little lady, more than a shade too heavy for her tiny, possibly swollen feet. While far from "seeming like yesterday" she felt that a whole century had ebbed away since she had last entered this entirely feminine drawing room, with its blend of prettiness and coziness which was altogether Miriam. At least a century. Yet, very pleasantly, she allowed Miriam to take her arm between soft, helpless little hands and to lead her like a trophy from one Swanfield to the other.

"You will remember Eunice?"

Barely. An abrupt, well-meaning woman who had burst into tears at her wedding and who now, to Claire's surprise, did not appear to have grown a day older, but rather to have taken on the appearance of a worn out, slightly apprehensive girl.

"Yes — indeed I do."

"And Toby," said Eunice, "my husband —" bringing him quickly forward before anyone could forget him, making absolutely certain that he had his share of notice, his rightful place beside his wife, presenting to Claire a pale, wispy, fine-boned man with an amiable smile who reminded her at once of a high-bred, high-tensioned, none too robust greyhound.

"How very nice to see you again."

"And Nola?"

She held out her hand to a woman who offered no more than the tips of lacquered, languid fingers in return, barely troubling to raise her painted eyelids to look the new arrival up and down, although her glance, when it came, was speculative, shrewd, rather too prolonged for good manners.

"Did we meet," she said, "when you were here before?"

Claire smiled. "I think so." Of course they had met. They both knew it. But Claire had been a child then, of no interest to Nola either as a rival or as an ally. She was a child no longer. The lacquered hand fell idly to Nola's side, her lean body in its narrow, grape-purple dress folded back into her chair, one leg thrown across the other, its shape perfectly visible through the thin, crêpe fabric in the manner which always made Miriam uncomfortable.

"Well, well — I suppose we shall be meeting again."

"Do come and sit by *me*," said Miriam, who had not for one moment relinquished Claire's arm. "Here, dear, on this sofa, while we are waiting for Benedict. My word, how very smart you look."

But, had she cared to tell the truth, Claire's dark red dress, cut like some kind of oriental tunic with a fringed sash loosely knotted around the hips was no more to her taste than it had been to Dorothy Lyall's, or Edward's. It was too plain, too severe, yet, at the same time, and although the word itself was in neither Miriam's nor Dorothy's vocabulary, too sensual; revealing not flesh as they themselves triumphantly revealed their nude arms and shoulders, but the whole of a long, supple silhouette, a new shape and concept of femininity which seemed alien to them and, therefore, dangerous.

But Dorothy, who had long since relinquished the dream of a ringleted daughter in white organdy, had made no comment when Claire had come downstairs that evening, having taken the precaution beforehand of pointing out to Edward that, since Nola Swanfield was famous for her outlandish wardrobe, the family at High Meadows must surely be accustomed to such things — might even like them — and would not take Claire's eccentricities amiss.

And indeed — although it was Miriam who noticed this, not Dorothy — there was something about the way Claire's slender body moved beneath that skimpy, *Ballet Russe* tunic which had a grace and softness lacking in Nola, an air of distance about her which was not cool — like Benedict — but composed of varied and subtle nuances, hints of sorrow and humor, of gentleness and firmness combined, which gave her smooth oval face a most decided fascination.

Miriam liked the composure of Claire's hands with their pointed, polished nails. She liked the long, jet earrings swinging from small lobes set close to the head, accentuating the elegant curve of the neck and jaw. Somewhat against her own better judgement she liked the dark, heavy hair cut in those geometric, vaguely oriental lines, woman's "crowning glory" shorn in a disturbing yet oddly piquant way.

Certainly not the well-mannered child Miriam had remembered. Nor the biddable, deceivable, uncritical companion she had imagined. Instead fate, as always, had been kind to Miriam and, understanding her needs better than she did herself, had delivered into her hands an attractive woman, interesting, unusual, resourceful, probably entertaining, who would suit her far better than any docile, grateful girl. And it was not until she had sat Claire down beside her and thoroughly contemplated this delightful turn of events, that she remembered Jeremy.

At once her eyes filled with tears and, her hot pink cheek coming rather closer than Claire liked, she whispered, "I have kept his room exactly as he left it. After dinner I will take you upstairs to see."

"Oh! Oh yes — thank you." And for a shocked moment, blessedly soon over, Claire had no idea what she could mean.

She had never seen Jeremy's room at High Meadows. She had never thought of it. For his mother's sake she attempted to do so now, to see him as a boy growing up, a young man, just to *see* him, her mind filling instantly, as she had dreaded, with Paul, a tremor of pain darting swiftly across her face which still looked for him in every crowd, hurting her beyond concealment so that she could think of nothing to do but convert it into an offering to Miriam who would naturally mistake it as grief for Jeremy. It seemed little enough to do for Jeremy's mother and she knew that Paul would not have minded the deceit. Would Jeremy? She had never known him well enough to judge.

"My dear child," gasped Miriam, totally convinced, immensely gratified, "we must not upset each other."

But Miriam's easy tears could not fail to communicate themselves to Eunice, her heart ever close to overflow, her sorrow graceless and red-eyed but utterly sincere.

"Poor Jeremy. How *dreadful*," she muttered, reaching out to her husband not only for the handkerchief which he automatically supplied, but to make sure that he was still whole and sound and safely *there* beside her; a gesture of tenderness instantly thrown into confusion as the door opened to admit her elder brother.

"Good evening," he said, speaking to no one, a neutral, entirely commonplace remark which nevertheless produced a tightening of the atmosphere, the slight feeling of alarm which Authority always arouses in those who expected to be caught out.

"Oh, Benedict." Eunice dropped her handkerchief on her lap, looking, for a desperate and foolish moment, as if she meant to hide it.

"So it is," murmured Nola, her long, supple body lounging in a slightly more provocative angle, her long eyes blinking lazily, nonchalantly, vindictively as a cat's, as her husband did not look at her.

"*Benedict* — my dear fellow," said Edward, his voice richly and triumphantly proclaiming his right to use that formidable Christian name.

"Oh, Mr. Swanfield," muttered Dorothy, who could never quite bring herself to do so, blushing as he took her hand and, becoming so flustered in her eagerness to make a good impression — for Edward's sake — that she misunderstood the commonplace remark he made to her, answering awkwardly and at random.

Toby Hartwell, finding nothing to say, swallowed jerkily, gave a nervous smile, a nervous cough.

"Benedict," murmured Miriam with the air of a sweet-natured child suggesting a party game, "do come over here, dear boy, and confess that you did not recognize Claire."

He came, shook her hand, agreed that she had altered. But somehow the compliment which Miriam had invited him to pay became overshadowed, in his cool clipped speech, by the implication that she had simply grown up. She had been very young. Now, four years later, she was less so. What could be surprising or even particularly interesting in that? Yet, smiling up at him in the open, friendly manner she used with everyone, she remembered that although he had been the only person who could have prevented her marriage to Jeremy, he had not done so.

She had been terrified of him then, her knees shaking, her stomach hollow, on the day he had sent for her to attend him at High Meadows and await his judgement. And he had shown her no kindness, offered no reassurance.

"My brother has convinced himself he cannot live without you," he had told her dryly. "Whether or not he has convinced me is another matter which need not — as it happens — concern you. Under normal circumstances I would incline to the view that you are both too young and my brother certainly too foolish to take any major decisions whatsoever. But the circumstances are not normal. And one can hardly declare a man who is shortly to lead other men into battle as unfit to take a wife. Evidently one must discount the fact that he has had no real training to do either. All I can say to you is that, in any eventuality, money will be made available."

Money will be made available. Suddenly, when she least desired to do so, she remembered how Jeremy had laughed at that. "Good old Benedict," he had said, his voice reaching her now through a long tunnel of time, far beyond the possibility of grieving. "That's his answer to everything. Money will be made available — or else it won't be — that's the way he operates. I'd better give you a baby Claire, now, before I go — just in case. A bonny little boy just like me, and then mother'll see to it that he refuses you nothing."

But there had been no child. There had been Paul. And still no child.

"Yes, I had an excellent journey," she said, in answer to his inquiry, her smile never wavering. "And what a lovely surprise to find the trains running on time, or very nearly."

He nodded. "Indeed. Although dinner at High Meadows, Miriam, seems to be a little behind schedule . . . ? Or am I mistaken?"

"Polly," Miriam told him, offering the name of her youngest daughter in explanation.

"Of course." It did not in the least surprise him. It did not please him either.

"She will be doing her hair," said Miriam, visibly brightening at his displeasure, "and re-doing it, and changing her dress. You know how these girls are."

"Yes. Unpunctual. Unfortunately — as you may remember — I have a train to catch later this evening. Had you forgotten?"

And Claire, sitting tranquilly among them, was at once aware of Eunice, her large pale eyes shooting wide open and naked with alarm; and of a gleam of something that might have been satisfaction, or malice, or some strange, angry pleasure in Nola. Clearly neither one of them had known that Benedict was going away. And for how long? Both his wife and his sister needed, probably for vastly different reasons, to know.

"Well dear," said Miriam, who had all the information she required and was not in the least concerned about train timetables or the lateness of her daughter, Polly. "I could send a message to her room asking her to hurry, although the chances are she would only get flustered and take longer. Don't you think so? Although if you would like me to send, then of course — at once, dear. What shall I do?"

"Just as you please," he might have told her once again, his manner curt or sardonic, but there came a sudden and rather delightful rustling in the doorway, a drift of perfume, an impression of color and warmth and whispering laughter.

"Polly," said Miriam, and at once all heads were turned, all eyes were fixed, with varying degrees of admiration or exasperation, on the young lady who stood there, tall, golden, effervescent, as innocently, artfully alluring as "pretty Mimi" had ever been.

"Am I late? Oh dear, yes — I'm late."

But that, most certainly, had been her intention and posing now in the doorway she sketched a curtsy and took a little dancing step from side to side, her sapphire blue skirt with its silver spangles swirling and glittering around legs which everyone supposed to be long and shapely and firm, her cloud of hair brilliantly gold, her blue eyes bright and sparkling and set wide apart like Miriam's, her radiant smile, revealing perfectly white, perfectly strong teeth, informing the assembled company that she was already well pleased with herself and that if they wished to make her gloriously happy — and she felt sure they must — would they please be so kind as to go on looking at her.

"Were you *waiting* for me?" she breathed.

"Well worth waiting for I'd say," obediently replied her brother-in-law, Toby Hartwell, who was good natured, sympathetic and fond of children.

"What an enchanting young lady you are, Miss Polly," said Edward, paying his courtly homage.

"Why, thank you kindly, Mr. Lyall."

Once again she sketched a curtsy, performed a little dance, coming to rest directly in front of Benedict, still preening herself with all the transparent vanity of nineteen, inviting him to see her as Toby and even Edward were seeing her, as very soon every young man in Faxby would be seeing her. A woman.

"I presume we may eat now," he said.

And Claire was in no doubt of Nola's intention to wound, to puncture Polly's brash but possibly fragile self-esteem, when she gave her low, throaty, and, in this case, thoroughly unkind laugh.

The dining room at High Meadows was high and square and of an overbearing splendor, furnished not with the floral coziness of Miriam but to suit the baronial inclinations of her late husband, the massive antique mahogany, the ornate Georgian silver, the strong dark colors and textures, the display of deep-rooted wealth that would surely endure forever; Aaron Swanfield's portrait still there above the white marble fireplace, scowling across the room at Miriam's impossibly angelic twenty-five or possibly thirty-year-old face, framed on the opposite wall.

The artist had given her a silvery fairness, huge, forget-me-not blue eyes, an unreal, fairytale beauty which could have been anyone. But she had been delighted by his meticulous attention to every detail of her dress and her jewelry and had employed him, later on, to reproduce surely not chaotic, kindly Eunice but a demure, quietly dreaming girl of fifteen, tapering hands which had never belonged to Eunice folded in an eternal restfulness she could not have sustained for a moment. Polly and Jeremy had been set in identical, oval frames, a handsome schoolboy, a dainty rosebud doll, Miriam's perfect family, all beautiful and brilliant, all three looking exactly as Miriam wished them to look, *being* just as she most desired them to be.

But Jeremy was dead. Eunice was miserable. Polly? Sitting now between Edward and Nola, hemmed in by the pomposity of the one, the brooding silence of the other, she had put her elbows on the table, her head drooping over them, her sparkle considerably dimmed. And understanding how thoroughly Benedict had deflated her, how hurt she had been by that low chuckle of Nola's, Claire smiled at her and, overhearing some particularly old maidish remark of Edward's, followed the smile with a wink. If she could make a friend in this house then the obvious choice would be Polly. Yet the four short years between their ages, which should have made no great difference at all, had contained the testing ground of war. And it worried Claire that, with the best will in the world, she could not stop herself from thinking of Polly as a child.

But Polly *was* a child. No one should grudge her that. Claire wished devoutly that at nineteen she had been allowed to remain a child herself. Abruptly, through the self-assurance of Swanfield conversation, the solidity of their possessions, she saw that line of shuffling, blinded men, clutching each other by the shoulders, stumbling eternally through her memory: and she shivered.

"Claire — dear Claire," said Miriam, who had been watching her fondly, possessively. "You are not eating. My dear, I know why. But it does no good — really it does not. He would not wish you to pine, you know."

What? Who? She leaned forward, smiling a polite inquiry and then, suddenly understanding, slid at once into the mold of social deceit, good manners, compassion, smiling now with a well rehearsed wistfulness so that Jeremy's mother, at least, would be satisfied.

"You must be so proud of your daughter, Mrs. Lyall," breathed Miriam.

"Oh," said Dorothy, considerably taken aback. "Oh yes — yes of course I am. *We* are . . . She has been very brave."

"Shocking times," said Edward. "Best forgotten."

"I absolutely adore your haircut," said Polly.

"Thank you," said Claire.

"I expect you'll have heard," said Toby Hartwell quietly, apologetically, "that they sent me off to manage a munitions factory. Pity to miss the show and all that but, absolutely essential work, just the same."

"Oh — absolutely," said Claire.

"And dangerous," said Eunice, looking hot and agitated, "*terribly* dangerous. There were explosions in those munitions factories, people killed, and the operatives turning yellow from the chemicals . . ."

"I dare say," said Benedict Swanfield, who had not appeared to be listening. "But at least they were kept in full employment, which seems unlikely to continue."

And for a while thereafter there was silence.

The custom of leaving the gentlemen alone in the dining room for their after-dinner port and cigars was still observed at High Meadows and as Claire followed Miriam across the hall she knew that her moment of maximum danger had come. There would be coffee in the drawing room, Miriam beckoning to her, "Sit by *me*, my dear," and then the photograph albums, Jeremy through every stage of his babyhood and his childhood, Jeremy on his first pony, his first and final motor car, Jeremy in his academic robes, his lieutenant's uniform, Jeremy the scholar, the sportsman, the gallant knight-at-arms, the beloved son. And then the unthinkable pilgrimage to his bedroom to intrude upon his hairbrushes placed exactly as he had left them, the bed unchanged since he had last slept in it, his cricket sweaters, the pipe he had never really learned to smoke, the odds and ends of his careless, contented youth. And no more than that, since manhood had been denied him, and she had killed him all over again by forgetting.

Perversely and dreadfully, a longing that was entirely physical swept over her for Paul, so fierce and basic a need of her body for his that it gave her actual pain. And how could she — with that pain still lodged inside her — go now and stand, with Jeremy's mother, among the remnants of Jeremy's life, and weep for Paul? Surely it would be indecent. Very likely. But it would also be kind.

Therefore, if it could not be avoided, it would have to be done. And how could she avoid it? She could not simply walk away without a word as Nola had just done, looking as if she needed air, or perhaps a cigarette. Nor could she rely on the speedy return of the gentlemen to the drawing room, thus necessitating Miriam's presence as hostess to serve their coffee, since she knew Edward would detain Benedict Swanfield, with his cigars and his importance, for as long as he could.

"Claire." Polly's light hand touched her arm. "Come upstairs and see my clothes."

Reprieve?

"Claire?" said Dorothy Lyall, glancing anxiously at Miriam, hoping it would be all right. But Miriam had been caught by Eunice who was muttering urgently, "He never *said* he was going away tonight. He never told Toby," followed by some quite frenzied whispering which, although clearly unwelcome to Miriam, diverted her attention long enough for Claire to make her escape.

Polly's bedroom was everything Dorothy Lyall had always wanted for Claire and probably for herself, an atmosphere of pink rosebuds and white lace, heart-shaped satin cushions and cheerful, if slightly cloying innocence: a room for easy, virginal daydreams, romantic flutterings of the heart, an Edwardian orchid house in which a young girl might bloom and ripen at her mother's leisure.

Yet Polly, of whose virginity there could be no doubt, barely allowed Claire to sit down on a low, padded stool before opening a drawer and offering her a cigarette.

"You *do* smoke, don't you?"

"Yes, thank you." And Claire realized with some amusement how deeply she would have disappointed Polly if she had not.

"I felt sure you would. It says so much about a person, don't you think?"

"Does your mother know?"

"Oh well," Polly pouted, shrugged. "She *knows* of course, because she's always having a good old rummage through my things the very minute I turn my back. But so long as she doesn't *see*, she needn't act. That's the rule isn't it? Silly really."

And she began to smoke with the self-conscious abandon of the novice, stealing sidelong glances at herself in the mirror, watching herself being wicked, daring, smart, as, with a great scattering of ash, she flung open her wardrobe doors and took out one dress after another, a rainbow of pastel gauzes and satins, brocades threaded with silver and gold, beaded chiffon, silk *mousseline*, the skirts cut not quite so straight as Claire's or Nola's but narrow enough to cause concern to Miriam who did not wish her daughter to acquire the dubious reputation of a "flapper," the flat-chested, lean-hipped, painted boy-girl of current fashion.

"I made them all myself," said Polly, quite certain that surprise and praise would follow. "In fact that's all I *have* done these last two years since I left school. That, and wait for the war to end. What a bore."

"Well, at least you kept yourself busy while you were waiting."

Polly shrugged again, indulged herself with another little peep in her mirror, too intent on her own reflection — looking twenty at least, she thought, with the help of the cigarette — to notice the slightly grim amusement in Claire who, during those same two years had dealt far more with shrouds than evening dresses, maintaining an intimate acquaintance with such things as fear and horror which, whatever else, had *never* bored her.

"What else was there to do?" Polly said, her voice suddenly quite querulous. "Benedict wanted me to stay at school, but even those dreary school-marms told him there was no point to *that*. So I just got out my sewing machine and cut and stitched myself all these dresses so I'd have something to wear when the time came. Because there's been nothing fit to buy in the shops for simply ages, I do assure you. Not that there's been anywhere to go either. It's been dull — *dull* beyond all telling. But now that things are getting back to normal and people are bound to start giving parties again — well, I'm ready. What do you think?" She held up a dazzling garment of emerald satin, rich with crystal beads and gold spangles, her face as vivid and excited as a birthday party child. "Come on — what do you think?"

"Lovely. Where on earth did you get that material?"

Instantly, openly, Polly became effervescent with delight.

"I knew you'd ask me that. There's been nothing like it in the shops has there since this whole dreary business started? Just serges and tweeds and miserable cheap linen. Well — I got it all from the attic."

And she paused, sketching one of her little curtsies, being perfectly prepared to applaud her own ingenuity should Claire be slow to do so.

"Yes. The attic. All my mother's old ball gowns are up there stored away in dozens. Cut to suit Queen Victoria, of course, or Boadicea, but wonderful, wonderful fabrics. My fingers just ached to start unpicking the minute I saw them, and she said if I'd promise to leave her wedding dress alone I could have what I pleased. So I took — oh — everything. Miles and miles of tulle and chiffon and these divine satins. Scarlet — look — and this absolutely sinful black and orange. When did my dear mamma ever wear that? Mind you she wore so *much* of it, and of everything else, that I could get half a dozen dresses out of one of hers. Why do you suppose girls are so much *thinner* these days?"

"Playing tennis in schools, perhaps, and riding bicycles."

Polly looked doubtful as if she had wanted the answer to be far more dramatic than that.

"Well, *I* never played anything at school except truant. And you wouldn't call me overweight would you?"

Claire shook her head.

"I thought not. A friend of mine says it's from not eating cream and sugar and butter during the war and running around selling flags for war widows and Belgian refugees. And that makes sense, I suppose, when you think that all our mothers used to do was sit around all day pouring tea and *guzzling* chocolate cake. You don't think my bust is too big do you? Oh good. I sometimes wonder."

Turning again to the mirror she stood for a moment considering her reflection in silence, concentrating hard on all the lithe, golden-skinned, golden-haired beauty for which, in her private thoughts, she was so grateful, until, frowning slightly, she caught a glimpse of Claire sitting quietly behind her, smaller, finer, not sparkling as Polly wished to sparkle, not setting out to attract as Polly did, yet, nevertheless, attracting, subtle, somehow, and memorable. Smart, thought Polly. Fashionable. And most of all — best of all — unhampered by the petty restrictions of mothers and brothers who wanted to keep her young and insipid and out of trouble when she so positively ached — had been aching for two long years now — to be daring and exciting, to have her rightful share of experiences and a great deal of style.

"You're so lucky," she breathed.

"Am I really?"

"Well yes — you're exactly the right age you see. Too old to be labeled 'the flapper' but young enough to wear all the short skirts and the cloche hats and the feather boas. I can't tell you how I longed for a feather boa. But Benedict — as you might guess — wouldn't hear of it. He said it made me look like a tart, or words to that effect, which was a hoot really, since Nola was wearing one all the time just then. And you've been married too, Claire, which means you can get away with things, can't you? I mean smoking and drinking cocktails and staying out all night. Not like poor old me with my man still to find. I have to be careful."

"I don't suppose it will take you long Polly."

"To find a man?" It was the greatest compliment Claire could have paid her and she was instantly aglow with it. "Oh — lots and lots I hope. I just had a slow start because of the war. All the interesting men went away and I wasn't quite old enough to go with them. So I just had to stay behind with the callow youths and the nervous wrecks and the old fogies — and good old Toby who tries to make out he'd have been a fighter pilot if only Eunice hadn't held on to him so tight and persuaded Benedict to stow him safely away on munitions. Poor Eunice. Everybody calls her that. I wonder why?"

"I hardly know. She seems — a good sort."

"Oh she's *that* all right," sighed Polly, dropping down on her knees beside Claire, her bright blue skirt swirling and settling around her to reveal long, coltish legs in blue silk stockings, the glimpse of a lace garter embroidered with blue rosebuds. She had been bored almost to the point of physical pain at dinner and had taken far more wine than had been good for her. A decent butler would not have allowed it to happen but Atkins, the head parlor maid, was always too preoccupied with the correct management of decanters and bottles and ice buckets to notice whose glass she filled, so that now Polly's head and her tongue were light and incautious, perfectly ready to join with Claire — a Swanfield herself after all — in the delightful pursuit of picking the whole family, and its skeletons, to pieces.

"Eunice means well," she said, clearly quoting her mother. "But Toby is the most hopeless creature imaginable. He's very sweet and all that, and quite witty and clever and he probably *would* have got to be a fighter pilot if Eunice had let him. But apart from cricket and rowing and driving fast cars there's absolutely nothing he's good at. Poor Toby. I quite like him really. I don't know why."

"Because he looks lost and sad, I suppose. A lot of women are attracted by that."

Polly considered, her head on one side, flinging one long blue silk leg across the other, stretching herself, almost purring with sheer joy in her own assuredly peaches and cream future, and the fact that Claire had just called her a woman.

"Well, yes — I do see that. But imagine being married to a man who just never comes out on top — never, ever. I'd hate that. I'm looking for someone enormously strong and sure, who'd just sweep me along — you know — and never take no for an answer . . ."

"Like your brother Benedict, perhaps."

For a moment Polly, who had been thinking of some blackeyed desert sheik, some aristocratic brigand of the high seas with gold earrings and a leopard skin rug in his cabin, looked comically but totally aghast.

"*Benedict!*"

And it was plain to Claire that she had never, for one moment, thought of Benedict as a man of appetite or emotion, but as a stark symbol of authority, the obstacle to most of the things she had wished to do with her youth and her vitality since her father died.

"Lord, no. Not Benedict. How could you ever think of that?"

"Because he's an autocrat I suppose. And that's what you said you were looking for."

"You don't know him."

"No. Not really."

"Then you'd better watch out. People say he's like my father — and he does look like him a bit. But that's as far as it goes. Father was strong all right and nobody would have ever dared to contradict him. But he never made me afraid. I always felt absolutely safe with him because if he said it was going to be all right then it certainly was — one *knew* that. But he liked to see me happy. He just adored giving me things. All Benedict thinks about is how much piano practice I've done, and how many French verbs I've learned, and not letting me go into town alone and then only ever to Feathers' Teashop, never to the Crown Hotel or anywhere else where there's music and *people*. And it's not because he cares about me, don't think that. He just doesn't want the trouble of putting me right if I go wrong, that's all. Benedict doesn't care about anybody. If she wasn't such a bitch I could even feel sorry for Nola."

"Does she feel sorry for herself?"

Polly shrugged, ungraciously like a child. "I don't know what she does. Nobody knows. But what I do know is that she never stands up to him — not really. Well, I can't blame her because neither do I. Neither did Jeremy. And even mother treads carefully with Benedict. He never listens to excuses you see. He just says 'Do this, do that' and walks away."

She tossed her head and blinked hard, another coltish movement but this time of distress, the wine swinging her abruptly from elation to a painful reminder of how much she missed the sure rock, the certain comfort, the fond audience that had been her father.

"Honestly, Claire it's been *awful*. I didn't think it could get worse after Jeremy was killed but it did. Because it went on and on you see. Absolutely on and on, day after day, with nothing to do but sit around waiting for something to happen — for life to get started I mean — and worrying that one would be just too old when it finally did. I don't know how to put this without sounding unfeeling — and I'm certainly not *that* — but there were times when I even envied the girls like you, who'd lost their husbands and fiancés. Wicked, isn't it! But at least they'd done something, *had* something — don't you see?"

"I see." Heartbreak. Disillusion. And now, in its aftermath, the disorientation, the bitter suspicion that one could feel more at home in the Flanders mud with one's own kind than here among the familiar gods — all false, she now believed — of tradition, society, the family.

But Polly, who had no thought of harming anyone, was smiling again, radiant and eager, possessed simply by the need to make up for lost time, to claim her season of youth and frolic while she still could. She wanted to flirt, to dance, to meet a wild young man or, better still, half a dozen, and then, when the fun had lasted long enough — a year or two she imagined — she would get married, have children, stay in bed all morning like Nola, give orders to her cook and her chauffeur and her gardener, like her mother. She had no desire to do anything in the least spectacular in the world, simply to fulfill the normal inclinations — as she understood them — of any ordinary, unacademic, healthy girl. But the war, by imprisoning her at High Meadows, had kept her a child too long, frustrating her abundantly natural instincts so that, of late, she had begun to experience strange sensations in the presence of elderly clergymen and "dugout" schoolmasters, to compete even for the attention of her sister's wistful husband, Toby Hartwell, and the irritable, asthmatic doctor who attended Miriam.

Now she could be free of all that.

"It's over," she said flatly. "And if they'd just stop talking about it . . . Well, I think it's positively morbid, don't you, the way they go on adding up the casualty figures and working out that at least three or four women in ten will have to stay single because there won't be enough men to go round."

"That happens to be true, Polly."

"Oh — that's what Nola says. She thinks we're moving toward a female dominated world — or says she does. But that's only because she used to be a suffragette."

"Nola? Was she really?" It was the first question she had asked, during her whole tête-à-tête with Polly, to which she really wished to know the answer.

"Well, not *really*, I suppose. Just dabbled, as she does with everything. One year it was sculpture, the year after it was botany, then religion and Greek dancing and Lord knows what else — then votes for women. She never marched or threw bricks or anything like that because Benedict wouldn't let her. She just talked about it when mother particularly didn't want her to. None of it amounted to much."

"I wouldn't say that. It got the vote for women last year."

"Oh *that*." All too clearly Polly was not impressed. "But only for women over thirty. And, I ask you, who'd want to admit it? I mean, to claim the vote you'd have to register, wouldn't you, so that everybody would know how old you were. And how many women would care to do that? Benedict says the government are banking on it not being many, which is why they set the limit at thirty in the first place."

"Very likely. But I'm not sure I think so poorly of women."

It was not the answer Polly had expected. She did not really understand it, and it was with a certain defiance that she said, "Well — mother says a clever woman can get what she wants without voting for it or getting up a committee to pass a law about it. And for once I'm bound to agree. You were never a suffragette were you, Claire?"

Slowly, suddenly quite weary, Claire shook her head.

"No. I was just too young for it. My mother wouldn't let me throw bricks either."

Had she ever wanted to? Theoretically, idealistically, yes she had. But mainly she had wanted to be admired and courted by Jeremy, loved and needed by Paul. And what had she ever desired from life more urgently than the chance — the time — to bear Paul's child? Her aims had been no different from Polly's. And therefore she had no right to resent Polly or to be irritated by her because her own lovers were dead and her own youth had been stolen from her, while Polly's was still there, rich in hope and opportunity. Yet Polly *did* irritate her. She *was* resentful. And feeling that her exposure to so much youthful exuberance had lasted long enough she got to her feet and calmly, pleasantly, put an end to it.

"Perhaps we should go down."

"Damn — I expect so. But we must see a lot of each other, Claire. And if Benedict should take it into his head to trust you with the car, as he absolutely never will trust me — I mean without the chauffeur — then we could absolutely go all over the place and no questions asked. Let's start by taking a trip over to Leeds and having a look at the shops. Tuesday? How's that?"

Agreeing sweetly, falsely, that Tuesday or any day next week would suit her perfectly, Claire inquired directions to the bathroom, needing a moment or two of her own company, and then went downstairs, reaching the hall as the gentlemen were coming out of the dining room, Edward still engaging Benedict Swanfield in what, to Edward, was evidently a most interesting conversation although Toby Hartwell looked thoroughly bored with it.

"Oh — *hello*," he said to Claire, not in the least flirtatious but simply relieved to be escaping from the weight or the chill of Benedict's company, until he glimpsed the presence of his wife standing like a sentinel in the shadows, which badly startled him.

"Good God, Eunice — must you give a fellow such a fright?"

But her mission was not with her husband.

"Benedict!"

"Eunice?"

"Could I have a word with you?"

"Now?"

"Yes. *Now*. Please."

And it was evident to Claire, who had herself approached hospital matrons in that same dry-mouthed agony with requests for leave that meant the difference between seeing Paul for a few extra hours and perhaps never seeing him again, that it would have to be *now*, at once, before the courage she had screwed up so tight to face her brother should explode, evaporate, and be all done.

He glanced at his watch, his face entirely without expression.

"Not the best moment, I'm afraid."

And although his voice held no particular curtness or impatience,

58

no threat, just words, in fact, spoken, with an empty clarity, in their correct grammatical order, he managed, nevertheless, to fluster her badly.

"But I've had something to ask — something to *say*, that is, for days."

"Yes. I do know that, Eunice."

"And since you're going to London tonight . . ."

"Exactly."

"Well then . . ."

"Then I have three-quarters of an hour before train time and rather a lot to do. Claire, I wonder if you could spare me a moment? In the study perhaps? I won't detain you long."

She paused on the bottom stair, her whole posture an inquiry. Why me?

"Ah yes," said Edward, answering for her in automatic self-importance. "You'll want me to be present, I daresay."

"Will I?" inquired Benedict Swanfield of his solicitor. "Should it become necessary, I will send for you."

Did he ignore — Claire wondered — or did he simply not wish to see the helpless gesture Eunice made toward her husband and the brave smile, the jaunty "making the best of it" air with which he responded? Could he have failed to notice the obsequious manner in which pompous, easily offended Edward, knowing himself to have been dismissed like an errand boy with a snap of the fingers, had smiled and hurried away? Did he not realize that those whom he treated in this scornful, cat-and-mouse manner would be unlikely to forgive him for it?

Smiling very calmly, she walked through the door he held open and sat down in the chair he indicated in a room that was dark brown, male, meticulously tidy, as impersonal as the man who took the chair behind the desk, its solid mahogany and gold-tooled red leather presence creating a physical distance between them which his attitude seemed well able to match.

"Very well, Claire —"

And once again he glanced at his watch, calculating with the thoroughness of a man of affairs who not only has a train to catch but to whom time is money in any case, the exact number of minutes available and how to employ them to their full.

"There are certain matters to be explained, I think."

"Yes." She was aware of it, did not welcome it, and now wished the matter over and done. "About my plans for the future, I suppose."

"Ah — you have made plans then, have you?"

"No. Not exactly. Not quite yet, at any rate."

It was not, she realized, an answer likely to please a man in a hurry although it did not appear to surprise him either, being the kind of reply, she supposed, to which he was accustomed from Polly and Eunice and Miriam. And, feeling no inclination whatsoever to be classed among the domestic herd of women who pleaded with him — or with any other man — for money or favors or attention, she felt her temper begin to stir a little, preparing itself to rise.

"I am not sure what I intend to do, Mr. Swanfield. I am in Faxby mainly to see my mother. Beyond that I am not yet certain."

The room was not well-lit, his dark face even further darkened by shadow, but she thought he smiled, briefly and with the fleeting degree of humor one might extend to a child experimenting with adult words and situations beyond its scope or its abilities. He was watching her in fact as she herself half an hour ago, had watched Polly smoking a cigarette, his condescension infuriating her. For she was not a child. Far — very far — from that. And, most unwisely, she felt a great urge, which she knew to be childish in itself, to tell him so.

"Well then," he said, clearly dismissing the matter as a formality which had already been decided. "Since your arrangements are uncertain and my time is limited, may I take it that you will be coming to live with us here at High Meadows, and make *my* arrangements accordingly? I know the suggestion has already been put to you. It seems perfectly satisfactory. Obvious, in fact."

Could he compel her? Suddenly, sitting before him in the dark-paneled, close-curtained room, the fresh Spring evening decisively shut out, an airless silence within, she felt herself weaken, falling victim once again to the confused and often illusory oppressions of her childhood, the bonds of straw which, nevertheless, had been so very hard and slow to break. Were they truly broken now? Once — rather long ago — Edward Lyall had controlled her easily and unscrupulously through Dorothy because, accepting the values of Dorothy's world, she had believed it necessary to obey them in order to be loved. But that tense and narrow time was over. That stifling, tightly structured world of Dorothy's and Edward's and Miriam Swanfield's, if it had ever existed at all beyond the limits of their small imaginations, their petty authority, was no more. She had seen it crumble. What had she now to fear?

"Mr. Swanfield," and she even smiled at him in her friendly, pleasant fashion, "I am sorry to appear ungrateful and I would certainly not wish to offend Jeremy's mother. But the arrangement does not seem obvious to me."

"Then — one assumes — you are considering the possibility of remaining at Upper Heaton with your own mother?"

"Oh no." And she smiled again, serene, good-humored, doing rather better than she had expected. "It would not suit my mother's husband to have me for very long at Upper Heaton. It would not suit me either."

"I dare say." Clearly the domestic tensions of Upper Heaton were not unknown to him. "Then where *do* you propose to go? Yes — yes — you have already told me you have not made up your mind. Then, may I suggest that while you are doing so — since the process may well be slow — that you accept Miriam's invitation? She seems keen to have your company, and since you have nothing else to do . . . Shall we consider it settled then — for the moment?"

How often, she wondered, had he used that phrase and then, rising to his feet, glancing at his watch, had walked away, canceling out the resentment, the opposition, the will to fight back of those left behind him by the simple and lethal process of ignoring it? Many times, she supposed. And, in the face of his absolute conviction that others — particularly his female relations — would obey him, it was not easy to resist.

"I'm sorry," she said quietly.

"For what?"

"For being a nuisance."

"The remedy for that, my dear, is in your hands."

"You mean that I should do as I am told?"

Yes. That was his meaning exactly. They both knew it. And while she digested it, pondering the consequences of her disobedience, there was no need for him to speak.

"I am in something of a hurry, Claire," he reminded her.

"Yes." But she was in no hurry at all. No one waited or watched for her return and she could think of nothing for which she cared enough to label "Urgent." "You are going to London, aren't you?"

What business was that of hers? His curtly raised eyebrow asked her the question and she smiled in reply, sensing the strength of his will, yet untroubled by it. What could he do to her? Many things, she supposed, which would have mattered to her once, as they mattered now to Dorothy and Eunice and Polly: which would probably matter to her still if she had her future with Jeremy or with Paul to fight for. If she was whole. Things which might matter to her again should the numbed and damaged part of herself ever heal enough to function. But, for the moment, perhaps for a long time to come, she was empty of needs and desires and therefore most amazingly at liberty.

"We are not offering you charity," he said tartly, "you do — as I am very sure you realize — have certain rights here."

Had he misunderstood her reasons? Did he imagine that, far from refusing his offer of comfort and security, she was simply being devious?

A scheming woman trying to put up her value? She believed he did and slowly, just a little sadly, shook her head.

"Rights? No — no. I don't think so."

"My dear girl," he said, curt, displeased, clearly suspecting himself to be face to face with a greedy woman but anticipating no real trouble in dealing with her. "I am not making suggestions. I am stating facts. You were my brother's legal wife. On his death you inherited both his place in this house and his share of the Swanfield estate. Of course you know that."

Again she shook her head, not denying the fact itself, of which Edward Lyall and her mother, as his emissary, had made her only too well aware, but the substance, the justice of it.

"I don't think so." And the tone of her voice, the gesture of her hand, palm outward, seemed to be pushing something away rather than grasping it, not disputing the truth of his statement so much as refusing it.

He leaned forward as she took out a cigarette and deftly, brusquely, lit it for her. "I would be obliged to you, Claire, if you could explain — as briefly as possible — exactly what nonsense this is. Has Edward Lyall never made clear to you the terms of my father's will, as they affect you?"

"He may have done."

"He *must* have done. Twice in fact. Once when you married and again when Jeremy was killed. Those were my instructions. Did he fail to carry them out?"

"No. Of course not. He told me. And then he wrote to me to make sure I understood."

"And did you?"

She sighed and then straightened her shoulders, her impersonation of a good child about to recite a lesson so exact that he frowned, only slightly, but enough, if she chose to see it, to give her a warning.

"Oh yes. Your father left everything in trust to be released when you choose, and in the amounts you choose. I understand the legal aspect at any rate."

"What other aspect is there to understand?"

He got up, walking a yard away from her into the deep gloom behind the desk where, from a massive silver box, he selected a cigar, lit it and remained that little distance away, looking at her in a manner which made her acutely uncomfortable, the more so because she could not see his face. But the moment had come to explain herself and although her mouth was dry and her head, in this smoky dark, beginning to ache, she would not permit herself to falter.

"Mr. Swanfield, I was your brother's wife for three days. I knew him for a few weeks before that and wrote to him for a few weeks afterward.

I cannot feel — really I cannot — that those three days should entitle me to the financial support of his family for the rest of my life. I did nothing in those three days — or certainly not enough — to have earned that much."

Was she talking to herself? Had he gone away, leaving her to drag these painful words through her parched throat and waste them in the empty dark? *How* did one reach this man? Perhaps, quite simply, one did not. And if it was his wish to be separate and distant and alone then she, of all people, would not question it. But after a moment his voice came to her, dry, disdainful; still wary, she thought, in case all this high-mindedness should be no more than a maneuver to get something extra for herself from the Swanfield will.

"An odd notion, Claire, if I may say so, and unlikely to prove generally popular. You will find that the law of our land, which is as adequate as any other, does not agree with you."

"I can't really bring myself to care about that."

"Well then — and perhaps more to the point — you will find that the Swanfield family does not agree with you either. Nor the Lyalls. Nor any other family with a daughter to marry. Do you care about that?"

"I think — well, I think on the whole not. You are entitled to your opinion — I to mine. And what I need most of all just now is some time alone."

"A convenient philosophy. Do I take it, then, that you mean to refuse the allowance which I may — or may not — be proposing to make you?"

She swallowed, rather hard, and then, raising her eyes, looked directly into his, meeting a keen, cool stare of assessment which, for all her resolution, disconcerted her.

"I had rather assumed, Mr. Swanfield, that any allowance you had thought of giving me would be conditional on my coming to High Meadows."

"Of course you did." And then, very abruptly, having made up his mind or, quite simply lost interest, he rapped out, "However — it does not. You may have — to begin with — two hundred and fifty pounds a year. Hardly enough to turn your head, I grant you. But sufficient to be alone on, in tolerable comfort. It is the amount Polly fritters away on intangibles, although a great many working men in this town have raised families on less. Do you want it? If not, it goes back into the estate until you find yourself in a more receptive frame of mind. Or until my death. In which case you will have a tribe of lawyers and bankers to deal with. So — and I really *am* obliged to hurry — what do you want me to do?"

"Why?"

He raised an inquiring eyebrow.

"You are being very reasonable, Mr. Swanfield. Why?"

"Do I have the reputation of an unreasonable man? Whoever can have told you that?"

"And there are no conditions at all? None?"

"There may be. In fact, yes, of course there are. I require proof of your fitness to handle money. I may require other things from time to time and it is only fair to warn you that I shall probably get them. Conformity to certain family traditions for instance. Because, having grown accustomed to even the small amount of security two hundred and fifty pounds can bring, you will find yourself very reluctant to give it up."

"And you would, of course, take it away from me whenever you pleased?"

"I have that power, yes. I would not use it lightly. I can be reasonable. I am not generous. Not in the matter of allowances and trusts, at any rate, since the money is not mine. But such conditions as it may occasionally suit me to impose will be mine, of course, and for my purposes, not Edward Lyall's. You may see some advantage to that."

He was offering her freedom. She was *almost* sure of it. Freedom from Edward, at any rate, from the degrading necessity of deferring to his opinions and stifling her own for lack of those few shillings a week which would buy a train ticket, a hotel room, a rented flat. With two hundred and fifty pounds a year she could breathe, she could choose. And following hard on her relief came a swift and unashamedly wicked rush of glee. For what would Edward say when he discovered that she had not only escaped his interference but that Mr. Benedict Swanfield had given her the means to do it? Suddenly, through the deepening shadows, she smiled, her whole face alight with the mischievous enjoyment of Edward's discomfiture, although she did not wholly relish the task — hers she assumed — of breaking the news to him.

"You are going to accept my offer then?"

"Yes. Thank you."

"Good — although I hardly doubted it."

"*I* doubted it. Please don't think me naïve or unappreciative of the things money buys or the freedom it bestows. But I *do* believe that it should be earned."

"Very well. Come here to keep Miriam company and earn it."

"You said that was not a condition."

"It is not. No doubt Miriam would like it to be, but I could hardly, with any justice, enforce it. I am simply suggesting how you might overcome your scruples."

"Please take me seriously Mr. Swanfield."

Once again she glimpsed his brief smile and then the deliberate withdrawal of his face into the shadows as if he chose to keep his amusement, like everything else, strictly to himself.

"I can hardly do that until you have learned to see beyond the superficial value of money — its purchasing power in goods and services and what you call independence — to its real meaning."

"Which is?"

"Power, Claire."

"Oh yes — so I have often heard."

"Then believe it. Ideals, philosophies, religious revivals may have their uses. But what really controls populations, families, you — and me — is money. It is the underlying reason behind everything which is done in the world. It is the only way in which one man, or one nation, can effectively manipulate another. What government would ever commit the extravagant folly of war unless there was a profit to be made somewhere or other? Mine, for instance, since my weaving sheds have been turning out uniform cloth by the mile these past few years. But never mind that. We are agreed, are we not, that until you have achieved your self-sufficiency, you will allow me to pay you?"

"You don't think I ever will be self-sufficient, do you?"

"No. I think that by this time next year you will very likely be married again and negotiating with me for the release of your capital."

She smiled, accepting his assessment of her aims and abilities without being in the least offended.

"Oh, I am not nearly so tempestuous as that, Mr. Swanfield. For the moment a small flat somewhere in Faxby will be quite enough for me to handle. That and some kind of work to do."

"Very well." There seemed nothing more he wished to say. "Miriam will be disappointed, of course. But I will explain as tactfully as I can."

"Oh — perhaps I should tell her myself. Yes. I suppose I should."

"What an active conscience you *do* have, Mrs. Swanfield."

"Yes. I know. It is a great trouble to me."

"Would it trouble you, do you think, to call me Benedict? On the whole — since I am your brother-in-law — it might cause less comment than Mr. Swanfield."

"Heavens," she laughed, returning to more familiar ground. "Benedict — I do apologize."

But her impulse of warmth, her sudden awareness of him as a human being, a *man*, was instantly chilled by his sardonic "No need to apologize. I notice your mother also has difficulty with my Christian name."

"My mother —" she began, and then, sensing the futility of it, turned her defense of Dorothy into a simple exclamation, rounded off by a shrug. Her mother was a timid, well-meaning, awkward woman. Benedict had noticed the awkwardness. He would not, she felt, have any interest in the rest. And how weary she was now, how perilously close to her limits, that sickening moment which assailed her from time to time when, instead of standing firm and continuing to wage her calm, well-mannered battle for personal freedom, she would infinitely prefer to run away, to find herself a quiet, secret corner and leave the explanations, the confrontations — as her mother and Miriam had always done, as Polly would do — to someone else.

But that was not the way she had chosen and if, perhaps, she would not be obliged to endure Miriam's reproaches tonight, she could not avoid Edward. He would be *there*, in the car on the way back to Upper Heaton, *there* once again tomorrow morning at the breakfast table, his nerves and his digestion deteriorating by the minute, as she revealed the full extent of her treachery.

She could endure it. She would have to. That, and Dorothy's recriminations and the pangs of her own troublesome, well-trained conscience. But she knew that even now she would find it hard.

"Thank you, Benedict."

"Quite. I have ten minutes left before I go. Would you be good enough to send Edward Lyall to me?"

"Oh, yes —" She would send Edward anywhere, willingly, preferably a hundred miles away. "May I know why?"

"Because someone should acquaint him with the details of your new financial status — don't you think?"

A burden had been lifted from her shoulders. Was he aware of it? Glancing at his guarded face she could not tell and, in her overflowing relief, she did not choose to investigate. But, as she crossed the hall, she was aware that her fatigue had lightened, her detachment and resolution had both returned, so that, as she entered the drawing room and beckoned to Edward, it occurred to most of the assembled company to wonder why, having been cloistered for so long with their paymaster, their taskmaster, their inquisitor, Benedict — she should be smiling.

4

IT was Nola, of all people, who found her the flat.

She had been prepared for overtures of friendship from Polly but Nola's husky voice, when it emerged from Edward's telephone, had startled her into the same brusque telephone manner used by Edward himself, who always picked up the instrument gingerly and put it down as soon as he could, in case it might explode.

"I wonder if you'd care to have tea with me? This afternoon? At three? The Crown Hotel."

And Edward had been so conscious of the honor done him by Mrs. Nola Swanfield in allowing her voice to enter his home that he had agreed, with only a mild degree of hysteria, to lend Claire his car.

The Crown Hotel seemed far from an obvious choice to Claire. The two station hotels, the Midland and the Great Northern, had always been respectable, if not much frequented by Faxby's ladies, existing mainly for the use of commercial travelers and the annual dinners of various commercial or charitable, but predominantly masculine societies. It would have been permissible — if only barely — for ladies to meet in the claret-colored plush and brown leather interiors of either of these establishments, although Feathers' Teashop with its pretty lace tablecloths, its waitresses looking just like parlor maids in their white caps and aprons, its discreet toilet facilities — unique in Faxby — which, on their introduction just before the war, had finally enabled Faxby's ladies to stay in town longer than the interval between essential visits to the bathroom, would have been far more usual. Even the tearoom, recently opened in Faxby's department store, Taylor & Timms, would have been allowable, although the tables were rather too much exposed to the view of anyone who happened to be passing through haberdashery or millinery, and the "powder room" door so publicly situated that nothing — not even the prospect of a hurried and uncomfortable journey home — could induce such ladies as Dorothy Lyall and Eunice Hartwell to pass through it.

But the Crown Hotel had always been a place of vague ill-repute, situated, perhaps appropriately, in an old, haphazard part of the town, once prosperous, but which had been left far behind when Faxby moved its center to Town Hall Square and the clearcut dividing lines of Providence and Perseverance Streets.

She had even some slight difficulty in finding her way through so much decaying grandeur, past so many tall gray houses standing, dilapidated yet still pointedly aloof, behind heavy, ancient trees and a curtain of fine spring rain. Yet the Crown, when it did appear, was very much as she remembered it, the still intriguing if considerably worse for wear relic of a past age and it was not until she had parked Edward's car directly outside the main pillared entrance, well away from the tramlines and the hooves of fractious horses as he had instructed her that she realized the hotel appeared to be closed.

She went in, nevertheless, treading carefully through a confusion of planks and stepladders and paintpots to be claimed at once by a small boy, posted, to her relief, as a lookout and who, paying far more attention to the processes of replastering and decorating than to Claire herself, took her along a passage, indicated a door and bolted.

She knocked and hearing first a movement and then a murmur went in, realizing at once that the man sitting a correct six inches away from Nola had only just moved there, while the tray in front of them, far from containing the teatime apparatus of china pot and silver kettle and wafers of bread and butter, was set with tall, fluted glasses, a box of Turkish cigarettes, an ice-pail sprouting the neck of a slender, dark green bottle.

"Oh, Claire — hello." Nola, reclining with her provocative ease and languor on the cushions of a low settee, blinked heavy-lidded, transparent eyes through the smoke of her cigarette, looking boneless, fluid, excessively smart in a narrow sage-green dress with foxtails loosely draped around her neck, her greeting so offhand that for a moment Claire wondered if the invitation had been forgotten, regretted, or had turned out not to be convenient after all.

But, if so, Nola quickly decided to make the best of it, bidding Claire to come in and sit down with a series of gestures acquired during the days of her enthusiasm for the *Ballet Russe*.

"Come and meet Major Hardie. Kit — this is my sister-in-law, Jeremy's wife. Now then, Claire, you don't remember Kit Hardie do you? No. I suppose he'd be just before your time."

His handshake was warm and firm and decided, his hands well manicured but hard, wholly masculine, wholly capable, Claire thought, of breaking in a horse to the bridle or whipping in a pack of fractious hounds. There was a humorous crinkling of fine lines, she noticed, at his eye corners while the eyes themselves were a bright keen blue, sportsman's eyes, accustomed to scanning the mists of Autumn mornings, for the early pheasant, the running fox. A country gentleman, to whom the command of soldiers in battle must have seemed as natural as the ordering of gamekeepers and hunt servants, his air of authority softened by the jaunty good humor, the slightly quizzical nonchalance of the leisured classes who quite simply do not expect to be disobeyed.

"Hello," he said, a pleasant modern greeting spoken in a rich, male voice in which she detected a trace, although only a faint one, of the far north. Scotland perhaps? Grouse and heather and malt whiskey with a veneer of cosmopolitan sophistication. A bankrupt laird, perhaps, as they all seemed to be these days, with a taste for *foie gras* and vintage champagne? It suited him. And as he took command of her, installing her in the chair he thought would best suit her, pouring her wine, she was aware of two things, her own leap of response to his charm and a pang of disappointment that it should be squandered on Nola.

"Yes," said Nola, who had seen the response and could easily guess the rest. "My friend, Major Hardie."

And suddenly shooting her lazy eyes wide open she smiled straight at Claire, put down her empty glass and laid her hand briefly on the Major's knee.

My friend. My find. My diversion. She smiled again. *Mine*, dear. Claire nodded. And there was no thought in either head of embarrassment or offended morality.

"I am an unfaithful wife," conveyed Nola's subtle mind. "Are you going to tell my husband?"

"No," answered Claire's. And reading very accurately Claire's unwillingness either to judge or be involved Nola's smile deepened into satisfaction. Good. She had expected no less. Not friendship of course and certainly not loyalty, Nola having encountered these things far too seldom to set much store by them. But an "arrangement" between two women who might — while the arrangement lasted — be of use to one another.

"Tell lies for me," said her long light eyes, her indolent smile. "And now and then, if I can remember, I might tell lies for you."

Claire raised her glass. So did the Major.

"Here's to — what shall we drink to?" he said.

Nola stirred slightly on the divan, rearranging her furs. He would drink to her, one way or another. She would see to that. For as long as it pleased her. *Diverted* her. And then, when it stopped mattering, as she supposed it would; *then*, when it had all turned stale and flat, both she and her Major could drink to anyone they chose. Anyone, she thought, who would have them. But not yet.

"Anything you like," she murmured as if she was making a promise. "Or to the Crown Hotel — which might save us from death by boredom next winter."

And when Claire looked her inquiry she added "Have you forgotten the Faxby winter, dear child? Long and cold and nothing to do but suffocate in the bosom of one's family? Kit is going to change all that — aren't you my darling. He has just taken over the management of this hotel and he's going to see to it — aren't you Kit? — that we all get our fair share of decadence and evil . . . Or, at the very least, rich food and fine wine and jazz. One should give him another medal for it."

He would have plenty of those, Claire thought, turning to him with interest and some surprise, wondering what a man like this one might know of hotels beyond the knowledge of a guest who would expect to be well served without caring or even thinking to inquire the ways and means of it. And what might he know of rich food beyond the pleasure of ordering it in a London restaurant? Throughout his youth an unseen presence named "Cook" would have encouraged his appetite with robust English flavors. Later a more voluble "Chef" would have emerged, at his command, from various famous kitchens to receive his praises or his blame. The army would have given him a servant to shield him yet again, not from danger or sudden death which were properly considered to be the business of gentlemen but from the tedious domestic mysteries of boot polish, the boiling of water, the frying of eggs.

What could he possibly know of the management of the crumbling, ailing, never popular Crown Hotel?

"The owners have given me *carte blanche*," he said, "which is very noble of them, or would be, if it wasn't pretty clear that they really haven't much to lose. I've got a year to make a go of it — hence the repairs and renewals. And if I fail, then the whole thing, including myself, goes under the hammer."

Already, on so short an acquaintance, she was finding it hard to associate him with failure. But, just the same, knowing Faxby as she did, the undertaking seemed risky to her, the kind of rash venture into which ex-officers all over the country for whom there was no peacetime employment were throwing themselves, taking the same mad chances with their savings and their wound gratuities as they had been trained to take with their lives in battle. And she had not judged this man to be reckless.

"Does Faxby need another hotel, Major Hardie?"

Who came to Faxby, after all, but commercial travelers with trains to catch who would have to be provided with very good reasons for deserting the station hotels?

"No," he said, his calm assessment taking her by surprise. "I think Faxby has just the number of hotels she needs and exactly the kind she deserves. The bedrooms are adequate and the service doesn't leave too much to be desired. But should you wish to take a friend out to dinner — well, the Great Northern serves thick brown soup and plain boiled cabbage, whereas the Midland — !"

He gave an exaggerated shudder, so that she was laughing as she asked him "And what does the Crown serve?"

"Nothing as yet. The kitchen ceiling collapsed the day I arrived, right on top of me, I might add, which wouldn't have mattered too much if I hadn't had my little Belgian friend with me. A chef of some ability, as a matter of fact, who didn't take it well when a ton of rotten plaster descended on him. I expect you know how these Latins tend to make a fuss. But he calmed down in the end — being a refugee and having nowhere else to go. So now, here he is with a brand new ceiling and brand new stoves to go with it, waiting for opening day. And I just think you might be tempted — if you *did* want to treat a friend to a good dinner — by his green turtle soup or his oyster soufflé. Followed by — well, lobster *à la bordelaise* — how's that? — or a saddle of venison. *Very* nice. And strawberries in Curaçao and brandy topped with a layer of *Crème Chantilly* a yard thick."

"Major Hardie — where can one get food like that these days?"

"Perhaps you'll just believe me when I say that one can. At a price, of course. But Faxby can afford it, with her textile magnates and iron-masters turned armaments manufacturers, and her engineers. They tell me there are more millionaires per acre in Faxby than anywhere else in the country, unless it should be Bradford."

"I dare say." And she looked, without her being aware of it and somewhat to his gratification, worried for him, anxious to put him right. "But they're not lobster *à la bordelaise* millionaires, are they? Major, how well do you know Faxby?"

"Oh — passably."

She very much doubted it. For one thing, had he spent any significant length of time in Faxby, where handsome, urbane gentlemen were never in great supply, he could not have remained unnoticed. He would have been sought after, invited everywhere, certainly to High Meadows. He would have been remembered. And since she had never heard of him, what more could he have done than pass through as someone's weekend guest, at the shooting parties perhaps which used to be held at one or two of the old estates beyond Faxby Green, before their owners went bankrupt or got killed? And knowing, by instinct, that the Major must be penniless too, suspecting that he was basing his judgement of Faxby's tastes on his own, acquired under far more sophisticated skies, she turned to him in alarm.

"People just don't dine out here, Major. In fact, where *do* people dine out except in London? And no one could call Faxby smart. We have no theaters here, except the Princes which is really only a music hall, so there's no need for theater suppers. And the cinema crowds could hardly pay your prices. While as for taking friends out to dinner, people in Faxby who can afford to entertain do so in their own homes, with their own staff."

"I know." The warm blue eyes seemed to twinkle. "It has been ever thus. But can it continue?"

"I see no reason why it shouldn't."

"Then let me show you one. We shall see an end to the shortage of cream and butter and the shops will be piled high with sugar again before long. But what about housemaids?"

What about them? She had been born into a world in which housemaids were so natural a part of the landscape that although women like her mother and Miriam Swanfield might spend cozy hours bewailing their inefficiency, their annoying tendency to take cold, or burst into tears, or get themselves seduced by soldiers, she had never for one moment seriously contemplated life without them.

"I'm not sure," he said, although she knew he was quite certain, "just how those girls will settle down again, now that they've found out they can get higher wages for shorter hours in the factories. And it takes a lot of housemaids to fetch and carry and do the dishes when madam orders dinner for twenty-four and breakfast for a dozen. She might find it more convenient to give her dinner parties at the Crown Hotel."

"I do hope so."

"Thank you. But you don't believe it?" She smiled and slightly inclined her head.

"Major Hardie, you are a brave man."

"Of course he is. He has a chestful of medals to prove it." Nola's voice sounded lazy, still half-asleep, her pointed face betraying some kind of secretive amusement Claire did not try to understand.

"Ah well — as to that . . ." But before the Major could brush aside his gallantry in approved heroic fashion there came a knock at the door, a respectful voice calling him away to more serious matters.

"Major Hardie sir, the builder's here."

He got up, excused himself for just a moment, and as the door closed behind him Nola opened her light eyes very wide and looking straight at Claire said flatly, throwing the words at her and bidding her make the best of them, "He was the butler at High Meadows. Naturally you didn't know."

Silence. A struggle — no easy one — not merely to speak, but for breath. Yet she knew she must speak, and she did so. For after all she had been shocked before, had been hit hard before, and in the gut, by women striking for their own amusement. Perhaps like Nola. Perhaps not.

"No. I didn't know." And why on earth should it matter? Surely the war had swept away all that nonsense about class, about knowing one's place and keeping one's place. Rightly so. She had never believed it, never liked it. Yet, just the same, from generation to generation, girls brought up as she had been, in households where young grooms and footmen were often handsome and therefore dangerous, had been fed a defense of prejudice and taboos. The traces — faint and unpleasant and furtive — remained. And while Nola's infidelity as such had seemed a matter of indifference, the fact that it should be with her husband's former butler troubled her. She knew, all too exactly, how Benedict Swanfield, Miriam and Dorothy and anyone considered by them to be "decent" people would react to it. And although she did not share their class loyalties, their class blindness, she was, nevertheless, uneasy. And, moreover, she felt a fool.

"Yes," said Nola flatly, "the family butler. What a scandal, eh! He enlisted in the summer of 1914, right at the start, so I daresay you never met him. Not that nice girls ever look at gentlemen's gentlemen in any case. But if the class thing should be worrying you — and I suppose it *is* — then let me put your mind at rest. I never noticed him when he was at High Meadows. I don't suppose Miriam ever really noticed him either until he left and she realized just how he'd been running the house like clockwork and making it all look so easy — which is what professionalism is all about. Or so he tells me, at any rate. I met him a year ago at a party in London and all I saw was a damnably attractive man — in uniform, of course, which always helps, especially when it has as many ribbons and decorations as his. You'll understand that."

"Yes. I do."

"And I meant what I said about his having a chestful of medals. They gave him just about everything they could give him for 'conspicuous gallantry in the field' and all that. Over and above the call of duty is the phrase they use, except with Kit the first thing one has to understand is that his duty is always and absolutely to himself. He got the medals and the prestige, but he survived. That's what Kit Hardie is. A survivor. And an opportunist. He takes advantage. So unless you *want* to be taken advantage of — and it *can* be rather fun — then beware. The owners of this hotel are called Crozier — my cousins Arnold and Bernard, who own an awful lot of things."

Once again she opened eyes that had a swift, feline gleam, allowing Claire to draw her own conclusions while telling her plainly that she did not care a fig for them. What did she care for? Many things, it seemed to her. But for how long? And shrugging, blinking, creating an impression of insolence half-felt, half-necessary to stave off the certain knowledge that she would not care about Kit Hardie, or any other man, for long, she reached out a narrow, listless hand to touch her amber hair, her amber furs.

"So . . . He takes advantage of me. I take advantage of him. He's ambitious. I'm bored. That's the extent of it."

She smiled almost brilliantly this time. For it was enough. It was as much as there had ever been. A handsome man who fired her senses and occupied her mind. *Now*. Today and, almost certainly, tomorrow. And when the trough of uncaring came, she would just have to deal with it, endure it until it could be filled all over again.

"Now then, Claire Swanfield," she said quite cheerfully, "and what do you think of that?"

"If it suits you, Nola, then what has it to do with me?"

"Suits me?" Nola was amused, a little scornful, remembering that this girl, for all her quiet sophistication, was still young enough to be sentimental. "Whether it suits me or not — and, as it happens, it does — my dear, what *else* is there to do?"

She meant it.

"I don't know," said Claire. "One hopes."

"But of course one does." Leaning forward Nola gave her throaty chuckle. "One hopes. Positively for miracles no less. Every time. My dear — isn't that the fun of it?"

And having stated, in those few words, the entirety of her way of life she came suddenly, almost briskly, to the true purpose of her invitation.

"I hear you are looking for rooms," she said.

"Yes. I am."

"You won't find it easy."

But Nola, Claire understood at once, would help her. At a price. And could the price be high? No more, she supposed, than her services as an alibi, a safeguard for Nola who, in a provincial town like Faxby where eyes are sharp, tongues long, and adultery still a serious business, must be constantly in need of excuses. And what could sound more valid — what lie more convincing — than a visit to the new little sister-in-law? Did Claire wish to play that role? Not particularly. Yet, on the other hand, did any sense of loyalty to the Swanfields hold her back? With a certain rueful amusement she doubted it. And, already quite desperately, she needed a flat.

"There's not much on the market," said Nola, telling her what she already knew. "All those wartime marriages, you see. And now with all our conquering heroes coming back to their war brides and their war babies, accommodation is like gold. Have you found anything to suit?"

"Nothing I could afford."

"Well — well — let's not despair. I have the very thing — just there, across the road and round the corner and — hey presto — a bedroom and sitting room and 'facilities' all your own. Kit Hardie moved out a week ago. He lives here now and the flat is still vacant. I'll take you over to have a look at it. It's in a lovely old house. My Crozier cousins, by the way, own *that* building too."

They stood up together, Nola having stated her terms, Claire having understood if not entirely accepted them.

"All right, Nola."

"Yes dear — so it could be. To our mutual advantage perhaps."

"I dare say."

"Let's go then, shall we, and see."

Kit Hardie, standing among the chaos of the vestibule, an agitated tradesman at his elbow, watched them come toward him, Nola, her fox tails swinging behind her, striding through the plasterer's rubble as if it did not exist, Claire walking carefully — thinking about her shoes — but without hurry, perfectly ready to exchange a smile in passing with the workmen Nola did not appear even to see. An attractive girl, this youngest Mrs. Swanfield. Not an obvious conquest, like Nola, who, in fact, had needed no conquering but had taken him by storm, on fire — he well knew — with the sheer novelty of a man like himself, a "common" man, he supposed the phrase still went, although even in his early days as a polisher of other men's boots, a scourer of their pots and pans, he had never felt himself to be common. While none of those who had called him so — and there had been many — had ever convinced him. Tough certainly and resilient with an awareness, acquired very young, of the need to guard his back, an ability to wring every drop of advantage from any situation with which he might be presented. But not common.

He had been, all his life, a hungry fighter, a clever fighter, not always a fair fighter of course — he cheerfully admitted that — having been brought up in a world where foul blows were only to be expected. A cruel place, the world of the "common man," harsh beyond the imaginings, it occurred to him, of those who had enjoyed the long childhood of the leisured classes. Jeremy Swanfield for instance who, cushioned from responsibility, would have remained a boy into his fifties. Nola, who could think of nothing to do with her privileges but squander them. All those lads who had called themselves captains and colonels in the first year of the war and had seen their first battle as an extension of the playing fields of Harrow and Eton. Rarely their second. Claire? And although his humble origins had never yet hindered him in his dealings with women he found himself wondering about Claire.

She would know, of course, by now that he had been Miriam Swanfield's butler. Nola would have seen to that. And while he had not deceived her he had done nothing to correct her mistaken impression of an officer and a gentleman born, not made; of privilege smoothly inherited rather than grappled for, cheated for, risked life and limb for, *earned*. Why should he? He was not ashamed of it. Yet how might this self-contained yet somehow fragile girl — this beautiful girl — react? Certainly she would not be excited by his plebeian attributes themselves as Nola had been, burrowing eagerly through his polish for the traces of roughness and coarseness which so intrigued her. No. He had no illusions about Nola. No illusions about anything. He had never been able to afford them. Yet it occurred to him that he would be — what? —disappointed he supposed should Claire Swanfield now be ill at ease with him like some prim little schoolroom miss or — even worse —should she be curious about the way a handsome, well set up, *common* man might make love. Like one or two of his commanding officers' wives, and Nola.

Yet her smile, when it reached him through the distractions of hammering and sawing and the muttered complaints of the builder, was as friendly and open as before.

"You look busy," she said, wanting simply to speak to him.

"So I am." And his voice too was easy, its tone warm, his eyes openly admiring, a little speculative, just a shade — because it was his habit to laugh at the world, or appear to do so — amused. "These fellows keep telling me they can't be finished on time. But I've got a higher opinion of them than that. I reckon they'll manage it."

"Kit," said Nola, cutting brusquely through this conversation which did not center on herself, "I want your keys."

"Yes. I'll send Euan to open the outer door for you. It sticks. Euan — get down here will you!"

And from a plank suspended at a precarious angle between two ladders, a young man put down his paintbrush, sketched a military salute and swung himself easily to the ground, a workman in paint-spattered cord trousers, stripped to the waist, until he said in the drawling accents of the Home Counties, public school and privilege which Claire still associated with Paul, "Yes, Major Hardie, sir. *At* your service."

"All right, Euan." Kit Hardie sounded tolerant, resigned, although with a faint suggestion behind his good humor that this form of greeting might one day fail to amuse him. "Just take these ladies over to the flat and do the necessary."

"Yes, sir. At the double, sir."

"Stop playing the fool, Euan, there's a good lad. And Euan!"

"*Sir!*"

"Put your shirt on."

He grinned and began to pull a flamboyant but exceedingly shabby blue and red check shirt over his head, the upward stretching of his arms revealing a rib cage with no flesh to cover it, just thin, fair skin which looked sickly pale beside the hard, bronzed fitness of Kit Hardie, a nervous, fine-drawn body from which Claire — because of Paul — quickly averted her eyes to the sounder, steadier, muscular figure of the Major.

And this time there could be no mistake. No possibility of error. No reason, even, for astonishment — nowadays — that a gentleman born and bred should be plastering a ceiling, presumably for wages, for a gentleman new-born and self-created.

"He's Euan Ash," explained Kit Hardie, "and harmless enough. Lieutenant Ash, he tells me, and I suppose I believe him, late of Eton and Oxford and God knows where . . ."

"*And*," said Nola tartly, "about the only drawback I can think of to the flat, since he'll be your neighbor. Although not for long, we hope and trust, since he's on his way — where is it, Euan? I forget."

Still buttoning his shirt, he turned his head and smiled at her with the deliberate sweetness and unconcealed malice of a fallen angel. "Do you know, there are times when I'm not sure myself. Edinburgh? Cape Town? Sidi-bel-Abbès?"

"Just over to the flat will do," Kit Hardie put in smoothly, swiftly. "Open the door, Euan. Put the kettle on. Watch your language."

"Don't worry, Major. If this is the lady we've been hearing about, who was a VAD, then bad language won't worry her. And in any case I think *this* Mrs. Swanfield and I may have met before."

It could easily have been true. For the past four years his face, in its hundreds of variations, had looked up at her from those hundreds of hospital beds, his eyes sometimes blue, sometimes brown, sometimes blind, his manner jaunty, defiant, bitter, his hand sometimes clinging to hers, sometimes pushing her away and damning her to Hell as he lost his limbs, his youth, his faith, his virility. She had escorted his broken body a hundred times over to hospital ships and collected it back again from the next convoy of wounded. She had received, in wooden huts and open fields and under canvas, the full impact of his delirium, his agony, his disillusion, his obscenities, his occasional outbursts of lust, his even more troubling moments of tenderness. He had once been — a long time ago — of the gallant company of knights-errant, the seekers of the Holy Grail, which had included Jeremy and Paul. And now, recognizing instinctively that he belonged, as she did, to that numerous band of half survivors, who — unlike Major Hardie — would be very slow to heal, she smiled at him and nodded, acknowledging their affinity yet not caring to make too much of it.

He was twenty-six, she thought — Paul's age — as tall as Major Hardie but pared down to the bone, a long lean body without substance — like Jeremy's — a narrow face with a high forehead, fine pale hair and light blue eyes, a hospital pallor she recognized about his skin, something behind his pose of heedless, even callow youth that was ancient and weary and totally cynical.

She knew, without asking, that he had gone to war — like Paul, like Jeremy — straight from the classroom. She knew that now, like hundreds and thousands of other young officers, he was rootless and unsettled, finding nothing in this safe, dull, *petty* peacetime world to hold his attention, drifting until such time — if it ever came — that he could take off his restlessness, his resentment, his disorientation as gladly as he had taken off his uniform, and put the war finally away.

More than that she did not wish to know. But, good manners allowing her no alternative but to go with him, she walked between him and Nola, keeping their animosity apart, for the five minutes it took to reach Mannheim Crescent, their destination. And, from the first moment, the house interested her. "A gentlewoman somewhat in distress, don't you think," said Euan Ash as he pushed open the elaborate but ailing wrought-iron gate and led her through the sad little garden with its tangle of shrubs and weeds, its overhanging screen of sinister, misshapen trees.

"It's not bad," she told him.

"Oh it's lovely. It's a little corner of paradise. Every frontline soldier's dream."

And he unlocked the door, wincing at the protesting creak it made as it lumbered inward on heavy, overburdened hinges.

The hall was dark, and had once been imposing, designed to suit the self-importance of some early textile baron, perhaps a century ago, and then abandoned when the explosion of industry had made life in the city center smoky and undesirable and he — or his good lady — had elected to follow their friends to the fashionable hills around High Meadows or the spacious levels of Upper Heaton. Mannheim Crescent, therefore, had lost its exclusivity and had become merely respectable, then tolerable, then finally, when its population of lawyers and doctors and small tradesmen had also moved away — either upward to suburbia or downward to social oblivion — had received the sorry classification of a "dubious address."

Its gardens, its paintwork, its drainpipes and guttering had become neglected. Its houses — too large to be properly maintained by the kind of people who were now willing, or obliged, to live in them — had been divided, first of all into fairly substantial flats and then subdivided, over and over again, into sets of rooms where dancing classes and music classes were held, where religious sects and political parties with unusual aims and short life-spans held their meetings and where people of no fixed abode and no serious occupation lived semi-vagrant lives of shared kitchens, inadequate plumbing, uncertain drains.

"Splendid, isn't it!" said Euan Ash, whose accent had certainly not been acquired in furnished accommodation in Mannheim Crescent. "You have what used to be the dining room, I think, and the back parlor. Anna Pavlova — or so she'd like us to call her — gives ballet lessons through there, which I suppose was the drawing room. And I have about two square yards at the end of the passage, opening onto the conservatory which I use as a studio. I paint — or try to — which is my excuse for not doing much else, except odd jobs for the Major. I'll do your portrait, if you like — which is my excuse for being alone with beautiful women."

"You'll be wasting your time, Claire. He's no good," said Nola, stalking past him with an irritable, predatory step, swinging her furs.

"I don't get many complaints," he breathed after her, smiling once again with his malicious sweetness as she came to a halt at the door of Kit Hardie's flat to which he now had the key.

"Open it," she told him curtly, making her voice a snap of the fingers.

"*Madam!*"

"How very nice," said Claire, walking into the room without looking at it, simply to get away from them, and then realizing, when her eyes began to focus, that far from the shabbiness she had expected, the room was clean, cool, well-proportioned, scented not with damp and age but with lavender and faint, by no means unpleasant, traces of tobacco. The furniture was plain, cheap she supposed, although she was not well acquainted with the cost of furnishings, but the two armchairs and the sofa stood firmly on their carved oak feet and, although of different shapes and styles, looked well matched in their covers of green and white chintz patterned with water lilies. There were bookshelves, a table and sideboard, a fireplace with a broad mantelshelf, all of them empty but immaculate, bearing no stain, no trace of dust.

"A tidy man, the Major," said Euan Ash, lighting a cigarette and tossing the match, still lit, into the empty hearth.

"Thank you," said Nola taking out her own cigarette case. "Claire?"

But she shook her head, having noticed the french window and the long, walled garden beyond it, two shallow stone steps leading to a tangled fairyland of wild and cultivated foliage missed altogether, shades of green from sage to laurel and on to emerald, pierced every now and then by the startling yellow of a daffodil, a branch of forsythia hazarding its starry, lemon blossoms between polished rhododendrons, swelling with buds. A fine, mild rain was falling, a fragile mist curling gracefully, gently around the topmost branches of a double row of trees, apple, she thought, and flowering plum, so old and so untended that their branches had interwoven into what would be a lattice-work of blossom.

No one was there. Beyond the mossy gray stone wall nothing could be seen but a low gray sky and the reassuring vastness of a giant elm whose summer foliage would provide an even denser solitude. She could be alone in this garden. In this house, with its drifting population, she could be anonymous. It was an approach to freedom, the nearest, perhaps, that she could hope to make at present, since the familiar web of her mother's insecurities had already reached out and entangled her far more than she had intended. Dorothy Lyall did not know that she needed her daughter. But Claire knew it. And until the need had lessened or settled, she understood that she could not leave Faxby.

"You'd better take it," said Nola from the armchair behind her. "You'll find nothing else at present. Nobody has been building houses during the war and now people are setting up home in barns and wooden huts and old railway carriages. So, unless you're quick about it, you'll find yourself stranded at Upper Heaton or High Meadows."

"And you ought to know," said Euan Ash, turning upon Nola a light blue gaze that was far too innocent, "that Nola *always* knows best."

"Didn't he tell you to put the kettle on?" she snapped. And laughing, he held out a hand to Claire, his touch surprising her by its coolness and the dry, slightly rough texture of his skin.

"Come on Claire. You'd better see the kitchen *now*, more or less as Kit left it. I just hope you can match his standards. We're supposed to share it, although I don't cook anything beyond sausages and beans. I might scrounge though, should you be kind-hearted."

The kitchen, at the end of a narrow, bottle-green passage, was square and plain and spotless, a well scoured wooden table placed directly in the center of the dark red linoleum floor, open shelves — mainly empty — lining the walls, a shallow stone sink beneath the clean, chintz-curtained window, a surprisingly adequate gas stove offering the welcome alternative, in Claire's eyes, to the huge black iron range with its boiler and coal ovens which dominated the entire inner wall.

"Do you understand that thing?" he inquired and sitting down at the table while he filled the kettle and turned on the gas, she smiled. She had never boiled an egg, never sliced a loaf of bread, certainly never lit a fire before 1914. And now, although eggs and bread and coal were well within her capabilities, she wondered how much time she was really willing to accord them.

"I expect I could manage."

"Ah well — I'm not sure that's good enough. Kit is an absolute wizard with such things. Seems a pity to lower the standard."

"I suppose he cleaned everything up here too?"

Grinning, he abandoned the spluttering gas jet, left the kettle to its own devices, and came to sit beside her.

"Who else? The place was a pigsty when he got here, although *I* never noticed it until he pointed it out to me. I moved in a week or two before him, you see — on my way to somewhere else — and since I wasn't staying, there seemed no point in changing anything. But Kit doesn't see things that way. He had the mice standing to attention before we knew where we were. I bet nobody ever got 'trench foot' in his Company. He'd make sure they all took their wet boots off and kept their feet warm with sandbags. He'd be the kind of officer who shaved, too, every night and morning — no matter what."

"And you didn't."

"Christ, no. I had a beard to my knees. Good camouflage."

"When did you enlist?"

"My dear child — in August, 1914. Didn't everybody?"

"Straight from Oxford?"

"I rather think it was Cambridge."

"Where did they send you?"

"Oh, here and there. It slips my mind."

Like Paul — like Jeremy — he would have been among those first zealous three million volunteers who, since the Government had only anticipated five hundred thousand and had nowhere near enough equipment to go around, had prepared for battle by drilling with walking sticks. And perhaps he would have missed the first confused weeks of war when two great armies had hurried here and there around Western Europe looking for one another, led by generals who understood war in terms of cavalry charges, sweeping maneuvers across open plains in broad daylight — preferably in good weather — and whose strategy in the main was purely and simply to keep moving. Occasionally the armies had met, taking it in turns, almost, to advance and retreat until, one late September day, the Germans who had been marching up and down, down and up, for weary weeks like everybody else, had paused for breath, dug themselves holes to shelter in, rigged up a barrier of barbed wire, a few machine guns, and stayed there, quite simply too tired to walk anymore.

Jeremy had still been in training — with his walking stick — somewhere on Salisbury Plain, Paul already on his way to France where the allied commanders, casting puzzled looks at these trenches had realized that, since men so dug in could not easily be coaxed out again, the best thing to do would be to dig trenches of their own. And for the next four years both sides proceeded to slog out the war knee-deep in mud, throwing bombs and shells at each other, discharging poison gas which, should the wind be in the wrong direction, blew back, as often as not, and killed its own keepers; rushing at each other, from time to time, over the top of their fortifications with fixed bayonets, doing bloody, repetitive, day-in, day-out murder for the sake of a yard or two of barren ground.

Had Euan Ash been anywhere in the region of Neuve Chapelle the following March when Jeremy — as Claire knew but Miriam did not — had been impaled by a rifle bullet on the enemy wire and had hung there, horribly crucified, until a sympathetic sniper had finished him off?

"The name seems to ring a bell," he said, his eyes full of their deceptive, light-blue innocence.

Had he been on the Somme where, in one single day of fighting — the memorable 1st July, 1916 — the British Army lost sixty thousand men, which did not deter them from continuing their attack until, at the cost of four hundred and twenty thousand wounded or killed, they had advanced, in three months, little more than three miles?

"Now do I look the kind of man who'd get involved in a cock-up like that?" he answered.

"Were you at Passchendaele?"

"Wasn't everybody?"

It had been a wet summer that year in Flanders, so that the campaign had begun on waterlogged ground into which, when it had been reduced to liquid mud by the traditional exchange of shells, men sank waist deep — in which wounded men drowned — and heavy artillery disappeared out of sight. Yet, nevertheless, notwithstanding the mustard gas used here for the first time, two sets of innocent victims stood firm and massacred one another, six hundred thousand of them bleeding into that unspeakable mud for an allied gain of five miles and the empty, abandoned village of Passchendaele which — being of no particular use to anyone — they soon gave back to the Germans again.

Had he been near Amiens the following September when, very early one morning, a British shell, falling short into No-Man's-Land had ripped Paul's legs apart and left him to lie there bleeding in its crater, until nightfall, the traditional gathering up of the day's wounded and dead, when it had been too late?

"I seem to remember that it rained a lot," said Euan Ash. "I had the devil of a job getting my boots off, once, after five days up to the ankles in trench water."

"What else did you do?"

"Oh — not much. Took care not to show any more gallantry in the field than I strictly had to. Not like Kit Hardie. Now there's a man who had a good war, there's no denying."

"Don't you like him?"

The light eyes became a shade more angelic, the smile sweeter.

"Now then, Claire — what a question! Even on a half-hour acquaintance you must know that he's an absolutely splendid fellow. I haven't managed so far to find a single thing he *can't* do — and by God I've tried. Our butler at home never seemed to get beyond answering the door and pinching the claret. And he wasn't even awfully good at that."

"Where's home, Euan?"

His smile, which seemed initially to be dazzling, was no more than a device to screen his face, a flash of brilliance used deliberately to obscure her vision so that she could not see beyond.

"A fair distance — quite a tidy step. I'm *en route* for Edinburgh to see a friend. Did I tell you?"

"Nola mentioned it. I can't help noticing that she doesn't seem fond of you."

He laughed dryly, his face, without its wonderful wicked smile, looking strained for a moment and — very briefly — much older.

"I dare say that just goes to prove her good taste."

"I assume there *is* a reason?"

"Oh yes — one or two. She may tell you herself one day when she's had her absinthe or her whiff of chloroform or whatever she's using now. But *I* can't say much, can I, because a gentleman's not supposed to talk about these things. I may be the Major's odd-job man, after all, but let's not forget that I was born and raised a gentleman."

"And the Major wasn't? Is that what you mean?"

"I try not to. Perhaps he's one of nature's gentlemen. Certainly he'll be a great success. I don't expect to be. But you'd be wrong to pity me — if you were thinking of it, that is."

"I wasn't. It's weakening."

"How clever you are, Nurse Swanfield."

"So are you. You managed to tell me you had an *affaire* with Nola without actually saying it — which wasn't very gentlemanly of you, after all."

"Oh — I do so agree. But I don't think Nola minds who knows, so long as it's not her husband. She was only filling in time, in any case, waiting for Kit. That's why she came here, to find him a flat. And what did she find to go with it but a poor, struggling young artist — or so she imagined — in need of a muse to inspire him and organize him and make a household name of him. And if I *had* wanted that, then there'd have been nobody better than Nola to bring it off for me. She made a lot of plans on my account. Good plans — except that no plans are good where I'm concerned. That's about it. Then Kit arrived. And plans are just his style. She got busy persuading her Crozier cousins to give him a decent salary and a percentage of the profits he's bound to make, and to let him tear the place to pieces and build it up again just as he thinks best. And she decided my pictures were no good. Let's say she's right. Will you take the flat?"

"I might."

The kettle boiled. He arranged a tray casually, quickly, and when they returned to the living room Kit Hardie was there, smiling, taking control, larger and infinitely healthier than Euan, calmer than Nola, more self-possessed than Claire; a man without formal education who was, nevertheless, far more capable of adding and subtracting life's complexities than any of them.

"Milk and sugar, Major?" inquired Euan, deliberately playing the servant. But it would take more than that, more than Euan whose own opportunities, Kit knew, had burned in the same fire as his illusions, to offend him. Kit had disliked the slaughter in France as much as anybody, had never, in fact, fired a gun at man or beast other than in the course of battle, whereas Euan, he supposed, must have brought down his share of partridge and pheasant every season and assisted at the ritual tearing to pieces of foxes which Kit himself abhorred. Yet Euan, who had gone to war a boy, had returned as a wraith inside a young man's body. Whereas Kit, already a practiced survivor, had survived.

When Euan Ash had strolled into the Crown, looking like a vagrant bricklayer, sounding like a young and by no means humble squire, offering to do anything that would pay for a night's lodging or two, Kit had had no need to ask why. And when he had subsequently offered to replaster and repaint the complicated hotel ceilings for a crate of whiskey, he had understood that too. If, tomorrow morning, Euan should not appear and should never be seen again, he would know better than to inquire. So too, he imagined, would Claire, whose experience of warfare must surely have taught her to recognize that wraith in Euan and to know that there would be no cure. Otherwise — already — he would not have cared to place her so much in Euan's company. He gave her time to drink her tea and then, having shown her the pale green bedroom, explained the window catches, the details of the rent, the disposition of the neighbors and of a certain stray cat, he managed to whisk her away into the garden without giving her time to make her own intentions clear.

Outside the air was cool, the earth damp and heavy, the tree trunks green with venerable antiquity, the clamorings of street and town, of loyalties and the emotional demands and posturings of others, dispersed, reduced, forgotten in this enclosed wilderness which even Kit Hardie had not tried to discipline.

"I find this very charming," he said, and she glanced up at him, surprised that he should think so, oddly pleased that he did.

"So do I." And they walked on a little way in silence, savoring an attraction that was, as yet, wholly physical — since he was an intensely physical man and her emotions were too scarred to be easily hazarded again — but which, far from alarming her, seemed to wrap itself around her like a warm blanket, softening the needle-sharp memories aroused by Euan Ash, protecting her from the groping tentacles of Swanfields and Lyalls which, if she could not keep her own annoying conscience under control would stifle her for their own purposes, their own convenience, with no conception of hers.

Kit Hardie, at thirty-six, was older than the other men she had known, infinitely steadier; self-seeking, she had no doubt, even coarse at times perhaps beneath his easy, polished charm. But assured, decided, strong. And how fascinating it might be — if only for a little while — to be younger and frailer, to be swept along, controlled, sheltered. How restful. How *easy*.

"Nola will have told you," he said, "that I was in service at High Meadows."

"What a dreary expression — in service. It doesn't suit you."

"No. It didn't. This suits me better. Will you take the flat?"

"Oh, I think — perhaps."

The blue eyes twinkled down at her, the sensual, yet humorous mouth curved into a smile which could only encourage her own.

"That's not an answer. Shall we try again? Will you take the flat?"

"Yes — I might."

"Claire . . .?"

It was the first time he had used her name.

"Yes," she said, "I will."

5

I_T was beyond the comprehension of Dorothy Lyall why anyone, who had been given ample opportunity to do otherwise, should deliberately choose to live in Mannheim Crescent, the self-same landscape, dingy, difficult, humiliating, of her own first marriage, from which only the intervention of Edward had saved her.

But Claire's behavior came as no surprise to Edward himself. Had Dorothy never noticed, he feebly inquired, the traces of instability in her daughter? An inheritance from the paternal side, no doubt, but which *he* — who had taken her into his home in good faith — was now being asked to bear. Was it really to be wondered at, that the whole sorry business was making him ill? In the grip of a particularly violent stomach cramp — and who knew what *that* might lead to? — he retired to his study, drew down the blinds, closed his eyes, and sank, a wronged and disillusioned man, into a chair.

Dorothy, her own stomach knotted with the panic he could so easily inspire, marched into Claire's bedroom and shrieked at her the old accusation, "Are you trying to ruin my marriage?" And when Claire took the precaution of locking the door, she lay in wait for her on the stairs, wringing her hands and asking, "Why are you doing this? Why?"

But in the end the only question which needed to be answered was "What will the Swanfields say?" And only when it transpired that their favor was not, after all, to be withdrawn, did Edward discover the greatness of heart to forgive his wife her daughter's trespasses and allow her to be at peace again.

Claire moved to Mannheim Crescent as soon as Edward's sulk was over, taking nothing but her clothes, Paul's letters, the volume of Rupert Brooke Jeremy had given her, no other memorabilia of the past, no bits and pieces of a suburban girlhood, no bric-à-brac to relieve the spotless anonymity of the flat. She desired, merely, to be quiet. To be, not physically perhaps, but emotionally alone. Yet she quickly gave into Dorothy's slightly hysterical insistence on accompanying her, that first morning, to "settle her in" and agreed without much resistance to meet her the following Wednesday — and every Wednesday thereafter — in Feathers' Teashop where, at their window table, the section of Faxby which mattered to Edward might see them sipping their tea in perfect harmony, an exercise invariably rounded off by a stroll around Taylor & Timms, a great deal of pausing and smiling and "I am sure you will remember my daughter — Mrs. Jeremy Swanfield . . ."

"Lord," said Nola, walking into the flat an hour after Dorothy had left it, her fox tails draped high around her neck, a jockey cap in orange and gold striped silk perched low on her forehead, "That mantelshelf looks damnably clinical. But no matter. It so happens that I have just acquired a friend — a sculptor — who does wonderful modern pieces. *Highly* significant. "Grief," he's working on at the moment and "Jealousy" — the darker emotions. Positively unknown, of course, which is criminal, and yet — well, it's so important, you know, and so *exciting* to be in at the beginning. I'll take you to see him. *Not* cheap. Not now, at any rate, since I pointed out to him what he's worth. But *what* an investment. You won't regret it."

"I'll give you some charcoal sketches," offered Euan Ash. "Perseverance Street on a wet Saturday night" — how about that for significance?"

"Mother says," beamed Polly Swanfield, turning up on that first crowded afternoon and posing gracefully in the kitchen doorway where Euan Ash could see her, "that it's the little things which make a home, and since we've got masses of things both great and small in the china cupboards at High Meadows, she says when you come to dinner on Sunday you're to take your pick. She's sending the car for you, by the way, at six o'clock."

And so, to avoid the deluge of unwanted gifts, the intrusion of other people's tastes and fancies, she spent a morning in the dilapidated arcade which housed Faxby's few and far-from-prosperous art dealers and antique shops, emerging with a collection of pure white figurines, nymphs of classical antiquity mass-produced, she rather imagined, in Birmingham, and several prints vaguely reminiscent of Renoir or Monet, sunlight dancing on pale green water; cornfields rippled by blue air; girls in white dresses lounging beneath striped umbrellas; a Parisian street leafy and dusty with high summer.

"Junk," declared Nola, who understood art that season only in terms of odd gyrations of metal and stone. "And cheap junk, too, I'm glad to say, which means you'll have some money left to spend on *art*, dear child — quality. I'm arranging an exhibition for my sculptor friend in June and I shall expect you to be generous. The boy is brilliant, that's all — totally original. I'm moving him into a studio not far from here so you'll be bound to meet him. In fact, I'll bring him over to show you, one afternoon next week. Tuesday? Good. About three. And need I add that Polly would be decidedly in the way?"

Yet Polly, to whom Mannheim Crescent seemed a place of wicked Bohemian excitements, was not easily to be discouraged, the more so since she came as the emissary of Miriam's generosity, the Swanfield chauffeur depositing her at Claire's door at least twice weekly, bearing some large, solid, expensive gift, each one intended — Claire realized — to anchor her ever more firmly to Faxby.

"Mother thought you might need cheering up." And Polly, with the exuberance of a Christmas tree fairy, would produce a fur rug, an exquisite Chinese screen which was "just dying of loneliness in the attic," a bedroom chair, a quilted counterpane.

"Mother thought you'd need some cups and saucers." And into the hall came a packing case, decorated with yards of blue satin ribbon containing a Crown Derby dinner service, which "absolutely nobody wanted," and a tea and dessert service in dainty flowery Minton.

"How can I ever use all these?"

"Well," said Polly who rarely thought of uses, "I expect you'll break a few. So *now*, since I have the car, just put on your hat and we'll go and watch the cricket on Faxby Green — or, rather more to the point, we'll let a certain fast bowler watch me."

"How very generous of the Swanfields," enthused Dorothy, gazing at the Crown Derby with relief. "Edward will be so pleased."

And it became difficult, therefore — because of Edward and Dorothy and because Miriam, after all, was Jeremy's mother — to refuse the bounty of the Swanfield fruit trees and greenhouses, dispatched in overflowing baskets as each luscious fruit or exotic bloom came into season; even more difficult to reject the almost apologetic little notes from Miriam which accompanied them, inviting her to tea, to eat strawberries and cream on the lawn, to play croquet or tennis, to "help me revive my poor little waltzing parties where you used to dance with Jeremy."

She had never waltzed at High Meadows, but she did so now with the very young men and somewhat neutered older ones Miriam considered suitable for Polly, making the easy, friendly, quite meaningless conversation with which she often defended herself, while Polly, in one of her own creations of gold-spangled orange satin, sulked by the piano, dissatisfied even with her own appearance, longing, now, for a dress that was no more than a slip of black net covered with jet beads like Claire's; for bobbed hair; a cigarette in an ivory holder; a negro jazz band from America; a lean, hard, *wicked* man to teach her the foxtrot and the tango.

"Claire, dear," murmured Miriam, "I wonder if I might have a word with you about Polly? Not here, dear — no, no, later and strictly between ourselves. She keeps asking me, you see, about her hair and her skirts — wanting to shorten both I'm afraid — quite drastically, and I am not at all sure how far one may decently go. So, if you could spare me a little half-hour, dear? Thursday, perhaps? At two o'clock? Or better still, come to lunch. I will send the car."

The car was sent, Polly continuing to sulk, Miriam to take the false and deliberately flustered view, "My dear, if you are so set on cutting your hair then I suppose *I* must be resigned to it. But what will Benedict say?"

"I don't care." But, caring or not, she certainly lacked the courage — as Miriam well knew — to take a pair of scissors to her golden head without her brother Benedict's consent, a state of affairs to which Claire, when it had called her at least half a dozen times more to High Meadows, attempted to put an end by tapping on Benedict's study door one morning and asking him.

"It seems that Polly wants to cut her hair."

"Yes. I know."

"Oh —" She had not in the least expected this. "Do you really? Then what do you think?"

"Am I obliged to *think* about it?"

"I suppose not. But she is getting quite agitated and — really — she just wants your opinion."

"I wonder," he said curtly, "why she should think me in any way qualified to give it."

Had he consented? Had he refused? Had he simply expressed a lack of interest so total that Polly might feel free to cut off her head, let alone her hair, so long as she did not annoy him with it? Claire, watching his blank dark eyes as they glanced at the clock, had not the least notion. But her own time was running short that morning, a Wednesday with Dorothy expecting her at Feathers, Nola requiring her help that afternoon to move her sculptor into his studio, Polly and Miriam waiting for her now in Polly's bedroom, the petty, time-greedy maneuverings of domestic life, the velvety, quite sticky chains which *must* be broken, so that she said quite sharply for her, "You wouldn't mind then?"

"What wouldn't I mind?"

"If Polly cuts her hair."

He smiled, not, she thought, particularly pleasantly.

"On an issue of such enormous importance perhaps she should do as her mother thinks best."

"He says you can," reported Claire falsely to an overwrought Polly.

"Did he really?" mused Miriam, knowing, or perhaps just hoping that he had said no such thing.

"Yes he did." Claire smiled, sweet, candid, looking as innocent, in her falsehood, as Miriam.

But the matter did not rest there. Polly's demand to be taken at once to a beauty parlor arousing a protest in Miriam that was as thoroughly overpowering as a barrier of eiderdown. A beauty parlor! Oh dear, no. My goodness. Neither Miriam nor her acquaintances had ever visited or ever intended to visit such an establishment, being perfectly agreed that, like certain other imports from America — the drinking of cocktails for instance and the use of lipstick — they ought not to be encouraged in good English society. Ladies had maids to do their hair. And if — as Polly insisted — no one at High Meadows was skilled in the entirely new art of cutting women's hair then Miriam really did not know how they were to manage.

"I'll go to a common barber," snarled Polly, mutinous, tearful.

"Claire . . . !" murmured Miriam feebly, closing her eyes. And, within moments, Claire found herself behind the Swanfield chauffeur on her way to town, returning with the obliging girl who cut her own hair, and then sat in exhausted frustration in Polly's bedroom while the deed was done, Miriam shedding sentimental tears at the loss of each long golden tress, Polly herself, who had expected her hair to lie flat and heavy and straight like Claire's, bursting into tears and hurling her hairbrush across the room in rage and panic when it became apparent that her own head would be a mass of curls.

"What have you done to me? What have you made me do?"

"What you asked for," said Miriam, producing her smelling bottle.

"It's lovely," said Claire, quickly ushering the startled hairdresser from the room.

"I'll just never dare go out again, that's all," sobbed Polly. "Never. I might just as well go and put my head in the gas oven right now — much the best place for it."

"Good Heavens," said Eunice Hartwell, coming unexpectedly through the door, her own long, pale hair uncoiling itself in wispy strands from an uncertain bun. "Polly — what have you done?"

"Get out," shrieked Polly, throwing yet another hairbrush across the floor at her sister. "Don't look at me. I've made myself plain, that's all — like you."

But, having contemplated those riotous golden curls for an hour or so from every angle, it occurred to her that their distinctly boyish look really did — as Claire had suggested — accentuate the undoubtedly feminine charm of the face and figure beneath, creating — on the whole — an impression that was piquant, original, above all *modern*.

"I know women who spend a fortune having their hair curled trying to look like that," said Claire, not from motives of kindness but simply to get away.

"It's very smart," said Eunice doubtfully. "Even too smart, I'd say."

"Oh dear," breathed Miriam. "I do hope no one could mistake her for a — what is that word they use — flapper?"

And thus encouraged, since to be called a flapper had long been the subject of her most cherished dreams, Polly fell promptly and head-over-heels in love with her new appearance, parading it for the rest of the day before an admiring chorus made up of housemaids, the garden boy and Eunice's obliging husband Toby who, very kindly, went through the performance of failing to recognize her. "*Who* is that stunning girl? It can't be Polly."

"The very same," she told him, sketching her little dancing curtsy, her elation lasting until she came face to face with Benedict who effectively, if perhaps unintentionally, quenched her ardor by the simple fact of not appearing to notice it.

"Benedict — I have cut my hair."

"Ah — then I assume that is why you have missed your piano lesson yet again?"

"Oh, Lord — *that!*"

"Yes, Polly. That. I have just come across Miss Peterson leaving by the back gate — having spent an hour waiting for you in the drawing room — and have sent her home in the car. And I am sorry to have to say to you once again, Polly, that if you feel obliged to cancel a lesson then it seems no more than common politeness to let your teacher know. I am surprised you should allow this to keep on happening, Miriam. The woman comes all the way from the other side of town by tram and, apart from her inconvenience, it seems nonsensical to keep on paying her for lessons Polly does not have."

"Oh Benedict, dear," smiled Miriam, "If you have sent Miss Peterson to Faxby in the car, how is Claire to get there? Poor Claire — you will just have to put up with us an hour longer."

And when the car returned, Miriam placed her gently inside it with a bouquet of freesias, a covered basket containing cinnamon buns and a large chocolate cake, and the information that she would see her on Sunday.

"Sunday?"

"Why yes, dear. We always dine together, absolutely all of us, on Sundays. And now that you've settled in you must be with us too. Family day, my husband always called it, and no leave of absence, no excuses. Such a *positive* man, my Aaron. They can eat where they like, he used to say, Monday to Saturday, when they're old enough. But one night a week they'll come home and eat at my table — since I pay their bills. Which was his way of saying, of course, how much it meant to him to see us united in affection — everyone — all together. My husband set great store by tradition — a nuisance sometimes, I do agree. But Benedict is so like him. And, as the new head of the family, he *does* insist upon it."

"I see."

"Yes dear."

And she knew she had been deliberately, almost caressingly reminded that Benedict was her paymaster too.

She attended the garden party held for Miriam's birthday in May, wearing a long, pale lilac garden party dress and a large hat with a floppy brim and a trailing, lilac chiffon scarf around the crown — an outfit of which even Edward approved — taking her turn at strolling around the garden arm in arm with Miriam who, in powder blue lace and pearls, was at her radiant best. The sun was shining, the massive hedge of rhododendrons had flowered overnight, in tribute to the occasion, with a glorious display of deep red, deep purple, lilac and white. The cherry orchard beyond it had been transformed, by the warm weather, into a fragrant cloud of pink blossom. There were bluebells raising their delicate heads beneath the wide arms of the chestnut trees, girls in pale dresses gliding like swans across the lawn and young men — *very* young, most of them — in flannels and blazers and public school ties reminding Miriam so forcefully of Jeremy that she was obliged, for a vulnerable moment to lean rather heavily on Claire's arm, regaining her equilibrium only when the raucous presence of Eunice's four sturdy sons and Benedict's two physically more fragile but uncomfortably correct young gentlemen — home from school for "grandmamma's party" — brought to her notice the more awkward realities of boyhood.

"Do go and *play*, children," she said quite nervously to Benedict's serious, silent boys, a suggestion she had no need to make to her four Hartwell grandchildren who, from the moment of their arrival, had been knocking one another to the ground and scuffling like boisterous puppies, ruining, in the first five minutes, the expensive new shoes and jackets Eunice had bought — but probably not yet paid for — from Taylor & Timms.

"Eunice dear, do you think — for just a little while — that they could be induced to keep their voices down?"

"They're only children, mother — boys, after all."

"Eunice dear — Justin is fifteen and Simon twelve — *big* boys, you know."

"Mother! They're only having fun. It's only *natural*." And Eunice flushed and glared hotly at Benedict's two immaculate, almost motionless sons who did not seem natural to her in the least.

There were little tables with organdy cloths set out on the lawn, beneath the trees, or simply dotted here and there about the rose garden. There was champagne, a heart-shaped birthday cake iced in Miriam's favorite sugar pink, cream ices, water ices, mountains of vivid confectionery, the string quartet from Feathers' Teashop playing in the trellised arbor by the goldfish pond. There were presents for Miriam, each one of her Hartwell grandchildren being dragged up to her in turn by Eunice, clutching a gift which Eunice had spent anxious weeks choosing, awkward hours packaging; Benedict's children performing the same office as correctly as little soldiers on parade, bowing gracefully and presenting parcels which had been wrapped by Taylor & Timms at Nola's laconic request, and which contained whatever the manager of that obliging store had thought appropriate. And — in accordance with Miriam and Aaron Swanfield's time-honored custom — there were also gifts for everyone else, the day ending with a vast treasure hunt all over the house and grounds, in pursuit of the brightly colored little boxes of treasure which Miriam had carefully labeled and hidden away for every guest.

"How exceedingly generous," said Edward Lyall in Miriam's hearing, knowing there would be a box of cigars somewhere with his name on it.

"What fun," said Nola sourly, having not the least intention of rummaging through redcurrant bushes or crawling underneath the dining room furniture for the sake of the silk scarf or the powder compact she would be likely to find.

"What *fun*," said Polly, devoutly meaning it, being ready to scale Everest should there be the chance of a surprise parcel at the summit.

"How lovely mother looks," said Eunice, needing an ally, since she would be unable to conceal from Benedict for much longer that her fifteen-year-old Justin had — fortunately without damage to himself — inflicted considerable and costly injury on a neighbor's property while borrowing "*naturally* without permission," Toby's car. Nor would she be able to explain to him, since she did not fully understand it herself, why Toby had seen fit to exchange the only slightly scratched and almost brand new car for a much more expensive model.

"Boys will be boys," she kept on muttering to herself, her glance straying, despite her goodwill and her better judgement, to Benedict and Nola's children who appeared to have spent the afternoon drawing out chairs for old ladies, behaving like perfectly functioning little machines who would grow into big, powerful machines, like Benedict, or would malfunction restlessly, maliciously, like Nola. Her children, at least — if a little out of hand — were *natural.*

"Come on lads. What about a scout round the hayloft," said Toby, sounding hearty, feeling resigned, having no greater inclination for party games than Nola but well aware of the need to distract his own four rumbustious boys from their proposed schemes of ducking one or other of their cousins in the fishpond.

"Happy hunting," cried Miriam, blowing kisses to spur them on and waving her tiny, sparkling hand.

"What a wonderful woman," said Edward.

"Tally ho," shrieked Polly, bounding away like a greyhound off the leash, followed by a crowd of eager, awkward youths and one exceedingly optimistic old man.

"Excuse me," said Nola, "I have a headache coming on."

Nothing at all — although one knew he *must* be there — had been seen of Benedict.

"My dear," called Miriam, beckoning to Claire, "come and keep me company. There's no need for you to go hunting. I have your gift ready."

And with an affectionate hand she gave Claire an antique gold and enamel locket which held the photograph of a handsome, unknown child and a lock of baby-fine, baby-blond hair which she understood, with alarm, had been Jeremy's.

"Wear it on Sunday dear at dinner, with your pretty red dress."

She doubted if she could ever bring herself to wear it at all. The chain burned her skin as Miriam fastened it fondly but firmly around her neck, telling her — as she had feared — that the locket had been Jeremy's birthday gift to his mother, long ago on a warm May afternoon just like this, paid for with the whole of his first schoolboy allowance, the photograph taken on a furtive trip to Leeds for which she, suspecting him of mischief, had punished him.

"And he just stood there and took the blame for something he hadn't done because he knew how much I loved my little surprises and he didn't want to spoil it for me. What a good heart he had."

"Yes." Claire knew no reason to doubt his goodness. Quite simply with sorrow and guilt and a familiar sense of futility, she could not remember it.

"And such a sparkle. Such a sense of fun and folly — like me, I fear."

She could not remember that either.

Returning to Mannheim Crescent she bolted her door, took off the locket and shut it hastily away in a drawer where, once out of her sight, it became a voice whispering to her all through the night to be let out, set free, *remembered*, so that her dreams were threaded once again with that terrible line of blinded men, shuffling toward the horrific, crucified presence she knew, without looking or daring to look, must be Jeremy. And even when terror jerked her awake and she lay in the heavy dark — clammy and weak with gratitude that the dream was over — she was so painfully conscious of the baby-fine hair in the drawer at her bedside that she had to get up and take it away into the other room before daring to sleep again.

Yet there were days when she succeeded in holding herself aloof from all Swanfield and Lyall intrusions, in the manner of a cat who can be seen and even touched but remains, nevertheless, quite separate. She had not yet begun to think about happiness. It was too soon for that and, in any case, she did not yet require it. She had already experienced great joy, albeit in difficult conditions, and although she had lost the source of it she did not believe that she had lost the capacity. Eventually it would revive. Already — and it did not trouble her to admit it — her sensuality was no longer stunned and dormant but stirring once more with curiosity, the sound, healthy impulses of a perfectly functioning female body which might hurry her — perhaps before her heart was ready — to take a lover.

But for the time being, and once again in cat-like fashion, physical sensations of a lesser nature contented her. After four years of personal discomfort, of cold water or contaminated water or no water at all, of cold feet, blistered hands, damp mattresses, dysentery, fleas, it was luxury enough to be warm and clean. After four years of personal danger it was a blessed relief to be safe. After four years of overcrowded huts, communal eating and bathing and breathing she was rich now in the possession of a door to lock, space in which she could move unquestioned and unobserved. After four years of belonging, by her own choice, to any man who cried out in pain, she was content now — for a little while —to drift, to evade, to rest on life's surface until, strengthened by solitude, she might equip herself to choose a new purpose. And until then, Mannheim Crescent with its motley population of drifters, evaders, solitaries, its prevailing winds of aimlessness and disillusion, seemed her rightful home.

There were rainy mornings when she did not get up at all, mornings of sunshine and warm breezes when, wrapped in a kimono which had seen better days, its embroidered dragons fraying at their seams, its gold threads coming loose, she would go out into the little walled garden, barefoot, her hair undone, and drink her breakfast coffee on a stone seat beneath the plum tree, smoking and reading, basking in the rich, sweet idleness of making no plans, journeying only from one moment to the next, a spectacle of Bohemian disarray which would have appalled her mother. She watched the plum blossoms open their eyes; absorbed through her skin, the fragrances of damp, growing green, of bluebells and dandelions standing companionably together, of ferns uncurling themselves in the sun. She listened to the rustling of leaves and grass, the movements and voices of birds and, every now and then, the notes of a hesitant piano from two floors above where a fragile spinster taught a limited repertoire of Strauss waltzes and Beethoven's *Für Elise*.

She took long walks in the rain, not always intentionally but because rain was a feature of Faxby she well remembered, fine, almost feathery rain in the summertime, drenching, stinging downpours at other seasons, a hint of it usually hovering somewhere above the hills by which the town was entirely surrounded, a clouded hollow, its cobbled streets gleaming with damp, curls of mist falling low, most spring evenings, to blend with the stridently swirling factory smoke. And when she had walked enough she lay in her green chintz armchair, her wet hair wrapped in a towel, put on her disgraceful scarlet and gold kimono and sometimes, but only vaguely, wondered about the future.

She had been educated, expensively and traditionally, not to work but to be married, not to earn a living but to provide domestic comfort and entertainment for the man who supported her. She had been taught not to cook but rather to select a well-balanced menu, to decorate a table with flowers and mosses and napkins twisted to look like swans. She could play the piano, speak French, write a well-worded letter to cover any of the eventualities her schoolmistresses — ladies of a gentler, pre-war era — had thought likely to come her way. Until Paul's death, she had given little, if any, serious thought to a career. She had planned only to be with him, to support him in any venture *he* might choose to undertake, to nurture *his* ambitions, which represented no great sacrifice since she had none of her own. And although she did not discount the possibility that she might marry again — in fact she rather hoped she would — she did not expect it to be soon, could no longer guarantee that it would be forever. The values of her girlhood had been swept away, she fully understood that, and, unlike Miriam and her mother, she had no inclination to cling to their wreckage. She was a "new woman" who, having rushed headlong to France, had acquired none of the new skills acquired by the regiment of women who had eagerly taken men's places when conscription had emptied the country of its able-bodied men. She had never learned to type or keep accounts and was consumed by no great fires to learn. She could, of course, dress wounds, bathe eyes, administer medicines, but since she desired most urgently never to enter a hospital ward again, what now?

"You're not much of a housewife are you," Euan Ash told her, watching her as, with complete unconcern, she swept up the broken remains of a Crown Derby saucer.

"No. So don't expect me to clear up your mess. I have more than enough with my own."

"Ah yes," he said, giving her his smile of impudent, decadent sweetness. "You're going to be awkward. I thought as much. But don't worry. We can get Kit Hardie to come over with his dustpan from the Crown, or send one of his minions. Not that I need much in the way of creature comforts myself, I'm sure."

She had seen his flat by now, just one small, square room leading to an old-fashioned, ramshackle conservatory, the room itself virtually empty except for a narrow bed covered with a gray blanket, two kitchen chairs, a heap of cushions thrown down in a corner; the conservatory cluttered with the messy apparatus of art, a huge work-table invisible beneath its burden of sketches finished, abandoned, just begun, canvases standing face to the wall in rows like naughty children, paints, brushes, pallet knives, tins and jars of varnish and turpentine, oily rags, dirty rags, piles of shabby periodicals and books, a cracked, vaguely oriental vase at least three feet high left behind by the previous tenant and which it had not occurred to him to throw away.

"What chaos you live in."

"Dear child — my natural habitat."

Yet his shared tenancy of the kitchen caused her no alarms, making itself felt mainly in the empty whiskey bottles he left on the table for her to throw away and, three or four mornings a week, the presence of a girl — scantily clad and rarely the same one twice — brewing his coffee, scrambling his eggs, washing out his shirts and socks in the shallow, stone sink.

"He has the morals of an alley cat," said Nola loudly in his hearing, having spotted one of these obliging, somewhat disheveled young ladies scurrying off through the garden gate at eleven o'clock in the morning. And with his deadly smile, he quite affably agreed.

"What's wrong with the alley cat? He makes love whenever he gets the chance because it just might be his last. So do I. What do you do with your life, Nola?"

She was sitting at the cheap lodging-house kitchen table, draped in her fox furs, a new double pelt this time joined by the front paws, two pointed foxes' heads hanging down her back, two sumptuous, russet bodies falling to her waist in front, two empty russet legs dangling, a cloche hat with a feather covering her ears, several strings of amber beads, several more of gold cascading to her elegantly crossed knees. She was rouged, perfumed, expensive, a cigarette holder with a jeweled monogram clutched in one nervous hand, a crocodile skin bag with a gold clasp in the other.

"What *do* you do, Nola?"

"Bastard," she said tonelessly and snapping open her bag, taking out her gloves, she got up and walked away.

"That was unkind," said Claire.

"Yes, I know. I'm not really a bastard either. Not in the eyes of the law, at any rate."

"We never supposed you were."

"What am I then, lovely Claire?"

"Oh — a young gentleman of good family, I think, with a private income so that you can afford to dress like a gypsy and do odd jobs at the Crown without losing face — or caste. Is that what you are?"

"More or less. A very small private income though — probably a lot less than yours. Just keeping-body-and-soul-together money really."

"Enough to let you waste your expensive education."

"If you like. What else?"

"How should I know?"

But she knew very well and incautiously she rushed on. "I expect your mother breeds pedigree puppies and organizes the hunt ball and everybody's morals and wins all the prizes at the local flower show. And your father will be a clergyman — the fashionable kind who understands good claret."

Without being aware of her danger until it was far too late she had described Paul's parents, Paul's background, exactly as he had once described them to her. And now, to complete her self-betrayal she realized with horror and with considerable surprise that her eyes had not only filled with tears but had let loose a whole fountain of them to pour, in embarrassing profusion, down her cheeks.

"Oh *shit!*" she said, flatly, distinctly, and he laughed with open, genuine delight.

"Well done, Nurse Swanfield. Spoken like a true VAD. Well — a fellow's supposed to have a clean handkerchief at times like these, I do know that. But I'm not sure I can manage it. Oh yes — here we are. I think it's Kit's but never mind."

And he dried her eyes deftly, with good humor, apparently accustomed to women's tears and disinclined to take them too seriously, his artist's eye, she rather suspected, far more concerned with the physical mechanics of weeping, the exact working of the muscles and the blotching of the skin and how to portray them on canvas than with the causes of her distress.

"I'm sorry," she said.

"So am I — I can't tell you. I rather thought I might have a chance of making love to you quite soon. But perhaps it won't be *quite* soon if I remind you so much of somebody else. I suppose that *is* the trouble?"

"Yes."

"And I also suppose — taking into account the time span and all that — *not* your husband."

"No. Not my husband."

"Fair enough. But it's a pity, though. I was looking forward to you, Claire."

"You make love to so many women, Euan."

He grinned, boyish suddenly rather than malicious.

"I know. It's just about *all* I do at the moment with any degree of concentration — and a certain amount of success. I wonder if it's the nearest I can get to not killing? Just about the exact opposite, I rather think."

"Do you? It seems a little — indiscriminate."

"So is killing — the kind I've done, at any rate."

"Don't tell me."

"You must know that I wouldn't dream of it."

She nodded and, leaning forward just a little, gave him the honest, open smile of a friend.

"I know. But the real opposite to killing would be to get all those girls pregnant. And I'm sure you wouldn't care to do that."

"Dear God —" he said, looking startled and then very much amused. "I hope you realize that you may, just possibly, have put an end to my virility. Because fatherhood . . . !" He shuddered. "No. Oh no, not that, I'd have to run, of course. Much kinder."

"Oh well — a convenient point of view, and *not* original. And, speaking of originality, is Nola right when she says your pictures are no good?"

"Come and see."

She went with him into the bare room, the cluttered studio and knelt on a lumpy, hessian-covered cushion while he uncovered the canvases stacked against the wall. She had already seen his sketches of Faxby's alleyways and the patches of littered wasteland in between where Faxby's youth, unable to afford the comfort of a cinema or a bar parlor, met to preen themselves before one another on Saturday nights. She had seen the satirical, sometimes spitefully accurate portraits he dashed off in the taproom of the "Rock and Heifer" just behind Mannheim Crescent, and sold across the bar for a shilling each. But she had avoided his real work, fearing — she suddenly realized — to see the distorted death of the trenches, to discover that the line of blinded groping soldiers which so sickeningly haunted her had somehow shuffled out of her nightmare straight onto Euan's canvas. But instead, to her infinite relief, her intense surprise, she saw first a leaf and then the petals of a flower painted with a botanist's exactness, a woodland world of small, wild blossoms and spiky grasses, water dimpled by rain, flat many-shaded pebbles, the life of the hedgerow, the river bank, the ploughed furrow as experienced and observed by a grasshopper, a speckled, self-important thrush, a bee lavishly exploring the universe of a foxglove, a cowslip, a cornflower.

It was the English pastoral of childhood storybooks, the small furry creatures, the muted colors, the mild weather, with the extra and startling ingredient of reality, the knowledge of the human rifle leveled at the happily burrowing rabbit, the mass-produced boot crushing the primrose, the natural cycle of birth and death, necessity and renewal — which was cruel enough — disrupted by the blundering presence of man.

It was beautiful and painful. Perhaps the blind soldiers would have been easier to bear.

"I don't know enough to judge," she said quickly; and kneeling beside her, his body composed of lean, hollow curves and brittle angles, he studied the canvases, his head on one side.

"Oh — I think 'mediocre' ought to describe it. As an artist I might just make a living painting pretty pictures of not so pretty women — if I cared that much about making a living."

They were kneeling close together and with no more than a slight inclination of his head, he kissed her, no other part of his body touching her except a cool mouth, a swiftly darting tongue, his presence light, elusive, uncertain even at this proximity; the man who, without appearing to resist, had slipped through Nola's possessive hands like water and who held Claire to him now not by the arousal of her sensuality but by a fragile shadow of the years they had unknowingly shared.

"Don't be alarmed," he said easily, amiably, "I don't want any kind of commitment that might expect me to look beyond tomorrow morning."

She got up smiling, easy and amiable herself.

"I'm not alarmed. I just don't want any complications. And you're complex, Euan."

"Lord no — not a bit of it. Just a straightforward sort of chap. I'm faithless, of course — or so I've been told — but I do give fair warning in advance. I can only offer what I have in me, you know, which isn't much and doesn't last, but if it fills the present need or the present pleasure then it's better than nothing, I reckon. And if it happens to be alive and kicking tomorrow — then that's a bonus — wouldn't you think? I'm just passing through, after all. I make no secret of it."

"Where *are* you going Euan?"

He grinned and got to his feet, tall but far too thin, too fine-drawn to offer any kind of physical menace.

"I'm on my way to Edinburgh — didn't I mention it? — to see a friend. Although whether or not I get there will depend on many things. The weather, for instance. If we have a good summer I may find myself in Scarborough or Whitby doing pencil sketches at sixpence a time on the beach. And even if it rains I might not get beyond Carlisle. No point in rushing things. Come with me, if you like. Traveling together might be fun. Not as lovers, of course — that's far too heavy. Just friends who happen to share a bed. Friendship doesn't scare me."

Was he going to see a girl? A wife? How long, she wondered, would it have taken Paul to return to Gwendoline, or Jeremy to her, had fate so decreed? And even should there be no wife, no unknown child, no tag-ends of half-remembered promises, how long did it really take — having learned without too much difficulty to obey the commands "Charge," "Fire," "Kill" — to adapt, with like obedience to the new orders of the day "Return to normal," "Settle down," "Be as you were," "Live"?

No one could tell her that.

Forever, she rather imagined. And there was nothing to do, therefore, but make the best of it.

"I don't travel well, Euan," she told him smiling, and returning to the kitchen she rinsed out her coffee cup, put on her hat and, looking poised, slender, admirably but far from totally self-assured in her gray *foulard* dress with its white lawn collar, her white silk stockings and high-heeled gray shoes, she went over to the Crown Hotel to drink a glass of early afternoon *Chablis* with Kit Hardie and give him her answer to a proposition he had recently made her.

6

SHE found him in the nearly completed lobby contemplating with sardonic eye a block of marble four feet square which — when one had looked closely and pondered at leisure — assumed the form of a pregnant, triple-breasted, faceless woman.

"Nola sent that," said Claire in high glee.

"She did."

"And you'll have to pay for it, I suppose?"

"I will — with her Cousin Arnold Crozier's money."

"Do you have any choice?"

"Not much. Only where to put it."

"The ladies' powder room, I should think — as a dire warning."

"Well yes — if you think any woman would really believe *that* could happen to her."

"Never mind, Kit. Sculpture may not last. Pastoral art — and Euan — didn't."

His tanned face crinkled with humor.

"Neither did I."

And he saw no reason to pretend a heartbreak he was far from feeling now that Nola, with the advent of Sculpture into her life, had tired of him as a lover. Good luck to her. Initially — and he was able to laugh at his own reaction — he had been flattered by her attentions, the wife of Benedict Swanfield of High Meadows meaning more to him in terms of conquest than the wives of other distinguished but unknown gentlemen who, in the frenzy of wartime London, had fallen eager victims to the cut of his uniform and his medals. He had known exactly what such women wanted and had supplied it. But Nola, stalking him through a weekend leave which he had promised to someone else, had carried things a stage further.

"I know what *you* want," she had told him. "Let me help you." And at once, in a fine flair of ardor, she had set about championing his cause, extolling him, presenting him, marketing him almost, until she had wrung from her less than enthusiastic Crozier cousins the promise of the Crown Hotel. Cousin Bernard had wished to knock the property down and build an arcade of shops. Cousin Arnold had considered converting it into flats.

"Stop," cried Nola. "I have found this wonderful man . . ." And Kit had been impressed by her, entertained by her. He had rather liked her too. During his service at High Meadows, knowing more about each member of the family than they knew about one another, he had watched the mad risks she took with her reputation, the punishment of fatigue and alcohol and nicotine she inflicted so casually on the long, supple body he had seen displayed in the lamplight of High Meadows a hundred times and never desired it. And on the night when she had first offered that body to him, throwing it down on his narrow hotel bed like a challenge, it had not been desire so much as status, not the thought of Nola herself but of her aloof, austere husband which had mattered. Kit Hardie had served nobler and wealthier families than the Swanfields. There had been a baronet, a Member of Parliament, a bishop, a transatlantic millionaire and, in the time-honored, only-to-be-expected fashion of servants he had cheated every one of them every now and again, cheerfully, scornfully, not thinking too much about it. Only in Benedict Swanfield, middle-class industrialist just two generations away from a factory floor, had he recognized real authority and, although he had neither feared him nor liked him, he had cheated him in nothing, until the seduction of his wife. Mrs. Benedict. A symbol of what? His leap over the barriers of class? His triumph over origins which, while troubling others far more than they had troubled him, had never operated to his advantage? But, very soon, she had become just Nola, turbulent, impossibly generous, impossibly wrong-headed, exciting and exasperating him both together. Colossal alike in her blunders and her good intentions. A good pal sometimes. A damned nuisance at others. Not lovable, of course, for love had had no part of it. But, just the same, he wished her well.

And he would not forget the doors her erratic hand had opened for him. Arnold Crozier's counting house. The Crown. Claire?

Like Euan Ash, Kit had enlisted in the summer of 1914, but for different reasons. Euan, he more than supposed, had gone out to France an idealist and a patriot, in search of that mystical, malicious Holy Grail which like so much else had drowned in the Flanders mud, disappeared in a cloud of poisoned gas; or — as Kit could have told him — had never existed at all. For Kit, although as prone to bullet and shrapnel wounds, frost-bite and rat-bite as any gentleman, had never suffered — having no ideals to lose — from disillusion. And what had mattered to him in the trenches was not the why and wherefore, the rhyme or reason — since he knew there would not be much of that — but the single process of staying alive.

He was the son of a hard-wearing Northumbrian woman, sixteen at most she'd been, he suspected, at his birth, possibly less, who had risen from kitchen maid to cook in the household of a coal-owning baronet. While as to his father, he had soon learned not to ask too many questions about that. A predatory young squire on the spree, he'd liked to think in his youth, although, on mature reflection, he was bound to admit — with a decided twinkle in his eye — that it could just as easily have been the butler. His mother had named no names, carried no grudges, and although it had never worried him, it may have been responsible — as a certain London lady had once pointed out to him — for his casual, cheerful attitude to sexual infidelity. Very likely. He had never analyzed it beyond the plain facts that in a world where menservants could expect to lose their jobs if they married and maidservants were not famous for keeping either their virtue or their heads, an enterprising fellow did the best he could.

"You have no morals," his London lady friend, the one before Nola, had told him. But he had always believed in giving good measure, paying the price when it was due, carrying his share — without complaint — of the corn. And whenever opportunities came his way he had not only seized them with both hands but had followed them through, progressing through the domestic hierarchy of under-footman to footman, under-butler to butler, not only by his shrewdness and deftness, private toughness and public charm, the ruthlessness of purpose to guard his own back and seek out the weak spots in others, but a simple understanding of consistent hard work.

And although — *of course* — a servant could never be a gentleman, he had learned, early on, that with a certain amount of good luck and a great deal of good management, he could contrive to live like one. And, without any false modesty, Kit knew of no better manager than himself. He had acquired his easy, open-air manner by loading the rifles of an employer's sporting guests. But when the shoot was over, the gentlemen in their baths, he had taken the pick of the grouse or the partridge for himself and had it cooked to the complicated recipes of a

French chef. He had gained his understanding of vintage port and claret from the painstaking process of decanting it for other men while taking what *he* considered to be his due, and had nurtured his palate since boyhood on anything his quick mind, his keen eyes and ears, had discovered to be fine or rare. He had learned about clothes from the wardrobes of men and women who, in that leisured pre-war time, had changed at least four times every day, and in his off-duty hours, had worn his own suits and overcoats — few but of excellent quality — with more dash and swagger than any of them.

He was not greedy. Not for food and wine, at any rate. Discriminating, rather. An expert in his own field. Damned good at his job. Did he enjoy it? Up to a year, perhaps two, before the war he'd been too busy — achieving it, staying there — to wonder. Certainly he'd always felt a step or two above his circumstances. And certainly — most certainly — he'd felt his employers to be more than a few steps below theirs. Except Benedict Swanfield of course. But wasn't that simply the way of a world where rich men were usually pompous, rarely handsome, their sons lacking in spirit or physique or just bone idle, their daughters vacant or giddy, their wives self-important or self-righteous? Or horribly frustrated?

He understood that. He had used it often enough to gain his rapid promotions. But having gained them easily, at a younger age than even he had anticipated, he had found himself plagued by a new, exceedingly persistent question. What next? *Now* that he had achieved expertise, experience, security, an adequate income except for the months when boredom lured him to the racetrack or the poker table, what else? And it had irked him consciously, sharply, to have his choice limited so severely by the class structure which, in the summer of 1914, no one had seemed seriously to question.

"Hardie dear, I shall expect you to stay with me for ever," Miriam had told him, sensing his restlessness and assuming it to be financial.

And there had been a woman that year, as there had always been a woman, the young widow of a local grocer who needed a capable man both to satisfy her colorful temperament and to run her business.

Either way had been open.

"Thank you, madam," he had told Miriam warmly when she had increased his salary.

"You're not going to leave me then, Hardie?"

"No, madam."

He had made the same promise that night to the eager black-eyed young widow and then, the next morning, on his way back to High

Meadows where blue-eyed Miriam just as eagerly awaited him, he had passed the recruiting office and enlisted. To Hell with it. And when both women had complained he had put his tongue in his cheek and called it patriotism.

"I'm just doing my duty, madam." An impulse he had instantly regretted on seeing the muddle of the training camps, the even greater confusion of the battle lines in France. During his first weeks in the trenches he had not had the least idea what he was supposed to be doing there. Nor what anybody else was supposed to be doing. Nor had he found anyone to tell him.

"You're doing your duty, lad."

His Captain had been nineteen years old, a boy from Harrow, surrounded by teenage lieutenants whose previous commands had been as prefects at a similar school. His Colonel had been a veteran of twenty-five, a graduate in philosophy, with a landed fortune, an inherited seat at Westminster, a whimsical disposition.

Duty, daring, *muddle* had killed them all by the month-end, and so many tommies with them that Kit had found himself one of the longest-serving soldiers in the Company. A good, steady chap, they were already saying. Calm under fire. Clean in barracks. The salt of the earth.

He had expected little in the way of medals or promotion. Officers, after all, were required to be gentlemen and one needed titled relatives for that or, at the very least, a private income to support all the things expected of an officer, the polo ponies and hunters and the ready money to treat one's brother officers properly in the mess. But in that winter of 1914 no one had really anticipated the extent of the carnage and although a common man had always remained *very* common in the armed forces of his or her Britannic Majesty, once those brave and brilliant captains and colonels lay dead in their hasty graves, a month or two, sometimes only a day or two after their promotion, who was left to take their place?

Kit Hardie had been among the first of his social background to be commissioned, created in the current phrase "a temporary gentleman," although he had always felt so at heart. And returning to London on leave as a Lieutenant, a Captain, a Major, his manners more perfect, his understanding of the social niceties more exact than many a gentleman born and bred, he had found all barriers of class and conditioning swept aside. Before the war there had been rich men and poor men, men who were noble and men who were common. But now, in this strange, uneasy year of 1919 there were men who had fought and those who had not. And Kit had seen the sense, on his discharge, of taking full advantage

of his glory while it lasted, of wringing as much as he could out of it —
and he intended it to be a great deal — before medals became unfash-
ionable and retired majors a bad joke.

The war, instead of killing him as it had killed Jeremy Swanfield or
scarring him as it had scarred Euan Ash, had been good to him. And
he saw no reason to spoil his present advantage by being ashamed of it.
The fact existed. He had not enjoyed the slaughter. He had killed when
necessary to prevent another man, who probably did not enjoy the slaughter either, from killing him. And having made up his mind to it he had
refused — as yet another tool of survival — to brood, so that he had
not been plagued and weakened by nightmares, nor haunted by the faces
of dead men at his window, as others had been. As Euan, he supposed,
still was. And, for all these reasons, he was and would remain grateful
to Nola for persuading her cousins to give him the chance and the
challenge of reviving the Crown Hotel.

Grateful. But not unreasonably so. Not to such a degree that he
could allow it to obscure his judgment or in any way alter his plans. Kit
Hardie wanted many things, status not least among them, and he intended the Crown to be his creation, *his* testing ground, not Nola's. And
their differences of opinion, although amicable and even exciting to
Nola while her infatuation was at its height, had proved impossible to
reconcile.

She had wanted the decor to be *modern*, plain walls, bare floors,
zigzags of black and white, the faint decadence of tiger skin rugs, wine-
glasses with transparent girls for stems, "amusing" little jugs and teapots
which poured out their contents from unusual apertures. He had given
her fringed cushions, soft pastel colors, the conventional elegance of the
gold-rimmed china and cut crystal she was forced to endure in Miriam's
cozy, pretty, *dreary* — "Don't you see that, Kit? *Damnably* dreary?" —
drawing room.

"Of course," he told her pleasantly. "And with good reason."

"What possible reason?"

"Because people like it."

"Oh — *people!*"

"Yes — since it's people who pay the bills. The ones who live at
High Meadows or somewhere like it, will feel comfortable here. And as
for the rest, I think you'll find, Nola darling, that most people who *don't*
live at High Meadows really rather wish they did. So they'll like it
here too."

"Philistine," she had accused him, still rather fondly, having not yet
lost her fascination for his skill and stamina as a lover, his unashamed
appetites and ambitions, the slight coarseness just beneath his charm

and polish which had caused him, once or twice, to treat her as she rather imagined a chambermaid might be treated: an experience she had found quite delightful. Yet there was no doubt that her desire for him was, in the end, greatly weakened by his taste in interior design.

She had expected — at the very least — that he would lower the shabby, shaky ceilings and cover up their impossibly baroque encrustations of plaster fruit and flowers with something flat and smooth and shiny; that he would throw out the dusty old chandeliers and illuminate his rooms with steel wall brackets of Art Nouveau pomegranates and lilies. Instead he had dismantled the chandeliers with his own hands and polished each crystal droplet until it gleamed, had cleaned and repaired every inch of plaster and sent Euan Ash up aloft to restore — for another crate of whiskey — the painstaking work of Regency craftsmen, re-creating rich squares of azure blue and old rose, garlands of acanthus leaves and flowers shading from the faintest pastel pink to crimson, each petal delicately, and perhaps miraculously — when one considered how rapidly the contents of those whiskey bottles went down — picked out in gold.

"Kit Hardie," said Nola, "you are a *conventional* man."

"Have I ever denied it?"

She had never thought to ask. She had simply assumed, planned, *needed* him to be different. She had wanted — what? As usual — of course — she had no idea, except that it was not this. She had seen the Crown as an experiment, an adventure, another snap of the fingers in the face of convention and authority. Futile, perhaps, in the long term, but exhilarating — *fun* — while the protest endured. To him it was a serious business, designed to suit neither his personal pleasure nor hers, but simply to succeed. And suddenly her nights and days with him, their present conversation, acquired a familiar, final ring.

"Oh well —" she said, shrugging her double fox pelt around her shoulders, adjusting her feathered Sherwood Forest hat. "You'll do all right with it, Kit, I'm sure."

"I'll do my damnedest, Nola."

She believed him and for a moment it crossed her mind to wonder how it might feel to desire something so bluntly, with such singleness of purpose; to be herself so desired. Might *that* not be the answer? But a few days later Sculpture had entered her life in the form of an intense, self-possessed young man from Leeds who offered a challenge she could more easily recognize. A great talent — not hers — for her to nurture. A studio to be found in Faxby or as near to it as possible so that the Genius and his Muse could be more easily together. An exhibition to arrange. Her Crozier cousins to be convinced of the soundness of investing in oddly interlaced twists of stone and metal, heads without eyes and a double helping of noses, apparently untouched blocks of marble or clay with grandiose titles. "Suffering." "Humanity." "Peace."

"Good luck," said Kit Hardie over the bottle of champagne they both believed appropriate to such occasions.

"That's noble of you, Kit."

And they had remained on easy, mainly friendly terms.

The Crown, therefore, just a week or so from its reopening had become entirely his own. A hundred years of grime had been removed from the exterior, a procedure considered by Faxby in general to be extravagant if not downright foolish since it was well known that the smoke from Faxby's mill chimneys could be relied on to blacken anything within a twelvemonth. The woodwork had been painted white, a matter for hilarity in Faxby although no one could deny how well it looked against the newly cleaned, mellow, light brown stone, and a bold new sign erected, bearing a massive golden crown with a white ground.

"First impressions *count*," declared Kit Hardie, sounding calm and cheerful although he was well aware that only a rapid accumulation of banknotes would impress the Croziers. The lobby, therefore, was aqua-marine and gold, and full of flowers. The main lounge with its mag-nificent baroque ceiling, had dusky pink walls, a rose-patterned carpet, wide-bottomed armchairs in floral chintz and pink velvet, a clutter — according to Nola — of plants and potted ferns, bric-à-brac of the nymph and shepherd variety, a great many portraits in oval frames of swan-necked Regency ladies displaying their bracelets, their cashmere shawls, their bare bosoms. Each chair had beside it a little table ready to hold a glass, an ashtray, a coffee pot. There were cushions and footstools and reading lamps, a writing desk fully equipped at all times with pens, ink, and paper. There was a map table, arranged in a good light by the window with sporting and fashion magazines and newspapers of adequate variety which would be ironed throughout the day whenever — to Kit's eagle eye — they appeared crumpled.

"It is the little things," Kit said, "that make the difference."

The dining room was starched white linen, Wedgwood blue walls, an Adam ceiling and, being connected by double doors to a room of equal proportions could easily be used as a banqueting hall or a suitable setting for the wedding receptions and dinner dances which, with house-maids not only in short supply but making strange mutterings about "regular hours" and "overtime," could no longer so easily be held at home.

There was also a second restaurant, smaller, darker, far more intimate than the first, the tables set very far apart in little alcoves where would be served the masterpieces of Aristide Keller, the thin, morose Belgian who, with his almost mute and skeletal wife, Amandine, was now installed in the superbly equipped kitchen, keeping a sharp, neurotic eye on his recipes which he believed the kitchen maids were conspiring to steal, and making sudden demands for more, or better, or simply different implements, which were always met.

"It pays handsomely," Kit Hardie told Claire, "to look after the staff."

And, without knowing quite how it had happened — whether he had put the idea into her head or she had thought of it herself — she had agreed to accompany Amandine Keller, who spoke only French, on a dozen shopping expeditions to equip the cottage which Kit had provided for them in a quiet street not far from the hotel; Madame Keller exhibiting a far more capricious side to her nature than Claire had expected.

"I must have sage green table linen," she said, the *only* shade, Claire noticed, to be unavailable in the drapery department at Faxby's Taylor & Timms. Bradford had no sage green tablecloths either; a journey to Leeds on a sultry, sticky day producing the right shade but not the right texture; Keighley, which had both, affording Claire a temporary relief, soon shattered when Madame Keller rejected the merchandise with a scornful gesture at its narrow, light brown border.

"*Plain* sage green," she said.

"Try Manchester," suggested Kit.

"Is she worth it?"

"Oh yes — because nobody else will go to so much trouble for her. And when her husband throws a tantrum one night and decides to walk out on me perhaps she'll remember it."

The trip to Manchester was duly made, the sage green linen — "not *exactly* what one had in mind. But, *enfin*, one should not be unreasonable. It will do" — duly purchased; Amandine Keller returning to Faxby as perky and voracious as a little bird, Claire in a daze of exhaustion finely balanced between laughter and tears.

"Why am I punishing myself like this?" she groaned, kicking off her shoes and sinking into the armchair beside Kit's desk.

"Because I ask you," he would have liked to say, knowing it was true. But not quite in the way he wanted. Not yet. No more than an act of friendship at present which she would have performed for many others. He was well aware of that. For Euan Ash, for instance. For anyone who touched her sympathies or who knew how to impose upon her. And although sympathy was not his style and no woman, that he was aware of, had ever felt sorry for *him*, he knew very well how to impose, carefully, gently, little by little, tiring her perhaps but amusing her, involving her, fresh every morning, with the new day's triumphs and disasters which, however they might sometimes exasperate her or wear her out, had the saving grace of not being Miriam or Edward — or Paul.

It was not guile. It was — ? He hesitated to name it. A tool of his trade, he supposed, when he applied it to other people, an ability not just to inspire confidence in those under his command but to arouse their enthusiasm; not just to get them going but to get them *interested* as well. A trick. A talent. A piece of professional expertise. Damned useful. But less straightforward, somehow, when applied to Claire. She was, of course, exceedingly desirable — the calm almost dreamy surface of a lily pond that had slow-burning fires set deep underneath, he was sure of it. And he had desired her on sight. Almost uncomfortably. He had *liked* her too. And recognizing the lost, uncertain facet of her nature, the broken wing, the bruised antennae, he had even understood how best to reach her. Strength was the card to play. And steadiness. His feet were set firmly on a sure path, hers were wandering. And perhaps, with a little amorous cunning, he could take advantage of her present frailty to make her follow him. But for how long? To other women he had given cheerfully, freely, generously of his charm, his stamina, his abundant sensuality, the pleasure of his company, and had thought it sufficient. Nor had he asked for anything else in return. *Now* — and he was often less than pleased about it — he wanted to give more than that to Claire. Conventional things like diamonds, which were also easy things since it only took money to buy them. And rather more complex things. Status, which for him could never be easily obtainable. An established place in the world for which he had still to fight. Security. The fruits of labors he had only just begun to sow.

And since these gifts were not yet his to make he did not — on her return from Manchester — take her slender, arched, undoubtedly aching feet between his hands to warm them, as he might have done, nor call for the champagne supper she might have accepted, but allowed her to go back alone to Mannheim Crescent where, later that evening, he sent a basket of cream-colored roses with his card bearing a briefly scrawled "Thank you."

It was not guile. It was not love either. Or, if so, then it did not seem to be the sentimental, ungainly thing he had imagined. He simply knew that if he could choose a woman to live and work beside him, to *be* beside him, then it rather looked as if it might be this one.

"It pays handsomely," quoted Euan Ash, his eyes on Kit's roses, "to look after the staff."

"I'm not staff," she told him, arranging the lovely bouquet in Miriam Swanfield's cast-off vases.

"What then?"

She hesitated. "A friend?"

"All right. And you must admit, he knows how to choose his friends, the Major. I work for whiskey. You work for a bunch of flowers."

"It's not *work* exactly, Euan."

He shrugged, looking out of temper and out of sorts. "Well, whatever it is, he's lost me for the moment. I've got a picture to do."

"A commission?"

"Hell, no. Just a picture — inside my head trying to get out. It might just make it too. Wish me luck."

"I do."

"Thanks." And then, almost hesitantly, he said "It's not easy — being alone with it."

"I suppose not."

Yet she had no true conception of the effort, the fever — for so he privately called it and suffered it — which proceeded to feed itself on his already fleshless body, paring him even nearer to the bone, blackening the skin around his eyes so that after two nights and then three spent nailed to his canvas by the anguished need to release in paint the very things he needed with equal ferocity to hold back, he looked like a man who has been sleepless for a month.

Disturbed by the light burning in his studio, the noisy forays he made into the kitchen in the small hours of the night to clatter pots and pans, bang doors, and — for all one knew — leave on the gas, the dancing teacher hastened to complain.

"Now listen here . . ."

He neither listened nor appeared to see her, looking through her, when she lay in wait for him by the bathroom door, as if her wiry, entirely earth-bound body had been made of air.

"Drugs," she declared darkly. "Did you see the color of him — that sickly yellow? I can always tell. He's not safe."

But Claire, translating the woman's meaning as "We are not safe with him" shook her head.

"He's painting, that's all."

And, having cleared away the mess of burned sausages and beans, the full mugs of cold black tea she found abandoned on the kitchen table, she knew that he was also starving, deliberately perhaps, consuming himself, flesh and fears together, in a soul-draining agony which might — or might not — end in renewal.

"Leave him alone," she said. He was burning himself in fires she understood, in which she had not dared, so far, to hazard herself; a self-

cauterization of withered hopes and maimed emotions, on the off-chance —
no more than that — that, from their stumps, a new whole feeling, a
glimmer of faith in life, might grow. And if he succeeded — !

He was laying his ghosts and conquering his demons. Casting them
out into paint and canvas. Exorcising himself; his face, when she glimpsed
it, and his eyes so emptied of their mocking sweetness, their angelic
depravity, that he seemed a stranger. A new man. Devoutly she hoped
so. Sprawling in her own shabby armchair, wrapped in her disreputable
kimono, she even prayed for him, without faith in any particular Al-
mighty, simply wishing to leave no stone unturned on his behalf. "I
don't know if You are there, but if You should be, then — really — since
You haven't done a lot for people like him and me up to now — !"
Very much as she had prayed for Paul.

"When are we to see the masterpiece?" inquired Nola who, despite
her scorn, would nevertheless have been more than ready to arrange the
unveiling herself, in the presence of well-prompted Crozier bank accounts
and suitably prepared gentlemen of the press.

"Leave him alone," said Claire.

"He won't answer the door," the landlord's agent grumbled, having
three times called to collect the rent. "I don't like it. Mr. Crozier won't
like it. It's queer."

She put a ten-shilling note and two half-crowns into his hand. "Please
leave him alone."

"You heard what the lady said," advised Kit Hardie, looking at her
from behind the rent-collector's shoulder in a way — knowingly, wryly —
which made her blush.

And then it was over.

Kit Hardie came upon him one morning sitting at the kitchen table
pouring the dregs of a whiskey bottle into his tea, a large canvas propped
behind him, its face to the wall.

"It's finished then?"

"It's finished." And, far from triumphant, he looked chalk-white,
fine-drawn, tight-stretched, breakable, disposable by the faintest breeze,
his voice weighted and slurring with fatigue.

"Mind if I have a look?"

It was the face of a young man, yet not exactly a face. Not Euan
himself, although very like him, a young gentleman, very blond, very
pure, a clean soul somehow in his eyes so that looking at them —
recognizing their blue — Kit, who was not much given to analysis, swallowed uncomfortably and felt that he ought to look away. A private face
and behind it, around it, the open faces of minute flowers, the texture
of cloud and sand and good plowed earth; eggshells in deep, soft nests,

114

cosseted by the tips of bird-feathers; the contentedly breathing flanks of a dog; swift striding horses; a smiling landscape of young manhood, half-lost and half-rejected, but still beckoning. Still there.

"I don't know . . ." said Kit who was rarely troubled, rarely at a loss for words.

"What don't you know?" The weary voice all too clearly did not care.

"I didn't have that kind of boyhood, Euan."

"What boyhood? It's a chocolate box picture of Sir Galahad in cricket flannels, looking at flowers."

Kit didn't think so. A lost paradise. A doomed paradise, its invitation, its soft beckoning a cruel illusion, hair-line cracks in the eggshells warning of dead chicks in those deep, cozy nests; a foam of madness, no bigger than a snowflake, on the mouth of the dog; blight on the dainty under-petals of a flower; disease in the horse's hoof, the seeds of paralysis in the bird; mounds of earth that could serve as graves as well as furrows; a film of poison on the land. Paradise destroyed, decaying from within, rotting before the candid eyes, beneath the unsuspecting nostrils of the fine, fair young pilgrim, the Believer, the pure-hearted.

And although this had never been Kit's paradise and he had never believed in anything beyond his own drive and determination he shuddered slightly, needing more than ever to look away.

"It's good, Euan," he said roughly.

"Christ." Weariness had hollowed Euan's voice now to a kind of hoarse whisper. "It's a story-book illustration — for children."

Kit shook his head and smiled grimly. No. He had had no place in that sunlit, ailing world, no innocence to be destroyed, no boyhood, as such, to be taken from him and trampled into the Flanders mud. He had never had to learn the casual, everyday brutality of man to man. He had always understood it, dealt with it, from the feckless unconcern of his own father — whoever he might be — to the last elderly, alcoholic colonel who had sent the last schoolboy conscript off to be killed in France. He had always known the world of Euan's young pilgrim to be false. Yet now he found himself growing angry with a strange need to defend it — or at least this heartrending, sinister, exquisite portrayal.

"It's good."

Euan looked too exhausted to shake his head. And in any case, what was the point of a denial. It *was* good. He knew that. It was what he had set out to do, to force out of himself, drop by agonizing drop. And so, measured by that yardstick, one could call it a success. Weakly, almost fretfully, he began to laugh.

"So you've come out of hibernation have you?" A broad bright voice spoke suddenly from the doorway and the dancing teacher came into the room, looking more like an athlete with her wide shoulders and short muscular legs — a tightrope walker — than a ballerina, her sharp eyes, on the lookout for drugs and debauchery, fastening themselves at once on the canvas.

"Oh I say — that's awfully pretty."

"Yes," said Euan smiling. "Isn't it."

"And what a good-looking young chap. Anyone you know?"

"An old acquaintance." And Euan's eyes which had been dull and void began to fill again with their malicious sweetness.

"Well — well — fancy that. And here was I thinking you were — well — well!"

"Taking cocaine," he supplied amiably, "and painting nude women."

She blushed very slightly and then, having lived in cheap lodgings far too long to be bashful, gave a loud, unmelodious laugh.

"All right. I'm big enough to admit it. An old friend eh? I wouldn't mind having him on my wall, I can tell you."

"Take him." And even Kit, for a moment, thought he was joking. He was not.

"Now look here," she said considerably startled, "I didn't mean . . . It's very nice I'm sure, but as to what it's worth . . . ."

"Nothing," he said, his fallen angel's smile breaking out of him like the poisoned sunshine dappling the face of his young pilgrim. "It's a gift — from me to you my darling — because you're beautiful and I'm generous. Just take it away. Something to remember me by when I'm gone."

Eventually, after ten flustered minutes, she took it, half-convinced, as she carried it through the door, that it might suddenly explode or squirt jets of water at her or give off a bad smell; that there was something odd about it at any rate. Yet, since it was free and large and might come in handy someday, especially if he ever made a name for himself — although she doubted *that* — she took it, leaving the two men in a silence that lived and almost moved with Kit's strangled pity and exasperation, an urge he recognized as crazy to defend that blasted painting — and Euan — coupled with another urge — less crazy he thought — to take Euan by the scruff of his neck and shake him.

"You bloody fool," he said.

"Very likely."

"You sweated blood over that picture."

Euan's listless shoulders sketched a shrug, the only substance in him, the only source of energy, his angelic smile and the innocent malice of his eyes.

"Oh — pretty thin blood," he said carelessly, "blue, of course, but past its best."

"And that silly bitch didn't even want it. I suppose you know that." Kit was becoming very angry.

"I know. I didn't want it either."

"Christ Euan — you could have done something better with it than that."

He got up, whistling a ribald soldier's tune, his pilgrimage, his time of innocence, very far behind him now, his search abandoned, cast off, the cauterized stumps of his past unhealed. It had all been for nothing. Never mind. He believed now that he had expected it.

"All right, Kit," he said, his blue gaze seraphic, "what *did* you want me to do with it? Give it to Claire?"

She came into the kitchen a few moments later, just as Euan had gone off, still whistling, across the back yard, her face saddened but not, Kit thought, surprised.

"I've just seen the ballet teacher," she said.

"Yes."

"Did Euan show you the picture?"

"He did. It was . . . I don't think I'll forget it."

She sighed. "Oh well —" And it was a relief, a *pleasure* to go off into the solid world of curtain fabrics and floor coverings with Kit, the down-to-earth, flesh-and-blood creature comforts of hotel bedrooms which, he decided over smoked salmon sandwiches and a glass of *Chablis* that afternoon, were to be given identity by their color. Blue fittings for the Blue Room, pink for the Rose Room, muted orange for the Tangerine Suite, pale green and lemon, lilac and cream to be dealt with in equally meticulous fashion. An attractive notion which absorbed her time and her energy and wore blisters on her heels all over again when he further decided that tangerine towels must be matched by soap of a toning tangerine, that even ashtrays in the Blue Room must be blue, in the Rose Room pink — she would never have believed pink ashtrays so hard to find — that the heart-shaped Victorian pin-cushions set out on the various toilet tables should not only contain needles *threaded* with suitable cottons but should fit exactly into the color scheme to which they belonged.

"You're absolutely right," she told him, kicking off her shoes again a week later. "Little things *do* make all the difference. Your little pink ashtrays are making a lot of difference to me."

"Then let me pay you for your trouble."

"Nonsense."

Nor would she accept anything more substantial than flowers, chocolates, wine, for finding, beneath a tattered shawl and a layer of dust in a Harrogate antique shop, the beautiful inlaid piano which stood now on a platform in the dining room, to be played each evening by a performer — and Kit had not yet made his selection — who would be expected not only to make sweet music but to look well-groomed and, if possible, attractive, the Major's own sensibilities having been seriously offended by the dandruff-speckled evening suits of the Feathers' Teashop string quartet.

Another piano of a similar type had been ordered for the smaller restaurant and, as a final innovation, to which by no means the whole of Faxby had taken kindly, there was to be dancing in a room which, being partly below ground level, could be reached clandestinely and thus rather excitingly, by a separate entrance at the back of the hotel. A public bar? Most hotels had them. But Polly Swanfield had heard, and reported half swooning with delight to Claire, that this was to be a real cocktail bar, the first of its kind in Faxby, with those fascinating new drinks from America all mixed up in silver shakers which her mother had warned her never to drink because they had gin in them and everybody knows that ladies are not supposed to drink gin. Was it true? And a jazz band, they were saying, not from America she supposed because that would be far too good to be true, but certainly not from Faxby either. A proper nightclub, in fact, like London, especially thrilling since no one ever seemed to be quite certain whether they were legal or not. What absolute bliss! And if it turned out not to be legal and one ended up getting arrested — what a lark. Benedict, of course, would get her out pretty quickly and hush it all up, but just the same . . . !

So? Was it true? She had just had her scissors out again and sliced inches off all her evening skirts and *slashed* the necklines positively to the waist.

"You're just so lucky, Claire," she moaned. "Why can't I practically live at the Crown, like you? And to think it's just Hardie, who used to look down his nose at me for leaving my tennis shoes in the hall and who'd never ever give me more than one glass of wine at dinner. Just Hardie. And my friend, Mary-Ellen Stephens, saw him in Town Hall Square the other day and says he's positively devastatingly *attractive!*"

Kit Hardie's office on the first floor of the hotel was light and sunny, his manner unhurried, quietly assured no matter what crisis might be on hand. A haven, Claire frequently found it. The easiest place, the most *breathable* place she knew.

"I want you to come and work for me," he told her.

"Yes."

"Is that an acceptance? Or just an acknowledgment of the fact?"

"I think it means — let's wait and see."

"Must we really? I can't go on asking favors, you know — can I?"

But, nevertheless, when his secretary developed a sick headache that afternoon, brought on, it seemed, by his insistence that in no circumstances would a semicolon do the same job as a comma, Claire, who had patience to compensate for lack of skill, tapped out with two fingers and a perfect understanding of punctuation, his letters, his bills, his sample menus.

"The Croziers are bringing somebody over this morning to take photographs and those flowers in the hall look positively mean. Is there another florist in Faxby, Claire, that one could trust?"

And Claire, who had been taught about flowers by Dorothy, did the arrangements herself and worried about them until the Croziers had emptied a final glass of *Dom Pérignon*, climbed into their Rolls and driven away.

And, quite soon, she began to wake up, more often than not, with a feeling — half uneasy, half excited, by no means unpleasant — that Kit Hardie would be expecting her, that there were things she had not exactly promised but somehow seemed committed to do, and that if she failed to appear he — and she — would feel that she had let him down.

What things? Of what real use was she? A cool head. A keen eye. Peacemaker, since the Major, beneath his urbanity, was always exacting, sometimes by no means gentle.

"Smile — damn you!" she heard him bellow one morning after the sullenly retreating figure of a new young chambermaid who, instead of dimpling instantly with the smiles Kit considered to be a first essential to the chambermaid's trade, burst into tears, muttering some tragedy of a sick headache or a sick mother in which he expressed no greater interest than a curt "Talk to her Claire."

And Claire, accustomed to hysteria in all its conditions, had explained quietly, sweetly, the Major's insistence that the staff of the hotel must control their own emotions like actors on a stage, that "the show must go on," that "the guest must always be right," that "Punchinello and even a little chambermaid called Mary-Anne must keep on smiling, no matter how sick the headache or how broken the heart."

"The training," said Kit. "*Any* training should be so bloody hard that the job itself should seem easy. If they ever get that far."

Not everyone did. Before a single guest had set foot in the hotel an under-chef had been chased from the kitchen by Aristide Keller who, in his incoherent fury, had failed to clarify whether he suspected the terrified young man to have had designs on his recipes or his wife. And there was, of course, the dangerous restlessness among the female staff caused by the arrival of the jazz musicians and of MacAllister, with his rakish charm and his silver shakers, behind the cocktail bar. But what, she asked herself, could possibly happen in a hotel kitchen or bedroom or stillroom which, after her service in France, could seriously unnerve her?

"Come and work for me properly," Kit asked her again, choosing his moment and she knew that her reluctance had nothing at all to do with the hotel.

"Heavens — I have nothing to offer."

"Yes, Claire. You do." And his voice was firm now, ready to persuade and then, if necessary, to push her not very far, perhaps, just one step at a time, but definitely, pleasantly, with immense anticipation, in the direction he wished her to go. "You have a deft hand with the oil on troubled waters."

"I dare say. But that hardly seems to equip me for a career."

"Don't be so sure. The cocktail bar is bound to cause trouble you know."

"Oh yes. So Edward — my mother's husband — tells me."

"He's right. Young ladies getting a drop too much gin and vermouth, and more than they know how to handle of MacAllister's blarney. I can see it all."

"So can I. Jealous scenes. Hysterics in the powder room . . ."

"Exactly. And I can't follow a young lady into the powder room, Claire, and tell her she'll feel better tomorrow. And then there's Mr. Clarence."

"Is there really? Do I know him?"

"I hope not. You shouldn't. He's the personable young fellow I've just hired to stand at the front desk. Very picturesque. I reckon he could charm the birds off the trees, which is what I hired him for. But on a bad day — and there's no doubt he'll have bad days — he just might book two complete strangers into the same bed. I feel I could rely on you to get them out again without too much embarrassment. I'm not inventing work, Claire, or anything else you might suspect me of. I need you."

"Yes."

"Now what does that mean?"

And she had known exactly what it was in his voice and his face and in her own rapidly, perhaps treacherously stirring senses which had made her blush.

She had promised to think the matter over. Today she had brought him her answer.

"Have you come to turn me down?"

"No."

She had not precisely intended to accept either — yet, oddly enough, it was a relief to find that she *had* accepted, his enthusiasm sweeping her far over the threshold of her uncertainty to the point of acknowledging that this, after all, was what she wanted. And, having qualified her thought humorously, ruefully, with the reminder that, for the moment it was all she could get, she sealed their bargain with a cheerful handshake, accepted a glass of champagne — the same vintage, she noticed with approval, that he'd offered the Croziers — and smiled.

"You won't regret it, Claire."

He would make it his business to be sure of that, and when she finally returned to Mannheim Crescent her head was too light to care whether or not she had done the right thing. It was not ideal, of course. But what could ever be that? And the word "ideal" itself, which she had been brought up to revere as noble, tended these days, having seen what idealism led to, only to repel her. She was no longer concerned, as she had once been — as Paul and probably Euan had once been — with taking up some significant work of serving and saving humanity. She was no longer certain that humanity could or indeed ought to be saved from its own nearsighted greeds, its puerile urge to destroy itself. And, that being so, since destruction seemed inevitable and would be no great loss — it often seemed to her — in any case, she might just as well serve champagne and dry the tears of debutantes and chambermaids alike at the Crown Hotel. Either that, or go on drifting like Euan.

And because she did not want to think too deeply about Euan, knowing all too well what she would be likely to find, she diverted herself with the idea that her employment at the Crown — and *paid* employment too — would at least make her less easily available to the Swanfields.

She was to dine at High Meadows that evening and, suddenly buoyant with resolution, the prospect no longer oppressed her. She had been weak with Miriam and Polly and Nola, had succumbed far too often to attacks of good nature and bouts of conscience. Now she must learn not only to evade but to refuse. And what did refusal consist of, after all, that was more difficult than saying no?

She felt no need of protection, no mad urge to barter her solitary, not always comfortable freedom for a secure place in that powerful, dangerously enticing family circle. She wished merely to remain the adult and separate woman she had been three months ago. And suddenly, checking her reflection in the looking glass and being pleased not only with what she saw but with her own natural, healthy vanity, she felt a quick surge of delight, an almost mischievous glee as she remembered Benedict Swanfield's dry cool voice informing her that within a twelve-month she would most likely be married again and knocking on his door with her begging bowl like the rest.

He had not, of course, used quite those words. But she had understood. He had seen in her the gold hunter, the husband hunter, the nuisance he appeared to see in every woman. And now the urge to prove him wrong, to fling her newfound employment, such as it was, at his feet like a mailed gauntlet became so pressing that it was a relief to hear the Swanfield car draw up outside her gate, an incredible although somewhat unnerving bonus to see not the usual impeccable chauffeur but Benedict himself at her door.

"Benedict!" she cried out unnecessarily, sounding, to her intense dismay, as eager and excitable as Polly. "This *is* a surprise."

"I dare say. I had the car and it seemed less complicated for me to come myself rather than drive home and send Parker back again."

"Of course." She knew he had found it irksome and unnecessary to make an explanation, that he was busy and bored and possibly rather tired and that she would do well, therefore, to spare him her girlish chatter. But she was not girlish, or at least had not felt so until she had opened her door to him and encountered his — what? — nothing positive, nothing to be grappled with, simply his lack of anything to encourage her in her good opinion of herself. But she had something to tell him. Clearly he did not care to listen. Nevertheless.

"Then may I surprise you in another way? I have just accepted an offer."

"Have you really?"

"Yes indeed — to go into the hotel business." And, totally unbidden, she could hear Polly's light voice chanting "Benedict — I have cut my hair," could see the golden head tossing, preening, clamoring for his admiration, anger, praise or punishment, anything so long as it was the *notice* which he had denied.

"Ah," he said now, denying her his notice too, although — she reminded herself — she had not asked for it and did not care. "Hardie has given you something to do has he. Very decent of him."

Hardie! And, behind his level, neutral tone, she heard, sharp and sardonic and very clear, the implication "my man, Hardie." The Swanfield butler who had poured Benedict's wine, brought him his letters on a silver tray, handed him his hat and gloves and who now, like the good fellow he was, had provided "young Mrs. Jeremy" with something to occupy her mind and keep her out of mischief until she settled down again. Very decent of him.

Remembering how Polly's triumphant, tousled head had drooped, she kept her own very high and, clenching back what she knew amounted to unreasonable fury — because *why*, of all things, should she wish to impress him? — she gave him her brightest smile.

"He is paying me, Benedict."

"Is he really. That is decent."

Was he amused? Certainly. But why? She swallowed hard, her elation ebbing as fast if not so visibly as Polly's had done, and then, feeling shallow, frivolous, naïve, when she had planned to be businesslike, competent, calm — when she *knew* herself to be all these things — she smiled again.

"I believe it makes me a woman of independent means," she told him, her voice ringing false and facetious in her own ears, the giddy woman she had never been, making the giddy declaration she had never intended. And why, under the pressure of those black, dark eyes, could she not now retract it? Why could she not prove herself to be a woman of sense, as she would have done easily and pleasantly with any other man, by admitting that although her salary from the Crown might pay her rent and keep a possibly none too robust wolf from her door, it would not be enough to free her from the financial pressures of the Swanfields. Independent means! Why on earth had she made such a stupid remark as that?

"I think," he said, "we'd better wait — don't you? — and see?"

7

THE family was already assembled in the drawing room at High Meadows, arranged, everyone in their accustomed places and attitudes in Aaron Swanfield's charmed circle, Polly irritable and bored, Nola half-asleep, Eunice keeping a watchful, nervous eye on Toby to make sure no one else was neglecting him, Miriam alone thoroughly at ease, with her life and with herself.

"Dear Claire," Miriam said, her sharp eyes fastening on the locket around Claire's neck with satisfaction, her soft hand overtly tenacious, but no more, no worse — Claire reminded herself — than the grip of any other self-centered matron, demanding far more than anyone should be entitled to receive. She had only, albeit kindly, to refuse.

"Dear Claire," mimicked Nola, brushing past her as they took their places at table. "Oh dear — dear Claire."

And not even Claire's unruly conscience felt any sense of obligation to Nola. Nor to Polly who must be allowed to make her own mistakes. Nor to Eunice whose mistakes, in loving too unselfishly, too frantically, could not be rectified. Nor to good-natured, weak-willed Toby who had submitted without any apparent struggle to the burden of that love. Not to anyone. She had no reason to feel committed. No one could force her to become involved. Or so she imagined until Polly, laying down her fork with a clatter, finding the roast beef as excellent, perhaps, but as eternal and therefore as *tedious* as everything else, suddenly announced, her clear voice cutting through the monotonous hum of dinnertime chat, and then silencing it, "I think it was mean of you, Claire, sneaking off to Manchester yesterday with Nola, when you know I've been aching to go over there and do some real shopping for ages."

Yesterday? Claire had spent the day with her mother at Upper Heaton, the evening in Mannheim Crescent being sketched by Euan Ash who, for reasons which had seemed clear to him after a tumbler or two of whiskey, had given her a mermaid's tail. What had Nola been doing? The answer leaped out at her so visibly that it seemed to be dancing around Nola's head — and her own — like a treacherous, telltale flame, branding them equally as conspirators. And, without needing to look at him, she was sharply, acutely aware of Benedict Swanfield sitting aloof and separate, at the head of the table.

Damn Polly. Damn Nola. Damn them both, one for a giddy fool who ought, at nineteen, to know better and the other for — what was she? A lunatic, surely, to take such risks, to put herself and others in this atrocious position.

"Manchester," murmured Nola smoothly, propping her pointed chin on her hand, her eyes barely open, "is for grownups, Polly. And since we missed the last train home, *what* a disaster, my child, if you had been with us. Don't you think so, Claire?"

But the thought uppermost in Claire's mind was how exquisitely satisfying it would be to strangle Nola. Or, failing that, to find the courage — the cruelty — to lean forward and state crisply and clearly, "Don't implicate *me* in your shabby love affairs."

"Oh yes, absolutely," she said.

"I don't see why," persisted Polly. "The Croziers would have been perfectly happy to put me up too wouldn't they? They must have at least a dozen spare bedrooms and heaps of interesting friends. It would have been *fun.*"

It had not occurred to Polly that Nola had lied. And indeed, even Claire was not sure where the lie began or ended. Perhaps she really had missed the last train. Claire thought it likely, for otherwise she would have had her alibi more carefully prepared. But why? For God's sake, why had she not warned Claire in advance? A whispered word before dinner would have been alarming, annoying, but possible, advisable, *sane.*

Claire was not, by nature, deceitful. But she had told lies regularly and fluently throughout most of her girlhood, from necessity, her life with Edward and Dorothy having thoroughly schooled her in the servile arts of falsehood, how to smile sweetly as her pulses raced with panic, how to speak smooth words — like Nola's — as her mouth turned dry, how to test the ground beneath her feet for the hidden pitfall, the sudden quagmire, the trap. She was, therefore, an experienced if unwilling ally who knew that in order to defend herself she must discover first and foremost and very fast who, if anyone, suspected her.

Miriam, her round blue eyes intent, it seemed, on the pattern of her plate, continued placidly to eat her carrot purée and her green peas. Polly had not and would not see beyond the purchases she had wished to make in Manchester, the wicked young man who *might* have been waiting for her at the Bernard Croziers. Eunice seemed puzzled but not suspicious. Toby, who so often had occasion to cover his own tracks, became suddenly very busy with the sauceboat. Benedict? She could not look at Benedict. *Must* not. Yet, sickeningly, she could look at no one else, her eyes drawn to his dark, distant face by some compulsion, whether of her guilt or his will she was uncertain. And although his expression had nothing in it that she could name, she felt the whole of her skin turn cold, the whole of her mind fill with the nightmare conviction that he could see right inside her head.

"Did you enjoy the play, at least?" he asked her.

What could she answer?

"Yes," she said brusquely, almost throwing the word at him, knowing it was not enough. What play? Which one had Nola seen, or said she'd seen? And why, in what seemed to Claire a thick, unnatural silence, could not Nola — who must surely know the answer — make some move in her own defense? Nola — for Heavens sake! But she remained motionless, hardly breathing, a listening, *waiting* figure, her chin still on her hand, an odd light in her eyes, her lips curved in a remote, peculiar smile which Claire had seen before, many times in France; the strange, almost sensual pleasure of those who have become addicted to danger. Damnable, treacherous woman! Was she worth this agony? Were any of them? No. Absolutely not. Yet — just the same — *what* play?

Abruptly her mind emptied and then, as suddenly, filled up again with a jumble of half-remembered conversations which — because she had to say something — forced her to take what could only be a chance.

"I have always been enormously impressed," she announced primly, "by the work of George Bernard Shaw."

Would it suffice? Was *Pygmalion* playing in Manchester, or was it next week, last week, had she only imagined it? Or had Nola been talking about the Russian dramatist Chekhov, the other day, and comparing his work with Shaw? Was it *The Cherry Orchard* then that Nola had pretended to see?

"Yes," said Benedict, his face telling her nothing, "I rather thought you might."

"Oh Lord — *that* stuff," said Toby Hartwell, coming, she fully under-

126

stood, to her rescue. "Too highbrow for me, by half. I'd as soon go over to Leeds and doze through *The Merry Widow*. How about it Eunice? It's on at the Grand."

"Oh yes," breathed Polly, claiming her place on any outing. "*Do* let's."

"Try waiting to be invited," snapped Eunice. "It happens to be our wedding anniversary next week."

"Oh well." Polly was unabashed. "I was at your wedding, wasn't I, all done up in my little organdy frills, so don't be mean with the anniversary. A box, Toby, shall we, since it's a special occasion, and supper afterward — you *are* an angel. And I'm just longing for a ride in that gorgeous new car . . ."

There was a sharp, nervous clatter as Eunice's fork struck the edge of her plate.

"Yes — yes — quite," said Toby, his glance flickering uneasily to Benedict.

"Oh — have you got a new car, dear?" murmured Miriam.

"Well — not exactly — I mean . . ."

"He means," said Nola, making a casual sacrifice of Toby, "that it hasn't been paid for yet."

"It means," flared Eunice, rising at once to Nola's bait, "that considering the amount of driving Toby does — because Benedict *sends* him — and the customers he has to chauffeur around all over the place — and the hours it takes in the evenings and at weekends too — that, well . . . It stands to reason, doesn't it, that he has to have something decent to drive in. Doesn't it? I should think we're entitled to that — aren't we?"

Benedict, beckoning to the parlor maid to refill his glass, said not a word.

The next morning, early for her, Nola came to Mannheim Crescent, not particularly to apologize but to explain. She had used Claire's name on impulse to get herself out of an unforeseen complication. She had even taken the precaution of calling on Claire, the previous morning, to give her fair warning but — Claire might remember — having exchanged a few sharp words with Euan Ash, she had gone off in a huff, why not admit it, and, what with one thing and another, had forgotten all about it until the brat Polly had come close to letting the cat out of the bag. And what a cat! Lowering herself with one supple movement into Claire's green chintz armchair she seemed only too ready to relive every erotic detail, graphically, greedily, taking her time over it.

"I don't want to know," Claire told her. "And don't ever put me in that position again."

"Oh dear — dear — we are offended?"

"Furious, Nola."

"Whatever for? We got away with it, didn't we? And you were splendid."

"I was terrified."

She smiled. "Yes. I know. So was I. *Quite* a sensation. Dear child — have I shocked you?"

Claire shook her head. "You can do what you like Nola — sleep with anybody you like — but don't involve me. Not in any circumstances and particularly not with your husband sitting there."

"Oh I see — pangs of conscience about Benedict. Well, you can't judge, Claire, can you, because you don't know how marriage works. You could hardly call those few days with Jeremy a marriage. Could you, now?"

"I don't pretend to."

"Exactly. So, on the subject of husbands in general and mine in particular let me put your mind at rest. He's as bad as I am. He has other women, you know."

"I know nothing about it."

"But he does. Or at least I hope he does, because he doesn't have me. Not since Conrad was born he doesn't, at any rate."

Claire did not want to know. And yet — ! Good Heavens! "How — old is Conrad?" she said.

"Thirteen. It's been a long time, Claire."

"Yes."

"So stop looking down your nose at me, dear, unless you're fool enough to believe what they taught you — that the woman is always to blame."

"No. I don't believe that."

"Good. Then you may not believe that other convenient little myth our mothers teach us either — that marriage is the ultimate, the only, fulfillment for a woman, that all one has to do is get a man to the altar and — hey presto — paradise lies at one's feet."

"Of course not."

"Lucky old you. Polly believes it. So did I. And my wedding, my dear, — I can tell you — was the social event of the Bradford season. White satin with a train half an aisle long and my mother in a Worth gown weeping all over the cathedral — from joy, one tends to think. And Benedict, handsome and rich and ever so faintly sinister, which always helps. Yes — I was as big a fool in those days as Polly about wicked young men. We had a Mediterranean honeymoon too. I was rather good at that. In fact I quite understood how to be a fiancée and a bride. It seemed to be leading up to something. Unfortunately, I never managed to find out just what — or just why — or what point there was to it. Have you ever felt like that? No. You weren't married long enough to have to wonder what to do next. The answer they give you is "Have a baby." I tried, and as a brood mare I was no one's idea of a success. I had a bad experience with Christian. Worse with Conrad. And when the doctors advised me not to risk it again — well, what is one's husband to do in a case like that? Assuming, of course, that he's a gentleman?"

"I suppose —"

"What do you suppose? I'll tell you this much. What you might feel *entitled* to suppose is that your husband would be upset about the loss of his privileges — his 'conjugal rights' don't they call them? Or that he'd at least go through the motions of being upset — of *missing* what men are supposed to set such store by. Wouldn't you?"

"*Nola!*" she said sharply, recoiling with a vehemence that she barely understood from this too personal glimpse of Benedict. "It's really none of my business you know — none at all."

But Nola, leaning forward, in the grip of something taut and angry which caused her to mock her own actions in the same breath as she sought to justify them, would have none of that.

"I daresay. But it's my business and if I choose to make it yours then I have every right."

"Why should you want to, Nola?"

"Oh — dear child — I don't ask myself these profound questions anymore. I just do what I can and what I like at the moment I like it. So if now I want to explain myself to you then you may as well listen. Why not? All right — when the doctors advised me against having more children they may not have meant for ever. And I may not have been so terrified about getting pregnant again as I made out. I may have been exaggerating the danger — for my dear husband's benefit. Now why did I do that?"

"Do you expect me to guess?"

She gave her deep-throated chuckle, leaning her head against the chair back, her eyes narrowed. "Dear Claire — I'm only guessing myself. I may have wanted to put an end to our sexual relations, of course. My own mother did that after my youngest sister was born and my father managed well enough. But on the other hand, I might — I'm not saying I did but I *might* — have wanted something quite different. Men desire what they can't have. We all know that. And how might have I reacted if he'd come tapping on my bedroom door one sleepless night? Men can be driven mad by lust, or so we're led to believe. Just think of it. He might have turned on me in a fit of violent passion and dragged me upstairs by the hair. What would I have done then, I wonder? But of course he didn't. He moved out of my bedroom very courteously — very fast. And that, my dear Claire, was thirteen years ago. Don't imagine I'm casting any slur upon his virility because he has plenty of that. He has a cottage in the Dales I believe — in fact I know he has — with a black marble bath and black satin sheets to match, I shouldn't wonder, where he entertains his passing fancies. That's how we live. He's discreet. So am I."

"No you're not."

"Thank you."

"*Nola!* Do you even realize the risk you run?" And since it was a risk which had just occurred to Claire, she looked for a moment, quite badly shaken herself.

"Oh quite. I told my husband I couldn't sleep with him for medical reasons. I convinced the doctors that my nerves wouldn't stand it. Presumably the doctors convinced him. Should he now discover that all this long while I have been sleeping with other men, what *would* he do? Murder me, do you think?"

It was evident that she expected him to make the attempt and would, in fact, be disappointed if he did not.

"Why don't you leave him, Nola?"

"Why on earth should I wish to do that?"

"Because you don't care for him. He evidently doesn't care for you. So where's the point to it?"

"You're not talking about divorce are you?"

And her supple body stiffening in the depths of the armchair, she sounded hostile, offended, quite — and most uncharacteristically — shocked.

"What else? I don't know how easy divorce is nowadays. But at least it's possible."

"Possible? So is bubonic plague, I suppose. Dear child — how many women do you know personally who have been divorced?"

"One."

"And what happened to her?"

But before Claire could dredge from her memory the face and the supposed fortune of a woman she had met three years ago in France, Nola stopped her with an unusually commanding gesture of the hand.

"I'll tell you what happened to her. She broke her mother's heart and her father struck her name from the family Bible and — rather more to the point — cut her out of his will. Her brothers' wives were too shocked to speak to her and her brothers too embarrassed. Her friends stopped inviting her because they thought she might pinch their husbands. Her children were taken away from her if they were small, and if they were older they blamed her for causing them so much inconvenience. She lost her home, her income, her position in society. And every man she met thought she was fair game and ought to be grateful. Isn't that what happened?"

"Perhaps."

"I'm sure of it. And your friend's husband probably did the decent thing and took the blame — hired himself a chorus girl for the weekend and went to Brighton so that his wife could divorce him. Benedict wouldn't do that. Oh, no. He'd make sure I emerged as the guilty party with nothing but a pittance to live on. And I have not the faintest notion of how one sets about living on pittances, dear child, nor the least desire to learn."

"It can be fun."

"Yes — at your age with family money sitting in trust for you, perhaps it can. But if you had nothing of your own — as I have nothing . . ."

"Surely, Nola — ?"

"What? The Crozier money? You don't know my father. He brought up his daughters to be rich and to be married. And all his financial settlements veer strongly in that direction. He will pay out whatever it costs to avoid a scandal. But if scandal should ever break out, then he would let whichever one of us caused it starve. We all know that. And whatever Benedict may be, he never questions my spending. No — no — I may not like High Meadows — but I have nowhere else to go, my dear. No one ever taught me anything else but how to be a rich man's wife. And how could I support myself now? Giving piano lessons at a shilling an hour like that poor old soul upstairs? Or German lessons? I wouldn't care to gamble on what would kill me first, boredom or starvation. Oh no, dear — the only hope of independence I shall ever have is to be a rich widow — like you. Except, of course, that Benedict, being a machine, will live for ever."

But Claire was in no mood, just then, to dwell on the deceits practiced by faithless women on faithless men. If Nola and Benedict enjoyed their adultery, and since they took so much trouble over it one must hope they did, then — for all she cared — they could get on with it undisturbed. Her aim was not to worry about the Swanfields but to avoid them, a policy she pursued with success until, returning home very late a week or so later she found the Swanfields' Bentley, Miriam's car, parked somewhat erratically outside her gate. Damnation. But Miriam, surely, had gone to Leeds, to see *The Merry Widow* with Eunice and Toby. Who then? Had Parker, the Swanfield chauffeur, a friend in Mannheim Terrace? Nothing to do with her, of course. Not even when she heard the bursts of tipsy laughter coming from Euan's side of the passage and recognized Polly's high, excited giggle among them.

She went into her own room, put on her disreputable kimono and sat down with a book, barefoot and naked under the scarlet silk. So Euan was having a party. Good. Since recovering from what he now termed his "attack of sincerity" he had been having a great many of those; rowdy, haphazard, spur of the moment gatherings of stray young girls and boisterous men who got drunk and used "language" as the dancing teacher put it, and often had to be stepped over the next morning, sleeping like logs on the hall carpet or the stairs. And Polly — she reminded herself — was simply not her responsibility. Yet, just the same, what was she doing with Euan? Rather more to the point what might he be doing with her? Was she safe with him? Of course not. But it had been Polly's ambition for so long to meet a wild and wicked man and that being so, ought she not to be allowed simply to get on with it? To make her own mistakes, find her own solutions, *grow* in her own way? But then — what of the car, which somebody — not Polly — would have to drive back to High Meadows? Let Euan drive it. But Euan would be even more dangerous by now at the wheel of a car than Polly. Should she telephone High Meadows? What if Benedict answered? Probably — since Polly was on the loose — he was not there. Very likely he was in London. In fact she remembered Nola saying so. But could one take Nola's word for anything? Leave it. Polly would get into trouble sooner or later. It might as well be now. But — nevertheless — oh *damnation!* And having read the same paragraph twice over without understanding a word, it was a relief to have her third attempt interrupted by Euan's sharp tap on the door.

He was drunk, or at least had consumed enough to make him drunk, a condition which he carried off with a flourish, his eyes a little glazed but his speech precise, his bearing steady, only his humor inclined to swing, at such times, with stunning rapidity from sweetness to malice. A wild and wicked man? Undoubtedly. And far more than Polly could hope to handle.

"I have a damsel in distress on my premises," he told her, leaning in the doorway, his eyes and then an inquiring fingertip moving to the open neck of her kimono.

"Really?" she said quite pleasantly, pushing his hand away.

"Really. Not that it seems to be bothering *her*. But do come and remove her."

"Why?"

"A number of reasons. She turned up — oh God knows — hours

ago, with some man she wanted to show to you. She showed him to me instead."

"And don't you like him?"

"It's not that. I have a little matter on hand of my own, you see, and although I'm not exclusive I do need to be private — you know what I mean? And, of course, she *is* in danger of losing her virginity on my studio floor. Thought I'd better mention it."

"She's nineteen, Euan. What were you in danger of losing at that age?"

"*Claire* — tut tut — my goodness. Only my life. The other is a fate worse than death, didn't they tell you that at school. But there again, if she doesn't mind, and you don't mind . . . You have lovely bones, Claire. Why don't we leave them to get on with it? I'll come into your room and discuss bones — and skin textures — shall I? Please, Claire?"

He slid both hands around her waist and smiling, she used no more than the pressure of two fingertips on his chest to push him away.

"All right. Then save me, at least, from the brat Polly."

She walked briskly across the hall and into the studio, smaller than usual without her shoes but tall in authority, intending — since she had not wished to do it at all — to get the matter over and done with as soon as she could.

Polly, spangled, tousled, adorable, lay on the floor on a heap of cushions, displaying bare dimpled arms and shoulders, long legs and silver stockings and silver lace garters which the handsome, anonymous young man beside her was trying clumsily to remove, greatly to the disgust — it seemed — of Euan's girl who sat prim and straight-backed at the table, her expression conveying that despite her cheap shoes, her secondhand evening gown and her board school education, *she* would never behave in this wanton manner.

"Good evening," said Claire, in the tones of an army matron to the considerably befuddled young man. "I am *Mrs.* Swanfield. And you, I think, should get up and go home."

They were drunk and taken by surprise. She was not. The boy was young and soft and did not want to cause any trouble that his father might get to hear of. Both she and Euan knew how to be menacing and hard. He went off, sullen, humiliated, wishing he had never set foot in Mannheim Crescent, vowing never to do so again. Polly laughed and then she cried, accused Claire of conspiring to ruin her life with her mother and Benedict and everybody — and aimed a blow at her.

"I'll stay here with Euan."

"Oh no you won't."

She lay down on the floor again.

"Move me."

Euan's girl continued to sit primly at the table, taking no notice.

"Oh come and lie down with me, Euan."

She rolled over on the cushions, amorous as a kitten, wanton and entrancing, arousing if not his sensuality then certainly far more of his curiosity than would have been good for her had they been alone. "Some other time," said Euan, glancing at Claire and his silent, disapproving girl who, quite suddenly, got to her feet and left the room without a word, letting the door fall shut with a final-sounding slam behind her.

"Polly," he said, "you have condemned me to a night of solitude and frustration."

"It will do you good," said Claire, returning to her own room and scrambling into her clothes.

"I want to dance," decided Polly and, with a lovely, childlike abandon, she danced out into the hall and through the outside door which Euan held open for her, performing a wild tarantella in the garden until she was sick, rather neatly — remembering even *in extremis* not to spoil her dress — under the bushes by the gate.

"I want to die," was her next decision.

"Die in the car," suggested Euan sweetly.

"I want my father," she said, swaying toward him, suddenly fragile, vulnerable, a little girl for whom the world had never been the same since Aaron Swanfield left it.

"Then, dear Polly," said Euan, backing hastily out of her reach, "you have certainly come to the wrong address."

She began to cry painfully now, huge sobs which hurt and frightened her.

"I want my daddy." It was the absolute truth. He would never have allowed her to get lost like this, to feel so dizzy and so astray, so sick in her stomach and sick at heart. She knew, suddenly and absolutely through the haze of alcohol which she had not really enjoyed — had consumed in such quantities only to impress the Charlesworth boy who meant nothing to her now — that she did not trust her mother, that she was terrified of Benedict, that even Eunice, who used to be kind to her had not wanted her company at the theater that night, had been glad when she had made a fuss and decided not to go. Who loved her then? No one since Aaron. Or not in the way she wanted. Since her father died she had never felt safe.

"I want my father," she wailed.

"For God's sake — get her into the car," said Euan, torn between irritation and amusement, irritation getting the upper hand.

"Into the back," said Claire, "in case she's sick again, since I suppose I'm driving."

"I do believe so. But I *will* start the engine for you. There — just don't stall it going up the hill. I'd come with you — in fact I realize I ought to come with you — but there it is. Better not. I expect you'll be all right."

"Thanks Euan — for having so much faith in me."

He laughed, saluted, and went inside.

The car was unfamiliar and heavy, the road dark and narrow. Through the glass partition separating passenger from driver she was aware that Polly had started to shiver and probably, although the glass obscured the sound as in a goldfish bowl, to cry again.

She had made no plan. It was simply necessary to get Polly safely home — to get rid of her in effect — and, concentrating on the car, knowing that there was far more likelihood than she would ever have admitted to Euan of stalling this venerable but sluggish engine, she did not at first pay too much attention to the car behind her, gaining on her from nowhere, a flash of headlamps in her mirror, an impression of power and speed greater than her own, a huge motor which ought to have overtaken her, but did not. And she remained unaware of the exact moment when she realized it was Benedict.

She saw through the glass that Polly appeared to be unconscious, or perhaps only asleep. The lodge gates of High Meadows were approaching and since the road led nowhere else she turned into them, parked the car as close as she could to the front door of the house, and stood on the gravel drive, waiting.

That he would be furious, scornful, abrasive, she was quite certain. That he would blame her for the whole episode and take the course he was always taking with Eunice and with Polly herself, of reducing her allowance, was not impossible. What he might do to Polly she could not imagine. But what alternative had she but to face him and tell him, not the whole truth perhaps, but enough to give an accurate picture of what had occurred?

But as he got out of the Daimler and came toward her, what she actually said was, "We thought you were in London."

"Yes. So it seems. I came back this morning. What happened?"

"Oh," and she had not intended her voice to sound so flippant, "Polly got drunk. She turned up at my flat and I brought her home."

"You make it sound an everyday occurrence."

"I don't mean to. It isn't. I'm sorry."

Was he angry? She had no idea. Stepping forward he glanced through the window at Polly and as he turned back to Claire again she realized that although she was looking at him she could not really see him, could make no assessment of his reaction because her own was too powerful to permit her to judge. Was she really so afraid of him? Blinking hard to clear her vision she admitted that it did rather seem that way.

"May I ask," he said, "what you intended to do with her? Get her upstairs with the help of the servants perhaps and ask them to say nothing to her mother? Was that it?"

"Yes. Something like that."

Very faintly, almost imperceptibly, he smiled.

"Then please do so. And, by the way, I suppose there is no need to remind you not to lay her flat? Good. I thought not. Come and see me in the study afterward."

The chauffeur, Parker, carried her upstairs, flanked by a pair of maids who clucked and cooed with sympathy, eyes gleaming at having such a good story to tell, although only in the servants' hall and not — they promised Claire — to her mother. She saw Parker from the room, stood back while Polly was undressed by skilled, impersonal fingers, supervised the arrangement of her pillows, instructed the girls to sit with her until she was sleeping naturally, and then went slowly downstairs feeling puzzled, distinctly uneasy as to just what might happen next.

"May I give you a drink?" asked Benedict.

She wrinkled her nose fastidiously, her nostrils remembering Polly's odors of whiskey and perfume and vomit.

"No thank you. Not right away."

"Then I'll take you home."

"Oh — will you? I mean — I suppose — Parker could do it."

"I suppose he could. Nevertheless . . ."

The Bentley had been driven away, the Daimler was waiting and she got in beside him, allowing him to negotiate the drive and the gateway before saying what could be said in Polly's defense.

"She may not have had so very much to drink, you know."

"I dare say. But it is unwise, to say the least, for a woman to be drunk in public. One could hardly let it pass."

"She became very upset. She was crying, quite dreadfully, for her father."

"Yes? There would seem to be very little I can do about that."

The car drew smoothly into Mannheim Crescent and suddenly, her social expertise deserting her, she had no idea what to do with him, whether to thank him or wait for him to thank her, whether to offer him coffee or simply walk away.

He came around the car and opened the door for her so that as she got out they were standing side by side, hemmed in between the car and

136

the gate, shrouded by its thick hedge and tall overhanging trees. The street was deserted, the houses dark, the moon just a trail of gray vapor in a heavy sky.

"Thank you, Benedict."

"Thank you, Claire."

"Good night."

"Good night."

His hand was on the gate but he did not open it.

"Would you like — well, coffee perhaps?"

"No. Not coffee."

"Then — some brandy?"

She thought he hesitated, briefly, and then shook his head.

"I think not."

"Well then — ?"

The gate remained between them, his hand still upon it, effectively, if in a most highly civilized manner, blocking her path, detaining her without laying a hand upon her as other men might have done. What could he want from her? With any other man she would have known.

"Claire, perhaps I ought to mention . . ."

"Yes?"

And looking swiftly upward, what she saw in his face was a glint of humor, faint and fleeting perhaps, not kind, not charitable, spiked at its edges, no doubt, with probes that were as sharp as needles. But humor, nonetheless.

"I had dinner at the Great Northern Hotel tonight with a group of businessmen and their wives — an annual occasion."

"Oh — did you?"

"Unexpectedly, too, since I got back from London a day early."

"Oh — oh, yes?"

"My own wife could not join me because she had a previous engagement. A pressing one I might add. With you, Claire."

She closed her eyes.

"I forget just where. But that hardly matters, does it?"

Her eyelids, slightly against her will, opened and she found, once again, that all she could see of him was a dense, overwhelming mass of shadow.

"Benedict — "

"Don't trouble. She needed a quick excuse and she will have had no time to come and warn you. When she comes tomorrow there is absolutely no reason to disillusion her. So — wherever it is she decided you have been together this evening you may confirm it to me — should I happen to ask. Is that understood?"

Mesmerized, her head jerking forward like an obedient puppet on a chain, she nodded, her mouth opening to produce one hoarsely whispered word, "Polly?"

But, of course, as she ought to have known, he had thought of that.

"Polly did not see me. And she wouldn't dream of mentioning tonight's little escapade to Nola. I shall manage to lecture her on the evils of drink and debauchery without mentioning your name, never fear. I shouldn't worry about any of this you know. There's really no need."

"No."

He opened the gate.

"Good night then." She walked through it, reached the door and then, fumbling with the lock, unable to turn it, dropped her keys with what seemed a mighty clatter on the path.

"Oh *damnation!*"

The dense shadow that had this powerful, complicated man at its center moved swiftly beside her, engulfed her, retrieved her keys and deftly unlocking the awkward, heavy door, held it open.

"Good night, Claire. Remember — don't worry."

Yet, as she walked hurriedly, gratefully inside, leaving him behind her, two things loomed large in her stunned head to worry her. First — and perhaps foolishly — poor Nola, feeding her craving for excitement, and perhaps for much more than that, on deceiving this man who knew himself to be deceived and did not care. How cruel. And then, on the other side of the coin, how merciful. How tortuous. First Nola. And then herself, her own part in this sorry charade; the awful realization that Benedict, only the other night, had sat coolly at his dinner table and watched her lie to him.

8

THE Crown Hotel opened its doors a week later to considerably less than universal applause, at least eighty percent of Faxby, who could not afford its prices, greeting the event with complete indifference; the remainder divided between those who disapproved of new innovations, those who disapproved of everything, and a minority — small but persistent — who simply wished to reverse the bleak coin of the past few years and enjoy themselves.

There were no residents on that first evening apart from Nola's cousin Arnold Crozier, wool merchant, property developer, *bon viveur*, a widower of few words and undistinguished appearance who had reminded Claire at once, and greatly to her discomfiture — since she had been warned to make herself very pleasant to him — of a benign and immensely shrewd black beetle. Yet the arrival of his Rolls had released the spring which set the hotel in motion, the doorman, a former sergeant of the Welsh Guards, descending the shallow marble steps with the air of a general to take charge of Mr. Crozier's car and luggage, followed by Kit Hardie himself, looking far better suited to the part of millionaire than shrewd, shrivelled, sallow-complexioned, presumably lonely Arnold Crozier. They had walked into the lobby together, apparently deep in conversation, Kit Hardie saying exactly — and only — the things which, in his assessment, Mr. Crozier would wish to hear. The receptionist, Mr. Clarence, had exuded the charm for which Kit Hardie had engaged him. The housekeeper had accepted Mr. Crozier's compliments with an air of efficient yet somehow maternal dignity, giving the impression — as Kit Hardie had instructed her — that she genuinely and deeply cared about the temperature of his bath, his supply of warm towels, the flask of iced water at his bedside, the positioning, to suit his exact convenience, of cushions and lamps. Young girls with bright fresh faces and handsome immaculate young men answered Mr. Crozier's bell throughout the duration of his stay, smiling, attentive, looking — as Kit Hardie had painstakingly taught them — as if nothing could delight them more than serving him tea, which he took every hour, replacing his ashtrays, which he filled as regularly, taking his telegrams to the post office, finding him a gardenia for his buttonhole, a copy of an Austrian newspaper, a manicurist who, it was noticed, stayed rather longer than anyone thought needful, a map of Northumbria, various railway timetables. Chef Keller, who admittedly had little else to do that evening, consulted him on the menu, serving in the otherwise deserted restaurant, a dinner of salmon trout on a bed of lobster mousse, chicken breasts poached in white wine with crayfish butter, and Mr. Crozier's favorite apple pancakes flamed in brandy. While the resident pianist, sloe-eyed, willowy, dandruff-free Miss Adela Adair, played soulfully and exclusively for Mr. Crozier and his guests; his party consisting of his much-married brother, Bernard, whose wife would be expecting him home in Manchester no matter how late the hour; two stately yet accommodating ladies whose acquaintance with the Croziers did not appear to be recent; two more prosperous looking men of affairs, one bald, one hairy, and Nola.

They drank large quantities of champagne and three different clarets, Arnold Crozier being in the mood for claret that evening and declining, since he was paying the bill, all suggestions of "white with fish, red with meat," even brushing aside the fears of Chef Keller that so robust a wine would swamp the delicate flavor of his salmon.

"He who pays the piper," said Arnold Crozier in his dry little whisper, "calls the tune."

"Absolutely right, sir," murmured Kit Hardie, pouring the claret himself, making sure the glasses were no more than half full to leave space for the aroma to collect below their rim, beginning a pleasant discussion on the respective merits of *Châteaux Lafite* and *Latour* while, at the same time, giving Claire a discreet signal to run down to the kitchen and pacify the chef.

The following morning, after a breakfast of scrambled eggs and smoked salmon, Arnold Crozier returned to his large empty house in Bradford, having reserved the Tangerine Suite for the following weekend, leaving an impression that he regarded the Crown rather as a convenient *pied-à-terre* of his own. He had left the hot water tap running in his bathroom and had not tipped any member of staff.

140

"Old goat," said Mr. Clarence, the receptionist, his voice charming now only from habit.

"Skinflint," said the housekeeper, no longer motherly.

"Dirty old man," declared the fresh-faced young chambermaids in chorus.

"Miser," shuddered Miss Adela Adair, the pianist, who felt entitled to something more substantial than a pat on the behind for sitting up half the night playing Viennese waltzes.

"Barbarian," muttered Chef Keller, not at all pacified.

"Agreed," said Kit Hardie pleasantly, firmly, "and we'll be just as kind to him next week, and the week after that. Agreed?"

The same courtesy, the same lavish attention was to be extended to every guest without exception.

"There is only one kind of tray," decreed Kit Hardie. "It is made of silver. A napkin is starched white linen. Ashtrays exist to be filled and then *immediately* to be emptied. Mirrors and windows are there to be polished. A guest is made of gold. Cherish him."

But, in the early days, there were very few to cherish, the bedrooms remaining in such pristine condition that the occasional occupant seemed almost an intruder, the restaurant serving no more than a nightly dozen; businessmen mainly, "trying the place out," their somber attire and heavy conversation creating an atmosphere which, although perfectly respectable, and producing nothing of which even the most careful of mothers or the most pernickety of town councillors or magistrates could possibly complain, was undoubtedly dull.

For ten days, fifteen days, a month, and then rather more, the beautiful rose-pink lounge with its baroque ceiling remained empty, Feathers' Teashop full. Yet, nevertheless, tea was there to be had should anyone require it, magazines and periodicals continued to be laid out on the map table, the flowers to be changed twice weekly, the lounge waiters to hover if not in attendance then certainly in anticipation.

"Is it looking very bad, Kit?" Claire asked him, wondering if she should offer to forego her salary, uncomfortably aware of the money which had been spent on decorating and furnishing, for which the Croziers would want a speedy return. But, whatever his private opinion, he remained outwardly of good cheer.

"No more than I calculated. But you could invite your mother to tea. And should there be the remotest possibility of Miriam Swanfield — ?"

Miriam, albeit most charmingly, declined — yet, since the Swanfields in a spirit of *noblesse oblige* felt bound to offer some measure of support to their former butler, Eunice appeared one afternoon and, sitting down somewhat gingerly at first in a pink armchair, was so impressed by the strawberry *mille-feuilles*, so delighted with the array of fashion magazines — having given up such luxuries herself in favor of Toby's motoring and racing journals — that she returned the week after, her approval obliging Edward to lift his ban on Dorothy, "ever setting foot in such a place," although of course, with his delicate digestion, he could not come himself.

"Who else can I invite?" asked Claire, looking extremely anxious.

"Who do you know? Look up the girls you were at school with — and their mothers. The kind who meet friends for tea. And we need women in the restaurant. I can manage the occasional celebrity from the Princes Theatre or the Grand, but a few smart young ladies — not too young mind — wouldn't go amiss. Women who wear big hats for luncheon and low-cut dresses at dinnertime."

And so Claire, who had not wished to play the game of old acquaintances, wrote notes to addresses of which she was no longer quite certain, made telephone calls which varied from the amusing to the embarrassing, catching in her net an assortment of women who had been girls when they had last met and who reacted variously to her approach. Yet there were some among them, comfortably married and slightly bored, or war-widowed and lonely who, once the lounge in the Crown Hotel had been pointed out to them, found it a more comfortable gossiping place than Feathers; others who, having admitted that the slaughter of their generation had made marriage a matter of chance rather than the certainty it had once been, were beginning to make lives and careers for themselves without men, and for whom dinner in town with friends was no longer improper.

"Well done," said Kit Hardie.

"What next?"

"Let's give some attention to lunches."

Claire telephoned Swanfield Mills and asked for Mr. Hartwell.

"Claire?" Toby's voice sounded nervous. "What *am* I guilty of now?"

"You haven't been to see us at the Crown, that's all."

"Can I afford you? I rather promised Eunice I'd economize, what with the new Merc. and well — one or two other things . . . A little flutter on a horse last week for instance that's still running . . ."

"Oh Toby, don't let me down," she said, sounding a little like Polly. "I suppose there must be an important customer somewhere that you'd like to impress. Come and see what we can do."

He came that same morning for coffee, glanced at the wine list, sampled a paté, disappeared into Kit Hardie's office to emerge, an hour later, openly savoring the after-taste of old brandy and looking well satisfied. He returned to lunch with a party of four others, a celebration, or possibly a consolation, lasting until four o'clock in the afternoon and, before long, had become so much a part of the hotel that his constant presence, always vague and sweet and half apologetic, popular with the staff, generous with tips he could not afford, ready at all times to drop everything and lend a sympathetic ear — or a five pound note — to anybody's problems, gave Claire a sharp pang of conscience. Did Eunice know how he spent his time and the Swanfield money? Did Benedict know? She supposed they did. And there was no doubt that his value to the Crown, if not to the Swanfields, not only on his own account but for the customers he introduced, was immense.

"What next, Kit?" she asked.

"We keep on giving good food and wine, good service, good value. The news will get around."

She sincerely hoped — for his sake at least and partly, already, for her own — that it would.

But from the night of its opening, a week after, the cocktail bar was filled to capacity, every table around the minute dance floor booked in advance, every seat, every bar stool, eagerly taken by young people not only from Faxby but from miles around who asked nothing more from life, it seemed, than to dance, all night if possible, to these sensual, staccato American tunes and drink these American concoctions of gin and vermouth, pernod and grenadine, green and yellow chartreuse.

The war was over. And half of the young men who came roaring up to the back door of the Crown in their dashing little roadsters had too many medals for gallantry under fire to be cautioned by parents on the evils of late hours and strong drink. The future, which had once seemed limitless, had turned out to be very short. And what mattered now was to cram its little duration, its insignificant span of time, with brief passions, temporary joys, to make a noise loud enough to echo when the voice faded, to paint colors vibrant enough to last at least the night; to be — in accordance with the latest fashion — both "crazy" and "smart."

"Sandwiches only in the cocktail bar," decreed Kit Hardie. "Dainty ones. Curls of smoked salmon, rare roast beef cut like paper, a dash of caviar, silver trays and lace doilies and plenty of garnish — tomato roses, cress, lemon wedges, black pepper, horseradish, all the trimmings. Very pretty. Looks a lot and pleases the eye but just *whets* the appetite."

"Darling — I'm hungry," moaned one liberated young lady after another. The restaurant, for those who could afford it, was close at hand, and since orders for dinner were not taken after half past nine, it soon became the fashion among that "smart and crazy" set, to dine first while palates were still sharp and heads relatively steady before drifting downstairs, replete, pleasantly tipsy, faintly amorous, to flirt and make promises, to drink fruit-flavored spirits, smoke Turkish cigarettes, and, above all, to dance.

There was the bunny hug, the shimmy. There was the foxtrot, the most perfect excuse yet invented for a man and a woman to embrace publicly. There was the tango. Girls danced without gloves, without programs and with complete strangers. The need to be introduced had become obsolete alongside the need to be chaperoned. Young ladies — and they made no bones about it — did not come to the Crown in search of husbands. They came, unashamedly and as young men had always been allowed to do, for the adventure, the amusement, the *fun*. The great thing was not to be bored. In some cases not to remember. And where better to blur one's sense of resentment of the past and futility at the future in a haze of tobacco, jazz music and alcohol, than the Crown?

"Nowhere," said Kit Hardie, "but if we could fill the bedrooms we'd be making money all through the night as well, while everybody's asleep."

"Major Hardie, do you think you could help me out?" inquired a bright but suddenly earnest young thing. "We're having a party for my twenty-first — marquee in the garden and all that, and what with our cutting down on maids and moving to a smaller house after the boys were killed, Mummy wonders if you could possibly put up about a dozen of our guests — just overnight for the 24th and maybe the 25th?"

"I only wish you had given me more notice," replied the Major, looking grave.

"Oh I say, Major Hardie, please don't let me down. If my friends can't come here then I'll end up with nothing but my cousins and brothers-in-law and old grannies at my birthday party. *Please* Major."

He hesitated, glanced upward speculatively, as if he just might have been deciding which of his numerous bookings could best be canceled. "Mr. Clarence," he said, "Mrs. Swanfield. Let's put our heads together and do a little juggling for this young lady."

"Oh, Major. Mother will be *so* thankful."

Would she convey her thanks in person? She came, a sensible, handsome woman dressed with unobtrusive elegance, the "first lady," despite her removal to smaller premises, of the village a dozen miles from Faxby where her family had been settled for several generations. Kit Hardie, at his most impressive, escorted her around the hotel, a grand tour culminating with the Earl Grey tea in floral Coalport china, freshly baked scones and raspberry jam, hot muffins, a traditional English plum cake, nothing too elaborate or suspiciously continental, Claire noticed, nothing, in fact, which the lady might not have expected in the country homes of her friends.

144

"This is really very pleasant," she said, relaxing into a chintz armchair, glancing with approval around the quiet room, perfectly at ease with its unostentatious, reassuring solid comfort. "Very pleasant. I had expected something rather more flamboyant, I confess. I am so glad. Do you have facilities for private parties, I wonder? I chair a number of committees and when it comes to annual dinners and the like it seems sensible, these days — when one is afflicted with a servant problem, as I am — to take the catering out of one's home."

She left with menus, brochures, prices.

"The word is spreading," said Kit.

Would it spread fast enough? But by the autumn, Claire no longer felt the slightest qualm about accepting her salary, being well aware that she often earned it twice over.

"You can't possibly enjoy it," said Dorothy, no question this but a statement she desperately wanted to be true, in order to assure Edward that her daughter's latest madness was over.

"It gives me a reason to get up in the morning."

"*Claire?*" Dorothy was plainly scandalized. "And you must know, I suppose, that — inevitably — there have been rumors. About your relations with that man."

"Inevitably?"

"Well, of course, since you are always with him, shut up together for hours in his office by all accounts. Claire *is* that necessary? And you were seen, you know, in his company at two o'clock one morning, walking in the direction of Mannheim Crescent. I really didn't know how to explain it."

"It must have been a fine night."

And then, seeing that Dorothy was sincerely upset, she said tartly, "Mother, whoever it was who saw me, must have been out in the streets at two o'clock in the morning themselves, you know."

"Yes. Yes. We all know about that." Dorothy's temper, under pressure from her nerves and from Edward, was fraying. "Just the same — since you are so clever — you should also know that it is downright foolish to allow yourself to be seen in compromising circumstances with a man to whom you *cannot possibly* be attached."

"Can't I, mother?"

"No, No you can't. Certainly not. Claire — for Heaven's sake — he was in service."

And had she said "in prison," "infected with a social disease," "insane," her expression could not have been more shocked and bitter.

"Yes, mother. But he was a war hero too, you know. You should see his uniform — absolutely covered with ribbons and medals."

"The war," snapped Dorothy in direct quotation from Edward, "is over. And now that things are back to normal again — well . . ."

"Yes mother. A lady is a lady. And a butler is a butler."

And what, she knew Edward had demanded, would the Swanfields say should she misbehave herself with theirs?

Did she care? No. Only insofar as it would hurt Dorothy. And both she and her mother — and Edward — would just have to live with that. If she decided, that is, to "misbehave."

Throughout Claire's life every one of her close relationships had been, to some degree, painful and she knew of no reason why her future ones should not follow suit. Intimacy, therefore, implied a certain amount of hurt and, still bearing more or less bravely the scars inflicted by Dorothy and Jeremy and Paul, what concerned her now was not to avoid wounds altogether but to make sure they were light, superficial, quick to heal. And in her present frame of mind, Kit — as he seemed to know — was too much for her. Not that he would hurt her. On the contrary, should she go to him now, this minute, she rather imagined that he would take her straight upstairs to the elegant little flat he had made for himself from the attics of the Crown and make love to her so thoroughly that she would have no breath left to worry about what anyone might say. And afterward she would be able to lean against him, firm hands upon her, a firm will to guide her, allowing him to blend her and merge her with himself until they became a couple. She was almost sure he wanted that. Not, of course — and she found herself smiling tolerantly, with affection — that he was prevented by anything he might feel for her from succumbing promptly and with a goodwill to any temptations strewn along his path by certain ladies from the Princes Theatre and elsewhere. He was a man of appetite who had never had any reason for restraint. She understood that. And until he *had* a reason it would not occur to him to be celibate.

Was it only a question of breaking the barrier between the warm camaraderie they now shared and the more exclusive passion of lovers? It could be done, she sometimes felt quite certain. And to be cherished by a man like Kit, who did nothing by halves, could be no mean experience. Yet what — at present — had she to give him? He would want a great deal. If he ever made a commitment he would expect, quite rightly, as much in return. And even on the days when it seemed to her that she would be glad of that, she did not feel fit for it. In her present state of mind it would be an act of weakness, not of giving so much as of surrender. So much less than he — or any decent man — deserved, that she could not really think of it. Not yet.

And in the meantime, since he was evidently in no hurry, she admired him, *liked* him, was very happy to learn from him. There were times, of course, usually early mornings following too little sleep, when she found him exacting, exhausting, over-meticulous, extravagant. Yet when, at his insistence, the silver which had seemed quite bright enough, had been polished once again, the flowers which, in everybody else's opinion, could easily last a few more days, had been replaced, when everyone had grumbled that it could hardly be necessary to rearrange those newspapers, empty those ashtrays, plump up those cushions so constantly over and over, there was — when one surveyed the final picture — no denying that the Major had raised the Crown a decided cut above the station hotels. And when tempers flared, crisis or panic or chaos broke out as it inevitably, and fairly regularly did, the mere appearance of Kit Hardie upon the scene provided instant reassurance, a speedy return to calm. *Here* was the man who would take the decision, provide the solution, shoulder — if necessary — the blame. *Here* was the man who would put things to rights, would save the day and everybody's bacon, reducing disaster to a little extra work and ingenuity and sending it tamely away.

"What name can one give for what you do?" inquired Dorothy. "We rather think you should be called an assistant manageress. At any rate, that is what we tell our friends. I don't see how you can object."

She did not object, thinking it as good a title as any for her range of tasks, for the miles she ran every day from Kit Hardie's office to every part of the hotel; to the lobby where Mr. Clarence, his charm being interspersed with brief fits of melancholy, could not always cope; to the little flower room to make sure the girls had remembered "blue for the Blue Room, pink for the Rose"; to the housekeeper's room to investigate an unaccustomed moodiness in a chambermaid, or a discrepancy in the linen stock. She calculated and paid out the wages, checked the bar accounts, arbitrated in Chef Keller's many disputes with tradesmen, kept within sight of the lounge at teatime and made herself pleasant to any solitary ladies. Three nights a week, often four, wearing a long tunic of black net covered with jet beads, she moved through the restaurant and the cocktail bar, available for conversation, compliments, complaints; ready to preserve order and keep an eye on the barman, MacAllister, an agreeable fellow but quite likely — said Kit — to give short measure at full price and pocket the difference if he could. She spent hours listening, with half her mind, to men who boasted of their virility and their bank balances and men who charmingly confessed that they had little of either; to the beginning and end of love affairs; to Arnold Crozier's discourses on the art of making and drinking wine; Toby Hartwell's abandoned ambitions to be a test pilot, a racing motorist, to ride the winner of the Derby; the claims of the restaurant pianist, Miss Adela Adair, that only the envy of her music teachers and her own generosity to a series of feckless lovers had kept her from the international concert stage. In obedience to Kit Hardie's instructions that the Kellers, upon whose culinary expertise so much depended, must be kept happy at any cost, she made frequent visits to the kitchen, where more often than not, she was able to convince Aristide Keller of his own genius, the high value the Major and the entire gourmet population of Faxby — never large — put upon him, and that no one was in the act of stealing his recipes which he kept scribbled down on scraps of paper and impaled on a spike behind the door, except for their one most vital ingredient which remained locked inside his shrewd, suspicious mind.

"Yes, mother. I think you might call me an assistant manageress."

"Oh — very well," said Dorothy doubtfully, still wondering how to convince Edward that one could feel proud of that. "But do you *like* it? Is it what you want?"

"It keeps me busy. It occupies my mind."

It also enabled her to stand back, not altogether but sufficiently, from the Swanfields so that, at this safer distance, she could see them in less threatening colors. Eunice and Toby had never alarmed her. Nola, she decided, must be taken at her face value, not high perhaps but often amusing, intriguing, more or less inevitable. To the enigma Benedict represented, she could find no solution and had concluded that it would be pointless, therefore, to study him too closely. While Polly, as Claire had always suspected, seemed more than able to look after herself, having solved the problem of her independence by the acquisition of a more acceptable chaperone than her mother, a young admirer, a possible fiancé, Mr. Roger Timms of Taylor & Timms, a weighty, amiable young man who had avoided conscription because of his weak eyesight and whose friendship not only enabled Polly to behave in a very queenly fashion in the Millinery and Perfumery Departments of his father's store but to visit, in the supposed security of his company, the hitherto forbidden Crown Hotel.

"I know I can *rely* on Roger," beamed Miriam, "to look after Polly." And if she knew that he seemed perfectly content to spend his evenings blinking owlishly into a whiskey and lemon juice while Polly flirted — never with him — and danced, then at least the conventions of escort and chaperonage were being observed and Miriam had no need to feel — no need to worry that anyone else might feel — that she was neglecting her youngest, never particularly her favorite, child.

"Roger darling — I'm ready to go now."

"Right ho, princess."

And short-sighted, muddle-headed, wanting nothing more, it seemed, than a pat on the ear like a good dog, he would shamble to his feet.

"What a devoted soul he is," mused Miriam speculatively. "Rather backward as a child, of course — I remember his mother being most anxious about it — but always sweet-natured. And very rich. Polly could do much worse."

So — for her present purposes — she could.

"Roger — pick me up tomorrow at two o'clock and don't forget to collect that hat I left for trimming. There's a picture I want to see at the Palace — a bit above your head sweetie but you can sleep through it — and then you can take me out to tea. Get me home by five, which leaves me plenty of time to change, and then pick me up again for — well — seven-thirty — no — eight. And Roger — don't wear that spotted tie."

She was imperious, occasionally indulgent, always decisive. He was dazzled, happy to be led, her dominion over him appearing to suit them both. Perhaps she would marry him and, if so, her wedding would be the most spectacular Faxby had ever seen, a fairy tale of tulle and spangles and white orchids. Or perhaps not, in which case she would live out some other fairy tale, would be swept off her feet by some man far less biddable than Roger, who might even hurt her a little but would, of course, be terribly sorry about it in the end. Perhaps.

Claire began to believe that, so far as the Swanfields were concerned, she was relatively, adequately free. But she had reckoned without Miriam and the war memorial.

Every town, every village, every corner of England was by then in the process of honoring its dead by some public inscription of their names, some piece of sculpture, to provide a focal point of remembrance. And Faxby had not lagged behind. A stone soldier leaning head bowed upon his rifle was to be unveiled that autumn in a memorial garden laid out with evergreens and sad pale lilies just beyond the floral clock in Faxby Park. His companion at arms was to stand on a stone platform in Town Hall Square where hymns would be sung and wreaths of poppies laid for the first time on the 11th November when, at 11 o'clock, a two-minute silence would be observed, as had been done daily in Cape Town throughout the entire war, as a tribute to the slain. Similar monuments, plaques, commemorative works of art were being commissioned everywhere by banks, building societies, regiments, colleges, railways, town councils and parish councils, commercial enterprises. An empty tomb was to stand in clean-lined, straight-hearted significance in Whitehall. At the suggestion of the Dean of Westminster in Whitehall, the bodies of six soldiers were to be dug out of their shallow, nameless graves, one each from Ypres, Cambrai, Arras, The Marne, The Somme, The Aisne, and taken to an army hut near Ypres where a blindfolded officer would select the coffin, containing an unknown man perhaps six years dead, which would be given a state funeral in Westminster Abbey.

And Claire, had her mind not been full of other things, should have known that Swanfield Mills, which had lost its quota of men at the front, including the founder's younger son, would be unlikely to shirk so obvious and so sacred a task.

A plaque, inscribed with those thirty or so names, headed by Jeremy's, would have been adequate in Benedict's opinion, situated in the marbled and extremely splendid reception hall of the mill. Perfectly adequate, agreed Miriam, provided some piece of sculpture could be added, a frieze perhaps, depicting a line of young soldiers looking noble and dedicated and sad.

"Then the list of names below it," mused Miriam, "and below that one of those wonderful phrases, in gold lettering, 'Their country called. They answered.' Or — yes, of course, best of all — 'Their lives were not taken but given.' "

"Try 'lambs to the slaughter,' " said Nola.

"And then," continued Miriam sweetly, taking no notice, "there must be a fitting ceremony for the relatives and some kind of commemorative medal or plate or beaker perhaps for everyone to take home."

Throughout those autumn Sunday evenings which Claire still spent at High Meadows she heard without listening until, one early November night, the truth burst upon her. Forty-two men of the Swanfield work-force had died in battle including Jeremy Swanfield, a garden boy and a groom. Forty-two bereaved mothers were to be assembled, therefore, at the mill, almost as many fathers, twenty-eight widows, thirty-four children, some of them still babes in arms, a great many sisters and brothers, a few grandparents, rather more fiancées than seemed reasonable although Toby Hartwell, who had organized the proceedings, had thought it ungentlemanly to inquire too closely. The vicar of Faxby Parish Church, a Methodist minister and an ebullient officer of the Salvation Army were all to say a few words, after which the plaque with its frieze of young warriors was to be unveiled by the joint hands of Jeremy Swanfield's wife and mother who would then present suitable mementoes to all those other wives and mothers, speaking a few words to each. There would then be tea, sandwiches and cakes, to the accompaniment of the Associated Textile Workers' Brass Band, playing their strident music in the mill yard.

Had she agreed to do it? No one had asked her. *Could* she do it?

Lying dry-mouthed and sleepless that night in her bed, fearing to close her eyes and succumb to the images which she knew were there, waiting behind her eyelids, the horror which, however firmly she suppressed it, still lurked in the recesses of her memory, she very much doubted it.

"We should wear black, my dear, with perhaps a shoulder spray of white flowers," said Miriam. "And I wonder whether one should consider mourning veils? What do you think, dear, since we were unable to hold a proper funeral?"

Smiling quickly, palely, she had no comment to make.

"A sad duty," sighed Miriam, "but I do believe it absolutely necessary to engage the families in conversation for just as long as one is able. It will be greatly appreciated. There is no need to memorize the names you know. Just call everyone 'my dear' as I do. And they will be very well satisfied."

"I don't think I can bear it," she told Euan Ash.

"Then don't."

"It's not so simple."

"Oh yes it is. All you have to do is say no."

"What would you do?"

"Ah — about the same as always — not much. Get drunk. Lock myself in my room for a week or two to think about it — until it struck me that none of it mattered a damn. Because it doesn't you know. That's freedom, Claire. At least I hope it is. Not caring. *That's* the state of grace I'm after. You should give it a try."

She had seen his painting by now, which the dancing teacher had sold, for the cost of the gaudy frame she had stuck around it, to the art dealer and pawnbroker just behind the Crown.

Euan, Claire supposed, must know it was there, propped up in the window, marked down at 12/6d among the brass Bombay elephants, the cracked Victorian china, the trays of old coins and Ashanti and Boer War medals. Had he stopped to look at it? She didn't think so. Yet she had looked herself for as long as she dared at that magical, beautiful, diseased world of Euan's boyhood and Paul's. Recognizing both of them in the face of the pilgrim. Knowing how total had been their faith in all the magical, beautiful falsehoods that world had taught them. Wondering if Paul too — had he seen the lies revealed — would have desired more than a temporary joining of hands, unable — like Euan — to sustain any relationship beyond the level of two companions traveling, for as long as it lasted, for as long as they could, along an open road.

Did she, herself, feel fit for anything heavier or more permanent than that?

Like Euan.

Yes. Very like him, sometimes. So that when her heart bled for him it bled for Paul. For the pilgrim. And for what had become of him. For her own kind.

"You're not helping me," she said quickly, dragging her mind back to the war memorial.

"I am not helpful, which is the same as saying I don't interfere. Do what is right for you. It may not be right for me. I don't know the difference between right and wrong in any case. Once *thought* I did, of course, but that was in prehistoric times when they were still teaching us 'Thou shalt not kill.' All that stuff about justice and mercy didn't stand the test of time too well either."

She endured another sleepless night, another evening at High Meadows where, quite suddenly, the weight and sweetness of Miriam's presence becoming unendurable, she jumped to her feet, found Benedict in his study and informed him "I'm sorry. I can't go through with it," her emotion so intense that she saw him recoil, not in alarm, she thought, but in pure distaste, his nostrils curling as if the odor of such hotly expressed feeling seriously offended them.

"You mean the Memorial Service, I suppose. I think you can hardly avoid it."

"Nevertheless — I can't go."

"I expect you're going to tell me why."

And, once again, at a moment when it was essential to be calm, to state her case rationally and precisely if there was to be any hope of him listening to it at all, she found herself overwhelmed by her own reaction to this passionless, haughty man, tumbled by the sheer force of it into incoherence.

"I can't take a leading part in a ceremony I don't — with which I can't be *at ease*."

"It seems harmless enough to me."

"You were a civilian," she said rashly, mulishly. "You wouldn't understand."

"Ah — yes. Naturally not. Would you care to enlighten me?"

"I don't want to be reminded, Benedict, that's all. It's not necessary. I can remember. Surely you can understand that?"

"Well yes — I *do* think my understanding might extend so far. But you have no monopoly on grief, you know. Every other woman present will have just as much to remember."

"I doubt that."

"Do you really? Well — yes — I suppose if one takes the view that, as a member of the educated classes, your sensibilities are keener than those of working women, then I suppose it follows that your loss must be the greater. Is that what you mean?"

"I most certainly do not." She was furious, her skin bleached by it so that her dark eyes, glittering with suppressed tears, seemed enormous.

"What I mean is — for God's sake Benedict — I *saw* it and they didn't. They can remember their boys as they were — decked out in their brand-new uniforms with the right number of arms and legs and eyes — and I can't. I saw what happened to them afterward and I don't want to think about it too often — not just yet. Those women weren't told . . ."

"I imagine they have a good idea."

"No they don't. They'll have had their telegrams from the War Office and those letters from commanding officers — and hospital nurses — saying he was shot cleanly through the heart and can have felt no pain — when it was no such thing — when for everyone who went like that there were twenty more who died in filthy, mutilated agony that lasted for hours and days — and others who shot themselves in their own trenches because they couldn't stand any more of it. Mothers and wives weren't told about that either."

"Do you think they should be?"

"Why not — why the hell not."

"To give them extra pain — like yours?"

"No — to stop them handing out white feathers the next time we go to war. To stop all this nonsense — like Miriam's — about 'Their lives were given, not taken.' Because it is nonsense — dangerous nonsense. It's just politicians making excuses. I've watched hundreds of young men die — boys, that's all — and not one of them was ready — or willing. They weren't making a sacrifice. They were *being sacrificed.* They knew it. It was horrible."

She was atrociously upset and wanting to take her distress as far away from him as she could, to hide it as animals hide when afflicted by disease, she moved over to the window embrasure and sat down on the padded velvet seat, shivering, sick at heart. It was not in her nature to make such outbursts and this one, as it tore her notions of good taste and self-restraint asunder, hurt her badly. She would not have cared to expose herself in this way to anyone. But particularly not to Benedict, whose own self-control was so absolute that he could only despise her for the loss of her own.

Yet, instead of the scorn she had anticipated and had prepared herself to meet, he simply poured out two glasses of brandy, put one into her unsteady hand and stood, very tall and very quiet, before her, hemming her into the window seat as he had done once before at her garden gate, but without menace this time, prepared, it seemed, to wait.

"I'm sorry," she said, not looking at him, her eyes fixed on the heavy crystal goblet, the amber spirit. "I don't know why the war started. I've never worked it out and, at the time, it never even crossed my mind to ask. When you're young you can accept that some things are just — *there*. You believe what they tell you and when they say 'do or die,' well then, that's what you do, because you're young and idealistic, which is the same as saying you're exploitable and a bloody fool. What mattered most to me in 1914 was getting away from home and the war was my opportunity. I took it. I don't know what I expected. Parade-ground soldiers in scarlet getting hit cleanly through the head or the heart like we said in all those letters and leaving dying messages to mother instead of cursing and screaming — or whimpering — because they didn't want to die at all. And, of course, as I got older they kept on getting younger. And they weren't regulars anymore or volunteers, who'd chosen to be there, just eighteen-year-old conscripts who were in the trenches, some of them, for one reason — and one only. We'd have shot them as deserters otherwise."

"We?"

"Yes." And the bitterness inside her was like venom, poisoning her veins, corroding her. "The generals, who kept well back — *well* back. Did you ever hear of a general getting hit by a shell? The politicians who sat safe at home and talked about it. Silly women who persuaded men to enlist and then went back to their own comfortable parlors, instead of going to the front themselves and doing something more useful — less obscene — than handing out white feathers. Old men who played games with young men's lives — nine million lives . . ."

"And war profiteers? Like me?"

"Very likely."

"Thank you. You have a point, I won't deny it. Trade in manufactured goods was not at its best in 1914. We had a great deal of competition from Germany you see. That, for the moment, has ended. The war brought a boom — full employment — high wages. That, I rather fear, has ended too. Had those men whom we are going to honor at our Memorial Service survived, then I'm not certain that I would have had jobs to give them. Not all of them, at any rate. And not for long. And Miriam was very embarrassed only the other day by an ex-officer — Military Cross, I believe, among other things, and several wound stripes — attempting to sell brushes at the back door."

"Yes. Miriam would be."

Raising her head to take a swallow of brandy she saw him smile.

"Of course. The man was clearly a gentleman, just as a brush salesman is clearly not. A year ago, when he was still in command of whatever it was he commanded, she would have entertained him in the drawing room. But a brush salesman, even with a Military Cross and a university degree, is hardly entitled to that. Nor could she even feel comfortable about buying too many brushes, since salesmen of this type abound, and what one does for one, etcetera, etcetera, one might feel obliged to do for the rest. She worried a great deal about it. I don't expect you to have any sympathy with her dilemma. I may not have too much myself. But — nevertheless — these attitudes of hers should not obscure the fact that she was sincerely attached to Jeremy. She *did* mourn him. If she now wishes to unveil a plaque in his memory then I wonder why you should grudge her what amounts to an afternoon of your time."

"I have told you why. Because he died for nothing."

He took the empty glass from her hand and, as she made the gesture of a woman looking for her handbag, gave her a cigarette, still keeping her there in the curtained recess, not captive in the sense of any actual restraint yet held there, just the same, until he — she was well aware of it — chose to release her.

"I might agree with that, Claire."

"Would you really?"

"I might. I might take the view that this war has been so rashly conducted on all sides, the peace so harsh and so nearsighted that far from being the war to end all wars, as they told us, it will simply go down in history as a stepping-stone to the next. I *might* take that view. You would obviously share it. Miriam and perhaps eighty percent of the women you are to meet at the ceremony prefer to think otherwise. A delusion, perhaps. But it would certainly be unkind and perhaps somewhat pointless to shatter it. Don't you think?"

And when she did not answer he said crisply, "The men are dead. It hardly seems fair to blame them for the inadequacy of the reasons."

"I don't. Very far from that."

"And the women are alive and have to make the best of it. We are saluting the dead, after all, not the generals and politicians you spoke of — and the profiteers —, since *we* are all still very much alive."

She sat for a moment, her head bowed, very still, and then, frowning with the intensity of her concentration, she looked up at him abruptly and said "Benedict, you are absolutely right."

"Yes, I know."

"And I still can't do it."

She had been taken by Miriam only the day before to see the plaque with the frieze above it, a line of chalk-white soldiers in single file, handsome, anonymous, dead men in dead marble, whose pallor had caused her to drop her eyes before she saw the carnage waiting for them around the corner.

"Beautiful," she had said hurriedly. She said now, just as quickly, "It has nothing to do with principles or ideals. I agree with you that the men should be honored. We could never honor them enough. But — whatever the rights or wrongs of it — I also know that I can't stand in that enclosed space with all those grieving women — I just can't. I couldn't breathe."

She ducked her head, awaiting punishment, dismissal, finding his silence so unendurable that she rushed headlong against it and broke it herself.

"I know Miriam will be upset. I know it will look odd and people will talk. Edward Lyall will never forgive me and he'll make sure my mother never does. I don't expect any of them to understand. And if you want to stop my allowance then please do — I wouldn't mind. In fact it might be a good thing if you did, and then I wouldn't have to worry about it — to feel that because I take your money I ought to do — well — as I'm told."

Let the punishment come *now*, she thought. Let him threaten her, offer some tangible intimidation with which she could grapple and have done.

"I didn't realize," he said quietly, "that you had retained so much feeling for my brother."

She got up then, almost without realizing her own movement, and walked away from him, not far, but no longer shut in between the window and his shadowy yet so powerful presence. And, with her back still toward him, she said "I can't even remember what Jeremy looked like — nor anything else about him."

And, the words delivered, the confession made into blank space, empty silence, she turned round — feeling a physical compunction to do so — and faced him again.

"I see."

"How can you?"

"Because you didn't know Jeremy and consequently what *could* you remember."

"So I tell myself. It makes no difference to the way I feel about it."

"Your troublesome conscience again? You should really take it in hand you know."

"I do know. I feel guilty already about not attending the ceremony."

"Then attend it."

"I can't."

156

"Very well."

He took a step toward her, looking — what was it? — not angry, not impatient, not *pleased* — Heavens, what could she possibly have said to please him? — but rather as if something had given him a measure of satisfaction, as if he had in some way been proved right.

"What do you mean by 'very well'?"

"Oh — simply this. If you can't — if you are not up to it — then I suppose you can't."

"That's right. I'm a coward. I agree."

"And you are shirking your duty. You do accept that it *is* your duty to make yourself agreeable, for a moment or two, to a handful of our employees?"

"Yes. I accept that."

"And that your refusal to do so would give them serious offense."

"Yes. That worries me most of all."

"How kind. Then may I suggest that you become a diplomatic coward and fall ill, tomorrow at the very latest. Influenza is always believable and, in view of last year's epidemic, I doubt that either Miriam or Polly would come near you to check. Should you then change your mind and attend, everybody will think you very brave and won't expect too much of you in the way of conversation. If not, then there should be no hurt feelings."

"I won't change my mind."

"We'll wait — shall we — and see."

She returned to Mannheim Crescent, her resolution firm, the weight of unease which had been burdening her for days already lighter. Right or wrong — she had at least made up her mind and, the decision taken, all that remained was to brace herself for its consequences.

Miriam would not believe in her influenza but would pretend to do so. Polly and Nola would not care. Eunice would simply be alarmed in case she had infected Toby. Dorothy, for her own sake, would do her best to convince Edward. What would Jeremy have wanted her to do? She had tried hard to avoid the question yet now, to her discomfort, it kept leaping out at her from a corner of her mind, taking her by surprise so that she was forced to admit that Jeremy, who had not lived long enough to lose his faith in gallantry and glory, might feel entitled to the sad little measure of immortality conveyed by his name in gold letters on polished stone, and a woman of his own to weep for him. Surely he had a right to that? Surely the young girl who had married him would not have had a moment's hesitation? Where were they both now?

"I am about to have influenza," she told Euan Ash the next morning.

"Ah — strategic influenza, I take it?"

"Yes. I'm not going to the service."

"Aren't you? Then come to Faxby market with me instead. I'm selling antiques — more or less — for a friend of mine, and doing sketches on the side."

"How can I do that with influenza?"

"Perhaps not. They'd stop your allowance then all right."

"Oh well," she said, speaking, she realized, mainly to herself. "I'm not going in any case."

But, a little before noon, a smartly turned out messenger boy from Swanfield Mills appeared at the Crown and put an envelope in her hands, marked "Private and Confidential," looking official, *feeling* through the high, smooth quality of its paper, a decided threat.

"Ah well," she said to Euan who had come over to beg a drink. "I rather think half my income has gone."

"Shouldn't be a bit surprised. It's not a bad life, behind a market stall."

"Dear Claire," wrote Benedict in an elegant, legible, neutral hand, "It occurs to me that the matter of your allowance preys somewhat unnecessarily on your mind. In order to alleviate this pressure and to make you fully aware that no course of action need be dictated to you by these financial considerations, I have today canceled your monthly payments and arranged for the full amount to be paid to you annually. Money to cover the period from November, 1919 to November, 1920 has, therefore, been paid into your bank. I trust you will find this convenient."

He had handed her the only tangible weapon he had ever had against her. He had given her — what? — complete freedom of choice and, with it, the responsibility of freedom. He had challenged her. "If you're not up to it," he'd said. And now he had taken away the one excuse she might have made to herself, her only chance to say, "He forced me." Now she could languish at home, making weak excuses, playing wily, feminine games like Miriam and Nola, or she could rise to the challenge and show him what a free woman was made of. He had planned it, of course. He had discovered the right way, perhaps the only way, to force her hand. By the time she had folded his letter and put it back into its envelope, she knew, with a little resentment, some amusement, and a certain grudging admiration, that he had won.

9

SHE wore a black wool coat with a velvet hem and a high mandarin collar, a cloche hat pulled low over her ears, her pale oval face looking tranquil if faintly untenanted, as it often did in her moments of stress. The day was drizzly and overcast, a mean-spirited November wind tossing sudden handfuls of rain at the brass band, not entirely protected by an open-fronted marquee in the mill yard. The reception hall was full of chrysanthemums, wide-spreading banks of dark red, rusty brown, deep mustard yellow, and of sober, sensible women in their Sunday clothes, some of them dyed black for the occasion, standing in quiet rows before the claret velvet curtains which concealed the roll of honor; the Swanfields first, then their bankers and solicitors, and behind them, in strict order of precedence, the families of shed managers, weaving overlookers, skilled operatives, unskilled laborers, an awkward line of girls who had been "walking out" or otherwise associated with one or other of the soldiers and, finally, a rearguard of the firm's military survivors, wearing their wound stripes and campaign medals.

Miriam, in floor-length black furs, looked quiet and sad and, somewhat to Claire's surprise, immensely dignified. Eunice, her muskrat coat — had it once been Miriam's? — looking rather too big for her, wept and would continue to weep throughout the day in an unusually quiet, oddly resigned fashion, not only for her brother Jeremy but for her son, Justin, who had been taking money from her purse lately for purposes she had not dared to investigate, and for her son Simon who had persuaded Toby to buy him a motorcycle. Nola looked peevish and out of sorts, Polly, leaning heavily on Toby's arm, so beautiful, her skin so white above her black fur collar, her hair such a halo of fine spun gold, her face so perfectly endowed with the sorrowing gentleness of a Botticelli angel, that even Claire — who did not believe Polly capable of any deep feeling — was touched by it. Toby Hartwell, who had not been a soldier, stood smartly to attention, an officer and a gentleman to the life. Benedict Swanfield, who had not been a soldier either, looked exactly as he looked in his study, his boardroom, his bank, the Wool Exchange, competent, controlled, fully in charge yet only barely, if at all, involved.

A few clerical words were spoken. A hymn was sung, a prayer said. Miriam walked forward slowly, her furs eddying about her, Claire playing the lady-in-waiting to a bereaved and sorrowing queen, and together they drew back the curtain to reveal the gilded names, the chalk-white, ice-cold frieze. There was a low gasp of distress, the sound of a woman hushing a child, a man clearing a dry throat embarrassed by its own emotion, a staccato, quickly suppressed bout of coughing, a shuffling of feet. Both Eunice and Polly burst into tears, Eunice angrily now and hurtfully — more like her usual self — Polly quite fearfully as if it had only just occurred to her that bodies as young and healthy as her own could really die, her burst of panic turning her hastily toward her brother-in-law Toby, against whose obliging shoulder she cowered like a child in terror of the dark, Eunice on his other side, standing her own, uncertain ground.

Miriam returned to her place to observe, with an expression of careful, gentle sadness, the two-minute silence inaugurated by the King. Claire followed her, her own face as carefully blank, her mind empty. But, as she stood patiently, quietly, between Miriam and Benedict, her nostrils were suddenly aware, faintly and incredulously at first, of an odor reaching her through the scent of the chrysanthemums, a whiff — just a whiff, but enough to turn her stomach — of gas, and obscenely entangled with it, the sweetish, sickening odor of human decay. From where, in this clean, marble hall, did it come? She did not — *of course* she did not — really believe it. Yet, nevertheless, something touched her, a chill breath, a dead hand, a fear too primitive, too deep-rooted to contain. A moment more and the smell was crawling along the surface of her skin, entering her pores, filling her lungs with a terror as filthy and fatal as a drowning in mud. And lifting her eyes to the frieze she saw that the first chalk-white soldier, then the second, then the one after, had started to turn a sickly, stinking yellow and then to swell to enormous proportions, a line of putrefying giants coming down from the wall and shuffling, shambling in single file, each man with his hand on the shoulder of the man in front of him, blind eyes staring at her from the two dozen ochre-tinted faces which became — each one in passing — the face of Paul.

She knew quite well that she was hallucinating. She also knew that it was neither uncommon nor particularly serious and that it would pass. On the last afternoon she had spent with Paul he had seen, very clearly, walking down a street in Boulogne, a man he knew to have been two years in his grave. Almost every soldier she had nursed with more than six months' service at the front had suffered delusions equally alarming and bizarre. Resurrected comrades had abounded in France. Ghosts had walked everywhere. Shell-shocked minds — and every man or woman, who had been exposed to months of constant fear remained in some degree of shock — had seen corpses piled up at suburban English street corners where none existed, had thrown themselves flat on the ground, when on leave in English gardens, at the sound of a popping cork, had turned sick at the faint hiss of domestic gas.

Her case was no different. She knew these yellowing phantoms existed only in her mind. Yet that did not prevent her mind from recoiling, cringing from them in horror, her senses dissolving in a panic far beyond her control so that the whole room began first to sway and then to heave, hurtling her with brutal precision toward the plaque and its empty frieze and then back again down some tunnel of the mind where, for a moment of pure terror, she saw herself shrinking into rapid oblivion.

She knew she was about to faint. Slipping her hands inside her sleeves she dug savage fingers with their pointed nails into her arms. It made no difference. She was falling, face down she thought, into that odor of gas and corruption and chrysanthemums until Benedict Swanfield put out an arm to bar her way and she sank instead into the shadow she had always sensed around him, where she remained, captive but safe, adapting her frantic breathing, her racing pulse to the steady rate of his, her still precariously balanced mind taking refuge in his logic, his cold realism, his power.

More clerical words were spoken. Another prayer. Another hymn. The heavy hothouse fragrance of chrysanthemums became, not pleasant, but innocent again. Her vision cleared. The festering giants shambled away, not far perhaps, but out of her sight. Sanity returned so gradually, so easily, that, once the hallucination had gone, it seemed of little importance, a matter to be shrugged off as she remembered Paul — and others — had always done.

"Christ — I see corpses walking sometimes. Doesn't everybody?"

Benedict released her.

"Thank you," she said. And, as if in answer to her unspoken plea that nothing more should be made of it, he nodded and turned his attention to the congregation, now dispersing.

"Are you all right?" hissed Dorothy from behind her, moved by her

161

daughter's collapse yet not quite certain what the Swanfields would make of it.

"Come dear," murmured Miriam, intending to make nothing of it at all, rather more concerned with Polly who having started to cry did not seem able to stop. "You and I must do our duty." And while Polly, her face white and drowning, was led away to the boardroom by Toby, Miriam moved forward to greet her fellow mourners, inquiring from every young woman the names and ages of her children, from every older woman the exact state of her health, even asking the occupations of the obviously single girls at the back; information to which, no matter how warmly maternal her manner, she barely listened and promptly forgot.

Claire followed her.

"I'm so pleased you could come," she murmured almost inaudibly, speaking the words in order to say something, meeting decency, curiosity, one or two faces that had remained stunned by sorrow, one or two pairs of resentful eyes, a pair of sharp ones which took in, at a glance, the value of Miriam's furs and Nola's rings.

"You were a nurse in France then, Mrs. Swanfield, were you?"

But it was no more than politeness, a safe topic rehearsed beforehand, and she knew they did not listen to her reply.

"Dreadful about young Mr. Jeremy," somebody mentioned.

"We have all of us suffered the same loss," said Miriam gently and — at that moment — sincerely.

The band began to play, a signal which obliged Toby Hartwell to leave Polly to her own devices while he, as official master of ceremonies, organized the distribution of tea, souvenir medals and cakes. Miriam, who had been prevented only by the bleak November weather from opening her garden to "her workpeople," smiled, made one of her expansive gestures bidding everyone to eat their fill. Polly, rather more terrified of solitude than of sudden death, appeared dry-eyed but very pale, a little girl again quite lost inside her smart, grown-up coat, overwhelmed by her elaborate hat, her sapphire blue eyes peering timidly from beneath the brim, still looking, perhaps, for her father and finding no substitute. Eunice continued to do her duty behind the teacups, one watchful eye on Toby, her mind's eye probing fretfully in the supposed direction of her sons. Nola, in a spirit of pure provocation, had summoned all three clergymen into a corner where she proceeded to amuse herself by asking the very questions that they would have preferred not to answer.

"Explain to me the differences in your creeds. Why do you think you are right and he is wrong? What is your position on divorce, illegitimacy, the afterlife, the social position of women? And, since we are all adults and have heard of Marie Stopes, what about birth control?"

Claire, half listening, half smiling, produced with deceptive ease the polite phrases her upbringing had taught her and then, when they had been adequately delivered, moved away. And although she remained calm and quiet in her manner, her face serene, she knew herself to be in urgent need, enormous need — of what? Release. That was the word her mind offered, repeated, retained. Yet, what form it might take she had no notion. She had simply fallen — fallen deep and hard — into a state of extreme restlessness, fine-strung tension, churning unease, the state, encountered in dreams, of knowing she must set off on a journey at once, that it was vital, essential, could not wait, that she must hurry — hurry — not a moment to lose. Run. Catch that train. *Listen* to the ticking of that clock. Go now. But where? For what purpose?

"Have you seen over the mill?" asked Benedict offering her — could it be intentionally? — the respite she needed.

Yes. One afternoon, long ago, in her first trance of adoration for the knight-errant Jeremy, he had brought her on a grand tour of the Swanfield Mills, almost as ignorant as she was herself of the processes by which his family's fortune had been made. And she had walked shyly beside him, still grateful to him for wanting her, not wishing to put herself forward or appear bold, trying to look serious, intelligent, *worthy*; on her best behavior, in fact, as her mother had told her. But her mother had also warned her to be pleasant to everyone, to make a universally good impression, and so she had smiled bravely and equally at every corner of the weaving-shed, trying not to recoil at the sour odors of raw wool and engine grease, the ferocious clatter of power looms, the dangers of straps and picking-sticks breaking loose; had watched, with more obedience than delight, the sharp-ended, lethally pointed shuttles flying back and forth the length of every loom, tended by scantily clad women who held voiceless conversations all day long, reading each other's lips from one loom-gate to the next.

"They all go deaf eventually, of course," Jeremy had casually mentioned. "But they can all lip-read so amazingly I suppose it's better than losing an eye. Although that can happen too, of course. Don't stand too near the looms, darling, because those picking-sticks *do* swing loose occasionally — quite hard enough to break an arm. And those shuttles don't always aim straight either. They fly out, sometimes, all over the place and if one happens to be in their way — well, what I said just now about eyes — !"

She had drawn hastily back, the noise of the machinery an assault in itself, lodging inside her eardrums, woven, by those vicious shuttles, into her mind so that even when it had been left far behind for the dignified silence of the burling and mending room, where better-dressed and, in their own view at least, better-class women sat at high tables, correcting faults in the unfinished cloth with meticulous hand stitches, she had heard it still.

But the weaving-shed was silent this November Sunday afternoon as she entered it with Benedict, the shuttles and the picking-sticks which sped them on their way through a web of yarn, no danger to anyone, the looms looking squat, sullen, but inoffensive.

And standing in the acrid silence beneath the grimy, industrial ceiling that, for all its squalor, was as high as a cathedral, they said nothing to each other of the least significance.

He made no reference at all to her distress, her near-collapse, at the unveiling of the plaque.

She did not mention his letter.

He did not mention his brother, nor she her husband.

She did not ask him why he allowed his wife to deceive him, nor why he pretended to be deceived.

Instead she listened, her head on one side, while he explained, crisply, concisely, and one by one, the processes by which the wool, once taken from the sheep's back, was scoured, then — if it was to become worsted cloth — combed into long-fibered "tops" and short-fibered "noils," or, if it was intended for woolen fabric, carded on rollers, then twisted, spun into yarn, woven into coarse, gray pieces which, having passed the scrutiny of the burling and mending room, would, by the miracles of dyeing and finishing, become camel hair, cashmere, mohair, high quality gentlemen's suiting, fancy dress goods for ladies, fabric to upholster the seats of motor cars.

"I have nine hundred looms in here," he said, "which can give me 22,000 yards of cloth a day — if I want it."

"Don't you want it?"

"Only if I can sell it."

"But surely — *everybody* wants to buy Yorkshire cloth. Is there any other kind?"

He smiled but not quite in her direction, just a little over her shoulder so that his amusement was not entirely shared, contact not fully made.

"So we were brought up to believe. So they are still saying — and rather proudly — at the Piece Hall and the Wool Exchange."

"Are they wrong?"

"No. Our product is excellent. But some of our markets are no longer there. Trade with Russia has collapsed since the Revolution. American import tariffs are discouragingly high. Germany has been reduced to bankruptcy and starvation. And as for the rest of Europe, including ourselves . . . Well, we *do* have a hefty war loan which America can't be blamed for expecting us to repay. We *do* have to look after our returned soldiers and our second army of munitions workers whose services are no longer required, but who have become accustomed to high wages. And if we can't employ them then we'll have to support them on whatever public money we have left, which can't be much when one thinks of the cost of all those shells."

"Oh dear. And I thought we were having a boom."

"So they say. So we are. The munitions workers still have their savings to spend, and the soldiers their gratuities. But when that's done — and if there's still no work — well, I suppose if the choice should be between paying the rent and buying a Swanfield camel hair coat, that any sensible man would pay his rent."

"So then you wouldn't need your 22,000 yards of cloth a day."

"No. Nor the workers to produce it. But don't worry. The trust funds are secure."

"That doesn't worry me."

"I know. Are you ready to go back now?"

"Yes."

But she did not move, feeling an odd reluctance to leave the shelter of this alien machinery, their two voices echoing in the vast, anonymous shed as they played their commonplace, yet so restful, game of question and answer.

"Do you know how to operate these machines, Benedict?"

"Of course."

"And the spinning-frames in the other shed?"

"Yes. Why do you ask?"

"Because Jeremy didn't know how."

"I see you remember something about him."

"Yes. That much. Shouldn't he have known more?"

"Why duplicate the same knowledge? I haven't touched a loom for years. But I know how it works and what can go wrong with it, and why. My engineers know that I know, which is the whole point of the exercise. Just as my accountants know that I can read a balance sheet — etcetera —"

"Yes. But do you *like* it, Benedict? Is it what you wanted?"

"Would you like to see the burling room?"

He had not ignored her question, far more than that. He had chosen not to hear it at all, no syllable remaining as he slid open the heavy doors and switched on the lights to give her a better view of the high burling-tables shrouded identically with pieces of gray unfinished cloth.

"It will all look the same to you," he said, accepting her ignorance very calmly. "But that's a heavy worsted — that's cashmere — that's mohair —"

"I see," she said gravely, seeing nothing of the kind.

"Do you? What else can I show you? Or does your conscience tell you that you ought to be listening to the band?"

She returned, refreshed, she thought, although she did not really know what had refreshed her, to the mill yard where the band was still valiantly playing and smiled warmly at Miriam, who pretended not to have missed her, and at her mother who all too clearly had.

"Where on earth have you been?" hissed honest, unwise Dorothy.

"Come and sit by me, dear," murmured clever Miriam, "and have a buttered scone."

The afternoon wore on. Confectionery continued to be eaten with the enthusiasm of squirrels hoarding for the winter, a great deal of tea to be drunk. How, Claire wondered, with a twinge of desperation, could it be brought to an end? But quite soon the sky above the bandstand grew heavy with the early November dark, a sugar-induced somnolence spreading itself with the consistency of a treacle tart over the gradually wilting throng. A child, stuffed to capacity, had to be led away in sudden *extremis*, several more began to whimper or look pale, men shuffled their feet, women gathered up scarves and purses and latch keys, averting their eyes in quick distaste from the remaining curd tarts and currant pasties and ginger parkin set out before them; while even the strident music began to curl slightly at its edges like a sandwich left too long on a plate. The time — at last, thought Claire — had come.

A few more clerical words were spoken, each reverend gentleman avoiding Nola's eyes as he took his turn and then, as a crisp and blessed finale, an address by Benedict who, by the simple procedure of thanking everyone for coming, indicated that the entire proceedings should now be considered closed. Miriam, rising slowly to her feet, still fully aware of the graceful picture she made in the midst of those eddying furs, held out both arms to indicate her readiness to shake hands once again with anyone who chose to approach her chair. Dorothy, at a signal from Edward, signaled to Claire that she should do the same. Nola retired to a corner to discuss the fundamental issues of organized religion, the human condition, and Doctor Marie Stopes with the Salvation Army minister, the only one to have stayed her course, his Anglican and Methodist counterparts having tiptoed rather gingerly away. Roger Timms arrived at the precise moment Polly was expecting him and drove off with her in his father's new car. Eunice's second son, Simon, put in a sudden appearance looking jaunty and sheepish, a combination which always meant trouble, and spent a long time whispering in his mother's ear. The bereaved families began to drift homeward in small, quiet groups clutching their medals and souvenirs and bags of leftover buns Toby had made up for the children; some of them to the nearby mill cottages they rented from the Swanfields, others to the tram stop, a long wait in the damp, cold breeze, a long walk over steep cobbles at the end of it.

Glancing at her watch, Claire was amazed to discover the hands standing at four o'clock. Surely it must be later than that? And what now? Hours more, she supposed, of Miriam's company before dinner, savoring and re-savoring every bittersweet drop of the afternoon, and the cozy chat afterward by the drawing room fireside, reminiscing over the coffee tray. How, without giving offense — without giving hurt — could she escape it? She was immune now — more often than not — to the photograph albums, the locks of hair, the boyhood escapades, even to the moment, once impossible to bear, when the round blue eyes began to brim with tears, the small chin to quiver, the even smaller voice to whisper, "If only *you* had had a child — a darling little boy like Jeremy — how wonderful." But not tonight. Assailed once again by that crashing wave of unease, the panic conviction of an urgent road to travel, a vital task to perform, a frantic sense of haste, speed, of stepping lively, taking wing, of rushing headlong toward no matter what — *whatever* it turned out to be — she knew that tonight Miriam would be a sore trial indeed.

Eunice, having seen to the proper disposal of the tea urn and the mill china, having even given some instructions about feeding the left-over milk and meat scraps to the mill cats, shepherded her husband and son into their brand-new, still controversial motor car rather quickly, before anyone should inquire of Simon the whereabouts of his brother.

"Can we give you a lift, Claire?" asked Toby hopefully, seeking to put off what, by the expression on his wife's face, looked like yet another day of reckoning.

"I hardly think so," snapped Eunice, flushing scarlet, her rudeness a sure indication of her agony. "Mannheim Crescent is out of our way."

Claire smiled at Toby and shook her head.

"I suppose you'll be coming home with us," said Edward Lyall un-graciously, having hoped for an invitation to High Meadows, and turning peevish now that Miriam's withdrawal to "powder her nose" for the homeward journey made it seem unlikely.

"Oh yes, *do* come to Upper Heaton," said Dorothy sounding much relieved, wanting her daughter's company and grateful, for her part, to be spared the ordeal of Miriam.

How could she refuse? Yet, on the other hand, how could she possibly endure Edward — and an out-of-temper Edward at that — in her present humor? Yet to decline his invitation would upset Dorothy. Therefore she must accept it, endure him as long as she could — not long, she suspected — and then surely, inevitably, annoy him, defy him, bring on an attack of his indigestion, so that Dorothy would be upset just the same.

"Oh Claire — there you are." Benedict's voice startled her and then, as she understood its message, utterly dismayed her. "Miriam asked me to find you. She is expecting you to drive back with her and have dinner, since Polly is out for the evening. If you'd like to wait over there I'll send Parker when the car is ready."

He indicated a chair in a deep alcove by a window and she sat down in it meekly, knowing herself to be caught, and watched as he put one hand on Edward's shoulder, the other beneath Dorothy's elbow and led them out into the mill yard, an attention which was clearly so gratifying to Edward that his temper and Dorothy's prospects of a peaceful evening, seemed much improved. Could Benedict possibly be aware of that, Claire wondered, leaning forward a little to study what she recognized as a cool and very deliberate display of charm? And if so was he being kind, or devious, or simply amusing himself with Edward's deference? Or was it simply that she herself was beginning not precisely to hallucinate again but to drift into some hazy no-man's-land between fact and fantasy, which might well be the prelude to hallucination? Very likely. Too likely. And she must not allow it to happen. She must get up now and go back to Mannheim Crescent alone and at once. Yet the prospect of her own company, her own undivided scrutiny, seemed no less an ordeal. What then? There was Euan who, having ghosts of his own, would not be alarmed by hers. There was Kit. Either one of them. She had no need for solitude. She could be with a man — either one of them — who, by the act of sex alone could exhaust her body and ease the restless aching of her mind. Was that, indeed, the root of her turmoil? Sexual desire, the altogether natural demands of a healthy body for a healthy body, of sound lungs for sound lungs; straightforward sensation — and gratitude — in place of complex emotion? Was that it? Was that *all*? And, if so, how obvious — how simple — how sad.

She saw Parker bring the car to the front steps, get out and salute Benedict with military smartness.

"Ready for the ladies, sir."

But instead of sending him to fetch her, Benedict simply nodded and began to say something about the running of the car which she made no effort to understand. Had he forgotten her? How marvelous if Miriam would forget her too so that she could just take a tram — something

Miriam had never done in her life — and *go*. Small chance of that. She heard the tap of Miriam's diminutive feet, the swish of her furs, saw her coming down the main staircase and across the hall, Nola stalking behind.

They did not see Claire. She realized, indeed, that sitting deep in the window embrasure, no one could see her. But it made no difference. In a moment she would be called for, sent for. Benedict would remember.

"Has anyone seen Claire?" asked Miriam, a little out of breath, since even for her it had been a long day.

There it was. Claire rose to her feet and then abruptly, incredulously, sat down again.

"Claire?" said Benedict, his voice so level, so neutral, that even Claire, who *knew* he was lying, could not quite believe it. "She went to Upper Heaton with her mother."

"She can't have done." Miriam sounded very positive, and then, as the effort of being cross proved too much for her, rather less so. "Didn't I ask her to wait for me? Well — perhaps not. Perhaps I just assumed she would. Are you sure she's gone, Benedict?"

"I'm afraid so. I watched them drive away."

And because it did not enter her head to disbelieve him, as it had not entered Edward's or Dorothy's a moment ago — since he had certainly lied to them too — she pouted a moment, shivered and, complaining of the chill, allowed Parker to drive her and Nola away.

Claire watched them go, at the slow pace appropriate to royalty, through the mill gates and up the rise to High Meadows. She watched Benedict get into his car and ease it forward to the exact spot which Miriam's Bentley had occupied a moment before. How strange. How extraordinary. How very *interesting*! What, she wondered, her mind hovering, quite feebly, between amusement and alarm, might happen next? Surely, on this most peculiar afternoon, anything was possible? And getting up, feeling like a sleepwalker who might at any moment succumb to a fit of wild, weak laughter, she went outside to the man who was waiting and, without a word, got into the car beside him.

"Benedict — have you rescued me?"

And she listened to her own voice, speaking a little off-key, as if it had been the voice of another person.

"I believe so. From Miriam and your mother at any rate. Are you in a desperate hurry to get home now?"

Home? What an odd word. Did she even know its meaning, or where to look for it, or how to recognize it should it ever be found?

"No," she said, answering her own question, not his.

"Good. I have a house in Wharfedale, a village called Thornwick — not far. The couple who look after it for me put on a very decent dinner. Would you care to join me?"

For a moment — not a long one — she allowed the silence to fall.

"He has a cottage in the Dales," Nola had told her, "with a black marble bath and black satin sheets to match, I shouldn't wonder — where he entertains his passing fancies."

Could Benedict regard her as a fancy, passing or otherwise? *Benedict!* Was it possible? Yes, of course it was. And having decided that much, she wondered why, being far from naïve, she had not suspected it before. Possible, natural, highly, terribly dangerous. She knew that she ought to be scared half to death. Yet she was not. She knew, far beyond supposition, that she would unhesitatingly have advised anyone else in her place to withdraw now — to bolt for cover — while it could still be done in a friendly fashion. Not — absolutely not, for Heaven's sake — to tamper with what any fool could see amounted to dynamite. She knew all that. But the temptation to observe this man at closer quarters, removed from the schemes and fears and frustrations of his family which so colored him, was too strong to ignore. Here, offered to her in the guise of a simple invitation to dinner, was the challenge, the contest, the dare, her overwrought nerves had demanded. She *knew*, with an amazing calm, that she could not resist it.

"Thank you Benedict. I am rather hungry."

She traveled a mile or so in a drowsy silence and then fell asleep abruptly, very deeply, a loss of consciousness rather than slumber from which she woke alert and — to her own amusement — eager; her restlessness having given ground entirely now to simple, healthy curiosity.

They were driving along a dark, narrow road, branches entwined overhead in a bare trellis through which she could glimpse a charcoal gray sky, a thin drift of cloud, an impression, on either side, of empty fields, cold, swift water, a land already drawing itself together to do patient battle with the coming winter.

She had been to Thornwick once before, she remembered, a long time ago, on a picnic with Dorothy, a holiday treat which, like so much else in childhood, had given little pleasure. For Dorothy, to whom "good impressions" were of greater importance than enjoyment, had, at some sacrifice, bought her daughter new shoes and a pretty new summer dress for the occasion, an outfit which, no matter how many compliments it had drawn from old ladies on the train from Faxby to Skipton, had made Claire look and feel like an overdressed doll. But Thornwick had been — *could* have been — an adventure, rural enough to seem quite foreign to her city eyes, a page from a *Girl's Own* storybook had it not been for the stiffness of her pale pink sash, the spotlessness of her white cotton gloves, the straw hat with its satin ribbon tied in a tight little bow under her chin.

There had been a village green, she recalled, a square of tufted grass, coarse and springy to the touch, with low, square stone cottages built all around it; a shop with a wonderful window like a patchwork of colored, dimpled glass; a public house that had worn a shuttered, sheepish look; a squat gray church with an ancient graveyard where Dorothy had set her to decipher the headstones while she rested in the church porch, out of the sun. There had been a river, fast-flowing, magical, strewn with flat, white stepping-stones upon which Dorothy would not allow the child to set her feet, because of those precious, black patent shoes. There had been a steep grassy bank starry with wild flowers, where Claire, because of the pink muslin dress, had not been allowed to sit down; a dozen stiles which dress and shoes and white gloves combined had forbidden her to climb. And so they had walked about all day, prim and awkward in their finery, eating their picnic on a hard plank bench near the station yard, Claire longing to be barefoot, hatless, "common," Dorothy longing simply for train time, home time.

Neither one of them had ever suggested a picnic again.

"I have been here before," she said cheerfully now to Benedict. "I was seven and wearing new shoes. They hurt abominably. I scuffed them too, which made my mother very cross."

They left the village behind, the road beginning to climb and to narrow until, for the last half mile it was little more than a cart-track cut by usage between two dry stone walls, a roofless stone tunnel down which the November wind hurried, cold and whining and then rushed back again toward the high moor. Yet, in the way of tunnels, there was a light at the end of it, a gate opening into a flagged courtyard, two houses, one long and low, the other, some distance away, much smaller, the traditional grouping of farmhouse and laborer's cottage with all the agricultural debris swept away, the yard no longer littered with the rusting tools and plowshares Claire had often seen in such places but neatly, expensively paved, the old wooden farm gate replaced by elaborately scrolled wrought-iron; an immediate impression, even in the fading light, of money well spent, good window frames, solid roof tiles, recently cleaned chimneys; a conviction that the plumbing would be advanced and efficient, the woodwork sound, that there would even be electric light.

She got out of the car and stood leaning into the wind listening to the muted, moorland voices of water over sharp, clean stones, the stirrings of coarse grass and autumn heather, the resigned bleating of a solitary sheep, the sudden, questioning bark from the nearby cottage of a dog.

"The good ladies who keep house for me," said Benedict, "have an ancient spaniel, hardly for their protection so I must suppose they are fond of it."

"And they live up here — in the cottage?"

"They do. And I live here, in what was the farmhouse — as often as I can. Shall we go in?"

The door was old, beautifully preserved, solid oak banded in black iron, so low that Benedict was obliged to bend his head slightly although she passed through easily enough into a long, surprisingly high room which may once, she thought, have been two, where the first and growing impression was of warmth and quality, restrained but impeccable taste. The ceiling was old too, its massive oak beams venerable and fragrant with woodsmoke and polish, the fireplace not original perhaps, but magnificent, an entire wall of rough-hewn stone bearing a blaze of vigorously crackling logs in a black iron basket. There were armchairs of dark brown leather with fringed, berber-striped cushions thrown against them, rugs of black fur over the deep reds and browns of the Persian carpet, cabinets filled with books and china, small tables bearing, each one, some object at which a first glance simply aroused the desire to look again.

"Good evening, Mr. Swanfield," said a plain, pleasant woman in her late fifties, taking Claire's coat as if she had been expecting her. "Can I get you anything, madam?"

"Oh yes — if you could just show me — ?"

She was longing not to use but to *see* the bathroom, to find out if it really was black marble and decadence as she had been told, and following sensible Mrs. Mayhew along a narrow but dimly lit, deeply carpeted corridor, she felt not in the least apprehensive as she knew she ought to have done, but buoyant, light-headed, *released* as she had longed to be all day.

The bathroom was everything she had hoped for, a bath of imperial proportions in black veined with white, white fur rugs on black and white tiles, startling at first until her eyes adjusted to these dramatic contrasts of color, enabling her to pick out the touches of elegance, the white opaline beakers threaded with gold, the slender nymph, long hair tossing in a sculptured breeze, holding out in naked, alabaster arms a fluted shell of pure white soap, the wall mosaics of delicate sea creatures swimming in a midnight-colored sea.

And, as she gazed at it, smiled at it, allowed herself to be just a little excited by it, one thought rushed into her head and lodged there. How Nola would have loved all this.

Returning down the same bright, lavender-scented passage she found sherry waiting, a chair drawn up to the fire, yet so entranced was she by his possessions — each one a clue, surely, to the truth of him, or something near it — that she made no attempt to stop herself from peering around the room with the open delight of a child intent on deciphering a party puzzle.

"Benedict — you have such lovely things."

And astonishing, delicate things. French paperweights, clear crystal encasing the petals of flowers or the jeweled wings of a butterfly; slender vases of cameo glass, white chrysanthemums engraved on amber, acanthus leaves on sapphire, classically robed goddesses on sepia, all of them intricate, exquisite, easily broken. And then modern things. A Tiffany lamp of colored glass panels, iridescent as a peacock's tail, a vase of Tiffany glass that had the pale sheen of a lily pond, another that was, indeed, the tail of a bird of paradise made of green glass feathers, all the opalescent enameled art-glass creations of Lalique and Gallé, the riches of Art Nouveau so despised by Upper Heaton and High Meadows. How Nola would have adored them.

How Claire adored them herself, this personal blending of styles — the traditional opulence of fur rugs and log fires and carved mahogany so perfectly balanced by the fragility, the frankly decadent, wholly bewitching allure of these crystal water lilies and peacock feathers — completely enchanting her.

"And your books, Benedict? May I look?"

Voluptuous poetry, she wondered? Swinburne and Dowson and wicked, wonderful Baudelaire, his "Flowers of Evil" matching the sensual iridescence, the delightful wantonness of the Art Nouveau glass? She hoped so. But they were volumes of political philosophy — another enigma — gold-tooled and richly bound but, to Claire, quite boring.

"Do you have any land?"

He drew back the curtains and she went to stand beside him at the window, peering through the gathering dark at a bare field sloping sharply toward a stream, naked trees erect and solemn in the distance, black, quiet hills beyond. A night wind, rising cold and stainless from the surface of the moor, hurled itself suddenly against the windowpane, making her shiver.

"Heavens — winter is coming on."

"Yes," he said. "I don't mind the cold weather. I was born in the winter. Miriam thinks it suits my nature."

"Oh yes — Miriam would. I've heard her theory. I was born in July and she thinks that makes me warm and sunny and easy to handle."

"And does it?"

She smiled, went back to the fireside, took a sip from her glass, feeling — how could she best describe it? — separate, individual as she was never allowed to feel at High Meadows; unhampered — and how delightful that was — by the flurried, anxious choices her mother wished to force upon her; fully and competently adult.

"Do you want to sleep with me, Benedict?" she almost said, could have said quite easily, for this was a situation she had met before, handled before, discussed in a perfectly friendly fashion with a dozen men between Jeremy and Paul, sometimes the decision going one way, sometimes another, encounters just as brief, most of them, as this one was likely to be.

Where were those men now? She blinked hard, reminding herself that she, at least, was here — *safe* — in a warm, clean room with nothing more dangerous to threaten her than a man's perfectly normal desire for her sound, whole, *living* body. She smiled at him, thinking she would have her dinner first and then talk about it afterward over a glass of brandy. Probably she would refuse. It seemed best.

The dining room was heavy English oak with one or two surprises, pictures of Chinese pagodas and willow trees painted on silk, pieces of frail Chinese porcelain in shades of rose and jade, a pale green rug patterned with delicate Chinese flowers which gleamed like velvet on the highly polished wood floor. The food was English, too plain for the exacting talents of Aristide Keller of the Crown Hotel, but of the highest quality, excellent beef and home-grown vegetables, harvested by Mrs. Mayhew's spinster sister, Miss Todd; well risen batter puddings and thick brown gravy; a fruit tart — a perfect combination of Mrs. Mayhew's pastry and Miss Todd's apples; a good Cheddar cheese and, as a sole concession to the gastronomic arts of France, a ripe *Camembert*. The claret was old and smooth and full, conversation easier by far than she had expected.

"You are very comfortable here, Benedict."

And he told her, pleasantly yet rather as if she had been a recent acquaintance with only a superficial knowledge of his status and circumstances, how he had found the house some years ago in an almost terminal state of decay and how, through what she assumed to have been an enjoyable summer, he had rescued and restored it, cleared the land, drained the marshy area around the stream, installed competent Mrs. Mayhew and energetic Miss Todd in the cottage, purchased his cameo vases, his Chinoiserie, his Art Nouveau glass. What had his wife been doing that summer? No casual acquaintance would have dreamed of

174

asking. Therefore — since in this atmosphere, his private place, they had not met before — she did not ask. Nor did she greatly care. She was having dinner with an intelligent, attractive, highly civilized man who would certainly make love to her if he could, and his identity as her brother-in-law, Nola's husband, the Swanfield paymaster — the colors in which other people had painted him — quickly faded before the stimulation of these exploratory approaches, the teasing preliminaries to the game of sexual love. She had not expected him to play it so well. She had always known him to be attractive but had never felt it, never actually *seen* it before. She realized now, with some amusement and a fresh upsurge of curiosity, that he knew it himself, not from any personal vanity or observations in a looking glass, she thought, but simply from the effects, the results, his appearance had produced, many times she supposed, on women. Seduction, evidently, had come easily, even regularly. It followed, therefore, to a man of Benedict's logical turn of mind that he possessed a seductiveness adequate to his needs. Did it seem to him as simple and straightforward as that?

In the oak-beamed, close-curtained living room, where coffee and brandy awaited them, the light from the Tiffany lamps was emerald and gold, the light from the fire a warm excitement of moving shadows, the armchair into which she sank was wide and deep, a nest of ease and forgetfulness, inviting her to repose not only her body but the bonds of social restraint, inducing a mood of companionable abandon in which it seemed quite natural to slip off her shoes, arch her back and *stretch*; her body, pampered by food and firelight, asking nothing better now than to drift mindlessly and gladly into love. Had she taken just a glass or two more of the claret then the outcome would have been quick and clear. She almost wished she had.

Seeking to divert her own attention she glanced swiftly around her and, attracted by a sudden blue reflection from the crystal paperweight on the table beside her, murmured "How pretty."

"Yes." And apparently understanding her need to talk about anything but the real issue, the real purpose of their meeting which seemed now to be lapping all around them like gently but persistently rising water, he added, with a calm voice and a distinctly dry humor, "Very pretty. *Millefiori* from the glassworks of Baccarat in Lorraine. About 1855. *Millefiori* meaning a thousand flowers. Hold it up to the light if you want to see them all."

She did so, already no longer certain whether she was playing for time or simply prolonging this delicious hesitation for its own quite separate pleasure, her hand suddenly full of jewels as fine points of light in sapphire, amber, amethyst, diamond, began to fly in all directions.

"They are made from canes of glass," he said, "in various colors welded together."

"No Benedict. They are real flower petals."

"I fear not. Just colored rods cut and molded and then fused into clear glass which magnifies them . . ."

"Oh no — !"

"Oh yes — I do assure you —"

"Benedict," and she was light and laughing, physically aglow, "I don't care how they are made, or who makes them. I'm just grateful somebody does — or did."

"I dare say." And as he leaned forward in his chair and looked at her with the keen, shrewd yet caressing eyes of a collector, a connoisseur, she knew, with the lurch of her stomach, the dryness of her throat, the sudden catching of breath which meant excitement, *sensation*, that the first stage was over and the time of question and answer had come.

"Those cameo vases are exquisite too," she said.

"So are you, Claire."

"And you want to add me to your collection?"

She made the gesture of reaching for a cigarette and, offering her one from a vibrantly enameled box, he lit it and then returned to his own chair, maintaining a physical distance which was in itself a provocation.

"Yes — setting collections aside — of course I want you, as you very well know."

"Would you care to tell me why?"

"Certainly. You are a very desirable woman. You must know that too."

"Well — yes. But I do hope you have rather more to say about me than that."

Did she actually like him? She rather thought that she could, or might. Certainly his capacity to intrigue her remained immense and, in that case, surely there must be *something* about him, some hidden key to his nature which she, like everyone else, had missed? And how clever she would feel, how rather like a cat with a cream pot, if she managed — when all the others had failed — to find it. Not a noble aspiration, she admitted, but better, surely, in this world of compromises, half-hopes, half-truths, than no aspiration at all. Did she even want to like him? Was it necessary that she should? She had great liking for Kit Hardie, the possibility of rather more than liking for Euan, and she had taken pains to commit herself to neither. She had come instead to this isolated place with a man who would not ask for commitment and could not, therefore, be in any way hurt by her unreadiness, perhaps her inability, to give it. Benedict's motives, she knew, were openly and entirely sexual.

Why should hers be different? Yet, as the last remnant of caution briefly reasserted itself, bidding her, albeit with a very small voice, to think again, she knew, with a shrug of resignation, that for her — perhaps for most women — the act of sex could never be so uncomplicated, so unentangled by feeling of one sort or another, as that.

Other men had said "You are beautiful." A few had said "I love you." Benedict Swanfield said calmly, "My dear — everybody at High Meadows wants you. For a variety of reasons. I think you must think mine more natural and acceptable than some others."

Just as calmly she nodded her head.

"And I also think you are looking for a relationship without permanency."

"Yes, I think so too."

"Otherwise I would not have brought you here. I am not inclined to permanency in these matters — for obvious reasons . . ."

And meeting his eyes she smiled very quietly and nodded her calm, neat head.

The paperweight still lay in her hand and taking it from her he put it back on its table.

"My possessions interest you, don't they? Let me show you more."

And taking her hand he pulled her to her feet slowly, gently, allowing her ample opportunity to resist him, waiting until her body had accustomed itself to the nearness of his before he put his mouth against her neck, the line of her jaw, the base of her throat, her ear, the lightest brushing of closed lips against her skin, the merest touch of a bee's wing, soon over, although the vibrations of pleasure — and danger — lingered on.

"The cameo vases are very rare," he said, as if he had not even touched her.

"Yes."

"Shall I tell you how many layers of glass it takes to produce them?"

"Please do."

"Then look closely."

But as she bent her head he slid a hand under her chin and kissed her on the mouth, parting her lips slightly and then releasing her before she had made up her mind whether or not — or how much — to surrender.

"The peacock vase," he said, "is by Tiffany. You can see the evil eye in the tail — if you turn this way."

And this time she was waiting to be kissed, a heady, reckless, enchanting little game leading to consequences it seemed wiser, as yet, not even to contemplate.

Yet there was no unseemly haste.

Picking up her glass she found it empty and accepted more brandy, sipping it slowly, knowing herself to be quite tipsy enough already, as he explained to her the somber gold icons on either side of the door, the remarkably English watercolors decorating the walls of the passage beyond, each one leading step by step toward his bedroom door until she stood beside him contemplating the jade table screen by his bed.

"Do you have black satin sheets, Benedict?" She rather wished she had not said that, but without the least sign of surprise or offense or curiosity as to why she should think so, he drew back the covers to reveal crisp white linen, a scent of fresh lemons.

"Do take off that heavy dress, Claire. It doesn't suit you."

"No. It doesn't."

The room was not cold, lit once again by colored glass lamps and a brightly flickering fire, but she undressed quickly for this was the moment she had dreaded. Nudity, in theory, did not dismay her. Nor, when she had grown accustomed to a lover, did it seem other than utterly delightful in practice. But not even her years of hospital training, her even too thorough acquaintance with human anatomy, had enabled her to overcome her shyness of removing her clothes for the first time before a man who, until that "first time" should be successfully over, remained a stranger. How wonderful, she had always thought — and more than ever now — to be transferred by some magic formula from the state of being fully dressed and flirting in an armchair to being naked and amorous in bed, some blessed act of metamorphosis which would spare her this awkward scrambling with buttons and belts and buckles, the embarrassment of looking or not looking as the jacket and shirt and trousers to which she had grown accustomed became the unclothed body of an unknown and physically excited man.

Four men before Benedict — no, five — had watched her perform this painful exercise and each one had spoken his version of "not so fast. Hey — let me do that." Benedict said nothing, allowing her to bolt for cover beneath his immaculate, fragrant bed linen, and to hide there until he joined her. But now that they were both naked her shyness evaporated and she lay passive for a while beneath his exploring hands, her eyes closed, her mind closing, yielding utterly and mesmerized with the yielding, until her senses sprang to life again and she was attacked — she could think of no other words for it — by fierce shafts of her own desire, the accumulated need of two barren years offered now to Benedict.

She could not say "I'm ready. Take me and please be quick about it!" Dorothy Lyall's daughter could never have managed to say that. But she could and did press herself against him with all the urgency that was now in her, her fevered body telling him plainly that on this first occasion there was no need for *finesse*, no time for the techniques of practiced sensuality, only for vigor and speed.

Her body erupted into orgasm the moment he entered it, a mighty upheaval that shocked her as, clinging to him, well nigh enduring the fierce joy he had brought her, she realized that while it thundered through her, renewing her, *releasing* her, it would scarcely have mattered whether or not she knew his name.

"It has been rather a long time," she said weakly ten minutes or so later, feeling the need to excuse herself since women were not supposed to take pleasure as men took it, for the sake of the pleasure alone. At least she had never before done so and was uncomfortable now with the aftermath.

"My dear — I do realize that."

But he lay for a while with his back toward her, tense she thought, presumably dissatisfied, the familiar air of distance about him — the shadow — which he had discarded on entering this house enveloping him again. Obviously she had not pleased him. Very well. It was regrettable, and awkward, and she had not the slightest idea what to do about it. But, she was, after all, no tame, domesticated creature who lived only to please a man. Nothing obliged them to see each other again except on the most public of occasions, and she had coped with worse disasters than this. Yet she had never before made love without some acknowledged degree of affection, had never suffered, afterward, the rebuke of silence, the insult of a hostile back. And although she could understand it and accept it and had not the least intention of making a fuss, it was, nevertheless, unfortunate. Disappointing? Embarrassing! Not easy to bear.

The answer was to get up, get dressed, make some cheerful remark and indicate her readiness to leave.

"I suppose it must be late."

"No," he said, turning toward her. "Not yet."

"Oh well — !"

She sat up and, taking her by the shoulders, he slid her down again so that she was almost beneath him.

"Not yet, Claire."

"I rather thought you wanted me to go."

"I know you did. I don't. Wait a while."

She waited, her head in the hollow of his shoulder, her body curving, fitting itself against his, adapting to him, so that when he entered her again, thoughtfully and slowly, taking time and care, exercising skill and imagination, her desire for him was wholesome, sound, no longer desperate, her vision of him accurate, her memory not of hunger slaked but of shared pleasure. And afterward, when he retreated into his distance and managed, with some effort, to ease himself only a little away from her, she fell asleep with perfect content, waking a half an hour later, to find him fully composed.

"Can you stay the night?"

"I'm afraid not."

He did not ask her why.

"Ah well — I suppose that means I have to dress and drive — !"

But he was perfectly pleasant about it, courteous, amused, as he had been at the start, certainly not tender, no longer amorous, but — how could she phrase it? — as if that hidden quality, that *something* which she knew to be there, wanted to be there, whatever it turned out to be, had somehow risen a little nearer to the surface.

"I'm glad," she said, "about the second time."

"Ah! Is that why you are allowing me to watch you slip into that delightful lingerie?"

"Heavens — I hadn't noticed."

"Oh yes you had."

"Well — that's all right then."

Yes. Perhaps it would be all right. She hoped so. Outside in the paved yard the wind was fierce and cold, threatening rain and the certain prospect — as she had already remarked once before — of winter coming on.

"Are you coming all the way back here, Benedict — or to High Meadows?"

"I really don't know."

She understood that he had not the least intention of telling her. Nor, when they reached Mannheim Crescent, did he seem at all disposed to linger.

"Good night, Claire."

"Good night, Benedict."

They had stood here before at her gate and spoken these same words on the night he had calmly admitted his knowledge of his wife's promiscuity. Calm because he had not cared. Calm now. And why not? She did not expect him to care for her. She would be surprised, alarmed, possibly inconvenienced if he did.

"Good night, Benedict."

Yet, just the same, she was glad they had made love that second time. Perhaps, in fact very likely, they would never make love again. But she would remember that.

10

STANDING in the kitchen the next morning, clattering the breakfast china Miriam had given her into the wholly unworthy lodging-house sink, she was painfully aware of Euan Ash, sitting at the wooden table behind her, ironic, far too knowing, sipping, with an air of spiritual sweetness, a mug of tea which even at this early morning hour he had laced — as one did in the trenches — with whiskey.

"Congratulations," he said.

"On what?"

"Well — I conclude from my observations that your life has been — entered, shall we say? — by a man."

"One could say that."

"So — congratulations. Can't say I'm surprised but I might be sorry. Anyone I know?"

She shook her head.

"Oh good." He gave her a seraphic smile, calmly pouring another tot of whiskey into his tea. "I was rather afraid it might be Kit."

"No. Not Kit."

"That's all right then."

"Why?"

"Because Kit is quite horribly tenacious, my darling — don't you know. Hangs on like grim death to anything he decides to call his own."

"Euan!" Slapping a Minton cup and saucer down hard on the chipped, wooden drainer, she swung round to face him. "Kit changes his girls like partners in the barn dance and makes no bones about it. Everybody knows that."

He shrugged and smiled again, the cruelly accurate light of the No-vember morning giving him a very brittle look indeed beneath a thin shirt, a gaudy, inadequate pullover. "Ah yes. But that's only one side of him, Claire. Maybe his best side and certainly his most natural, I agree, but he's on the verge of something else just now. Haven't you noticed it? I rather think he's going to turn respectable."

"Oh — for Heaven's sake, Euan, don't be clever."

"Darling, one is what one is. I just use my trained eye, that's all, and draw conclusions with my expensively educated mind. And if Kit isn't heading for a bout of morality then I'll be very much surprised. It was all right for Kit the butler and Kit the gallant major to be promiscuous, because butlers are expected to deflower all the maids — it's a perk of the job — and we all know what soldiers are. But Kit the hotelier will have to mend his ways, or at least look as if he has, until he gets rich enough to please himself. Stands to reason. Only overbred aristocrats like me and those jolly chaps who drive dustcarts can afford to be open about their depravity. Middle-class gentlemen have to be very careful. And once he gets his hands on a nice middle-class young lady like you, then he may not let go. Not in time for me, I mean."

"Are you in such a great hurry, then?"

His smile, this time, was deliberately boyish and sweet.

"Well yes — I've got to be on my way soon, you know. To Edin-burgh — or somewhere near it."

"To see your friend?"

"That's right. Naturally you'll miss me."

"Oh yes — naturally. I might even come with you."

"Good Lord — you *did* have a bad night then — didn't you."

She hardly knew what kind of a night it had been. Nor did she wish to think about it in too much detail. She would treat it, she decided, as a temporary imbalance of the mind, a direct result of that dreadful unveiling ceremony which he had forced upon her, *maneuvered* her into attending. He had taken advantage of a vulnerable moment . . . *No!* To think such nonsense was to return to the philosophies of Dorothy and Miriam, the level of the dewy-eyed milkmaid seduced by the squire, and she would not sink to that. He had been perfectly honest. He had wanted sexual gratification. So had she. And it would, therefore, be unjust and slightly hysterical to blame him because she had turned out to be less sophisticated, less seasoned, than she had herself imagined. He had taken her at her face value. She must take him at his. And stop playing the innocent led astray when she was no such thing. There would be no awkwardness. He was far too experienced for that. When they met again he would behave as if nothing had happened. Nothing — of any real significance — had. And for one thing at least she was thankful. He had not insulted her by sending her flowers this morning, via a casual command to his secretary. "Oh, by the way Miss — whatever the woman's name might be — get some flowers delivered to a Mrs. Claire Swanfield this morning, will you? The usual thing." Or had he? She put on her hat and left the house at speed in case the offensive tribute should still arrive and ruin her entire day.

Kit Hardie was in the hotel lobby, having already completed his first "commanding officer's inspection" of the morning, looking sound, handsome, blessedly familiar.

"Ah — the light of my life," he said, kissing his fingertips in the gourmet's gesture of appreciation as she hurried through the door, and then glancing at his watch, just to let her know that — light of his life or not — he *had* realized she was late.

But he was feeling cheerful this morning, experiencing a moment — rare with him — that was almost content. For the first time, that weekend every bedroom in the hotel had been occupied. All sixteen tables in the restaurant had been fully booked and could have been booked twice over on Saturday night. Sunday lunch — a recent innovation — had aroused more interest than expected. And had Mr. Clarence not been standing there behind his reception desk, keenly observing, drawing swift and salacious conclusions, he would very likely have kissed Claire's cheek — or perhaps just the corner of her mouth — and ruffled her hair. For, although he knew quite well that neither one of them was ready yet for the other, it did no harm to establish the habit of touch, no harm at all to let it be understood, in the hotel and elsewhere, that she was spoken for.

"Good morning, Kit. You're looking well."

Wonderfully well, in fact. So very much the rock to lean on that she felt an undeniable temptation, on this uneasy morning, to lean. Yet, just the same, she had made him no promises. There could be no obligation. He had no right even to inquire how she conducted herself, much less to feel hurt by it. She repeated that, loud and clear and several times over in her mind, furious with the rush of altogether unnecessary guilt which made her smile brighter, her manner rather warmer than anyone could be entitled to expect on a dreary November morning. Where had *he* spent the night for that matter, she wondered? Judging by his geniality and his air of well-fed content it seemed unlikely that he had slept alone. A mature, probably wealthy woman, she rather imagined, or, on the other hand, some scatterbrained little chorus girl from the Princes Theatre, according to his humor or his opportunity. But, nevertheless — right or no right, promises or not — she was slightly uncomfortable with him for the rest of the day.

The weekend's cherished guests departed, escorted tenderly to the door and then forgotten, their rooms cleaned and aired and refurbished for the "cherished guests," whoever they might be, who would occupy them tomorrow. The weekend's flowers were thrown out with the debris from the breakfast trays and replaced with the best Claire could find on a November Monday. Lunchtime was so quiet that Aristide Keller went home to preserve his artistic talents for evening, leaving Amandine to cater to the needs of Toby Hartwell and Nola's cousin, Arnold Crozier, whose weekends at the Crown had a habit, sometimes, of extending to Wednesday. The two men lunched at their favorite tables in opposite corners of the dining room, Toby alone and rather wistfully, still suffering the aftermath of a weekend at High Meadows, Arnold Crozier with a girl, very young and very blond as all his girls seemed to be, a "flapper" with a short skirt, a cloche hat, a glazed expression, quietly sipping her champagne and fingering the new gold bracelet on her wrist while he, in his black beetle's whisper, lectured her on the exact number of millimeters per day a white wine should be turned when left to mature in its bottle.

"Creepy old man," said Polly Swanfield, appearing at Claire's elbow as Mr. Crozier, giving his young lady a final word of advice about the new season's *Beaujolais*, climbed into his Rolls and was driven away. "He got me one night in the cocktail bar — you know how he sits lurking in his corner and then just *pounces*. Lord, what a scream — he just went on and on about some kind of a beetle that came over from America on a Californian vine, years and years ago, and ate up just about every vineyard in Europe. Isn't that just the kind of thing you'd expect Arnold Crozier to know? As if I cared. What mattered to me was keeping a straight face because all I could think of was that this beetle — phylloxera or something I think he called it — must have been his brother. And since he *is* Nola's cousin and owns half the hotel and half of Bradford and Leeds to go with it, I suppose mother wouldn't like me to laugh at him. Anyway, Claire, how about giving me a cup of tea? I've been rummaging through Taylor & Timms all morning and I *am dead.*"

Installed in a corner of the empty lounge, few of Faxby's ladies sharing her enthusiasm for Monday morning shopping, Polly shrugged off her coat and shook the raindrops out of her hair, small parcels in the silver gilt, blue-ribboned wrappings which meant perfume, lace garters, embroidered Swiss handkerchiefs, anything she could find that was pretty and expensive, tumbling to the floor one after the other around her feet.

"Tea and sandwiches," she called out to the waiter, scarcely looking at him, certainly not seeing him, yet smiling at him nevertheless as if she thought him the only man left alive in a world of amorous women. "In fact — lots of sandwiches. Lovely roast beef with mustard and then a whole plateful of sticky buns. *You* know what I like, Peter" — the man's name was George — "and then a slice of Normandy apple flan. Oh yes, *of course*, with cream."

"Didn't you have lunch, Polly?"

"Oh yes —" She looked puzzled as if she could scarcely remember it. "Ages ago — twelve o'clock and now it's half past three." And she proceeded to eat not just with relish but as if the food before her might suddenly be snatched away, leaving her no option but to cram herself with its richness here and now, while she could.

"Peter dear — may we have another pot of tea? Oh bless you, you've brought a mince pie. How adorable. My first of the winter. Mother never serves them until Christmas Eve. Well yes — all right then — I'll have two."

"You'll get fat," warned Claire, remembering Polly's anxiety, only six months ago, about the size of her bosom. But Polly, who had once bandaged her chest every night to flatten it, had clearly resolved the issue entirely to her own satisfaction.

"Oh no I won't, because I don't sit still long enough. I don't walk, I run. I play tennis, I skate, and I dance — and dance. You've seen me."

"And you walk miles every day around Taylor & Timms."

"All right. So that way I can eat and drink what I like. And nobody gets fat on champagne. By the way Claire, do you happen to have come across Roy Kington yet?"

The question seemed artless, airy, a chance remark which simply could not matter less, although Claire, meeting the full impact of Polly's most dazzling smile, knew better than that. Roy Kington? Surely she had heard the name before? And recognizing Polly's careful nonchalance for what it was she hardly knew whether to feel glad or sorry for Roger Timms.

"Yes, I suppose I know him. He hangs around with you doesn't he?"

"My dear —" Polly sounded infinitely tolerant, just a shade conde-scending. "That's Rex, his younger brother. Roy is — well, you'll see — *older*, darling. About your age. He was in the war and then, instead of coming home, he volunteered to go and fight for the White Russians against the Bolsheviks. Not that I understand White Russians from any other color — except that it seems to be the Bolsheviks who shot the Tsar and the Whites want to shoot them, which will hardly bring back the Tsar and those poor Grand Duchesses, I know . . . But anyway they shot Roy at Archangel or Murmansk or some such place, so he had to come back home. He looks like Rex but he's taller and thinner and altogether more — Are you sure you don't know him?"

The question now was sharp, a little accusing, determined — if Claire was entertaining thoughts of getting Roy Kington for herself — to put a stop to it.

"No. I don't know him."

"Well then —" She was not wholly convinced. "You will. And it seems only fair to warn you that at the moment he's heavily involved with Sally Templeton — *you* know — that insipid beanpole with the red hair and the silver lamé stockings. But that won't last, of course, as I happen to know, because — well, he and I had a talk about it the other night."

"You mean you're next in line. Poor Roger Timms."

"It has nothing to do with Roger."

"It has nothing to do with me either, Polly. You seem to be warning me off, I can't think why."

"Because you're always here aren't you for everybody to see. And because — well, for Heaven's sake — you don't seem to realize what a gap there is in my generation."

"Of course I realize it."

But Polly was too painfully entangled in these first anguished stirrings of jealousy, the turmoil of what might be first love, first heartache, to notice the coldness in Claire's voice.

"All right, Claire. But it's not the same for you. You've been married. You were old enough, before the war, to have your pick and I wasn't. And it's different now. Oh yes — I don't do badly. I'm popular. There's no need, *ever*, for me to stay at home any evening of the week. I can have Roy's little brother Rex whenever I want him, positively eating out of my hand. He'd do anything for me. But he's seventeen, Claire, and I'm nearly twenty. Or I can have old codgers over thirty telling me their troubles. Or I can have Roger Timms. The rest of them — the ones who are really the right age for me — are either dead or wounded or nervous wrecks or have fiancées to come home to or they drink too much like Euan Ash, or else all they want to do is go off to the wilds of Africa and grow tobacco or some such thing, absolutely miles from anywhere, with no facilities and no fun. Or else they're so depressed there doesn't seem much point to their being alive at all. You know that, Claire."

"Yes Polly."

"So when somebody like Roy Kington comes along, handsome and clever and wanting to get on in the world — *and* twenty-five years old — well, one can't be blamed for putting up a little fight. Can one?"

"No Polly. I'll keep my distance."

186

She smiled. "I thought you'd understand. Fair's fair, after all. And you'll like him. Everybody does. The family are bound to. What do you think, Claire? Should I get mother to invite him to something or other now, or wait until Benedict gets back?"

"Is Benedict away?"

She had not intended to ask that question, could have bitten her tongue now that she had. But Polly, her ears attuned solely to pick up vibrations concerning Roy Kington, heard nothing amiss.

"He went off this morning, I don't know where, and you wouldn't expect him to tell *me*, would you. But Nola was looking very pleased with herself at breakfast which probably means he's not going to hurry back. So perhaps I'd better not wait. Claire?"

"That's right. Don't wait."

Polly got to her feet, gathering her parcels, already poised for action. "I won't. He's had dinner, once that I know of, at the Templetons — and tea half a dozen times. I'd best have a word with mother."

"Yes Polly. I'd do that."

"Right." She glanced at her watch. "Oh Lord — is that the time? I'll be off, Claire. Roger will be waiting."

So he had gone away. It made absolutely no difference. She walked with Polly to the front entrance, down the immaculately scoured front steps to the Timms' Mercedes and watched smiling while young Mr. Timms drove off, at Polly's urgent insistence, to High Meadows so that she might confer with her mother as to the best method of making herself Mrs. Roy Kington.

She had a drink with Nola that evening in the bar, accompanied her, a night or so later, to a performance of Swan Lake at the Grand, without once hearing or mentioning Benedict's name. She dined the following Sunday at High Meadows, observing Miriam's "family Sunday" with less resentment now that she could so easily invent some crisis at the Crown to cut her visit short.

"When is Benedict coming home?" asked Eunice tersely in the middle of the meal, evidently needing to know.

There was no answer.

But she saw him herself the next morning in the lobby of the hotel, or rather heard his voice and Kit Hardie's as she was coming downstairs, her arms full of Monday's wilting flowers.

"Just ten bedrooms," Kit was saying, in answer to Benedict's question. "And sixteen tables which gives me a maximum of sixty-four diners. Small, of course . . ."

"Yes," said Benedict, "but manageable. Would you care to show me round?"

"Delighted, sir."

Hastily she retreated, handed her burden of dead flowers to a far-from-gratified chambermaid and managed, throughout the morning, by accurately guessing the route Kit would take, to keep herself busy and out of sight. So he had come to the hotel. It made absolutely no difference. High time, in fact, that he *had* made up his mind to condescend — for what else was it? — and give Kit the accolade he deserved. She was glad he was here for Kit's sake. She insisted on that. Yet when Kit sent a waiter to tell her that he would like her to join him and his guest for lunch her immediate instinct was to lock herself in the bathroom if necessary and refuse. Yet, as she knew quite well, there was no way to do that. For if she could invent pressure of business to excuse herself to Miriam or to her mother, she could use no such ploy with Kit who knew exactly and to the minute how she filled her working day. There was nothing to do, therefore, but smile, run a comb through her hair, and walk, still smiling, into the dining room, the composed, efficient, resourceful woman who was pleased and even proud to be an employee of Major Hardie of the Crown.

"Good morning, Benedict. How very nice."

"Good morning, Claire. How very nice of *you* to join us."

The atmosphere was deferential, almost caressing; Gerard, the head waiter, discreetly overseeing his minions who, trained to the precision and grace of a *Corps de Ballet*, deftly and almost lovingly served the "light luncheon" of lobster *mousseline*, chilled *vichyssoise*, chicken breasts in white wine and cream and truffles. Sitting between them, making her professional small talk — very small indeed — she sensed both the immense satisfaction in Kit, the honest, cock-a-hoop triumph that he the son of "common" and in the case of his father, unknown parents should be entertaining in his own premises the son of Aaron Swanfield; and, once again, a deliberate exercise of charm in Benedict, the calculated art of pleasing for a purpose. And she was forced to concede his performance to be impressive.

"Excellent," he said with decision whenever comment was required. "Very well done. Now tell me —?" And the question would not only be pertinent but phrased in a skillful manner which enabled him to call Kit nothing at all, since "Hardie" would have been condescending and "Major," now that everybody's medals were losing their luster, could so easily have been misconstrued.

"What about these new Licensing Laws? Are you managing to find your way through them?"

"Oh — I keep to the very letter, as understood by Faxby Town Hall, that is."

"Very wise. I take it you have a good friend on the Licensing Committee who can explain it all to you."

And they smiled at each other, men of the world who perfectly understood the needs and nature of such friendships.

Toward the end of the *Chicken Suprême* Kit, after whispered consultation with Mr. Clarence, was called to the telephone, excusing himself with just the right degree of reluctance at leaving his guest.

"It will be Mr. Crozier, I expect," said Claire brightly, knowing — because where Kit was concerned she always seemed to know these things — that it was far more likely to be his latest and more than usually persistent entanglement, a mezzo-soprano from the Viennese Operetta currently on tour in the northwest.

"I wonder," said Benedict, without altering the restrained cordiality of his voice, "if you are free tonight . . . ?"

Perhaps she had expected it, or something like it, but had prepared no reply and was saved from doing so now by the arrival of the head waiter, with a flourish of white napkins and the clinking of ice, to refill her glass.

"Thank you, Gerard." And when he had bowed, spun round on a polished heel and gone away, she sipped her wine and smiled with a brilliance worthy of Polly at her best.

"This is a very unusual wine, don't you think, Benedict?"

"Delicious."

"Very delicate and fresh, yet *definite* — very individual. Don't you agree?"

"Absolutely."

She sipped again, savored, offered another radiant smile.

"It comes from a little place called Vouvray — do you know where that is?"

"Yes."

"Oh — do you really?"

"I do. Near Tours in the Loire Valley."

"Quite right."

"I know." And they exchanged small sharp smiles that were the acknowledgement of duelists before swordplay.

"Have you been there, Benedict?"

"Not recently."

"Kit was on leave there once, during the war — I suppose he must have been visiting a girl — and, whatever happened to the girl, thank goodness he discovered the wine."

"Very astute of him."

"Well yes — because it's not at all well known in England. You may

find it in London, I suppose, but where Faxby's concerned it's a rarity —
I am pleased to inform you — only to be enjoyed at the Crown. We're
very proud of it. Oh, Kit — there you are! I've just been telling Benedict
about the *Vouvray*."

And as Kit took his seat, smiling urbanely, betraying no hint of the
tirade he had just received from his excitable Viennese prima donna,
the conversation embarked smoothly, safely, on a wine-lover's tour of
the Loire Valley — from subtle *Vouvray* to pale dry *Sancerre*, spicy *Pouilly-
Fumé*, the rich dessert wines of *Anjou*, gentle *Muscadet* — which would
have delighted Arnold Crozier and soon left Claire behind.

Brandy was offered to the gentlemen, *Cointreau* to the still brightly
smiling lady, and then coffee in the dusky-pink Baroque lounge where
once again, for a moment, she was alone with Benedict.

"Is the coffee from Brazil?" he inquired pleasantly, "or from some
little plantation in the heart of Africa?"

And she knew, with regret, that the complex tangle made up of anger
and offense, bruised pride, natural caution, simple common sense, was
rapidly melting away.

"Cream?" she offered, as wide-eyed and innocent as Miriam, "and
sugar?"

"*Are* you free tonight, Claire?"

She smiled and shook her head.

He would not ask again. She had put an end, as graciously as could
be expected, to something which should never have started, a decision
she knew he would respect. The matter was closed. She had done the
sensible thing, the *right* thing. They both knew that. She walked with
him to his car, utterly convinced of it.

"Goodbye, Claire."

The afternoon was very cold, the white sky of winter already promising frost, a razor-sharp edge to the wind.

"Tomorrow perhaps?" she said.

The back gate of the house in Mannheim Crescent could be reached
only by Claire's garden. The alley beyond it, cut between two high stone
walls and further obscured by old, overhanging trees, was unlit and just
wide enough for Benedict's car to pass. Why had she agreed to meet him
there? Better not to think. Standing in the bitter cold wind outside the
hotel he had been neither angry nor distant, evidently prepared to take
her refusal well. And, reminded too closely of the frail and mysterious
quality of their second lovemaking her resistance had quite simply collapsed. She had agreed to see him again because she had wanted to see
him. It was as straightforward as that. Very well. Once more, and only
once. An indulgence. After which she would have to take herself more

seriously in hand. The time had come to forget her old wartime attitudes of living for the day, somehow getting through the night. One had to plan now for tomorrow, even the day after. The war was over. Dear God — how many more times would she have to hear that?

Her heart did not leap as she saw Benedict's headlights entering the lane. Having spent the day burdened by the prospect of the night ahead she was already heartily sick of it and simply wanted it over and done. That he was married and that she had been married to his brother did not greatly trouble her. She would have considered herself unduly sentimental if it had. Paul too had been married, legally although in no other fashion. Nola's marriage to Benedict was a sham. Jeremy was dead. No hearts were likely to be broken. Yet even so, this was a small town where adultery remained adultery and she could not ignore the damage she would do to Dorothy should she be discovered. But what likelihood was there of that? Who cared enough to make a fuss? Certainly not Nola. And who, in the event of gossip, would have the nerve to do other than take Mr. Benedict Swanfield's word that there was nothing in it? But the thought of Dorothy remained, a pale but persistent shadow at the back of her mind, accompanied by the anxious prayer, inevitable at such times, that the techniques of Doctor Marie Stopes in which she, like Nola, had placed her trust, might continue to succeed.

Yet the dread of untimely maternity had never been strong enough to hold her back from those war-torn encounters before Paul, when it had seemed right to give what she could. It had not been strong enough tonight even to force her into plain underwear and a sensible coat and skirt instead of her seductive French *lingerie*, her black lace garters, a black silk dress that had no sleeves, no back, a low neck beaded with jet, a costume which openly acknowledged her expectation of making love.

It was, after all, what he had asked for, what she had asked for herself, although, as she put on her coat, it seemed to be the last thing her body desired. But once inside his car, already his private place, she entered his atmosphere so instantly and so completely that it seemed impossible to carry the consequences of anything she did in his world back to her own. And although of course she clearly recognized the dangers of such a philosophy, it did wonders both for her nerves and for her conscience.

In the farmyard the wind, howling down from the moor, seemed colder than ever, the house warmer and even more enchanting, the pattern of their meetings already taking shape inside her head. The drink by the fireside. The expensive, well-cooked dinner. The brandy. The act of — what? Sex she had better call it. It seemed wiser. The silent drive home. How classic. How commonplace. Except — ? And how terrible, how truly destroying if he turned out, after all, to be a common-place man.

He took her coat and poured out her sherry, not touching her.

"Thank you, Benedict."

He drew out her chair, unfolded her napkin, served her from the dish of smoked salmon pâté Mrs. Mayhew had left with hot brown toast on a side table.

"I'm hungry," she said.

"And thirsty?"

"Oh yes."

"Good."

And from its bath of ice he drew out, without the least show of ceremony, a bottle of the pale, subtle, unobtainable — in Faxby — *Vouvray*.

"*Benedict*, how clever." She was delighted and more than ready to give him full credit for it. "How on earth did you get it?"

He smiled, filled her glass and his own, and took his first reflective sip.

"Yes. It is just possible that, of the Loire Valley wines, the *Muscadet* may do better with fish since it grows near the sea. But the *Vouvray* is very pleasant, I don't deny it."

"Pleasant! It's wonderful. I could drink it all day and nothing else. But you *are* going to tell me how you got it?"

"I rather think so."

He passed toast and butter, lemon-juice and black pepper for the salmon.

"Well then?"

"Yes — well then." He looked quietly amused, separate still but not distant. "I could say that I have had it maturing in my cellar for twenty years waiting for the right moment."

She nodded, her elbows on the table, her eyes shining.

"Or I could say that at great trouble and expense I ran a bottle to earth somewhere in St James or the rue St Honoré or a *cave* on the banks of the Loire just for you, my dear."

"Yes — I'd quite like that."

"Or, of course, I could tell you that I bought a case of it from the Manager of the Crown Hotel."

"I'm surprised he agreed to sell it to you."

"Are you really?"

She looked at him a moment.

"No. I suppose not."

Mrs. Mayhew came in, removed the salmon and brought roast partridges, game chips, a purée of root vegetables, returned a moment later with a cold lemon soufflé, curd tarts and cheese, and closed the door firmly behind her to indicate that she would not trouble them again.

"How discreet she is."

He looked almost surprised.

"Yes, of course."

The wine — *her* wine — was sparkling inside her as she returned to the fireside, the armchair, to what had already begun most incredibly to seem the long wait before he could decently suggest making love. How sad, how silly, that, as Dorothy's daughter, she knew she could never manage to suggest it herself. Yet she wanted him now, had wanted him throughout the lemon soufflé, the cheese, the coffee, and was not ashamed of it, recognizing that only in this way could she ever hope to know him. He would continue to guard his speech, his manner, his waking face or, being skillful and astute, would offer to her any image of himself he chose to create. But he could not be so inscrutable — she thought — in the vulnerable, revealing act she had decided to call sex but still thought of as love. No one could. And the last time, the second time, she had detected no meanness in him, no coarseness, no lack of physical sensitivity. Yes, it was certainly her surest means of getting to know him. She smiled, thinking that as an excuse for wanton behavior it was as good as any other. It also seemed to be the truth.

"Do you play backgammon?" he said.

"Oh Heavens — do I? Yes, I think so."

"You can hardly think so. You either do — or not."

"Well, yes, then. I was at a mess party once, in a château somewhere or other — rather drunk I suppose as one tended to be in those days — and for some reason somebody taught me backgammon. You'll beat me into the ground of course — no contest."

In fact she played quite well when she could be bothered to put her mind to it, a fast chancy game which was no match, as she had expected, for his deadly accurate calculations.

"Benedict, I don't even understand what you're doing, much less how to stop you. If you ask me to play chess next I shall go home."

"I don't think I shall do that. I'm *very* good at chess."

"Yes — it did occur to me that you would be."

He glanced down at the board and then, with his dry smile, looked full into her face, his expression speculative, amused, not at all sorry to see that she had not the slightest chance of defeating him.

"Why take so many risks, Claire? Do you enjoy them?"

"Heavens no. I don't even think about them. It's only a game."

"Games, my dear, are to be won."

"I dare say. I can't seem to take them seriously, that's all."

"You should." And he was no longer, perhaps had never been, talking of backgammon.

"To leave oneself so wide open — dear Claire — amounts to an invitation to be taken advantage of — imposed upon. Don't you see that?"

She smiled. "Oh — well — but at least I do *know* when people are taking advantage of me."

"And you are good-natured enough to let it happen."

"Good nature — or laziness perhaps. Most of the time I don't really mind, you see."

"You're not hard enough, Claire."

"I know. I should have thought you'd be glad."

"Of course. It pleases *me* very well."

The pattern, therefore, was fixed. Two or three times a week through November and December he would drive her to Thornwick where, after whatever civilized preliminaries he had devised in the way of food and wine, teaching her chess, listening to music she found too difficult for pleasure, he would make love to her, enjoying her body to the full extent of their shared capacity and then, for a silent, hostile quarter of an hour, he would turn his back to her until whatever troubled him had passed away. He was older than the other men she had known, his experience infinitely more varied, his patience — since he was patient in nothing else — amazing and moving her sometimes more than she thought wise. Each time she left his bed it was with a sense of every nerve deeply at rest, every muscle purring with content. And her body would hum sometimes for hours afterward like a finely strung instrument replete with remembered harmony.

She had never experienced so much unmixed sensation. Yet, beyond his ability to thrill and explode her senses into the kind of orgasm which had somehow never taken place in her past experience of young bodies in cramped and hurried conditions, thinking more of loving and parting than of satisfied desire, she seemed no nearer the truth of him than before. She continued to enter his world at times of his choosing, a clandestine, entirely sensual relationship between accommodating mistress and powerful lover which, had she not been the mistress in question, she would have declared distinctly old-fashioned.

And she was not the stuff of which good, old-fashioned mistresses were made. She spent many a long hour pondering that. She needed friendship and partnership from a man. His confidence, a certain amount of laughter, above all frankness. The relationship, she knew, with a wry shaking of her head had to be waiting for her with Kit Hardie. And

Benedict, apart from an occasional flash of dry humor, gave her none of those things.

Yet she was still curious about him. Sometimes she could readily admit his fascination. Sometimes she could go further still and acknowledge both the physical hold he had established over her and her own perverse delight in surrendering to it. She had detested, more than anything in her life, her mother's complete surrender to Edward. With Jeremy and Paul the question had never arisen. But if she had inherited enough of her mother's nature to enjoy being what amounted to the plaything of a man like Benedict, then she would just have to come to terms with it and keep it under control.

She continued to see him because she wanted to see him. It was no longer either simple or straightforward. It puzzled her a great deal, often alarmed her, yet it persisted. And, as December brought its rush of seasonal business to the Crown, obliging her to work longer and later, she soon found herself living her life, not for the first time, frantically and against the clock.

"Are you free tomorrow?" Benedict's voice would ask, sounding curt on the telephone.

"I should be. It's supposed to be my night off."

"Eight o'clock then."

"Fine. Oh Lord — just a minute — perhaps we'd better say nine. It gives me time to change.

But nine o'clock, more often than not, would find her racing like a hare through the back door of the hotel, shrugging on her coat as she ran, her feet and her stomach aching, having eaten nothing all day, in the midst of rich food, but whatever she had been able to snatch on the wing. Late, of course, however fast she ran; and still in her working clothes, either her daytime uniform of narrow dark gray dress with its white collar or the long net shift covered with jet beads she wore in the evenings, both of which Benedict detested.

"I see you decided not to change."

"I'm sorry." And she was always irritated by her own apology. "I've had no time even to wash my face — which makes me bold enough to beg the use of your gorgeous bath."

"Of course. Can you stay the night?"

This, for reasons she was uncertain, was the one request she would never grant. It would have been easier, of course, particularly for Benedict, had she been willing to stay. It did not please him, she knew, to get up from a warm bed in the middle of a winter night to drive her to Mannheim Crescent, particularly when there was no real need for her to go there. Yet she resisted his attempts to keep her at Thornwick as firmly as Miriam's hints about the spare bedrooms at High Meadows. She had a room of her own, a cherished measure of independence, and so long as her dresses and shoes remained in her *own* wardrobe, not a change of clothes here, a change of clothes there, she felt far more certain of keeping it.

And so she made excuses.

"Oh no — I have to be in early tomorrow. We have sixty-four for lunch and then a Townswomen's Guild Christmas Teaparty . . ."

"Splendid. I'm flattered you found the time to see me at all. And you'll want to be home early, I suppose, to get a good night's rest."

He was not accustomed, it seemed, to working women. But she had been crossing swords all her life, here and there, with autocratic men.

"Well — yes," she said, as sweet and innocent as Euan Ash, "but if I had a husband, of course, then you would have to take me home even earlier still."

A pause. And then his quick, dry smile.

"*Touché,*" he said.

But, once at Thornwick, lonely miles from anywhere with no transport of her own, no telephone, she was very much at his disposal. And quite often when she had finally cajoled him or teased him or had allowed him to condescend to take her back to Mannheim Crescent, it would be so late that, with the prospect of that Townswomen's Guild Teaparty looming before her, a silver wedding dinner-dance, a coming of age, the very private little parties which taxed the limits of everybody's discretion, given by Arnold Crozier in the Tangerine Suite, the eternal racket of the Cocktail Bar, she could look forward to no more than four or five hours sleep.

"This impermanent relationship of yours," Euan told her, "is doing you no good."

"That's my business. Not yours."

"I absolutely agree. I suppose you know you've got dark shadows under your eyes?"

"Will you leave me alone?"

"I only mention it because Kit is bound to notice. And apart from the fact that the customers won't like it, he'll know, won't he — perhaps a bit too well — just how one gets that kind of washed-out, wrung-out look."

"It has nothing to do with him either," she snarled, gritting her teeth.

"He won't think so."

"Then why the hell doesn't he do something about it?" Passionately, desperately — from time to time — she wished he would.

"Oh I see." Euan's face flooded with his honeyed mischief. "You want rescuing, do you? Well then, my darling, if Kit's too busy at the moment — what with the Christmas rush and his Viennese tart — I'd be only too pleased . . ."

She banged the door very loud as she went out into the street, marched to the Crown looking as if she meant to burn it down, glared at dapper Mr. Clarence at his front desk, who, being by no means averse to glares since at least they meant "notice," mildly said, "You've only got one glove. And the Major was looking for you — half an hour ago."

Damnation! But when she hurried to Kit's office it was to find him well rested and well content, wanting neither to reprimand her for late-ness nor to accuse her of breaking promises he had not yet asked her to keep, but simply to share with her the pleasure of his November audit, his financial forecast for December, his growing freedom from those long, cold interviews with the Croziers now that he had a credit balance to show them.

"Just look at that." And sitting her down at his desk, he spread the figures before her. "I'll say this to you, Claire, and to no one else, certainly not the Croziers. It's better than I expected. A damned sight better."

She studied the balance sheet for a moment, not understanding it but wanting to invest the moment with as much importance as she could, to give him the full measure of appreciation which she knew he deserved.

"Kit — this is wonderful." And although the meticulous columns of figures swam meaninglessly before her eyes what she saw was his unflag-ging energy, his cheerful despotism, his flair; her voice sounding deeply impressed because the man himself, rather than his neatly penned arith-metic, impressed her.

"Yes — although I say it as shouldn't — so it is. Bernard Crozier went away happy and even Arnold managed to smile."

"Did you ever doubt it, Kit?"

"Christ yes — all the time."

"I didn't. You said it was sure to be all right and I believed you — which goes to prove —"

"What a good liar I am?"

"No. I wouldn't say that. What a good leader."

"You're flattering me."

"Of course. What's wrong with that?"

"I'm not complaining."

"I'm just so glad for you Kit."

"I know. That's why I thought we'd open a bottle of champagne."

"For breakfast — ?"

"Of course — with a few other little things."

A beaming Gerard wheeled the breakfast trolley into the room, champagne in a silver bucket, the tall crystal glasses reserved for Arnold Crozier's private suppers, plates of smoked salmon with eggs poached in cream and butter, hot *croissants*, French bread from the Keller's oven, Amandine's apricot preserve, clover honey, a pastry rich with almonds and cinnamon and icing sugar.

"What fun," she said weakly, her stomach still heavy with Mrs. Mayhew's steak and kidney pie, eaten in haste very late the night before, her head still aching from the white wine she had gulped rather than tasted in order to keep pace with Benedict who, preferring claret, had opened the *Vouvray* specially for her. And now, at half past eight in the morning, on top of her undigested dinner, her uneasy breakfast — only twenty minutes ago — of burned toast and black coffee, she was being asked to drink champagne.

"Here's to the Crown."

She desired with her whole heart to drink to that.

"To the Crown."

"And to you, Claire."

He had not said "To us" but, just the same, as her stomach mustered its resources to meet this fresh onslaught of cream and spices and wine, her smile flickered uncertainly, went out for a moment to be swiftly rekindled, and she lowered her eyes.

It was a reaction she experienced often enough that winter at High Meadows, an uneasy blend of apprehension and unreality, of looking through a veil as she watched Benedict, on those interminable "family Sundays," take his place at the head of the table, detached, aloof, contributing nothing to the conversation but an occasional sarcasm, a hint that of those present somebody had been found out in something; retiring to his study afterward where, sooner or later, the "guilty party" would be sent for to make whatever defense they could.

"Poor Toby," drawled Nola, smiling at Toby's pallor as he emerged from judgement on one such occasion, his hand visibly trembling, tears so near his eyes that he went out into the garden and stood for a long time in a bitter wind. Or "Poor Eunice. I suppose you've heard that they've sent her darling Justin home from school because they found him in bed with one of their chambermaids?" or "Poor Polly. She wouldn't take it from me that Roy Kington is a fortune hunter. Let's see how she takes it from Benedict."

And Claire, sitting quietly, her apparently tranquil hands folded in her lap, her glossy dark head turning obediently wherever it was directed to look, would give that brief, flickering smile.

Yet what cause had she to feel guilty about Nola who, still obsessed by sculpture in the shape of her hollow-eyed, almost cadaverous lover, could think of nothing but escaping to be with him in Leeds where, unable to settle in the larger and far more comfortable studio she had found him in Faxby, he had sullenly returned. She had arranged an autumn exhibition for him in Manchester, had taken him to London to consult a specialist about his weak lungs, had spent three nights with him, on some flimsy pretext or other, in a cottage in Ambleside which she had loathed but had suffered gladly, having been told that fresh air was good for him. She wrote notes to him every morning, whether she expected to see him that day or not, and letters on violet-colored paper about him to other people, acquaintances who might buy his work, art critics who might review it, the owners of galleries from Edinburgh to New York who might one day be grateful to her for drawing him to their attention. And even on those tense and often morbid family Sundays she survived his absence by lounging, in her long sage green or dull purple dresses, on Miriam's sofa, a sequined turban wrapped around her head, smoking Turkish cigarettes and stroking the pages of an album containing photographs of his work.

She had made him her sole occupation. Claire was only too well aware of it. Guilt, therefore — in theory — was unnecessary, irrelevant even with regard to Nola. Yet, in practice, she found it to be quite different, her logic and sophistication easily giving way before the simple teaching of her childhood that one did not steal another woman's husband, particularly a woman of whom, in a very odd and annoying fashion, one happened to be fond. And she *was* fond of Nola. Nor could Dorothy Lyall's daughter fail to be acquainted with the double standard of her mother's world which, while utterly condemning her for "carrying on" with Benedict would, in the same breath, congratulate him for seducing her. She did not believe in that double standard. But Dorothy believed it. And she had an uneasy suspicion that Nola, beneath all her *avante-garde* posturings, believed it too.

Yet, one thought could still console her. It was to be such an impermanent relationship after all, so very unlikely — like the war — to last beyond Christmas that surely, with care, the risk was not too great.

The Sunday before Christmas almost proved her wrong.

Interminable "family Sunday." Her only free day of the week claimed by Miriam, a claim much reduced, almost broken by her first months at the Crown and then calmly renewed by Benedict. She had once been expected at High Meadows on Sunday afternoons. "Keep some clothes here dear, so you can change for dinner. You shall have the blue chintz room, and I shall put a little china nameplate on the door like Polly's. 'Claire's Room.' " Instantly, the alarm bells Miriam touched off so easily in Claire's ears had sounded. Once her name went on that door, her clothes in the wardrobe, a spare set of brushes on the dressing table, what next? And she had managed with great skill and not a little embarrassment, to delay her arrival until dinnertime.

"What do you do on winter Sunday afternoons?" Benedict had asked her.

"Recently I stay in bed."

"Then come and stay in mine."

"How can you get away?"

"My dear — by the simple process of walking through the door." How wonderful, she thought, how lordly, was such simplicity. How rare.

"I go to the office on Sundays," he said, "or so one supposes — often enough to arouse no suspicions. I take the car, Sunday being Parker's day off. Therefore, since I am at the office anyway, it would seem practical and obvious — to all concerned — to collect you on my way home. If you appear with me at seven o'clock in evening dress who is to say that I didn't? All you have to do is bring a change of clothes to Thornwick, whereas I — having been hard at work all day — can have no scruples about keeping everybody waiting for dinner while I change at home. Quite simple."

"Are you much troubled by scruples, Benedict?"

"Oh — I think I can safely leave such worries to you."

And because he had made it sound like an adventure, an extension rather than a curtailment of her freedom, she had agreed.

The first time it had worked smoothly. The second time Euan, seeing her leaving the house with a small bag, had called out "Have fun." The third time, twenty minutes before Benedict's car was due in the back lane, another car, small and asthmatic, jerked to a halt at the front gate and Nola got out, standing for a moment posing beside the little vehicle, overpowering it almost in her long nutria coat and her skullcap of pale gray feathers designed for a Russian ballet swan, the wind making floating banners of the various chiffon scarves around her neck. But, as she walked into the flat, her eyes were too full of her own images and urgencies to notice either the telltale bag with Claire's gold evening sandals and black *crêpe de Chine* dress folded ready beside it, nor Claire's embarrassment.

"You'll have to back me up that's all," she announced, clearly carrying on a conversation she'd been having for some time in her head.

"Oh Lord — I suppose you want me to say I was with you somewhere or other last night."

And the irony of the request struck Claire unpleasantly. What a devious tangle this had become! How — yes, how *sordid*. But for once Nola was not in search of that particular alibi.

"The car, my dear — the *car*," she said impatiently, wondering why Claire had not understood it at once. "Benedict won't like it. He'll say if I wanted a car why didn't I tell him, and the answer is that he'd have got me something enormous and expensive and a chauffeur to go with it. And since my particular way of life couldn't accommodate that sort of supervision the only way was to get myself a little runabout that no self-respecting chauffeur would ever sit in. Toby found it for me, bless him, but in view of Toby's record I'd rather not tell Benedict that either. So can we say you did?"

"Yes — yes all right." She was ready to promise anything.

"Belonged to a friend of yours — one careful owner — absolute bargain? Yes?"

"Yes — fine."

"And I'll make it up to you one way or another when my dear husband growls."

In ten minutes, perhaps less, her husband would be here at the end of the garden, waiting — not patiently — until whatever business his wife and his mistress might choose to conduct together should be over. If he caught a glimpse of them through the long windows he would probably smile. Claire could find nothing in this situation — *nothing* — to amuse her at all.

"Is that all you want me to do Nola?"

"For the moment darling — yes. Unless you'd care to make me a cup of coffee."

"Not desperately."

"Oh — I see. You're up to something aren't you?" And, her eyes sharpening, looking so intently for signs of a hidden lover that she quite missed the significance of the folded black dress and the gold sandals, she said, openly inquisitive, quite ready to be pleased about it, "Are you expecting somebody? A man, I mean?"

"Yes — I am."

"Well, there's no need to snap my head off, darling, because I'm absolutely in favor. In fact I can't think of a better way to spend a Sunday afternoon. And in your case, Claire, it's high time. Far be it from me to cramp your style. Well then? — come on. Don't be shy. Just tell me who he is and I'll be on my way."

"*Nola* — for heaven's sake." And she was as near to squirming with humiliation as she had ever been in her life, feeling her own worth — even in the presence of this other unworthy woman — melting rapidly away.

"Is it Kit?"

"I'm not saying."

"Ha!" Nola's pointed face acquired a knowing look. "But you're not saying it isn't either."

"I'm just not saying."

Not saying, perhaps. But, foolishly and cruelly, she had allowed it to be understood. And what was there to prevent Nola from going over to the Crown, this very afternoon if she had nothing else to do, and teasing Kit. Nothing prevented her. It would be like her. She would see no harm in it. She would enjoy it. "Congratulations, Hardie my man. I hear you've woken up our sleeping beauty at last — with rather more than a kiss I do hope and trust." And Kit would know that Claire had used his name to cover up an *affaire* with somebody else. She couldn't do that to him. Do what, for God's sake? It had nothing to do with Kit. Nothing to do with anybody except herself — and Dorothy.

"It's not Kit," she said too sharply, Nola's throaty chuckle telling her at once that she had only made matters worse.

"There — there — of course not, my pet. Even though it's been on the cards for ages. I'll believe you where thousands wouldn't. Pity really, because — as I remember him — he makes strident physical harmonies — *most* impressive."

"Nola, you're not to say anything about this — to Kit I mean."

"Why ever not?"

"Because, for one thing, I won't back you up about your rotten little car if you do."

"Goodness gracious me!" Nola, stepping back a little, was amused, surprised, intensely curious, the wheels of her mind spinning rapidly in their own complex patterns. "What *are* you up to? Could it be that you've been having an *affaire* with Kit for quite a while and yes — tut tut — you're being unfaithful to him, you naughty girl, aren't you? Is that it?"

To Nola, it seemed very likely. It was a thing which Nola herself might easily have done.

"It might be," Claire said sharply, unwillingly. Very well. To spare Kit's feelings she had deliberately descended to Nola's level. What else could she have done? And until Nola had forgotten all about it, and Kit was safe, she would have to stay there. "So if you say a word to him, Nola, I won't do another thing to help you."

Benedict had been in the lane for fifteen minutes when she finally threw her bag into the back seat of the car and got in beside him, having no more desire for his company at that moment than she had for Miriam's.

"I'm late," she said crisply, "Because your wife came to see me."

But he showed no sign of being disagreeable about it, negotiating the narrow tangle of Faxby's ancient center before remarking, as if it were a matter of casual conversation, "She wanted you to give her an alibi, I suppose."

"Yes. She wants me to say she's spending the afternoon with me, so she can go to bed with her lover while I'm in bed with you — which makes it all rather crowded, or incestuous, or some other damned ridiculous thing."

She had not intended to say that. But now, with the angry words spoken, the angry tears in her voice quite audible, it seemed a regrettable but perhaps appropriate, certainly a timely ending. The last thing Benedict Swanfield wanted from any woman was an emotional scene, she knew that very well, and now it would be a relief to her if he turned round and drove her back at once to Mannheim Crescent. And then, if nothing else, at least she — and Dorothy — would be safe.

He did not turn the car. Instead he drove for a while in a silence that seemed reflective rather than hostile and then, without looking at her, laid one hand on her knee, a light touch which, because he had never touched her before in this reassuring manner — had never touched her at all except as an approach to making love — had an impact far beyond reassurance, a *weight* far greater than any hand could reasonably possess, releasing throughout her body the dangerous, languorous impulse of yielding. She was rootless and uncertain. He was a man of fixed direction and great possessions who liked to possess. He knew — in her case at least — exactly what he wanted. She was struggling merely, and vaguely, for a kind of freedom, a kind of healing. It seemed likely, therefore, in case of conflict, that he would win.

"Did my wife upset you?" he said.

"No. I did that."

"Of course."

He removed his hand, her body instantly wanting it back again, although she knew quite well that she would be able to explain herself — defend herself — much better without it. And, brooding on the need for self-defense, the absolute necessity of breaking through this trance of amorous bliss he kept inducing in her to obscure her judgement, she was taken unawares by the offer he suddenly made her.

"What would you like me to tell you, Claire?"

He had never invited her to question him before. Had he ever explained himself to anyone else? Truly — she hoped not.

"I think — about Nola?"

"Yes?"

"I — oh Heavens — I don't know what I want to say . . ."

"That you rather like her and it troubles you? Is that it?"

"I expect so — which makes me something of a hypocrite."

"Possibly."

"Thank you. I do realize that how *I* feel about your wife can hardly be *your* problem."

"Quite. But 'my wife' as we keep on calling her knows very well about my — what shall we say . . . ?"

"Impermanent relationships?"

"If you like. After all, who suggested to you that I might have black satin sheets on my bed at Thornwick?"

"Nola."

"Exactly. And if it amuses her to keep her own impermanent relationships secret then I see no harm in it. It is a game she and I play together — the *only* game we play — and it should be no concern of yours. We married young, to suit the convenience of our families, although neither of us objected. We might well have grown together. Many do. We did not. We had what seemed the right number of children and went our separate ways. Not an uncommon story. Perhaps not one to be proud of either but — as I said — quite usual. We do each other neither good nor harm. And why should she raise objections in your case when she has never objected in the least to anyone else? Friendship can hardly enter into the matter, can it?"

"Can't it? Shouldn't it?"

He gave his dry smile. "My dear — in your place do you think consideration for you would make Nola hesitate?"

"That hardly excuses —"

"Are we really looking for excuses? I think you ought to be content with the simple assurance that whatever Nola might do or threaten to do, there would be no scandal."

And once again she was astonished and delighted, dazed almost, by the light yet somehow decisive pressure of his hand on her knee.

"Dear Claire — I am not much given to making promises in these matters, but there is not the slightest danger that Nola would ever tell tales to your mother you know. I do feel I can promise you that."

She had not expected to find room or reason for laughter but now she found herself laughing, just a little weakly, with self-knowledge and a keen, disturbing pleasure that he had come to know her so well.

"I think I am ashamed to say how much that troubles me."

"Why? It proves you a dutiful daughter. And I am sufficiently acquainted with Edward Lyall to understand your anxiety. But don't you know that he would deliver you to me bound hand and foot — if I asked him. And that your mother would hold you down while he tied the cords."

She shivered.

"I don't want to think that about my mother."

"It happens to be true."

"Yes. I know. I also know the reason."

"Does that make a difference?"

"It seems to. Can we talk about Nola?"

"Indeed — what else?"

"I suppose I ought to tell you that she didn't come to me for an alibi this afternoon."

"If you really feel in honor bound —"

"Oh Lord — don't tease me about honor. She came to show me her car . . ."

And once again she hesitated, floundered, unwilling to be Nola's go-between, Benedict's spy, carrying tales which, in this instance, might cause trouble for Toby, who had trouble enough.

"Ah — she has bought a car has she? What about it?"

Claire drew a deep breath. "Yes. Quite a bargain. She got it through a friend of mine. Awfully good condition."

"I see. And might your friend also be a friend of Toby Hartwell's?"

"How can I say?"

"How indeed?"

"Do you object to her having a car, Benedict?"

"No. I don't even object to her buying it from Toby, nor even to the commission one can safely assume him to have taken. And, as to the condition of the vehicle, I imagine Parker can put that right."

"Then why — ?"

"A game, Claire. Nola's game. The family game, if you like, since they all play it to one degree or another. I believe my father started it. He was a man who said no automatically to everything — except to Miriam. He *knew* what was best for everybody, you see, and became terribly enraged whenever one asked for something different. Nola's father is much the same. And so she is comfortable with deceit. She enjoys it. My dear — I realize that you don't."

Perhaps, later on, when she had the time to analyze and pull apart exactly what he had said to her, she would find it to be very little indeed. Certainly he had said it cynically and coolly. Yet, even so, despite the crisp tone, the air of faintly amused detachment, she had been aware of *effort* of the labor it had somehow cost him to say anything at all. Not from lack of fluency, not from shyness, not even from a natural coldness.

What then? A simple inability to open the doors of his nature, to let himself out or someone else in? And how terrible a confinement that must be if he *wanted* to unlock those doors.

She returned to Faxby some hours later bearing her physical content like a warm fur around her bare-shouldered black *crêpe de Chine* dress, having left her best knitted jumper suit and hat in his wardrobe at Thornwick; the concession she had refused to make to Miriam.

"I didn't mean to enjoy myself this afternoon," she murmured, drowsy and incautious with pleasure.

"I know. You were on the point of telling me it had gone on long enough."

"Has it?"

"I dare say. I dare say it should never have started."

"Benedict — ?"

His hand descended once again on her knee, reassuring her, reaffirming his possession.

"No," he said. "Not yet."

They reached High Meadows and walked, not merely through a door, but into another identity. "Good evening, Marton," he said, tossing his coat to the butler as he had once tossed it to Kit Hardie. "I'll need twenty minutes to change." And he went upstairs to a room she had never seen, leaving her to face the dreaded half-hour before dinner when, since no one else came down until the gong sounded, she would be alone with Miriam.

"My dear, how pretty you look." This much was routine. "Do come and sit down beside me, so I can have a good look at you." This, too, and the plump little hand reaching out like a velvet clamp, a jeweled anchor, was just as usual.

"Now then, dear child," and suddenly the blue eyes were far too full of innocence, as Euan's often were in the moment of implanting a deadly dart, "There is something I must say to you."

"Yes — ?"

"Claire dear — I know exactly what you are getting up to."

"I beg your pardon."

"Of course I do." Both small, soft hands were in action now, one holding her arm, the other stroking, kneading, *smothering*. "Of course — how could you hide anything from me? Running around at all hours as you do, wearing yourself out for that terrible man who never wore himself out for me. Your job — your nasty old job, dear — what else could I possibly mean? What else!"

"Oh — yes."

"And I am about to declare war on that job, my child. Your mother and I are quite agreed. It is not good for you. What have you to say to that!"

Very little.

"You are too pale — too thin — you need looking after, Claire."

"Not really."

"Oh — much more than that. If I cannot persuade you then I shall get Benedict — yes, Benedict — to do it. He is very fond of you. But, of course, you know that. So are we all. Ah — Eunice. You are very prompt tonight. I had expected at least another ten minutes with Claire. But never mind. I have just been begging her to take better care of herself — or give in like a good little girl and allow those of us who love her to do it. Remember, my dear, there is a room in this house with your name on the door. The blue chintz room, Eunice. You know, the one between Nola and Benedict."

What had she said? No more than her usual artless rambling which was never, in fact, so artless as it seemed. What did she suspect? And, her blood running cold, Claire knew it was certainly something. No proof, perhaps, but it had been all there in her pretty raindrop patter of words, the slight emphasis to "your *mother* and I are quite agreed," meaning "what would your mother do if she knew what I know?," the sharp touch in her face when she had distinctly pronounced "but of course you know that."

How did she know? It made no difference. What did she want? Like Dorothy, Miriam had been brought up to believe in virginity, perfect fidelity, absolute virtue. But, unlike Dorothy, Miriam cared not a fig for any of it. And looking now, in growing alarm, at the candid blue eyes, the air of a kindly, slightly anxious tea-rose in full and stately bloom, Claire knew that Miriam, who fussed so earnestly about white gloves and dance programs, who deplored short skirts and flushed a pretty pink at even the slightest reference to human anatomy, could not be shocked by adultery, although she could never actually bring herself to speak the word — and would happily condone it under her own roof, by the simple process of refusing to notice it, if it meant that by doing so her own aims might be satisfied. What *did* she want? Claire knew. And once again that day she shivered. "There is a room in this house with your name on the door. 'Claire's Room.' The blue chintz room between Nola and Benedict." Had she now found the power to force her inside it and turn the key?

Benedict came into the room looking like a man who has been at the office all day.

"Good evening, Miriam."

And she smiled at him sweetly, his father's wife who had been brought up to believe she had a right to his service. How much power did he really have over her? Claire had no doubt at all of his abiity to control Edward or Nola. He had set her mind at rest as to that. But if Miriam threatened to make a scandal could he prevent it? Or indeed — and the idea lashed out at her suddenly — if that blue chintz room next to his own appeared desirable to him, or convenient, would he even wish to?

"I have been telling Claire she is not looking well," said Miriam.

"Perhaps not."

And, for a sickening moment, behind their voices she could hear the blue chintz door gently closing, the well-oiled click of a key in the lock.

11

SHE had not expected Christmas to be easy and, having decided that much, she further made up her mind — as she had done in France — quite simply to get on with it. This was not the first time in her life she had had too little sleep, too many cigarettes, too much alcohol; not the first time there had been too many calls on her time, too many demands — all of them urgent to those who made them — too much to do, a constant, hectic changing of place and mood and rhythm. She had done it all before in France and, compared to that, *this* — she told herself — was easy, often pleasant, unlikely to be fatal. Her body adjusted. Her nerves adjusted. Like a great many others who frequented the Cocktail Bar of the Crown Hotel she embarked on this hot tide of pleasure with the bracing of her spirit, the gathering together and seasoning of her physical resources which had been necessary to endure the thunder of the guns.

She fell into bed on Christmas Eve blessing Faxby's Licensing Committee for its insistence on respecting the sanctity of Christmas Day and then got out again since no civic authority had been able to control the alcoholic intake of Euan Ash whose voice very soon awoke her, raised in no Christmas carol of love and peace and good cheer, no "Sleep Holy Babe" nor "God Rest Ye Merry, Gentlemen" but a song she had heard many a time above the sound of wet slogging feet on muddy roads:

> "If you want the old battalion
> We know where they are.
> They're hanging on the old barbed wire."

She closed her eyes, hoping she might ignore it. But his voice went on and on, high and eloquent with the whiskey which would have stupefied any other man. Or at least, any man who had not used it day in day out in the trenches to blur his sensibilities and reinforce his desire to stay alive. Claire understood that. But others — the older and rather more substantial residents of Mannheim Crescent, for example — did not and, hearing him pass vigorously from song to verse, she turned over on her back and groaned.

> " 'Good-morning, good-morning!' the General said
> When we met him last week on our way to the line.
> Now the soldiers he smiled at are most of 'em dead,
> And we're cursing his staff for incompetent swine.
> 'He's a cheery old card,' grunted Harry to Jack
> As they slogged up to Arras with rifle and pack.
>
> But he did for them both by his plan of attack."

She heard a window open on the floor above, a man's gruff voice and then more than one growling something that was not applause in the street outside, a rumble of dissent as Euan, having finished one poetic rendering, launched into another; a deep-throated muttering through which his clipped public school accent, trained to be heard above the din of rebellious natives or across the floor of the House of Commons, suddenly broke free.

> "Men marched asleep. Many had lost their boots
> But limped on, blood-shod. All went lame; all blind;
> Drunk with fatigue; deaf even to the hoots
> Of gas-shells dropping softly behind."

She had heard the poem before. She knew the poet was dead, killed by by machine-gun fire in the last month of the war at the ripe age of twenty-five. She knew that if she heard any more she would not sleep again that night but would sit, her eyes aching and burning, avoiding that line of shuffling, yellowing men. She put on her coat and shoes and ran outside.

> "Gas! Gas! Quick boys! — An ecstasy of fumbling,
> Fitting the clumsy helmets just in time;
> But someone still was yelling out and stumbling.
> And floundering like a man in fire or lime . . ."

He was standing on the garden wall, precariously balanced, looking, brittle, insubstantial, a wraith through which the cold Christmas wind could easily blow when one compared him to the thick-set, middle-aged men — the grocer from the corner, the coal merchant, a short-sighted but burly bookkeeper — confronting him.

"Euan," she called out. A moment longer and other burly middle-aged men — the local constables — would be called to take him away. And in any case, she couldn't bear it.

He smiled at her sweetly.

> "Dim, through the misty panes and thick green light,
> As under a green sea, I saw him drowning."

"Euan!"

> "In all my dreams, before my helpless sight,
> He plunges at me, guttering, choking, drowning."

In her dreams too.

"Euan, come down."

"There are children in bed up there," growled the coal merchant, "And women. It's not decent."

"It's Christmas Eve," said the grocer, as if he had found a talisman.

"He wants locking up," said the bookkeeper, "and in a straitjacket too if you ask me."

"Why," inquired a female voice from a high window, "doesn't somebody send for the police?"

"If," quoted Euan, still in good voice and by some miracle keeping his balance,

> "If in some smothering dreams you too could pace
> Behind the wagon that we flung him in,
> And watch the white eyes writhing in his face."

She got him down the only way she could, by standing behind him and tipping him over so that they fell together in the garden on a heap of rotting leaves which broke their fall but did nothing to dampen Euan's poetic ardor.

> "Fat civilians wishing they
> Could go and fight the Hun.
> Can't you see them thanking God
> That they're over forty-one?"

211

But he was on his own ground now, behind his own garden gate and since no one really wanted the trouble of the law and the inconvenience it entailed on Christmas Eve, the woman up above shut her window with a sharp crack, the trio of honest tradesmen contented themselves by growling "Bloody lunatic."

Sitting up on the compost Euan smiled at them angelically. "Oh absolutely — Lieutenant Euan St John Bardsley Ash, Military Cross, at your service."

She got him inside the house, her flat not his, since he had no heating and she did not expect to leave him straightaway.

"Do you really have a Military Cross, Euan?"

"Yes. Or I did. I put it down somewhere and never picked it up again. God — I feel awful."

"Yes — I know."

He had been drinking heavily for days, cooking eggs and beans and dubious sausages and leaving them uneaten on greasy plates for her to throw away, and now, through his thin shirt, the hollow wall of his chest, she could hear the rasping labor of his lungs, recognizing the scarred legacy of gas which would return every winter of his life.

She brought blankets, pillows, pushed her two armchairs together and deftly made him a bed into which he allowed himself to be placed, wrapped up, "settled down," and then, with an alcoholic flash of urgency, jumped to his feet.

"I'm just on my way to Edinburgh —"

"No — Lieutenant Euan St John Bardsley Ash — you are not! Get into bed."

"Ma'am!" He sketched a military salute, overbalanced and fell back giggling and shivering into the careful nest she had made him.

"I'm cold."

"Yes. Are you going to be sick?"

"No — no — old soldiers never do that. They never die either, they just —"

He became graphic, bitter, obscene and she ignored him, cocooning him in blankets, raising him on the pillows just in case, checking his temperature, listening only to the effort his breath had to make — would have to make every winter now, every damp spring, every humid summer — as it forced a passage through the clogged debris the gas had left behind.

Somewhere, not too long ago, a trench had filled up with gas not necessarily discharged by enemy hands but British gas — quite possibly — blown back on a neutral wind, to clog British chests, blind British eyes, cause the fumbling for gas masks which did not always work, the

212

choking and the green drowning of the poem he had thrown so defiantly a few moments ago at those men, all of them safely over forty-one, who wished to see the war dead and buried — like the youth of those who had fought it — and forgotten. She knew he would not tell her where the attack had occurred. She did not wish to know. She waited, listening to more snatches of verse, an occasional ribald marching song, until he fell suddenly asleep in the middle of a word, as she had seen men die.

"Good night, Euan."

There was no answer. She put his cold hands under the covers, noted that the shivering was less violent, his temperature not alarming, that he was drunk which did not particularly require her attention rather than diseased which might, and went to bed herself just four hours before it would be time to get up again.

It was not Benedict as it turned out but Parker, the chauffeur who came to fetch her to High Meadows, rather fortunately perhaps, since she was cooking an omelette for Euan when he arrived and made no bones about asking him to wait, giving him a mug of coffee and leaving him to draw whatever conclusions he liked as to what this thin young man with a bricklayer's flamboyant check shirt, a public school accent, and a hacking cough might be doing in her flat.

"You'd better stay tonight as well, Euan. It's warmer. I won't be back until tomorrow."

And no doubt Parker, she thought, would also feel free to put his own interpretation on that.

She had managed to avoid the blue chintz room on Christmas Eve, pleading pressure of work, but Faxby's Licensing Committee, by offering her a day of rest to follow and Kit Hardie by extending it to Boxing Day, had made it impossible for her to upset Miriam's plans. She was to spend Christmas Day with "the family," on Christmas Day night she was to be tucked up, warm and snug and safe, in the blue chintz bed, to be served a leisurely breakfast on Boxing Day, an ample lunch, and to be released to the world outside Miriam's charmed circle as late as possible on Boxing Day Afternoon, not a moment before "that nasty old job" reared its ugly head to claim her.

"There is simply no one to drive you into Faxby any sooner," Miriam had told her gently, not caring in the least how little time these arrangements allowed Claire to spend with her mother. "Parker is not on duty after twelve o'clock on Christmas Day, you see — and I don't like to ask Benedict."

The blue chintz room, therefore, awaited her, bearing on its door a pretty china plaque with her name in blue letters surrounded by blue flowers, a fire beaming a cheerful welcome from a blue-tiled fireplace, a little maid in starched cap and apron beaming just as cheerfully as she arranged Claire's dressing table, tucked her nightdress under the pillow, hung her clothes in the wardrobe, calling her "Miss" instead of "Madam," as befitted a young lady of the house, permanent, dependent, rather than a visitor.

The day was cold, clear, lightly frosted, perfect Christmas weather, the house a giant Christmas grotto of tinsel and holly in bright, sturdy branches; pale, strategic mistletoe; a Christmas tree from a Dickensian fantasy, laden with parcels, red candles, tinkling gold and silver bells, crowned by a fairy in a white crinoline, golden-haired, blue-eyed, a foot tall, made specially and secretly, long ago, on the instructions of Aaron Swanfield, from a portrait of Miriam.

She had worn a white crinoline herself that year for her Christmas dance and had posed charmingly — so everyone had said — beneath the Christmas tree to receive her guests, Aaron so proud of his "portrait fairy" that he had refused to offer a cigar to any man who did not immediately notice its resemblance to his wife.

She had been twenty-eight that Christmas Day, ten years married and still able to wear silver-spangled white satin and a white rose in her hair, still "pretty Mimi," the sole object of her husband's romantic adoration. She was fifty-three now in well-corseted powder blue as Claire caught her first glimpse of her, coming back from church, her cheeks pink with the weather, her carefully assembled flock behind her, Polly in a gray velvet cloak and hood trimmed with white fur looking pointedly angelic; Nola, the eternal huntress, draped in her double fox pelts; Eunice in the black fur coat which always looked too big for her, surrounded by her four sons, two large, two small, Justin in a sulk because his escapade with the school chambermaid had not, after all, won him a permanent aura of wickedness, Simon in a sulk because he had not yet had an escapade at all, the two little boys simply bored; Toby and Benedict walking behind immaculate and neutral as men often seem on these traditional occasions. And Claire, hurrying into the hall to greet them, was aware, quite suddenly, of the two strangers, two neat, dark, slender young gentlemen — she could not call them boys — keeping themselves courteously but decidedly apart, Nola's children — Benedict's children — home from school for the holidays and finding it, as she had always done herself — an uneasy and unfamiliar place.

"Claire," Miriam was at her most endearing, "you will just have to forgive me. I told you to be here in good time — yes, I know I did. I was even a little sharp about it — and now here we are, late from church, held up, dear, quite against *my* will, by all the young men who just had to come and whisper some nonsense or other to Polly — and one or two good souls who were kind enough to offer the season's greetings to me. Give me a kiss, dear. There now everybody — off coats and hats."

Coats and hats were removed.

"Sherry," she said, beaming benignly, "by the drawing room fire, as we *always* do."

Glasses were brought and raised, the toast was drunk. "Merry Christmas."

"Many of them."

"What a lovely morning."

"What an excellent sermon."

"The same as last year," said Nola.

"Not so fast," said Eunice as Justin defiantly emptied his glass.

"Why not?" murmured Nola "— now that he's a man."

"And don't put your glass down on that polished table, Simon," snapped Eunice, who was in fact so mortified by her son's public loss of virginity that she could not have discussed it rationally had she tried; certainly not with Nola.

"Can I have another?" inquired Justin of his grandmother.

"No, dear." She was affectionate but very firm. "One sherry before lunch on Christmas morning — that is our tradition. Grandpapa used to pour it himself — and serve it from this very tray. One sherry each."

"And a very sweet sherry at that." Nola's grimace made no secret of her preference for dry.

"I like sweet sherry," Eunice, who missed her father and needed her mother, spoke hotly. "It's a lday's drink, after all — so Father said."

Nola looked amused.

"Can't we have champagne instead?" breezed Polly.

"It is time now," said Miriam, still smiling, "to run along and tidy ourselves up for lunch."

Claire had not expected to change but the maid, who evidently knew better, had laid out the cherry red jumper suit she had planned to wear the following day but which she put on now with red silk stockings and black shoes with patent buckles, brushed her hair into its gleaming Chinese fringe, wound a length of black and red beads around her neck and ran downstairs again, feeling late, to find herself alone, for five painful moments, with those strange, silent young men — her lover's sons.

"Are you home for the holidays?"

Of course they were. Any fool must see that. But, with scrupulous politeness, they supplied her with the exact date and time of their arrival, the duration of their visit — as "visit" it was, no one being under the impression that they lived here — the train they would be most likely to take on their departure.

What else could she say to them? She could have asked Eunice's boys about their Christmas presents, but realized at once that with Conrad and Christian Swanfield she dare not raise a subject so trivial. She could have talked cars, motor cycles, dogs to Justin and Simon, books, the cinema, and they would have answered ungrammatically perhaps or thoughtlessly — but at least with some enthusiasm.

"Do you like your school?" she asked feebly.

"Yes," said Conrad, "It is a very good school."

"Yes — very much," said Christian.

She understood that they were bored with her, and, hearing a step in the hall turned toward the door, her hope of a reprieve fading before the renewed awkwardness of Benedict.

"You're down early, boys," he said.

"Yes, sir."

She saw that he did not know what to say to them either, and that they were bored with him too.

Lunch was enormous, lengthy, the traditional roast turkey with a special chestnut stuffing — "special" because Aaron Swanfield had chosen to call it so — plum pudding flamed in brandy, eaten with plain, honest custard because Aaron had disliked rum sauce, the same meal that was being eaten in every middle-class house in Faxby that day, except that at High Meadows it was grander, there was more of it, and Miriam could never quite stop herself from pretending that she and Aaron had invented it. And afterward, abandoning port and brandy which could be consumed at leisure all afternoon, the family — in memory, Miriam insisted, of her father — gathered around the tree for the distribution of presents, Eunice restraining her brood with difficulty, Conrad and Christian standing with the grave composure of twin bishops, while Miriam gave the signal for the scramble to begin.

Claire had brought her own gifts that morning and placed them under the tree without much interest, simply a family duty meticulously done with nothing personal or significant about it since Miriam had calmly handed her a list, early in November, not merely of appropriate gifts for every member of the family but of colors, sizes, flavors and in which department of Taylor & Timms they might be bought.

"I always do a list for everyone, dear. It saves disappointment."

And so she was able to say "Thank you, Benedict," knowing that the expensive but markedly unoriginal scent spray he gave her had been chosen by Miriam too.

Within moments the hall was littered with Christmas paper, tinsel ribbons, Eunice's four boys and Polly down on the floor squealing like happy, excitable little pigs scrabbling for trinkets which Polly, at least,

216

could have twice over, any day of the week, from Roger Timms: their cousins, Conrad and Christian, gravely comparing the Latin Grammar, the leather-bound Shakespeare, the books on antique coins and industrial architecture their grandmother had thought suitable — and apparently rightly so — for them.

"I say — thanks awfully," said Toby to the company at large, clearly embarrassed by Eunice's compulsion to check that her own children had been given full measure, that Toby's collection of cigarette cases and silk scarves and tiepins was of comparable value to Benedict's, that the scent spray she had herself received from her brother was exactly the same as Claire's and Polly's.

Nola, leaving her own presents in a careless heap on the hall table, her mind on her sculptor alone in his chilly flat eating his Christmas dinner of cold beans and pickled beef out of a tin, slipped away to inform him by letter that Christmas — as she had long had reason to know — was hell for lovers.

Benedict went into his study and closed the door.

"Merry Christmas," said Toby, feeling the need to say something, giving Polly a resounding kiss under the mistletoe which caused her to swoon most endearingly into his arms, her lithe, boundlessly enthusiastic body and long, silk-clad legs proving rather too much for his peace of mind.

"Toby," said Eunice sharply, "take the boys outside and race them up the hill or something."

"It is time," said Miriam, happily pronouncing her traditional formula, "for the punch."

The door bell rang.

"Quickly, Charlesworth — the punch."

And for the rest of the afternoon she served it with her own hands, Aaron's recipe, no innocent brew but "a punch that had punch" as Aaron had always said, good claret, whiskey, a bottle or two of champagne, the best fruit in season, no more lemonade than was needful, offered with hot mince pies, slices of Christmas cake and cheese to the upper echelon of Swanfield employees, the departmental managers, accountants, secretaries, who had all been required by Aaron to walk up the hill to High Meadows on Christmas afternoon, no doubt at great inconvenience to themselves, to drink a toast with their master.

Traditional "high tea" of raised pork pies, cold ham and tongue and turkey, a baron of beef, pickles, salads, another mountain of hot mince pies, a chocolate log, more dark exceedingly alcoholic fruitcake was served at five, after which it was time to rest and change for the evening, when there would be more guests.

"I feel sick," said Polly, walking into Claire's room and flopping down on her bed.

"I'm not surprised. You've eaten too much."

"So I have. What else is there to do? I just *loathe* Christmas Day."

"You liked getting your presents."

"Oh — that part's all right. I took Nola's lot as well. Why not? She just left them there, in the hall, so she obviously didn't want them."

"So now you have two of everything — two scent sprays, two silk scarves, two pairs of gloves, two beaded evening bags."

"What's wrong with that? I *like* having lots of things. I notice she didn't leave the emerald ring Benedict gave her last night lying around. *That's* on her hand, all safe and sound. Cost a fortune, I expect."

"Yes — I expect so."

"I'm going to have diamonds."

"Good."

"This time next year, Claire, if not sooner — a diamond like a pigeon's egg and a wedding ring to go with it. I could have had the engagement ring today if I'd wanted."

"From Roger Timms?"

She nodded, curtly, dismissively — poor Roger — and stretched herself, flexing her muscles, holding her long arms in the air and turning her wrists this way and that, badly crumpling the blue chintz quilt and then, suddenly sitting bolt upright, her whole body bristling with dissatisfaction.

"Do you know how many parties the boys have been asked to today?"

"Which boys?"

"*All* the boys, silly. Every single male of the species who's old enough to leave his mother's apron strings. Even Justin got a couple of invitations although Eunice, as you might expect, wouldn't let him go. *We* have to sit at home and wait and look pretty, because there's no shortage of us. But *they* can go where they please. And so what they've decided to do is go everywhere — sharing out their valuable time a little bit here, a little bit there, so that everybody gets at least one dance. What fun! That's why mother wouldn't give a ball this year — not enough guaranteed partners and not enough staff. You can't imagine what it used to be like here on Christmas Eve when we had our dance — fairyland, that's all. Heaven. Christmas 1913 when we had the last one — I was thirteen years old, the same age as the year, and too damned young to do anything about it but sit on the landing in my frilly nightgown and *watch*. But — well — I thought there'd be another one, you see, the year after, and the year after that — every year — and now I'm not sure — I just don't think there ever will — not *just* like that. Hell —

218

how I loathe Christmas Day. The Templetons are having a big party. I suppose you know that?"

"No."

"What they call a dancing party, whatever that means."

"A ball, I suppose, without guaranteed partners and not enough staff."

Polly made a face. "Clever, aren't you. Mother just wouldn't take the risk. But I suppose Mrs. Templeton has to do something with all those gawky girls on her hands, Kay and Margot and Jane — and *Sally*. Mrs. Timms has made Roger promise to call on his way here — to support Mrs. Templeton in her efforts. If he stays more than half an hour he'll have me to answer to."

And she had no need to add her almost visible fear that Roy Kington might well stay there the whole evening.

"Well," she said, getting up, flexing her long golden arms and legs once again, tossing her cropped golden hair, "I hate it — that's all — dreary old Day — and the part I hate most of all is *now* when they all go off and shut themselves up in separate rooms. You can see the tobacco coming under Nola's door. Mother's fast asleep and snoring. Eunice and Toby are having a blazing row, or at least Eunice is because Toby won't fight back, you know; wouldn't hurt a fly, poor lamb. It's about Justin, I suppose, who isn't a bit sorry for what he's done. Or about Simon who's just longing to do the same. Or else about why can't he buy her an emerald like Nola's. Benedict's gone out —"

"Where!" But Polly did not notice how sharply Claire had spoken.

"Lord — how should I know? Just *out*. He probably hates Christmas Day as much as I do."

Had he driven over to Thornwick? Alone? She refused to think about it, having no inclination whatsoever to face up to the sensations her suspicions might arouse. Yet, suddenly, in this hot and heavy place, she was caught unawares by an acute longing for Benedict's beautiful, tranquil house which, when coupled by a sharp spasm of desire for the man himself, dealt her a telling blow. How foolish. How wrong. He had not spoken a dozen words to her all day and she, oppressed by the sheer weight of High Meadows, the silent presence of his children, the blue chintz bedroom, had had little to say to him. Now, the suspicion that, in order to escape that weight, that presence, and for his own particular pleasure on Christmas Day, he had taken another woman to Thornwick, did not surprise her. It seemed entirely possible, quite natural, only to be expected. It seemed exactly the kind of thing Benedict would do and had been doing for years.

It hurt.

She did not hurry downstairs, waiting until she had heard several cars come and go on the drive below her window before she put on her long black dress, her rope of pearl beads, rouged her lips and walked into the drawing room smoking a Turkish cigarette in an ebony holder, a woman without a care in the world, as anyone could see. Benedict was not there to see it. She had not expected him to be. Nor was Roy Kington, although Roger Timms had arrived looking heavy and amiable and just a little sheepish as if the flattery of the four Templeton girls made a pleasant change, now and again, from Polly's scolding. Nola's cousin, Arnold Crozier, was there too, up from the Crown where he had taken the Tangerine Suite for Christmas, having got out of the habit, since the war, of spending December in Cannes. "A poor old widower who needs cheering up a little," according to Miriam, although she knew quite well about the young "flappers" who passed in and out of the Tangerine Suite door in such rapid succession; cheerful young things, scarcely identifiable one from the other, as tiny and blond and feather-headed as his late wife had been sallow and stately and shrewd. Of course she knew. One simply did not *talk* about these things.

Arnold and Roger and Toby. Eunice, looking sick and feeling blinded by the headache which always followed a quarrel with her husband. Nola in a green sequined dress which, with the green turban around her head, gave her the air, if not the look, of a snake, a large emerald ring on her hand at which she glanced occasionally. Polly in scarlet silk, vivid, almost painfully beautiful, concealing, just beneath the golden skin, the careful nonchalance, a scared little girl who believed her youth to be ebbing away. Claire, who had lost her youth with Paul and did not even want it back again, trying not to wait for Benedict, not to look at Nola's ring. Miriam, surounded by her family as she had fully intended, sitting at the center of her charmed circle yet quite alone in her perfect content. And, apart from that, a collection of second cousins, obscure uncles to whom something was due at Christmas, all of them with daughters, sisters, a generation of wallflowers who seemed resigned to sitting patiently together in quiet conversation; and a sprinkling of very young men — too young — sixteen and seventeen-year-olds who pestered Polly for mistletoe kisses boisterously, but with no less enthusiasm than some of their fathers.

Not that Polly had the least objection to kisses — nor to sex in general, recognizing how badly men wanted it. Although, being completely unaroused herself, she saw little point to it beyond the power it gave her. She enjoyed being kissed and tickled behind the ears and rumpled a little as one would play with a kitten. *That*, particularly when she had had a cocktail or two, was great fun, a game she would have loved to spin out for hours and hours had it not been for its alarming effect, after ten minutes or so, on her partners. Men wanted more. She understood that now, although she had been shocked to begin with, considerably scared the first time she had slipped out of the Crown to spend a cramped and frankly distasteful half-hour in the back seat of a parked car, having agreed to go out in the first place only because the girls with the shortest skirts, the most dashing haircuts, the "sophisticates" all did so. She had to force herself the second time too. But, like cigarettes which had made her very sick to begin with, she had persevered, had soon acquired the habit, soon learned the rules which, in her case, were very simple. She would give what had to be given, as little as she could get away with, as much as seemed necessary, to prove her own sophistication or to avoid being labelled a prude, a cold fish, a poor sport, Heavens — one could never survive that. And, should the pressure become sufficiently great she was ready to go even further, to do anything in fact, and even pretend that she had done it before, so long as if it would not make her pregnant.

Contraception did not interest her. She still planned to be a virgin bride, with a dozen bridesmaids and a white satin train six yards long. But, having accepted that in these changing times her blue and gold looks alone would not hold the attention of a man, or at least not of the men she knew, unless they could also be touched, even Roger Timms was allowed to kiss her with open mouth and unbutton her blouse from time to time; while others had been rather more fortunate than that. But Roy Kington, hard young warrior whose appetite for battle had taken him straight to revolutionary Russia from France, had acquired more knowledge of her eager, golden body — without in any way awakening it — in one short, blunt half-hour than anyone else had managed after months of persuasion. And while he had been clutching her breasts and biting them and forcing her legs apart she had consoled herself for all the discomfort and embarrassment he had been causing her with the thought that, for the sake of all this nonsense — and not very *nice* nonsense either — he had left Sally Templeton puzzled and lonely, waiting for him with a dry martini at the Crown.

But he was at the Templetons now, she had no doubt, dancing with Sally who was desperate enough to give him anything in order to escape that household of women, a domineering elder sister who would never find a man, two others who had lost theirs in the war, a widowed mother and a pair of spinster aunts who would all need a great deal of looking after one day. She had once felt sorry for Sally. Now she condemned her to something far worse than death and damnation — eternal spinsterhood.

Naturally she did not herself intend to suffer that dire fate. "Roger," she said, "do light my cigarette." Yet each time an engine was heard on the drive, each time the gravel crunched under the weight of a man, her stomach lurched, as Claire's did, her breath caught sharply and her ears strained — like Claire's — her eyes darted to the doorway — as Claire's did not — her impatience visible — Claire's perfectly controlled — to be replaced, as visibly, by disappointment, peevishness, when the door opened to admit another middle-aged businessman, a cleric, a youth.

"For God's sake Roger can't you sit still — you're crumpling my dress."

Where was he? He had promised to come. She had promised to make it worth his while, knowing full well that their ideas of "worth" would not be the same. Yet she had been ready to promise anything in order to see him, tempt him, relying heavily on her belief — learned from her mother — that men most want what they cannot have.

Where was he? She heard another car, approaching at speed, driven as one might expect a wild young warrior to drive and leaping to her feet, causing Roger Timms to spill his drink, she ran out into the hall fleet-footed as a virgin huntress of ancient Arcady, calling out "We have company."

It was Benedict.

"Good evening," he said, looking at no one in particular.

"Good evening, Benedict," a chorus of voices replied, not Claire's, not Nola's, who, in spirit, was in a cold Leeds attic eating beans. Not Polly who, caught now under the mistletoe, stood like a stag at bay surrounded by a pack of boisterous puppies and a few aging hounds clamoring for Christmas kisses.

"It's my turn. Come on Polly — be a sport. Oh, I say, Polly, give me another one."

"Leave me alone will you — all of you —"

"You don't mean that, Polly — does she chaps?"

And immediately there was a chorus of "Stop it, I like it."

"I've had enough," she struck out wildly, catching a young cousin a hefty blow across the head, pushing a much older gentleman, who should have known better, so that he stumbled against the Christmas tree, bringing down a shower of tinsel.

"Let go of me — grinning bloody monkeys . . . Just leave me be —"

"All right, Polly," Toby Hartwell, moving quickly to her side, put both arms around her, easing her slowly backwards so that no one could see the tears pouring down her face: away from her tormentors.

"What is it, old girl? Got something in your eye? We'll soon fix that."

And deftly, being a man whose wife was very prone to sudden outbursts of weeping, he dried her eyes, telling her soothing nonsense all the while, calling her "pretty Polly" again, as everyone used to do when she had been a child.

"Toby — I do love you."

"Well, I hope so. You've always been my best girl. All right now, princess? Ready to go back and dazzle 'em?"

"What that girl needs," said Eunice, who had heard nothing beyond her sister's use of "bloody," a word she had never pronounced in her life, "is a good spanking."

"I think I may get rather drunk," said Nola who had heard nothing at all. "Claire — how about it?"

Smiling, Claire nodded.

"It is time," said Miriam pleasantly, "for supper. Come children — there may even be surprises — and prizes — under the plates."

Nola was carried to bed at two o'clock that morning in exactly the kind of stupor she had intended, Claire following a few moments later, too tired and rather too tipsy herself to grapple with what she ought to be feeling about sleeping in the room next to Benedict, and the suspicion that Miriam had placed her there deliberately to show her how easily and in how socially acceptable a manner even adultery might be managed. She decided, therefore, not to think about it at all, falling asleep so deeply that it seemed only a few moments before the maid brought her breakfast tray and a piece of information which promised her release from High Meadows earlier than she had expected. Miriam, it appeared, was unwell and would not be coming downstairs that morning. Going to her room to inquire Claire found her suffering from a slight cold and a great deal of fatigue, wanting sleep for once in her life rather more than company. No, she would probably not get up today. They must manage luncheon as best they could. Nola did not get up either. Christian and Conrad — God help them, thought Claire — had gone to spend the day with Eunice.

"I'll drive you home," said Benedict. "Parker's not here." And before they had reached the main road he had slipped out of his role as Chairman of Swanfield Mills and, smoothly — almost imperceptibly taken up the part of cool, attractive stranger.

"Have you half an hour to spare?"

She nodded and he drove up the hill away from town, quickly and quite dangerously, she supposed, considering the steepness of the road and its sharp corners, the thin layer of frost just covering the puddles so that they released showers of needle-fine ice to mark their way. The air was crisp and snow-scented, a streak of winter sun low in the sky, painting the clouds a soft rose-pearl tipped at their edges with pale gold. Below them the town was a black smudge in the valley bottom, nothing but the factory chimneys and the tip of one church spire breaking through the eternal pall of smoke.

Getting out of the car they stood for a moment at the top of the hill, a bare place with nothing to shelter from, nothing to disturb them but a bird rising suddenly from the bare field beyond, beating its charcoal wings for a moment against the pink-streaked sky.

"Whatever your feelings might be about silver-topped scent sprays," he said, "perhaps you might prefer this." Quickly to her initial embarrassment, her sudden flash of delight, her anxiety in case her cold fingers might drop the lovely things, he gave her, or rather tossed in her direction, a pair of antique earrings, clusters of amethysts, opals and pearls in an elaborate Victorian setting marvelously crafted like no others she had ever seen. And she was amazed and a little alarmed at her own exultation in the sure knowledge that although anyone, who had the money, could go into a jeweler's and order an emerald ring, it had taken time and skill and taste to find jewels like these.

"Benedict . . ." She breathed out her pleasure and, with a movement of her whole body as spontaneous and eager as Polly's, walked, for the first time without invitation, into his arms.

"I see you like them."

"Much more than that. I saved your real present for your birthday next weekend."

"I shall be away for my birthday. I always am."

"Oh — why?"

"To avoid Miriam's overflowing enthusiasm for birthdays. You could come with me."

"No I can't."

"I'm not going very far."

"How far?"

"A little place called Thornwick, perhaps?"

She laughed, still leaning against him, her body so much in tune now with his, so finely adjusted to his rhythms — so dominated by them — that desire could be awakened by a touch, a memory, a suggestion, her whole mind accepting that whoever he was, whatever he turned out to be, she had never felt so powerful, so well nigh unmanageable a physical need for any man.

"We're not far from Thornwick now," he said into her ear.

"I can't." But it was no more than a token.

"Yes you can."

"No. I'll be late for work."

"What time are they expecting you?"

"Five o'clock." She had promised Kit she would be on duty by seven but it seemed wise to allow a safety margin.

He glanced at his watch. "Then you can."

The house was tranquil and strange as she had longed for it, her mood one of sheer release again, of taking flight, her body dissolving beneath his into a physical plane which made nonsense of reasons, identity, consequences. Giving herself wholly, setting herself adrift she allowed herself to be carried beyond every barrier she had set herself, every barrier which had been set for her by her mother's conditioning, until she had been drenched by sensation, saturated: dazed afterward and bemused by sheer satisfaction so that, in her trance, she was able to say, "Did you come here yesterday?"

"Yes. Even I couldn't think of a believable excuse to bring you with me."

"So you brought someone else?"

"Of course."

Perhaps he had — or not? It made no difference. It hurt.

"Oh well — she can't have been much fun or you'd hardly have felt — well — so energetic just now."

And she added quickly, "I don't really expect you to answer that."

"Very wise."

"And I have to go now anyway."

"Yes."

Would he go back to High Meadows? When he had left her at the Crown to take up her life again, the Boxing Day Dinner for sixty-four, the private party in the upstairs reception room, the usual pandemonium in the cocktail bar, what would he do then? She had never asked herself this simple question before. She had thought of him either at High Meadows with Miriam — never with Nola — or else here, with her. What happened in between? What *now* tonight? Was there someone in his life, not a simple sexual diversion like herself, but someone real, someone who knew him as she did not, someone so well established with him that she could even be called on at short notice on Christmas Day, someone who, after Claire was gone, might come here this very night and say, "Tell me about her. Is she doing you good?"

She could not bear it.

Was this jealousy? And if so, how ridiculous.

"Benedict —?"

"Yes."

"Is it time to go?"

"Yes. Very nearly," he said.

12

*H*IS birthday was of no importance to him, she saw that much quite clearly. Falling as it did in the trough between those glittering peaks of Christmas and New Year it could easily have been forgotten by everyone else, could have passed unnoticed, overshadowed by the tinsel and holly and silver bells, had it not been for Miriam's devotion to the cult of birthday treats. Therefore, by absenting himself from home that day, he allowed Miriam to forget it too. "Benedict has never liked a fuss," she told Claire, "It is his December nature, you see. If one makes a fuss of him then he has to — well — *thaw* a little, doesn't he. And I suppose if one happened to be December, one could hardly wish to melt."

Yet, just the same, she had spent time she could not afford to find him a gift and, in the end, money she could not really afford either when Euan Ash, through friends in Faxby Market where he displayed his pictures and assisted in the sale of usually dubious antiques, found her a piece of art glass, a bowl shaped like a lily, the petals shading from a pale opalescent green to a strange blue-white with the head of a woman at their center, long green eyes half-asleep, a long mouth half-smiling, opal-tinted hair floating gently on green glass water, a tranquil, dreaming lily-face in deep repose.

It was so very right that she could have wept tears of relief — and joy.

"He matters to you then, this bloke of yours," said Euan, "whoever he may be?"

She shrugged, would have liked to deny it. "No more than he ought to matter — at this stage."

"Does Kit know?"

"Don't start that."

But did Kit know? He had promised her some free time after Christmas but when she had asked for the afternoon of the 29th until the evening of the 30th he had subjected her to a long, level scrutiny which had left her considerably ill-at-ease, and then had nodded quite curtly, warning her — with none of the easy generosity to which she had grown accustomed — that he could not spare her until after lunch. And on the morning of the 29th, when Mr. Clarence sneezed twice behind the reception desk Kit, who would normally expect his staff to keep on their feet and *smile* through anything from a broken heart to pneumonia, sent him home and put Claire — who else could he trust? — in his place.

"Can't risk an epidemic among the guests. Think of the size of the doctor's bills."

"Yes, Kit."

She stood in the lobby, her stomach in hard knots, her eyes on the French porcelain clock heedlessly ticking away her chances of getting home in time to bathe and do her hair; in time just to change her clothes; just to pick up her bag; her chances of getting home at all.

Benedict had originally planned to take her out to lunch somewhere in the country, at a sufficiently discreet distance from Faxby, she supposed; and she had had to decline.

"I can't get away until three o'clock."

"Can't you really?" He had taken no pains to hide his displeasure.

"No — I'm sorry." In personal matters she was often weak but where her status as a working woman was concerned — or her conscience — she could be firm.

"Very well. But please be realistic about the time. If you tell me to meet you at three o'clock then I shall be there at three o'clock precisely. If there is any possibility that you cannot . . . ?"

"No, Benedict. Three o'clock I can easily manage."

Lunch then, was unavoidably — although he clearly thought she could have avoided it — canceled. They would go out to tea instead at a place he knew which might interest her, then Thornwick where, for the first time she was to spend the night. Interest her? Indeed it did. Where might a man like Benedict take a lady to tea? No conventional teashop, she was quite certain, but a converted abbey at the very least, some mysterious, faintly sinister hotel. She was childishly eager to know. Nor could she avoid just a whiff — and she felt she could allow herself that much — of excitement at the thought of waking up beside him on a clear morning with leisure to observe, to assess, hopefully to talk. It was not at all the same as the many other occasions when he had asked her to stay the night, simply to suit his own convenience. This was part of the gift she wished to bring him, no curtailment of her freedom but a holiday.

She knew he did not care about his birthday but she wanted to mark it, in her own mind, as a special occasion. She wanted to give him the lily bowl and her own self for a full day, a full night, for no other reason than the pleasure of giving. She knew how rich he was. She had good reason to know how powerful. She knew he could buy what he wanted, or take it or *get* it one way or another. Yet, increasingly, her instinct toward him was one of impulsive generosity. And on his birthday night she wanted to give him the lily bowl which had cost her hours of in-decision and the equivalent of two months' wages and herself at his dinner table dressed to please his *Art Nouveau* tastes in dark, supple crushed velvet, his grape clusters of opals and amethysts in her ears; generous with her whole mind, her undivided attention, her good humor; generous with her body afterward in his bed, giving herself freely and in double measure since he did not, or could not give himself at all.

It was not the first time in her life she had felt such liberality. She had given Jeremy as much as her limited experience had allowed in the time at their disposal. She had lavished the whole of her deep-rooted, female bounty upon Paul. To the five, half-remembered lovers between them she had given affection; had not loved, of course, but had cared. Why she should feel the same anxious caring for Benedict, who was neither young nor uncertain nor under sentence of death in battle as they had been, she could not tell. She was simply aware that she felt it and, that being the case, concluded that on his birthday night at least, he might just as well enjoy it.

Yet she knew she had calculated finely. The hotel was quiet. Lunch-eon, which began at noon, ought to be over by two o'clock. Plenty of time, in theory, to go home and change into her cherry red jumper suit, pack her treasured crushed velvet dress, her lovely earrings, her wicked black silk lingerie, the lily bowl, *arrange* herself, and be ready to stroll to the garden gate, as cool as a cucumber, on the stroke of three. In practice, there was Mr. Clarence languishing in bed, Kit hard-eyed and cool, Amandine Keller, who rarely spoke above a whisper, suddenly rearing up and spitting venom at her husband, French venom at that, so that when she proceeded to have a fit of voluble French hysterics, Claire had to be called to restore order, hysteria in confined, culinary spaces being highly infectious: and at the same time to rescue from incineration an order of lamb chops. Lunch, therefore, was late. The dinner menus could not be completed because Aristide Keller, having discovered his meek little wife to be a snake in the grass, could not decide what his shattered sensibilities would permit him to cook. And

Kit who would normally have dealt with the matter in his own cheerful, persuasive fashion, merely raised his shoulders and said, "Talk to him, Claire."

She talked. It was half past two when she came back to the front desk to learn that the relief receptionist had not arrived. Had he even been sent for? Something in Kit's manner, and her own overwrought nerves, made her wonder.

"You could hang on — I should have thought — for another ten minutes," said Kit, sounding pleasant, looking like a man it would be unwise to cross. Ten minutes passed.

"I'll go and find him. Don't leave the desk until I get back." And entirely ignoring her startled exclamation he strode outside, purposeful, extremely angry, leaving her anchored by the responsibility of money, the lunch bills, the bills for last night's accommodation, the bar takings.

Nothing kept her there, of course, but her own conscience. It was sufficient. Irresponsible behavior in another person — in Kit — did not excuse irresponsibility in herself. The whole discipline of her childhood had taught her that. And although something inside her was about to burst — she could feel it swelling inside her head, overheating toward explosion — Dorothy's daughter could not desert her post, the stepchild of Edward Lyall to whom Money and Duty were both Divine could not leave those bar takings unguarded.

He came back a minute after three o'clock, alone.

"I don't see how you can go, now."

She walked out from behind the desk and faced him, deeply hurt by his hostility but not prepared to put up with it, no matter what, or who had caused it.

"Are you ordering me to stay?"

"Oh no." Even in a fit of cold jealousy, something he had never felt before and was uncertain how to handle, he knew better than that. "But I might be asking you."

What had Nola said to him? Enough, she supposed, to tell him that she had a lover. Could he possibly have discovered the rest for himself? She hoped not. She did not want him to know that it was Benedict, his former employer.

"I'm sorry, Kit."

"But not sorry enough to stay and give me a hand. I'd make it up to you later."

"You can manage, Kit."

"That's hardly the point."

"No." And her voice, to hide the proximity of tears, was very sharp. "The point is that I've been working here since you opened without a break, and without a complaint either. I asked you, well in advance, for this afternoon and tomorrow. You promised. I made my arrangements. And that's that. If you don't like it —"

"All right," he said, capitulating abruptly, totally, hearing the threat of resignation loud and clear. "All right. I can manage — enjoy yourself."

It was ten minutes past three.

She ran out into the street, angry with Kit but horribly upset at being on bad terms with him, at losing even briefly his steady, cheerful support which she missed as acutely as the turning out of a light. And now, although he had probably ruined her day and her fingers still itched to slap him, a familiar uneasy brew of guilt and sadness was already stirring inside her. She knew he wanted her himself. Sometimes she thought it might be rather a good thing if he had her. What a tangle.

But what mattered now was getting to Benedict. No time even to go through the house and get her bag. She would have to run straight to the car and ask him to wait a moment longer, dash into the flat and back again, his impatience snapping at her heels, and spend the first half-hour apologizing. It had happened many times before. This afternoon she thought it a pity. The traffic, of course, was heavy and darting incautiously through it she misjudged the pace of a pair of heavy horses pulling a brewery wagon, stepped hastily out of its way and out of her shoe, her stockinged foot meeting, with revulsion, a slimy cobble, an inch or two of dirty water. That too had happened before. She reconnected wet shoe to wet foot and ran on, the hands of a giant grandfather clock beating time behind her forehead, a pain starting inside her chest, her face flushed, she supposed, her hair certainly a mess. Twenty minutes past three. The corner of Mannheim Terrace, thank God for that. His car in the alley. Her arm waving and then dropping, a dead weight, to her side as she watched him drive away.

"Benedict!" She knew he could not hear her. But surely he had seen her running along the road, turning the corner. Surely. He must have done.

She went into her flat, thankful to meet no one on the way, and flinging herself down on the bed smashed her fists hard into the pillow, over and over again. It did no good. For perhaps ten minutes she was so shattered by the sheer size of her frustration, the bitterness of her disappointment, that she could do nothing more than suffer it, allowing it to engulf her and to some extent abate before her mind could function or her eyes could see. And what they first looked at was the lily bowl, beautifully wrapped in pale green paper, waiting serenely to be given.

She shed a few tears then, lit a cigarette, took off her stockings and dried her feet, and paced the floor for a moment or two, thinking it over. Why? He had seen her, she was almost sure of it. Why then, having waited for twenty minutes, had he driven away? Had it been simply to punish her? But that was illogical, emotional. It was not Benedict. She wanted to know the answer. She also wanted to go to Thornwick, to wear her crushed velvet dress and her lovely earrings, to enjoy the evening she had planned. Underneath the affront, the wounded pride, the conventional side of her nature which believed a woman should preserve her dignity at such times, should never make the first move nor any move at all for that matter, what counted was being there.

And there were trains to Thornwick.

Naturally — she had better not. Much better. Not that the journey itself troubled her. In France she had found her way to remoter places than Thornwick in far worse conditions, on roads pitted by shellfire, walking alone, eight miles, ten miles, through landscapes of devastation, to meet Paul. If she could do that then getting to Thornwick was an easy matter and, once there, she could make some arrangements, no doubt, about the three miles or so of moorland track up to the farm. And what then? An exchange of barbed words, a cool dismissal? Very likely. She had no guarantee that he would even be there at all. But she had stopped believing in guarantees so long ago and so completely that they played no part whatsoever in her calculations. And this way, at least, she would have made the gesture, the effort, would have held out a hand. She hoped he would take it. She supposed he would not. But, when one stripped away the inessentials, it was the outstretched hand that counted.

She was fortunate at Faxby Station to find a train for Skipton just about to depart. It was her only piece of good luck. At Skipton she had to wait a full and extremely tedious hour for a connection, leaving her bag in the station but carrying the fragile lily bowl with her as she walked up and down the Main Street of the pleasant market town, held now in the state of suspended animation which falls between Christmas and New Year's Eve. She walked because it was slightly more bearable than sitting on a hard bench in the station yard, carrying her prettily wrapped gift in hands which soon grew numb, feeling the harsh dry cold like a knife between her shoulders, her red knitted suit and black wool coat no barrier at all to the wind which stung her and bit her as it spitefully chose. Yet as her discomfort increased, so her determination enlarged with it. It would be easier, of course, to go back. It might even be wiser to return to the Crown where she was needed than to press on to Thornwick where she was not. Yet, having endured ten minutes, twenty minutes, half an hour of this bitter wind, of these hard cobbles that were already silvering with frost, she could surely survive another ten, another twenty; could hardly, in any case, get much colder. So she imagined. But the little asthmatic train, when it finally came, was in no hurry, pottering here and there among apparently deserted villages, jerking to sudden halts which caused her anguished moments for the lily bowl, its wrapping crumpled now from all her frantic clutching. And ten minutes before Thornwick she heard, against the ill-fitting window, the persistent tapping of rain, soon thickening to snow.

The village was pitch dark, empty, its single street awash. Could anyone be found who might drive her at least part way to the farm? The publican could give her little information beyond his opinion that no sane person would be out on a night like this; an attitude she fully shared. And since it was not his custom to serve alcohol to unaccompanied women she thanked him kindly and went out again into the night. Was there a vicarage, she wondered, and a clergyman to take pity on her? But clergymen, she reminded herself, had a tendency to ask questions, draw conclusions, and to be acquainted with other clergymen who might, in their turn, be acquainted with Miriam. Better not. The blacksmith then? There was a light in the forge, used nowadays as much for the repair of motor vehicles as for the shoeing of horses, and picking her way through the litter of scrap metal in the yard, an old wagon wheel, a tangle of rusty harness, a brand-new petrol pump, she walked in and managed — as she had often done in France — to beg a mug of hot tea in this predominantly male atmosphere and eventually to come to an arrangement with a farmer who, when the sleet had somewhat abated, would be travelling roughly in her direction, leaving her with only the walled track to negotiate on foot.

The farm cart was unsteady, open to every gust of wind, every stinging handful of rain the night saw fit to fling against it, the farmer a dour, dispirited man who, throughout the three jolting miles she rode beside him, spoke not a word.

He halted at the beginning of the track and, fearful for the lily bowl, she threw her bag to the ground and jumped down after it. "Thank you." He drove on. Ah well. The last lap. And there had been no point in dwelling on how much she had dreaded it until now. But here it was, perhaps a mile of rough going, the ground iron hard with winter, treacherous with a frost so bitter now that it froze the sleet as it fell, the narrow path set between high stone walls which, rather than giving shelter, became a wind trap, a sinister, shrieking tunnel where dire things — to anyone of a nervous disposition — might spring out of the dark. Was she afraid? It occurred to her that she ought to be. There might well be a madman — and *only* a madman — at large in this desolation, with rape or murder on his mind. Yet the possibility alarmed her rather less than the certain menace of the cold, the molestation of the sleet as it inserted icy fingers down her back, the absolute necessity of holding onto the lily bowl so that even if she turned her ankle on one of these damnable stones or fell into a bog, as seemed quite likely, she might salvage it. She was no longer quite certain whether she would give it to Benedict or not. That — like much else — would depend. But unless she should succumb to the growing impulse to throw it at his head — very unlike her — she did not want it to break. And if it turned out that she felt unable to make him the gift, or he did not want it, then she would just take it away and give it — to whom? Not to Euan, who would stuff it in his kitbag, or leave it somewhere on his way. Not to Kit nor to her mother, who would think it bizarre. To Nola. How very apt. The thought enlivened the last scramble to the gate, the scraping back of the bolt with fingers she could hardly feel, the rather terrible moment of realizing that the quite stimulating ordeal was over and what she now had to do was face the awkwardness of her arrival.

His car was in the yard. Good. Naturally she no longer had the least wish to see him. Probably never again. But, having a fairly accurate knowledge of how much exposure her body might be likely to withstand, she knew she required a warm towel, a brandy, a lift into town which she preferred to take from him rather than throw herself on the mercy of Mrs. Mayhew and Miss Todd. But — oh dear — how very embarrassing. Ah, well —! She found the door unlocked, pushed it open and walked in. "Happy birthday, Benedict," she said.

He was standing by the fire, his back to her, about to put on a log which, at the sound of her voice, fell heavily from his hand straight into the blaze so that he seemed to spin round toward her in a shower of sparks.

And for a moment, while the fire behind him, unsettled by the falling log, exploded unevenly into flame, he stared at her without a word.

Then, curtly she thought, which was much as she had expected, "How did you *get* here?"

Was he angry? A little stricken in his conscience? Glad? But she was sick and tired of guessing games. Life was too short, too precarious, quite complicated enough without that.

"Magic bloody carpet," she said. "What else?"

"You walked up from the village!"

"Yes."

It did no harm to let him think so.

"Why?"

"Oh — I'm just delivering a parcel." She put the lily bowl down on a table, a disreputable, dripping bundle now but still apparently intact.

"Don't look at it now. I think you'd better wait — probably until I'm gone."

And when he gave no answer, when the silence lengthened and thickened and he seemed to her, once again, so wrapped in shadow that she could see no more of him than a dim outline — had she ever seen more than that? — she rapped out "You saw me running up Mannheim Crescent, I damn well know you did. Well — didn't you?"

"Never mind that."

"I do mind."

He made an exclamation of impatience with his tongue and, striding to the inner doorway, called down the corridor "Mrs. Mayhew, would you run a hot bath please." And turning back to her he made a gesture of pure authority, his manner not even taking into account the possibility of being disobeyed.

"Get into the bath and soak. Then come back here."

The water was deep and fragrant, and losing herself completely in the luxury of warmth after cold, the body's ease after hardship, she was content just to bask, to float; grateful to be no longer in that acrid smelling little train, on that hard road; to be *comfortable* while Mrs. Mayhew made discreet murmurings from behind the door about her bag and her clothes. It was now half past six o'clock. She had been three hours on her way. Dinner would not be ready until nine. Would she like a snack? Thank you Mrs. Mayhew. She ducked her head under the water, washed her hair, wrapped herself in a warm towel and wondered vaguely what to do next. He had said "Come back here." Very well. Mrs. Mayhew had whisked away her jumper suit, her wet shoes and stockings, her coat which, for all Mrs. Mayhew's domestic magic, would probably never be the same again. Could she afford a new coat? Remembering the lily bowl she thought not. But now all she had to wear was her evening dress, her gold sandals, or her night things. And because it suited her mood of resigned defiance, her conviction that since she seemed unlikely to please anyone else that night she might just as well please herself, she slipped on her old scarlet kimono with its threadbare gold dragons and went barefoot into the living room.

Her chair and its footstool were drawn up to the fire, a tray beside it holding sandwiches, a coffee pot, a glass of brandy. She sat down, stretched out her bare legs to the stool, and lay at ease, or apparently so, in the lamplight.

"Coffee?" He filled her cup, placed it so that she had only to reach out a hand, and sat down on the stool at her feet, one hand on her ankle, a contact which, half-closing her eyes, employing fatigue as a convenient device, she chose to ignore.

"Thank you, Claire."

She had been a long time in the bath and whatever he had felt or would have preferred not to feel was perfectly controlled now, his voice even and neutral, only his hand on her ankle a shade less than calm.

"For what?"

"Several things. The bowl, for one."

"Oh — you like it then?"

"Yes, I like it. Enormously. I also know how hard it must have been to find."

"Well, that's all right then."

"Is it?"

She had kept her eyes half-closed, filling her obscured vision with the glow of the fire, the emerald and sapphire reflections of the Tiffany lamp. But now she opened them and looked at him, finding his expression grave but as unfathomable as it had ever been.

"You did see me in Mannheim Crescent, didn't you?"

He nodded.

"Then why did you drive away?"

"Would it be enough to tell you how much I regret it?"

"No. Tell me why."

"I am not given to explanations, Claire."

"Very convenient for you. I shall just go on asking, you know . . ."

"I know."

And closing her eyes again, feeling the pressure of his hand around her bare foot, she was aware of a tightening in the air between them, of strain emanating from his body to pluck, quite painfully, at her already overwrought and therefore unsteady nerves; a moment laden not only with stress but with hard-dragging, bone-wearying effort. *His* effort. *His* struggle to force something from himself, or to hold it down.

"I saw you coming," he said slowly, "I may have been rather too glad of it. That is all I can say to you."

What he *had* said — if she had understood it rightly — was amazing, tremendous, more than she had ever hoped to hear. She sat up to think about it, her kimono falling open a little, disarranged by her own movement and by his hand, travelling now from her ankle to her knee.

"I never expected, Claire, for one moment, that you would come here alone."

"What did you expect?"

"Annoyance. Indifference. It would have been appropriate — wiser. It never entered my head that you would put yourself in danger."

He was concerned for her. He was even attempting to apologize. She heard it in his voice, loved it, ardently desired it to continue. But she answered him airily, knowing from some deep instinct, that it was essential to make light of it; knowing for certain, without knowing how she knew it, that he could not cope for much longer with even this small and only partially revealed degree of emotion.

"What danger? They're not much given to rape, are they, in Thornwick?"

Instantly, and with relief, he gave her his dry smile. "Silly child. You might find pneumonia rather more fatal."

"More run of the mill, I suppose."

"Quite. What an odd little garment you are wearing."

"Yes. I put it on when I am in a dangerous humor. But the point is Benedict — are you glad I came?"

Leaning over her he undid the sash which only loosely held the scarlet silk together, drew it apart so that she lay naked in the firelight, and put his mouth to her shoulders and to her breasts, to every line and hollow of her outstretched body, long, deeply considered kisses of possession to which on an impulse of absolute yielding, she responded by pressing his face against her stomach and holding him there in the shielding, nurturing embrace of a woman to whom love came easily, generously, as naturally as the breathing of air.

"It never occurred to me that you would do this," he said again, pulling her forward and lifting her from the chair.

"Oh Benedict —" And she was sighing and smiling. "Are you going to *carry* me to bed? I do hope so."

He carried her from the room and down the passage as carefully as if she had been an invalid or a child, and then dropped her from a height onto the bed, himself on top of her, so that she shrieked and giggled; sounds, she thought, which may not have been heard in that house before.

"That was savage of you, Benedict."

"Yes. Wasn't it? A side to my nature, perhaps, that you didn't expect."

She reached out slender arms with finely turned wrists and capable, gentle hands and he came to her, allowing her for the first time, she thought, to enfold him with her own lovemaking, to give pleasure in her own way rather than as the vessel in which he manufactured it for them both, so that when it was over, her body still vibrating like an overstrung harp, her senses still afloat, and he turned away from her as always with what had often seemed to her a shudder of disdain, she dared to invade the shadow which had fallen around him, the feather-light pressure of her fingertips on his chest and his back turning him toward her until her head was in the hollow of his shoulder, their bodies clasped in the lose, friendly embrace which she had always believed to be the right thing, the only thing to do after making love. So far their *affaire* had proceeded entirely at his direction. She supposed all his *affaires* had done so. She wondered why it meant so much to her to show him that there was another way. An "impermanent" way, of course, but one which had meaning as well as sensation, a way in which they might learn from each other as she believed lovers ought to do.

Life so far had taught her to snatch at whatever might turn out to be happiness without asking too many questions; simply to be grateful. And, therefore, for the rest of that evening she was happy, wearing her crushed velvet dress and her antique earrings, drinking *Vouvray* and champagne, saying whatever came into her head to a man who responded with charm and wit, who did not tell her she was beautiful but looked at her as if he thought so, who touched her, from time to time, as he filled her glass or lit her cigarette, with the same appreciation of her value and her rarity, the same instinct to cherish and possess which he accorded to the lily bowl and to his cameo glass. She was happy sleeping beside him that night in the wide deep bed, happy the next morning when he brought her toast and marmalade, new-laid eggs and home-cured bacon, on a tray.

"Benedict, you are spoiling me."

"Yes. But my purposes are entirely sinister."

"Oh — you are going to seduce me afterward, I suppose. Please do."

He clicked his tongue in mock reproach. "My dear young lady, have you no shame?"

"None."

"And no fear?"

"Very little. Not much sense either."

He smiled. "But a great deal of —"

"Don't stop. That sounds like a compliment."

"Yes. It might have been. Don't let me exploit you, Claire."

"That is not what you started to say."

"No — simply what I ought to be saying."

"This is very good coffee, Benedict."

She was still happy.

There had been a light snowfall in the night, pure white fields and a pale gray sky, cold, quiet air streaked by their breath as they strolled as far as her shoes could manage along the road and stood for a while looking across the steeply sloping land which led eventually — inevitably perhaps, she thought with a shiver — to High Meadows.

"Where do they think you are today, Benedict?"

"London."

"Do they believe you?"

"My dear — they don't care." It was a statement of fact, spoken without rancor, which seemed quite natural to him. Why should they care? It suited him far better that they did not. Yet it hurt her. Did he care for them? It seemed unlikely.

"Were you born at High Meadows, Benedict?"

"Yes. My father built the house for my mother — with her money, of course, since he had none until he married her."

"So that is why it belongs to you now instead of — the others?"

He smiled down at her, delighting her with a rare moment of confidence, "I believe my father saw 'the others,' as a kind of diversion, a pleasant little fantasy. Whereas I, of course, was the not quite pleasant reality."

"Were you fond of him?"

Rather desperately she wanted him to be fond of somebody.

"No. Not at all. I worked for him. I made sure he paid me." He smiled again. "I was the poor little orphan, you see, sent to work in the mill while 'the others' stayed at home eating strawberries and cream. And now I have the house and the mill and all the money — and the woman I want. Do I have her?"

"Yes, you do."

"Then let me take you out to lunch, since Mrs. Mayhew has worked such wonders with your coat and shoes."

She was happy now.

And afterward, no matter how carefully she looked for it, she could never quite place the exact moment that she lost him.

The drive across the Pennines to the moorland heights of Lancashire was pleasant enough. The inn, set in apparent and very lofty isolation, although it was reasonably accessible from several large towns, was famous both for its wine cellar and its history, and every bit as luxurious in its dark oak and tobacco-brown leather fashion as she had expected. Bandits and smugglers had done dark deeds here in bygone days. A highwayman of great local repute had been shot from his saddle in the stableyard. There had been elopements or abductions, according to taste, of highborn women and the last act of a tragic love story played out in the barn when a local Romeo and a Juliet from the Colne Valley had chosen to die in each other's arms. There had been the whispering of conspirators, Cavaliers and Roundheads, hiding from one another, both finding friends among the hard-headed, fiercely independent moorlanders. There had been supporters of catholic royalty hiding, in protestant England, from the protestant English, since the landlord of the day had been willing to give shelter to anybody of any persuasion who could pay his price.

There were ghosts, of course: young Juliet in a white nightgown wringing her hands, a murdered man — a supporter of Bonnie Prince Charlie it was said — looking for revenge on Christmas or on Midsummer's Eve, no one was absolutely certain. But on most days of the week the present landlord — aware of the commercial value of ghosts and legends — was pleased to serve ample luncheons of roast beef or game or venison in season in a low-beamed room full of horse brasses and weaponry, pikes and muskets and broadswords in gleaming, good-as-new condition, the food so exquisite and the light so dim that it had become fashionable and convenient for gentlemen who could afford it to lunch here with women who were not their wives.

Therefore, since many people would prefer not to be seen at the Gamecock, it was considered good taste, good manners not to look. Yet as they walked into the bar a woman, emerging from shadow across the room, called out "Benedict — how very nice."

Was it then?"

She was tall, not young to Claire even though she knew better than to underrate the charm of mature women like this one who, accustomed to the command of large households and the spending of a husband's income, were imperious, elegant, superbly dressed.

"Edwina," he said, "*what* a surpirise." And he went over to greet her, holding her in a familiar embrace. Not passionate of course. Claire noted that. But Edwina Challoner who was thirty-nine and exceedingly well-married, did not expect passion from a man she had known for ten years, during which he had been her lover for several short, highly civilized periods, each one of them beginning most agreeably and ending entirely without rancor. If, indeed, they could be said to have ended, for on no occasion had either one of them felt deeply enough or found it in any way necessary to speak the dramatic words "We must part." Other things had simply and quite naturally intervened. Social obligations. Business commitments. The claims of family and one's other friends. She had spent last winter in Egypt, for instance, on account of her husband's bronchitis and had certainly not expected a man like Benedict Swanfield to be available when she returned. She was, at present, rather heavily committed herself. Yet, just the same, she was rather more than surprised to see him in the company of a girl like Claire. A "flapper" no less, in Edwina Challoner's view, with her short hair, her legs crossed high as she sat down calmly on a bar stool showing her knees and lighting her own cigarette: thin as a stick, or slender as a reed, of course, should one wish to be charitable, a temptation to which Edwina Challoner, when it came to "flappers," did not succumb. And although she did not want Benedict herself — not just now — the sight of this far too obviously *modern* girl, smoking her cigarette with the matter-of-fact enjoyment of a man, obscurely worried her. All Edwina Challoner's *affaires* had been with men like Benedict Swanfield; wealthy, influential, hotblooded, cold-hearted, discreet. All his *affaires*, she'd assumed, since several of them involved her own acquaintances, had been with women like herself. And, with the approach of her fortieth birthday, she could only view with alarm any indication that the tastes of one of her "circle" might be veering in this odd direction.

She put her mouth close to his ear, looking over his shoulder at Claire who was very deliberately not looking at her. "Darling," she murmured, "Quite a poppet, of course. But really — one might almost call it corruption of our tiny tots."

He laughed, his arm casually around Edwina's shoulders, a laugh which, had Claire been able to hear it, she would not have recognized.

"My sister-in-law, darling."

Edwina laughed too, leaning against him.

"Benedict! You wicked creature. Your brother's wife. How very — well — how Biblical."

"Among other things. You must meet her." And he spoke the words as if they — or some possibility they contained — had just occurred to him. "Yes, Edwina. It might — interest her — to see me in another light. It might even do her good. Come and meet her."

"Benedict dear," she said, knowing him as well as anybody, "what *are* you up to?" And then, because whatever it was, it was hardly likely to hurt her, she brushed her cheek against his and smiled. "I'm just dying to, darling. But before I do you must meet *my* friend. You don't know Lois Chiltern do you?"

"I don't think so." But his greeting for the woman who now held out a large, well-manicured hand to him, puzzled the by no means insensitive Edwina. Not warm precisely but oddly satisfied, rather as if this friend of hers, this beautifully plucked and painted but otherwise quite unremarkable Lois Chiltern might be the very thing he needed.

And so, when he returned to Claire a few moments later there were two women beside him, Edwina very dark, Lois very blond, with nothing more than that — Claire at once decided — to tell them apart, the same long athletic limbs used to walking their dogs and riding to hounds, the same loud, toneless voices which they used to effect when opening their local flower show, the same diamonds on strong fingers, the same unshakable self-confidence. They were groomed to the shining perfection of racehorses, had wonderful clothes, Edwina a dark mink, Lois a pale one, which they wore casually, arrogantly, around broad shoulders decorated with diamond brooches like military medals.

"Shall we have lunch together?" suggested Benedict.

"Lovely idea," in chorus. And Claire, sliding down from her bar stool, displaying her legs — all she had to display — instead of diamonds smothered her disappointment with a smile.

Did she lose him then? Or was that the first moment of suspicion and unease, a warning that this sense of alienation, of being totally among strangers, would not only continue but increase.

In the dining room they out-maneuvered her, or thought they had, although she knew that if Benedict had wanted to sit beside her he would quite simply have done so. But instead he allowed Edwina to take his arm and lead him to the table, Lois close behind, and sat down between them not even glancing at Claire as she sat in the remaining chair, placed somewhat awkwardly for conversation. Not that she could have taken any part in it, in any case, since it was a deliberate — entirely deliberate, she felt — recital of the dinner parties and bridge parties, the amorous in-fighting, the marital deceptions of a series of men and women Claire did not know and did not care to know, which lasted through the soup, the turbot, the roast duck, terminating with the pears in red wine when Benedict, turning quietly but very definitely toward Lois, made some remark or other in a low tone to which she replied with an excited chuckle, a satisfied intake of breath. And thereafter, through the cheese, the coffee and brandy, he talked to Lois, her blond head close to his, her pale fur still thrown negligently around her shoulders, her large, light blue eyes watching his mouth and not listening to a word since she knew, from long experience, what he was really asking and had already decided on her answer.

Claire knew it too. Yet, in that critical, hostile company she could not afford to *feel* anything about it. At all costs she must remain smiling and calm, must let nothing show. Yes. He was hurting her, punishing her, and in a quite masterly fashion, with a kind of deadly brilliance which took the breath from her body like a foul, physical blow. And the only defense she could think of was to pretend not to notice, to go on smiling until her cheeks ached, to go on producing some trite little remark every time Edwina took pity on her and asked for one.

"Do you play bridge, dear?"

"Oh no. I couldn't sit still long enough."

"What a pity. Benedict plays superbly."

What game was he playing now? Edwina felt inclined to ask herself that question too, wondering just what there might be in beautiful, brainless Lois to arouse the desire — and so *obvious* too — of a discerning man like Benedict, who was not in the habit of behaving so amorously; not in public, at any rate. And the answer came to her quite suddenly, as she was making up her mind between *Roquefort* and Brie. Nothing. It was not Lois at all. How could it be? There had been a dozen women like Lois in his life, white marble statues with wide blue eyes and not a great deal behind them, and watching as he went through the motions of losing his head over this one, she did not believe it.

"Do you ride, dear?" she asked Claire, quite kindly.

"A little — when I was at school."

And watching him too, feeling with every humiliated inch of her own body the raw sensuality that was brewing, thickening, over-heating between him and this woman who seemed half-naked already in spirit, she went on smiling.

After all, in a dreadfully twisted and perverted fashion, he was giving her exactly what she had asked for. She had wanted to see him in different surroundings, to discover another facet of his nature. Very badly she had wanted that. But this calculated charmer, this out-and-out sensualist, this sophisticated, cold-blooded man who slept with these horsy women not in affection but as an exercise in sexual expertise, was a man she did not like. Did he know that? Fervently she hoped so.

The meal eventually would be over. That much was certain and she thanked God for it. It ended. They stood up to leave, Claire feeling small and shabby, wondering why she had ever imagined that her youth alone could really compete with all this well-groomed *hauteur* any more than her plain wool coat against Lois's mink.

"I must start giving my bridge dinners again," said Edwina. "I shall rely on you Benedict. You'll just have to get into the habit of hopping over the Pennines again, as you used to. Charles will be so pleased."

And kissing him with a calm, deliberate relish, she took Claire's arm and walked her briskly away, allowing Benedict all the time he needed to make his arrangements with Lois.

She got into the car and waited while he assisted them, one on each arm, across the frozen yard to their car, Lois looking undeniably magnificent wrapped like an empress in her pastel furs, what looked like several yards of blond hair bound intricately around her head, a heavy, probably quite glorious bosom which Polly would have declared old-fashioned but which few men of Benedict's temperament would be likely to despise. Very far from that. And closing her eyes she began, with the strength and the cruelty of desperation, to shut off her sources of tenderness, pride, affection, caring, loving, suffering — particularly that one and the one before it — numbing them, squeezing them into a state of precarious non-being until — as soon as possible — she could be alone with them.

"Benedict dear," said Edwina, detaining him a moment once Lois was in the car, "I am not deceived you know."

"Are you not?"

"Definitely not. You were very brutal with that poor girl, you know."

"Yes, Edwina. I know."

"You won't tell me why, of course?"

"Darling — you must know me better than that."

She smiled and slipped her arm through his, rather pleasurably aware of the two other women watching them through separate car windows, the suffering, oddly appealing girl who had been so publicly abandoned, and beautiful, bovine Lois who — Edwina felt sure of it — had been used.

"All right then," she told him, "let me guess. I think one can take it that our little Claire will never want to see you again?"

He smiled. With some difficulty, she thought.

"More than that, Edwina. She ought to consider herself well rid of me. Wouldn't you?"

And realizing that he wanted to know she glanced at him keenly.

"Good Heavens — Benedict! — can one believe it? I could see at once that she was fond of you and probably needed discouraging. Too young, of course, to take these things — well — as reasonably as we do."

She paused a moment, frowning, working it out. "Well — what can that mean, Benedict? Unless it should be that you don't want to lose her at all. One quite sees, in that case, that you'd have to break it off in such a way that it couldn't be mended. No going back. Goodbye for ever. And the girl thinking you an absolute bastard into the bargain so she wouldn't cry too long. My dear — it looks to me as if you care about that girl."

"Well — shall we say the danger existed. And one simply could not let it get out of hand, could one, Edwina my darling?"

She shook her head and taking her large, jeweled hand he gave it a companionable squeeze. "Ah well — let's put it down to old age, shall we? I was forty yesterday. A difficult time of life, they say. And I really think my sister-in-law has suffered enough. She ought not to be involved for too long with a man like me. I thought I'd better see to it."

Returning the pressure of his hand she kissed him lightly on the cheek, realizing that in their ten years of casual lovemaking she had never felt so close to him before.

"Benedict — how devilish of you." Brave too, although she knew better than to tell him that. And generous. He had made the girl suffer now in the hope that, in the long term, she would suffer less. Noble, really. One would never have thought of it. It had taken a great deal out of him too. Really — how very tired he looked.

"Do come to dinner, darling," she said. "Next Thursday, perhaps?" She felt fairly certain that Lois would be over by then.

He was smiling as he drove out of the inn yard and up the narrow moorland roads which were already disappearing beneath the snow, the afternoon fading into a damp, misty gray.

"Nice women, those two," he said.

"Nice?"

"Obviously you didn't think so."

"Well — a little — elderly — weren't they, Benedict. *Passée*, in fact, it rather seemed to me."

He laughed, not pleasantly, but as if her remark had given him satisfaction.

"My dear child — don't underestimate the appeal of the older woman. And don't believe all she has to offer is gratitude. Enthusiasm, perhaps. Certainly expertise, which counts for a great deal."

"I've never had much to do with older women, Benedict. So I'll leave you to judge."

"Very wise."

He allowed a mile or two to go by.

"What time," he inquired politely, "would you like me to take you back to town?"

She smiled at him sweetly, as she had smiled at Edwina a little while before, her whole body ice-cold.

"Oh," and she sounded very nonchalant "if we call at the farm to get my bag, you can take me now."

The farmhouse was warm and very quiet. Her bag was ready, neatly packed by Mrs. Mayhew, and she picked it up, her hands quite steady. She would not be coming here again. Whether he had decided that in advance or had simply taken the opportunity of Lois and Edwina as it came, she did not know. But the result was the same. It had happened sooner than she had wanted. It was happening in a manner which, she knew, when she relaxed her control, would give her pain: a manner which would remove every vestige of her pleasure in him, every shred of illusion. She probably would not like him very much after today. But, since it had to happen eventually, perhaps it would be easier to remember him with Lois, with Edwina, to remember him as they knew him, as she had seen him for the first time and — she hoped — the last time, today.

Catching sight of the lily bowl sitting serenely on an inlaid table by the fire she was not sure whether she wanted to snatch it up into her arms and protect it or smash it into pieces against the hearthstones.

"Goodbye, Mrs. Mayhew. Thank you."

She got into the car. Very soon now it would be over. The sooner — for so many reasons — the better.

"I suppose they are your standard types, are they, Benedict — Lois and Edwina?"

He smiled. And once again she felt that she had given him a cue.

"I suppose they are. But I diversify, of course, from time to time — as you know. Everyone should."

"Oh — should they? I'll remember that."

"Yes, do. But you haven't found your type yet, Claire. One always goes back to it."

"And for you that's Edwina, or Lois. Or both."

"Not both together darling. They have their principles."

He had never called her darling before. And inserted into that deliberately suggestive phrase it offended her. No, she didn't like him. Not like this. And if this was the truth of him, which she had looked so hard to find, then he had used her very coolly, very finely, very cleverly indeed. She didn't blame him. She blamed herself.

It was conveniently dark when they reached Mannheim Crescent and leaning across her he opened the door, an indication of haste, no time to spare in leave-taking.

"Here we are, Claire."

"Yes."

And, this being the moment when they usually made their arrangements to meet again, there was an awkward pause.

"What shall we say then, Claire?"

"I don't know. Anything you like."

"Perhaps it had better be lunch on Sunday at High Meadows — don't you think so?"

"Yes. I think so."

She got out, and he drove away.

"You're back early," said Euan. "How did he like his lily bowl?"

"Very much. It was a great success." She was friendly, very calm.

"Thank God you're back," said Kit, "Clarence really does have the flu. And look here, Claire, I'm sorry about yesterday — making you late and being a swine generally . . ."

"That's all right, Kit. I wasn't late. And it wouldn't have been that important anyway."

She was cheerful, friendly, calm.

She saw no point in being otherwise. She would not allow herself to be otherwise until, returning the following evening from the Crown, she found waiting on her doorstep a stiff, florist's arrangement of hothouse flowers, expensive, impersonal, even a little ostentatious, bearing a glossy white card with the printed name "Benedict Swanfield" and a scrawled message which might have said "In Memoriam" but, actually read "Good luck. Many thanks."

And, gathering up the innocent, overbred, overpriced blooms in savage hands she took them into the backyard and murdered them, shredding them one by one into the dustbin and then ramming on the lid, holding it down so that no particle of anything she had ever felt, or thought she had felt, about Benedict Swanfield could ever escape.

Thank God it was over. Thank God. She had been on the verge of falling in love with him. And now she could only regard it as a disease from which she had been cured just in time. A terrible disease. And what stung — what scorched — was what a gullible, romantic fool she had been.

13

POLLY Swanfield set out, deliberately and exuberantly, on New Year's Eve to create a sensation; to drink more champagne, eat more Russian Caviar or *foie gras* or anything else that was rare and expensive, to steal more kisses, arouse more desire in the loins of men and more jealousy in the breasts of women than anyone else in Faxby. Wearing a slip of orange satin covered in gold and silver butterflies with a transparent overskirt of gold-spangled orange tulle, her long bare arms jangling gold bracelets from wrist to elbow, a rope of gold beads swinging wildly around her neck, the stroke of midnight found her on the little postage stamp dance floor of the Crown Hotel, dancing alone with a circle of men around her, improvising her own tipsy ballet to a blare of smoky jazz, her eyes glazed with alcohol and an inner vision of her own glorious, still virgin body as it bent and swayed to each man in turn, her movements amorous and coy both together; "making an exhibition of herself" thought Miss Sally Templeton from the table where Roy Kington had once again abandoned her; "looking for trouble" thought Miss Adela Adair from her piano stool; "quite likely to find it" thought Claire from behind the bar where, the whole raucous night long, she had been assisting MacAllister with his cocktail shaker.

"Happy New Year." Polly flung her arms into the air in a gesture that cried out "Look at me. Look at me," paused a moment under the light so everyone — absolutely everyone — could see the sparkle of her gold butterflies, the rich sheen of the satin as it clung to her splendid, supple — still virgin — limbs, the daring, audacious new tint of her hair, bleached several shades lighter by some "miracle of nature" according to Miriam, and then fell into the arms of her admirers one after the other — Rex and Roy Kington, Roger Timms, a trio of Peters and Anthonys and Stephens, even MacAllister, the barman and Arnold Crozier emerging spider-like from his corner — giving them all long, noisy kisses, biting earlobes, throwing back her sensational, platinum head and listening to her own laughter.

Tonight she wanted to be kissed. For whatever one happened to be doing on New Year's Eve as the clock struck twelve one could expect to do all year — wasn't that so? — and 1920 was to be just not *her* year but a pattern for the years to come. Kisses, new clothes, everybody being kind to her, a wedding ring. And if she had not precisely made sure of Roy Kington yet — what with Sally Templeton still running after him in her shameless fashion and putting about rumors that he was thinking of going off to Ireland to join the Black and Tans — she was relying on 1920 to take care of that.

"MacAllister darling — why aren't you a millionaire instead of a barman and then I could fall in love with you? No, Mr. Crozier, I suppose you *are* a millionaire, but I won't come up to the Tangerine Suite, thank you very much. Roger — I *did* ask you to look after my bag. Now just stop that, Anthony — or Roy?"

"She's ripe for it, that one," said MacAllister, the barman, to Claire as they watched Polly convert the ritual of Auld Lang Syne into a scramble to hold her hand, "begging for it. And, by God, if she were to ask *me* — !"

"No, old chap," swinging around on his barstool, Toby Hartwell, who should not have been there at all, fixed MacAllister with a cold eye, an unusually pugnacious set to his jaw, "I wouldn't think of it — really not — if I were you."

"Just a passing remark, Mr. Hartwell, sir."

"I dare say. Not one I'd repeat though — old chap! Goodnight Claire. Happy New Year."

"Goodnight Toby. The same to you."

"Quite the Sir Galahad," shrugged MacAllister as Toby, having kissed Claire's cheek, slid off his stool and walked away; and she smiled and nodded, thinking how well the role of Knight Errant might, in other circumstances, have suited Toby.

Eunice Hartwell spent the evening at home nursing a heavy cold, feeling feverish and plain and thoroughly miserable because Toby had gone out and left her. Naturally she had told him to go. They had received half a dozen invitations to "see the New Year in" with friends, and she knew how much Toby loved this annual parade from house to house, a drink at every punchbowl, "first foot" over half a dozen thresholds, so much more fun than Christmas, which was always dominated for him by High Meadows. No reason, therefore, to spoil *his* enjoyment because *she* had a cold. Naturally, she had meant what she said the moment she said it. Naturally — to begin with — he had said "Wouldn't think of it, old girl" and had offered to give it all up and stay at home. Naturally, she had insisted. And now, sitting alone in the house they had bought to suit Toby's notions of what a family home should be — enormous — she was thoroughly wretched. She had no idea where he was. Not that she suspected him of intrigue or even of flirtation. She just wanted his company, wanted him to want hers, would have liked, for once, to be alone with him.

She had no idea where Justin was either, nor Simon, only where they had told her they were going — a milk-and-water party at a school-friend's house — which had not even sounded true. She could telephone, of course, and find out. In fact she knew quite well she ought to have telephoned earlier in the day to make sure. But if she had done that and had discovered that there had been no party, what then? If she had forbidden the boys to go out she was no longer sure they would obey her. The last time she had attempted to exert her authority and had confined Justin to his room, he had simply climbed out of the window and broken his ankle and a great deal of guttering besides. And, apart from the danger and the expense, his defiance and the fact that she seemed unable to do anything about it, had wounded her deeply. How did one discipline a boy of that age? She wished she knew. Scolding was no use. Nor pleading. She had tried both and he had either laughed or walked away. How could one punish him? She could neither slap him nor in any way physically compel him. She had stopped his allowance once and he had simply helped himself to money from her purse or taken it by force from his younger brothers. It had taken her a long time to recover from the shock of that. In fact, she never had got over it. And now, to stop it from happening again and to avoid the horrifying possibility that he might steal from somebody else who might inform the police, or Benedict, all she could think of to do — against her better judgment, well aware that she had lost her nerve — was to give him money whenever he asked for it; as much as he asked for; often a great deal.

What else could she do? Could Toby have done better? She had no idea because she had never asked him. Knowing how deeply Justin's pilfering would have shocked and sickened Toby, she had kept it to herself. She did not want Toby to know that his son was a thief. She did not want him, with his old-world notions of courtesy and honesty, to bear that burden. Toby might give things away, in fact he frequently did, and was often far too ready to pay the bill in restaurants and to stand round after round of drinks so that people took advantage, but he would never take a penny which did not belong to him. Ardently, she believed in that. And she had flown at Benedict like an angry cat, not too long ago, when he had suggested that by taking his lengthy lunches, his trips to York and Doncaster for the Races, his golfing afternoons, Toby was stealing time — which was the same as money — from Swanfield Mills. How that remark had incensed her. She had been so beside herself with fury that she had shrieked all manner of things at Benedict which she would not have dared otherwise to mention. She was angry about it still. How dare he? For Toby was a gentleman. His standards were finer, more complicated, different. She had always been impressed by his social superiority, although Toby himself never made much of it. But it was there. Good breeding. A heritage of good manners, a tendency — which had always charmed her — to think it only natural that one ought to rule the world. And she had never ceased to marvel at the innate superiority which had made Toby's gentle, scholarly, penniless father think of her own father — the great Aaron Swanfield — as a tradesman, in no way different from a grocer or a haberdasher except that he had more money.

Toby, in his heart of hearts, thought that too. To him, as to his ancestors, money was for spending, to create pleasure rather than to purchase power, to give away as *largesse*, *noblesse oblige*, assistance to the needy, rather than to accumulate in bank vaults or stocks and shares. Justin — and Simon — thought the same, except — and she had long known the difference — Justin and Simon were not, by nature, gentlemen. She must never allow Toby to discover that.

At midnight the maid came in to make the fire. "Happy New Year, Madam." But the girl, who had wanted the night off, was sulky, had already decided to give in her notice and get a job in a factory, and did not feel that Eunice's future happiness or lack of it, had anything to do with her.

"Thank you, Betty." She suspected the girl would be leaving and had already started to convince herself that there would be no need to replace her. She had a cook, a girl to do the laundry, a woman who came in twice a week to scrub, a woman once a month to sew. Surely she could manage without a parlor maid? It was quite the fashion now just to hand dishes round at dinner or to take one's guests to a restaurant. Or at least she could say it was the very latest London thing and insist she preferred it. And Betty's wages would be a useful addition to the money she had started to put by like a frantic, October squirrel, to be used for the rescue — whenever the need arose — of Justin or Simon.

On the nursery floor above her head her two younger children, her *little* boys, were not asleep perhaps, had quite possibly raided the larder for nuts and raisins and the dreadful concoction of sugar and cocoa powder mixed up together which they would be bound to spill all over the bed. But at least she knew where they were. Where was Justin? Enjoying himself in a way she would have found gross in anyone else's son. Drinking spirits, ready to repeat his misdemeanor with that chambermaid — that little slut — or with any girl foolish enough, or tipsy enough to let him. And if he succeeded, as he probably would, since he was handsome and could be persuasive as she had every reason to know, then it could only be a matter of time before he started a baby on its way. The thought struck her like a hammer blow and was followed instantly by another thought, equally compelling. She must save him, somehow, from all those little flibbertigibbets, those featherheaded, silk-stockinged girls who were nothing, when all was said and done, but temptation. Girls no longer conducted themselves as they should, as she had always done, *that* was the real trouble. They allowed liberties to be taken, led men on — only look at Polly! — and then, when the inevitable happened, set up such a caterwauling! She recognized her own injustice, of course. She even knew quite clearly how differently she would have viewed the matter had she been the mother of daughters. But she was not. And she would defend her boys, her own flesh and blood, through anything, always, to the bitter end. Her boys, and Toby. She had been unable to conceal from him that sorry business about Justin and the chambermaid. Justin's headmaster had seen to that. But any further indiscretions she would do her utmost to handle alone. And if it became too much for her, if it turned into some sordid business of paying off or hushing things up in a way she could not manage, then she would rather endure the scorn of her formidable brother than upset Toby.

Yet, where was Toby? She had told him to go out and enjoy himself. She had been glad to make the sacrifice. But, just the same, she knew he should not have left her. She knew that in his place she would never have left him.

Miriam Swanfield spent the last evening of the year at a civic banquet in Faxby's Town Hall where she herself had once reigned, for a glittering year, as Faxby's Mayoress. Aaron, of course, had not wanted in the very least to take office, she fondly remembered that. He was a businessman, accustomed to what he had called the "real world" of gigantic profit or loss and had no inclination — he had grunted — to waste his time arguing about the siting of park benches or what to do about the odor from those pig pens on Faxby Green. But he had looked very splendid in his mayoral robes and she had brought not only dignity but graciousness and style to her position as consort. She remembered that *very* well. She had worn enormous French hats, tight-corseted gowns that had nipped in her waist and pushed out her bosom, had presided at this very banqueting table in all the lavish silks and satins, the billowing lace and tulle which Polly had now cut up into these scandalous chemises she called evening dresses. Ah well. The times were changing. But not necessarily for the better. And she saw no one at the Mayoral table tonight who could in any way compare with the luscious, *clever* woman she had once been.

The present Mayoress, she noticed, was large and dowdy and had never learned the art of concealing her own excellent opinion of herself. The Councillors' wives were either serviceable and plain or aggressively smart; or, in two cases, indecently young; a pair of "old men's darlings" wearing too much paint and too much jewelry and thoroughly bored with these pompous, self-indulgent, elderly gentlemen who had condescended to marry them.

The wife of Councillor Greenwood was visibly younger than his unmarried daughter, Miss Greenwood, who liked it to be thought that she had lost her fiancé in the war, although Miriam knew it was no such thing. Poor Miss Greenwood, sitting now with a somewhat pained expression between the newly married pair, probably worrying — thought Miriam — about who, in the event of her father's death, would be likely to inherit his spinning mill, particularly since the other "civic flapper," the new young wife of Councillor Redfearn of Redfearn's Hardware — such a *lucrative* chain of shops — was expecting her first, his second child. Although Councillor Redfearn's daughter, of course, was another matter from poor, plain Miss Greenwood. A capable woman, Elvira Redfearn, a widow now of ample means and abundant energies, who would stand no nonsense from anyone, not even from her portly, pretentious father, much less his twenty-year old wife. Yes. A *clever* woman, Elvira Redfearn. Perhaps even a shade too forceful. A friend of long standing — as Miriam well knew — of Benedict's.

He had accompanied her tonight, his position as Chairman of Swanfield Mills amply justifying his place at the Mayoral table and she was bound to admit that the dignity sat well on him, rather better, in fact, than it had on Aaron. Her husband, even beneath the gold mayoral chain, the scarlet robes, the London tailored suits she had insisted upon, had retained a certain earthiness — she did not care to say coarseness although it had been exactly that and more attractive, too, than one would ever have imagined — whereas Benedict had always possessed a natural refinement, not merely an appreciation but an expectation of the best. Elvira Redfearn had once been the best catch in Faxby. But

Aaron — with his "earthiness" and his certainty of always being right — had looked farther afield and discovered Nola. And what a disappointment she had been.

"Happy New Year, my dears. Many, *many* of them." Miriam raised her heavy, long-stemmed wine glass, engraved with Faxby's civic arms in gold and ruby — the civic crystal which she had had designed for her own year of office and then presented to the town — her round blue eyes shining, a sentimental tear lightly beading short, pale lashes, to be quickly whisked away by a square of embroidered cambric held in a plump, helpless little hand. An elderly lady who had been very pretty, still looked very sweet, offering to one and all a verbal overflow of seasonal good wishes as she coolly considered — since in her private thoughts she made no bones about such things — how very much it would please her should Nola be so obliging as to drive that nasty little car of hers into a lamppost one of these dark nights, thus setting Benedict free to bring home a more comfortable daughter-in-law. Elvira Redfearn had once been her favorite. But now she much preferred Claire. She did not know for certain what had happened between them. She had simply assumed, knowing Benedict's temperament — so like his father's until she had tamed it — that he had taken what she archly and laughingly called "his evil way." Claire's reactions to her probing had confirmed it. And Claire suited her. She needed Claire. And if Benedict could oblige her in this — then she would be very ready to smooth away whatever needed smoothing from the path of what she preferred to call his "affections."

She was, therefore, a little put out to see him taking advantage of the dignified, civic chimes of midnight — the Town Hall clock booming out the hour from its spire directly above their heads — to make what she instinctively understood to be an assignation with Elvira Redfearn.

"Benedict, my dear," she sweetly inquired on their way home, "Forgive me, but are you not in danger of becoming something of a — well, I believe libertine is the word which springs to mind?"

"No Miriam." He sounded in no way put out about it. "Not 'becoming,' as I think you know — it has been ever thus."

"Yes dear. I know. How sad. Your father was just the same until I took him in hand. You need a good woman, dear boy."

"I think not, Miriam."

"So you say now. But as you get older you will find it hard to be satisfied by these casual encounters. They will bore you and they will exhaust you. You may take my word for it. That is what your father discovered, in any case, and he had every reason to know. Nothing could be compared to the pleasure of his own fireside, he often used to say, once he had found the right woman to light the fire. And if that sounds a trifle *risqué* then I must ask you to remember that I am simply quoting what your father said."

"Quite so," murmured Benedict, his eyes on the road ahead. "Perhaps one should also remember that when my father found you, Miriam, he was no longer a married man."

Nola had taken considerable trouble, put herself — or so she imagined — at considerable risk to avoid Faxby's Civic Banquet and watch the dawn of the New Year with her lover.

She had lied, dry-mouthed, to Benedict about a visit to the Manchester Croziers which ought not to be neglected. They were not only celebrating the New Year, she told him, but a whole batch of family anniversaries which involved presents, congratulations, Nola's presence, since one really had to say things like "Happy Birthday," "Happy Silver Wedding," "Happy Eightieth, Auntie Trudy" in person. So she would just have to be and do her duty.

"Certainly you must go," Benedict had said dryly. "So, it appears must I."

She had blinked rapidly, her eyelids which she had smeared heavily with vaseline to make them glisten, looking heavy and a little swollen beneath the scarf of black and purple striped chiffon wound several times around her head in Egyptian fashion. "Must you?" she had said, understanding only that she had been challenged, lowering her gleaming eyelids still further to hide the excitement she still so regularly felt in this fearful game of deceiving him.

"I think so, Nola. If it is so important a family occasion as all that, then shouldn't I — as your husband — accompany you?"

"Not necessary, darling."

"Why is that?"

She believed he wanted to know. She always believed him. And triumphantly, because the reason had just leaped into her mind, she told him. These anniversaries were not actually Crozier anniversaries, hadn't she mentioned? No, no. They were all relatives of her cousin's wife, Nanette, which made it remote enough for Benedict not to trouble. Although for Nola herself, of course, who had known Nanette for ever — almost like a sister — it was another matter. And he had arranged — hadn't he — to take Miriam to the Town Hall? She had been relying on that.

He nodded. She had won. And then — how predictable, how stimulating — not quite.

"You'll be taking the afternoon train? Then you'll need Parker to take you to the station or I'll drive you myself."

She would not be going to the station. She would be driving to Leeds in her own car. What now? Could she pretend she was taking her car to Manchester? No. Benedict would know quite well that neither her driving nor the shaky little motor could ever achieve that much. What then? She lowered those heavy eyes again, thinking it over, and smiled.

"No need to trouble anyone," she said brightly, knowing it would not be enough, simply playing for time. "Now that I have my own sweet little car I can just catch the train all by myself."

"On the contrary." She had known, with the odd undercurrents of dread and exultation these encounters always aroused in her, that he would say something like that. "What is to happen to your sweet little car when you get on the train? You can hardly abandon it in the station yard. Or at least, one can offer no guarantees that it will still be there on your return."

"But I don't mean to leave it there." What did she mean to do? The answer flowed suddenly into her mind — it always did — and as she spoke to him there was a note in her voice which was almost a chuckle. "It's all arranged, my sweet. No need to fret. I've promised to lend the car to Claire. She *did* ask me, you see, and with all the running about she has to do is it any wonder? So I'll just drive over to Mannheim Crescent and pick her up, she'll drive me to the station, keep the car and meet me the day after from the train. Now — isn't that clever?"

"My dear," he said, "very clever. Although no less than I expected. Enjoy yourself. Give my regards, of course, to Nanette."

It had gone well. She drove over to Leeds, therefore, with a sense of achievement, losing her way several times since no part of her ladylike education had encouraged a sense of direction, but very pleased with herself just the same, very excited. She was going to her lover, bringing him her devotion, her great faith in him, her burning ambitions on his behalf, a huge wicker basket full of cold roast turkey, *foie gras*, a trifle in one of Miriam's best crystal dishes, a bottle of Benedict's champagne. She was going to spend the night — all night — with a man of talent who needed her. She had planned it, dreamed of it, gloated over it for days. Now — now at last — it was in her grasp. Yet somehow, perhaps from too much anticipation, from having missed him so atrociously throughout that tedious family Christmas which had imprisoned her at High Meadows, her rush of exultation on reaching his door was just a fraction less than she had hoped, her thrill when he opened it falling just short of electrifying.

But it was too soon, of course, to grow desperate. She brought out her basket of goodies and set them on his table, put a solicitous hand to his forehead to check his temperature, listened to his cough and then, in great detail, to the progress of his current masterpiece; the ritual of nourishing, healing, inspiring which she always performed. Yet something was lacking. What had altered? The man himself was just as usual, lean, self-absorbed, self-tormented. Certainly the cold, cheerless room, a bare cell, she had always thought, in which to do penance rather than make love, was no different. What was happening to the lovely havoc, the sweet uproar this man and this room together — this atmosphere of frustrated genius — had for so long wrought in her? Clutching desperately she retrieved it and held it fast as one holds a warm quilt on a winter night, only to feel it sliding away again.

It had happened before. Each time she never expected it to happen again. This time she had been quite certain. But she opened her champagne — what else could she do? — realizing that his insistence on drinking it out of tin mugs which she had once thought so significant — but of what? — now slightly annoyed her.

"Happy New Year, darling." For him she knew that it would be. He would continue to live here with his dust and his mouse-droppings, his deliberate cultivation of hardship, eating his cold baked beans out of their tin, never combing his hair, carefully preserving his misery because every struggling artist worth his salt had to be miserable and unkempt. Suddenly she understood that this *vie de Bohème* was all he wanted. He had neither the desire not the talent for success. She had been wrong again. But, since she *was* here and had nowhere else to go, she undressed him as she always did at the appropriate moment, took off her own clothes while he kept warm under the thin blanket and then held him obligingly for the moment or two it took him to discharge his passion. He was not a good lover. She had always known that. But she had found her own pleasure in accommodating his need. She had always felt uplifted by his quivering, clumsy helplessness at such moments, perversely satisfied by his physical inadequacy, making a sacrifice of her own orgasm on the altar of his genius. Now, lying in the cold dark on his hard, far from spotless bed, she felt irritable, disappointed, *sad*.

"I have to go now, Roland."

He did not question her, and she had reached the dank, deserted alley behind the studio, alone at two o'clock on the first morning of the New Year, before it occurred to her to wonder just where she could go. Not home to her husband, certainly, since he had accepted her tale of family obligations in Manchester with Bernard Crozier and Nanette. Where then? No Leeds hotel would admit her without luggage at this hour, not even taking into account the huge emerald on her finger and her extravagant red fox furs. And she had an idea that if she attempted to sleep in the car then the police might question her and end up escorting her home for what they would call her own good. The officious fools! Yet — just the same — what conclusion might she draw herself at the sight of a woman of her age and class wandering alone in such a place? A sudden wind arose, sorting through the debris of the festive season, the cans and bottles, the rotting peel of brussels sprouts and mandarin oranges, the gaudy, empty shells of Christmas crackers dumped in the alley, lifting an abandoned newspaper which flew mournfully out of the dark like a giant bat. For an instant, Nola, fending off the soggy newsprint and kicking it aside as it began to wrap itself around her ankles, felt utterly forlorn.

But she had no time for that and there seemed little point to it anyway. The thought of Kit Hardie and his clean, comfortable bed at the Crown came briefly into her head. But there seemed little point to that either. What mattered first of all was getting this foul little motor started. *Damnation*! Supposing she couldn't? What then? What *did* one do when a car broke down, other than call Parker to come and put it right? She was chilled to the marrow and had split two of her long pointed nails by the time she finally jerked and labored her engine through those narrow, identical streets of industrial Leeds. She had even shed a tear of pure frustration by the time she had passed the same dingy warehouse four times, distinguishing it from the dozens of others only because the chains hanging from one landing to another to hoist up the bales of cloth had been painted an astonishing, sickly green. But having found her way to the main road and a miraculous signpost announcing Faxby, she drove on without taking any conscious decision about it to Mannheim Crescent and, pushing her way round to the back of the house through the shrubbery of tangled, dripping trees, stood for what seemed to her a very long moment knocking on Claire's garden door. She had never been so cold, rarely so miserable. She felt weak, which was unlike her, and — to which she was rather more accustomed — dispirited and low. Yet, when Claire drew aside the curtain and began hurriedly to unlock the bolts, nothing could have exceeded the flamboyant gaiety of Nola's greeting.

"Happy New Year, Claire — shall I be the first wet foot across your threshold this year — or shall I? You *are* alone? Ah well — poor you. As it happens, so am I."

She went inside, shaking the drops of icy water from her furs, tossing off her hat.

"Are you all right, Nola?"

"Not really. Are you?"

"About the same."

"Let's drink to it then."

"All right."

"Happy New Year."

It was the second year of the peace that would — who had told them that? — be everlasting, the year when the frenzied spending of gratuities and pensions, the "getting back to normal," "making up for lost time," the "boom" began to stop.

But waking up cold and stiff on that first dismal January morning, having spent the last few hours of the night in an armchair pushed up by the fire, Claire's first thought was of the wife of her former lover who had commandeered her bed by the simple process of falling into it, drunk and almost fully dressed, having taken off, in fact, little more than her furs and her shoes.

Yet Nola's presence troubled her, if at all, rather less than her own aching head and the stark treachery of the fire which, after all her ministrations, all the coal and wood she had lavished upon it, had gone out. The room, therefore, had acquired a temperature which threatened her survival as, with a cricket sweater — whose, she wondered? — over the heaviest flannel pajamas Taylor & Timms had been able to supply, a blanket over that, she went through the hated winter labor of attempting to light a new fire on the ashes of the old.

"Shouldn't you clean out the grate first?" inquired Nola from the relative warmth of the bed.

"Yes, Nola."

"So that the air can get through and ignite the sticks —?"

"Yes, Nola."

"And if you dump your coal like that on top of the wood you *have* got burning then — surely — won't you put it out?"

"Yes, Nola."

She drove a poker viciously into the grate, attempting to clear the ash — yesterday's ash and the day before's — which clogged it and, unable to face the task of sweeping it into a dustpan and carrying it, through a high wind, into the icy yard, she ran to the kitchen instead, teeth chattering, eyes watering with cold, returning with a can of paraffin with which she liberally soaked the coal and sticks.

"You're not going to set that alight, are you?" Nola sounded alarmed.

Claire struck a match, and, standing back a little, tossed it into the grate, retreating further still as the hearth exploded into a fierce, malodorous blaze.

"Good God," said Nola, putting a hand to the space between her eyes which clearly ached. "You live dangerously, my pet — I'll grant you that."

"Nola — do tell me — have you ever actually lit a fire yourself?"

258

"Lord no. Don't mind me. I live in a world where fires light themselves, we both know that. But, jaded as I may be, I do retain my capacity for astonishment . . ."

"Oh — ?"

"Those pajamas, Claire!"

"Campaign pajamas, Nola. We had bad winters in France."

"Chaste winters too, one supposes — in those."

"I wouldn't say that. Are you getting up today, Nola? When I've got the fire going and put the coffee on I shall want to make my chaste bed — unless, of course, you would care to volunteer?"

"No — no, I won't, thank you very much. I'll just lie here and work on my list of New Year resolutions. A New Year, a new opportunity, after all."

"Do I take it that sculpture is over, then?"

Nola shrugged, making the best of it, knowing that she was probably to blame.

"Ah well — on reflection it strikes me that Roland's work is not particularly original."

Had he ever told her it was? Or had she seized upon it — and him — and made them both up as she went along to suit her own need? Very likely. But if Roland was gone, the need, the hollow space he had filled, existed still. Covering herself with Claire's quilt she closed her eyes, realizing that her head, either from alcohol or simply from the biting cold, was truly aching.

"I believe I have caught the Spanish influenza," she said with a note of interest in her voice. She had never caught an infection before and at least it would pass the time while she thought of something else with which to replace Roland.

Euan Ash, whose cough had quite ruined the ballet teacher's Christmas, disturbing so many of her nights that she had finally seen no alternative but to complain, packed his kit bag that day. A New Year, a new opportunity.

"I'm off to Edinburgh," he told Claire.

"Are you really?"

"Well, I'll just go down to the station and see what trains are running. North, at any rate."

"With that chest, Euan, you shouldn't travel in this weather."

"With that chest, old girl, I shouldn't really be alive to tell the tale. I can hardly travel without it. The thing is I can't take my canvases — too bulky, too many. Will you hang on to them for me until I send. And if I don't send then just keep them in memoriam."

Of course she would. Of course. That was the very least — And then, suddenly thinking of something else she could do for him, she said, making her voice casual, "All right. Although God knows where I'll put them. Unless — Yes. There's an idea. You only pay a few shillings a week for that room of yours, so it might be worth my while to keep it on, just for the use of the kitchen. I'm not keen to share with a stranger."

And then, at least — at need — he would have a roof to come back to, a corner to call his own which, even if she never saw him again, he would *know* was there. An alternative to whatever he might encounter on the road.

"So your canvases can stay where they are."

"Right-o," he said.

She was immeasurably and amazingly distressed to see him go. She felt, standing on the wind-raked station platform, her teeth chattering with cold and heartache, like a woman sending out some delicate knight-errant to slay a dragon. She felt, as she had felt the night she had seen Jeremy off to France, as she had felt a dozen times, waving and smiling to Paul.

"I suppose you have enough money?"

"Oh — *I'm* all right. There's a money-tree at the bottom of my garden. Always has been. I just have to hold out my hand."

He held it out now and she clasped it, his fingers thin and brittle and very cold.

"You don't want to worry about me, you know," he said.

"No. You're right. I don't *want* to. Not at all."

He smiled and slid a thin arm around her, drawing her toward a body without substance, or any aspiration, submitting with the patience of a well-mannered child as she began to tuck the woolen scarf she had given him into the collar of his shabby trench coat.

"I'll be all right, love. Honestly."

"No you won't."

He sighed. "But I will. In my fashion."

"What's in Edinburgh, Euan?"

"I'll tell you when I get there."

"*If —*"

"Well — yes. But don't worry. You don't want to care about me either."

"Oh — now *there* you're absolutely right. Not in the very least do I want to care."

His arm tightened and flinging both her arms around him she hugged him, possessively, protectively, *angrily*, knowing that even if she might be able to guard him from the world with that surge of fierce, female strength, she would never manage to guard him from himself.

"I'm sorry," he said.

So — from the very core of herself — was she.

He had said goodbye to no one else, not to Kit or Nola or his associate stallholders in Faxby Market Place. He simply boarded the train, his kit bag on his shoulder, and went away, leaving her with two dozen canvases of fragile woodland creatures peering at one another between the fine-veined stems of English wild flowers; more empty cans and empty whiskey bottles than she had ever seen gathered together in one place; a huge oriental vase and, by arrangement with the agent of her landlord, Mr. Crozier, a kitchen of her own.

She missed him. And, in a way, she was glad of it, one sense of loss blending with another, so that it became difficult to know how much of it was for Euan, how much for Benedict.

A New Year, a new opportunity: and the war was over now — *over* — had been over long enough to be bearable, manageable, no longer the all-embracing alibi for irresponsible or erratic behavior which until now it had been. Unless she organized herself, *stirred* herself soon, she would run out of excuses. Unless she moved, and moved quickly, she would be — perhaps for ever — at a standstill. Paul was dead. Euan had gone. Benedict had been a dreadful mistake, a stupid mistake for which she could not forgive herself. But if she had failed to understand him, she had at least learned something about herself. He had used her as a sexual diversion and the role neither suited her nor sufficed her. She would never play it again. It was over. And she felt nothing — very little at any rate — except hostility and contempt for him now, finding his way of life distasteful, futile, *old-fashioned*, based as it was on clandestine encounters with those eternally, interchangeably "smart" women who took lovers in secret because they lacked the courage to stand alone. She did not think of such women as "smart," or clever, or daring, as they certainly saw themselves. She thought of them, quite simply, as out of date. She had nothing to say to Benedict now beyond the essentials of those "family Sundays" which still brought her to High Meadows. "Good evening, Claire. Are you well?"

"Good evening, Benedict. Very well, thank you."

"Splendid."

And if it was not quite splendid it was simple enough since she had always found it far too easy to separate the stern and critical master of High Meadows from the man who had made love to her at Thornwick. What she no longer wished to do was to separate that mysterious and challenging lover from the straightforward sensualist who had talked bridge and seduction across the luncheon table to those beautiful bovine women.

She wished them well of one another, or at least as well as they deserved, which could not be much. Lois, and Edwina, and Elvira, the handsome, officious daughter of Councillor Redfearn, who never failed to mention Benedict in a manner Claire recognized whenever she came to the Crown. And if Benedict was wasting himself, as she still sometimes believed, then it was not her concern. She had her own life to lead. And in the damp, unkempt wasteland of January and February when the hotel was quiet she had ample time, as she took stock of linen and silver and glassware, to turn the same scrutiny upon herself.

Euan and Benedict — and Paul — were gone. Kit remained. On New Year's Eve, dispirited, sick of her own indecision and the gross error she had just committed, feeling the need of a strong shoulder, a steady hand, she had welcomed Kit's arms around her, albeit in a public crowded place and would — or so it seemed to her now — have gone willingly upstairs with him to his wide, comfortable bed with its bolsters and double mattress and feather-filled quilts, to consummate what had been hovering between them for so long. But Arnold Crozier had required Kit's presence in the Tangerine Suite at a private New Year's Eve party, a rowdy affair of chorus girls, still in their pantomime costumes from the Princes Theatre, "flappers" wearing very little at all, a few mature ladies of local reputation, which Claire would not have attended even if she had been invited and to which Kit would have forbidden her to go.

"I'll come round in the morning — if I may," he'd said. "We could go out somewhere."

But the next morning had brought Nola. Euan had gone off to Edinburgh, or at least had taken a northbound train, in the afternoon. Kit's own physique, after a night of keeping pace with spidery little Arnold Crozier, was by no means in the peak condition required for any significant act of consummation. The moment had not yet come.

Yet what, if anything, was he waiting for? One evening, not long afterward, he told her. The Mayor of Faxby and his large, self-important little wife had dined at the Crown that February night, with a party of civic dignitaries, vying in size and self-esteem with one another, including the Mayor Elect, Councillor Redfearn, his new young wife and his handsome daughter, Elvira who, in view of her stepmother's youth and the advanced state of her pregnancy, had consented to be her father's mayoress. A great many compliments had been paid. The food. The wine. The service. The décor. All had found civic favor.

"You've done us proud, Hardie," the Mayor had grunted, choosing to forget his former and loudly voiced opinion that in the "good old days" when a man could protect his standards in any way he chose, "sharp customers" like the Croziers and their dubious, jumped-up hire-lings would have been ordered, none too politely, out of town.

"You have made this place a credit to Faxby, Major," murmured Elvira Redfearn, choosing also to forget *her* former view that the sordid little hotel be leveled to the ground to make way for a much-needed secondary school.

"It must be great fun," breathed her pretty little stepmother wistfully, having heard the strains of jazz music from the downstairs bar. Looking at her warmly, understanding exactly why girls like this with not much education and little else to rely on but big blue eyes and lemon yellow curls, chose to put up with these pompous, elderly husbands, Kit smiled his sympathy.

"You have exquisite taste, Major." Elvira — as Mayoress Elect — did not intend to be outdone, not by her father's fluffy, anxious, twenty-year old wife at any rate. And Kit, understanding this too, smiled at *her* — at once — in a fashion which adequately conveyed his appreci-ation of her well-groomed maturity.

The mayoral party would come again. There was a satisfying amount of handshaking and cigar offering in the lobby, the Mayoress and the Mayoress Elect both realizing simultaneously what an excellent idea it would be to meet one's friends — regularly in fact — in the rose pink lounge for tea: the wife of the Major Elect still glancing sadly in the direction of all that smoky, tantalizing, *youthful* jazz.

"Major — it has been a pleasure."

No reference was made to his service at High Meadows, although he had held hats and gloves and evening cloaks, opened doors, drawn out chairs in the past for all of them and — by each and every one — had been ceremoniously ignored.

Who remembers the face of a butler? He had been Christopher Hardie then, of course, having acquired the name "Kit" only later, in the officers' mess. Was Christopher Hardie forgotten? Kit remembered him.

Claire came to join him on the front steps as the Redfearns and the Greenwoods were driven away.

"One of these days," he said to her, ruefully smiling, "I'll stop feeling like the son of a daily cook."

"And what does *he* feel like?"

"Ridiculously pleased with himself when an old goat like Arthur Redfearn pats him on the head."

"Arthur Redfearn can't hold a candle to you, Kit," said Claire, mean-ing it.

"I know."

"Well then?"

He laughed. "Knowing is one thing. As I said — one of these days I'll start to feel it."

She received a postcard from Whitby toward the end of February with no message, just Euan's name scrawled across the back. Seven weeks and he had got no further than that; a lovely old fishing port, as she well remembered, but bitterly cold, surely, at this season, and shrouded so often in a fine, damp mist from the sea.

"Why worry about him?" said Nola. "Why worry about anything?"

Nola had made up her mind, this year, not to take life too seriously. What could one really say about life, after all, except that it was short and uncertain? So it may just as well be merry. Yet her decision to be carefree and obsessively light-hearted had to be postponed after a day or so, due to what she chose to announce as the breakdown of her health. She had caught a severe chill over the New Year — the lousy weather in Manchester, and Nanette Crozier's meanness about her fuel bills — from which she had been slow to recover. She had stayed in bed for the first two weeks of January, her bedroom like an oven, shivering and burning, drinking whiskey for her throat, brandy for her chest, gin to make a change and scandalize Miriam. And she had not really felt well since. She could not get herself going somehow these winter mornings. More and more she felt herself succumbing to a dangerous attitude — oh yes, she knew the danger — that since she had no specific reason to get out of bed, why bother at all? And when she did, she was lethargic, uneasy, had lost her appetite, could not make up her mind whether to sit down or go out and stand in the rain.

"I am having a mental collapse," she told Claire. "You will oblige me by making a list of all the most expensive asylums in the district. When the time comes I would like to be in a position to select the one which will cost my husband the most money. I am also suffering from chronic indigestion. Could Miriam be trying to poison me, I wonder?"

"Either that," agreed Claire obligingly, "or alcohol."

"My dear — I am just a poor invalid drowning my sorrows."

Early in February a slight improvement occurred, Nola looking almost as usual, swinging her red fox furs, her Egyptian head swathed once again in layers of striped chiffon, gold chains and chains of amber beads around her long neck, long legs in green silk stockings casually suspended from a bar stool, she entertained Claire and Kit, her cousin Arnold Crozier, MacAllister the barman who heard and often repeated everything with the details of her latest find, a schoolmaster no less, not from those unfrocked monasteries where they taught Greek and Latin and arrogance to the sons of gentlemen but a real teacher, a man who, having fought for his own education, was fighting now to extend the privilege to everybody.

"A man of the people," said Kit, the familiar blue twinkle in his eye. "You've had one of those before, Nola."

"No darling," she told him earnestly, "he is nothing like you. He is not like anybody else at all."

Sculpture was over. Education had begun. And then, swiftly and suddenly, it too had ended.

"What happened to the schoolmaster?" asked Claire.

"What schoolmaster?" Nola, who had just walked into the flat, looked around as if she had, in fact, mislaid something and then walked out again.

"What's the matter with Nola?" asked Kit. "She was in and out of here three or four times yesterday looking — well, looking like a lost soul if you could apply that to Nola — beneath the paint and the furs and the clever remarks, I mean."

Yes, increasingly Claire could apply that description to Nola.

"I suppose she's drinking too much."

She was.

That same night, in the downstairs bar, she became so drunk that Polly, who never liked Nola to trespass on what she considered her territory, went off in a huff, taking a half dozen young men with her, while Claire commandeered Nola's car keys and drove her home.

She came back to the hotel the next afternoon at teatime, looking sallow, brittle, utterly worn out, refusing offers of cakes and sandwiches with a disgusted shake of the head.

"I'd just throw it up darling. And Kit wouldn't like that. One must have regard for his powder-room carpet."

"I don't suppose you've seen a doctor?"

"No I haven't."

"I'll come with you if you like."

She shrugged, looking, Claire suddenly felt, like a sketch, a caricature of her nonchalant, free and easy self.

"That's very decent of you, Claire."

"All right. Any time. Today?"

"No." It was a sharply ejaculated command. And looking at her keenly, Claire saw a fear she recognized, just a glimmer but enough to tell her where and how often she had seen it before.

"Nola? You know what's wrong with you, don't you?"

There was an instant burst of laughter, one long, green silk leg thrown rakishly over the other.

"Of course I do. It's Miriam, my love, and her slow poison. She wants rid of me so Benedict can marry Elvira Redfearn. She wants to be mother-in-law to the Mayoress. I shall give you a letter, to be opened after my death, incriminating them both. Anyway — I've got to be off now — I'm meeting someone."

"Look — just chuck him whoever he happens to be. He can wait can't he?" Perhaps a doctor could not.

Nola, with a bold swirling of red fur, got to her feet. "My word — what an impetuous creature you are. Thanks Claire — but no. Not today. There's this man, you see . . . Somebody *rather* special."

"Oh — Nola. Not again."

And looking down at her Nola chuckled and gave a racy, impudent, reassuringly familiar wink.

"Again. The love of my life, darling — again. So I have to hurry. Don't worry about me, Claire. You know what they say about the bad penny. And I'm such a nuisance, aren't I, to certain of my kith and kin that it stands to reason that nothing could happen to me. I'll let you have that letter, by the way."

What letter? Claire remembered only how ill Nola looked, beneath the paint and the furs and the clever remarks. Ill and scared.

"Kit, did you see Nola just now?"

"Yes," he said, looking puzzled. "She kissed me — I mean really kissed me. Came stalking into the office and just — She hasn't done that — well, you remember when. Then she took off at speed. Do you know where?"

"She said to meet a man."

He shrugged, shook his head. "I don't know. She couldn't be eloping could she? Or going off to drown herself?"

"*Kit!*"

"Look — I'm just going round the back. She parks her car in the alley and the chances are she hasn't got the damned thing started yet."

But there was no sign of her in the street.

Claire left the hotel toward the end of the afternoon, taking her dinner home with her in a covered basket, having reserved the evening for washing her hair, writing to Euan who had finally sent her an address, plucking her eyebrows, giving herself a manicure and then going to bed early with a glass of brandy — to keep out the cold — and a book.

Such evenings of comfortable solitude were, from time to time, most welcome but if she felt a twinge of displeasure at the sound of her doorbell such a tame emotion was instantly obliterated by the first shock of seeing Nola. For if she had looked ill and scared before, she was plainly terrified now.

266

But not broken, of course, still ready to make fun of herself — and *it* — if she could, in the hope that a surfeit of clever remarks might cover it up, or even — did she still have any hope — send it away. Whatever it might be.

"Sit down," said Claire.

"I think I will."

"You look terrible, Nola."

"Yes. It's a guilty conscience, my dear — nothing worse than that. But one doesn't die of guilt. Does one?"

Claire had never been too sure of that.

"Are you going to tell me?"

A nervous smile flickered on and off Nola's face and then back again like the smile of a mechanical doll, her lips dry and swollen as if she had bitten them, her face quite gray. Her eyes, her whole expression, her whole mind — Claire knew it — saturated with fear, her precious nonchalance just a few rags and tatters to clutch around her.

"Oh yes — I've come to confess, since confession eases the soul. Isn't that what they say? I'm pregnant Claire. Isn't that rich? Isn't that a lark?"

Silence. And then Nola's throaty chuckle attempting with the courage of desperation to retain the character of laughter but deteriorating rapidly, painfully, into a cackle of hysteria which seemed to fill the room.

"Isn't that just — I wonder what Doctor Marie bloody Stopes would have to say about that. What do *you* think, Claire?"

She had thought, all afternoon, of terminal disease, a lingering, wasting death or an abrupt cessation of the heart; she had thought of melancholia, chronic nervous collapse, even suicide. She had not, incredibly as it seemed now, thought of this. But she had nursed men. It struck her now how little she knew of the ills of women.

"Whose child?" she asked because she had to say something, had to remain calm, and it seemed a logical question.

"Well, not my husband's, that's for certain, which wouldn't matter a damn except that I can't convince him otherwise, can I. I haven't slept with him for years, you know that. And I can't jump back into bed with him now and hope he won't notice when the baby comes two months early — because he wouldn't have me."

"*Nola!*" And all the pity, the sadness, the understanding Claire felt was in her voice, so strongly and deeply expressed that tears suddenly poured out of Nola's eyes like the switching on of a tap.

"Oh God Claire — don't do that to me. Don't be kind. Just tell me I'm a stupid bitch who deserves every foul thing that's got to happen — a whore and not even a good one. Call me names. Everybody else will. And then I can shout back at you."

"What good will that do? Nola, you're shivering — and sweating. You're in pain, aren't you?"

"No — no. Me? Never. Just give me a cigarette."

And as she leaned forward to take a light Claire saw that her hands were clammy, her forehead beaded with moisture that was dripping now into the mixture of tears and vaseline and kohl oozing from her eyes. The face of a tragic clown emerging from underneath the paint and the furs and the clever remarks that had been Nola. But when she reached out her hand and touched her arm Nola shied away.

"Nola —"

"No. Don't sympathize. You'll make me cry again. I'll tell you something now to make you laugh. New Year's Eve this happened to me. Would you believe it? While I'm lying there making up my mind it's all over with Roland, what is Roland doing? Impregnating me. Now isn't *that* a hoot."

Once again her voice cracked with raucous laughter and swallowing hard she closed her eyes for a moment and clenched her fists, the muscles and veins of her throat knotting with the effort of control.

"I know it was New Year's Eve, you see, because I was out of action the week before Christmas. I spent Christmas at home. And apart from the one time there's been nothing since. There's no doubt."

"Have you told him?"

"Of course I haven't told him." She sounded hard suddenly and scornful. "It's none of his bloody business is it."

"Isn't it?"

She swallowed again. "No. But the real reason I haven't told him is because he wouldn't want to know. He'd bolt like a scared rabbit — I know that. I don't want to watch it. Do you understand?"

"Yes. What *are* you going to do?"

Once again Nola lay back in the chair and closed her eyes, her body stretched out in a posture that was stiff and awkward, another clenching of muscles that were released abruptly on a long, hollow sigh.

"Yes — what to do? I know how caged mice feel now on a wheel — you know — round and round and round — and ending up in exactly the same place. There's a doctor, Claire — in Faxby — who says he can put things right —"

"No." She was so horrified that it became, for just a moment, a pain in her own abdomen, a spasm of revulsion that probed her very deep. For she had heard of these doctors before. And she had a woman's body too.

"No, Nola. You mean there's an old woman in a back street with a knitting needle —"

But Nola, her eyes closing again, smiled and shook her head.

"No, Claire. I went to see the old woman first and, desperate as I was — well, I could think of a more comfortable way of committing suicide. Although she can't kill everybody she touches, since her business is pretty brisk."

"They don't die on her premises, I suppose, and not always straight away."

"I suppose not. But there *is* a doctor — or so he says. One could hardly ask to see his qualifications. Not with the risk he's taking. He'd go to prison, wouldn't he, if he was caught?"

"Yes."

"Would I?" She opened her eyes wide and it seemed to Claire that she could see straight through them to the naked fear, the panic.

"I don't know. If he got caught you'd probably be dead anyway."

"Oh — thanks. That cheers me up no end. Is abortion so dangerous then — ?"

A long time ago, in Upper Heaton, there had been a fourteen-year-old scullery maid, Claire remembered, who had bled to death in a coal-shed. In France, a nurse she knew slightly had poisoned herself in her efforts to procure a miscarriage. Through long generations she knew that desperate women who, for whatever reason, did not wish to bear a child, would not do so, no matter how great the risk of pain or punishment, deformity or death. She knew that a great many of the unregistered midwives still practicing among the laboring classes continued to offer abortion as they had always done, as the only contraceptive available in the mean streets and overcrowded hovels of any city, where penniless, under-nourished, ill-informed women conceived annually like cattle. And when one, or several of those women died, who cared to ask too many questions? She knew that mill girls and shopgirls, refusing, like Nola, to beg from an unwilling lover, would submit themselves to this furtive, often fatal surgery for the simple reason that they had been told by generations of fathers and mothers "Don't ever bring trouble home to me"; not for moral reasons alone but because the family could not bear the burden of another mouth to feed. And so they bled to death in coal-sheds, sometimes, at fourteen. Or they sat, laughing and trembling and talking of death and prison at thirty-eight, like Nola. At Upper Heaton, all those years ago, no one had shown the slightest interest in discovering the identity of the dead girl's lover. Nola herself, in this case, did not wish to involve Roland.

"Don't do it, Nola," she said.

"Darling —" And, again, she unveiled those transparent, terrified eyes. "What else? Let's be sensible. What else is there — except the river? Naturally I've considered that. And what it comes down to is this. Drowning is certain death. My doctor friend may kill me or he may not. So I'll just have to take my chance . . ."

They faced each other in silence and then, quietly and slowly, Claire said.

"You don't want to consider having the child?"

"Are you mad?"

And Nola's voice was equally quiet and slow.

"It could be arranged."

"Yes. I could go abroad for my health, and come back in nine months' time looking much better — leaving a little bundle behind me in a convent or somewhere to be adopted. I know. But I'd need help for that. And money."

"Yes."

"And who has money? Cousin Arnold, of course. He might even lend me some. But he'd talk about it in the Tangerine Suite, to his flappers, to prove how generous he is and how safe they are with him. Cousin Bernard? Nanette wouldn't let him. She's a good woman, you see, which means she doesn't help people in trouble. She finds it too shocking. And my mother — Could you go to your mother, Claire, with something like this?"

"No. I couldn't."

"Exactly. You'd get a warmer welcome from the river. So would I."

"But you could get money, Nola."

"I daresay. But what I can't do, my sweet, innocent child, is get away from Benedict. What do I say to him? I'm just off to Cannes for a few months, darling. He's no fool. He'd know."

"Yes."

And once again they looked at each other long and levelly, eye holding eye.

"You're not suggesting I should tell Benedict?"

"Yes."

"I'd prefer to die." It was a statement of fact, delivered coolly, without drama. Claire believed it and, shaking off the silence, the false calm, she threw herself suddenly forward and took hold of Nola's hands, holding them fast, propelled to make this contact by a rush of compassion, the desperate need to prevent Nola's life, and the life it contained, from being thrown away.

"Tell him, Nola. Yes — you can tell him." Suddenly, almost joyfully, she was sure of it. "And whatever he does — whatever he says — oh good Lord — what *can* he do to you?"

The panic which had been simmering, waiting its moment, broke free with the force of an underground torrent spluttering through Nola's pores, pushing her over the brink of herself into raucous hysteria.

"Tell him? I'd jump in the river *now* before I'd do that. I've made a fool of him for years — years — you know that. He'd — oh God knows — he'd crucify me, one way or another."

And because she knew how much Nola had enjoyed believing that, had somehow needed it as an essential spice to all her untidy, often pointless adventures, Claire hesitated and then, in her determination to keep Nola safe from that unkempt, unsterilized surgery, she took a deep breath and went on, "Nola — I feel quite sure that he knows — about you and Roland, I mean — and the others . . ."

"*Knows!*" Nola was so shocked, so scornful, so completely aghast that it could, in less potentially fatal circumstances, have been comic. "Of course he doesn't know. Come on, Claire, let's not be naïve. It's all right to talk modern — look modern — but in the end — well — rules are rules. And when you're a woman the rule is not to get caught. My mother taught me that. And when you are caught — like I am now — then the thing is to cover your own tracks, clear up your own mess, have the good taste not to be a nuisance or an embarrassment to one's kith and kin."

"I suppose your mother taught you that, too."

"Yes — didn't yours?"

"Yes."

"Well then — ?"

"All right." And she was treading very warily on eggshells now. "Nola — I think —" and she was conscious of weighing every word separately on her tongue, "now — for this — you can trust Benedict."

"Do you really?" She might have been in a dream, her voice coming through a haze of distance.

"Yes, I do. You don't have to go to that doctor, Nola — really you don't."

"Fancy that."

"Nola — I mean it."

"Yes, I know you do. I'm sorry."

"For what?"

Taking another enormous swallow, her throat contracting again, Nola sat rigid and very still for a moment, allowing the quietness to return before she said, "Because the bastard cheated me — oh God, Claire —!"

Her body reared backward and upward in a fierce contraction of pain, her teeth sinking into her lower lip, her eyes staring.

"*Claire!*"

"Yes. Hang on to me." There was no point now in recriminations. She saw that the damage had been done. And what mattered was giving aid to whatever remained.

"The bastard said —"

"Never mind, Nola."

It was too late for that.

"I believed him. I thought he could *do* it, then and there, and it would be over. That's what I paid him for."

"This afternoon?" Of course. She understood it all now, the jaunty swing of furs, the talk of Miriam's slow poison, the sudden throwing of her arms around Kit, the story of rushing off to meet the love of her life — again. Of course.

"And then, when he'd put me through the hell of it — Dear God! I thought it was over and it was just beginning. He said "Go home and in a few hours you'll have a miscarriage. If the pain gets too bad or the bleeding won't stop call your doctor." He said *that*. "Go home to your husband and call your doctor" — oh — the bastard! I can't do that Claire. It's one thing I can't do. That's what I paid him for. And now — look at me, Claire — look —"

"Yes, I know."

She had seen, moments ago, that Nola was sitting in blood.

14

SHE had never nursed women. But, throughout the ages, one woman had always helped another in childbirth with no greater skills than the example her own body had taught her, and enough instinct remained for Claire to get Nola to bed, to prop up her legs, to calm her with false reassurances "It's going to be all right. Yes — yes — of course I know what to do" and, so far as possible, to keep her warm, and clean.

Blood in itself did not trouble her. Men's blood, that is. But this blood, containing the particles of an unborn life, was different. Very different. So far removed, in fact, from her previous experience that she felt compelled to treat it with tenderness, to remove each gore-soaked towel with care, to fold it gently instead of bundling it hurriedly away.

She had seen so many men in pain that even her compassion, at certain times, had blunted. Female agony was new to her and because it was *this* agony, this deliberate turning of birth into death, it entered her own body, the muscles of her own abdomen contracting with Nola's, her own womb forced open, straining and laboring to deliver these gouts of blood which had been — which were — a human child.

She understood wounds inflicted by guns and shells and gas. She did not understand wounds like these. She did not know how to stop the bleeding nor how long, without fatal results, it might be expected to continue. She did not know whether Nola was dying or not.

And Nola did not care.

No doctor must be called. She was adamant, hysterical about that, crying out and choking, her throat full of tears, making herself worse. A doctor would admit her to a hospital. Questions would be asked and even if the police were not informed, then her husband certainly would be. This was not London or some other big city where she could give a false name. This was Faxby. Two years ago she had herself officiated, with Miriam, at the opening of the new General Infirmary, wearing an oyster satin turban with an ostrich feather pinned to the front of it, a yard long. And somebody there would be sure to remember her. Which meant, of course, that by tomorrow morning everybody would know.

No doctors.

"I can't manage alone, Nola."

"It doesn't matter. I'll take my chance."

She had set herself to endure pain and the risk of death and endure it she would. It was not courage. She had gone far beyond that. For when no alternative existed, neither courage nor cowardice had any meaning. And this afternoon, when she'd gone, dry-mouthed, light-headed not from gin but from lack of food, to that prim little house with its potted plants and lace curtains, even the offensive cordiality of the "medical practitioner" who lived there, his hands folded together like two plump, white slugs, had seemed better than the disgrace of discovery. Men were *allowed* to treat themselves to their little sexual fads and fancies. Men — her own mother had made clear to her — were made that way. Women were made differently. Or at least — since men wanted it so — pretended to be. It followed, therefore, that if a woman *had* to sin — and, really, the sin itself never seemed to matter much — she either covered it up or paid the price. And paid it, of course, alone. Silently. Fatally, if necessary. Any way she could, so long as the good name of her family and her lover's family were not dragged through the mud. *That* was what mattered.

And so she had gone with that cordial, furtive little man into his back parlor, lay down upon his sofa and allowed him to rape her with cold steel, her skin crawling with disgust for the man himself, those fat slug fingers on her bare skin, that oily smile, until the sweat of pain and blind terror wiped her revulsion away making her weep and plead for him to stop — dear God how had she sunk so low? — and then sob with the heartbreak of bereavement when he had told her why he could not.

Bereavement! Why had *that* word, for God's sake, written itself inside her head?

Even now. *Bereavement.*

"No doctors," she said, rearing backwards again in her extremity, her whole body rigid with hurt and horror. Her other pregnancies had been luxuriously drugged and distant. This was her first acquaintance with raw pain and she had not expected it to be so ferocious. Nor had she expected to feel so debased, so filthy. It made no difference. "No doctors."

"All right. But listen, Nola — I'll have to leave you for a minute —"

"No — why? No you won't."

"Yes. I have to."

"No. Why? To call a doctor?"

"*No*. If you want me to look after you then I need the things to do it. I'll have to run to the chemist —"

"No." And she dissolved, almost faded into weak and angry tears.

"Listen, Nola. I have to look after you properly, don't I — for my own sake as well as yours."

"Oh God! I never thought of that."

"So — you lie still. Very still. *Please*, Nola."

"Yes — but *promise*. No doctors."

"I promise." And quickly washing her hands she ran across to the dentist on the other side of Mannheim Crescent, begged permission to use his telephone, and when, with considerable suspicion, he showed her to the instrument and stood back, not quite out of earshot, to make sure it really was the matter of life and death she had described, she could not, for a moment, remember the all too familiar number of High Meadows.

She had no guarantee that Benedict would be there. None. It was seven o'clock. An hour before dinnertime. Miriam, who never answered the telephone in any case, would be upstairs changing. So would Polly. Benedict, just as likely as not, would be at Thornwick or dining out at the Redfearns. What then? There was no telephone at the farm. Dare she contact him at the Redfearns, who would want to know why? Yes. Of course. She would have to. And if she couldn't find him, if he had gone into Lancashire or God knew where, then she would have to get medical attention as best she could. She would call Kit. He would help. She would call him *now*. It was a reassuring thought, instantly wiped away by the realization that she could not take the risk of implicating him in what might well become Faxby's greatest scandal for many many years. No. She must find Benedict. Or she would have to cope alone.

She asked the operator for his number as quietly as she could, although it seemed unlikely that either the dentist or his sharp-eyed wife would recognize it, enduring a long wait before a dignified voice announced himself as "The Swanfield residence"; and then more agony as no firm promise could be given as to whether Mr. Benedict might be at home or not.

"One moment, Madam. I will inquire."

"Please hurry."

"Certainly, Madam."

But the house was a large one, its pace leisurely. And Nola should not have been left for a moment, much less the time it would take for that cadaverous butler to walk upstairs and down that interminable corridor to Benedict's bedroom door. She went with him, every ponderous step of the way, willing him to walk faster, to be propelled by her own fierce urgency. Dear God. And if Benedict was there — if — then he would have to come all the way downstairs himself to take her call. Please hurry. Certainly, Madam. She had never before in her life felt so compelling a desire to scream.

"Swanfield here."

She had found him. And now, how did one convey to a man on a far-from-private telephone, that his wife had taken refuge in a common lodging-house and might well be bleeding to death.

"Oh, Benedict."

"Claire?" She had never telephoned him before.

"Yes. Could you come to Mannheim Crescent at once, please. Nola is with me. You must see her."

There was a slight pause.

"Can you be more explicit?"

"I'll try. She's been taken ill. Very ill."

"Have you called a doctor?"

"No. One would have to — choose discreetly."

This time the pause was imperceptible.

"I see. Yes — I'll be with you in fifteen minutes."

"Thank you."

What else could she say?

Nola was barely conscious when she returned, her breathing labored and guttural, her cheeks already sinking, her face fleshless, assuming the mask of bones and hollows Claire had seen so many times. Men wore this mask before they died. So, it seemed, did women. Automatically she performed the routine gestures of care, checked the pulse, the temperature, smoothed the brow, made the patient and the patient's bed tidy, tidied herself, sat down and waited for a higher authority. The doctor. Or Benedict. Or something even more final. Whichever should come first.

Not long. Benedict. Entirely composed, rock hard, she thought, but no rock to lean on; a rock, rather, on which vessels would break themselves if they ventured too close. Once she had almost — almost — sailed too near to him herself. Never again.

"Did I understand you correctly, Claire?"

276

"Yes." And as he entered her flat it was no longer her own, his presence filling it, arranging it, disposing of her time and ingenuity — her services — in a manner best calculated to suit his needs. He had already arranged for a doctor to attend. Since he was himself in evening dress she realized he must also have canceled a dinner engagement somewhere or other, before setting out. Had his memory stumbled with shock as hers had done so that he had been unable to recall a familiar telephone number? She doubted it. She could, with very little effort of the imagination, even hear his voice making cool explanations, "I do apologize — something has just come up — no, no, nothing serious — just a slight hitch." And even Elvira Redfearn would be unlikely to question him as to what sort of hitch it might be.

"I don't think you should go in to see her before the doctor comes," she said, standing between him and her bedroom door.

"Do you not?" He brushed her aside somehow without even touching her, opened the door, went in and stood for a moment looking down at his wife. Claire did not see his face. She was looking at Nola. Nola was looking at her. "Judas," she said.

The doctor came.

"Ah — doctor." Benedict turned from the bedside, his manner serious but affable and a little relieved — exactly right. "Thank you for being so prompt. As you see, my wife has suffered a tragic accident."

"Quite so." It was not, Claire noted, the comfortable little man who looked after Miriam's coughs and colds, but a younger, smoother, even more elegant individual of the type known as "a man of the world."

"An accident, you say — ? Indeed?" And even at a quick, preliminary glance, his manner implied that one could see accidents like these in the charity ward of the General Hospital every night of the week.

"Yes," Benedict replied. "An accident — I did say that."

"You were aware then, Mr. Swanfield, of your wife's condition?"

"Naturally."

And it was very clear that, whether or not he was believed, he did not intend to be contradicted. "As aware, that is, as she was herself. We had begun to hope. But, after fourteen years, one tends to hope with caution. Rightly so, in this case, as it has turned out, I regret to say."

"I see," said the doctor.

"Then please do what you can — regardless of cost, I need hardly add."

Nola closed her eyes.

Claire, feeling herself dismissed, went into her living room and sat down. She had done what she could to save Nola's life. And now the responsibility was no longer hers. She knew the doctor did not believe Benedict. She also knew that Benedict did not care whether he was believed or not, so long as he was obeyed. She thought there was every chance of it. Taking out a cigarette she smoked for a while, looking at her hands, noticing traces of blood around her nails, a streak of it drying a dark, brick-dust red along her arms. No doubt, that was why the dentist and his wife had looked at her so — what was it? — so *avidly*. She had seen that look before. The savoring of secondhand tragedy, other people's pain. The look of the Roman arena.

She finished her cigarette and lit another, leaning back in the chair and closing her eyes, her body feeling limp, depleted, as if it had been wrung out like a wet towel. She had no idea what would happen now. Benedict would decide. And she was quite simply too tired to grapple, just now, with her own complicated reactions. Her first desperate instinct had been to call him. Standing in the dentist's dingy hall with the telephone clutched in her hand she had suffered an agony of apprehension in case he could not be found. Benedict would know what to do. And here he was, doing it, coolly, efficiently, extremely well. His performance made even more impressive, perhaps, by the hard fact — in which she was in no doubt — that he did not actually give a damn. What more could she expect? He had acknowledged paternity of his wife's child, knowing it could not be his, as Paul had once done. She knew that Paul had acted from compassion. Had Benedict felt even remotely sorry for Nola? Did he understand now, as he stood at her bedside purchasing the silence of her doctor, that she had submitted herself to this butchery through fear of him? He was a clever man. His mind far more highly trained, experienced, seasoned than Nola's. And she concluded, therefore, that he did.

Her bedroom door opened and he came through it, the doctor a discreet pace behind him, continuing his low-voiced discussion without even appearing to notice her, the doctor looking professionally bland yet sounding just a little alarmed, like a man who has been maneuvered perhaps a shade too far.

"Very well, Mr. Swanfield, if that is your wish."

"It is."

"Quite so — but just the same I feel compelled to point out to you —"

"I believe you have already done so — several times, in fact."

"Then allow me to repeat once again — to stress — so that my own conscience may be clear —"

"Conscience?" And Benedict's cold sarcasm cut the air like a knife. "Good Heavens, are we talking about conscience? I beg your pardon. I rather thought we were considering the risk. Yours. And mine, of course — which amounts to much the same. Well — doesn't it?"

There was a slight pause. Not long.

"Mr. Swanfield — nevertheless —"

"Yes?"

"In view of the precarious balance of your wife's condition —"

"Yes, doctor — in view of exactly that, perhaps we might incline ourselves to speed. There is a back entrance to this house through the garden. You have a private ambulance, have you not — unmarked?"

"I do."

"Good. The turning is very narrow but you will just manage it. I see no reason to alarm my sister-in-law's neighbors by carrying a stretcher through her front door."

"No, indeed."

"So — perhaps we could say — rather soon."

The doctor took his leave. Claire went into the bedroom to look at Nola who was professionally sedated and packaged now, her unconscious face too helpless and too naked to be stared at for long. And coming back to find Benedict standing on her hearthrug lighting a cigar she said very coldly, "You must be paying the good doctor very handsomely."

"Am I in a position to bargain, do you think? I hardly think so."

"And you are moving her against his advice, aren't you?"

"I see no alternative."

"I do."

"Very likely." And his tone said "Spare me the details. Don't try me any further than you must." It was the tone he employed with Eunice.

"She can stay here. I see no reason against it."

"No — I suppose you wouldn't."

"You do, of course?"

"Yes."

No more than that! Just a single word of dismissal, reducing her to the level of a busybody, a scatterbrain. How dare he! She could not allow him to get away with it. But, as she drew breath to tell him so, he added, with visible impatience, "The reason is, my dear, that her life is still in danger. Were she to die here then you would no doubt have cause to regret your generosity. And even if *you* are willing to take the risk then *I* have other matters and other people to consider."

She moved a step or two away from him.

"What you are saying, I think, is that if she dies at High Meadows you can hush it up, but if she dies here there might be a scandal. So she will just have to go and die at High Meadows."

And throwing his cigar into the fire he spat out the one word, "Precisely."

She moved away from him again, slowly but very surely, wanting distance between them.

"What an icy bastard you are, Benedict," she said, her voice pitched at the level of casual conversation.

"Yes," he answered quite pleasantly, "it has taken you rather a long time, hasn't it, to reach that conclusion."

The journey to High Meadows was not the worst she had undergone. Very far from that. She had spent weary hours and days, unspeakable nights, in hospital trains packed like sardine cans with wounded. She knew the sounds and the smells of hospital ships, both in the flea-plagued heat of August when wounds festered and the murderous winter cold when they froze. This was by no means so terrible. But it was bad enough.

"My dear young lady, you have been most helpful." But the doctor had his own nurse with him now, a competent, astringent woman, a professional "civilian nursing sister" fully trained in the care of ladies and gentlemen, very much inclined to look down her nose at a common, war-time VAD. And Claire got into the ambulance only because she did not care to drive with Benedict or to leave Nola.

"There is a danger of infection, I suppose?"

The two civilian practitioners of medicine exchanged amused glances above her head.

"My dear — she is in excellent hands," Sister Cardew said, smiling reverently at her employer in a manner which irritated Claire. Yet, knowing she had been reminded of her inferior professional status, told to "keep her nose out of things which nice young ladies ought not to understand," she contented herself by holding Nola's hand and wondering out loud, from time to time, whether it should really be so hot.

"Her head is very hot too."

Sister Cardew, pointedly ignoring her, smiled once again, with enormous trust and admiration, at her doctor who, for his part, smiled benignly into space.

Benedict had arrived before them. Nola's room was ready. Her maid in attendance, Parker standing by to fetch and carry.

"My wife has been taken ill." It was as much, in his view, as they needed to know. It would not be worth their while or their jobs either, his manner implied, to find out more.

"Do you have everything you need, doctor?"

"I believe so."

"Should any need arise, no matter how great or small, then naturally, you have only to let me know."

"Quite so." There could be no doubt that the need — whatever it happened to be — could be supplied.

Claire could not tell whether Nola had suffered from the journey or not. She had been quiet in the ambulance, barely stirring in her drugged sleep, silently burning, and bleeding, Claire supposed, beneath the red hospital blankets, her life-flow restoring itself or ebbing away. Who knew? But she looked like an image of wax as they carried her upstairs. Old wax, its edges blurring away.

"Go with them," said Benedict, issuing a curt command.

"Oh — they don't want me to interfere —"

"I dare say. But *I* do. You'll understand enough — won't you — to judge."

"Perhaps."

"Perhaps isn't good enough, Claire. Better than that."

She had never in her life felt so hostile and bitter toward anyone.

"All right, Benedict. I quite understand your need to be kept informed. You'll have to be ready, won't you, to talk to your friends in high places — if she dies."

"Claire," he said, "if you wish to be useful then no one will complain. If not, then I am sure Parker will find the time to take you home."

Polly was out for the evening, would return late and too wrapped up in her own doings to notice anything amiss. Miriam had gone to the Princes Theater to see *No, No Nanette*, and it would be Benedict's task to welcome her home, not Claire's. What would he tell her? The smoothly contorted version of the truth which he had offered his doctor, and which Miriam, in the same knowing manner, would pretend to believe.

"My dear boy, how sad. I had really not the least notion that you were hoping to be a father again."

"Quite. One must accept these things stoically."

"How very true."

And Miriam would trip off to bed thinking that really, if one absolutely had to be adulterous then at least one might do it with style and, above all, with care.

Claire entered Nola's bedroom without knocking and closed the door firmly behind her.

"My dear young lady — ?" said the doctor, pronouncing a stock quotation.

"Mr. Swanfield asked me to come and help."

"Really — !" He exchanged a meaning glance with his nurse and lifted his shoulders in a shrug of resignation.

"If you should feel faint, dear," Sister Cardew said very sweetly, "do remember, if you can, to fall away from the patient."

Claire told her she did not think there would be any danger of that.

Night-watching was not new to her. She had sat, more nights than she wished to remember, in a hut full of dying men, "using her own initiative" as the phrase went, alone because there had been an epidemic of influenza among the nursing staff and because, since the men were dying anyway, no mistake could actually be fatal. She submitted herself now to the authority of this supercilious but — she gladly admitted — skillful pair, fetching and carrying, the "probationer nurse" again whose job it is to bear the brunt of temper and bring the tea. She became a pair of hands in the service of "the patient" who could have been anyone. And eventually the crisis was over, the hemorrhage under control, Nola's heart still beating, although her face had not lost its yellowing waxen look, its nakedness.

The patient was "comfortable," "as well as could be expected." No firm promises, mind. The words "infection" and "relapse" hovered on the brink of the surgeon's tongue, for women's bodies were unpredictable and the instruments used on this one may not have been clean. But he felt quite safe now in leaving the matter in Sister Cardew's capable hands. He would return in the morning, except that it was morning already, of course. Perhaps around eleven o'clock. Unless there should be a turn for the worse, in which case he would come at once. He begged Claire to rely on Sister Cardew's judgement about that.

"Is she going to be all right?"

"My dear — dear — young lady —"

"You should get some rest, dear," advised Sister Cardew, "or I shall have two patients on my hands."

The house was strange with early morning quiet when she came downstairs for the last time, a pearl-gray light just visible behind its curtained windows, not even the chambermaids about yet, with their ashpans and coal scuttles, just Benedict, his study door ajar, sitting alone at the vulnerable hour of five o'clock, smoking, waiting, she thought, with the intent, calculated patience of cats who are only patient for a purpose.

But she was no longer angry. Perhaps she had needed anger to carry her through. And now that the danger seemed over, her strength had gone with it. Now, she was weary. Only that.

"I think I could go home now, Benedict." It was all she wanted. Solitude. Silence. But it was not to be.

"I don't see how you can. There is some tidying up to be done — isn't there — in your bedroom in Mannheim Crescent. I think you will have to sleep here."

Oh Lord. She had forgotten that. And she had no stomach now for the soiled sheets Nola had left behind, nor energy to tackle their disposal. She sat down suddenly in the chair facing his.

Damnation!

"How is she now?"

"Still quiet. And Cardew looks very smug. *She* thinks it's going to be all right."

"Yes. So it seems. The doctor had a word with me here before he left."

But would it ever be all right for Nola? What would happen to her now? Would be punish her? Or, as always, would he simply allow her to punish herself?

"Claire . . ."

She looked up in surprise, wondering what more they had to say to one another and remained, for a moment of absolute shock, with her eyes fixed on his face. "Benedict, you look — *ghastly*."

"Do I? Why ever can that be, I wonder?"

His voiced was clipped and cool as always, Benedict at his efficient, sardonic best. But his face, in the hesitant light of a February dawn, looked hollow with strain, his eyes sunken and black, fine lines she had never seen before, or never noticed, fanning outward from their corners. He had been up all night, of course. And he had been drinking too. Yet — even so. He did not sound drunk. He did not look drunk. He looked as weary, as sickened, as she felt herself.

And as their eyes met they began to speak both together, his voice rising above hers, dominating it, forcing her to listen.

"I feel under no obligation to explain myself to you — none whatsoever . . ."

"Benedict — I haven't asked you —"

"But did it never cross your mind when you were standing there accusing me of — well, what *was* it exactly?"

She had never seen him even slightly moved before. He was moved now, perhaps only to anger, but moved nevertheless as other men could be moved, leaning toward her, his eyes narrowed, his mouth a thin line spitting out words she knew he did not want to speak, something inside him that was both enraged and enormous, hurling itself against his iron-held control. If it broke through then it would hurt him. Her too, perhaps. But she could cope with her own emotion. Already she was afraid for him.

"Accusing you?" she said carefully. "It seems a long time ago now."

"Not to me. So I'll ask you again. Did it never occur to you, while you were playing Joan of Arc, that I have two children to consider? Safely away at school, I admit, but nevertheless — Would *you* have cared for the job of telling them that their mother had died in suspicious circumstances in a lodging house in Mannheim Crescent? They are just old enough to understand those circumstances. Too young to be charitable about it. And the other boys at their school — bearing in mind that school is their home, their real life — would not have been kind."

"I'm sorry, Benedict."

"I *had* to move her."

"Yes — yes. I *do* understand now. I understood at the time. It was just that I felt so *sorry* for her and — and —"

"And I didn't feel anything at all? Is that it?"

"I suppose it is. Were you sorry?"

"No, of course not. Machines don't feel. But they function damn well in a crisis — for that very reason. They don't feel pity at the time, or guilt afterward — well, do they?"

"*Do you?*"

She saw that he did, and it was sufficient. It put everything, Edwina and Lois and that offensive bouquet of flowers — everything — right. Far more than it should have done and far too soon. Already, before he had asked for it or proved to her that he deserved it, she had forgiven him.

"I had to get her here. Yes, there was a risk. And yes — I did weigh her in the balance against my sons, and certain other things — Played God, if you like. And if she'd died in the ambulance then I'd have been to blame. The doctor made that clear enough. Obviously you imagine I found it easy."

"I thought so. I'm glad you didn't."

He leaned back in his chair, in shadow as she had so often seen him, and then emerging from it so abruptly that his face seemed very white, his eyes black hollows, he brought his hand palm down on the table beside him, setting the decanter and the overflowing ashtray dancing.

"For Christ's sake, Claire — how can you take so little care of yourself? Don't you even know the danger you were in? If she had been found in your bed they could have arrested you. And they'd have had a decent case. You were a nurse, you little fool. You could have done it yourself."

"Benedict — I could not."

Once again his hand descended palm down, with violence, on the fireside table.

"I know that. Of course I know it. But if they'd put you on trial for manslaughter what could I have *done* about it? An expensive barrister, certainly — or two — or any number. Yes — But could I have kept the news reporters and the scandalmongers and the hysterics away from you? Could I have made confinement in a prison cell anything other than unendurable? I doubt it. Could I have made it easier for you to stand in the dock and be accused of something you hadn't done and wouldn't do — ? You never gave it a thought, did you? You just stood there with blood on your hands worrying because I didn't look *sorry*. I intended to save Nola if I could. I was determined to save you, whether you liked it — or understood it — or noticed it — or not. Draw what conclusions you like. They'll be the wrong ones, no doubt. You were like a child, Claire, sitting on a railway track. Thank God you had the sense to call me."

"Yes."

And it was then, her mind racing, reeling from one conflicting thought to another, that she turned her head — seeking a respite perhaps from looking at him with her whole vision, the full measure of her concentration — and saw the lily bowl.

"What is that doing here?"

"What?"

She pointed almost accusingly and barely looking round — knowing full well what she had seen and its significance to her — he made a gesture of forced nonchalance, shrugging himself quite visibly back into his cynical aloofness, like a garment which, just as visibly, no longer altogether covered him.

"Ah — *that*. Did you want me to return it to you?"

"Of course not."

"Then why shouldn't it be here?"

"I don't know. It just shouldn't. It doesn't fit."

"How clever of you. No — no — it doesn't."

Once again he was moved, not this time to anger: and hearing the crack in the ice she reached out to steady him, not caring whether or not she was rebuffed.

"No," he said, throwing the word at her, "it doesn't belong here. Neither do I. So we may as well keep one another company."

"I don't understand you, Benedict."

"Good. That has always been my intention."

"You say you don't belong here. But High Meadows belongs to you."

"Does it? Oh yes — since they buried me alive under the foundation stones. Yes. One would have to call that belonging . . ."

It was her own childhood nightmare of suffocation, of Edward Lyall burying her in sand while Dorothy stood by, fondly smiling. She shivered, her hands — when had they become so cold? — twisting together in her lap, her whole mind straining toward him.

"*Please*," she said. "Just tell me."

Silence. And then an irritable hand reaching for a cigar, his eyes, blackened by fatigue, closing in a head that had started to ache. And in that bleak hour of winter daybreak, as she felt him weaken, so she felt her own strength return, a female strength, quieter but deeper than the male, far less spectacular than the armed warrior yet infinitely more dogged, more patient, longer-lasting.

"Benedict?"

The fire was burning low, gray morning tossing handfuls of rain at the windows, waking the household to activity. Soon there would be a tap at the door, an apologetic voice asking permission to draw the curtains, lay a new fire, inquire about breakfast. Soon there would be Polly's exuberance to contend with if Roy Kington had smiled at her, or her clamoring misery if he had not; Miriam's knowing sympathy; Eunice, hurrying up the hill to see what she could see. And, leaning forward into the quietness which had fallen, thick and heavy, between them, he began to speak quickly, curtly, anxious to get it over. "All right. Very well. There's no mystery about me, Claire. None. I am just as you have seen me. There is no more. I am a man who enjoys sex with strangers and then turns his back on them. Not for any of the complex reasons you may have imagined but because I want them to remain strangers. That's all. I also rule this family with a rod of iron because that is the way my father taught me. And to make sure I obeyed him he tied me up so tight that in fact — although they don't realize it — the family control me. I can't get rid of them, Claire — any one of them. In simple terms, they're entitled to annual payments which I have to earn. I can't pay them off in full because the business couldn't stand it. No business could. My father knew that, of course, and in effect, he gave me to Miriam, and the rest of them, for life. I resent the position in which I find myself. But I accept it. It makes me responsible, you see, not only for the family but for the livelihood of several hundred employees. And one can imagine rather too well how they would fare at the hands of Polly or Toby. So I am bound — absolutely — to this house and this family and the marriage which goes with them. Why should you be interested in such a man?"

He paused, but she had no time to answer before the rapid, toneless flow of words began again.

"God dammit, Claire, you know well enough the man I am outside this house. I made sure you knew it. It was the kindest thing I could have done for you. The best gift I could have made you. Don't deceive yourself. I enjoy women like Lois Chiltern. They suit me and satisfy me to perfection. I don't want anything more."

"I don't believe you."

"Claire." And the desperate sincerity in his voice claimed and held her own attention. "They are the truest words I have ever spoken. *I — want — nothing — more.* I am not equipped for anything more."

She shook her head.

"Then let me put it this way. I can afford nothing else. When one is a prisoner, of circumstances, or of one's own nature, or whatever, and one knows escape to be impossible, then the trick is to stop wanting to get away. My particular prison is very comfortable. I have made sure of that. Don't trouble me, Claire."

"Tell me why the lily bowl is here?"

"To remind me —"

"Of what?"

"How wrong I was. Of what a mistake you were. Of how much better off I am with women of my own kind."

"I very nearly fell in love with you, Benedict — so nearly that I think I did."

"How can you say that?" he said, aghast. "How can you admit it?" And it was so clearly beyond him how anyone could admit to such an enormity that she found herself smiling.

"Well — I felt it. So why waste it by pretending I didn't."

"I can't," he said. "You find it all so very simple, don't you — opening yourself up, lowering your guard. I can't."

She waited a moment. "The lily bowl."

"Damn your lily bowl, Claire, and damn you. I should have left you alone in the first place. And you should leave me alone now."

"Benedict — the lily bowl."

He swung round toward her, his eyes black slits in a white face which seemed leaner than she remembered, fiercer than she had ever imagined and, with one lightning movement, came at her so fast, so violently, that she braced herself instinctively for a blow. "Because I need it here," he snarled at her, "I look at it, like the fool I swore I'd never be, and think of you. I sent you away, didn't I, for that very reason — because I was thinking of you too much — and you damn well know it. And when I want you back badly enough, which happens fairly often —"

"I'm here," she said.

"What a fool you are. What a selfish brute you make me."

She smiled. How little that seemed to matter.

"Benedict — I'm here."

15

FOUR weeks had passed, leading them to the gentle beginning of April, cool sunlight from a sky washed pale blue-white by showers of fine, mild rain; fluted carpet of daffodils. Nola, accompanied by her Cousin Bernard's capable wife, Nanette, had set off for a month's convalescence in Eastbourne. There had been no scandal. Miriam herself, to whom scandal was indeed a fate worse than death, had seen to that, soulfully informing an assortment of Greenwoods and Redfearns and Templetons just enough of the truth to cover herself, should the real truth ever come to light and then obscuring it, bending it with consummate artistry into what was never *quite* — never completely — a lie. It had been unwise of Nola to attempt an addition to her family so late in the day. Mrs. Templeton who, had produced her daughter, Sally, at the surprising, embarrassing age of forty-two, and Elvira Redfearn who had conceived once when she had been well under thirty and never again — one child being all that was needful to prove herself as capable of conception as anyone else — both nodded their heads. Nola's miscarriage, therefore, was not to be wondered at, particularly when one remembered the difficulty with which she had brought Conrad and Christian into the world. Elvira Redfearn who had given birth to her own handsome, healthy, highly intelligent son as efficiently as she did everything else, and plain little Miss Greenwood to whom all bodily functions seemed dangerous and distasteful, both smiled their agreement; Elvira feeling rather pleased and very superior, Miss Greenwood simply relieved that there seemed little chance now of it ever happening to her. Miriam, of course, had warned Nola to take care, to little avail.

"I do understand," sighed Mrs. Templeton, reminded of how little attention her own daughters ever paid to *her* advice.

"A little late in the day for taking care," murmured Elvira Redfearn.

What could she mean? wondered Miss Greenwood, whose narrow education had allowed no room for the lectures of Doctor Marie Stopes.

"Quite so." Miriam, who knew nothing about Doctor Stopes either except that one did not discuss her in polite circles, gave them all three a sad, sweet smile. "Poor Nola. Poor Benedict. One tends to forget the feelings of the father in these cases. But — in the strictest confidence, of course, Benedict was greatly disappointed. Naturally he will put a brave face on it — one would expect no less. But can one blame a man with two sons for wanting a daughter? *I* cannot blame him."

Yet, by accepting responsibility for his wife's pregnancy, Benedict had condoned her adultery, canceling out any possibility of divorce. And the thin, empty-eyed, washed-out woman who had gone with Nanette Crozier to Eastbourne had looked unlikely to be committing adultery in the foreseeable future — perhaps never again.

But divorce, in any case, had never been Benedict's intention. Nola would remain his responsibility. He made that much very plain, both to her and to Claire.

"Yes, of course," Claire had answered.

Nola had simply closed her eyes.

"What is he going to do with me?" she asked Claire. "Find out for God's sake!"

And she had reacted strangely when the answer seemed to be that he was sending her to Eastbourne to convalesce and then — nothing.

"I think my father would have starved my mother to death if she'd done this to him."

"Hardly practical these days, Nola."

"Better though — I told you it would be."

Her physical weakness had made her tearful, suspicious, prone to a melancholy in which she took refuge, almost welcomed as a friend. She had made up her mind to die. She had been ready for it. And it would have been easier, too. After all, *she* would not have been expected to cope with it, recover from it, sit up and eat her dinner, draw some kind of conclusions about what to do next. Therefore, she would be ill. Very ill. And from there, as this most unmaternal of women began to realize that she had taken a human life, it was only a step away from believing she deserved her sickness. The reaction took her completely by surprise. Until now it had been a matter of *her* life or *her* death. Not the child's. Yet there were times during the long hours she lay in bed with nothing to do but brood, dissect, turn her mind inward, when that dead child seemed to be a symbol of her own failures, the chaotic, self-destructive impulses she had allowed to rule her life. And waking suddenly in the night or the dawn of a chilly day, finding herself still captive in the house she had never recognized as home, still the wife of the man she had never felt to be her husband, two thoughts would flash into her mind, one after the other, "I shall have no luck now" and "I shall never be forgiven."

She had not wanted the child. She had not even thought of it as an identity. Had she given birth to it she would have paid it no more attention than Christian and Conrad, which was no attention at all. Yet, just the same, it seemed to her now a damned shame that the poor little mite had never had a chance. And perversely, perilously, since no one cared for her and she cared for no one else, she began to identify with it.

She blamed herself. Yet she also blamed others for making her as she was. When her father, a gentleman of imperial dignity, arrived from Bradford she refused to see him and, when he insisted, lay back on her pillows, eyes closed, defeating him by the very qualities he had wished to instil into his daughters. He had declared women to be weak. Very well. She was too weak to be disturbed for more than a few moments. He had insisted upon bashfulness as an essential to femininity. She was too bashful, therefore, to answer his questions. She was in no hurry at all to get out of bed. Her room became her refuge, "her lair," said Polly where she lay all day long staring at the wall or at books she often held ostentatiously upside down. And when the doctor advised her most strongly to come downstairs, her appearances were erratic and eccentric, causing alarm to Miriam who, several times, found her stretched out on the drawing room sofa fast asleep, wearing an assortment of flimsy draperies with a lighted cigarette in her hand.

Nor could one be certain just when or how she might make an appearance. Miriam's tea party guests might welcome the diversion of Nola stalking into the room and out again without speaking a word, but Miriam did not. Roy Kington may have promptly forgotten his reference to Nola as "that elderly Ophelia" when he came across her one afternoon wandering about the garden quoting aloud from a book of German poetry, but Polly burned for the rest of the day with the shame of it and was at great pains to explain to everyone that she and Nola were related only by marriage which did not transmit hereditary madness, rather than by blood which probably did. She upset Eunice too, by staring at her in what she felt to be a most critical fashion; and upset her even more by staring at her children so that the whole of Eunice's protective instincts were hotly aroused, leading to something of a scene between her and

Toby when he expressed the view that if Nola really *was* planning to kidnap one of the boys, which seemed unlikely, then so far as he was concerned, she would be welcome.

Yet, perhaps worst of all, was her humble manner with Benedict, her air of walking barefoot along the convent wall in penitence whenever he appeared, her instinct being not only to fly from him but to let him see her in flight, waiting, at the sound of his car on the drive, until he had entered the hall before she came bursting through the double doors from the drawing room, draperies flying, and dashed blindly yet all too visibly upstairs, out of his way.

It had been something of a relief, therefore, certainly to Miriam and to Polly, when practical, bustling little Nanette Crozier had arrived to take Nola to Eastbourne.

And on that following Sunday afternoon of early spring, a young, uncertain sun just keeping the rain at bay, Claire sat once again in Benedict's study watching the sky mellow toward dinnertime, perfectly at ease with him now as they sat by his open windows, enjoying the hazy ending of a fragile day.

He was not yet her lover again. She had simply made it clear to him that when he wanted her she would come to him gladly and at once. She had said "I am here" and it had been a promise. She would keep it for as long as their being together retained its significance. And she had not the least idea how long that might be. She was, quite simply, filled, sometimes to a point which overpowered her, by generosity, a rich overflow of warmth which kept on rising and spilling over. He could not give himself. She understood that. Therefore, what prevented her, except mealymouthed pride and timorous convention, from giving enough for two? One gave what one could, after all. One gave what one wanted to give. For the first time since her return from France she felt herself stretched to her limits, functioning at top speed, maximum capacity, making the best use of herself that she knew how. And she was glad that she had no woman friend left who was close enough to confide in and who would be more than likely to call her a fool, as Benedict himself had done.

She had spent the morning at Upper Heaton, doing her duty, accompanying her mother to church, receiving afterward from the congregation of full-bosomed matrons the details of Nola's "sad accident" which they had heard, in confidence of course, from someone who had heard it from Miriam.

"The sea air will do her good."

She had smiled her agreement, smiled and agreed again when Edward, on the walk home, had lectured her on the need for a purpose in life and the general aimlessness of her own.

"One could hardly wish to see you waiting at table at the Crown for the rest of your life, my dear, in the company of one who — well — to whom waiting at table must come far more naturally."

"Oh — quite." She made her voice very sweet, for Dorothy's sake and because Edward no longer mattered to her one way or the other.

"And since — let us face it my dear — remarriage in these times with such a surplus of ladies, many of whom have both position and money, seems hardly a possibility, one feels bound to stress, Claire, that time is not on your side."

But she had a far more intimate acquaintance than Edward with the vagaries of Time, the cruel tricks it played, the promises never kept, its treacherous habit of simply running out.

"Do you know," she said now, smiling at Benedict, "how much Edward Lyall worships you?"

"A man of good taste then, wouldn't you say."

"No. Because it's all for the wrong reasons."

"Ah — yes — ?"

"It's because you're rich and powerful and so terribly impressive."

"And you don't worship me for that?"

She smiled at him again, thinking about Time. "I don't know. Shall we go up to Thornwick after dinner and see? If you want me, that is?"

"Of course I want you."

He had no need to touch her. They sat, their chairs well apart, and smiled at each other, acknowledging what had become a simple fact.

"Should you really offer yourself so freely, Claire?"

"I suppose not. I ought to be mean and coy and make you run after me — which I expect you would."

"I expect so."

"So why pretend to run in the first place? Isn't it just a waste of time?"

"Is there so much need for hurry?"

"Yes," she said, "There is. Always. When you're lucky enough to find something you want — and it *is* luck, because you can go on for ages and ages without managing to want anything — then you take it. You jump at it. Now. Today. The world may be over tomorrow."

"My dear — I doubt that."

"Don't ever doubt it. It ends for somebody every day."

He smiled, quite gently. "Yes, Claire. I know. The philosophy of the returned soldier. Then we'll go up to Thornwick, shall we, after dinner — if we can get away early enough?"

No difficulties were put in their way, both Eunice and Polly being concerned only with their separate determination to monopolize the telephone, Eunice in an attempt to locate her eldest son, Polly to keep the line clear for Roy Kington who had promised to call her. While Miriam, who might have put in a bid of her own for Claire's time, seemed wholly distracted by Eunice's constant departures from the dinner-table— "I've just thought of something. He's friendly with the Cartwright boys. I'll give them a ring" — bringing a wail of protest from Polly — "Mother — she'll gossip for ages and it's not *her* telephone. Tell her, mother!" — followed, when Miriam failed to oblige, by a sullen "The little beast is probably down at the police station — or in the river."

"How dare you talk about Justin like that," shrieked Eunice from the hall, the telephone still in her hand.

"Because it's true." Polly could shriek even louder. "And you think so yourself. Why else are you making such a fuss?"

"Girls — girls," murmured Miriam, glancing hopefully at Benedict who appeared to have noticed nothing amiss.

"Downright rudeness," said Eunice, coming back to the table flushing scarlet, "that's what it is. And I don't see why I should put up with it, mother, from a girl her age."

"*Mother!*" This time Polly, hearing what she thought might be a bell, had dashed into the hall, "Mother — now see what the silly bitch has done. She's left the telephone off the hook, that's all —"

"How dare you call me that," gasped Eunice, jumping to her feet.

"You did it on purpose so he couldn't get through," hissed Polly. "You wanted to spoil *my* fun because you never get any of your own."

"Ladies — please," said Toby nervously.

"I think," sighed Miriam, "that I will take my coffee upstairs."

The dessert over, she tiptoed off to bed, looking fragile, leaving Polly and Eunice glowering at each other as they circled the telephone, Polly willing it to ring, Eunice waiting her chance to seize it and put through another call, Toby keeping his distance, apparently engrossed in yesterday's copy of The Times.

"Shall I take you home?" said Benedict.

"Oh — yes please," said Claire.

No one watched them go. Not even Miriam's bedroom curtains twitched as they drove away. The night was fine, star-lit, so clear that one could see for miles, had one desired to do so, from the brow of Thornwick Hill. The farmhouse, in the springtime, had a different fragrance, crocus scents, open window scents instead of the woodsmoke and beeswax and hyacinths of the winter. And standing before the great stone hearth she put her arms around him before she had even taken off her coat, her cheek pressed against his, and held him for a long, uncomplicated, friendly moment.

"Let's not think too deeply about it yet, Benedict. I know we'll have to start talking about right and wrong and how long it can last. But not now. Let's just *live* it now. Then we've *got* it. And it can't be taken away. Let's just be happy about it — put into it as much as we can."

He smiled, his arms tightening around her, "I know. Before the bombs start to fall."

Her body had missed him. He had been very far from celibate yet her welcome enchanted his senses, precipitating them both very quickly into pleasure, after which she kept her arms around him, holding him fast.

Having made up her mind to live for the moment, to snatch it and savor it and be grateful — *very* grateful — for as much as it gave her, she was happy and told him so.

"And have you *nearly* fallen in love with me again?"

"Oh, yes." She snuggled against him, giddy with love and pleasure, able to say anything, to be as outrageous as she chose. "Tell me about your first girl, Benedict."

"Claire — for Heaven's sake." But he was smiling.

"Why not?"

"Because gentlemen don't tell about such things."

"Oh, that doesn't matter. It must have been so long ago. And it hardly seems fair, since ladies are entitled to tell as much as they like. How old were you?"

"Sixteen, I think."

"Shameful. Don't let me hear you say another word about Eunice's Justin. And she?"

"About twice that age."

"My word — how thrilling."

"Yes, she was. A schoolmistress of independent manners and advanced views. Eccentric, I suppose. Unpredictable. Very beautiful."

"If you are trying to make me jealous then — yes, you are doing it very well."

"I am simply answering your question."

"What did you do next?"

"I traveled a little, for the firm, and one makes acquaintances on the road. And then I had a long flirtation with Elvira Redfearn and almost got engaged to her."

"I'm not too keen to hear about that."

"Why not?" His dark eyes were frankly teasing her. "There's nothing in it to distress you. And it was *you* after all who started me talking. In the end my father decided against it."

"Benedict!" She sat up straight in her astonishment. "I can't imagine you allowing anyone — not even your father — to decide a thing like that."

"You didn't know me when I was twenty-five."

Looking down at him, his head still leaning against the pillows, she brushed a fingertip against his lean, slightly hollow cheek, his long mouth, the arch of his brows which she had once thought supercilious, the Roman curve of his nose.

"No I didn't know you then. I wish I had. How were you?"

He caught her hand and held it a moment, the texture of their conversation becoming denser, rather deeper than either of them had wanted.

"I was short of cash. That's what I remember mainly about being twenty-five. A deliberate policy on my father's part, of course. A traditional policy, as a matter of fact, in this area. How else can any self-respecting millmaster work his son as hard as millmasters hereabouts have always tended to do, unless he keeps him short of ready money? A young man with a pound or two in his pockets might not be so ready to get up at half past five every morning. And he might not do just as he's told in other ways either."

"You mean he might not let his father choose him a wife?"

"Yes. I'm afraid that's just what I mean. It may not be the right moment to talk about it. And it's certainly not the right place — but — since we've approached it so closely — ?"

"All right. I don't mind."

"When I was twenty-five it was decided that I needed a wife. When one attains a certain position in life it is just as well to be married. One looks askance at bachelors, particularly in small provincial towns. They arouse too much speculation. My arrangement with my father was that on my wedding day I would become a director of the Mills — in effect to receive official recognition for the job I had been doing for years. I was also to be paid a reasonable salary. And Elvira Redfearn had a certain amount of capital. So had Nola. My father decided that the Crozier warehouses and construction companies and their reputation in the wool trade far outweighed the Redfearn chain of hardware stores. I was in no position to disagree."

"You didn't mind?"

"I had known Elvira for a long time. Nola was a very recent acquaintance and because of that I may have found her the more attractive of the two. To be honest, she rather reminded me of the schoolmistress I just told you about — or rather as I thought my schoolmistress might have been as a girl. Unusual. No one's idea of pretty. *Uncoordinated.* But then, in my schoolmistress's case, when she'd pieced herself together, "uncoordinated" had turned out to be "original," "exciting." Well — in *our* case, Nola's and mine, it didn't. But, having said all that, I feel obliged to confess that what really mattered to me at the time was the authority I'd be acquiring in the business, and the money. If my father had withdrawn his offer then I would certainly have withdrawn mine."

She released his hand and brushed the tips of her fingers once again across his face.

"I'm twenty-five now, Benedict — or very nearly."

"I know. I'm forty. So this really is ridiculous —"

"Yes. Quite ridiculous. Because I *am* jealous."

"Of what — for God's sake?"

"Original, unusual women. All of them. Because I'm not."

"Claire," he said, his voice only just neutral, "I have never met anyone even remotely like you — never."

She slid down on top of him and kissed him for a long time, her hands on either side of his head, the length of her body curving against his in a gentle, supple, loving line, until his arms came around her, imprisoning her with such unrelenting strength that she was finally obliged to cry out "Darling — you're hurting me." And even then he did not let her go.

"Of course I'm hurting you. I'm bound to hurt you, aren't I, one way or another. How can I avoid it now? You should have disliked me when I gave you the opportunity. You should have seen the sense to it — as I did."

"Yes — flirting with abominable Lois, and those insulting flowers the next morning."

"I've done more than flirt with Lois, you know."

"You're boasting again."

"No. I'm making it plain to you that I tried — for your sake, not mine — to convince you that I wasn't a man you could possibly care for. *Your* sake. Because what have I to lose? Nothing. And everything to gain. I want you with me, Claire. I know how to keep you. I have only to exploit your sweetness and your generosity and I think you'd stay with me for a very long time. Permanently, in fact — and in the blue chintz room too if it seemed most convenient, as it probably would. Make no mistake about it, Claire. That's what I want. The first time I realized it I drove off and left you in the snow. I wasn't abandoning you that night. I was saving you, from yourself — not from me. But you wouldn't be saved would you? You did the generous thing — the original thing. And I couldn't resist. I lost the will to resist — until the next morning when I made the best use I could of Lois and Edwina. I hurt you deliberately and I didn't find it easy. I probably won't find it any easier when I *have* to do it again."

"We agreed not to go too deep — not yet."

"One seizes the moment. You, of all people, must know that. And you don't really want to end your days in the blue chintz room, do you Claire? I have nothing to offer you but that. At the moment I can still see how wrong it would be to impose such a future upon you. I may, eventually, lose sight of that."

"Not now, Benedict — please."

"No. Can you stay the night?"

"I shouldn't."

"That means you can. And when you see your employer tomorrow tell him you need a holiday — a fortnight starting not later than Monday next. He owes you that."

She sat up again. "Are we going away together?"

"Yes. Shall I take you to France? No, no, don't wrinkle your nose. I'm not talking about the grand tour of the battlefields. I thought you might like to see where the *Vouvray* comes from."

She clasped her hands around her knees, excited and apprehensive as a child at Christmas.

"Oh yes. Yes please. Could we manage it?"

"Of course. We have only to meet in London and then travel home to Faxby on separate trains. A reasonable amount of discretion covers the rest. I shall probably leave a day or two before you and stay in London a day or so longer. Quite simple."

"So simple that I am bound to think you have done it all before."

"Naturally."

"Oh — naturally."

They smiled at one another as they had done at the beginning of the evening, acknowledging a closeness which had nothing to do with touch.

"But not to Vouvray. The Edwinas and Elviras of my life have always preferred Paris or Cannes."

Two weeks in France. The prospect shone before her like a glittering prize, filling her with the total, unmixed longing of childhood. And, as children feel, it seemed to her that if she could just get to it, touch it, *have* it, then she would be content. Nothing must stand in her way. She would give up anything for it and count her losses afterward. And, sensing this, Kit Hardie bowed graciously to her demands. She had worked, after all, for eight months without a break. She needed a rest.

"But why France?" asked Dorothy, who simply knew, without at all knowing *why* she knew, that her daughter was up to something. "I know people do keep going out there to look at the graves, but surely you must have had enough of that?"

"Yes, mother."

"Then why not the south coast, dear? Edward and I stayed in a charming guesthouse in Bournemouth — oh, some years ago. I'm sure to have the address somewhere."

"No thank you, mother. I'm going to France."

Miriam, on the other hand, was all sweet encouragement.

"My dear, how very nice. I have been thinking for some time that you needed a rest. Benedict is going away too. Oh — didn't you know that? Indeed — why should you? I am not sure where, of course. A mixture of business and pleasure I expect and one would really not care to pry. Perhaps you could travel together, as far as London, at any rate. Oh, I see. You are leaving on Monday and he is going tomorrow. What a pity. Perhaps you will run into him somewhere. Who knows? These odd little coincidences *do* happen. Between ourselves — *strictly* between ourselves — Benedict often worries me."

"Oh — ?"

"He is far too solitary, my dear."

"Is he really?"

Miriam smiled fondly, a little archly. "Ah well, you naughty girl, I suppose you have heard whispers about him and his various *amours*, haven't you? Of course you have. And I shall shock you, I suppose, when I say they are all true. Why not? In view of Nola's sad experience I really don't wish to pass comment on the state of their marriage. Suffice it to say that when a man is less than satisfied at home he usually feels entitled to look elsewhere. Certainly my own husband, during his first wife's time, was exceedingly promiscuous. In fact, I was warned against him, my dear, in most explicit terms. Fortunately — young as I was — I understood how meaningless these fancies can become, how stale. Oh yes — a man can repeat himself so often with women of a certain type that in the end . . . Well dear, my husband who had a very direct turn of speech sometimes, told me that before he married me he had seen so many faces on his pillow that he could hardly distinguish them one from the other. It troubled him. I wonder if it is starting to trouble Benedict?"

"I really — I couldn't say."

"No?" Miriam smiled again, very sweetly. "Of course not. I am trying to put old heads on young shoulders, aren't I dear? Never mind. Experience matures very slowly and I have really so little to do these days but sit and *observe*. You do know, of course, that Benedict is a very difficult man?"

"Yes." She could not have answered more than that one word no matter how hard she had tried.

"Far more difficult than his father. Aaron was hard. Benedict is cold.

By their own choice, of course. Hardness was the character my husband selected for himself and hard was how he wished to appear. Benedict is the same with his coldness."

"Oh — I see."

"Perhaps you do. You remember my theory, child, about the children of the seasons?"

"Oh yes." Could she possibly distract her? "You said because I was born in the summer I must be lazy and easygoing from having had nothing to do in infancy but bask in the sun. And that I must be inclined to give things away, because there would have been so much fruit on the trees and so many flowers."

But Miriam was not to be distracted.

"And are you not like that, Claire? Generous — even a little wasteful — of your summer bounty? Unguarded because no cold winds threatened you in your cradle, so that you never learned how to cover yourself, not even saw the need for it? How very alarming all that must sometimes seem to a man like Benedict. He was born on a bitterly cold night, you see. His mother died. And no one had the time even to wrap him up. How very shivery and how very threatened he must have felt. Is it any wonder that he threw up so many defenses? There was no one else, after all, who could be bothered to defend him until I came along. And by that time it was too late. He was already living behind a screen. I failed him. How sad."

"Yes — yes, quite —"

"My goodness, what a pair they were, father and son. What they both needed was a sunny nature to warm them up — like yours dear, and mine — I could see that at once. Aaron was much simpler, of course. Solid rock. And what harm can the sun do to rock? None at all. It warms it. It makes things grow. And Aaron wanted to be warmed. One could see him, dear, positively basking — loving it. It did him immense good. Now think of Benedict."

She was thinking fast.

"Any man, Claire, who feels the cold must wish to warm himself. He may even long to do so. But think, dear, what the sun does to ice. And if he has used that ice, for so many years, as a protection . . . Well — in order to be warm he will have to watch his defenses melt away. How that must alarm him. He may even bolt back under his glacier from time to time, don't you think? Wouldn't you? But perhaps he may meet a summer woman one day, with enough patience to keep on coaxing him out again. I do hope so."

"Yes. That would be nice."

"Do have a pleasant holiday, Claire. It may help to settle your mind.

And then, I have a little scheme afoot to persuade you to spend a week or two here, in your own little blue room. In May, I thought, to celebrate my birthday and Polly's — something rather special, since she's bound to be married next year with no time to spare for her mother."

Nonsense, of course. And romantic, sentimental nonsense too, typical of Miriam. Yet Miriam, in fact, was shrewd, sharp as a razor, steely of purpose beneath all her frills and flounces, as Claire well knew. And there had been times — she could recall every detail in her memory — when Benedict had seemed to reach out toward her and had then retreated exactly — she could not help but see it — as if she had burned him. "I can do you no good," he had told her often enough. The danger had seemed to be wholly hers. Now the possibility of harming him simply by loving him was presented to her forcefully, getting into her dreams where, for three uneasy nights in succession, she saw him evaporate in her arms, to be, most horrifyingly, not there. An addition to her stock of nightmares which she did not welcome, the more so since it had been conjured up by Miriam, whose sole concern was to secure a more agreeable companion for her old age than Eunice and Nola.

Yet the holiday in France still waited, just visible, just a little way ahead, beckoning and dazzling her like a pole-star. She would have just that much, then perhaps only a little more or nothing more, but at least *that*.

They met among the indifferent, anonymous throng of Waterloo, seeing each other instantly as if by some magnetic empathy of thought and desire, which stopped Claire in her tracks and held her motionless as he came toward her. He was the tallest man in the crowd, his cashmere overcoat, woven in Faxby, tailored in London, swinging stylishly from wide shoulders, his hat tipped forward at a sporting, almost Newmarket angle, the same air about him of good quality, tip-top condition, the very best, which she had first noticed about his house at Thornwick. Had he been a complete stranger she would have been aware, at a single glance, that his shoes and gloves must be of the finest leather, his shirt and tie of silk, his cufflinks and watch-chain of pure gold. She would have been happy to look at him — simply to look at him — all day, gloating with contented pride on his clothes, his air of authority and quiet elegance, the set of his chin, the dark hair curling very slightly into the nape of his neck, the black tilt of his eyebrows, a hundred more tiny, tremendous details which, as she stood there breathless and tremulous with a new emotion, had each one the power to turn her knees to water.

And it *was* a new emotion.

She loved him.

She had thought so before. But what she felt now, what seemed to have suddenly fallen full upon her, was not the same. Before — before what? — just *before*, love had come easily to her, a feeling which rose quite naturally and flowed quite smoothly and which she had experienced certainly once in the past. But this was serious. Terribly serious. She knew that one recovered, eventually, more or less, from that smooth, natural, free-flowing emotion which was undoubtedly a kind of love. She had no way, yet, of telling if one recovered from this.

"Hello," she said and could say no more.

"Hello." His eyes touched her and then his hands, drawing her toward him and holding her in what they both knew to be an act of complete possession, complete surrender. She was his now, absolutely; abandoning herself to his desire, his love, his need, without reserve or restraint on conditions. His — to have and to hold, in unstinting, unbounded bestowal. For as long as she could. For as long as it lasted. Until the week after next.

It was, from the start, a perfect experience. A life within a life, wholly apart from what — for as long as it should last — she was no longer forced to call reality. The sun shone. The sea was calm. And for two fine, dry weeks every train ran on time, every arrangement they made proceeded smoothly and without a hitch, every hotel was warm and delightful, every moment separate, distinct, acutely memorable.

France. The country where she had grown, by force, to womanhood, where she had first loved and suffered and where Paul was still lying in a neat grave set among tidy rows of others which she had no wish to visit, content to leave this ritual to his wife and mother. She had accepted, at once, for a hundred brutal reasons, the decay of his body, knowing too well how soon and how irrevocably death had eaten it away. But his spirit had remained for a long time at the edge of her vision, unreachable of course but *there*, if only just, if beginning to fade mercifully from an almost visible presence to a memory. She had begun to release him, to allow him — and herself — to rest. Yet he entered her deeply dreaming mind that first night in Paris, gently and kindly, so that she knew he pitied her. Human emotion no longer touched him. Desire was over, and longing, all the frantic needs of one human body, one human heart, for another, the joy of a lover's caress, the warm handclasp of a friend in the dark.

For him all that was ended. Yet for her the rejoicing and the suffering was to do all over again. *Here*, in this land of France where she had learned to live only for the moment, to absorb the measure of happiness it gave with the gratitude and despair of a desert traveler tasting a raindrop, knowing there may never be another.

Live now, the dream told her, there's no time to spare. There never has been.

"I love you, Benedict." Had she really spoken? Or was it simply her arms, on waking, which had conveyed the words to him as they reached out to find him? And found him. Not only that morning but the next one and the one after, the sheer delight of such a little thing — such a miracle — coloring the day with gold and scarlet excitements, deep blues and lilacs of profound content.

She had everything she wanted. The whole of life's bounty. In one man. How perilous. But the peril was for tomorrow. Today was the leafy enchantment of the grand *boulevards* where she walked with him in a haze, a trance made up of the blissfully replete love of the body and the rich, deep-flowing love of the heart. It was the *cafés* where they sat under striped awnings, letting the world go gladly by, watching only one another. It was the smile always there to meet her smile, the hand always ready to clasp her own so that she could reach out blindly, eyes closed, confident of his touch. It was the constancy, the trust, so that she could have leaped out into space, knowing he would catch her.

That was today.

She knew tomorrow would come.

They took another train and traveled southward to a gentle green velvet landscape threaded by the broad, pale ribbon of the Loire. A land mysterious with deep woods, generous with vines and vivid with flowers, set here and there, at sudden turnings, with gingerbread houses of storybook illustrations, Cinderella's palace glimpsed, delicate and magical, through a pattern of rich foliage, Beauty slumbering for a hundred fragrant years in every tall, enchanted tower.

And here she dreamed no dreams of any kind.

They visited the castles of France's kings at Chenonceaux and Chambord and Amboise, and strolled in the soft air through royal forests. They stood for the whole of one afternoon beside a château the color and texture of white smoke, rising spire upon fairy tale spire from a lake of pale green water. They climbed the steep medieval streets of Chinon, topped by its battlements, once the court of England's Henry Plantagenet, where his lion-hearted son Richard had made himself a lair in which to die after his last crusade. They followed the course of the river, finding it placid, at this season, its surface the texture of silk scarcely ruffled by an almost amorous, lemon-scented breeze. They inspected the vines at Vouvray and the *caves*, cut into the earth beneath the vineyards, an ice-cold, rough-hewn womb where the wine lay maturing in giant casks and miles of dusty bottles. And, emerging from the chill dark of the cellars into the trumpet blare of light and heat, they sat in the sunshine tasting a wine that placed all the flowers and spices of the region, all the green enchantment, the silken beauty of the river and the fine fragile romance of those enchanted castles, on Claire's tongue.

A life within a life. A green glade in the dust bowl that was often reality. From the moment of setting foot in France they had not spoken one word of Faxby or anyone connected with it. It had seemed unnecessary. Nor did the necessity arise on their return to Paris. Not immediately. But on the last morning but one she went alone to the *Galeries Lafayette* to buy presents for Dorothy and Edward to ease her conscience, thereby creating the necessity of taking something for Miriam, something for Polly, something for Eunice who could hardly be left out. And, since she was buying for everybody else, could she forget Nola? Or Kit? Or Mrs. Tarrant, the housekeeper at the Crown, who had always been so kind to her. Or Adela Adair, the restaurant pianist, who always hung around, sad-eyed and dejected like a hungry dog at a banquet, when other people were unwrapping presents? And if she included Adela Adair and Mrs. Tarrant, then what about MacAllister who was a rogue, of course, but would usually change shifts with her when she wanted to get away early? And Mr. Clarence?

It took longer than she had expected and hurrying down the *rue de la Paix* and across the *Place Vendôme* to the hotel she saw Benedict walking toward her. Nothing more extraordinary than that. Yet it stopped her in her tracks, her heart and her pulses leaping from sheer delight in him, and a great and wonderful surge of pride and pleasure.

She loved him.

She told him so.

"Thank you," he said. An odd reply. And then "So you'll do something for me, will you?" That was better.

"Yes." Whatever he wanted, no matter how immense, her answer, at that moment, would be yes.

"Well — since you're in a shopping mood — I want to buy you something. Something expensive and very extravagant. Will you accept it?"

"Oh no," she said, ridiculously disappointed. "Why should you want to?"

"Because it would please me. Don't you want to please me?"

How could she deny that?

"Then listen. A woman can express her feelings by giving her body. It's what the world sees as her greatest asset, after all. A predatory male can hardly do that. So, when he wants to make a gesture of affection, he can only give *his* greatest asset. Money, if he has any. Preferably money he's worked for. Earned with the sweat of his brow if possible. That makes the gesture particularly tender. And I'm not twenty-five anymore, you know, and short of cash."

Her throat, for just a moment, was too tight to speak and then, sounding gruff and uncertain, she said, "What do you want to buy?"

"Anything you like. With the *rue de la Paix* just there, behind us, it shouldn't be difficult."

They took a great deal of time in the choosing, for she knew it was something she would treasure for the rest of her life and he stipulated only that she must be able to wear it openly and often; something, in fact — although he did not say this — which she could explain to her mother and to Miriam. A ring, therefore, of the value he insisted upon, would have caused too much comment. Several of the necklaces and bracelets which pleased her were, on reflection, too elaborate for Faxby. Earrings she already had. In the end, without daring to convert the francs into pounds, she chose an oval ruby, her birthstone, on a gold chain sprinkled with diamonds like tiny stars.

A lovely thing.

"It suits you," he said, fastening it around her neck that night as she was dressing for dinner. "I'm just sorry I couldn't bring it to you in some spectacular manner — like walking through the snow. As you did."

She felt his hands tighten on her shoulders, sensed a corresponding tautness in his chest as he suddenly pulled her hard against him, holding her from behind so that she could not see his face.

"I can't forget that night, Claire. Have you any idea how terrible it was for me?"

"Darling — ?"

"I was forty and falling in love — It was like the onset of a disease I'd believed myself immune to. I didn't want it. God help me, I want it now."

"You have it. I love you, Benedict."

"Hush," he said, "In my better moments I know. In my better moments it's not what I want for you."

They had dinner in a silence which became tender and afterward, walking through the evening stillness of the *Tuileries* Gardens to the *Place de la Concorde* and the leafy beginnings of the *Champs Elysées*, she became aware of a feeling of shared sadness, a regret so gentle as to seem sweet and which settled around them like mist. It entered their bedroom that night, hovering over the luggage already packed and labelled "Mannheim Crescent," "High Meadows." It sat, visible as a heavily veiled mourner, between them as they took that last, painfully cheerful breakfast before hurrying to the train. It seeped into the empty compartment and sat down before them, easily distinguishable from all the other mournful steams and vapors of the *Gare du Nord*. It accompanied them on board the channel steamer, wrapping itself around them like a sorrowful caress as they stood on deck, close together, in the sharp wind. It grew heavy, and thick, the mist becoming a fog through which they smiled at one another. And as the coast of France melted into the haze and the chalk cliffs of Dover gracefully emerged from a separate haze of their own, he took her hand and pressed his mouth very briefly against it.

"Are you saying goodbye to me, Benedict?"

"It would be sensible."

"Yes. Wouldn't it."

It seemed pointless to say more than that.

She was to go directly to Faxby. He was to stay the night in London. She thought it likely that he would then go down to Eastbourne to see Nola. She had no reason and no right to object. But when they reached the impersonal bustle of the city their plan to separate at once no longer suited him.

"I shall take you to King's Cross."

"There's no need."

"I didn't say that. I said I'd come with you and put you on the train."

"Benedict — the Faxby train. With the Leeds train on the next platform, I shouldn't wonder. Dozens of people could recognize you."

"Yes. They'll see me putting my sister-in-law on the train. What of it?"

"Just take me to the station then. Don't come on the platform."

But at King's Cross, having commandeered a porter and selected the first-class compartment into which he wished her luggage to be placed, they remained together, not saying a word, waiting with the dense melancholy of partings which may or may not be final, for the train to pull away, so that the slamming of the doors, the shrilling of the whistle, was both a relief and an agony. She had parted in this way from Paul. Only two years ago this station platform and every other had been taut with partings such as this, hands clasped tight through the carriage window, the silence vibrating and choking with the things one had left unsaid and which could hardly be called out now above the racket of the engine, the callous conversations of passers-by. Things which would sound small and foolish anyway to young men and women facing death.

It was not death this time. Unless it was the death of a future which had been forced as stillborn into the world as Nola's child.

"Are you going to Eastbourne now?" she said.

"Yes."

It was as if she had asked him if he was on his way to Passchendaele.

"I thought you would."

"Yes. She is my responsibility."

"And you're also quite fond of her. So am I."

He smiled and lifting her hand pressed it again to his cheek. "She would give up nothing for either one of us you know."

"I know."

"So — it seems we have turned out to be rather nicer than we thought."

The journey was over-familiar, very long, not particularly cold although, having begun to shiver, she found she could not stop; no more tedious than usual except that she came to believe it would never end. The last time she had traveled alone to Faxby on this train Edward had been there to meet her, peevish, unwilling, self-obsessed. Now there would be no one. Never mind. She would be better, tonight, on her own. Far better. And tomorrow she would go and make her peace at Upper Heaton, bearing gifts, telling lies, being pleasant to Edward for her mother's sake. She took a cab from the station, knowing she was lucky to get it, and let herself into the empty flat. Home. How ridiculous. She had better unpack, light the fire, read some of the letters which had been pushed under her door. All that seemed ridiculous too. Perhaps she should go over to the hotel and get drunk, which seemed marginally more appealing. But, instead, she lay down, not even taking off her shoes, and smoked a cigarette, utterly disconsolate, watching the evening draw in.

There was no need to be alone. But, nevertheless, she lay there for a long time accustoming herself to the fact that "alone" now meant to her the condition of being, not without company, but without Benedict. Once it had meant being without Paul. But Benedict was alive. Not far away. She had wanted to make him happy. She understood that she had not, could not. Of what use was it? None whatsoever.

She dreamed for three nights of his face as it had been at the station, taut, grim, gray as dark skin can appear under stress; just his face, disembodied at the train window, the train hurtling through blank darkness at perilous speed. Her own fear, for herself speeding down that aimless track and for him, outside in the cold. And the fourth night she dined at High Meadows, finding him there brisk and cool and sardonic as she had always known him, back from his unexplained journey about which no one had thought to question him.

"Shall I take you home, Claire?"

"Yes please."

"Early?"

"As early as you can."

The cold dream was over.

16

EVEN so, loving Benedict could not, and would never be easy, the difficulties lying not only with his closed, intensely separate nature but in a new and often fierce reaction of her own. She had once found it easy to accept his dual identity, to watch him playing his various roles at High Meadows without any particular pain or confusion in her own heart. But now, as the spring weeks tripped by, sparkling, insouciant, thinking only of their own brief, never-quite-to-be-repeated loveliness, she found it hard indeed to tolerate not only the deceit they were obliging themselves to practice, but the waste of their time, the draining away — to suit the convenience of Miriam and Eunice, the follies of Nola — of this precious substance which was their most certainly unrepeatable life.

What prevented her from leaping to her feet one stifling "family Sunday" and stating, loud and clear "I am in love with Benedict. Why should I sacrifice that love for any one of you? You don't deserve it. And since we shall all be dead in ten years, twenty years, even tomorrow, then none of you have the right to interfere"? Several times she dreamed that she had done exactly that, towering over them, six feet tall, eight feet tall, shooting upward like an underground torrent suddenly released from bondage, as they sat mute and astonished at their dinner table, until, rising as one body — Miriam and Dorothy leading them — they had smothered her with quilts and eiderdowns and soft, clinging blankets, pressing her down — "For your own good, dear. Because we need you. Because we love you. Because what will people say?" — into the earth again. A terrible dream from which only the fight for breath, the struggle to unclog her nostrils and her eyes from cold earth, the wholly primitive fear of burial alive, awoke her.

To begin with High Meadows had bored her. Now she hated it with a passion that was almost juvenile in its ferocity. If High Meadows should burn down, she would dance on its ashes. Yet, occasionally, and then rather more often, Benedict allowed her to see his desire that she should join him there.

The blue chintz room.

"We have one life," he said. "That is *your* philosophy, my dear. I was quite patiently and not unpleasantly getting through mine until you began to worry me about wasting time — about seizing what one can, while one can. And we are wasting a great deal of time, you know. The solution is in your hands."

"Benedict — I can't breathe at High Meadows."

"How unfortunate. I would like to look after you, Claire. Is that wrong?"

"What you mean is that you would like me to depend on you."

"Yes. That is just what I mean."

"To give up —"

She had intended to say "To give up my independence. My individuality. Many things." But he cut her short with an impatient exclamation, an irritable clicking of the tongue.

"To give up what? A menial job in a seedy hotel with a man who used —"

Perhaps he had been going to say "who used to clean my boots" but he had stopped himself in time. He was jealous and she saw how much it hurt and offended him, how resentfully he bore the pain, how contemptuous he truly was of this mean and savage feeling; far more contemptuous of himself for feeling it.

"I do love you, Benedict."

He passed a hand over his eyes and shuddered. "I know. Forgive me. And it comes easily to you, doesn't it?"

"I don't find it difficult."

"It even strengthens you, I think. How different we are."

They knew, and usually bore in mind, that fate had never intended them for one another. Yet Claire had still not managed to cross the limit of present joys and sorrows, the attitude of her generation that the future would be taken care of when, and if, it came. While Benedict, to whom the future had always been the subject of cool calculation, grew prone, for the first time in his life, to sudden and alarming swings of mood, becoming by fits and starts, intensely jealous, impossible to please and then, when the venom had coursed through him, just as impossibly charming, tolerant, urbane.

"Why do you put up with me, I wonder?"

"I wonder. Perhaps because, however bad you are — and you *are* bad sometimes, you know — it would be worse without you. Is that a good reason?"

"Hardly."

"Better than nothing though."

No. They were not made for each other. They had themselves chosen, contrary to the dictates of fate, or the natural order of things, to be together and not even Benedict himself was entirely on their side.

At the beginning of May — Miriam's lovely birthday month — Claire received a cool note from the matron of a hospital near Carlisle informing her of the sorry state of a Lieutenant Ash, who, when asked to reveal the identity of his next of kin, had eventually given her name. Could she, therefore, the matron wondered — wife, sister, cousin or *whatever* she happened to be — please communicate at once, since decisions both of a medical and personal nature ought not to be delayed and, one way or another, would have to be taken? Evidently Lieutenant Ash was proving something of a handful in Carlisle.

"I have to go to Carlisle," she told Benedict, dry-mouthed but lightly. And because he did not ask her why — being in a rational humor that day — she told him, making it clear, albeit calmly and sweetly, that whether he liked it or not, go she must.

"Of course," he said.

"I'll come with you," offered Kit and when she shook her head he shoved a fairly bulky envelope into her hand. "Well — he'll be short of money won't he. There'll be medical bills. And if there's any change buy him a decent overcoat or something. Don't tell him it came from me."

She found him in the bleak, cheerless ward of a charity hospital, wearing charity pajamas of coarse flannel several sizes too big; little of him left, as he lay in the narrow scratchy bed, but bones and the deep hollows they made in him, a six-foot skeleton with fine, flyaway hair and that fallen angel's smile.

"Here comes my darling Claire to the rescue. Didn't I tell you, matron — my sister would never let me down."

"Yes, Lieutenant Ash, you did tell me that — several times!" And the matron's sharp eye and small, pinched smile made no secret of how little family resemblance she could trace between the fair-skinned, fair-haired Lieutenant and this exceedingly dark-eyed brunette.

He had been very ill. The matron, in an initial interview which had made Claire feel as if she had not come so much to inquire about a patient but to apply for a job, had made that very clear. He had been conducting his life in a most peculiar manner, sitting all night in public houses, it seemed, drawing sketches of the taproom customers, to be paid in drinks, the good lady supposed, and sleeping in damp lodgings, taking no sensible, God-fearing precautions whatsoever. And in view of the existing condition of his lungs pneumonia had been no surprise.

"He was gassed in the war," said Claire.

"Quite," replied the matron who, being narrow in her views and near retirement, did not consider that an adequate excuse for sleeping rough or drinking alcohol. "He is lucky to be alive."

"Yes. He is."

But they were not thinking of the same reasons.

"And now, Mrs. — ah yes, Mrs. Swanfield, isn't it? — what is to be done with him? He is ready for discharge in the sense that we can do no more for him here. Yet it would suit neither my conscience nor the policy of this Foundation to turn him loose into the streets. Dear me no. Someone must take responsibility. And should you feel able to do so, Mrs. — Swanfield? — you and your husband? — then your — er, brother? — could be discharged today."

"In other words," chuckled Euan when Claire, sitting by his bedside, repeated the conversation, "Pack him up and take him away before he dies on us. The poor old girl was worried stiff that I might do just that and she wouldn't know what to do with me. Awkward for her, you see, if she'd shoveled me into a pauper's grave and I'd turned out to be a prince in disguise, or if she'd wasted hospital time and money keeping me on ice and I'd been a real pauper after all — since I claimed to be both. Big relief when I remembered my sister Claire. I expect she's given me to you, hasn't she, with both hands and not *too* many questions asked?"

"More or less. You look dreadful, Euan."

He grinned engagingly. "To tell the absolute truth I don't feel so good. Whitby was very cold all winter. Fun in parts, but bloody freezing. I did some lovely pictures of sea mists though and gulls and crabs and grains of sand. I think I almost got the texture of the wind on one particular canvas. I got quite excited about it. Pity I can't show you. My last landlord kept it in lieu of rent — I think."

"You didn't get to Edinburgh, then?"

"No." He smiled sweetly. "I got pneumonia instead — in Carlisle. Not a bad try, really. There's a direct train."

"Do you want to get on it?"

"Well — yes. But not right away. Pneumonia is a big event in a fellow's life you know. One has to give it some consideration. I rather thought I might go and consider it somewhere beautiful and quiet, like Ambleside or Grasmere."

"It rains a lot there."

"That doesn't bother me. Rain falling on still water. And have you any idea how many textures and shapes you can find in a puddle? It's another world."

"I expect so — especially when you're feverish and drunk."

"I expect so. What *are* you going to do with me then? I'm too deliciously weak to resist and wouldn't, in any case."

She had kept on his room in Mannheim Crescent to avoid sharing the kitchen with a new tenant and she took him back there, spending Kit's money on coal, blankets, a mattress they picked up cheap from a market trader, a store of wholesome food.

"I'll pay you back of course, like the gentleman I am —"

"Of course." She knew, as a gentleman, that he would find it easier to use what he believed to be her money, than Kit's.

"I can't say when — naturally. Next week if I can get myself fixed up again with a stall in the market and sell a picture or a few quids' worth of junk."

"All right, Euan."

"Well, you know how it is. But before I set off for Edinburgh again, at the latest. All right?"

"I said so. Just keep warm. And eat. Try not to drink."

"How is your brave Lieutenant?" inquired Benedict some little time later, his voice very neutral, his manner perfectly composed.

"Oh — as well as can be expected, I suppose."

"I'm glad to hear it. A young man of good family, I understand — and it would be a pity to lose any more of those."

"I don't know anything about him, Benedict," and she was speaking with great care. "Do you?"

"Oh yes." He smiled quietly, dryly, as she had seen him smile so often, so impersonally. "It has to be my business to know at least the essentials of any man who associates himself with any woman involved in the Swanfield Trust. No responsible trustee could do less."

"Benedict — you had him *investigated?*"

And although his smile remained dry, ironic, and she was doing her best to make light of it — to make fun — they both knew how deeply he had shocked her.

"Of course. Two young warriors, in fact, both together — Lieutenant Ash on your behalf and Roy Kington on Polly's. Regrettably Captain

Kington did not pass muster. One heard rumors of debts — and only rumors, since the people to whom he owed money seemed afraid to say so. I didn't like that. But the family of Bardsley Ash is very well established in Sussex."

"I'm not sure I want to know."

"Oh yes you do. His father is a high church cleric — very high."

"A bishop?"

"I thought you didn't want to know."

"Well — you've just proved yourself right again haven't you — as always."

He smiled, a shade less dryly.

"Yes. A bishop. A younger son of the nobility making what sounds like a noble living in the church — although he's quite an old man now, rather older than you'd suppose. I expect aspiring clergymen don't have to marry young."

"And does his mother ride to hounds?"

"Very likely. Her family tree bristles with masters of foxhounds, at any rate. So Euan Ash is extremely well-born and well-connected. And, furthermore, owing to the death in battle of four, or is it five, of his cousins, he's also heir to his uncle's baronetcy. So he'll be Sir Euan one day — if he lives long enough."

He paused, giving her time to ponder about the future baronet she had just rescued from a charity hospital, possibly from a pauper's grave: although nothing he had said surprised her.

"Poor Euan. I'm sure he can't want to be a baronet."

"He has no choice. One can't refuse a title. So — your lodging-house duckling has turned out to be something of an aristocratic swan. Just think of the pleasure it would give your mother, in Upper Heaton, to talk about her daughter, Lady Ash. Only think how pleased Edward would be then."

She swallowed. "I wish you wouldn't say these things."

He shook his head, looking taut and grim as he had done that day by the train; looking gray. "You will marry somebody, Claire — someday. I prefer to keep reminding myself of that. It is unlikely to be me, after all, and so I think it wise, at the very least, to be ready. Don't you?"

Unless, of course, she would accept the compromise of the blue chintz room. If she loved him as deeply and courageously and generously as she said she did, then surely she would bring herself to do that? Sometimes he certainly thought so. Sometimes she almost thought so herself.

Waking abruptly in the night, startled by the force which had propelled her straight from deep sleep to a state of acute consciousness, she knew how much he needed her. And to be needed was the grace note of her nature, the source of her most profound fulfillment. She wanted to be needed. She always had. Perhaps High Meadows needed her too. And it was then, as she turned to a shallow, secondary slumber, that she first dreamed of suffocation beneath soft, high-quality blankets, of earth covering her living face.

Nola remained in Eastbourne until the end of April, her return causing a surface ripple of minor inconvenience since in her telegram asking to be met in Leeds she had neglected to give the exact time of her train and then, when she finally did appear, had mislaid several small items of luggage, some of it being discovered in the restaurant car, some of it — the very things she needed most — having gone on to Manchester with Nanette.

"I'm sorry. I'm sorry," she kept saying.

"There's no need to be sorry," Benedict kept on answering.

"I do apologize."

"It really doesn't matter."

And so it went on, through the station to the car, all the way from Leeds to Faxby, Nola asking forgiveness for the loss of her dressing-case, her umbrella, her hatbox, Benedict politely requesting her not to worry, assuring her that only a minimum of inconvenience had been caused. It was only a year since Claire had first met Nola. Yet now she looked ten years older, smaller, oddly and tragically *unremarkable*; the plain, uncoordinated, uncertain woman she really was, had always been, beneath the dashing fox furs, the sequined turbans and trailing chiffon, the bold, careless swagger. For so many years she had stalked around High Meadows like a scornful, half-broken thoroughbred contemptuous of her captors, had used the house as a stage, making grand, eccentric entrances and exits through its doors, revelling in the consternation she aroused. She came in quietly now, not wishing — for the first time in her life — to make a fuss, her flamboyance all gone so that even the feather in her hat appeared to be wilting, her sage green coat with its massive apricot mink collar to have grown dowdy, somehow, and a size too big for her, as Eunice's coats always did.

"My dear, how *well* you look," cooed Miriam, quite delighted to see she didn't.

"I've been using your car," said Polly. "Well — it was just standing there. I suppose you *do* want it back again?"

"Lucky about your ring," said Eunice, who had already written Nola two long letters about her emerald which had been discovered in the bathroom by Justin shortly after she had left for Eastbourne, "What a good thing Justin has such sharp eyes." It was clear that Eunice, having got over her relief that Justin had not kept the ring and made some shameful, certain-to-be-detected attempt to sell it, now expected Nola to give him a reward.

Nola smiled politely, went upstairs, lay down in her armchair, her body still fluid in fatigue, and lit a cigarette, her fingers nervous and yellow with nicotine, her nails jagged at their edges and none too clean.

"What is he going to do with me now?" she asked Claire.

"Oh — I think — nothing — nothing terrible I mean."

"Why?" She was speaking through clenched teeth. "Dear God — *why?*"

"Because — I suppose — haven't you been punished enough? I expect he thinks so."

"But he hasn't *said?*"

"No. But then he doesn't say — does he?"

Where Nola was concerned it was true. He had said nothing to Claire. He had said nothing to Nola either. Visiting her in Eastbourne he had talked about the hotel, the quality of the food and service, the pleasant view of the sea, the number of small dogs one saw strolling about the town. On the way from the station they had talked about her hatbox and her umbrella. At dinner that night they listened to Miriam's enthusiasm for the forthcoming civic banquet, Elvira Redfearn's inaugural function as Mayoress, which they must all attend; to Polly's intense and detailed dissertation on what she should wear; to Eunice's equally rapid response, her eyes on Benedict, that *she* certainly could not afford a new evening dress.

"Polly," said Benedict as the meal ended, "would you come into the study please." And the rest of the evening was absorbed by Polly's fluctuations from hysteria to sulky defiance and back to wild tears again as he laid before her his objections to Roy Kington, warning her bluntly that if she succeeded in marrying him — which seemed blessedly unlikely — he would not release a penny of her capital.

"You have ruined my life," she shrieked at him.

"He has ruined my life," she shrieked even louder, running into the drawing room where, standing in the very center of the floor, she began to sob like a very small girl. "Mother — *tell* him. Father wouldn't have let him do this to me."

"Oh dear," said Miriam.

"Father would turn over in his grave," said Eunice bitterly, for once in full agreement with her sister, "if he knew the half of it."

"Steady on," murmured Toby, who, having steeled himself for days to make an appointment with Benedict to discuss his salary, was now most anxious that no one — particularly Eunice — should put him in a bad humor.

"Your father," said Miriam hastily, still sweetly, "did the best he could for you."

Once, a month ago, an age ago, Nola would have lowered her glistening eyelids and murmured, "Don't you mean, dear Miriam, that he did his best for *you?*"

Now she got up and went to her room, unnoticed, unquestioned, and lay once again in her armchair where, since it seemed pointless to do otherwise, she spent the night.

There was to be no retribution, no restrictions, no conditions, it seemed, of any kind. *What* was there to be? The same as before. He had set no limits around her. No one had. Benedict, she understood now, had never limited her, never controlled her, never attempted to impose his will upon her at all. It had been — like so much else — an illusion. She had assumed herself to be his captive, imagined it, *needed* it, and now how solitary, how very frightening it was to realize she had always been free. It meant — what? That now she had no one but herself to blame? That she could no longer hide behind that stock figure of comedy, the heavy husband — for what else had her life been but a farce? — and say "He made me as I am. I had no choice — no chance."

Now the terrible specter of choice loomed ahead of her — choice and freedom — and she had no equipment to cope with either. Her father had taught her obedience. Her mother had shown her how to get around it by stealth. Marriage had clamped her awkwardly but firmly — or so she had believed — into a mold which at least she understood, setting recognized boundaries to her behavior, limiting her opportunities, but giving her something tangible, something solid to fight against. But she had imagined that too. She had known how to be a captive and a rebel. Now she could do as she pleased. And she was terrified.

"I think," Claire told Benedict, speaking almost gingerly since it afforded her considerable embarrassment to talk to him about Nola, "in fact I *know* she would like you to punish her — quite violently even."

"I dare say. Unfortunately it is quite beyond me. You must know that."

"Yes."

"Well — what can I do? If she needs my forgiveness then — good God Claire, there is nothing to forgive. And who am I to judge, in any case. Can you find a way to tell her that?"

She tried, knowing that if Benedict made the attempt himself, it would sound in no way forgiving but uncaring, harsh, dismissive. "Pull yourself together. Don't trouble me."

But Nola was not seeking pardon.

Nor punishment — or not precisely. An answer then? Although, in her anguished prowlings around High Meadows, she did not even know what questions to ask. She had been caught in adultery and no one had cast a stone. She had aborted a child and instead of being confined to a prison or packed off in disgrace to whatever might pass these days for a nunnery, she had been taken to a comfortable Eastbourne hotel. And although she *knew* she had taken the only course she had believed open to her, *knew*, moreover, with a flash of self-knowledge, that she would do the same again, she *felt* that she had committed a crime. She had done an evil thing. Why, instead of talking of hatboxes and civic functions and the poor state of trade in Faxby, would someone not look her in the eye and admit that?

"How well you look, dear," Miriam told her absently every morning. She felt — *unreal*. Who was she? She had never known. Did anyone? She reclaimed her car from Polly, drove into town and spent a disconsolate hour in the lounge bar of the Crown, filling herself with alcohol to combat a sudden delusion that she had become invisible. She was transparent. Hollow. For one, brief moment of panic she believed that she had no real, living substance whatsoever.

"If it isn't my darling Nola," Kit Hardie called out to her through the open doors. Had he really seen her?

"You're looking blooming, Nola." No. He had not.

She went out into the street, feeling nebulous, vaporous, found her car, started the engine and drove aimlessly for a while, round and round. Where was she going? What a terrible question. Once it would have been to Leeds — quick! No time to lose! — to do all the busy things so vital to the nurturing of artistic genius. Once it would have been to Kit. Before that — how many others? And what she remembered most was how dull or how tawdry, how commonplace each *affaire* had seemed the moment it was over. Turning abruptly into a side street and coming to a halt not a moment too soon before a high, soot-blackened wall, it came to her, like the tolling of a mourning bell, that she had lost not only her nerve but her taste for lovers. She dare not involve herself with another man. Far worse than that — she did not want to.

What she sought now was something else — something tremendous. God perhaps? Or perhaps not. Yet no possibility ought to be neglected and Faxby, no matter how sparse in culture or social refinements, abounded in religion, the Church of England in all its aspects, high and low, broad and narrow; Methodism of both the Wesleyan and the Primitive variety; Baptists, Christadelphians, Unitarians, Episcopalians, Congregationalists, Presbyterians, Quakers, the supple Church of Rome, an ebullient Salvation Army Citadel, a small, discreet, but well attended Synagogue, a Spiritualist. Nola, in the first fortnight after her return to High Mead-

ows, visited each minister in turn, explained her crime and asked forgiveness which, in her view, was far too hastily granted. Go home and
sin no more. It was far less simple than that. She did not want to go
home. She never had. What astonished her now, was that she did not
want to sin either, a problem which caused some embarrassment to the
less experienced of the reverend gentlemen when, with alcohol on her
breath and nicotine stains on her hands, she tried to explain how deeply
this troubled her. She had always been a sinner. It matched the furs and
lipstick and the clever remarks. Now that she had nothing to hide, no
desperate lies to tell, no tracks to cover, no glorious, ridiculous dreams,
what was left of her?

"I do hope," said Miriam, "that she will manage to cheer herself up
in time for my birthday."

There seemed little chance of it. She took to staring again, intently,
critically, in excruciating, almost accusing silence at anyone and everyone, alarming Eunice, unnerving Polly who absolutely could not stand
it, embarrassing her sons when they came home for the Easter holidays,
her eyes unblinking, penetrating sometimes and a little glazed at others,
invariably so odd that Miriam felt obliged to whisper to Mrs. Timms, in
the sure knowledge that she would whisper it to everyone else, that she
put it all down to Nola's "time of life" and one had had ample experience
in Faxby of the peculiarities of menopausal women.

But, rather worse than that, she began to speak the truth.

"That young man won't marry you, Polly. You'd do well to settle for
Roger Timms while you can still get him."

"Why don't you make a bolt for it, Toby."

"Miriam, I believe you are getting old."

But Miriam who, in her youth, had been *very* young was now graciously and serenely ready to be old. And, moreover, without any advice
from Nola, she had made up her own mind about Roger Timms. Both
she and Polly had used him as a convenience long enough. He had done
well and now, in her favorite role of Good Fairy, Miriam had fixed upon
her birthday as an appropriate time to give him his reward. To tell the
absolute truth — and Miriam never told that kind of truth to anyone
but herself — she was growing out of patience with Polly, tired *by* her
and tired *of* her to such an extent that marriage to amiable, tedious Roger
seemed the only answer.

And so, most adroitly, she began to lay her plans.

She made it clear to Mrs. Templeton, for instance, over a slice of
simnel cake and a cup of Earl Grey tea, that although Polly very likely
did have more money than Mrs. Templeton's Sally, it was so regrettably
tied up in the business and the whim of her brother Benedict that one

might almost say the poor dear child had nothing to call her own but her pin money and a natural — oh yes — a positively frantic extravagance. It was, therefore, *rather* necessary for Polly to choose a husband with money of his own, unless, of course, she wished to be wildly romantic, love in a cottage and all that which — well — one knew only too well that when poverty came in at the cottage door how quickly love tended to fly clean away through the window.

Would Mrs. Templeton, surrounded as she was by her four daughters and her two spinster sisters, a woman badly in need of at least one man in the family, repeat the gist of all that to Roy Kington? Miriam certainly thought so. And to make absolutely certain or, being certain already, perhaps only to see the matter through, Roy Kington was invited to dinner the following Sunday when, quite predictably, Benedict stared coldly through him; Eunice, just as predictably, voiced her loud and incautious grievance on the subject of Toby's salary; while Miriam, at her fragile, fluttery best, leaned rather heavily on the young man's arm, making him sit beside her in the drawing room and showing him, with appropriate reminiscences, her photograph albums of Polly and Jeremy.

He was not particularly patient about it but Miriam, telling her happy little tales of life at High Meadows with all its quaint traditions in which *everyone* was expected to take part, appeared to notice nothing amiss.

"Really?" said the lithe, whipcord young warrior, bored to distraction and showing it.

"Oh yes. Unity is strength, isn't that it? My husband always said it was. He did so love us to be united, and he made his little arrangements, of course, to keep us together — *afterward*, I mean. So thoughtful."

And when Benedict appeared for a moment in the doorway and said "Toby — spare me a minute, there's a good chap," Miriam gave a start of unconcealed distress and, well aware that Benedict, who was taking Claire home — *how kind!* — merely wanted Toby to move his car, she put a hand on Roy Kington's arm and murmured "Poor Toby — in disgrace again, I suppose. Oh dear — and coming so soon after that fearful row about his salary. Eunice was so upset. But if I have told her once I have told her a hundred times — when Benedict says 'No' then his word — of course — is final. Absolute. Case closed. Oh dear — do forgive me for running on. It must be because you already seem like one of us. Tell me dear boy, what is it that you do? Remind me. Ah yes — you are selling cars at present, are you? What fun. Although I really must implore you not to sell one to Toby. It would make Benedict so cross. I wonder, although it is probably a little too early to tell — how have *you* been getting on with Benedict?"

Badly of course. She had known she could rely on that. And with Toby?

"He wanted to be a pilot," she said shrewdly, quite wickedly, having picked up the information somewhere or other that flying — along with several other pursuits equally chancy — was one of Roy Kington's ruling passions, "but of course any such dangerous sport must be out of the question. Eunice's nerves could never stand the strain and Benedict would never sanction the expense. My girls are very much alike — Eunice and Polly — have you ever noticed?"

She saw, with satisfaction, that he was noticing now. And having thus discouraged Roy Kington the next step must be a tête-à-tête with Roger's mother, Mrs. Timms.

"Clever women like ourselves, Edith my dear, have always managed to arrange things to our liking — haven't we?"

Edith Timms was, in fact, a clever woman. Her husband was a clever man. Just how it was that Roger, their only child, had turned out such a dunce, likable, of course, and well-meaning, but *slow*, remained a mystery and a sorrow to them both. Yet it had to be faced. Roger was *not* clever. Good-natured, certainly, and generous and his mother loved him — although she rather suspected that her husband did not. Yet Mrs. Timms had once been Miss Edith Taylor, daughter of the senior partner of Taylor & Timms department store and the thought of everything her father and her husband's father had worked for being placed in the hands of her son, Roger, often caused her to tremble. The thought of Roger in the hands of some scatterbrained young hussy did not greatly please her either. And she had, therefore, extended only a cool welcome to Polly, being altogether immune — unlike her son and, rather regrettably, her husband — to the girl's glorious golden looks.

"Old Mrs. Timms doesn't like me," sang Polly whenever the subject of her engagement to Roger was mentioned.

It was a state of affairs Miriam had now set herself to put right, by explaining to a fascinated Mrs. Timms in precise, easily assimilated detail not only the full extent of Benedict's control over Polly but the promise he had made his father to retain that control for as long as was needful: for ever, more than likely, in the case of her pretty, extravagant, lovable Polly. And it did not take Mrs. Timms long to realize that in matters of finance and disciplined spending, the handling of investments and allowances, the future good management of Taylor & Timms, one could rely absolutely on Benedict.

She went home to discuss the matter with her husband who, in addition to his partiality for long-legged blondes, had the fate of his family business very much at heart and suddenly the cry "Old Mrs. Timms doesn't like me" no longer applied. Suddenly, in fact, no day was complete for Mrs. Timms unless she had spent part of it pampering and praising her Polly.

"What a lovely dress. How graceful you are, dear. What natural style. Just come into the Millinery Department and try on the new hats. Oh dear — I thought as much — I think you'd better keep that one. It will never look the same on anyone else."

To begin with, accustomed to coldly raised eyebrows and a pinched smile whenever Mrs. Timms came across her in the store, Polly was startled, puzzled rather than pleased. But Edith Timms knew very well how to indulge the young — after all, she had always indulged her Roger to what some thought a fond but foolish degree — and her wily expertise, assisted by Polly's almost puppyish desire for affection, soon won the girl over.

She was invited to dinner where the entire Timms family, mother, father and son, looked at her, listened to her — a pleasant change from High Meadows — which made her feel witty, sophisticated and smart. And although she was accustomed to feeling clever with Roger, his parents, suave, dapper Mr. Timms and Edith Timms with her quiet, sharp-eyed elegance, were another matter. She was invited to stay the night — a considerable step forward in the game of matrimonial noughts and crosses — and positively encouraged to linger as long as she liked in bed, to eat chocolates from large Taylor & Timms' boxes all day if she pleased, to browse at her leisure through catalogues of next season's furs and evening dresses of which, it was discreetly implied, she had only to make her choice.

"I do believe," said Edith, "that your fingers as as small as mine. Or perhaps not? I know — let's see if they can fit my rings." And, for a heady afternoon, Polly decked herself in the jewels which had been collected by Edith's mother and mother-in-law, two of Faxby's greatest ladies, and by Edith herself, a treasure chest, a glittering enchantment which entirely dazzled Polly's never particularly clear vision and took her breath away.

Edith, of course, did not give her even the least valuable of the stones, nor the least considerable of the gold chains and bracelets, of which there was a goodly number. But it was nevertheless understood that as she had inherited them through the family, so too could they be Polly's.

"They make you look like a queen, dear." Edith Timms was making her feel like a queen and it was that, far more than the promise of chocolates for breakfast and furs and jewels, which inclined Polly to look again at Roger. Not that he was ever very much in evidence during the afternoons she had begun to spend with his mother.

"Run along, Roger. There's a good chap." And when, in his amiable, shambling fashion he had gone away, Edith would murmur, not with Miriam's sugary sweetness, but pointedly, woman to woman, "So biddable our Roger. Brought up to do as he's told and positively enjoys it, Polly dear. Pity one can't say the same for his papa."

No one had ever been so kind to Polly. No one had ever approved of her so warmly, nor shown so marked an inclination to treat her not as a featherbrained child but as a woman. No one had ever asked for her opinion before and then actually listened to it. And it seemed wonderful to her that the person who had finally taken her seriously had turned out to be Roger's mother of whom, until recently, she had been rather afraid. But she was afraid no more. Quite the contrary. She had found — incredible as it still seemed to her — a knowledgeable entertaining friend. How very pleasant life could be here in this cozy, easymannered house, with Edith Timms. And she began to forget, or perhaps simply no longer to pay attention, to the part Roger Timms must unavoidably play.

"Do you think your mother could spare you to me for a few days? After her birthday, needless to say. I have rather a fancy to take you to London. Oh yes — just the two of us. We can manage very well without our menfolk in Harrods and Selfridges and Fortnum and Mason. Would you like it?"

"Oh yes please — yes I would."

How perfect, or at least how perfect it might be, could be, if only she could fall in love with Roger. If only he wouldn't try to kiss her so often. If only he wouldn't tremble so much and look so red and heavy and awkward. If she married him she'd have to come to terms with that, every night. No doubt she'd get used to it. Her mother said so and Edith had hinted at it. She'd learn to put up with it as they had done — as women generally did — which was all very well until she remembered the lean, steel-hard beauty of Roy Kington and the sensations it aroused in an as yet entirely unexplored part of her abdomen.

She believed she *had* fallen in love with him.

"Prove it," he told her. "Words are cheap. I need more than that."

"*Much* more?" She knew what his answer would be and she was dreading it.

"A hell of a lot more, darling. Your brother doesn't like me. Your mother treats me like a fool. So give me something to prove you're not making a fool of me as well."

"Oh Roy — if we were just engaged?"

"Oh Polly — we won't be engaged, not ever, unless you do."

"*Why!*" She sounded desperate.

"Because I don't want to risk waking up one morning married to a cold woman, that's why."

"I'm not."

"Prove it, Polly."

There had been a supper party at High Meadows, a little treat for Polly, Miriam had called it, to which she might invite all her friends. And although she had scattered invitations like raindrops in the cocktail bar at the Crown it had, nevertheless, surprised Polly how many of those "friends" had turned out to be smart, up-to-the-minute, unfamiliar girls who — although this had not surprised her at all — had hung on Roy Kington's every word when, with a glass of what she feared to be Benedict's best brandy in his hand, he had talked rather more than she actually liked about the excitements he had known and clearly missed in wartime France. Where had these girls come from? She couldn't imagine. Nor, since she was neither particularly observant nor particularly deceitful herself — not bright enough to be devious, thought Miriam — had she noticed how often, on Miriam's instructions, Roy's glass had been filled so that now, as they stood face to face in the garden by the dark of the rhododendron hedge he was quite drunk in the manner of trench soldiers — as Euan Ash was often drunk — without showing it, or at least not to a girl with so little real experience as Polly.

"Well, Polly, what's it to be? Are you going to prove it? Or not? In which case — You know what I mean."

She knew. Sally Templeton who was so cheerful and good-natured and would do anything to get a husband. Supposing she *did* get him — this way. Supposing this was all it took? What a fool Polly would feel then? And if not Sally, then how many of those smart, modern girls who had suddenly invaded High Meadows could be trusted to turn him away?

"Well Polly?"

The teasing glow faded from her abdomen as she hung her head.

"All right."

"You'd better mean it. Don't lead me on."

"I do. But where?" He made a sudden lunge at her, taking her like an adversary, seeing no reason, after all these weeks of blowing hot and cold, to waste more time.

"Good Lord, not here — for Heaven's sake." Gasping for air between his kisses she was horrified.

"Come to my car then."

322

"*Roy!* It's parked on the drive. They'd see us from the windows."

"Where then? Is that a summerhouse down there?"

"Oh — *that.* It's filthy."

"Listen," he was out of breath, pugnacious, "are you backing out? You said you would. I won't ask again. I'm a man, Polly — not a kid like brother Rex or a simpleton like Roger."

"Oh yes I know. And I will — I want to . . ."

She had never wanted anything so little in her life.

"That's my girl — and you'll be my girl, you know, afterward. You'll like it, Polly."

She doubted that.

"I'm sure I shall. But we can't manage it here — can we?"

"Anywhere, Polly."

He leaned her back into the rhododendron hedge, the thick, old branches giving way just sufficiently to support her body half reclining, and leaning over her — knowing he had no time to lose — began to uncover her shoulders and slide her skirt up until it was waist high and he had bared her breasts.

"Isn't this fun, Polly?"

It was terrible, humiliating, something — a twig she supposed — was sticking into her back. She felt intolerably exposed, ridiculous, horribly upset. And what, at the end of it, if she had a baby?

"Yes. It's lovely," she said.

"Then do something about it, Polly. Answer me."

Whatever could he mean? All she really knew of lovemaking, from the mutterings of Eunice and her mother, was that women lay on their backs in bed in the dark and endured it. Like childbirth! Dear God!

"Touch me, Polly."

He had shrugged off his jacket and his shirt and although she would really have preferred to use her hands to cover her eyes she put them hesitantly on his bare skin, palms flat down and then stroking a little.

"That's nice."

"You do love me, Roy, don't you."

"Yes — I'm just going to show you, aren't I."

Suddenly she felt something strange against her leg — oh God, she *knew* what it was and at the same time could not imagine it, was just thankful, unutterably thankful, that she couldn't see it, couldn't be expected to look.

"Roy —" And she was pleading, imploring him.

"You'll be all right, old girl. Won't hurt a bit — not much at any rate — so they say —"

"No — please don't."

"They say that too."

Sliding a hard, cold hand between her knees he began to force them apart. That had happened before, with him, with others, but only her body had been uncovered, never his, never theirs; there had been no raw and crude exposure to this implement of procreation, this — the only name she knew for it had been learned in the nursery. And she had been too young to share that nursery with her brothers.

Now she was sick with terror, trembling from head to foot, caught in a double trap since she could neither go through with this nor bear to lose him.

"Darling." She flung her arms around his neck, kissing him wildly and talking very fast. "Not here, not here, no, it's too special to waste like this. Let's do it properly the first time . . ."

He swore at her viciously but she ignored it — she had not understood the words in any case — and rushed on. "I know what we can do — yes, yes I know. Tomorrow, at my mother's birthday party, when the house will be full to bursting, we can get into my bedroom — yes we can — easily — and nobody will know. Oh darling — just think of it . . ."

He swore at her again and still she went on talking, kissing him.

"But I want to give myself to you properly, Roy, don't you see that — in my cozy bed, absolutely without anything on — the two of us — and the door locked and the bottle of champagne hidden in my wardrobe for afterward . . ."

"Now," he said.

"Tomorrow," she told him, meaning it desperately, sincerely, genuinely believing that tomorrow it would be all right. He could do anything he liked with her tomorrow. Anything. She told him so. He told her graphically — his temper rising partly from natural peevishness, partly from a physical distress she did not understand — exactly what he intended to do with her now. She panicked; pushed him away.

"That's the end of it," he told her.

"No," she said, "tomorrow. I promise. Cross my heart I do."

"All right. I'll come to your mother's party for that and if I don't get it you'll never see me again."

She was in a fever the next morning.

"A great day for it," said Miriam archly. "Who knows what it might bring?"

It brought Claire, coming early, in a garden party dress of black georgette patterned with pink tea roses, bringing her small traveling bag since she was to stay the night.

"Give me a kiss, dear," said Miriam. "Your dear little blue room is ready. It pleases me so much to think of you making your nest — if only a weekend nest — there, especially now that I have a feeling Polly is about to fly away."

It brought Eunice in last year's blue silk dress and old cream straw hat and a new blue ribbon, her boys each one in a brand-new bespoke suit, handmade shoes, spotless linen, carrying their beautifully wrapped "presents for Grandmamma." It brought Edward Lyall, still suffering on this bright May afternoon from his winter cold, and Dorothy suffering with him, his medicines and nasal sprays and handkerchiefs taking so much space in her handbag that she had had to leave her own "essentials" behind. It brought Benedict for perhaps ten minutes and then, after an hour or so, for a brief appearance of ten more. It did not — although no one appeared to notice it — bring Nola. It brought Redfearns and Greenwoods, Templetons, that whole bevy of girls from the Crown — "My goodness, Polly, you *said* they were your friends!" — the Swanfield doctors and lawyers and bankers, Edith and Roger Timms. It brought Roy Kington and, on his arm, a sultry, willowy brunette Polly had never seen before but whom she recognized instantly as "a tart."

"Hello Pol — this is Natasha. I'd say we met in Russia at the Bolshoi Ballet if I thought you'd believe me but, failing that, I suppose the City Varieties will do."

How could he bring a girl of this type to her mother's house? How could he hurt her so deliberately?

"It's no worse than what you did to me last night," he hissed in her ear as Natasha, for just a moment, was called away. "You castrated me. Now I'm doing the same to you."

She didn't know what he meant. Only that she was losing him and she couldn't bear it.

"I promised you — today."

"I don't trust you."

"Give me another chance."

He hesitated, made her wait. It seemed a long time.

"All right. Only one." She told him how to find her bedroom and at what time.

"Be there, Polly."

"Yes — I will." She was feverish again.

"Polly, come and join the treasure hunt." Toby's voice was familiar and kind, so kind, so fond of her — calling her a "good girl," his "princess" — that she swallowed hard and turned away.

"Polly, you're not eating. Are you ill?" Claire sounded friendly, amused. Perhaps Claire would understand. But before she could blurt out anything of significance, ask her, tell her, beg advice, Miriam had intervened.

"Polly do go and talk to those two dear old ladies over there — I forget their names. Nobody has been near them for ages. Claire is to help me with the treasure hunt parcels. Come dear."

"Polly." What now? "Have you seen Roy?" It was Sally Templeton. Poor girl. How desperate she must be.

"No, I haven't seen him."

"Polly." It was Edith Timms. "I do believe you're neglecting me." She could never wish to do that. But Roger was with his mother, looking good-natured as he always did, and plain, and Edith would be sure to notice the flush in her cheeks.

"I'm just on an errand for mother," she called out and ran into the house and across the hall.

"Dear God," said Benedict. "Is there to be no privacy today?" Dear God indeed. What was Benedict doing here? But after a moment of pure unease when he *might* have been making up his mind to question her, he suddenly lost interest and walked away.

Only the stairs remained, and the bedroom corridor. No one saw her. And then, reaching her door, she halted, stood awkwardly for a moment hanging about the passage like a stranger and then made a dash for the bathroom. But it had to be done. She had made up her mind to it. The only question to be answered was whether or not she loved him. She did. And if he required this kind of proof then yes — it was un- derstandable, natural, modern. He had been a soldier, after all, was still a soldier-of-fortune at heart, and if she wanted to be a soldier's wife she would have to be more daring, broaden her outlook a little. It was not as if she doubted his intention to marry her afterward. It had not occurred to her even to question that. It was just — just — ? Yes. She would have preferred it to be truly afterward — after that lavish white satin wedding — rather than before. She wanted to float down the aisle to him like an angel, bringing him the gift of her purity, as her mother had taught her, not already deflowered and damaged — why did she persist in thinking of it like that? — as he wanted. But then — if he wanted it. And she knew full well that her mother was not only old-fashioned but dishonest. How could she trust Miriam's judgment? She knew, vi- olently, that she could not. Could she even judge her mother's motives or understand them? No. And only look at what Miriam's values had done to Eunice and to Nola. Such a fate was not to be hers. She was a "new" woman, a modern woman. Like Claire, perhaps. Would Claire do this? Would Sally Templeton? Yes — of Sally at least she was cer- tain — and that settled it.

She closed the bathroom door behind her and walked slowly down the corridor, going to the man she loved as if to the scaffold. And she was feverish again. Oh Lord — there was her hand turning the door handle. She saw it. In half an hour — did it take so long? — she would be a different person. For better or for worse — but that was the wedding ceremony. What was this? At least nothing would ever be quite the same again.

She pushed open the door, fixing her smile in case he had arrived before her, and saw him, lean and hard and beautiful, stretched out on her bed with a girl who could have been anyone — her eyes refused to tell her — but was probably the sultry, unknown Natasha. "Hello Polly — where's the champagne?"

She ran. She could think of nothing else to do. There was no feeling, no tears. Nothing. Not yet. She ran downstairs, across the hall, outside, her eyes focusing at last on something which turned out to be the amiable, awkward bulk of Roger Timms.

"Polly — I was looking for you. Benedict told me you'd gone up-stairs."

He looked plain and safe. She needed that.

"I don't feel well, Roger."

"Here — steady on."

He put his arms around her and she collapsed against his chest, an embrace which looked sufficiently amorous for his mother and hers, both spotting it together, to converge upon them, laughing coyly, a little excitedly as women do at the distant tinkle of wedding bells.

"Roger, dear boy, is this seemly?" inquired Mrs. Timms.

"Polly, dear — such a public show of affection. Or are you simply hiding your blushes?" cooed Miriam.

"Could it be," Roger's mother wanted to know, "that they have something to tell us. I do hope, my son, that your intentions are honorable."

"Come on, mother," muttered Roger, turning a hot scarlet, "you know I want to marry Polly."

"And does Polly want to marry you?"

"Of course she does," said Miriam.

Polly did not deny it.

"Congratulations," bawled Eunice who had been told by her mother exactly what to do.

"A wedding — a wedding," chanted Sally Templeton's spinster aunts, having grown accustomed to the fact that it was never Sally's.

"May I be one of the first to kiss the bride?" beamed Edward Lyall who had also been warned by Miriam to keep his eyes open.

"Marriage is regarded as a sexual refuge by most men," said Nola who had just arrived, very obviously quoting from a book, "whereas it irrevocably diminishes most women. I read that somewhere, just the other day."

"I didn't think she'd go quite so far as that," said Roy Kington who had heard the commotion from Polly's window.

"Be happy, Polly," said Toby who was looking pale and far from happy himself.

"A September wedding," called out Miriam clapping her hands as ecstatically as if she were herself to be the bride. "How does that suit you, Polly? Can you wait so long?"

Polly made no reply.

"I won't stay the night," said Claire. "In fact I don't think I'll stay much longer."

"No," said Benedict. "I understand. Shall I take you back now?"

17

THE engagement was duly announced through the proper channels, The Faxby Echo, The Yorkshire Post, The Times; a special journey was made to purchase a large diamond ring in Leeds. What the happy couple needed now was the sanction of an engagement party and Polly's, somewhat surprisingly, was to be held at the Crown, a concession, Miriam called it, to her daughter's modern notions although the truth was that she no longer cared — now that they had served her purpose — to fill High Meadows with her daughter's modern friends.

Miriam had begun to value not her privacy since she still did not like to be lonely but her tranquillity, the unblemished pile on her probably irreplaceable carpets, the delicacy of her Waterford crystal and her nerves. Therefore, since they thought it smart and modern, Polly's rowdy friends with their outrageously exposed knees and their terrible haircuts, their negro dances and their fatal-to-upholstery cigarettes might just as well make their noise and do their damage at the Crown.

"Certainly madam — with the greatest of pleasure," Kit Hardie had told her on the telephone, even putting himself to the trouble — which he would have done for no one else and slightly despised himself for doing now — of going to High Meadows for her instructions. An intimate dinner for twenty-five, no, perhaps to be on the safe side one had better say thirty. And then afterward dancing for the "dear young things" and somewhere just to sit and chat, rather comfortably of course, for those who were merely young at heart. A colorful summer menu, lots of strawberries and pyramids of cream whipped up with white wine — you know, Hardie dear, like we used to do in the old days — or a strawberry trifle perhaps with macaroons and ratafia biscuits and a gorgeously rich custard — *rich*, Hardie! — flavored with brandy. Yes, she would rather like that. And as to the rest — oh, something fishy in cream and wine and mushrooms. That seemed straightforward enough. Or a crab pâté would do. Both? Why not. Then chicken, she supposed, if one could think of something original to do with it since chicken, although terribly safe — as, alas, it was — could also be terribly boring.

"Leave it to me, madam."

"Very well, Hardie."

A celebration cake, of course. Very large. Very ornamental. Something people would *talk* about afterward. "You do see what I mean, Hardie — a cake really has to cause conversation, otherwise who remembers?" "Perfectly, madam." "Good. I will send you a sketch." Champagne — naturally — in rivers. Wines and brandies and those terrible cocktails as seemed appropriate. And then a little supper at midnight for the dancers of smoked salmon, lobster, something — not chicken again — in aspic, and those delicious little cheese savories they had always served, before the war, at High Meadows. Did Hardie think his chef could manage that? Hardie thought so.

And flowers? She paused, looking doubtful, clearly uncertain as to whether or not flowers grew in hotel lobbies. Certainly. Would madam care for orchids, perhaps? Madam would not. "Natural flowers, Hardie dear, the kind one might expect to see in the drawing rooms of one's friends. And — oh dear, I really don't wish to be a nuisance, but *not* in those stiff, professional arrangements — *florist's* arrangements. Just naturally put together as any lady would do in her own home. Is that — *all right*, Hardie?"

"Quite all right, madam."

She had, of course, reminded him with a dozen little velvet-clawed touches of his former position in her household. But he had expected that, and stifling an impulse to give her the party free of charge as his personal gift to Polly, he returned to the Crown in great good humor. The evening of the fourth of June, the date Miriam had fixed upon, would be a landmark in his life as a hotelier, a show-piece for his skills which would give Faxby's élite far more to talk about than a cake. He was not precisely excited. Jubilant came nearer, brimful of confidence and ready not just to rise to the occasion but to surpass it. His food and wine would be superb, his service faultless, but Faxby had grown used to that. Extra details were required, extra attentions, an extra stretch of the imagination. Very well. She had expressed a desire for flowers which looked as if they had been arranged by a lady and he knew plenty of ladies, in these days of shrinking incomes and investments, who would be happy to earn a discreet pound or two. He hired three of them to transform such areas of the Crown as would be brought to Miriam's notice into a garden of her favorite shell-pink roses — Madame Pierre Oger, by name, he had not forgotten — alongside a profusion of the considerably more homely larkspur, love-in-a-mist, blue cornflowers and white daisies, sweet peas in all their tender colors. She had mentioned the cheese savories once served at High Meadows quite mischievously, assuming their recipe to have departed with the morose little woman who had been her pre-war cook, long since retired and now quite possibly dead. But, at some inconvenience, Kit eventually discovered her as alive and melancholic as ever in a Humberside cottage where it cost all his charm and persistence and a five-pound note to obtain her recipe from her. The fish and the pâté and the trifles presented no problem, but Miriam had complained of the tedious reliability of chicken. He called Aristide Keller to his office and convinced him that not only Miriam Swanfield but the world in general were ready and waiting now, all agog, for the creation of *Chicken Suprême Aristide, Poulet Keller*, whatever he chose to call it so long as it ensured that Miriam would never be bored by chicken again. She had spoken of a cake. Who better than Amandine Keller, pastry chef *extraordinaire*, to bake and decorate it? She had wrinkled her nose at the thought of cocktails. Had she ever tasted one? He doubted it. And he called another conference, with MacAllister this time, asking him not only to create a special cocktail for Polly, which was always done for brides and fiancées in any case, but also for Miriam, called a "gracious lady," he rather thought, in a wide-brimmed glass, a dash of well-spiced sweet Jamaica rum and apricot brandy, a dark color to it, something purple, vaguely imperial. She wouldn't be able to resist a sip or two of that. She might even mellow sufficiently to be impressed. And if that happened it would not spoil his pleasure one little bit to know that he was charging her royally for it.

And then, two days before the great event, a bolt from the sky which, a moment before, had been a limpid, unruffled blue. "Where is my wife?" Amandine Keller's husband wanted to know.

Amandine Keller, pastry chef, was found in the stillroom, not busily icing Polly's cake as she ought to have been, but in compromising proximity with the fishmonger who supplied the best turbot and sole and shellfish to be had in Faxby, to the Crown.

"I am going to kill you," announced Aristide Keller, *chef de cuisine*, to his wife who promptly threw a pastry fork at him which lodged in his temple, although without doing too much harm; and then, while first-aid was being administered by Claire, went off to pack her bags and take refuge in the fish-shop of her lover.

"I'd take it easy — wouldn't jump to any quick conclusions. There *could* be another explanation," said Kit who certainly could not think of one himself, being simply thankful that dinner, at least, was safely over. But Aristide Keller, knowing himself betrayed, shook off the false reassurance of false friends and set off at speed, muttering fiercely of what one could only assume to be revenge.

"It might be as well to follow him, Claire," said Kit. "I'd go myself, but I've got the Mayoress in my office, waiting to book a banquet and overnight accommodation for a Mayor and Corporation from somewhere in the Colne Valley. And in the state he's in, he might think *I* have an eye on Amandine myself."

She followed apprehensively, soon lost his trail without too much regret, so that she was neither present nor particularly sorry to have missed the fun, when he physically attacked the fishmonger's shopfront, causing so much grievous bodily harm to plate glass windows and counters and then a certain amount to Amandine herself, that he was locked up in the cells underneath Faxby Town Hall and sentenced the next morning to three months in Armley Gaol.

So much for *Chicken Suprême Aristide*. So much, too, for Polly's party cake already baked, of course, but still waiting for Amandine's magic to transform it from three square dark slabs of fruit and spices and cherries to an enchanted icing-sugar tower.

So much, too, for today's luncheon, today's dinner. And what of tomorrow? How would it affect the reputation of the hotel? And what about Arnold Crozier who, with no reputation of his own, set high standards for everyone else? What would he have to say about adultery among the *Crème Chantilly* and *Poires Belle Hélène*, and headlines in the local press?

"One thing at a time," said Kit who had spent most of the night attempting without success to persuade Amandine and the police to drop their charges and then, when he finally admitted there was no chance of it, doing what he could — not much he feared — to keep the affair out of the newspapers. "Let's think about breakfast first, shall we? You all know you can manage that. And put a little posy of fresh flowers on the trays — in case things don't improve throughout the day."

He went into his office, spent a long time on the telephone, sent a few telegrams and then called for Claire.

"I have to go down to Kent."

"Kit — at a time like this!"

"Exactly. I need a chef. I know where to get one. In Kent."

"Can't you just send for him?"

"Claire — if life could only be so simple. As it happens he has a job. I've no reason to believe he doesn't like it. So I have to go and convince him he'd like this one better. And apart from that — well, he's a fairly peculiar fellow. I worked with him once before, years back, and he was odd then — worse now I reckon."

"Why worse?"

"Because of the war — no, not shell shock or gas — nothing so straightforward as that really. He was a conscientious objector."

"I like him already."

"I thought you would."

"Did he go to prison?"

"Oh yes. He says, at one point, they shipped him and some others over to France. Told them the Government had signed their death warrants and staged a mock execution. Stood them against a wall, blindfolds, guns, the lot. That's what he *says* — !"

"I believe it."

"*He* believes it. He's never got over it. So — he is somewhat on the twitchy side and the kitchen maids won't love him. But he can cook."

"What are the chances that he'll come?"

"Enough to take me down there. After all, as a conscientious objector his days in the kitchens of the aristocracy are over. Perhaps he's not doing too well. He needs looking after in any case. I'll have to find out what he wants and convince him I can supply it. And while I'm away do you feel up to going on your knees to Amandine about Polly's cake?"

"Pound notes would do it better."

"Whatever it takes to get her back."

"Which means — ?"

"That if I get John David, this bloke in Kent, I can manage without Aristide. So, if the Kellers won't work together again — and they probably won't — I'll take the pastry chef."

"And the fishmonger."

"Well yes. I suppose he is part of the deal. I can't see him delivering his merchandise to our back door again — can you? — until he knows there's no chance of meeting Aristide with his meat cleaver. And I wouldn't know where to go for better turbot."

"How long will you be away?"

He put a steady hand on her shoulder, gave her a steady smile, showing more faith in her than it would have been reasonable for anyone to feel.

"From now until tomorrow afternoon."

Her mouth went dry.

"That means today's lunch and dinner. And lunch — at least — tomorrow."

"I'm not worried about it Claire. I know you'll cope."

"No you don't. Without a chef?"

He smiled. She wondered how he possibly could.

"It's midweek. We're quiet. Get the kitchen staff together and ask them what they can do. Then use your own judgment. Don't let anybody try to prove himself another Escoffier. Simple menus, and plenty of stand-by dishes in case something goes wrong. I went to the vegetable market on my way back from the cells first thing this morning. The meat has been delivered. Get the under-chefs to have a look at it before you put the menus together. No point in promising *Escalope Marengo* if there isn't any veal — and no tomatoes. Try and keep the waiters calm."

"Is that all?"

"Yes — except that you're a lovely lady."

"I'm terrified."

"Oh — you're not really you know. Once you get going you'll be fine."

He smiled again, picked up his bag, touched her arm and her cheek.

"Don't miss your train."

"No. And — by the way . . ."

"Yes Kit?" She had heard his "by the way" so many times before and she knew she had good cause to dread it.

"It's midweek as I said. We *ought* to be quiet. But with Aristide's little mishap on the front page of the Faxby Echo — oh yes, it's bound to be. Well — the Lady Mayoress might cancel but other people might just want to come and see how we're managing without him. I'd rather you didn't turn any bookings away."

"Yes Kit."

"No man is indispensable, Claire."

"So I've heard. As a theory it never quite convinced me."

Now she knew why.

Lunch which amazingly, gratifyingly, *did* prove quiet was an anguished rehearsal for dinner.

"Can I do anything to help?" asked Toby, stopping by for his prawns poached in white wine and cream, his Wednesday bottle of *Chablis*.

"Yes. Come to dinner tonight and keep on singing our praises very loud."

"So I will. Not that anybody listens to me. And as to the spot of bother with Aristide — well — nine days' wonder you know. Front page news this morning. Nobody can quite remember just what it was all about the morning after."

Yet several people telephoned, quite early, to voice vague apprehensions about future bookings, including Miriam — the telephone held at least four inches from the delicate mechanism of her inner ear — who informed Claire, in a flustered, desperately well-meaning voice that there was a horrid rumor in circulation about the Crown. Was it true? And, if so, she hoped it would not be allowed to cast any kind of a shadow on her party. Claire — her eyes on the undecorated slabs of birthday cake — assured her that it would not.

Predictably the Mayoress canceled her table for that evening, not wishing, with true political instinct, to associate herself with an establishment which might now have started on its downward path, particularly as the bench which had sentenced Aristide Keller that morning had consisted of an uncle and two cousins of hers. But others proved more curious, happier to take a chance, less fickle, and it soon became terribly clear that the restaurant would be full.

"Excellent," said Claire, smiling brightly, and having made sure that everybody was gainfully occupied in obeying Kit's instructions to the letter, she dashed off, her arms full of flowers, to plead with Amandine.

She had no time for diplomacy.

"What do you want Amandine?"

Revenge first of all. For a moment Claire was at a loss as to how she could supply that.

"Well, he's in prison. And when he comes out, the Major doesn't want him. He wants you." Amandine gave a thin, peevish shrug. Her husband would not be returning to the Crown in any case. He was planning to open a restaurant in Town Hall Square. It was all arranged. Claire wondered what the Major would have to say about that.

"All right Amandine. We need you."

"I know," said Amandine, her mind playing happily around those large plain squares of fruit cake. And what it came down to in the end was how much. She named her price. Claire halved it. They haggled, settled. She would come back and ice the cake and then they would see. Perhaps she would stay, because of the Major, who had always been good to her. Perhaps not.

"Detestable woman," thought Claire.

"Do not imagine," said Amandine, from her new position of power," "that the Major will marry you. He will not."

Dinner approached.

"That's delicious," said Claire, standing in the kitchen in her evening dress of beaded black net, smiling serenely, having passed the barrier of tension to an unnatural, exalted calm. "It's going very well — coming out just right."

The menu was smaller than usual but the portions larger, four vegetables instead of three, potatoes in many guises, less complicated main dishes but a larger variety of cheeses and cold desserts, little extras slipped in between courses, a champagne sorbet to follow the fish, crystallized fruits and what remained of Amandine's dainty confectionery with the coffee, lashings of cream.

"Yes — that's exactly right. You're doing fine." She hardly knew what she was praising. She simply praised, soothed, spoke calm, cheerful words, was simply *there* — as Kit was always there — to be referred to, to make the decision and take the chance, to keep on repeating, until she had almost convinced herself, that everything was going well, would be perfectly all right.

One spark of panic, only one, and she knew there would be no putting out the conflagration. Therefore, there must be no panic. When a sauce curdled and a cry was raised, "What do I do?" Claire, who had never made a sauce in her life, looked into the pan with wise appraisal, and said "Oh, that's not serious. You'll easily put it right." When a kitchen maid burned her hand on an oven door and, jumping backwards, collided with a waiter and his tray of, fortunately, iced *vichyssoise*, she moved like lightning to put herself between them, converting what might have been a flare of highly infectious temper, a burst of demoralizing tears, into a simple matter of clearing up broken china, cold leeks and potatoes and starting again. When too many waiters brought in too many orders and shouted them all at once she did not interpret the jumbled, abbreviated culinary terms which, in fact, she did not fully understand. She simply stood between the two opposing forces, those who cooked the food in shirtsleeves in hectic, stifling obscurity and those immaculate dignitaries who carried it condescendingly to table, her cool presence keeping them apart.

"Let's just get on with it shall we?" And they submitted to her composure, her good humor, her fierce determination that none of them — absolutely *no one* — should let Kit down.

She went into the restaurant and, a smiling, unobtrusive presence, made her rounds. "Is everything all right for you, sir — madam — ?" In most cases it was. "What's all this we've been hearing about?" somebody wanted to know. "Jealous husbands, eh, and meat cleavers — very continental." But what did anyone really know of Aristide beyond his *Veal Marengo* and his *Lobster Bordelaise*, or of Amandine that was of greater interest to them than her *mille-feuilles*. And if those things remained more or less unchanged, who really cared?

"Is everything all right for you, sir?" In one instance, and fairly loudly, it was not, Claire's apologies falling sweet and fast as she whisked away the offending *Steak Chasseur*, although very little remained on the plate to judge whether or not it had really been tough, and replaced it with the lobster the gentleman now considered he should have ordered at the start.

She slept in the hotel that night, having spent a long time cashing up, tidying up, giving praise generously where it was due, and was downstairs early, as Kit always was, to make sure that everybody else was at his post and that all the early morning requirements of the guests were promptly and cheerfully met.

"Will the Major be back today?" Mr. Clarence and Mrs. Tarrant both wanted to know.

"I expect so."

She sounded admirably unconcerned. If he came, all well and good. If not then what of it? They would just carry on.

Mrs. Tarrant sorrowfully shook her head. Mr. Clarence gave a nervous smile. Adela Adair, the restaurant pianist, who had no reason to be in the hotel so early, her red hair looking very red indeed in the unaccustomed daylight, her long face a year or two older, heaved a sigh and began to talk of her long association with disaster. Gerard, the head waiter, kept glancing at his watch, and MacAllister, despite Claire's vigilance, had consumed far more of his own rum punch than had been good for him.

Could she hold them together through another dinner? Could she convince them — if Kit did not come today — that their jobs were still secure, still worth the effort? And today was Thursday. Tomorrow, possibly this afternoon, Arnold Crozier would be here. She sat in Kit's office and spoke to each one in turn, privately, confidentially, appealing to the mother in Mrs. Tarrant and perhaps in Mr. Clarence too, to the good sport in MacAllister, the supportive, masculine rock in Gerard although she would not have cared to lean on it too long, her message essentially the same. "The Major has treated you well. Don't let him down. Do your job as he trained you to do it. That's all you have to do." And she would be here to coordinate, to join each well-polished, well-ordered piece to the perfect whole, so that when he returned he would find palatable food emerging from his kitchen, contented guests availing themselves of fresh linen and hot water, Mr. Clarence smiling urbanely behind his desk, MacAllister as sober as could be expected behind his bar, even Amandine herself in the still room busily creating her pyramid of pink sugar and marzipan.

She got up, still calmly smiling, and began to walk around, unhurried, unflustered, pausing to chat to a guest — all the time in the world, nothing pressing, absolutely nothing burning — making sure everyone had seen her and knew where to find her in case of need. And, preferring to assume that he would not come, she made her arrangements accordingly, constantly bearing in mind how easily, how rapidly they might fall apart. One little snag would be enough to do it. And so she continued to walk upstairs and down, to look and feel and listen, to anticipate that snag and deal with it before it arose.

He came striding into the lobby late in the afternoon, a thin, quiet, ungainly man at his side. John David? Fervently she hoped so.

"Hello, Major," she said, casual and friendly, the lobby being full of departing and arriving guests and Mr. Clarence's eversharp eyes. "I'll be with you in a minute. Had a good trip?"

And, with new guests to welcome and old ones to be waved farewell, it was half an hour before she saw him again.

"Your chef came then."

"He came. He's gone straight to work. Doesn't want the Kellers' cottage, didn't even want to see his room. Just had his bag sent upstairs and went straight to the kitchen. Like I said — odd sort of chap."

Leaning against his desk, Kit looked tired but very well pleased.

"You did a first-rate job, Claire."

"Thank you. Do I get a raise?"

"We'll talk about it. I knew you'd cope."

"You knew no such thing. You just took the gamble."

"Call it a calculated risk. I'll bet you didn't even miss me. You looked as cool as a cucumber when I came through the door."

"Kit — I have never been so glad to see anybody in my life."

"I wish you meant that."

Yes. She could wish that she meant it herself. Yet now that the crisis was over, now that she could bask a little in her small moment of triumph, it was to Benedict that she longed to tell the tale of her agonies and her achievements. He was the audience she wanted. His was the approval she wished to gain. How monstrous that she could not share this with him *now* while it was still vividly alive inside her. By Sunday afternoon she would need to re-kindle it all over again and would have remembered by then, in any case, how little her overnight management of a small hotel could really impress him when he was struggling, day in, day out, to fill the dwindling order books of Swanfield Mills, to fend off for his employees the dreaded specter of short-time, half-pay, no time and no wages, for some of them, ever again.

He would soon have to go out looking for new markets himself, he believed, North America, South America, Africa, anywhere, to keep those looms ticking over; or would have to start cutting back, turning men off and running the risk of bringing the rest of them out on strike. Possibly he would be abroad a great deal during the next year or two. If nothing else it would be an escape, as Thornwick had been an escape.

338

Did he want Claire to go with him? In the silence that fell between them she could feel her heart swelling, thudding painfully against the wall of her chest. Yes, of course she wanted to go. Of course. Particularly at a time of trouble. But could he promise her — did he even wish to promise — that her commitment, if she made it, would not end sooner or later at the blue chintz door?

"I'll go with you," she said.

"Oh — I don't think you really want that."

"You're wrong."

He shook his head, his dark skin looking gray again, his face somber and grim, a private face, older and far more heavy-laden than the cool mask he used for public display. She would do anything for him when he looked like that, would throw away, without permitting herself a backward glance, all those things which seemed to her, by fits and starts, to have so much importance. Freedom, for instance. Self-determination. The notion, which seemed odd to her in this mood, of limiting her own development by tying it to his. What heights did she wish to reach other than her natural fulfillment as a woman? What gifts had she, what talents, other than generosity in love?

"I'll come, Benedict."

"I don't think so," he said.

Polly's engagement party, arranged to suit the exacting standards of Miriam, Kit Hardie, and the nervous but highly original John David, was as extravagant and elegant as an Ascot hat, Polly in gold and silver spangles, Miriam in old rose and pearls, Edith Timms in saffron trimmed with exceedingly costly *Valenciennes*, Roger Timms beaming cordially but otherwise not much in evidence, having been warned not to draw attention to himself, so that when Benedict proposed the toast to the happy pair it was Roger's father who replied to it.

The future, he declared, for this couple at least, could only be made of pure gold. The girl was beautiful. The boy his only son. A piece of land had been purchased on their behalf. A villa of the very latest design, a marvel of modern plumbing and advanced domestic technology, was to be built upon it. The happiness, therefore, of his heir and of his old friend, Aaron Swanfield's youngest daughter, could not fail to be complete, as perfect in its entirety as this evening had been, since what could have exceeded the sparkle of Polly's celebratory champagne, her wonderful cake, three icing sugar baskets of pink and white roses one on top of the other; the dinner itself which had introduced "Empress Chicken" to Faxby, breasts hammered thin and rolled up around a stuffing of chicken liver pâté and herb butter and Heaven knew what, except that

Mr. Timms had tasted nothing like it and would be more than ready to taste it again? The sauce, too, had had the texture of velvet, the aroma of a vineyard and a herb garden enticingly blended together. And the cheese savories, light as a feather, with just the right amount of onion and a hint of — what had it been? Tarragon?

Her smile never wavering, Mrs. Edith Timms caught her husband's eye and gave a sharp cough.

"Oh yes," he said, reminded of what she had instructed him to say, although his mind still visibly wandered through that herb garden, wine glass in hand. "My wife and I shall be delighted to welcome Polly as a daughter."

Polly smiled, showing her perfect white teeth and her diamond ring.

"And I shall be only too happy to welcome into my family another young son," said Miriam, wiping away a tear, letting it be known that she was thinking of Jeremy.

Eunice, knocking over a glass, scrambled to her feet and rushed across the room to kiss her sister. "I hope you'll be as happy as Toby and I have always been."

"Hear, hear!" quickly muttered kind-hearted Toby.

There was a pause. No one had anything more to add. And then a voice was heard, husky with tobacco and alcohol. "Marriage as an institution is unlikely to survive the century," said Nola.

She had improved in the sense that she was no longer quite so much trouble to anyone. Had she met another man, Claire wondered? Yes, in a sense, at a rather different level, perhaps she had. Wandering disconsolately one day into Faxby Park, vaguely the worse for the brandy she had taken at breakfast to get herself out of bed, the gin and vermouth which had served instead of lunch, she had, in fact, come across the schoolmaster who had once, in his role of Education been intended to replace discredited Sculpture in her affections.

And, expecting nothing to come of it, she had accompanied him on a visit to Faxby's Probation Service, a converted warehouse in a particularly unholy part of Faxby named All Saints' Passage, and had there encountered Mr. Kilmartin, Miss Pickles, Miss Drew; and Doctor Sigmund Freud.

Faxby's magistrates had seen no reason to spend lavishly on their Probation Service, a peculiar institution at best in the opinion of those local stalwarts, who would have preferred, one and all, to sentence an offender to a flogging at the cart-tail or deportation to Australia — had such things still been possible — than to the reforming zeal of Miss Pickles or Miss Drew, in the forlorn hope that a pair of well-meaning spinsters might somehow cure them of their villainy. Yet, in these unsettled times, with the jails full to bursting, the newspapers setting up a constant caterwauling against long sentences, particularly if the prisoner happened to be a woman; and with the vote extended to women over thirty and to *all* men, it was as well — if one wished to seek election — to avail oneself of what these newspapers and those women considered to be a human alternative.

An old warehouse, therefore, was discovered — with no great difficulty since it had been in the Greenwood family for a couple of generations — cleaned out and painted, not too thoroughly, of course, for the reception of Faxby's socially inadequate and socially sick — according to Miss Drew; a dumping ground — as many Town Councillors saw it — for those who were neither quite vicious enough to lock away in prison, nor quite mad enough to commit to an asylum for the insane.

Which did not, of course, rule out the possibility of meeting, in All Saints' Passage, a number of people who were very vicious and extremely crazy. A circumstance — perhaps to be encountered in any dumping ground — which brought added unpleasantness to the equally large number who were naturally just a little feckless and slow; those who would not have been feckless at all had they been able to find work; those who had lost nerves or limbs or faith in France and could not come to terms with it.

To Mr. Kilmartin they needed fatherly, slightly embarrassed advice which he gave, in clerical fashion, from behind the pulpit of his office desk and in carefully phrased terms which his clients often failed to understand, although they would agree to accept his advice, whether they had grasped his meaning or not — and the shilling that sometimes went with it — because anyone could see he was such a decent chap.

Miss Pickles was made of sterner stuff, a stocky woman of boundless energy and unshakeable belief in the universal panacea of soap and water treating her particular area of Faxby as, for generations, the squire's lady had treated her manorial village, seeing cleanliness as next to godliness and expecting her "people" to be very godly.

But Miss Drew, as spinsterish as Mr. Kilmartin in her manner, had read the works of the father of psychoanalysis, Sigmund Freud, and knew, therefore, about the problems of repressed sexuality, the intensely sensual feeling of the girl-child for the father, the boy-child for the mother, which, if wrongly handled, or only slightly misunderstood, could scar the infant's emotional judgment and stability for life. And since this delicate infantile passion for a parent invariably was mishandled and often savagely misunderstood — perhaps no one should doubt that — Miss Drew believed, quite simply, that nobody was to blame for anything. Ever.

She invited Nola to tea in a frilly, pink and white flat, all organdy tablecloths and lace doilies and explained, in her piping, old-maidish treble, the terribly story of Oedipus, Prince of Ancient Thebes, who had murdered his father and married his mother, a tragedy used by Freud, said Miss Drew, to illustrate the quite passionate love a baby boy could feel for his mother, the equally savage jealousy he might entertain for his father, and how desperately that jealousy might terrify him since, when it came to any kind of contest between a powerful adult male and a toddling infant — particularly for possession of the resident female — it would seem unlikely to the child that he could win.

"Therefore," murmured the prim and entirely passionless Miss Drew, "our early years seethe, my dear — positively *seethe* — with jealousy and desire and a most volcanic sensuality which, since of course it can have no physical outlet, turns inward and causes — Heavens, such a multitude of problems in later life. A girl, my dear, will only take as husband or lover a man who either resembles her father as closely as possible or is his exact opposite, depending on what her relationship with him has been. Likewise a young man's choice of partner is entirely dictated by how well or how badly he has got on with his mother. Therefore, you see one cripples one's children simply by existing. How sad, yet how inescapable, I fear."

Miss Drew, in her broad outline, was probably quite correct yet, having had no lovers of her own, no husband, no children, only an invalid mother who had faded quietly away without too much trouble, her view was entirely academic and she was a little alarmed to see Nola suddenly turn pale.

"May I give you some more tea, Mrs. Swanfield?"

"I killed one of my children," said Nola, her pallor quite ghastly.

"Oh dear." Miss Drew did not, at first, know what to make of that and even when the facts were put before her could think of nothing very explicit Freud had ever said about abortion. Perhaps the ladies of nineteenth century Vienna had not gone in for it overmuch, or, if so, had had the good taste to keep quiet about it.

"Oh dear." Yet one thing Freud did believe in was the easing of the soul's burden by confession, his and perhaps the Church of Rome's version of "a trouble shared is a trouble halved." Remembering this, she brightened.

"Would you care to tell me . . . ?"

Since that atrocious morning when she had woken up, neither in hell nor in oblivion, but in her own room at High Meadows surrounded by bright smiles and a conspiracy of polite silence, Nola had been consumed by the need to tell somebody.

"These little accidents do happen," the nurse had said. Miriam had come tripping in behind the tea tray to pronounce her version of the same. Claire, smiling vaguely, had let her talk but had not listened. "Nothing," Benedict decreed, "has occurred."

But now.

"I can't get over it," she said, "I don't know why I can't. I *ought* to be the kind of woman who wouldn't let it worry her. But I'm not. It's on my mind all day. I can't get rid of it. It *follows* me. I can hardly believe it myself. All I cared about at the time was getting myself out of trouble. I expected just to go and have it done and pay for it and then, if it didn't kill me, never give it another thought. Why can't I do that?"

Miss Drew had not the least idea. "Just talk, dear," she said, to give herself time to think it over.

Nola talked. The next day she came back and talked again.

"Oh Lord — am I boring you?"

But Miss Drew, to whom nothing of any significance had ever happened and, therefore, had no problems of her own, was fascinated by the agonies of others.

"Just talk, dear. It will do you good."

She talked.

"I wonder," said Eunice, "what Nola is up to now?"

She had been ripe for conversion to something. An extreme and possibly harsh religion of the walking-barefoot-on-broken-glass variety, had one been available. A political discipline of the far left perhaps? But the Labor Party had grown quite respectable now and Communism had not yet come to Faxby. The sudden naming and acknowledging of her own neuroses sufficed her admirably. Freud — as interpreted by Miss Drew — did not forgive her sins. He explained them. He told her it had never been and could never be her fault, thus making forgiveness unnecessary. Yet, if it were true that each generation unknowingly mutilated its young — and it seemed to be true — then what had she done to her own living sons? And although her neglect of them had its roots in her own childhood, now that she had been made aware of it, now that she knew that she had rejected parenthood because of her disastrous relationship with her own parents, it must surely be her duty to put things right. As their mother she was the first woman in Christian and Conrad's lives. Their relationships with other women would depend on how they had fared with her. And so far there had been no relationship at all, no living, caring female at the center of their lives, making of herself a bridge over which they could, in time, successfully cross to the love of other women. What had she done to them? No bridge. No hope of reaching love or even recognizing it if they should happen to encounter it by chance, as she herself had never reached it; never known how to distinguish the true from the false. No ability to feel love, or — perhaps worse — to show it. Like Benedict.

The warehouse in All Saints' Passage became her Mecca. She had found something to believe in. More incredibly, she was on the threshold of finding something to do. And she was in a receptive mood, therefore, when she learned that her younger son, Conrad, had run away from school.

Benedict set off at once for Cheshire to see the headmaster. It had not occurred to him to ask Nola if she wished to accompany him. While the headmaster himself, who was a bachelor and highly nervous with women, was positively gratified by her absence, preferring to deal with any issue of importance, in fact with any issue at all, strictly man to man. No, the boy had shown no signs of being unhappy or unsettled, no sign of anything very much at all. Never communicative, alas, and with such boys it was always hard to tell. Well behaved, of course, co-operative, academically sound, slightly above average and under no pressure, no strain. Nor had there been any "incident," any quarrel, any "spot of bother" of any kind. he had simply told his brother he was "getting out" and had gone. His brother, not being particularly communicative either, had not thought to ask him where or why. Unfortunate really. And so near the end of term too. Clearly the headmaster thought it a great pity that Conrad had not had the courtesy, the consideration, to wait a week or two longer after which it would have been a simple matter of going home for the holidays.

Benedict spent ten minutes alone with his elder son who had nothing to tell him, checked with the local constabulary, the stationmaster, certain shops in the village and came home.

Eunice's boys were called into the study one at a time and taken to task. Had Conrad made friends locally during the holidays or spoken of friends elsewhere? A girl? They looked amazed, would have been inclined, before anyone else, to giggle. No. Conrad did not make friends. Rather to their surprise their stern uncle accepted that.

"The poor lamb," wailed Miriam, "how am I to sleep tonight, thinking of him wandering about just anywhere?"

"At least my boys have never run away from school," murmured Eunice.

"No need," snapped Polly, whose temper had been very uncertain since she became a fiancée. "They got rid of Justin, didn't they, before he had the chance."

"If I can help at all, Benedict, just let me know," said Toby.

Nobody had anything to say to Nola.

Where could he have gone? Remembering her own boarding schools and her own uneasy childhood home, Claire thought it would be as far away as he could manage from High Meadows. The family closed ranks as families do in times of disaster, Miriam drawing them all around her, looking on the bright side, refusing even to hint at all the dire fates which might befall a boy who was, in a manner of speaking, on the run. "At least we are all *together*," she murmured, "which will make it — whatever it is — easier."

Nola went outside, through the garden, across the sloping meadow which gave the house its name and found her son trudging up the road from Faxby, looking more like a boy, less of a little gentleman, than she had ever seen him, with dust on his shoes and his shirt collar undone, and with no more idea than she had herself of how to get comfortably home unless Parker was waiting at the station.

"Hello, Conrad."

For a moment he looked appalled and then, "Oh — hello."

He had no idea what to expect from her nor she from him. They were strangers to each other. And Nola knew there was nothing he could possibly do about that. The lead would have to come from her. Was she up to it? Probably not. Nevertheless, *now* she would have to try. Now — perhaps never again — was her chance to free herself just a little from the guilty voice which was so continually whispering to her; so persistent and shrill, so difficult to silence, these days, even with alcohol. Now — not easily but just possibly — she might redeem herself.

"You look tired, Conrad."

"Yes."

"I suppose running away takes it out of one rather. Bit of a lark though."

He looked at her as if her words had suddenly been translated, as she spoke them, into Chinese.

"Aren't you — angry?" Even now in his amazement and his confusion, possibly in his hunger and thirst and his aching feet, he was a boy of clipped speech, few words.

"No. Not now when I can see you're not dead in a ditch. I wouldn't have taken kindly to that."

Yet what would it really have meant to her? Last year, very little. With her new soul-scouring honesty, she was forced to admit as much. And now? Yes — now she hoped that it might come to mean a great deal.

"Why did you do it, Conrad?"

"I don't know."

She knew. He had wanted his mother and father. Not her, of course, and not Benedict, but real parents as neither she nor Benedict had ever been; that warm, caring woman to be his bridge to womankind, that approachable, interested, interesting man with whom he could identify. She could not change Benedict. But — *now* — she could make anything she chose of herself.

She was right, of course. It was, therefore, extremely unfortunate that she had not the least idea how to cope with these new revelations and opportunities other than to be carried away by them, to lose her head over them so that her "rightness" sounded wrong, felt wrong, galloped off at once too far and too fast.

"Do you want to go straight up to the house? Look — hang on a minute — I'll go fetch my car and we can go out to tea somewhere. All right?"

"All right." She was his mother and although he was not in the least acquainted with her he did know that a mother ought to be obeyed.

"Good. I won't be a tick."

And in her excitement, her great desire to talk to him, to become his friend, his confidante, his healer — to become his mother — all in the space of one afternoon, it did not enter her head to tell anyone that he was found.

It was some two hours later when they returned from the Crown where she had crammed him with pastries and ices and strawberries and cream, watching his enjoyment, hesitant and quiet though it was, with an intent delight.

"This is my son."

He was a boy to be proud of. He deserved at least that. And now, if she did nothing else of use in her life, she would — in accordance with the code of All Saints' Passage — advise, assist, and defend him.

Claire was present when she walked into the drawing room at High Meadows, her hand on his shoulder.

"This is my son."

"Oh thank God — thank God!" Miriam's collapse onto a sofa had at least the advantage of occupying Eunice.

"Let's talk about it in the study," said Benedict, not unkindly, to Conrad, as the family, with appropriate cries of relief and curiosity, began to press in. And it was very evident, almost comic, that neither the father nor the son expected Nola to go with them.

"I am his mother," she said.

"Yes — of course you are. I beg your pardon."

The three of them walked out of the room and closed the door.

"I really can't stay," said Claire, "there's no point — I mean now that he's safe — now that everything's *all right*."

All right? Very far from that as she might have known, did know perhaps, as Parker grudgingly in case there should be any "fun," drove her home.

"Thank God that's settled — if it is settled," said Toby Hartwell, coming into the lounge bar the following morning.

"Oh — has he gone back to school then?"

"Well yes — don't they always? Benedict took him back this morning. Although what Nola means to do about it I wouldn't care to say."

Claire's smile flickered on and off her face.

"Why should Nola do anything?"

"My dear —" Adding a splash of water to his whiskey, Toby swallowed liberally and shuddered. "Last night, for a moment or two, it looked as if she rather meant to shoot him. Benedict, I mean. A lioness defending her young no less — teeth bared, claws out. Not Nola, I grant you. Or so you'd imagine. But it *was*. Never thought she'd even noticed what was happening to those boys, much less cared about it. But last night, once he'd turned down her offer, she went wild —"

"Offer?"

"Oh yes — she made that calmly enough. Came straight out with it. Took my breath away, I can tell you."

"I see."

"Shouldn't think you do, old girl, for a minute. Not the kind of offer I've ever heard before. Never thought I'd feel sorry for Benedict either, but there it is. One can see he had to turn it down — one *has* to see that. But, just the same, he might not have wanted to. Perhaps I ought to be ashamed to say how well *I* understand that. Freedom — and no strings . . ."

"Toby — ?" And she was too aghast to wonder why he was smiling at her so very kindly. "Could you — just tell me — I mean, what happened — and how — and *where?*"

His smile, releasing dozens of fine lines and crinkles around his mouth and his eye corners gave him the face of a wise and kindly elf.

"Yes Claire. I see what you mean. In the drawing room would you believe. Not Benedict's idea, of course. He was all set to hold his usual audience in the study but he couldn't keep her there. Or at least not long enough. All of a sudden, just when I'd got Eunice into the frame of mind to go home — leave well alone and all that — there she was, *filling* the hall — believe me, that's the only word for it, because she took it over as if she'd grown — *expanded*. I've had nightmares about women who did that — giant Miriams and Eunices haunting me all through the night. But never mind that. Asked him if he'd said his final word and, if so, then she was going to say hers, but not shut up in the dark in his study where nobody could hear or judge who was right and who was wrong. She wasn't going to hide the Truth away. Rather sounded to me as if she thought she'd just discovered it — the Truth, I mean — and so she felt under an obligation to tell the world. Poor Nola. Ignorance is bliss don't they say? Or what's that about a *little* knowledge?"

"They say it's a dangerous thing, Toby."

"Quite. So that's what she did. Told the world. Or rather told Benedict, all over again, what she'd obviously told him once or twice already in the study."

"With Conrad there?"

"Oh yes. With Conrad there, pale as death, taking it all in and wishing he'd stayed at school I expect. *And* Eunice and Polly with their eyes popping and Miriam pretending it was all being forced on her attention when really she wouldn't have missed it for the worlds. And Nola, of course, at the center of the stage, causing a sensation — except that, funnily enough, I don't think she was trying to shock us. No, I don't. I'd say — and you may smile — that she was trying to educate us. Getting it wrong — yes — and fighting a losing battle . . . Well. I suppose nobody was in the mood to learn."

"Toby — ?"

"Yes my love. I'm getting there. She stood in the middle of the drawing room with her hand on that poor lad's shoulder and told Benedict he could divorce her and she'd supply him with the evidence in triplicate, or words to that effect. Said their marriage was a sham and everybody knew it. Not his fault. Not hers. Sounded as if she rather thought Aaron Swanfield and her own lady mother were to blame. But be that as it may, she'd had enough of it. Wanted to live clean and honest. Turn a new leaf and all that. Don't we all? And she wanted her sons. Just give me my children and I'll be on my way. Little house in the town, local school, heavy diet of good friends and good conversation — had it all worked out. Kind of *avante-garde* Utopia it sounded to me. And being Nola, of course, she didn't specify just who was to pay the bills. Benedict took her up on that, of course, straightaway. Tried his dismissive approach, but she wasn't having it. Got curt with her and tried to walk away, but she just followed him. You'd expect that I suppose, now that she's seen the Light and he hasn't. You know what converts are. In the end he turned on her — one could see it coming — *I* hadn't got the heart to blame him — and told her straight. She'd gone through Greek Dancing and Pottery and Music and Sculpture and the Family Butler and a few other detours on the way — raked the whole lot up and threw it at her — and if she thought she was going to play Motherhood in the same fashion, then she had another thing coming. He told her what the law allowed him to do and what he *would* do to stop her. Wasn't pleasant. Had to be done though. I wouldn't describe myself as a fond father but even *I* could see how downright dangerous it would be if all a young fellow had to rely on was Nola. And a bit risky for Nola too, of course, if she had to start relying on herself. Don't honestly see how she'd manage it at this late stage. No halfway decent man could discount that, you know."

"Yes, Toby. Thank you."

"There's a bit more, Claire . . ."

"Yes?"

"Something — *odd* I'll have to call it. You might know more about it than I do. Don't ask me why I should think that because I'll never refer to it again, you can rest assured."

"All right, Toby."

"It's like this. She started to say something — about crime and punishment, it rather sounded. Not clear to me. But Benedict understood all right. Whatever she had on the tip of her tongue he didn't want his boy to hear. *Her* boy too, although one does tend to forget it. He told her to shut up — snarled at her in fact. Very nasty. Even Miriam changed color and it certainly made Eunice's knees and Polly's turn to water — nobody with even half an eye could miss that. But, you see, Nola had all this Light and Truth in her eyes, and I suppose it does tend to dazzle."

"What did she say?"

"Nothing, Claire, that made much sense. She tried, jolly hard though. Guilt and shame and punishment, words like that — something about being pregnant which, of course *must* have been a long time ago. He tried to shout her down but she wouldn't have it. One could see that she was going to come out with it, whatever it was, or choke. Couldn't help herself."

"And then?"

"He hit her I'm afraid — hard too. Knocked her clean off balance, in fact. Good thing she was standing by the sofa. It broke her fall all right and no harm done, although you could see Miriam was getting worried about her china bits and pieces —"

"*Toby!*"

"Yes. The awful thing was, of course, that one had to wonder what Conrad would do. Not easy for a chap to watch his father knock his mother down, even if she has — or hasn't — deserved it. Looked to me as if he might just have a go at Benedict, which would have been pretty terrible, because then Benedict would have had to thrash him. Benedict thought so too, because he whipped round on the lad like lightning and told him to pick his mother up and help her to bed. Hard I thought, at first, but it gave the boy something to do —"

"And Nola?"

"Went off like a lamb — to the slaughter that is. Never seen any thing like it. Head down, barefoot certainly in spirit. If she were in the Middle Ages and he'd said 'Get thee to a nunnery,' that's how she'd have looked. Eunice kept on telling me all the way home that she couldn't understand it."

"Could you?"

He smiled his wise, kindly smile again.

"Well — she'd been talking about punishment. He'd punished her. Could that be it?"

She got down from the bar stool carefully, slowly, feeling stiff in the joints like an old woman.

"Are you having lunch?"

"Yes," he said, "Care to join me?"

It was a long afternoon, Benedict's voice on the telephone toward the end of it, arranging to pick her up at eight o'clock. She glanced at her watch. A quarter past five. She did not want the intervening two and three quarter hours to pass.

He looked — what? Old? Yes. She could not mistake it. Grim and taut and gray as he so often did these days. Weary. That was it. Bone-weary, heart-weary. His energy drained away.

She felt at the far end of herself too.

"There was no choice," he said. "None. There never has been. Do you believe me?"

"I try to."

"The boys are my responsibility. So is she. The only way I can control her is to live with her — insofar as I do live with her. There is nothing new about that."

"I know."

"And she would never have gone through with it, Claire — do you know that too?"

She nodded her head.

"So it would have been cruel, wouldn't it, to my boys, to you — to myself — had I done other than put an end to it? She may have meant everything she said, Claire — as she said it. But the plain fact is that she doesn't know the first thing about *doing* any of it. And I can't let her practice on my sons."

350

"No you can't — I agree."

"And you weren't — disappointed shall we call it — when you heard I'd refused her a divorce. Tell me the truth."

"Yes. Bitterly."

"And now?"

"I've had it all out with myself. I see that you couldn't and I see why you couldn't. It would be like turning her loose to destroy herself. I wouldn't expect you to do that."

"My dear — I know you wouldn't expect it. But, just the same, don't you wish I had? Do you really think she's worth the sacrifice? Haven't you said to yourself that my boys will grow up and lead their own lives without even realizing that there *was* a sacrifice? Haven't you asked yourself all that?"

"Yes. I have."

"And where does it leave us. We've been offered two partial solutions, the blue chintz bedroom and this. If we can take advantage of neither, then what else is there?"

She refused to answer him.

"Is Conrad all right now?"

"Not really. He didn't want to go back to school. I didn't particularly want to take him. Unfortunately I could think of nowhere safer. He was intensely miserable. So was his brother. Naturally, being my children, they refused, or didn't know how, to talk about it. I can't leave it there, can I, since they *are* my children? I shall have to discover the cause and provide some kind of a remedy. All I can say for certain is they're better off then they might have been had I not played the villain, as usual, before Conrad's horrified eyes, threatened his mother with exile and starvation unless she did as she was told. I doubt if he understands the law well enough to know that I couldn't really have carried out those threats. Neither does she. And then, of course, I had to knock her down. He'll never know why. He'll just remember seeing it happen. His instinct was to defend her. One can hardly disapprove of that."

"No. He seems a good boy."

"I shall have to find out — or try to. Won't I?"

Yes. She could not allow herself to be other than glad of that. And, with a boy whose instinct was to defend his mother, she knew she could have no part of it.

"You will have to help me, Claire."

"Yes — of course — anything."

There was an aching silence, a weight of dread on her heart although she had known all day what he was going to say to her and had no defense against it.

"Benedict — ?"

But his taut face was again in shadow as she had first known it, inscrutable, obscure, observing her carefully, thoroughly, while concealing everything but a bare outline of himself.

But he had asked for her help.

"What do you want me to do?"

"Leave me," he said. "Just that. And a little more. I rarely fail in my resolve but if I should ask you to come back to me, don't come. Can you promise me that?"

It was the first promise she had made him.

"You do understand," he said, "that it is the best we can do now — all we can do."

She understood.

It made no difference.

18

SHE agreed that she had to leave him. There were times when she even wanted to do it. It became an act of love and salvation — both his and her own. She tried.

She spent the following Sunday afternoon sitting with Euan Ash in his cold and dusty studio watching in careful silence as he painted minute petals and humming birds and butterflies on plain white china, small masterpieces created for his pleasure which he would then sell without a backward glance in Faxby Market for a shilling or two. "Take what you like," he offered, and, feeling stunned, her whole mind out of focus yet still continuing, as a result of thorough training, to go through the motions, she thanked him and selected, by no means at random, a cup and saucer alive with bluebells and perfect if improbable blue-winged sparrows.

"Thanks, Euan. I'll always keep it."

"Whatever for? I suppose you'll hang on to that piece of red glass round your neck too."

"I suppose so."

How calm she was: as from a hammer blow to the head: as from the freezing or the simple sweeping away of sensation by a disaster too great to be endured and, therefore, at its first shock, not even felt. How calm she was, preparing for dinner at High Meadows that night, wearing his ruby, smiling at Parker as he came to fetch her and then, fifteen minutes later, smiling at Miriam and Polly and Eunice, at Benedict himself; doing all the things she had promised, of which she had assured him she was capable. Since — of course — for Dorothy's sake, for everybody's sake, for her own self-esteem, she must get used to seeing him again as her brother-in-law, a Swanfield, an acquaintance. No friendship. He rejected that utterly and she did not really think it possible herself. They must be together, or not together. Very well. They could not be together. How calm she was, how very pleasant at the dinner table, how wonderfully empty and absent, talking neither too much nor too little, not looking at him yet not ignoring him, except for that single moment when, getting up from her chair to go into the drawing room, she caught his eye. But apart from that one brief moment when her stomach *had* lurched and her breath *had* got stuck somewhere like a barbed fish-hook in her chest, how well she was doing. How calm, even when he appeared in the drawing room door, looking for his victim, and said in his curt, judicial "Family Sunday" manner, "Would you come into the study please, Claire."

"Poor Claire," gurgled Polly who had been expecting a summons herself. "What *have* you been up to?"

She got up and followed him, across the hall, into the study and straight on like a sleepwalker to wind her arms around his neck, sensation returning to her body as it made inch by inch contact with his.

"You shouldn't do this," he said roughly into her ear. "You shouldn't come when I call you."

"You shouldn't call me."

So it went on. Partings leading only to reconciliations which, in their turn and just as swiftly, led to fresh partings. A painfully revolving circle shading from moments when separation seemed possible to moments when it did not. The summer was hot, torturous, unbearably prolonged; sultry, airless days which brought Claire a succession of blinding headaches — what else could it be, she told her mother, but the weather? — and which produced in Benedict a loss of weight and appetite, a deplorable shortness of temper, attributable, of course, to the sorry state of trade in Faxby and to the recurring problems of an unstable wife and two withdrawn, unhappy children home from school for the holidays. His Sunday afternoons were spent with them now, inspecting abbey ruins or Roman remains at York, uneasy outings made partly to keep them away from Nola who, at every opportunity, took them up to her room and, through a fog of tobacco, questioned them about their dreams, shaking her head wisely, prophetically, as she uncovered in each one the seeds of a dozen neuroses.

That she bewildered and embarrassed them was very certain. That they were ill at ease with Benedict was equally clear. While the presence of both parents, when Benedict invited Nola to accompany them on a visit to the Roman Wall at Hexham, produced verbal paralysis in Christian and Conrad and an unfortunate incident with Nola who, declining to "walk the wall" on a particularly sultry afternoon, remained at a local hotel to be retrieved by Benedict in a condition which even her well-wishers could not have described as other than very drunk. She had expected motherhood to be romantic and was finding it far more *irksome* than she had supposed, revolving far more around dry socks and regular supplies of beef sandwiches than any grand emotional rescue, of filling their stomachs in a perfectly conventional fashion rather than making of herself a bridge for the passage of their liberated feet. While Benedict, who could supply sandwiches in any quantity or variety and held the view that, at present, his duty was to keep them safe rather than set them free, returned from the company of the silent, critical youngsters looking jaded and worn out.

Yet he continued, regularly and rigidly, not only to perform his duty — as he saw it — but to hold Nola, so far as he could, to hers. It was a situation from which Claire could only keep her distance. Her own childhood, stifled by her mother's obsession with Edward, had made her unusually wary of finding herself in the same position with regard to other children. And she had no desire to complicate the already taut and complex lives of Christian and Conrad Swanfield, who had no real relationship with their own mother, by expecting them to form a relationship with her. She was neither emotionally prepared nor physically old enough to be their mother. What could she ever seem to them but an intruder, as Edward had always seemed to her? Once or twice, meeting them by chance, she tried to talk to them and dismally failed; not, she imagined, because they disliked her but because they had never given any thought to her at all. She did not concern them. Did she wish to bring herself to their attention? Was she up to it? She thought not. Benedict did not disagree.

"Let's not prolong the agony," he told her. "Where's the sense to that?"

"No sense."

"Then keep your promise this time, Claire. Don't come back to me."

She promised. Six times, in fact, from May to August, a promise six times broken.

"You shouldn't come to me when I call."

"You shouldn't call me."

So it went on.

What they needed now was an event, an accident, an intervention from outside either to force them apart, which they freely admitted would be for the best, or to bind them irrevocably together, taking the decision out of their hands. She had lived her whole life according to the whims of such accidents and interventions, making the best or enduring the worst of what happened or of what had been done to her. He had lived his life, retained his impeccable composure, by ensuring that very little happened to him at all. And there were times now when the great defense of that composure began to crack, or perhaps even worse, to melt away.

One night at Thornwick it ebbed far enough to provide a moment of destiny, one of those small vital lapses into what may afterward be seen as a great folly or great wisdom, one of those short half-hours or less which can change, sometimes in one direction, sometimes in another, the whole course of lives.

The black marble bath was not quite big enough for two and so, whenever the day had been long and hot, they bathed quickly, separately. Benedict usually first, Claire second since it was then, in the expectation of making love, that she prepared herself with the sponges and creams, the paraphernalia of caution and commonsense which she kept, carefully wrapped and disguised, in his bathroom cabinet. But this evening, meeting her in the bedroom doorway as he came from the bath, finding her undressed and waiting her turn, he did not move aside but stood for what seemed a long while looking down at her intently, examining her body in a manner which suddenly embarrassed her.

She spoke his name in inquiry. He shook his head, dismissing, denying whatever had been in his mind and then, very suddenly, as if the thought had refused its dismissal and come rushing back again, lifted her onto the bed and, covering her body with the greater strength and heat and weight of his own, filling her nostrils with the particular scents of his skin and hair which could only be Benedict, began the slow process of possession to which she surrendered at once, until the memory of her contraceptive gadgetry still reposing in his bathroom cupboard caused her a thrill of alarm.

"Darling — I have to go to the bathroom —"

"Ah yes — Doctor Marie Stopes is waiting is she?"

Yet still he held her.

"Benedict — ?" Her voice, to her own ears, sounded small and bewildered.

"Yes. I know."

"Then let me get up."

"Yes." But he continued to make love to her, his recklessness — and when had he ever been reckless in his life before? — producing no further alarm in her as it should have done but a warm, rapidly stirring excitement: a glow of wonder.

"Shall we take the risk just once, Claire — and see?"

Had he really said that? She wound her arms around his neck and kissed him slowly, taking time as well as pleasure, because she wanted to think about it, to bask for as long as she could in this perilous, tantalizing madness. For of course it *was* madness. Wonderful and incredible but totally insane.

Her struggle, throughout her adult life, had been against pregnancy not toward it, but now, flooding her awareness, came his entirely primitive, entirely natural male desire to fertilize, as an act of perfect union and possession, his chosen woman. Of course he would not do it. But by allowing her to see that he desired it, he had given her a treasure. She would always remember it.

"Oh Lord — what am I doing?" she said.

"Loving me."

Yes. That was it. Loving him. And hazarding her future, as she had always done, on an act of chance or fate, risking herself, once again, on a throw of the dice and making the best she could, afterward, of the way they fell. Loving him. Trusting him. Giving herself in full. A mood of absolute abandon possessed her, going beyond sensuality, beyond all desire for such refinements as orgasm to a basic and far more primitive need. He wanted to make her pregnant. Her body was aching now and greedy to conceive. She had never, in her whole life, been so touched by madness, so aware of danger yet dazzled by what she recognized and continued to think of, long afterward, as glory. And it was the glory that mattered. She belonged now entirely to him yet, at the same time, she had never felt so totally in possession of herself. She had agreed, by this act, to belong to him. She had consented. They had chosen to be together. All that remained to be decided now were the practicalities.

"Lie still," he said and she obeyed him, curled warmly against him while his seed completed its journey through her womb weaving, beyond any question, the irrevocable pattern of their lives. It was the seed, she realized, which would decide.

"Have we gone crazy, Benedict?"

"Very likely. One learns odd things about oneself. I ought to be ashamed, I suppose."

"I suppose so. I ought to have stopped you."

Hearing the clock chime she got out of bed feeling strange and shy, a little unreal, and, holding her for a moment in what seemed a delicate embrace, he began to dress her very carefully and thoroughly, fastening every button, smoothing every fold, tucking her into her clothes and keeping her warm as if she herself had been a helpless, precious child.

The night had turned cold. He buttoned her coat, turned up her collar, wound his scarf around her neck, clicked his tongue in indulgent reproach because she had no gloves, tilted her chin and kissed her lightly on her nose and her forehead while she leaned against him, weak and dizzy with this new depth of emotion. And, still safe in her sweet and wonderful madness, she believed that she was already carrying his child.

"If you are so careful with me now," she said, still leaning against him, still safely and warmly insane, "how will you treat me in six months' time?"

And, his mouth against her hair, he made, gravely and precisely, his first and only declaration of love.

"I will look after you, Claire, and cherish you as much as I possibly can. It will be a great deal."

Yet the folly, was not repeated. And when, after two weeks of suppressed agony, she was able to tell him that she had not conceived, she understood that they had reached the end. The sweet madness had become an act of gross irresponsibility for which — once he was quite certain that there would be no consequences for her to bear — he now felt able to apologize. There seemed no longer the remotest possibility that he would ever lose his reason in that way again. They had taken their gamble. Had they won or lost? It made no difference now. He was going to Italy in a week or two with his sons to encourage their taste for pictures and statues and grand opera. Nola, just possibly, would go with them. Claire smiled. Yes. She hoped so. Quite definitely it would be for the best. And, as for herself, she would stay in Faxby until Polly's wedding at the end of September, and then . . . ? Well, as they had so often remarked, the world was full of opportunities for an independent and not precisely dull-witted woman. She would find plenty to do.

They were very careful with one another now, elaborately courteous, so anxious to be helpful and cooperative and never — in any circumstances — to blame or criticize each other for anything, that their reticence was sometimes deeply moving, while at others it grated on their nerves.

They no longer made love. This too, they both hastily and frequently agreed, was for the best. For if she had not conceived by intent on that strange wild night, it did not follow that she could not conceive now, by accident. The following "Family Sunday" which now invariably included Roger Timms, also brought Elvira Redfearn to High Meadows at Benedict's invitation, her presence in his car that night preventing him from being alone with Claire. Yet the next time they were alone together, when he took her to Thornwick to collect the odds and ends which Mrs. Mayhew could easily have packed and sent on to her, she was aware not only that he wanted her but that if she moved only half a step toward him, he would not resist.

But she experienced no feeling of power, nothing but a deep, damp sorrow clinging to her like seaweed, slowing her down as she went to the bathroom for her toothbrush, the bedroom for her black silk night-gown, her wispy *lingerie,* her perfume and powder, her discreet little embroidered wallet of contraceptive sponges and creams, all the essentials of a love affair which, when hastily bundled together, did not even fill a small bag.

It was over. Five minutes to pack it away, zip up her bag, and go. She sat down on the bed, feeling the room around her, remembering almost to the point of seeing and hearing herself and Benedict together here, tense sometimes and often anxious, so often in that aching state of half-happiness, of not quite daring to be happy, that terrible sense of time lost, time running out, which had been the most unbearable of all.

They had been cruelly, mistakenly right for each other. Only the time had been wrong and the location; and the crowding demands of others. Left alone together they would have been perfectly and deeply content. He would have filled her life. She would have warmed and broadened and delighted his. In a world of half-unions and decaying unions, half-commitments and unwilling commitments, of falling stan-dards and failing virtues, they could have been whole together, honest, and sound.

"I will look after you and cherish you as much as I possibly can. It will be a great deal."

What a monstrous waste. What a criminal squandering of time which ought never, *never,* to be squandered; what an unpardonable throwing away of life and of the love which was its greatest privilege. She had seen too much of that. The door opened. "Are you ready, Claire?"

"Yes." She got up, feeling light and faintly unsteady, a note or two out of tune with herself, unable to remember just where she had put her bag. Yes — there it was, at her feet. She would never come here again. Somehow she must make herself believe it. She smiled, held out both her hands to him and, lifting her off her feet and onto the bed again, he made love to her like a man in deep water struggling for air, her body unresisting, passive, while he raged over it and then, his needs spent, shuddered and turned his back to her with a long sigh.

It had been for both of them a terrible experience, an act of extreme compulsion beyond any control she had ever learned to exercise and beyond his entirely, it seemed. He had not intended it and now, as in their first days together, he had turned away from her, leaving her alone.

"Benedict —" She had not expected him to answer her.

She had eased his bodily tensions, his inbred guilts and remorse so many times after making love with little more than the soft pressure of her fingertips. Dare she touch him now? Gingerly she reached out a hand, feeling the muscles of his shoulder contracting hard and rigid beneath her palm. "Leave me alone," he snarled and she drew back her hand as if his skin had burned her.

He got up without a word, dressed, went out of the room and after a while, her head and her bones aching, her skin sore in patches, hot in others, she put on her clothes very neatly she thought when one considered how badly her hands were shaking, and followed him.

He was sitting by the great stone hearth, no fire in the grate, the lamps unlit, the room, without its familiar illumination of jeweled glass, the glow and crackle of pine logs burning, looking shadowy and vaguely sinister, feeling chill, giving her the uneasy impression of a stage set when the audience and the players are gone.

This was not the house she knew. Nor the man. Or had the house ever been more than an illusion which had now lost its point and its purpose, which he was just too weary now to create?

Had *she* done this to him?

He did not speak to her.

"Are you blaming me?" she said, sitting down in her usual place by the burned-out fire.

"You?" He looked up, hard-mouthed and stern, although his contempt, as it turned out, was not for her. "Of course not. I have been at fault in every respect from the start. You have done nothing against your nature, Claire. I have violated everything I have ever valued in mine."

She heard him and understood. She knew exactly what he meant. But all she saw, with the shock of knowing she ought to have seen it much sooner, was the grayness in his face, the loss of color and energy and substance.

"Benedict, you're not well are you?"

"No." He seemed surprised that she thought it necessary to ask.

"What is it?"

"My disease?" He shrugged. "Of the mind, I suppose. One could call it irresponsibility, indecision, self-disgust — the inability to do what I know to be right. One could call it loss of faith, in myself and my own judgment — or loss of control. A damnable set of symptoms for a man like me. Loss of resolution. Misery. Take your pick. But I rather think . . ."

He paused. And when he spoke again his voice seemed to be rising from a chasm. "I think that it will very likely — No, Claire, I think *you* are killing me."

She heard her own breath catching somewhere in her chest, a startled strangled sound, soon over, and then, folding her hands, she bowed her head a little and sat quietly, back straight, ankles neatly together, with nothing more to say or to do, with nothing to hope for and nothing to offer him now but the strange gift of her absence.

"Don't you know what has happened to me?"

He had not said, "Don't you know what you've done to me?" But she understood.

"I was not unhappy when we met. I was not happy either. Few people are. I had everything I wanted, or everything I allowed myself to want, which amounts to the same. I was — *satisfied.* I don't expect to be satisfied again. But what I must do is function. It is essential to me — imperative. Perhaps you will believe me if I tell you that without that ability I am like a child in the dark. And I am not functioning, Claire. Because of you. I am not as I intend — and must — and wish — to be."

He was speaking through clenched teeth, painfully, the effort beading his forehead with sweat, the veins at his temples swollen and blue, his voice still rising to her from a hollow distance. "I can't resist you, Claire. And I doubt if you can comprehend how much that appalls me. Please — *resist me.* If you force me to go on like this, then I believe you will break me. I know you don't want to do that."

The possibility had never occurred to her. The danger — of discovery, of disgrace — had always seemed to be hers. The likelihood of heartache had seemed hers too. But now . . . "I will look after you and cherish you as much as I can." He would have kept his word. It was much too late for that. Too late even for the blue room at High Meadows. And it was her nature to heal, not to hurt. She closed her eyes, clasping her hands tight together, bowing her head still further, as she took into her mind the stark knowledge of how much she had hurt him. "You have done nothing against your nature," he had said to her. But by wounding him, by reducing him to this despair, she too had violated everything within herself she valued. She had believed love, any kind of love, to be a blessing, well worth the price one had to pay. Or the sacrifice. But she had loved him and harmed him.

"I'll get my coat," she said.

Outside the wind, howling down from the moor, seemed very cold, her lips stiff and heavy, difficult to manage, as she got into the car, trying to smile at him, to make a sign, since she had no voice to tell him that he, and she, and everything, so far as possible, would eventually — possibly — be all right. She would never come here again. She was leaving in sorrow and leaving sorrow behind her. It was another death, another France. She had endured another battle, emerging alive as she always seemed to do, but more than ever defeated.

"I wanted —" she faltered, speaking each word as if it were made of glass, "I thought — I might make you happy —"

"It was never really a possibility," he said.

She dreamed that night, once again, of blind soldiers, not shuffling in line this time but inflicting destruction on other blind soldiers, two battalions of sightless men killing without knowing whom they killed, as Paul and Jeremy had died, as she — without seeing — had wounded Benedict. She woke, her heart pounding, feeling his ruby around her neck like a talisman to call him back. But she must never do that now. Never again. Lying in the dark, her vision distorted by dreams and shadows, she knew herself to be dangerous to him, felt herself to be cruel and crying herself back to sleep, dreamed of him again, sitting at the dinner table at High Meadows, stern and rigid until, with the sudden horror of dreams, his skin began to crack and to let out not blood but cold gray water, the brackish, grimy liquid that city snow becomes at the thaw.

"He is melting," said Miriam placidly, employing a napkin to mop up the mess. "I told you so."

"Can I have my money now?" said Eunice, her mouth full of sherry trifle.

"What shall I wear," said Polly, "for the funeral?" And they continued to eat their dinner with that terrible gray water spilling all over the table, over their hands and into their laps, making puddles around their feet, a great stream of it, a flood which had been Benedict and would not stop coming.

She woke with a mighty jerk in such a state of terror and confusion that, leaping out of bed, needing air and escape and daylight, she could not find her bedroom door, nor the light switch, stumbling around the room with the winged panic of a bird which has flown in through a window and hurls itself upon the glass in its frenzy to get out again.

She spent the next day going about her normal business at the Crown in painfully suppressed agitation, startled by the sound of the telephone, the appearance of a telegram boy, a footstep at her door, fearing and hoping for a message from him, ashamed of the hope, feeding the fear.

She spent her free evening writing notes to him of desperate apology — the last thing in the world I ever meant to do was hurt you — which she then tore up and threw into the fire. She must not contact him. No matter who she offended in the process she must not see him. She must not set foot in High Meadows until he had left for Italy and, on his return, if any danger still remained of doing him further injury, then she would simply give up her job and move away. It would not be easy. Dorothy would be hurt by it. And Kit. She had never meant to harm them either. Guilt, a familiar companion, began to nudge up to her, its whine filling her ears, its sticky hands clinging to her as Miriam clung, its weight dragging at her heels. Another death. And what had she done with her life, since Paul's death two years ago, but cause damage to everyone she cared for? Benedict. Dorothy. Kit. None of them had anything to thank her for. And perhaps what hurt her most was the knowledge, acquired from past griefs, that she would recover. She was not only free now to begin again but *could* begin again, would assuredly do so.

Yet it did not make her sorrow any less because the war had taught her that no sorrow lasts for ever. And whatever else she had to face, there remained the problem of Miriam. There were ten days to be got through before Benedict's holiday, ten days of letters on lavender-colored, lavender-scented paper, Miriam's dainty little summonses to "Come and help me choose a hat for the wedding," "Darling, do give me some moral support about the *trousseau*," "Dear Claire, I am not well enough to go to Leeds with Polly today to match the bridesmaids' taffeta, and since you are to be her matron of honor —" Ten dangerous days, including one "Family Sunday" which must be avoided at any price. She would have to cancel at the last minute, she decided, so that Miriam would have no time to contact Edward who would be sure to send Dorothy at once to inquire just what she meant by so outrageously neglecting her duty.

What excuses could she make? She would need a great many. She sat down at her kitchen table to ponder, her hands clasped tight together, jaw clenched, eyes clouded over with concentration so that she paid no attention as Euan Ash came into the room and, watching her for a while with wry amusement, sat down beside her.

"Pardon me, my dear young lady . . ."

"Oh —" He had startled her. "Euan! Yes? What did you say?"

"Nothing desperately vital. I just wondered — would I be right in thinking that you were having a crisis?"

"Quite right."

"And not enjoying it?"

"Not much."

"Broken off with your bloke again, have you?"

She nodded, finding that she did not wish to say it.

"Oh well — you've done that before, haven't you?"

"Yes, but now I have to mean it."

"So —" He gave her a radiant smile, "if it's true that practice makes perfect — and you *have* put in plenty of practice — then there should be no problem."

"No."

"But of course there is. Shall I solve it for you?"

"Don't be stupid, Euan."

He produced a battered packet of cigarettes, took one and pushed the packet towards her, a gesture not of man to woman but of camaraderie.

"Help yourself." She did, realizing as she leaned toward his match that the sky behind the ill-fitting kitchen window had turned dark. How long had she been sitting here, brooding, regretting?

"What time is it, Euan?"

He shrugged. "Well, you wouldn't expect me to know exactly, but the pubs closed about an hour ago so I suppose it must be late. Why? Have you anywhere to go?"

"Just bed."

"Well yes — I was rather hoping you'd see that the time has come at last. And don't give me that 'Control yourself, Lieutenant Ash' look either, Claire. It's all for the best. I'm really rather positive about that."

"Euan — please don't be so —"

"Absolutely sensible, my darling. You want a reason not to go back to this bloke of yours don't you? All right — come to bed with me and that's sure to do the trick. Not, I hasten to add, because I'm such a perfect lover but because you wouldn't feel right about more than one at once — if you see what I mean." Shaking her head, she smiled in spite of herself and then, meeting those deceptively candid blue eyes, paused, stared at him, her gaze held for a long steady moment by his.

"You mean it, don't you?"

"Oh yes. I mean it."

Leaning forward, the table between them, not even their hands touching, he lay his cool closed mouth on hers and then opened her lips gradually with a cool tongue, an exchange not yet of passion but of expertise.

"Do I pass the test?" he said.

"Magnificently. But then — just think of all that practice."

"I know. So — do I graduate to my night of ecstasy in your arms? You must admit I've been awfully patient."

She shook her head. "How can I Euan? I'd be using you."

"Oh — my dear girl — don't worry about that. I've done the same myself many a time. I'd be the very last to complain. Use me. Feel absolutely free. What are friends for?"

"Not quite to be used like that."

"Nonsense. If this were the night before Passchendaele and something had whispered to me that I wasn't going to make it over the top tomorow, can you honestly say that you'd refuse?"

"No. I wouldn't. I didn't. But it's not Passchendaele tomorrow."

364

"Oh yes it is, Claire. It's always Passchendaele."

Not for *them*, of course. But for him and for her. For *us*. So it was. Of its own accord her hand found his and clasped it with the pressure of the initiated, of those who, having passed through the same fire, have acquired the same scars.

"Good," he said. "I do believe I'm starting to convince you. Let's have a cup of tea while you're making up your mind."

He scraped back his chair, easy in his movements, still very thin, she noticed, his fine hair too long and straggly, his bricklayer's shirt a disgrace, frayed at the collar and cuffs but faintly scented nevertheless with a sharp, mossy cologne, his manner, as he filled the kettle and went to light the gas, almost debonair. He was even whistling under his breath, something vaguely familiar to her, most probably vulgar when, she wasn't sure what happened, a draft from the ill-fitting window, water spilling from the kettle which he had filled too full, perhaps a combination of both which, as he turned up the burner, put out his match, leaving naked, malodorous gas spluttering, beneath the kettle, from unlit jets.

It was not serious. He had only to turn off the stove or strike another match. She knew, instinctively, that he could do neither.

"Christ," he said, his face chalk-white, his hand trying to go forward toward the stove and then, like the rest of his body, cringing away from it, "Oh Christ —" And with a movement of total, terrible panic he threw himself back onto his chair and cowered there shaking, his face pressed hard against the table, his arms over his head in the position of a man protecting the more vital parts of his body from shells.

She ran to the stove and turned it off, smelling the gas herself now, and then ran back to him, finding him, as she had expected, still shaking, his shoulders, as she put her arm around them, ice-cold. And although his lungs had sounded clear and unclogged a moment ago he was struggling in hard agony for each breath now.

She got him with some difficulty into her flat since he was violently unwilling to go, wanting to be alone to see it through, to hide somewhere as animals do in their extremity, and either cure himself or not. But she had tackled larger men than Euan in states of far more chronic delirium and eventually, by the simple procedure of tugging and pulling, threatening and cajoling, she got him as far as her living room. And, when he absolutely refused and she failed to compel him to get into her bed, she brought her quilt and blankets and pillows and made a nest for him, as she had done once before, on her hearth rug.

"Oh — Christ —" It was all he could say. It was all he had said on that other pleasant summer night when the gas had started to seep up the trench toward him. It was the last thing he remembered, his own voice screaming a blasphemy not a prayer before the poison had ripped the lining from his lungs, torn out his eyes, or so he'd thought, drowning him in a thick, stinking obscenity which had lived in his nostrils ever since. One whiff of domestic gas and he was drowning again. And with it came the great cold, the trembling of limbs, the chattering of teeth and bones, the terrible fear that the bowels and the bladder as well as the rest of him would lose control. She knew that. If it happened she would do her utmost to convince him that she hadn't noticed. But now all she could do was keep him warm and, the summer night turning chill, she got under the quilt with him and held him, using her body heat to little avail against the bitter inner cold, the freezing sweat, which assailed him, talking and saying nothing, simply keeping up the murmuring of reassurance until the ferocious shaking eased, a little warmth returned, and he was no longer blind with remembered terror but merely exhausted, sickened, angry, horribly ashamed.

"Oh Christ — why *now*." Lying back on the pillows, his thin face eaten half away by the black smudges which had started to spread beneath his eyes, he became fluent and excessively obscene on the subject of his ill-timed attack of "neurasthenia" and of all that had caused it.

"You should take your clothes off," she said calmly. "Your shirt is soaking. And sweat can probably give you pneumonia, like rain, if you let it dry on you."

But when she began to unbutton his shirt he said, "No Claire — don't nurse me."

"All right." She bent down, kissed his mouth instead, went off to fetch him a dressing gown and then, while he changed, made him a mug of hot tea.

"Did you put a tot of whiskey in it?"

"I might have done."

"You did — bless you. I'm still cold. Do your small magic with the bedclothes again, Claire — and the pillows."

Once more she built a nest around him, got in beside him and stayed there, the two of them drinking their tea and huddling together like orphans of the forest beneath a covering of leaves.

"Well," he said, "so now you know the ghastly truth about Lieutenant Ash. *Not* the young Lochinvar exactly — not by a long chalk. Clapped-out lungs. And his own particular brand of St. Vitus Dance. About the only thing I haven't got, or haven't had, is syphilis."

"Well of course not, Lieutenant. Didn't the officers have a better class of camp follower?"

"Not so you'd notice. But about the neurasthenia —"

"Is that what they told you to call it, Euan?"

366

"Is there another name?"

"Shell-shock."

"Well yes, love. But that's what the Tommies have. I *was* an officer. And at that level it's neurasthenia."

"We all have it, Euan — to some extent. All of us who were over there for more than six months, I mean. That's what they told us in the hospitals. They told us to watch ourselves because nobody knows how long it's likely to last or what it might do."

"I haven't noticed you shaking and having cold sweats, Claire."

"No. But I dream. I do irrational things. I can't make up my mind to anything. Once — just once thank God — I hallucinated. I suppose it could happen again."

He lay back into the pillows, his breathing easier now but his face drawn and spent.

"I hope not. I saw a corpse at one time, in a bonny old state of decay, grinning at me whenever I looked in the mirror. Perfectly ridiculous. I knew the bloody thing wasn't really there. But it stopped me from shaving for a month or two. I'll bet nothing like that ever happened to Kit."

"He's older," she said, feeling in honor bound to defend him. "And he was probably a good bit steadier in the first place than us. I suppose he had to be. And he wasn't gassed either."

"No." He closed his eyes, his breath rasping again for just a moment at the memory. "It was the thing I dreaded most. I didn't even like the look of our own gas-men. Peculiar crew they were. Made me downright uneasy. But my first wound was nice and clean. A wholesome piece of shrapnel in the groin. An inch or two to the right, of course, and my voice could well have been several octaves higher. But never fear. Those two inches were the salvation of my race — or would have been if I intended to be the father of children, which I certainly don't."

"Don't you really — not ever?" She had remembered, with affectionate, tolerant amusement that one day he would be a baronet, a man with titles and lands to inherit.

"Christ, no. Have you read the terms of that Peace Treaty they've concocted? Twenty years from now they could go to war again. I don't feel much inclined to breed sons for that."

She shivered. She would be forty-five by then. Young enough to suffer the same agony all over again.

"Don't think like that, Euan. We need some kind of faith in the future."

"Have you found any?"

"Not much. I've tried too — pretty hard."

"Poor Claire. You need a good man with a firm hand."

"Yes. I know."

And leaning her head beside his on the pillow, their faces turned toward each other, almost touching, she told him about Paul, everything she knew, everything she had hoped for, all the memories she had guarded in silence because no one else but an initiate, a survivor, one of the walking wounded like herself, could have understood them.

"Oh yes," he said. "I'm very comfortable with Paul. I know him well. What about this other bloke — the one who's been crucifying you lately?"

She told him rapidly, explicitly, easing her burden just a little by an act of confession which she knew would wash over him and be quickly set aside.

He whistled and shook his head.

"Well, you said it yourself, Claire my love. We've all got shell-shock to some degree. You don't shake, but could you be carrying a death wish do you think? I had one once. Lots of the chaps did. When they sent me home after the shrapnel, I volunteered for service overseas again. Went back to get killed, I suppose, and got myself gassed instead. Don't let that happen to you."

She shook her head, the movement bringing her face closer to his, his hand coming to rest on the nape of her neck, his eyes half-closed and screened by long pale lashes, their blue insolence dimmed.

"What a damnable thing to happen," he said. "Just a bloody gas jet blowing out and all of a sudden I'm impotent."

"Not for long."

"I dare say. I'm sorry, Claire. You've had no real luck, have you, with your men."

"Have you — with women?"

He smiled, his eyes still closed, not his usual smile of malicious sweetness, not his look of a depraved angel to which she was accustomed and against which she knew how to defend herself, but an expression of genuine amusement.

"Doesn't apply to me, my darling. I've never been in love — with a woman."

"Oh — !"

He sat up, still pale, but grinning.

"Oh — she says. And what she doesn't say, because she's a lady, is whatever can he mean, I wonder? Could it possibly be the worst — the thing they locked Oscar Wilde up for and Mummy would never talk about? Could it be that beastly nonsense — whatever it is?"

"Could it?" If so then she would take it calmly, might be disappointed but would learn to understand. She could think of many other things she would find harder to forgive than that.

"No," he said, bathing her now in that brilliant, beautiful smile which was his self-defense, "not exactly."

"Do you want to tell me?"

"Why not? I've heard your confession. You may as well hear mine. I had a friend. Naturally one jumps to the obvious conclusion, the famous homosexuality of our public schools — all those lovely beatings and rolling about together on the rugger field. But it wasn't that. We were at school together, of course. What else did any of us have the time to do before the war but go to school? And then Cambridge. We had our first girls together — so our mating instincts were in the right direction — and we swapped notes afterward like proper little gentlemen. Quite a lot of girls, in fact. It was just that the best relationship we had was with each other. More than brothers. His father was a judge in India who hadn't seen him since he was eight. My family were only in Sussex but it might have been the moon for all the difference they made to me. Good people, of course. Just didn't believe in molly coddling their offspring with affection. And I was a pleasant, affectionate sort of a lad in those days. Am I making sense?"

She nodded and brushed the tip of her nose very lightly against his.

"Yes. You're saying you had a friend who loved you and that you loved him."

"That's right. And that we didn't love anybody else. Didn't need to. And there was nobody else we considered fit to love in any case. We were very much admired at school, my friend and I, I can tell you. Particularly him. He was handsome and witty and clever, and rather more than that — something extra about him, an ingredient nobody could ever name but that everybody knew was there. Charm doesn't go halfway to describe it. He was arrogant, of course. But so was I. He got away with things — always. I managed it most of the time. Everybody knew that whatever he made up his mind to do in life it would be a splendid success. He'd make his first million as soon as he felt like it. Marry the girl he wanted when he wanted. One could see it written all over him, somehow. He was generous too. He always gave away more than he could afford and it was the only thing he did quietly, so nobody would know. You'd have liked him Claire. He was the face in that picture — you know — the one I gave to the dancing teacher."

"Yes." She had understood.

"We joined the army together in 1914, as soon as we could. Took our degrees and applied for commissions straightaway. Everybody expected that of us. We couldn't wait to put on those uniforms, believe me we couldn't, and set off looking for that Holy Grail. What a pair of gallant, pure-hearted knights we were. My heart would bleed, if I still had one, when I think of it — dedicating our swords and our souls both together to the cause of Justice and Freedom and Right. "Now, God be thanked Who has matched us with His hour." Those lines were written for us. We were told by some doddering old pedagogue or other, just after we were commissioned, how lucky we were to be young in the glorious year of 1914, how privileged to be able to take up arms in this glorious crusade, and we believed him. We were going to ride into battle together, chaste and valiant warriors, trumpets sounding and banners flying. We didn't know we were giving ourselves up to be slaughtered by incompetent fools who'd buy a few yards of ground with thousands and tens of thousands of our lives and then give it back again the next morning, when they'd cleared the corpses off it, because it didn't suit. And when it comes to the incompetence of officers, I reckon I can say as much as I like. I was an officer. I was incompetent. *I* knew that. The men knew it. The only person who didn't seem to know it, or didn't care — apart from the fools who gave me my commission in the first place — was the bloody company commander. And what possessed him to think that because I knew Latin and Greek I knew how to lead men into battle I can't imagine. One learns, of course, by one's mistakes. And since one buries one's mistakes — in the trenches — one gets away with it. But I don't have to tell you what kind of a hell it was — what kind of a bloody cock-up they made it —"

"No, Euan."

He had started to sweat again and she wiped the moisture gently from his forehead with a corner of the blanket, removing it drop by drop, taking time and care, giving him her patience and her attention.

"They murdered us Claire."

"I know."

"For fun, it seemed to me. Just playing games."

"Yes."

"And where was Sir Galahad then — ?"

She knew he was going to tell her, needed to tell her. And when she saw that, despite his need, he couldn't quite speak the words, she said quietly, believing she knew the answer, "What happened to your friend?"

"He's in Edinburgh," he said. And the effort of bringing out that single sentence, of making that one short admission exhausted him, taking what little remained of his energy clean away.

"I didn't realize —" Nor, in fact, did she know what to make of it.

"No," he smiled, very weakly, "I suppose not. You thought I had a wife tucked away up there, didn't you?"

"It crossed my mind."

"Naturally enough. A lot of the chaps did get married on leave and then couldn't remember why. But no — marriage wasn't precisely my style even then. There's a hospital up there — a special kind of place. Do you know it? Bad cases. The ones who really aren't fit to be seen. Good Lord — we've got to put them somewhere, haven't we? Can't have the poor blighters running about the streets and frightening the horses. Not that any of them can run."

"*Euan.*" She put her hand into his, her cheek against his cheek, feeling a moisture on his skin that could have been sweat but which was probably tears. And she was crying anyway.

"He's paralyzed and blind. And burned of course. He's twenty-six. He's been in that hospital bed since he was twenty-three."

For a while longer they remained close together, hands clasped, cheek against cheek, their breath mingling, two lives barely salvaged, remembering those other lives, younger than theirs, which had been thrown away.

"Have you seen him?"

"No." That, most of all, he needed to say.

"Will you?"

"I'm trying. At first it was out of the question, of course, because I was in a bit of a mess myself — what with the gas and the nerves all shot to hell. Shaking and sweating all the livelong day just then. And afterward — when I got on my feet . . . Oh — I've got as far as Edinburgh twice. But I came away again. I tried all winter in Whitby to get myself on a train. I had to change at Carlisle. You know the rest."

"Does he know — ? I mean that you might be coming?"

He gave a short, harsh laugh, masking what could have been a sob. "I don't think he knows anything very much — or cares. His father died a couple of years ago and there didn't seem to be any money. I pay for certain things. I have an allowance from home. Not much because they're trying to get me back again. Most of it goes up there, which is why I'm usually short of the readies. What I can't do is go and look at him. He was — rather glorious. I can't somehow manage to go and face up to what's left of him. Feeble of me, don't you think? Though pretty much what you'd expect from a chap who was never keen on cricket or rugger or letting his dogs tear pretty little woodland animals apart."

"It's not feeble, Euan. I'm not sure I could go either."

"Oh — I think you could. I really think so. I think he could too — in my place — for me."

"What good would it do?"

"None to him, I suppose. It might, just possibly, set me right with myself. On the other hand, it might send me completely round the bend.

I shall have to give it a try. Can't say just when of course. But I'm working on it. I've already been two years on my way."

"If you have to do it, Euan, then I wouldn't wait much longer —"

"Why ever not, Claire?" Sitting up again he gave her a dazzling smile. "He won't die you know. Mark my words, nothing so pleasant as that is likely to happen to him. He might get worse — in fact, one could even rely on it. But he'll get old. He'll live. Seems a pity the poor bastard hasn't got a friend with the decency to hold a pillow to his face."

He began to get up and she said quickly, "You don't have to leave, Euan." And taking her hands he pulled her to her feet and held her for a moment, the feel of his body sharp and cool, angular, twenty-six years old.

"Thank you, Claire. That means a lot to me. Rather more than I'm comfortable with, truth to tell."

"What does *that* mean?"

"I'm not sure. It might mean I shall ask you to come to Edinburgh with me. Would you come?"

"I'll know when you ask me. If you ever do."

She walked with him across the hall to his chilly, dusty room, turned down his bed, arranged his pillows, tucked him in.

"Kiss me goodnight."

She kissed him, a sister's kiss — or a mother's — and then, his hand in her hair, a lover's kiss.

"If we make love now," he said, "that's all we'll do, and all we'll think about. Lovers come fairly easy in any case, don't they? I need a friend."

She smiled and kissed him again.

"I'm here, Euan," she said.

19

RETURNING from the Crown the next afternoon she found three notes from Miriam in her letterbox, delivered by Parker at intervals throughout the day; and Parker himself at her doorstep bringing a fourth, a gentle almost kittenish bombardment of arch little words and phrases begging her attendance at High Meadows on Wedding Business, "Claire, dear, I believe Polly is having a Crisis, as one would expect. And please dear, you cannot have forgotten the great Mystery of the Lace Garters. You must have been among the last to see them, darling. So it follows, therefore, that we cannot start the Great Garter Hunt without you. And on Wednesday next we are having a special little farewell party for Benedict and Nola and the children. You cannot wish to miss that."

She thanked Parker for his trouble, told him there was no reply and, without even opening the door of her flat, went straight back to the hotel and informed Kit Hardie, in a manner which greatly alarmed him, that she must get out of Faxby for a while. Personal troubles, she said, family troubles at High Meadows and with her mother at Upper Heaton, Polly's wedding taking everything over and getting on everybody's nerves, Miriam commandeering every minute of her free time to match samples of taffeta for bridesmaids' dresses and go looking for lost garters. And she was tired. The hotel was busy, she knew, but surely no crisis was brewing? John David, in his morose "neurasthenic" fashion had settled down well enough, and if he *did* have a tendency to upset the kitchen maids, more by what he did not say than by anything he said, so that they became nervous and dropped things and then burst into tears when he "looked" at them, only two of them had actually left and had been easily replaced. And Amandine Keller, who could be morose and difficult herself, was still there, putting up the price of her lover's fish, one noticed, but turning out her full quota of cakes and pastries, more delicious than ever since she had fallen in love. Nor had Aristide Keller proved much of a threat since his release from jail, his plans to open a restaurant in Town Hall Square having run into trouble due to objections from the Town Hall itself about the conversion of the premises he had chosen for culinary use. Had Kit had a hand in that? Possibly, since the Crown had seemed unusually full of Redfearns and Greenwoods lately. But she had no time to wonder about it now.

"You could spare me, Kit. Just a week or ten days at the most would put me right."

"You're wrong. I can't spare you at all," he said. But for ten days he would let her go.

She told no one else but Euan to whom all departures seemed quite natural and her mother who, sitting in Feathers' Teashop the next morning, aware that her daughter's bags were already packed, raised an immediate and entirely predictable objection. Edward would not like it. Miriam Swanfield had already mentioned — just a hint, really, without the least wish to cause any trouble — that Claire had been neglecting her lately. No, she hadn't been angry, nothing like that. Sad. And disappointed. And Edward had taken it very much to heart.

"She wondered if you weren't well," said Dorothy fiercely. "And then — I could hardly believe it — she suddenly looked quite shy and timid and asked us if we thought she'd done anything, unwittingly, to upset you. One could see she was really worried about it. Just imagine — Mrs. Miriam Swanfield upsetting herself over *my* daughter. Edward was badly shaken."

"Yes, mother. He would be."

"And he's not well at all — really not."

"No, mother."

"He can't seem to shake off that cold. And his digestion of course is terrible."

"And his temper?"

Dorothy flushed, bit her lip and then, deciding there was no time to argue, shrugged her still handsome shoulders.

"I don't like ingratitude that's all, Claire — *we* don't like it — and the very least you could do for Mrs. Swanfield, in return for all her kindness to you, is to give her a hand with the wedding. It's only three weeks away."

"Five, mother."

"Five then. And a million things to do. Weddings don't arrange themselves, you know."

Dorothy was fond of weddings, had dreamed in her youth of a white satin crinoline of her own and had had to make do, at her first hasty, romantic marriage to Claire's father, with a party dress she had worn twice before, and for Edward, a sensible, matronly outfit of dark blue. And Claire, her pretty daughter — for Claire *was* pretty, she had always thought so — had rushed to church like a schoolgirl in flowered summer muslin and a graduation day straw hat with long, pale pink ribbons.

Remembering it, and the new white gloves left in the taxi, the posy of lilies-of-the-valley which had shaken a little in Claire's pale, young hands, her pale, young face above them, so serious, so very determined to do her best — so young — she smiled at her daughter.

"I'll be back in plenty of time, mother," said Claire, instantly responding, "and then we'll have a morning together — or even a day in Leeds if you like — to choose your wedding hat."

"That would be lovely, dear." So it would, except that Edward would probably not allow it, finding, just as Dorothy had put on her coat and gloves, that some new pain had developed, or that he could feel one of his old and various attacks just coming on. No, no. He didn't wish to alarm her. If she felt it necessary to go off to Leeds then of course she must go. Perhaps if she left his study window slightly ajar and then, should he have cause to cry out for help, somebody — although, of course, one wondered just who — might hear. And Dorothy would buy her wedding hat in ten minutes, the day before the wedding, at the far from fashionable little shop in Upper Heaton or would ask Claire to fetch her whatever seemed suitable from Taylor & Timms.

"Edward," she said, by simple association of ideas, "has ordered a new morning suit. I just hope he will be well enough for the fittings."

"I expect he'll manage it. What have *you* ordered, mother?"

"Oh — don't worry about that. I suppose you'll look very smart."

"I doubt it. Polly won't let anybody outdo her. So she's wearing encrustations of pearls and floating panels of lace and chiffon and yards of embroidered net in her veil, and the poor bridesmaids have to make do with skimpy little frocks in sweet pea shades of taffeta. Mine is lilac and hideous. I shall give it to a jumble sale afterward."

Dorothy was horrified.

"Claire — everybody who is anybody in Faxby will be able to recognize those dresses. Everybody will be at the wedding. And if one of them turns up at a church bazaar then they'll *know*. And if each dress is a different color they'll know it's yours, too. What an insult to Mrs. Swanfield and to Mrs. Timms."

Edward, clearly, would be *very* upset about that.

She left that same afternoon for Scarborough where MacAllister's sister had a boardinghouse, a small, unpretentious establishment in the old town with no particular view of anything but a row of houses like itself, and into which she was "squeezed" good-humoredly, the month being August, simply as a favor to MacAllister. Her room was small and clean, a slope-ceilinged attic painted a pretty rose pink with the kind of narrow, decidedly single bed she had not slept in since her schooldays. The food was simple, ample, appearing regularly and piping hot. Her landlady was pleasant, incurious, had her own life to lead and wanted nothing from Claire but payment in full at the end of ten days. And by then Benedict, and presumably Nola, would have left for three weeks in Italy. Time — her ally now she hoped — would have passed; enough of it to enable her to follow him calmly down the aisle when he gave Polly in marriage to Roger Timms; enough of it to wish him well, with all her heart, if it turned out that he had found a way to live on easier terms with Nola.

She took long walks on the cliffs above a gray, northern sea shrouded more often than not in mist like a finely beaded curtain, escaping the August crowds and setting her mind in order, coming to a halt only when she realized, with love and pain and a certain amount of wry amusement, that everything she did and said, her attitudes and postures, the way she smiled or held her head, her manner of walking, were being played out, each and every one, before an imaginary audience that was Benedict. And she was glad therefore, on the seventh of her ten days, to see Euan Ash, his kit bag on his shoulder, standing at her lodging-house gate.

"Thought I'd have another crack at getting to Edinburgh," he said. "I've left you my canvases and most of my stuff like last time. If I get there I should be back in Faxby in a few days. If not, I'll let you know."

He left his bag with MacAllister's sister who had a fondness for soldiers, and they walked out onto the cliffs as high and far as they could go, moving at their leisure through gray air above gray water until the town disappeared and they were enclosed in a cloudscape of mist, patterned by the swooping and crying of the gulls.

"Look —" he said, and for an hour or more he showed her, as he had once promised, the enchantment of a puddle, the patterns made by rainwater in soft earth, the textures and colors, the rich variety of pebbles, a leaf like a star of pure amber floating beside a tiny white feather tipped with black and streaked, so minutely one had to *think* to see it, with gold.

They looked at tree roots, tangled and thirsty in the salty air; stirred through a windfall of broken branches to release the crushed face of a small blue flower; stood quietly, hand in hand, to observe the comings and goings of a mouse, a frog, a ladybird. They came down from the cliff and looked at the sand, a universe of seaweed and shells, each one with its own face he told her, each bird with its own voice, the sky and sea, which she had thought simply and starkly gray, revealed by his artist's eye as muted layers and shadings of a dozen colors.

"Don't you see the pink and the primrose?"

"No."

"Look — and think. You'll see."

She saw.

They walked back toward the town along the beach, wet and no longer very clean, streaks of damp sand on her skirt from kneeling down to acquaint herself with the mayor and corporation of a rock pool, her shoes never to be the same again, her nails grubby from scratching under rocks for the pleasure of holding a probably indignant shellfish in her hand. Saddened and contented both together. At peace with his companionship yet knowing that when he turned the next corner or the brow of the next hill she might never see him again.

"Are you staying a day or two, Euan?"

"No. I just wanted to tell you I was off. I can get to Carlisle tonight. And from there it's a straight run."

"Euan!" She stopped in her tracks so that he walked a step or two ahead of her. "Don't just try to go this time. Get there. Resolve it."

She could not bear to think of him for what could be his lifetime hesitating at that hospital door, his life's energy absorbed by the need and the fear of going in. Or skulking for ever — and how long could that be? — through northern winters, eternally "on his way," eternally impeded, eternally caught in the nightmare of running without moving, of tunnels leading to blank walls.

"Euan! *Please*."

And, to the consternation of several plump young matrons surrounded by infants and sandcastles and small dogs, he turned, came back to her, put his hands on her shoulders and drew her toward him, watching her come to him, his face intent, engrossed, *looking* at her in depth, in total, in keen, clear-sighted pleasure as he had looked at the pebbles and the grasses. And she let him take her and hold her as if they had been standing not on a beach but a battlefield, a welcome and farewell both together.

"You have to go, Euan, and get it settled. Otherwise I think you'll die of it."

"Yes. Kiss me goodbye."

The plump mothers, to whom sex happened quickly if regularly in the dark, gathered up their children and their yapping little terriers and herded them away, looking back over scandalized shoulders at this odd couple, the tall, young man in the shabby trench coat — a gentleman of course, one could always tell — and the brazen hussy — they knew the type at once — with her short hair and her indecently exposed legs, so busy plying her sinful trade that she had not even noticed them.

"All right," he said, having claimed his kiss and several more for good measure, "that's me sorted out. What about you?"

"Something will turn up."

"I don't doubt it. But listen, Claire, could you — well, not *promise*, of course, I wouldn't go so far as to ask that — could you just hold on a bit? Not make any decisions — of a fairly permanent nature, I mean — until you see me again?"

"And if I don't see you?"

"Lord — don't worry about that. I may be asking you to wait for ever but with a chap like me one can count for ever in months, you know — not years. I just have this uneasy feeling that I might get back to Faxby one day, all eager and bright-eyed and fighting fit, and find you gone."

"I'd leave an address, Euan. Plenty of people would know."

"I dare say. But it wouldn't be much good to me, would it, if you'd just walked down the aisle with some worthy chap — or done something final with your brother-in-law?"

"I suppose not."

He smiled, failing for the first time since she had known him, to produce quite the degree of dazzling waywardness he had intended.

"All I can say just now, Claire, is that I *would* like to see you again."

"That's a lovely thing to say, Euan."

They had a good Yorkshire high tea with MacAllister's jubilantly Irish sister — cold ham and tongue with mustard pickles and salad, pork pies with brown sauce, currant teacakes, malt bread thickly buttered, custard tarts, several pots of strong tea; Euan, who put down an enormous meal to settle his nerves rather than fill his appetite, affording great satisfaction to black-eyed Teresa MacAllister who liked nothing better than to see men eat.

He got his bag.

"I'll be off then."

He knew better than to ask her to come with him to the station. There had been too many trains, too many desperate last embraces for both of them. He would not put her through that again.

"I'll be seeing you — I expect."

"I expect so."

She smiled, very calm, very steady, nothing on the surface to betray the sudden reemergence of an old superstitious dread which had filled her, flooded her, every time she had said goodbye to Paul. "If I keep on smiling he won't get killed." It had become a jingle, repeated over and over in her head as she had watched all those trains pull hideously away, tapping it out with her heels as she had made her way alone through those identical, heart-rending station yards. She had kept on smiling. He had died.

"Goodbye, Euan."

She let him get to the gate and then, snatching her coat, ran after him. "I'll just walk with you to the station."

"Thanks Claire."

He held her hand through the compartment window, very tight, his fingers cold, his body so taut that she could feel the uneasy, overstrung vibration of his nerves, the beginnings of revulsion and panic, of pity too deep to be endured: and the inevitable, ineradicable hate.

"I think I'm up to it," he said. "It helped — telling you."

He had not asked her to go with him. But she had only to get into the train, now, as she was, and she thought he would be glad. Why not? A reckless, ridiculous step perhaps, but her spirit was poised to take it. The open road, perhaps, without hearth or anchor, but a part of her nature responded to that. Euan — if he managed to come to terms with the destruction of his faith and love — could offer her freedom. What could she offer him?

"See it through," she told him.

"I'll try. You're right, of course. If I don't, then it's bound to finish me off."

The whistle sounded, its screech unnerving her, throwing them fiercely together.

"Wait for me, Claire."

"Yes I'll wait."

Time had reeled backward, two years of it, three years, and one promised anything when those whistles blew. He smiled, still clutching her hand.

"I told you Claire — it's always Passchendaele."

"I'll come with you," she said. Had she spoken aloud? Had he heard? It made no difference. The train was already pulling away. "If I keep on smiling then he won't get killed — he won't die of wounds — he won't be paralyzed and blind — he won't be crippled and castrated, neither in his body nor in his soul."

Her smile was fixed and set when she turned the corner to the boardinghouse and saw MacAllister's sister standing at the gate, shading her eyes, looking for someone.

"Mrs. Swanfield — oh Mrs. Swanfield —" The hand began to wave in evident agitation, a square of orange paper clutched within it. Claire came nearer, her smile deepening, becoming as blank and brilliant as Euan's.

"God love you, Mrs. Swanfield, you'd been gone no more than five minutes when they brought you this."

She held out the telegram as gingerly as one might handle dead vermin and for a moment Claire went on smiling, as incapable of taking it as Euan had been incapable of turning off the gas.

There had been too many telegrams.

"Bad news, I reckon," said Teresa MacAllister, stating a fact, not asking a question, since she had lost two brothers, numerous cousins, in France and knew what telegrams were for.

Yes. Bad news. Not Euan, at least she could be sure of that. Not yet. Nor Kit either. Somehow she knew that. But Benedict was traveling in Italy. If there had been an accident, if he had been taken ill — and remembering that drawn, hollow look she knew it was possible — would it occur to anyone to let her know? Yes. Toby would think of it. Then it must be Benedict. How could she get to him? Color left her so rapidly that Teresa MacAllister put out a hand expecting her to fall in a faint, and then, as she snatched the envelope and tore it open, her pallor changed, beneath the Irish woman's kindly, incredulous eyes, from chalk to rose; her expression of horror changing too, to what *could* have been — although Miss MacAllister was ready to give her the benefit of the doubt — a kind of wondering, excited delight.

"It's Edward," she said, "my mother's husband. He died this morning."

And crumbling the dreaded orange envelope in her hand she went on down the street, walking with a decided bounce in her step, toward the sands.

She was free. It was the only thought in her mind. Absolutely free. And through the sheer, lark-soaring delight it aroused in her she was unable to feel anything else. No pang of guilt came near her. How could she bring herself to grieve, in any case, for an old man dead in his bed of natural causes when she had seen others blown to pieces at nineteen, burned and blinded at twenty-three? Nor did she hate him. She was simply overflowing with gratitude, burgeoning with gladness, that he was gone. She had never, for a moment, expected it. She had thought him indestructible, that his whine might grow thinner perhaps, but that Edward himself would continue to cast his shadow through her life, to hold her back, keep her down, manipulate her through Dorothy, for ever. Now she could go back to Faxby and lead her life as she pleased. Now she could go to High Meadows when and if she chose, with no fear of what Edward might do to her mother should she decide not to go at all. Now — for the first time in her life — it no longer mattered what the Swanfields had to say. She was free. She was her own woman. Had she even been consciously aware of how much he had oppressed her until now when the crushing burden of him had been lifted? But she was very light now, floating in blue air without it, possessed by an impossible, probably — she supposed — an indecent joy which carried her buoyantly along the sands to the post office where, having composed herself sufficiently to request a black border without offending the clerk she sent an answering telegram, solemnly worded and correct, promising to return on the next train.

The funeral was not conspicuously well-attended, Edward having had few relations, no personal friends, and, in view of his long retirement, only one or two colleagues and clients who remembered him well enough, or kindly enough, to make the journey to Upper Heaton. The neighborhood, of course, did what it could, curtains remaining drawn as a sign of respect for the whole afternoon, a gesture which, the weather having turned unseasonably cold and rather more than usually wet, most people considered to be adequate. Miriam sent a lavish wreath of lilies and white roses, and her excuses. She was not quite well herself and funerals depressed her in any case. Poor, dear Mr. Lyall would not have wished her to court pneumonia trudging behind *his* coffin, she felt very sure of that. Benedict was still in Italy. No one expected Polly to stand at a graveside. And so the Swanfields were represented by well-meaning Eunice and easily set-aside Toby, the very ones Edward himself had least regarded.

"I think Miriam might have made the effort," said Claire because she knew Dorothy thought so and would not say it.

"Oh no — not at all." Dorothy had not yet convinced herself that Edward could no longer hear, and was visibly intimidated by the presence of a pair of Lyall cousins who much resembled him. "Her flowers are very fine."

"Just a quick 'phone call to a florist, mother. Not much recompense for all of Edward's frantic devotion."

The Lyall cousins, one male, one female, exchanged pained looks. Dorothy flushed and bit her lip, knowing that in their eyes she had remained no more and no less than the young governess Cousin Edward had so surprisingly taken it into his head to marry.

"I am pleased to see," said the female Lyall, "that you have kept the silver in good condition."

"Tell me," said the male, "should there not be two of these *Cloisonné* vases? The value diminishes considerably unless they are kept in pairs."

"Certainly there were two," his sister answered him, both of them turning to Dorothy with the air of those who feel entitled to an explanation.

"Oh —" she said, badly flustered. "I don't remember. Could one have got broken, do you think?"

"Hardly — since they are made of metal. Someone could have dinted it, of course. Did someone do that?"

"Does it matter?" said Claire coldly, rudely. "And even if it did, I rather think my mother has more important things on her mind just now than Chinese vases."

"Indeed," snapped two pairs of thin Lyall lips, two pairs of small, black eyes, wintry with disapproval, looking Claire up and down.

"Indeed," she said.

"Oh dear," said Dorothy, flushing scarlet as the Lyalls proceeded outdoors to assess the condition of the garden. "I think you have offended them."

"I certainly hope so. They were talking to you like a housekeeper, mother, and not a particularly good one either. Why on earth do you put up with it?"

"Oh — don't make a fuss, Claire, please. They are Lyalls, after all — Edward's family."

"And you were Edward's wife. This is your house now and if they start bothering you again about vases or silver spoons or *anything* then just tell them to leave."

"Claire! I can't do that." For a moment Dorothy looked terrified.

"Mother — ?"

And when there was no reply, "Mother — what is going on?"

"Nothing. What should be? And what a vulgar expression. It's just that — well, this is a family house. The Lyalls have always lived here — and —"

"Do they want to buy it from you? That might be a good idea."

"No they don't." Dorothy's temper was flaring to cover her embarrassment. "This house has never been bought or sold since Edward's grandfather built it."

"And now it's yours — isn't it?"

Not even Claire thought so poorly of Edward as to believe that he could have left his wife without a roof to shelter her.

"Yes, of course it's mine. At least . . . Yes it *is* mine. For now, at any rate. And some money to look after it and live in it. For my lifetime, I mean. And then it's theirs."

"*Theirs!* Mother — they're older than you."

Dorothy gave her heavy, exasperated shrug, her cheeks burning. "Well, I can't help that, can I? And they have a nephew, Edward's — I don't know — second cousin, I suppose. He's only thirty. *He'll* outlive me. Oh, for Heaven's sake, Claire, it was all agreed before we were married — what I was to have and what was to be kept in the family."

"It's a strange family, mother, that doesn't include a man's wife."

"Just don't make a fuss. It was all agreed — all signed and sealed years and years ago — and that's that. I was so much younger than Edward, you see, and he'd been a bachelor for so long. It just wasn't fair to the Lyalls — I understood that. I shall have quite enough to live on. A nice little allowance and all the household maintenance to be paid out of the estate."

"Mother!" And now it was Claire's turn to be horrified. "Do you mean to say you've been working all these years, *slaving* in this house, at the beck and call of that man, just for an allowance?"

Cornered, well aware of the awkwardness of her position but refusing wildly to admit it, Dorothy rushed to the attack. "I mean nothing of the kind. It's all quite usual with second marriages — in good families, that is, where there's property — it's the way things are done. If you don't believe me then ask Mr. Duckworth, Edward's solicitor — he'll explain it all to you."

Herbert Duckworth, a slight, bone-dry little man who had been practising the law so long that he no longer troubled to conceal how very much it bored him, gave Claire five minutes of his time the next morning, yawning behind a thin hand as, tonelessly, tediously, he confirmed her fears. Dorothy was to have nothing outright but the use of her late husband's home, the enjoyment of its contents and a certain monthly income.

"How much?" asked Claire.

He told her.

"Those are housekeeper's wages," she said.

Nevertheless, Mrs. Dorothy Lyall had agreed to them. Eighteen years ago perhaps the sum concerned had seemed more satisfactory. He had explained the agreement to Mrs. Lyall himself and she had made no complaint. Young brides outlive their elderly husbands. More often than not, they marry again. Mr. Lyall had merely taken the precaution of ensuring that should his widow choose to bestow her hand and heart on another man she could not include the Lyall property with it. Quite usual. No more than prudent, particularly as Mrs. Lyall had a daughter of her own to whom she would naturally wish to bequeath any inheritance she might acquire on the way. Hardly fair, thought Mr. Duckworth, yawning again, to the remaining Lyalls, three in number, Miss Richmal and Mr. Charles and their nephew Mr. Henry, the son of their late elder brother. A charming young gentleman, soon to be married. In the course of time the house and its contents would go to them. Mr. Duckworth supposed there could be no objection to an inventory of those contents being taken? Miss Richmal Lyall had asked for it and it would probably save awkwardness later on. Miss Lyall had also put forward what seemed the entirely reasonable proposal that certain items, the silver for instance, and a particular dinner service — far too large, Miss Lyall thought, for a woman alone — might be given as a wedding present to the Lyall nephew, of whom Miss Richmal Lyall was very fond. And since the matter *had* arisen, Miss Lyall had expressed the view — a view only, he hastened to add — that certain pieces of furniture, Mr. Edward Lyall's desk and bookcases for example, might be of greater use to young Mr. Henry Lyall, at present bearing the heavy cost of setting up a home, than to Mr. Lyall's widow. Bedrooms too.

"Bedrooms?" asked Claire.

Yes, indeed. How many bedrooms would Mrs. Dorothy Lyall be likely to need? Miss Lyall thought it could hardly be more than two. It had, therefore, occurred to Miss Lyall that there would be beds and sideboards and some rather splendid carved mahogany wardrobes to spare.

"I see," she said.

Mr. Duckworth, understanding that she saw very well, shrugged shoulders as narrow and brittle as a bird's.

"There is also a question of linen. There is a great deal of it, Miss Richmal says. Rather more than would seem necessary for your mother's needs. It would be a kindness, in view of the exorbitant cost of matrimony, to offer a portion of it to young Mr. Henry."

"He was not at the funeral."

"No. He is on holiday, somewhere in Austria, I believe, and in view of the suddenness of the event . . . I think it safe to assume that his aunt, Miss Richmal, will speak for him."

She returned to Upper Heaton to find Miss Richmal Lyall busy in the china cupboard, listing individual items of Worcester and Crown Derby, Dorothy upstairs, not in the room she had shared with Edward but sitting, tense and frayed, on the edge of what had been Claire's bed.

"Mother, what is that woman doing?"

"Listing the china — every cup and saucer. All of it. What does she think? That I have to pay for anything I break?"

She was trying hard, for Edward's sake, to keep her temper and not quite succeeding.

"And what do you think?"

"That she can have it — take it away with her now — the lot —"

"Mother — how could you?"

"What?"

"Sell yourself so cheap."

She had spoken in sorrow not condemnation and Dorothy, hearing it, gave a sudden start, squeezed her eyes tight shut, clenched her hands, caught her breath in a great gulp and then let it out in a gasping, jerky sigh.

"Because I was frightened and I was thirty-two and he was the only one who asked me," she said.

She burst into tears then, mighty sobs which set her shoulders heaving, made her eyes smart and her head ache but ultimately did her good.

"How stupid," she said, blowing her nose hard, apologizing because Edward had always been seriously offended by tears and she had trained herself to please him so rigorously that she could not break the habit all at once. "I'll be all right, Claire. I just wanted a roof over my head — and yours — that's all, and enough money to pay the milkman and the coalman, so I didn't have to hide when they rang the bell. At least I'll never have to do that again. I've got a home —"

"If that woman downstairs leaves you a chair to sit on."

"I don't care. She can take the lot —"

"No she can't."

"Claire — she's — she's just looking after her nephew — her own flesh and blood."

"So am I."

"Yes — yes I know — but don't fuss — please don't. If Edward had never married me then Henry Lyall could have moved here straight after his wedding — that's what they all want. And there's a housing shortage too, because of the war. Old buildings not repaired and new ones shoddy and costing the earth. She keeps telling me that."

"Then tell her to go to hell."

"*Claire!*"

"Mother — he married you. You were his wife not his housekeeper. And a damned good wife."

"Please don't swear, dear — not so *she'll* hear you, at any rate."

"Mother — stop being so humble. Stop it — *now* this minute — there's no need. Do you want that woman to count your china?"

Dorothy shook her head.

"Do you want her sorting through your linen?"

"No."

"Do you want to give the silver away?"

"No — I don't."

Dorothy had spent hours, which added up to months of her life, polishing that silver, deriving comfort from its possession.

"And do you want to end up camping out here in one half-furnished bedroom and the kitchen corner?"

Dorothy shivered, hating unfurnished rooms for the sparse memories they aroused of a past when bailiffs, not acquisitive spinster cousins, had taken the furniture, rolled up the carpets, unhooked the curtains, and carted them away in payment of debt. She had married Edward to escape from that.

"No, I don't."

"All right, mother."

Claire went downstairs to the china cupboard and said coolly, "Miss Lyall, I would like a word with you."

Miss Lyall, however, had nothing she wished to say to Claire.

"As you see, Mrs. Swanfield, I am rather busy."

"Yes. I do see. May I ask what you are doing in my mother's china cupboard?"

"I am making an inventory."

"Who asked you? And for what purpose?"

No one had ever spoken to Miss Richmal Lyall in that particular manner, a hospital matron issuing crisp, no-nonsense commands to a probationer nurse. And, although it was, of course, a tone she regularly employed with others, she was taken aback at being so addressed herself.

Claire gave her no time to recover.

"If my mother wants an inventory then she will probably make one."

"It is hardly what your mother wants, Mrs. Swanfield."

"It is *entirely* what my mother wants, at this stage, Miss Lyall. She lives here. You don't. I really must ask you to leave her cups and saucers alone."

For a moment Miss Lyall, of whom even her peevish, spinster brother was slightly afraid, did not know what to say. Such a thing had never happened to her before.

"Really! Indeed!" giving herself time to think of a truly crushing retort which, when it came was simply and lamely "How dare you speak like that to me?"

"Easily," replied this cool, faintly amused young woman. "Because you are behaving badly and I don't see why you should be allowed to get away with it."

Edward had got away with it all his life. How she wished she had had the courage to tell him so. But this narrow, greedy woman was a fair substitute, so mean and petty and self-righteous, so thoroughly hateful, so like him, that Claire smiled at her almost fondly as she implanted her next dart.

"Let me make my mother's position clear, Miss Lyall." This too she had longed to say to Edward. "She is not a flighty seventeen-year-old who caught your cousin's eye for a month or two and is trying to feather her nest out of a passing fancy. She lived with him as his wife for eighteen years. She nursed him when he was unwell which he usually thought he was. She had patience with his fads — and he had plenty of those. She *put up* with him. She worked damned hard for him, Miss Lyall, and she's earned her place in this house. She's *earned* her mahogany sideboards and her silver candlesticks *and* her china cupboard. She deserves her peace of mind and if you try to bully her into giving anything away or make her feel guilty for keeping it, then I shall not take it kindly."

"You are an insolent young woman." Richmal Lyall had pronounced those same words on many occasions to house maids who had been reduced instantly to tears; to shop girls who had humbly begged her pardon and, at her recommendation, had often lost their jobs; to her neighbors who knew better than to allow their dogs to stray in her garden or their children to indulge in noisy play. But this terrible person with her painted lips and her cropped head simply looked her up and down and *smiled* at her.

"Just listen to me, my girl." Miss Lyall had never been flustered before and did not know how to handle it. "When your mother prevailed upon my Cousin Edward to marry her —"

"Prevailed?" To Miss Lyall's amazement, Claire's smile deepened to a beam of sheer delight. "Is that what he told you? That she'd *prevailed upon him?* Yes, I can just hear him say it. But are you really so naïve? He couldn't wait to get his hands on my mother. He was — well, you're a spinster lady and so I won't embarrass you — although so was he. Just a fussy old spinster with his knitting. At heart, that is. Certainly not in other directions. Perhaps that was what made him so — oh good Lord, he was a *joke*, that's all, and rather a poor one. I should have seen it years ago."

Suddenly she was laughing.

"I won't listen," said Miss Lyall, rooted to the spot, like a small rodent fascinated by a shaft of light.

"I don't really care, Miss Lyall. There's not much more to be said. Just don't disturb my mother again, there's a good lady. I daresay you would like her to move out of here and save your nephew a lot of expense and a lot of trouble. Probably Edward would have liked that too. But she's not a housekeeper to be dismissed with a reference and a month's wages. She'll go when and if she's ready. If Edward didn't want to pay for the pleasures and services of a wife then he should have made do with a whore. It would have killed him sooner and cost him less."

"We haven't heard the last of it," said Dorothy when, having escorted Miss Lyall off the premises, Claire found her mother on the landing, half-defiant, half-defeated, succumbing to mild hysteria whenever the thin specter of Edward inserted his whine of reproach into her mind.

"You've not heard the last of it," said Kit Hardie, smiling across his desk at her as they checked the bar takings. "Not by a long shot. Hell hath no fury like an old virgin, mark my words, when it comes to the family silver. I've seen it time and again in the families I've worked for, gentle old tabby-cats growing claws like tigers over who gets the monogrammed towels and the apostle teaspoons. You know, Claire — if your mother needs a change of scene she'd be welcome here for a week or two. There's nobody in the Rose Room just now and the staff would look after her."

"That's kind of you, Kit."

"Then bear it in mind. Or take her to Bournemouth or somewhere, if she fancies that. You can have the time off."

"Kit — you're generous too."

"Yes. In fact I'm a very decent chap — more often than not. I'd expect you back, of course, before Aristide opens his doors and does his damnedest to close mine. Didn't I tell you? He's found himself a place in Petergate — used to be a chip shop, so one couldn't raise objections at Town Hall level about the cooking smells . . . There's to be a gala opening, mid-September. Won't affect our business, *of course*. He won't poach any of our staff either. *What* an unlikely notion. But, just in case, if you should happen to hear of a decent pastry chef, you might let me know. Come to think of it, Bournemouth could be just the place to find one."

"You'll pay my expenses then, will you?"

He smiled. "We'll talk about it. Just look after your mother."

She would have to be in Faxby by mid-September, in any case, for Polly's wedding.

"Dear Claire," wrote Miriam in several coy variations of the same demand. "I simply cannot understand why you have not been to see me."

"Dear Miriam," answered Claire, in a bold, free-flowing hand. "I will come when I can. But, at present, my mother needs me."

What would the Swanfields, or the Lyalls, make of that?

Miriam, agile and supple as ever, sent Dorothy chocolates in gold boxes and a basket of crystallized fruit decorated with pink satin ribbon.

Miss Richmal Lyall, considerably more upright but far less intelligent, sent Mr. Herbert Duckworth with an official proposal that Dorothy should give up the house and contents at once in favor of Mr. Henry Lyall, and install herself in "alternative accommodation," a flat or perhaps a boardinghouse in some quiet seaside town, the rental of which would be met, throughout her lifetime, by the Lyall estate. Could it be denied that the house was far more suited to the requirements of an ambitious young couple and their future children than a woman alone? And since that woman was merely a custodian, not an owner, holding the property in trust for them, was it just or even sensible to make them wait the duration of her lifetime — twenty years Miss Lyall estimated — at the end of which the Lyall children would be grown up, away at school, gone, and half the Royal Worcester would probably be broken? Miss Richmal Lyall appealed, through Mr. Duckworth, to Mrs. Dorothy Lyall's sense of justice or, in more basic terms, her sense of right and wrong. Could it even be denied that if Edward could speak to her from the grave, he would be urging her now to give up her claims?

Dorothy, falling immediately into panic, did not deny it. Of course he would. He may even have suggested it to her during his lifetime, in fact she rather thought he had, although she hadn't understood at the time and he, not expecting to drop dead so instantly of a heart attack, had not insisted. Probably, if he had lived long enough, he would have brought the matter up again. And since she would have agreed to it then, she might just as well agree to it now. She had done her best for him but he had always despised her. She was no fool, whatever anyone else might think, and no milk and water innocent either. He had despised her and had despised himself for wanting her so badly. It was true — her daughter had said it, and seen it — that he hadn't known how to keep his hands off her. And had she been to blame for that? She'd simply put up with it, like everything else, and now she was glad to be rid of it — yes, very glad — just as she'd be glad to get out of this dark, dreary house and see the last of those moldy old wardrobes and sideboards that had always given her nightmares.

"Let the Lyalls have them," she shrieked. "I don't want them. I'll take an axe to the lot if I have to stay here. And as for that china, all Edward ever let me do was take it out twice a year and wash it and then put it back in the cupboard again. Let Richmal do that from now on. I'll just get a room somewhere, anywhere — I don't care — back where I started. I'll leave today."

Left to herself Dorothy would assuredly have signed each and every one of her rights away, succumbed to every pressure, agreed blindly to a lifetime of genteel poverty in a rented flat and ended up thanking them for it. Mr. Duckworth certainly, Miss Lyall probably, were both well aware of that.

"No, mother," said Claire.

"I have to," said Dorothy. "They won't leave me alone until I do, and I can't stand it."

Claire called once again to see Mr. Duckworth, conveying to him very pleasantly her mother's readiness to leave Upper Heaton.

"Very wise, my dear. These family squabbles do tend to drag on so, you know — rarely worth it, one finds in the end. So I may close my dossier, may I, on the affair of Lyall v Lyall before it has really started?"

He looked infinitely relieved about that.

"Not quite, Mr. Duckworth."

He sighed.

"Since there is a great deal of money in the estate I think my mother's allowance should be increased annually. Not a great deal but enough to accommodate these rising prices one hears so much about."

She smiled at him kindly, knowing as he did not, that there was worse to come.

"I would need, of course, to consult the family."

She nodded. "And I would need their agreement before allowing my mother to move an inch."

"Yes — quite so. And — if there should be any other matters arising?"

"Well yes, Mr. Duckworth. You don't really expect to get away so easily as that do you? My mother would like a small modern house in one of the new estates near Faxby Park. You might have seen them, very light and bright, two reception rooms and a kitchen downstairs, two bedrooms, boxroom and bathroom above, no attics or cellars, just enough garden to grow a few flowers and keep a cat. Ideal for a lady living alone. She could manage easily with a gardener twice a week and a daily woman to clean and cook. Most economical."

Mr. Duckworth closed his eyes as if in prayer, searching his soul, it seemed, while she, still floating on the bliss of no longer being afraid of Edward, calmly lit a cigarette.

"My dear young lady," he said at last, clearly hoping for a miracle, "those houses you speak of are *for sale*."

"Yes. I know."

"Whereas the family, I believe, had rather visualized . . ."

"Yes. I know that, too. A furnished room and a shared kitchen and bathroom in a lodging-house. I live in such a place myself. At twenty-five it can be amusing. At forty-five, or fifty-five, it must be very sad. I don't intend to let my mother find out."

He closed his eyes again, hands clasped together in the post of spiritual devotion, feeling, since there was to be no miracle, that a loophole would do. Predictably, since he was a man well-versed in the arts of evasion, one occurred to him. Not foolproof, of course, but possibly enough to save him from Richmal Lyall's wrath. Emerging from meditation, he smiled.

"You mean, I take it, that a house should be purchased by the Lyall estate and maintained for your mother's use during her lifetime? That *is* what you mean, dear lady? Yes? Isn't it? And then reabsorbed into the estate after her death? Do you know, I believe something might possibly be achieved in that direction. Not Faxby Park, perhaps, but something — quite suitable."

"Smaller, you mean, and cheaper? A back-to-back mill cottage with an outside toilet down a passage? What a pity they have no rooms to rent at the workhouse."

"Mrs. Swanfield — really — there is nothing to be gained, you know, in these domestic disputes, from bitterness."

She stubbed out her cigarette, offending Mr. Duckworth mightily since he did not care to see women smoking in the first place and could not abide the sight of a dirty ashtray.

"Probably not. So I'll state my case, shall I? My mother does not intend to be greedy. She does feel, however, that adequate recompense should be made to her for the eighteen years she endured with Mr. Lyall. A house in Faxby Park, furnished to suit her requirements, and an allowance, as we discussed, should just about cover it. The new house and contents, of course, to be her property absolutely and entirely."

"Yes," said Mr. Duckworth, "I was afraid that was what you meant. Miss Richmal Lyall will never agree to it and she will never allow Mr. Henry or Mr. Charles to agree either. It would mean money permanently leaving the estate. What reason could I possibly put forward to get her to consent?"

"That, otherwise, my mother will remain at Upper Heaton. I may even join her there. Nothing in Edward's will forbids it. And since my friends are mainly war veterans who drink and smoke a great deal and get up to all sorts of pranks, there might not be too much left in the china cupboard, after twenty years or so, for Mr. Henry."

"Mr. Duckworth swallowed hard. "That could almost be a threat, my dear young lady."

"A promise, Mr. Duckworth. Make sure Miss Lyall understands it."

"Yes, indeed. But she is a stubborn woman, my dear, and perhaps not always a wise one. Where a matter of principle is concerned she will rather tend to soldier on regardless. And, of course, in this case she not only believes herself to be in the right but is fairly certain of being able to wear your mother down. I think she probably can."

Claire thought so too. She also thought, had been thinking all along, how swiftly and surely Benedict would have dealt with this situation, how rapidly, after ten minutes exposure to his abrasive presence, even Miss Richmal Lyall's resolution would have crumbled away. Could she bring herself now to use the threat of him? Could she even manage to speak his name?

"Please tell Miss Lyall," she said, "that I shall expect an answer by tomorrow morning. Should she find herself unwilling to meet my mother's terms then I shall simply place the matter in the hands of my brother-in-law, Mr. Swanfield. You are acquainted with him, I suppose? Good. Then you are in a position to explain to Miss Lyall just what her chances are of wearing *him* down."

"We'll never get away with it," said Dorothy, utterly horrified. "She'll never consent. I'll have to stay in this mausoleum for the rest of my life."

She wanted nothing better now, although she still did not like to admit it, than to put Upper Heaton behind her. She had never, in her whole life, *chosen* a house to live in. There had been her childhood home, the lodgings she had shared with Claire's father, other people's houses in which she had been an uneasy visitor, including Edward's. Faxby Park would be a dream come true. And, therefore, impossible.

"She'll never consent. And if she did, how do you know I could get a house in Faxby Park? They could all be taken."

"Let's go and see."

"No." Dorothy was shocked. "That's tempting fate."

They went, finding the only house Dorothy had ever wanted until they found one she preferred next door to it, a plain, clean box with two bay windows, two small square rooms behind them, a bathroom with blue tiles, a handkerchief of a garden back and front. And then, around the corner, its twin sister except that the bathroom had a painted panel of tiny blue fishes and there was a large elm tree in the garden.

"Which one do you want?"

"This one." Dorothy had never been so happy.

"We'll take it."

"We can't."

"Why not? We'll call round and see Mr. Duckworth on our way back and make the arrangements."

He received them almost at once, looking increasingly small and bored.

"You are very prompt," he said.

"Are we?"

"Indeed." He had dispatched a note by messenger to Upper Heaton only an hour ago but did not wish to go into that. "Yes, very prompt, although the Lyalls, as you will readily concede, have not been tardy. Now then — all that remains to be settled, so far as I can see, is the matter of the furnishings. Your daughter, Mrs. Lyall, specified that the house be furnished to suit your requirements. Miss Lyall and her brother found this wording somewhat vague — not that anyone suspects you, dear lady, of extravagance. It is simply that Miss Lyall would feel happier if one could fix a certain sum — ? She suggests that you might make a list of what is needed, room by room . . ."

"Oh yes — I will," said Dorothy.

"No list," said Claire, knowing that Dorothy would not list half the things she wanted and would not dare to buy anything she had forgotten to put down. "I think my mother can get everything she wants from Taylor & Timms and there would be no difficulty in arranging for their bills to be sent to you."

Mr. Duckworth, who had been expecting this, sadly nodded his head.

She had dinner with Kit that night served in his office on a trolley, fillets of sole from Amandine's fishmonger poached in *Chablis*, a plump duckling in a sauce of oranges and lemons, an apricot *soufflé*, and then, the feast over, the hotel all around them starting to fill up with diners and revelers who would soon claim his attention, he said "Look — I'd better show you this." And opening a desk drawer he took out a telegram. It had not recently been delivered she could see that. It had been opened, crumpled, whatever evil news it contained had been dealt with by now, could not — or could it? — affect her. Yet, nevertheless, her stomach lurched and, through the glow of not fearing Edward which freed her from fearing anyone else, she turned pale.

"Don't get alarmed. This came for Euan, the day of your stepfather's funeral I think. The dancing teacher took it in and then gave it to Adela Adair to give to me. I can't make anything of it and I don't know where he is, in any case — do you?"

She held out her hand, adjusted her eyes, and read "Regret to inform you Captain Roderick Manners passed away this morning. Please communicate."

"Oh — Christ," she said.

About a week later, very early in the morning, she heard movement in the kitchen and found Euan there as if he had never been away, upending a whiskey bottle to put the last few drops into his tea.

"There was a telegram," she said.

"Yes. Yes, I know."

"You got up to Edinburgh then?"

"Yes. In time to bury him, which was something, I suppose. He hadn't really known what was going on around him for ages — so they made out. Said if I'd come sooner he wouldn't have recognized me — wouldn't have made any difference. That's what they said, at any rate."

"If that's what they said, Euan, then they'd mean it. It sounds very likely."

He smiled. "Yes — well, never mind. There was just me at the funeral and a couple of nurses. All over in ten minutes. Odd really, when you think he was all set to be Prime Minister. He'd have made it too — or something like it."

"Yes."

"So here we are again. Just came to get my canvases together. Care to give me a hand?"

They went into his cold, untidy room and worked for an hour, making small impression on the chaos of what had been his camping place, his bolt-hole, while she told him about Edward and her mother and waited until he could tell her about himself.

"Did it help, Euan?"

"Seeing him? Yes. He was dead, of course, so we didn't have to ask each other why. I didn't have to feel that he was blind either, or that he couldn't move, or that his brains had turned to scrambled eggs. *You* know — because one could hardly expect great things from a corpse. But it helped. Yes — stands to reason. All I've done these past two years is try to get there. Now I've been. I don't have to go again. So I can give my mind, such as it is, to something else."

"Painting?"

"I doubt it. I might get too emotional about it — ambitious I mean — and I wouldn't like that. I don't want to want things. Nola, in the days when she wanted to make me famous, could never understand that. I expect you can. It's a form of cowardice, I readily admit. It comes from having wanted rather more than my share at one time. I might get over it."

"And in the meantime?"

"I'm going home for a while. Not long. I couldn't promise that. But they haven't seen me since I got out of hospital myself at the end of the war and it's always been on the cards that I'd have to show my face. Now that I've been to Edinburgh I think I can. *Not* a totally joyous

394

occasion, I hasten to assure you. They live pretty close together, my people and a whole batch of uncles and aunts and lesser connections. And all the young men got killed except me. So there's nobody left to be the next Master of Foxhounds and Chairman of the Bench of Justices and captain the local cricket team and marry the Squire's daughter . . ."

"Except you. And you won't, will you."

"No, Claire. No chance. The line ends with me. I told you."

Another death. She shivered and he took her hand, his face very pale, very tired, very still, the ordeal over and nothing, as yet, to occupy the void it had left behind in him.

"There's a jolly old Manor House as well for me to inherit. I'd even like to live in it. I'm sure I never will."

"You have to do something with your life, Euan."

"Why? That's what they told us when we were young. And there aren't too many of us left now, you know, to tell them they were wrong. I'd like to marry you Claire, and make you the Lady of my Manor. But you'd want children and I couldn't — absolutely not. I've thought about it more than somewhat and — well — I couldn't that's all. And it wouldn't be fair to you. So I'll just keep on seducing the village maidens and — I love you Claire."

"Thank you. I love you."

But it was in the past. It had never happened and it had always been too late.

Quietly they began to organize his leaving.

"Keep the canvases will you. Or let that bloke in Faxby Market sell them for you. They might raise a pound or two. Buy yourself something outrageous with it."

"Will you give me an address?"

He scribbled it down on a scrap of paper which, his angelic, wayward smile just breaking through, he stuffed down the front of her dress between her breasts.

"I could be back, of course. Will you keep the room for the kitchen?"

She heard a step, the sound of the door opening, and without looking round she knew it was Kit who stood there.

"Well, well," he said, "the prodigal — or the bad penny —"

"That's me, Major sir — at your service."

"I've just been through the vegetable market and I heard you'd been seen with your kit bag on your shoulder — coming or going nobody could say."

And Claire knew that beneath his easy cordiality he was alarmed. That he'd come to see her, not Euan; to make sure she hadn't suddenly taken it into her head to go off with him.

"Bit of both, Major. Just arrived — just leaving."

"Want a lift to the station?"

Euan's smile suddenly broke free again, dazzling now, and as wanton as before, "No Kit, thanks awfully — but I'll walk down to the train with Claire. Come on Claire — get your coat and hat."

She went off to change and Euan stood for a long moment staring at the door. And then, turning to Kit a thin face emptied of everything but weariness, the effort — not always worth the trouble to him — of just keeping going, he said, his voice as light and mocking as he could make it: not a great deal, "I suppose I can rely on you, Major — *sir* — to look after her?"

"I reckon you can." Kit's voice was rough, his throat dry, anger in him and a wry affection it exasperated him to feel. Pity. An urge to shout "For God's sake pull yourself together lad" while knowing far too well — remembering those corpse-littered trenches, the fair face of the pilgrim — why he couldn't.

"Will you marry her, Kit?"

"Yes. If I can."

"Oh, you'll manage it, old chap — if you set your mind to it. You'll get there. You always do."

"It won't be for want of trying."

"That's right. So — carry on. I won't say goodbye to her. Cowardly of me, I suppose, but one may as well stay in character to the end. And there are some injuries one just doesn't inflict on oneself."

Shrugging on his trench coat, hoisting his kit bag on his shoulder, he went to the back door, poised to make his escape across the kitchen yard, and then, hesitating, smiled with such natural sweetness, such pain, that Kit — remembering the pilgrim again — was forced to look away.

"I love her you know. Pretty badly. Too much to risk it. So I won't be back. That's — that's the best thing I can do for her. The only thing, really. Tell her — Christ, tell her I'm going home."

"Are you?"

"Well — south, anyway."

"Damn fool. Have you any money?"

Kit had money to give, food and shelter and warm fires, and he could not have expressed how deeply it grieved him that Euan would accept none of these things.

"I'm all right, Kit."

"No lad — far from it."

"Well then — so long as *she's* all right. And there's a better chance of it with me out of the way."

He held out a hand, thin and cold against Kit's square brown palm, and clasping it for a moment, still struggling with the tightness in his throat, Kit suddenly threw an arm around him and hugged him in a hard, speaking embrace.

"Bloody idiot. You know where I am if you need —"

"Thanks Kit. She'll be fine with you. Better than with the other bloke. Do you know about him?"

"Yes. I know."

"So — put your mind to her, Kit — there's a good fellow. That steady mind of yours and those sound nerves. She needs that."

"So do you."

"I daresay. But it's not likely to happen. Just tell her — well — thanks Kit."

And sketching his mocking military salute he was off across the backyard, balancing the half-empty kit bag easily on his shoulder, whistling a ribald soldier's song.

"Good luck," said Kit through an aching throat, speaking to empty air. And then, his own feet on firm ground, he closed the door, swallowed hard, took Miriam Swanfield's flowered cups and saucers from their shelf and put the kettle on.

"Has he gone?" She looked pale, on the threshold of tears, *anxious* — pitifully so — but not surprised.

"Yes. It seemed best."

She nodded. Bit her lip.

"Oh well —" And he not only desired to comfort her but knew how it could best be done.

"He said not to follow him Claire. He also said goodbye and all that. It looked to me as if he didn't mean to come back. If it hurts you, I'm sorry. I've put the kettle on. Drinking tea doesn't solve any problems but it gives you something to do with your hands."

She sat down at the table, her hands clasped in front of her, worrying already about his homecoming and how long he would be likely to endure it, how long it might take him to get home at all.

"Thanks Kit."

"Don't mention it. I keep on telling you I'm a decent sort of chap."

"Yes — you are."

He went on talking, telling her easy, uncomplicated, amusing things about the Crown, the Kellers, Faxby's mayoral family, the new blonde Arnold Crozier had discovered selling newspapers behind a station bookstall and who was reputedly costing him more than his Rolls Royce to maintain.

"Here — drink your tea. And talking of flappers, I suppose you've heard the Swanfield wedding is off? For the time being at any rate. Poor

Roger Timms. Appendicitis, they're saying. A bad attack. A big operation. They say he'll be laid up for some time. So Polly's on the loose
again."

"Hardly. They'll watch her."

"I dare say. Now come on, Claire — drink your tea."

"Do you think he'll be — all right? Euan I mean?"

"I shouldn't think so."

Sitting down beside her he put one large square capable hand over
both hers — a small, but in its way complete, possession.

"Probably not. But there's nothing you can do for him, Claire."

"Oh — I know that."

"And since we're on the subject — why don't you move over to the
hotel now that he's gone? Better for everybody I'd say."

"Would you, Kit?"

"I would."

"I'll think about it . . ."

The pressure of his hand increased slightly.

"I want you there, you know."

"Yes."

She looked up and warmly, quizzically, he smiled at her. "I told you
one day I might stop feeling like the son of a cook."

"And have you?"

"No. I've done better than that. I've learned to be proud of it."

20

THAT Roger Timms had almost lost his life was not disputed. The attack had been ferocious, the operation highly dangerous — his mother believed she would never get over it — while his own recovery to good health continued sure, perhaps, but slow.

Too slow for Miriam.

"Perhaps we could have the wedding just before Christmas?" she suggested hopefully, wanting Polly off her hands by then.

Edith Timms did not think so.

"Roger is far more delicate than he looks."

But to Polly, as she sat by his bedside on what should have been her wedding day, he looked like nothing so much as a slightly perspiring whale washed ashore in red and blue striped pajamas and amiably gasping for air, lacking the sense, she thought, to know that he was choking to death. Glancing at her watch — an engagement present from Roger in platinum and diamonds — she realized two things, that, had it not been for the intervention of his appendix, he would have become her legal husband ten minutes ago, and that apart from the time spent in his car, when he was either driving or trying to kiss her and unfasten her blouse, she had never been alone with him.

And at no point, either during those clumsy, easily called-to-order attempts on her virtue, or among the crowded excitements of cocktail bars, nightclubs, houseparties, had they ever had a conversation.

"How are you feeling now, Roger?"

"Oh — getting along nicely."

He said the same thing to her every day.

"I've brought you some chocolates."

What else could she bring him? What else would interest him or please him?

"You could give me a kiss, Polly."

She smiled. And shivered. Had he become her husband, ten minutes ago, she would have been obliged to give him much more than that.

She went home and stared at her wedding dress, hanging in splendid isolation in a special wardrobe. It was her own design, the most wonderful Faxby had ever seen, except, of course, that no one, not even the maids at High Meadows, not even the bridesmaids, had seen it yet in case its impact should be spoiled by gossip. She had given hours of thought to each floating panel, some of them stiff with seed pearls, others gauzy, diaphanous, taking wing on the slightest breeze so that she would appear to be moving in the center of a jeweled cloud.

The bride of the season. The most beautiful bride of any season drifting down a red carpeted aisle, mighty organs playing, to a bridegroom she knew to be Roger, had to be Roger — podgy, amiable, slow — but who, in her mind's eye, so easily became the hard, lithe young warrior who had not even cared whether or not he broke her heart.

Had he done so? There had seemed no point in thinking about it. He had left Faxby shortly after her mother's party. She had got engaged to Roger. Today she would have married him. It had all been arranged. No doubt it would be arranged again.

But in the meantime there was Roger's convalescence to be got through, the tedious business of sitting at his bedside trying to think of something to say, trying not to look at him too often since the sight of his plump body in those loosely fitting pajamas made her think of herself in bed beside him, having made her promises to honor and obey.

And she did not like it.

She arrived a little late the following afternoon, later still the day after.

"My dear." Edith Timms immediately took her to task for it. "Roger has been fretting for you."

She had seen in Edith Timms the mother she believed she had wanted. But she was Roger's mother, after all.

"Roger darling — here is Polly for you. I feel sure she won't keep you waiting again."

Here is Polly for you. Once she had given him a pony, a Persian kitten, a bicycle, a motor car. Now — prettily wrapped in her best silk nightie — here is Polly.

Fixing her eyes on the sparkle of her diamond ring, she smiled — and shivered.

Claire wrote to Miriam expressing regret at the postponement of the wedding and offering the information — of no particular interest to Miriam — that Dorothy was now comfortably installed in Faxby Park. She sent a basket of fruit to Roger Timms, a short note to Polly, and then, without a word to anyone but her mother, gave up her flat in Mannheim Crescent and moved to the staff wing of the Crown, a small bedroom and sitting room next to Mrs. Tarrant's and directly below the very comfortable attic flat Kit had arranged for himself.

Dorothy, who still knew exactly what Edward would have thought about it, was not certain whether she approved or disapproved herself.

"It means I'm always on the spot, which can be important. It means I don't have to think about cooking my own meals or lighting fires."

It also meant she would be closer than ever to "that man."

"I don't sleep with him, mother," she said bluntly.

"Oh," Dorothy looked surprised. "Do you think you will?"

Had Dorothy really said that? Edward — poor old soul — would have been horrified.

"I don't know, mother." Claire was delighted. "Do you think I should?"

"Just don't get pregnant," said Dorothy, feeling oddly wise and rather peculiar but suddenly very sure of herself. "*That's* what I think."

Claire had no reason now to see the Swanfields. Only Toby still came to the Crown as he had always done for his leisurely luncheons, lingering until long past teatime, more often than not, over his Napoleon brandy, offering snippets of information which she received with a flickering smile, swiftly rekindled each time it went out. Polly, alas — clearly Toby thought it a pity — was still chained to her fiancé's bedside by command of their respective mothers. Eunice was busy with the children, fussing over Simon's examination results — or lack of them, that is — and positively fuming because Benedict seemed a lot less than keen to take Justin into the business. One quite saw her point of course. It was a family business and Justin, as Aaron Swanfield's eldest grandchild, had certain rights. So Eunice was insisting, at any rate, and certainly, if his Uncle Benedict refused to employ him, nobody else would. Eunice had even tried to call a board meeting to get Benedict overruled, but of course there'd been no chance of it. All she'd managed to do was upset herself and make things rather more awkward than usual for Toby at the office for a day or two. Benedict had even told him to keep his wife in order which was pretty rich, after all, coming from a man whose own wife spent her time traipsing around the town rescuing young girls from sin, with a bottle of gin inside her and another in her handbag. She'd have been drunk in charge a dozen times over by now if she hadn't been Mrs. Benedict Swanfield. But Toby, of course, hadn't thought of that while Benedict was berating him and freely admitted he would have been too scared to say it even if he had.

Good Lord — was it really four o'clock? Toby shrugged frail shoulders and smiled. Not much point in going back to the office now, he supposed. Not much point in going home either, with Justin lounging about all over the place sulking because his mother couldn't get him a job as a managing director or a cabinet minister or something, and Simon bickering with Eunice because neither of them could work out how to do his sums, and the little boys making one hell of a racket now that Eunice had got rid of their nanny and decided to look after them herself. No — he wouldn't go home. Not yet. No point really, with Eunice so set on protecting him from the boys' bad behavior that it was quite a strain pretending he didn't know all about it. Particularly these days when Justin — and Simon too he supposed — had gone a step further than pinching the loose change from his pockets and had started helping themselves to his silk shirts and ties and cravats which Eunice kept on frantically replacing. Poor Eunice. She'd do better to buy herself a new dress. But if he suggested it — well, he'd tried once or twice and she wouldn't have it. Wearing herself out of course. Wearing him out too if it came to that. Sometimes his heart bled for her. Not much use in that either. No, he wouldn't go home. He'd sit in the lounge for a while and glance at the newspapers, if that was all right? Quiet as a mouse he'd be. In nobody's way. And then, when MacAllister opened, he'd have a Martini or two in the cocktail bar, although even that didn't seem the same somehow — these days.

Claire realized that he meant "without Polly."

The postponement of Polly's wedding had also put off the ordeal of seeing Benedict again, although Nola still slipped into the Crown from time to time for a quick drink before dashing off to analyze the dreams and, therefore, pinpoint the neuroses of some harassed and penniless mother of twelve whose main obsession would probably turn out to be how to borrow a shilling or two to pay the rent.

The holiday in Italy had not been a great success. Nola had embarked upon it as upon a crusade, in search of the maternal instinct which her own self-analysis, conducted in accordance with Freudian practice as laid down by Miss Drew, had taught her that she did not naturally possess. Her intentions had been of the noblest and the best. She wished to sacrifice herself entirely for her children, even if it meant returning to a husband who made her feel uneasy and ashamed. She knew he did not like her. She hoped he never would. It was her way of walking barefoot on hot ashes in penitence for her infanticide. She followed him, head bowed, through Rome and Venice, as extreme in her obedience as in everything else. She followed him through Florence and Pisa, as silent as her increasingly bewildered sons. "Where would you like to go now?" he asked her. Once, only a year ago, she would have gone rushing off alone to Vienna to find an analyst of the Freudian school and lay herself, an ardent disciple, at his feet. The thought entered her head and went out again. She was too tired.

"Anywhere," she said.

"Home?"

Thank God. These self-contained, critical boys did not want her sacrifice. They wanted — yes — money, that was it. Like herself they had been brought up to understand affection in terms of what it cost, and it was their father who held the purse-strings, their father who paid for all this first-class travel, these luxurious hotels, this rich living, as her own father had done. She saw, somewhat dimly, having dined rather richly herself, that Christian and even Conrad, who was deeper — her own son, she'd thought — admired this in Benedict. What did they admire in her? It struck her that she was an embarrassment to them, a person for whom, should they ever become articulate enough, they would feel bound to apologize. And what better service could an embarrassment perform than remove itself? She went down to the Arno that night rather thinking she might drown herself but, confused by Chianti and Cointreau, did not immediately notice that the river was dry, returning to the hotel not as some cold, dead Ophelia in the arms of pallbearers, but on her own exceedingly muddy feet.

Even suicide, it seemed, was more difficult than she had expected and by the time she had scraped the mud from her shoes and the hem of her dress and then, realizing the futility of the task, had thrown them away, she had lost the urge to try it again in any case.

"Home," said Benedict, looking as if his perseverance too was deserting him.

Home. But not High Meadows. Going at once to All Saints' Passage she rushed straight into the cubbyhole of an office occupied by Miss Drew, completely ignoring the several dozen people who had been waiting, some of them all morning, on the benches outside.

"I am quite desperate," she said.

"Oh dear —" Miss Drew, accustomed only to desperation among the lower classes — "ladies" usually have been brought up with the good taste not to mention it — looked startled.

"I thought, if I could just devote myself to them that I'd get over it. But they wouldn't let me. I got drunk and fell in the river and they were polite to me. I was supposed to be committing suicide. I couldn't even manage that."

She burst noisily into tears and Miss Drew, finding herself unable to cope with hysteria in a woman wearing fox furs and emeralds rather than the more usual apron and blanket shawl, called on the stalwart Miss Pickles for assistance who, looking Nola up and down, pronounced at once, "The trouble is, my dear, that you haven't enough to do. Work is the thing, you know. Care to give it a try?"

They set her to filing their papers to begin with until Mr. Kilmartin voiced timorous doubts as to her "suitability — "These are *confidential* documents, ladies, containing the most intimate details of our clients' lives, *not* to be bandied about in a cocktail bar" — after which they released her, in small doses, upon the clients themselves who, in general, were quite happy to tell anybody anything.

Not their "best" clients, of course, not the "interesting" cases, not the girls who were best responding to Miss Pickles' methods of scouring front doorsteps with pumice stone or baking ginger parkin, not the tortuous, emotional webs Miss Drew was so expert at untangling; not the girl in St. Jude's Terrace who was in love with her mother's husband; not the musician at the end of Taylor Street who had developed hysterical paralysis of the hand which had been convicted of a minor forgery: not the bold young harlots who might, one never knew, turn "theatrical" and whose conversation, even now, was entertaining: not those who challenged or intrigued Miss Drew, nor any of those who, in the opinion of both these ladies, might, with careful handling, be encouraged to adopt better ways.

But Nola, perhaps, might care to interest herself, not in the stars of Faxby's criminal community, but in certain minor members of its chorus, the hopeless cases who, being incorrigible or incurable, could not really be made worse by anything Nola did to them; the dull cases; the pettier of the petty thieves; the commoner of the common prostitutes; the inarticulate, the sub-normally intelligent who — after so many years of them — frustrated Miss Pickles and bored Miss Drew.

Nola was not ideal. They were well aware of it. But they were overworked, hardly paid at all. And she was willing.

"Mrs. Swanfield, would you be so kind as to deliver this dear old gentleman to the Salvation Army?" The man was abusive, had a most suspicious tendency to scratch, and filled Nola's car for hours afterward with an odor of unwashed skin and sweat-soaked, very probably urine-soaked cloth which stung her eyes. When he asked her for "beer money" meaning a few pence at the most, she gave him a five-pound note, having nothing less in her purse, with the result that he walked away from the Salvation Army Hostel and never came back again.

"Nola dear, could you be a love and take this old granny to wherever it is she lives? She's had a drop too much, you see, and if the police should pick her up — for singing or shouting or for just falling asleep in doorways again — then the magistrates have faithfully promised to send her to jail."

"Granny," who looked at least ninety and as frail as a half-drowned sparrow, was not only drunk but could not remember her address.

"Oh dear," said Miss Drew when Nola brought her back to All Saints' Passage. "Just drive her around the town a little — it might jog her memory. If not then — well, I don't suppose the Salvation Army will take her after last time, so you'll have to drop her off somewhere, as far from the police station as you can."

Neurotics were Miss Drew's speciality. Not vagrants, who took their neuroses away with them, nor drunkards who had forgotten theirs.

"Do the best you can, dear," she said, never for one moment expecting that Nola would take the old woman to the kitchen at High Meadows, causing what would have been a complete walkout of the staff had Benedict not put a stop to it, and hysterics in Polly and Miriam who went about for days afterward searching the entire house for fleas.

"Mrs. Swanfield — could you just *talk* to this woman?" That seemed safe enough. But the woman in question was voluble, psychopathic, making up a new life story every day of the week, boring but harmless to Miss Pickles and Miss Drew who had met the type before and knew all she really wanted was an audience to play to. But so plausible, so fascinating to Nola, who was so utterly convinced by the image presented to her of a gentlewoman down on her luck, that she took her to lunch at the Crown, offending Councillor Redfearn who happened to be at the next table and had once "sent her down" for something or other, and considerably embarrassing Kit when it was discovered that all the toilet soap and towels and somebody's chinchilla wrap were missing from the powder room.

"Now then, Mrs. Swanfield, this is Patsy who is terribly lonely. Could you keep her company — shall we say once a week, for an hour or two?"

Patsy was pale, depressive, ready to talk all day and all night in a toneless whisper about disaster, misery, suicide, about how no one, anywhere, had ever cared for her or understood her, or given her a chance. She believed it. Nola believed it.

"I need you," said Patsy.

"Any hour of the day or night," said Nola, writing down her telephone number and her address so that one never knew, at High Meadows, after that, just when the telephone might shrill out in the middle of the night to release the hysterical babble which was Patsy's cry for help — instant and immediate, "Come at once" — to Nola, or when

Patsy herself might be discovered in the early morning, curled up against the kitchen doorstep, wraith-like and scantily clad, having waited there, with the eerie patience of a cat, all night.

"This is Ginny, Mrs. Swanfield — a likable soul, except that please don't give her money — *ever*. Our aim is to help our clients to stand on their own feet, not ours. So no money. Please."

Ginny was small, quick-witted, apparently fertile although the children who hung about her were not always her own. She was also prone to pains in her hands, a condition caused by the cold, and considerably aggravated by the fact that she had no gloves. Nola at once took off her own — expensive, hand-stitched doeskin — and would have been saddened and surprised to know, although Miss Pickles and Miss Drew would not, that they fetched five shillings that same evening in Faxby Market Place.

"God love you, Mrs. Swanfield," said Ginny, trundling to market week after week with the blankets her "bairns" — neighbors' children hired for the day every one — had needed to get through the winter, the boots in assorted sizes without which they could not go to school, the pots and pans to "help put a morsel or two in their little bellies," the cradle for the "next poor little bastard" she alleged to be on his way.

"I feel," said Miriam, looking seriously upset about it, "that I am under siege."

"Don't ever borrow her car or let her give you a lift," warned Polly who, having encountered something she recognized instantly as a louse, although she had never met one before, on Nola's passenger seat had just consigned to the kitchen fire a nearly new silk *foulard* dress.

"I have caught scabies from somebody," announced Nola as if she expected congratulations. "Look — in the joints of my hands."

"Don't come near me," shrieked Polly.

"Don't go near Justin or Simon or my little boys," said Eunice.

"Oh dear," said Miriam, suddenly sitting down. "Oh my goodness — Not a word — absolutely not a word of this to anyone."

"It's only a matter of time," Toby told Claire, entirely without malice, "before she falls in love with a housebreaker. And what are the Greenwoods and the Redfearns going to make of it if they happen to be on the bench the day she marches into court and asks for him to be released into her custody, swag-bag and all, because she's the only one who understands him?"

What would Miss Pickles make of it — and Miss Drew? What would Benedict make of it?

Claire preferred not even to wonder, going about her business at the Crown as untroubled by the memory of him, as could be expected, until the night when Elvira Redfearn's penetrating voice reached her across the restaurant, its "I declare this meeting open!" quality rising far above the discreet murmurings of the other diners as she informed her companion, a woman as overbearing as herself, "My dear, if you are thinking of a little place in the country, then I believe I can point you in the right direction. Benedict Swanfield has just put up for sale an absolutely delightful Dales farmhouse — presumably someone left it to him since the contents are up for auction too — next Saturday, I believe. Yes indeed, I *shall* be attending the sale. Perhaps we could go together. Lovely pieces of art glass."

Claire went to the powder room and leaning hard against the wash-basin stood for a while, her eyes tight shut, her forehead pressed against the mirror, her body alternating for long, sickening moments between flushes of damp heat and the freezing chill.

He was selling the farm, the Tiffany lamps, the cameo glass, the Chinese rugs, the memories. Had he found it impossible to take another woman there? Triumph and despair tore at her both together. Where would he go, then, not for sex which he would always find easily at-tainable but for peace and rest and his illusion of freedom? The farm had been far more to him than a convenient place to entertain women. It had been his escape from High Meadows, a sanctuary. Her eyes still closed she felt the tranquility of that low, oak-beamed room wash over her, remembered how, in the midst of Miriam's gold and scarlet Christ-mas, she had longed for it. Now she had robbed him of that too.

Some days later a messenger from Swanfield Mills brought her a parcel on which an imperious hand she recognized had scrawled "Fragile. With care." She knew it was the lily bowl and, taking it up to her room that night, found that she could not open it. It sat on her table, staring at her through its brown paper wrappings while she drank her bedtime cocoa. It was there, waiting for her, the next morning when she got out of bed. And when she put it away in her wardrobe out of sight, barricaded into a corner behind a heap of sweaters, it still worried her. She could neither give it away nor keep it. She could neither unwrap it nor bear to think of it, never more than a few yards away from her, suffocating beneath its sawdust and somebody's old cricket sweater. In the end she took it to Dorothy's spare room in Faxby Park.

"What is it?"

"Just memories, mother."

"Oh well — let's close the door on it, shall we, and go down to Feathers' to tea."

But, quite often these days, Dorothy could be persuaded to have tea at the Crown, one place at least where she could be sure of not meeting

Richmal Lyall, and where, sitting at ease in the baroque lounge, she was able to see Kit Hardie no longer as "that man," as Edward had taught her, but as the Manager of this comfortable establishment, a figure of authority and considerable charm.

"The Major is looking well today."

"He always looks well."

"These pastries are delicious."

"They always are."

But was it true that Amandine Keller was showing signs of discontent with both her lover and his fish shop, particularly now that her husband's restaurant, *Chez Aristide* was about to open its doors? Kit rather thought so.

"It may be only a *bistro*," he said, "but at least she'd be *La Patronne*. Any idea how to make *mille-feuilles*, Claire?"

"No thank you. And a bit more than a *bistro*, don't you think? A red and gold awning over the door the last time I was passing."

"Don't pass next time," Kit said. "Walk in and see what he's doing. You could probably get away with it. Drop a hint that you might be looking for a job and see if he jumps — and how much. Get him to show you a menu."

"You're not worried are you, Kit?"

"Good Lord." He gave her his cordial, professional smile, his eyes twinkling. "*Worried!* What a very peculiar idea. As if *my* customers could be enticed away."

"I expect they'll all come back again."

"I expect so. I'm not even sure it matters."

"And what does that mean?"

"That I might be thinking of moving on."

Consternation struck her a hard blow.

"*Kit!*" And what she meant was "How can you leave me?"

"Not yet," he said, "but this was never more than a proving ground, you know. And I've proved myself, I reckon."

"So what next?"

"When I've made up my mind I'll let you know. Strictly between ourselves, of course. I wouldn't want the Croziers breathing down my neck until it's all arranged. And I can't see me giving it much attention until after Christmas at the soonest."

"Is that all you can tell me?"

"It won't be in Faxby. To tell the truth I think Faxby may well have had its day — for a place like this I mean. And a place like Aristide's. Once trade gets really bad the Redfearns and Swanfields and Greenwoods aren't going to feel comfortable sitting here eating their *Contrefilet* and drinking their *Moët & Chandon* with the unemployed on the prowl outside. They won't want to be seen, which means secluded little places well away from tram-stops and railway stations. Converted country houses in the Dales or up in the Lakes, only available to the carriage trade in their new horseless carriages. Fairly easily accessible too, these days, now that the roads are mended and all the village blacksmiths have turned themselves into motor mechanics."

"Sounds risky."

"So did the Crown. And you joined me here."

"Are you asking me — ?"

"Of course I am. As soon as I can. Just a few minor details to settle first, like raising the money . . ."

"Ah yes — ! Your bank manager *has* been dining here rather often lately."

"He has. I hope we've impressed him."

"I'm sure *you* have."

"Then let's make it a good Christmas. I could use the bonus."

It was around Christmas time that Polly, with her fiancé once again in tow, returned to the Crown, causing offense both to Roger's mother and her own; Edith Timms insisting that her son was by no means sufficiently recovered for all this drinking and dancing and "gadding about" to keep up with Polly; Miriam offering her tart opinion that if he was well enough to "gad about" at all he was well enough to get married.

But a few small problems had arisen with the house Aaron Swanfield's money was building. Delivery dates had been postponed and then, in one or two cases, forgotten. Work had not been done. And, in any case, Edith Timms did not think it advisable for Roger, in his weakened condition, to move into a new house in the frozen depths of winter.

"You do see, Polly dear, that it wouldn't be wise. So much better for both of you when the sun is shining."

Polly, who had become very docile since Roger's illness, very much inclined to sit for hours on end in what Edith called a daydream and Miriam a trance, smiled and nodded her platinum head.

"Yes, whenever you think best."

What a *dear*, sweet girl, thought Edith, an opinion swiftly revised when her son came home with the milk one morning, looking not so much in a state of trance as in shock, having followed Polly from the Crown to no fewer than three different parties where he sat, as he'd always done, talking to Sally Templeton or buying an occasional drink for the restaurant pianist, Adela Adair, watching, waiting, nodding off over his whiskey sour while Polly danced.

She had not danced since the beginning of September. And now she was making up for time lost, time which might hang heavy on her hands next year when she would be Roger's wife, rushing in frantic haste in every and any direction, piling up memories of folly against the day, not far distant, when Edith Timms, who had seemed to be her friend, would oblige her to be serious: a fragile, frenzied butterfly settling everywhere and nowhere until the day — quite soon — when Edith's net would force her to be still.

It did not occur to her to cancel her engagement. Such things, without serious provocation, were simply not done — particularly now when fiancés were not easily replaceable. And Roger had done nothing to provoke her except come down with appendicitis, for which she could not blame him, and show himself to her — no worse than she ought to have expected — in those crumpled striped pajamas. She had agreed to marry him — and everybody else, her mother, his mother, her brother Benedict, the authority figures of her life, had taken her very seriously. Money had been spent. Benedict had made certain arrangements, in agreement with bankers and lawyers and Mr. Timms, about her trust fund. There was the new house on Lawnswood Hill, filling up with carpets and furniture as if by magic before her eyes. There was her wedding dress. And what of the cupboard on the top landing at High Meadows, crammed full of wedding gifts which had already started to pour in before Roger's illness, and for which she had already written notes of thanks? It was simply not in her to call a halt to all that. And far better, in any case, to be the wife of a rich young man, dull and podgy and *balding* she'd noticed lately though he may be, than face a lifetime of spinsterhood — resigned like Sally Templeton, embittered like Adela Adair —at High Meadows.

She was, without really being aware of it, quite desperate, wearing an aura of abandon well suited to the mood of the times. She was a flame in the process of burning out. She was self-destructive, unstable, at the end of her tether. Irresistible.

"What a treasure," said Arnold Crozier, gazing at her speculatively across the pale blond head of the girl he had taken from a station bookstall and was already thinking of putting back again.

"What a waste," said Toby, looking sadly at Roger Timms who, once again, had become a feature of the cocktail bar, sitting placidly among the wallflowers like Sally Templeton until the stroke of whatever hour their mothers had specified called them home, and then, when the jazz band had left too, buying the musical talents of Adela Adair for Polly, plying her with drinks and Turkish cigarettes to keep her at the piano while Polly danced.

Christmas passed in a sleepless haze. January and February, cold and gray for everyone else, were cold and hard but golden for Polly. And it was in this mood that she met Roy Kington again.

She had not forgotten him. She had simply been too proud to talk about him and had made a point of *not* inquiring his whereabouts from his brother, Rex. Although, since Sally Templeton — showing what Polly considered a notable lack of self-respect — had taken pains to find out he had been staying in Cheltenham with his former company commander, naturally Poly knew it too. He had hurt her. He deserved her hatred and she desired that he should have it. Yet when he appeared in the cocktail bar doorway one February night and paused there, lean and hard and arrogant, surveying the scene, she had felt his presence nevertheless like a blow that had reopened both old wounds and deep-rooted, far-better-forgotten delights.

She had not forgotten. She had not forgotten the shame either, the rough handling and the final degradation to which he had subjected her. But what mattered — instantly — was that he should pay attention now to *her*, not to Sally nor hopeful, greedy Adela Adair, not to anyone in that line of wallflowers he had set so badly a-quiver.

And, to that end, while Sally enthused her joy at seeing him again and Adela Adair dipped her red head and her bare freckled shoulders into the lamplight for his perusal, Polly ignored him.

She danced.

He stood, leaning against a pillar, allowing Sally and Adela to watch him: watching her.

He went away and, although she was very sweet to Roger on the way home, she managed to excuse herself from permitting him what had become the usual, clumsy liberties.

"I'm so tired Roger — and I have a headache."

Fortunately, or perhaps not, Roger Timms was somewhat in awe of headaches, his mother having suffered from them at every crisis point of his life and her own, and believed — as Edith had taught him — that at such times a man must tread very warily.

"Beastly old headache again," she told him the following evening at the Crown. "It's so smoky in here. I'll just step outside for a breath of air. No. Don't come with me. I want to be quiet."

"All right, Polly." He smiled, resumed his seat again, having heard his mother use the same words a hundred times and when Edith did not wish to be disturbed one did not disturb her. All women, it seemed, were the same.

"Where's she going?" asked Sally Templeton sharply.

"For a breath of air." He believed it. And although Sally Templeton probably knew she had gone out to meet Roy Kington, she was a "lady" and did not know the words to say so.

She met him in the alley behind the hotel, coming to deliver a message of contempt for him, to pronounce a final, scornful goodbye to which he replied, "I couldn't forget you, Polly."

She had not expected that.

"I left Faxby because of you. I couldn't stay once you'd got engaged to that chap. I've just come back to see my mother and then — well — no use in hanging around now, is there?"

He had, in fact, left Faxby because he had been promised a job in Cheltenham and would not have returned had it materialized. He had remembered Polly as a flighty bitch who had led him on, had tried to make a fool of him, and upon whom the tables had been turned. Seeing her again, sensing the desire she was arousing in other men, he had made up his mind to have another crack at getting her himself.

It meant no more to him than that.

"I couldn't stop thinking about you, Polly."

He had, in fact, met a woman in Cheltenham, older and wiser than himself who had taught him a certain amount of amorous expertise, explaining to him that the female of the species can more easily, and sometimes *only*, be aroused by affection, by making her promises not of orgasm but of love.

"I — I've missed you Polly."

The effect on her was everything and more than he desired.

"I don't believe you." But, because believing him was what she wanted most that moment in the whole world, it would only take another word or two to convince her.

"Why did you bring that dreadful girl to my mother's party?"

A natural soldier he moved at once to the attack in order to defend himself. Revenge, he told her. Madness of course but then, who was to blame for that but Polly herself who had hurt him, driven him half-crazy? He'd been ready to kill her. He'd thought he probably might, and if it were true what the poet said and each man kills the thing he loves, well then, he'd leave her to draw her own conclusions.

Leaning against the alley wall she gazed at him, mesmerized.

"Kiss me goodbye," he said curtly, throwing the command at her with pain — he hoped, she thought — at the edge of his voice, letting her know that it was her fault he was abandoning his comfortable home and his widowed mother and possibly his native shore, although in fact he had already quarreled with his mother, was at present living in furnished accommodation with a trio of like-minded bachelor friends and had made no firm plans to go anywhere.

She swayed forward, a gorgeous prize rabbit, he thought, into his snare but remembering the advice of his friend in Cheltenham, all he did was kiss her, as gently as he could, his self-control made easier than it might have been by the fact that he was due to meet a girl of exceedingly available virtue at her flat in an hour or two.

"Roy darling — don't go."

"Why?" And he sounded harsh. "I have nothing to stay for. Have I?"

Had he indeed? Later that night when Roger Timms parked the car a discreet few yards from the front door of High Meadows and put a damp, plump hand on her bare knee, her revulsion was so great that she leaped out of the car and ran from him, crying out over her shoulder no more than the shocking truth that she was going to be sick.

She spent the next day cowering in bed, tearful, feverish, her head aching and her stomach queasy, unable to bear either the smell of food or of the flowers her fiancé — or perhaps her fiancé's mother — had sent her.

"Wedding nerves," said Miriam cozily, wondering, in fact, if her daughter had rather anticipated the wedding and might already be pregnant. "Won't be long now, darling." She would see to that.

No one else came near her. There was no one she wanted. The only woman she had ever trusted was Edith Timms and she could not confide in Roger's mother that the physical proximity of Roger made her ill. She had never relished it. She had simply believed she would get used to it, that it was not even particularly important for women. She understood now that it would be unendurable. She could not marry Roger. And since she could not withstand, alone, the combined family pressures of Swanfields and Timms and the condemnation Faxby had always accorded to "jilt," she would have to rely on Roy Kington to take her away.

The fever with which he had infected her before struck her again, its delirium lasting through the last dull days of February to a suddenly crisp and daffodil-colored March.

"If I could believe you," he told her. "After what you did to me last time, how can I believe you? How do I know you won't lead me on and let me down again? You hurt me, Polly. You really hurt me. I couldn't risk going through it again."

If she loved him she would give herself. Why not? Even clumsy, amiable Roger had tried the same thing and there was no doubting his sincerity. And she was asking a great deal of Roy. He had no money and, if Miriam and Benedict so decided, neither had she. Surely it wasn't too much to ask — was it? — for a little proof of her affection, something to keep him warm while he was facing up to the chill of Benedict? He no longer tried to force her. "Please Polly," he said. And afterward, when what had become such an enormous obstacle in her mind was finally got over, they could decide whether to run off and get married or whether to go straight away and brazen it out at High Meadows.

"*Please* — Polly."

"Please Polly. Please, please —" muttered Roger Timms nightly, for ever, unless she did something to put a stop to it now.

"All right then — I'm leaving," said Roy Kington. She threw her arms around him in panic and despair and would have given herself then, pressed against the alley wall, had they not been disturbed by a noisy, inquisitive crowd spilling out of the hotel.

"Come to my lodgings — it's only across the street." He had invited her there before and she had always resisted. But now her body was so close to yielding, as desperate and unafraid as it would ever be.

"Yes Polly — do come. You're ready. You love me — I can almost believe it — I'm very near —"

She had left Roger waiting for her in the cocktail bar, drooping as always over his whiskey sour, blinking owlishly at Adela Adair and Sally.

Roy Kington put his mouth against her ear. "What does that matter, Polly? Once you belong to me you won't be going back to him."

The glow of that declaration carried her across the street, its radiance obscuring the dinginess of his room, the staleness of old cigarette ends and beer bottles which filled it, although she was uneasy at the way he immediately peeled off his clothes and attacked hers. Polly cared about her dresses. She didn't want to see this one crumpled and flung to the ground. She was also very cold.

"I'll warm you." But he did not. His experience of women was extensive, his experience of virginity limited to the losing of his own on a drunken spree ten years before, while still at school. And what he had learned in Cheltenham about a woman's need for tenderness and romance he had understood to be a preliminary no longer required when fulfillment was so close at hand. He had waited a long time for Polly Swanfield, had endured frustration and loss of face on her account — having expressed too much confidence to too many friends in his ability to get her — and now his first concern was speed, before she changed her mind and then, having achieved the tight entry and ruptured the membrane that constituted her maidenhead, what mattered to him was stamina. Since he would certainly talk about it afterward he assumed she would do likewise and wished to give her cause to speak of him as virile, accomplished, more than able to stay the course. He did not understand orgasm in women, assuming it came with his or, in the case of "ladies" like his mother and sisters, not at all. He had thought no more about it than that.

"Isn't this great," he said.

414

"Yes." It absolutely *had* to be. And gritting her teeth, lying beneath him on a thin scratchy blanket, she endured not the disgust she had expected to feel with Roger but a physical outrage just the same, a hard, *unloving* object penetrating her body, since nothing that loved her could give her such pain, an ugly intruder taking satisfaction from her in this gainly, unseemly fashion.

She did not like it. She could not shut out of her ears the sounds of the lodging-house going on all around her, other people — strangers — talking, listening, through that thin wall. If she could hear their voices, their footsteps, that spate of coughing, those bursts of laughter, then surely they could hear the agonized creaking of Roy's bed springs, the awful puffing and panting he was making. She had never realized that lovemaking was so noisy, although it had struck her, from the start, that in a place like this, it was probably against the law. Hadn't she heard that? Yes, of course she had — of hoteliers refusing accommodation to couples who couldn't produce a marriage certificate. It must be illegal then. And what if someone knocked on the door, or suddenly burst in and accused them of immorality? What if someone threatened to fetch the landlord, or the police, or Benedict?

She did not like it at all. It hurt her, and scared her, and puzzled her too since in what had been done to her so far she could see not even the possibility of pleasure. Yet if he wanted it, as he all too evidently did, then she would bear it gladly. And she would find her enjoyment in his. She loved him. She had given him the precious, unrepeatable gift of her virginity to prove it. No woman could ever give him more than that. And in a few moments — could it last much longer? — she could get dressed and plan their life together. Perhaps he would want to go and see Benedict tonight and get it over with, throw his cards on the table and be damned? Or perhaps he would want her to elope straight away, creep home and get her things and run away with him? But either way she didn't despair that Benedict, when he realized they had already done this thing which so absolutely bound them together, would see reason, make the best of it, and let her have her big wedding. The house on Lawnswood Hill had been built, after all, with her money. Why shouldn't she live there, after a discreet interval, with Roy? Would he like that?

He shuddered suddenly, groaned, clutched her more wildly, hurt her for a moment quite badly, and then rolled aside.

"Wasn't that bloody marvelous?"

"Yes it was. Wonderful."

And now, having won his bet with himself and with his mates, it was time to extricate himself from the consequences.

"You don't really think so, Polly. You're lying to me."

"No I'm not." Having undergone the ordeal, paid the price, she had been looking forward to affection, tender little speeches, all those happy exciting plans; and she was horrified.

"Yes you are. I can tell. You think I'm a lousy lover — well, if that's it, then I don't care. I won't plead with you."

For ten minutes she pleaded with him, wept, wrung her hands, vowed — no longer caring who heard her through those thin walls — that he was magnificent, thrilling, beautiful, that she adored him.

"I don't believe you."

What else could she do to convince him? She had given him everything. And now he was everything to her. She had no one else. A shaft of raw fear entered her heart, a terrible thing, so that she began to weep again, cry out to him again how much he meant to her.

"Do shut up," he said. "For God's sake, Polly — these walls are thin you know. No point in providing entertainment for all and sundry."

"You didn't care who heard you a while ago."

"Well, that was then and this is now, Pol. Makes a difference. I'd get dressed if I were you old girl. The chap I share with should be back any minute now."

She got dressed, her hands shaking, her skin crawling, sobs catching in her chest, her head teeming with snatches of thought which must be — *had* to be impossible. She had to be wrong. Nothing so terrible as this could possibly happen.

"Sorry it didn't work out," he said.

What did he mean? Staring at him, her mouth opened soundlessly, stupidly, her eyes glazing over.

"Well it didn't, Polly. You must admit — That's why one has to do it, don't you see? I'm sure I made it clear enough. Dreadful business if one went ahead and got married — like our parents' generation used to do — and *then* discovered that one didn't suit in the things that matter."

He had mortally wounded her, that much was clear, and quickly — since the friend he was expecting any minute might have other friends with him — he gave her the *coup de grâce*.

"Pity really. We could try again if you like when I get back from Ireland — if I ever do. No — I know I didn't tell you that I'd joined the Black and Tans, but all's fair in love and war, don't they say? And since I'm off to war again — ! Need I say more? That's why I came back, of course, to make things right with my mother and put my affairs in order, Ireland being a pretty dangerous place. Yes, I've joined up again, Pol. I'm off to enforce British rule on our nearest colony."

She hurled herself at him then howling, not caring what he did to her so long as she could fasten her nails or her teeth on some part of him and claw it to death, squeeze it to death, destroy it; not caring if he murdered her, so long as she could damage him first.

"Oh what fun," he said, holding her away, but she was strong and he had to hit her hard to stop her, and even then, when he knocked her down, she kept on getting up again and throwing herself back into the attack.

"My word, Polly — what a girl you are."

He had never found her so attractive.

"Bastard," she shrieked, going for his throat, his eyes, his groin, the shrapnel they hadn't been able to get out of his chest, so that he was rather more relieved than he would afterward admit when his friends arrived.

They were hard men, like himself, all bound for Ireland and the Black and Tans.

"I say — is this just between the two of you or can anybody join it?"

"Help yourselves," said Roy Kington, laughing to disguise a serious shortness of breath.

There were three of them. Polly stood for a moment, horribly at bay, and then, leaving behind her coat, her bag, every penny she possessed, every cherished illusion, ran down the creaking stairs and out into the street.

The cocktail bar was not crowded that night, Arnold Crozier in his usual corner stroking rather absent-mindedly the arm of his blond, Toby leaning against a bar stool making up his mind to go home, two or three young couples, and Claire tidying up, glancing at her watch, wishing them all away, since she was going up to Westmorland the next morning with Kit Hardie to see a house he thought suitable for conversion to a hotel. And with Kit on her mind — the day and night she had agreed to spend with him — she had noticed nothing amiss. Polly had been here, she remembered that, mainly due to the familiar sight of Roger Timms patiently waiting, treating Sally Templeton to gin and vermouth and Adela Adair to neat *Calvados* in exchange for their conversation. Since Roger was no longer here, she supposed Polly had come back to be taken home. And so closely were they bound together in her mind as a couple, that she even looked for him behind Polly's back as she suddenly appeared in the doorway, badly disheveled, and walked unsteadily across the floor.

Was she drunk? It certainly looked like it. Had she fallen down somewhere and hit her head? Having seen the beginnings of a black eye before, Claire thought it likely. And it would also account for the state of her dress.

"Are you all right, Polly?"

But Polly brushed her aside and marching directly to the table where Roger usually sat, as if drawn to it by magnetism, said in an odd, disjointed fashion, "Roger." And when there was no answer, when he failed suddenly to materialize from thin air at her call, "Where's Roger? Where is he?"

"I don't know Polly."

Who did? The circle of her intimates, Arnold Crozier, Toby, Kit Hardie himself, were converging upon her, each one of them drawing his own conclusions about the bruises and the streaks of tears and mascara on her cheeks, the terrible shuddering which had started very deep inside her and was now spreading all over her body, jerking her like a demented marionette.

"Where's Roger?"

"He left," said MacAllister.

"He wouldn't leave me." And even in her hysteria her tone said, "The poor fool."

MacAllister, no stranger to hysteria in women and not particularly impressed by it, raised scornful shoulders.

"Have it your own way, pretty Polly, but I heard him with my own ears offering a lift home to Adela Adair, and saw them go through that door with my own two eyes."

Nothing had prepared her for this.

"Good," she said. "I'm glad. Good riddance — to me I mean, not him. Good riddance to me. I'm not worth a damn —"

And dragging the diamond ring from her finger, realizing now with bitterness that it *was* too tight as Miriam had always told her, she flung it wildly to the floor, somewhere underfoot.

"Good riddance. Good riddance —"

Several hands reached out as she swayed forward but it was slightly-built, easily-set-aside Toby who caught her first, holding her firm and fast as she collapsed against him sobbing, muttering, accusing herself of every heresy and disgrace, every hideousness, which his soft, generally unreliable voice covered with a lullaby of "It's all right now Polly. You're safe now Polly."

"I'm no good, Toby."

"You're my Princess Polly — always have been. My best girl."

He took her, still leaning against him, still sobbing, through the hotel and to his car, Claire walking behind them, vaguely uneasy, suffering one sudden pang of alarm which made her turn hastily to Kit.

"Shouldn't somebody go with them?"

He shrugged, his mind too on their lakeland journey, not really caring.

"Who? You're the only one who could go with them to High Meadows, Claire, and I wouldn't care to suggest it."

"Just the same . . ."

"Come on Claire — that's good old Toby over there putting her into his car and tucking his traveling rug around her knees — not Arnold Crozier. I reckon she's safe enough with him, don't you?

"I suppose so." The idea that it might be otherwise was, she agreed, ridiculous.

"And in any case, Claire, it rather looks to me as if the damage has been done. And not by Roger either, the poor bastard —"

"Yes, it does look that way. Poor Polly."

"Yes — poor Polly, since once gets the distinct impression she didn't enjoy it. But it's not our affair, is it, love?"

"Not really."

"And might it not pay us to remember that there's a valuable diamond lying about somewhere under one of the bar tables? Might be as well to get to it before MacAllister. Polly may not want it again but Edith Timms certainly will."

She smiled and nodded.

"All right, Kit."

And they were both thinking about tomorrow.

21

*T*HE journey to Westmoreland was accomplished easily and pleasantly, by train to Windermere and then the jolting, shawl-wrapped delight of a pony-trap between banks of rhododendrons just in bud and
rippling waves of daffodils to the village of Wansfell; a dozen low slate
cottages, their walled gardens making a purple and yellow patchwork of
spring flowers beside a stretch of smooth, quiet water. And on the hillside
above the lake the great house of Wansfell Howe, turreted, aloof, in its
several wild acres of broom and lilac and giant rhododendrons, huge
conifers standing sentinel at its gateway, last year's dead leaves still
drifting in the breeze of a new spring, the leaves of two years past, or
more, lying sodden beneath them.

"I used to be under-footman here," said Kit, smiling at his own past
without regret. "Then footman. Then butler in all but name since the
old boy who was supposed to be doing the job was getting a bit past it.
It was a good house to work in — decent people. Three very lively little
boys running about and raising hell all over this garden in my day — and
in the lake. We had to fish them out many a time. Very pleasant place
to grow up, it always seemed to me. And Madam had no edge to her
either. Nice woman. An earl's daughter, married a bit beneath her, I
suppose, since he had no title — although nobody ever denied he was
a gentleman. Scholarly sort of a bloke, liked his Wordsworth and his
Coleridge and his De Quincey. He died about a year ago and the house
has been empty ever since. She wouldn't see much sense in living here
alone."

"The boys?"

"All gone.

"Killed?"

He nodded, his eyes on the glint of water just visible through the thickly tangled trees.

"Yes. In the first year of the war, so the housekeeper tells me. Three telegrams in the same month. Julian would have been about nineteen, which would have made the twins twenty-one. Nice lads."

"That's why the house is up for sale?"

"Yes. Nobody to inherit it. I reckon there are a lot of houses like this, up and down the country, right now, in the same position. Nobody left. Madam's living in London — thank God. I'm not sure I could face her. Not as a prospective buyer, at any rate. She'd be very gracious about it, of course, and wish me well. But it would be bound to hurt. All the housekeeper said when she recognized me was 'I see *you've* come through it all right, Christopher Hardie.' "

"You're not ashamed of that are you?"

"No — damned glad."

"Me too."

The house had been left fully furnished with old, comfortable sofas and chairs made for the sprawling of growing boys and heavyweight hound puppies, massive sideboards scarred by time and the whittling of a careless penknife, venerable carpets cheerfully threadbare, a great deal of blue and white china which had been meticulously glued together, a library with leather armchairs and oak tables from which only the books had been taken, the bare shelves as shockingly bereft as the house without its children.

"I do the best I can, Christopher Hardie," said the stiff-backed, pinch-lipped housekeeper, "but the dust settles. Madam said you'd be staying overnight. Will it be one room for me to get ready or two?"

There was a short pause.

"One room will do nicely," Claire said.

"Very good." She was far too accustomed to the promiscuous habits of under-footmen to be in any way offended. "And dinner at seven o'clock. Does that suit?"

"Yes," said Kit easily. "I've brought some wine in the trap. Would you put it to cool?"

He had spoken with cheerful authority and for a moment her obedience hung in the balance, promiscuity being one thing, the order of command quite another. And she had commanded Christopher Hardie often enough, and sharply enough too, impervious to that charm of his that had wheedled the virtue out of more than one of the parlor maids and always kept him on the right side of the mistress. Master Julian had always liked him too, the young scamp — the young hero. Master Julian shot through his fair curly head. And Master Stephen, "missing believed killed" the telegram had said, blown to pieces by a shell more like with not enough of him left to identify. Master Granville. What had happened to him? There'd been a letter from his company commander saying he'd died instantly and felt no pain and nobody had ever been able to find out anything more than that. His father had tried, gone to Whitehall and waited about in drafty passages, and then he'd given up. He'd spent his time sitting in the overgrown garden after that watching the boathouse, that the boys had started painting in June 1914 and never finished, fall into decay. She knew he'd been glad to die. And now here was Hardie and this pretty, clear-eyed, cropped-haired young woman. The survivors.

"The wine, Mrs. Roe."

"Certainly," she said.

For the purposes of a hotel the house was big enough, two spacious drawing rooms overlooking the level stretch of Wansfell Water and the bare slopes beyond, the library with long windows leading to a covered verandah and descending in their wild tangle to the lake. The kitchens were old-fashioned but ample, the dining room conveniently placed and, close beside it, a billiard room which could be converted with ease to accommodate forty or so extra diners. There was a sufficiency of bedrooms on two floors requiring a great deal of taste and a certain amount of careful planning. The views, in every direction, took the breath away. The gardens, as Kit well remembered, had once been something of a horticulturist's paradise. The village of Wansfell was charming. The surrounding countryside was probably the most spectacular in the land. There was exercise to be had, climbing the fells or strolling the relatively gentle path around Wansfell Water, and culture — the poet Wordsworth and his sweet sister having lived the most intense idyll of their lives in a cottage not many miles away.

"Can people get here?" Claire wanted to know.

"Yes. If they know where to come. I haven't committed myself yet. I just think it could be right. For me — and for you. What do you think? Or would you rather wait and tell me in the morning? I didn't bring you here you know for that . . ."

"Oh dear." She laughed and tucked her arm through his. "Have I been too forward? I wouldn't want to seduce you, Major, against your will."

"I expect I'll give in gracefully."

"I expect so."

They walked down to the village, still arm-in-arm, a fresh breeze ruffling the surface of the water, just tossing the heads of the clustering daffodils, and bought newly-baked gingerbread at a cottage doorway, old companions chatting easily together as they strolled the single, winding street and the ancient mossy churchyard, none of the villagers who nodded to them with incurious courtesy recognizing in this soldierly, affable gentleman, the young under-footman from Wansfell Howe.

"How would they take to a hotel on their doorstep, Kit?"

"Badly," he said, "at least to begin with. Not even the village shop-keeper would like it, since I'd hardly be getting my *foie gras* from him. But when the old boy retires he might sell the business to a younger man who'd start selling things I might find handy — or my guests would. Picture postcards, cigars and cigarettes, the old lady's gingerbread nicely packaged — and they do a very decent rum butter hereabouts. Pack it in fancy jars and I believe you'd be on to a winner. I might even buy the shop myself. And I'd give employment, of course, up at the hotel to all the young girls who have to leave home now, when they turn fifteen, because there's no work for them in Wansfell. Most of them never come back. So if I'd be changing the village, I'd also be keeping it alive."

"And you'd be the new Lord of the Manor wouldn't you." She gave his arm a tolerant, affectionate squeeze and laughing he dropped a kiss on her forehead.

"I saw Mrs. Roe thinking just the same and hating me for it."

"Don't let that worry you."

"It doesn't. If she can bring herself to realize that she's never going to see Julian and Stephen and Granville running down the hill at teatime shouting for her muffins and her oatcake, then I might offer her a job. She's got nowhere else to go. Neither has Wansfell Howe. And better common young Christopher Hardie than genteel woodworm and dry rot. I'd like her to see that."

They walked back up the hill, through the towering rhododendrons, somber now but soon to be glorious, widespread masses of pink and purple, white and red, and through the crumbling stone gateway of Wansfell Howe, Kit's eyes busy now on the structural details, on how much was wrong and how much it would cost to put it right. The building itself was gratifyingly sound and the interior not much shabbier than he remembered it. Take out all the old furniture, strip all the walls, give some thought to the plasterwork and it wouldn't be too bad. The end product — and there was no doubt he saw it very clearly — would be a country house as one had always imagined country houses ought to be and never really were; traditional comfort far better maintained than any earl's daughter he'd ever come across ever managed to do it; the plumbing in first-rate order which was not always the case, he'd found, among the gentry; boilers and stoves that worked, so that his guests would never be exposed to those public school hazards of eating cold food and washing in cold water. Local labor would be cheap and convenient, local tradesmen reliable. The area was no longer so remote as it had been, and all he really needed was a reputation for good food and gracious living in a world growing every day plainer, sparser, meaner of spirit. And those who could afford it — and, however bad the times, they would remain numerous — would come not only from nearby Lancaster and Carlisle but from Edinburgh, Manchester, London, every city and country in the land. Naturally he would be risking his own money and the bank's money this time, not the Crozier's. But already he wanted to do it.

"Then do it," said Claire.

They went over the house again, taking each room at a time, planning it, seeing it. No cocktail bar, of course, although cocktails would be served in a profusion, deferentially and individually, on silver trays at the touch of a button. No, he was not thinking of asking MacAllister to join him, nor Mr. Clarence, two city-bred types who would only upset the locals. But he would bring John David who could blend very well into all this green solitude and whose creative flair would be wasted, Kit thought, on the sirloin steak and dover sole future he envisaged, in the long run, for the Crown. He might ask Mrs. Tarrant, but he'd see what he could do first with Mrs. Roe, one of the dragons of his young manhood that it would give him satisfaction to tame. He would have no use for Adela Adair but Gerard, the Crown's head waiter, was a competent fellow who could be trusted to knock the local girls into shape if it turned out they'd have to use waitresses, rather than waiters, as they probably would. No harm in that, since the gentry were accustomed to being waited on by parlor maids. If he could get Amandine Keller he would be well-pleased although, with the opening of *Chez Aristide*, it seemed unlikely. But by the time the place was ready for opening he'd have found somebody else.

"What about you, Claire?"

His enthusiasm reached out to her, easily kindling her own.

"I'm asking for a commitment," he said. "It's lonely up here. We'd be close together."

"Yes."

" 'Yes' you will or 'yes' you'll think it over?"

"I can't make decisions easily Kit — I never learned how. During the war there seemed no point to it and before that I suppose I was too young."

"Too sheltered?"

424

"Too smothered."

"You need a good man to look after you."

Euan had said the same and now, smiling, she made the same reply.

"Yes, I know."

"I'm here, Claire," he said.

Mrs. Roe, correctly interpreting the requirements of her former under-footman, had given them a room with a balcony which seemed to hang, in the twilight, above the still surface of the lake, the high, old-fashioned bed smelling of old-fashioned flowers, honeysuckle and lavender and clove pinks from the sachets of potpourri underneath the mattress and the bolsters, the hand-embroidered counterpane a little worn in patches so that Claire folded it carefully, recognizing it as someone's labor of love, a personal treasure.

She was not in any way shy with him. She had consented to this, in her own mind, months ago. He had needed simply to choose the moment. He had chosen it now and she was ready — just that — not eager nor inflamed but deeply, gladly prepared; her body too well acquainted with his for reticence, her mind reading between the lines of his too well for fears. They were friends who were about to be lovers. Perhaps that was the right order, the way it should be done. Opening her arms to him, allowing him, with none of the awkwardness she had felt with other lovers, to remove her stockings and to kiss her ankles and her knees, she hoped so, smiling with comfortable ease, with sheer coziness, as he undid, one by one, the tiny pearl buttons of her blouse, in no hurry himself, taking time and thought over each one — a hundred would not have been too many — until the garment parted and he removed it carefully, his fingertips caressing with delicate, infinite leisure every inch of skin as it was revealed to him. He had wanted her for a long, patient, wary time and now he rewarded his patience minutely, tenderly, turning her body around in his arms and back again, exploring the whole of it with unhurried hands and mouth and eyes, not once only but again, as often as he chose, the whole night before him, a whole new day in which to possess and repossess her tomorrow. He had had sex with more women than he could remember. He had never made love before and recognized it, like the natural *gourmet* he was, as being far too rare and precious for haste. It was to be tasted drop by drop, held on the edge of every appetite, absorbed, luxuriously and totally enjoyed. And when he had done all that so often, so thoroughly that he could hear her very bones purring, he entered her still very slowly and gently, with no thought of all the sexual techniques, the prowess, the erotic games of skill and stamina which had made his reputation with other women, seeking only — with this woman — to join his body to hers, feeling her pleasure grow beneath him with triumph and with gratitude, nurturing it, coaxing it to its conclusion and then releasing his own pleasure into it, through it, with an urge to possess and protect her, to enslave and enthrone her which he knew to be wholly primitive.

"I love you," he said.

"Kit." She was laughing, but so was he. "You don't *have* to say that — really?"

"I know."

Was it even true? He rather hoped so. He would like it to be.

"I don't suppose you'd marry me would you Claire?"

"I — I hadn't thought of it. Is it necessary?"

"If you come up here with me the locals might prefer it. So would I."

Lying on her back among the fragrant pillows, shafts of moonlight drifting like pale feathers through the open windows and across his handsome, easy, familiar face, she raised her hand and trailed lazy fingers along his cheek.

"You'd be unfaithful Kit — you know you would. From habit. All those pretty barmaids and voracious opera singers and adoring mayoresses. You couldn't resist."

He thought she was probably right. Perhaps not.

"I'd try," he said, kissing her hand.

"That's honest."

"Of course. I can promise to be that. Perhaps it's better that way, Claire. Honesty rather than the crazy promises youngsters make, which nearly always get broken. You're right about me, of course. I 've been a faithless man with women all my life. I never promised to be otherwise. It was just part of this life below stairs. The wages were poor but the living was good. A magnum of *Moët & Chandon* here, a parlor maid there, and move on. The army was the same, except that the parlor maids got to be stockbrokers' wives. You know how it was. And so I'm not by nature or by training a marrying man. I don't want a wife to cook for me and keep my house clean. I can make other arrangements for all that. I've no particular opinion either way about children. If they come I reckon I can cope with it. If they don't I wouldn't fret. I'm not on the lookout for somebody — wife or child — to prop me up when I'm old. If I ever get that far I'll see to it myself. No child of mine would stay at home so long anyway. But I'd like to be with you, Claire. I'm not saying I need you in the sense that I couldn't manage without you. But I don't want to be without you. If I can have you and keep you then I'd be a fool to throw it away for a night at the Viennese Opera, wouldn't I? And I'm nobody's fool. We could have a good life together, Claire."

"I think you're right."

426

In the feathery moonlight, lulled by the fresh breeze from the fell and the nearby lapping of clear water, she was sure of it.

"But you can't decide."

She smiled, sighing and snuggling against him ready for sleep.

"Perhaps you should drag me off by the hair — except that I suppose it's not long enough."

"Don't let that worry you," he said, folding warm, firm arms around her, "there's enough to get hold of. And I won't let go."

They made love again in a fragile daybreak, pale-gray light falling in patches across the counterpane, another leisurely exploration leading to a slow building, deep-rooted joy.

"Shall we stay another night?"

"Won't the Crown fall down, Kit, without you?"

"I'd like to think so. Probably not."

They stayed, looking over the house again as a token gesture to Mrs. Roe's conscience, walked the lake path and spent an hour throwing pebbles in the water, Kit's skimming boldly half way across, Claire's sinking fast. They had a ham and pickles and gingerbread lunch and spent the afternoon in bed, Mrs. Roe's grim smile when they appeared for dinner indicating that the lecherous inclinations of her under-footman had not, in her view, improved one bit.

"She knew my mother," he said, when she had set plates of roast duckling before them and gone off to serve their bread and butter pudding. "That's how I came to work here. My mother and Emma Roe came from the same village in Northumberland. There was never a Mr. Roe, of course. Mrs. is just the courtesy title they give to housekeepers. There was never a Mr. Hardie either. My mother had to go home in disgrace for a while to have me. But Emma Roe didn't go in for that sort of thing and so she got on quicker and better. My mother brought me here when I was sixteen with everything I owned in a carpet bag. She'd come down in the world by then, poor old girl. She'd worked in some big houses, cooked quality for the quality all right, but her health had started to let her down and she was cook-daily to a clergyman, while Emma Roe was housekeeper at Wansfell Howe. My mother was nervous. Emma was patronizing. Couldn't resist it. I suppose, since my mother had always been the best-looking girl in the village and even if she'd got into trouble — well, let's hope she had fun doing it. So Emma looked down her nose and my mother let her do it. She wanted to see me in a good place and she needed Emma to put in a word for me with the butler. I got the place and she died a month after. I'd like her to see me now. I'd like that a lot."

Leaning across the table she kissed him, a friend's kiss of understanding and sympathy and then a lover's kiss, disarranging the cutlery and almost putting out the candles, which said to him "I wish I could give you that."

"She'd be proud of you."

He sighed wryly and shook his head. "No she wouldn't. When I was butler at High Meadows she'd have been proud of me then. She'd worked under butlers all her life and she understood that. But now all she'd see is that I'm doing something above my station which is the same as heading for a very bad end. She believed in knowing one's place and keeping one's place, my mother. She'd die all over again with shock if she heard me offering Emma Roe a job. And as for being so bold as to lay a hand on you Mrs. Swanfield . . ."

"Lay a hand on me again, Kit."

Emma Roe, standing in the doorway with a hot dish of bread pudding in her hands, raised pained eyebrows, set the dish down between them and marched off, her stiff back registering only token outrage, accustoming herself slowly in this tragic, tumbledown new world in which she served duckling to Sally Hardie's bastard son and had been glad of the five-pound note he gave her.

They walked the lake path again after dinner in the dark, waiting to make love, drawing out the moment of their return to make the anticipation finer, the appetite keener and then lingering on the verandah so that the waiting became a longing they had only to climb the stairs to satisfy.

"Lay a hand on me, Hardie."

"With pleasure, madam. And I'll take you by the hair too when I'm ready — and force you."

"I expect I'll come quietly."

"My mother would never believe this, Claire, but I'm the right man for you."

"I think I'm beginning to believe it."

"Good. So what we have to do now is decide the ways and means."

They made love and then, lying on his back, his arm across her stomach in a gesture of possession which did not press heavily upon her but was not, for all that, in any way casual, he swiftly outlined his plans. He would buy the house as soon as he could raise the money. And then he would make it *his* house. Wansfell Howe, rescued from decay to make, not his fortune perhaps, and certainly not at once, but an ample living, a satisfying living, chancy — like everything that was worth anything — but rewarding, challenging *fun*. And for the first time in his life he'd be his own master. That was what mattered. He'd always kept faith with himself and he wouldn't let himself down now. This was what he wanted. He was going to have it.

"You really don't need me, do you?" she said.

"I want you. That's better. Come adventuring with me, Claire. I suppose that's what I'm asking."

"It's a fair offer."

"I've never made it to anybody else. Shall I make you take it when the time comes?"

They slept late the next morning, Mrs. Roe having failed to call them early because, she explained primly to Kit, she had judged them to be tired out after their "exertions," walking up and down so much on the lake path.

He smiled, gave her another five-pound note for her trouble and her impudence and — although he did not say so — in memory of his mother and asked her to make sure the pony-cart was ready to take them to the next train.

"Why don't you ask me to stay another night?" asked Claire pertly, knowing his answer.

"Because, my darling, I have an urgent appointment at my bank."

Once again Mrs. Roe, who had thought his mother a flighty, feckless woman and had not judged Kit himself, in his youth, to be worth much, raised her eyes to Heaven.

"The pony-trap is waiting — *Major* Hardie."

What a world, she thought, although gradually, grimly, she was becoming resigned to it, where all three of her young gentlemen, had they lived, would have been obliged to salute Sally Hardie's son.

The journey in every way had been a success. They had put into it all they had intended and got out of it everything they had desired. A rare achievement, one of life's bonuses which did not come readily to hand and for which — knowing such bonuses to be in short supply — they were properly grateful. And returning to Faxby, it did not surprise them to see the Crown still standing, nor did it interest them quite so much as it would once have done. They had other concerns now. They were, imperceptibly but surely, not quite the same people who had left Faxby three mornings ago and so, walking back into the full flood of a chaotic Friday night, it took them a moment to register at any significant level what Mr. Clarence and Mrs. Tarrant, then Gerard and a badly shaken, far-from-sober MacAllister all whispered to them.

The Swanfield engagement had been broken off.

And Toby Hartwell was dead.

Claire knew she would have to go to High Meadows. In common

decency and humanity she could do no less than that. She also knew that Kit, who would never be a Major to Miriam, could not go with her. Who then? Dorothy perhaps to provide the safeguard she ought not to need — not now — against Benedict. Borrowing John David's old Talbot she drove to Faxby Park finding her mother more than ready to pay a visit of condolence, sorry for Toby of course who had always been very kind to her, but all agog at the rumors that were flying around all over Feathers' Teashop and every department of Taylor & Timms about Roger and Polly. And there seemed no doubt that Roger Timms' desertion of glorious, golden Polly for a brazen harlot, well over thirty they were saying, from the Crown, had moved Dorothy rather more than the lonely ending of Toby Hartwell early that morning on the road to — well, Dorothy could not say just where he had been heading.

Neither — when they were shown into the drawing room at High Meadows — could Miriam. It was inexplicable. Dreadful. Sitting alone in the middle of a wide sofa, perching rather on the edge of the cushions like a child, her diminutive feet just touching the ground, she looked smaller than Claire had ever seen her, the rouge and powder she was supposed *never* to employ quite visible on her round, smooth cheeks, her need for a mask outweighing, today, her concern for propriety. Yet, however badly shaken, she was able to offer a choice of tea or sherry, perhaps a wafer of fruitcake, not only to Dorothy and Claire but to the elderly second cousins and aunts and "dear friends one has known forever" who were gathering like crows behind a storm, her brave smiles, the grave but steady tone of her voice, making it clear that the social niceties of bereavement would be obeyed.

Eunice was upstairs in what had been her girlhood bedroom, heavily sedated, a nurse in attendance. Polly, too, had collapsed at the tragic news and was, therefore, better off in bed, particularly as she, poor child — and here the elderly relatives pricked up their ears like so many inquisitive terriers — had suffered a setback of her own. Benedict was — well, at the *scene*, ten miles away, taking care of the appalling details, doing what had to be done in cases of accident where . . . Oh dear. It was by no means so straightforward as when one died in one's bed. And for a moment she sounded just a little aggrieved with Toby for driving that extravagant, highly-powered car of his off the road and over the edge of a disused quarry instead of "going" more conveniently at home, like Edward Lyall, of a heart attack.

No. She had no idea where Toby had been going at that hour of the morning. Perhaps Eunice, when sufficiently recovered from the shock, would be able to throw some light on the matter. No one else knew anything about it. *Most* distressing, the more so since Toby had spent his last evening here, in her house, at High Meadows. Yes indeed. He had come specially to cheer up Polly who — well, perhaps it was no longer a secret — had good cause, alas, to feel down in the dumps. A shocking business. How could they, she wondered, have been so mistaken in that young man? She could only feel that Edith Timms, his mother, had a great deal to answer for. But there it was, and she saw no point, now, in being other than brutally honest about it. Her daughter had been *wronged*. What other word could one use to describe it? The young man had promised marriage and had then jilted her in the most humiliating fashion, had gone off with a *person* about whose reputation all that seemed certain was her lack of it. Perhaps Edith Timms would know how to deal with creatures of that class. Miriam rather prided herself on the fact that she did not. Polly, of course, had been distraught. Utterly and absolutely shattered. Her mother had found her, in the early hours of yesterday morning, pacing about the upstairs corridors in her dressing gown, staring and wringing her hands and weeping — such tears, good Heavens — looking for all the world like that tragedy queen — whoever she was — oh yes, Lady Macbeth. Such grief. One wondered really, how *any* man could possibly be worth it. Particularly someone so — well — *ordinary* as Roger Timms. And she had kept it up throughout the day, pacing and moaning and staring so that Miriam had been quite worn out by it and rather grateful when Toby had arrived at about five o'clock to take the strain. Miriam remembered the hour because it had been her teatime and such a relief, after that long day of storm and tempest, to be able to drink her Earl Grey and eat her buttered scone in peace, and then close her eyes for half an hour or so while Toby bore the brunt of Polly. The dear man. He had always been so kind to Polly and so understanding, so ready to put up with her whims and fancies and those occasional little tantrums, Polly's mother being quite ready to admit that Polly could be difficult. When she had woken up, with rather a start, about an hour later it was to find that he had taken Polly for a drive, an excellent idea she'd thought, the very thing to distract her and draw her out of herself. But when they came back — oh, she supposed about eight o'clock — Polly had looked worse than ever and Toby himself a little strained, which was not to be wondered at surely, after a three-hour exposure to Polly's heartbreak? Miriam, having endured a whole day of it, had felt much inclined to sympathize, had thanked him for his trouble and stood, waving at the doorway, until his car was out of sight.

That he had gone home then was quite certain, all the boys had seen him and presumably Eunice herself, although she was too incoherent at present to say so. He had gone up to his room without speaking to anybody, presumably to change for dinner. And then, at five o'clock this morning, his car had been found horribly smashed to pieces in a Pennine quarry. No. No one knew for certain. His car had left the road at a particularly dangerous bend and had been spotted by another motorist — hours later one supposed — who had noticed that the quarry fence had been broken down. He had alerted the local constable who, very fortunately, had in turn alerted someone in the Faxby constabulary who had had the good sense to inform Benedict, not Eunice. He had gone at once to confirm that it *was* Toby — unnecessarily painful, she'd thought — and then, of course, Eunice had had to be told. Benedict had brought her back to High Meadows in a state bordering on insanity. Miriam, for as long as she lived, would never get over the sound of those terrible cries. They had pierced her — how else could she express it?— through the heart. Indeed, she had had a pain in that region ever since. And then Polly, too, falling down right there in the hall by the main staircase and banging her head, over and over again, against the banisters. What a spectacle! Miriam, as perhaps her friends would readily admit, rarely encountered a situation she could not command. But standing there, watching Polly smash her head repeatedly against solid wood, she had not known what to do. It had shocked her deeply. The memory of it shocked her still. Yes, she was rather tired. How kind of everyone to notice. Perhaps if she could just close her eyes for awhile, dab a little cologne on her forehead, she would be quite refreshed.

Claire attended the funeral not as a member of the family but as an employee of the Crown, preferring, since it was there she had known Toby best, to stand at his graveside with Kit and Mrs. Tarrant, MacAllister and Mr. Clarence, and the considerably subdued Adela Adair who had got much more than she'd bargained for by accepting a lift home from Roger Timms. Under the circumstances neither Edith Timms nor Roger were present, the family being represented by Mr. Timms who stood about awkwardly, clearly feeling at a serious disadvantage in the presence of the girl his son had jilted and the woman — definitely over thirty — Roger had so suddenly taken it into his weak head to marry. Greenwoods and Templetons and Redfearns were there, quite naturally, in force, along with the departmental managers of Swanfield Mills and certain other gentlemen of a more sporting appearance, Toby's bookmaker among them, sincerely mourning the loss of favorite client.

"A bad business." Everyone said it, agreeing absolutely with each other, declaring him to have been an excellent fellow, no one wishing to be the first to wonder just what he had been doing on that lonely road.

It was a bleak March day, a cold wind blowing. A bad business. Bury it then, quickly, and get it over. Much better so.

Claire, her arm through Kit Hardie's, raised her eyes and looked across the open grave at Benedict, seeing him, for the first time in months, surrounded by clutching, clamoring women as he had always been; Miriam, invisible beneath her old-fashioned mourning veils, leaning heavily against him at one side; Polly, likewise invisible, collapsed against the other; Nola hovering just behind, unsuitably dressed in a tweed suit and cape and a strange deerstalker hat, refusing to interest herself in any grief which did not emanate from All Saints' Passage, her conversation liberally peppered now — to the dismay of Greenwoods and Redfearns and Miriam — with references to "one of my prostitutes," "one of my pickpockets," "a girl of mine who was so brutally raped by her father at thirteen."

Eunice, shocked by laudanum into silence, stood rigid and ghastly, propped up like a tragic wooden doll between her elder boys, Simon embarrassed by grief, Justin embarrassed by his mother. He had heard of women — only in books perhaps, but nevertheless — who threw themselves into the grave when the coffin was lowered, refusing to be parted from their husbands. Might his mother do that? The suspicion that she was quite capable of it haunted him. And if it happened — with Uncle Benedict's hands full of Polly and Grandmother — would he, as her eldest son, the senior male of the family now present after Benedict, be expected to cope with it, go down there and get her out? With everybody who was anybody in Faxby watching him? If she did that to him he would never forgive her. He would hate her, like poison, for the rest of his life.

But, to his infinite relief, when the ceremony was over and those terrible shovelfuls of earth had started to fall, she came away with him jerkily, but obediently, blank eyes fixed and unblinking, looking quite demented he thought, *dangerous* even — someone he might actually be scared of if she weren't "just Mother" — but at least not making a fuss, leaving it to Polly, who had always upstaged her, to fall down very suddenly, the moment Benedict let her go, and there, kneeling at the graveside, to be violently sick.

"My goodness — the poor child." There was an immediate thrill of interest, curiosity, speculation, running from Templetons to Redfearns to Greenwoods, ending at the embarrassed figure of Roger's father, Mr. Timms, and the bowed, flame-colored head of Adela Adair.

They had broken Polly's heart, between them. Whoever would have thought it? Whoever, if it came to that, had ever credited her with a heart to break? Yet seeing her now, her silk stockings and fine muskrat coat daubed with graveyard mud, vomiting and shivering and howling, no one could possibly doubt it.

"Polly." Claire made a move toward her but Kit, tucking her arm firmly in his, said, "Leave it, love." And it was Benedict who picked her up and carried her through the cemetery to the waiting car, her pale head hanging over his arm like a broken lily.

Eunice returned to her own home that night, her decision to "start as she meant to go on" unopposed by Miriam who really was very tired and who knew that Eunice's departure would also include her noisy sons. Delightful boys, of course, but only in small doses, smaller than ever just lately when she had not been feeling *quite* so well as usual. And their presence in the house, these past four days, *had* been irksome. They were always so hungry for one thing, demanding enormous teas and suppers as well as those terribly inconvenient cooked breakfasts, at a time of sorrow when Polly was apparently intent on starving herself to death, Benedict had made his own arrangements, and Miriam herself should have been content with something light and easily prepared, on a tray. Neither she nor the servants ought really to be troubled with steak and kidney pies and suet puddings at a time like this and she made no objections, therefore, when Eunice decided to take her hungry boys home.

"Much better, dear — that's the only way to get over it."

But Eunice's purpose was not to "get over" Toby but to build him a shrine, thus causing considerable disappointment to Justin who had expected to be given the first choice of his father's wardrobe for himself. Toby, in his eldest son's opinion, had been a "natty" dresser and it gave Justin great offense to think of those silk shirts and pajamas, those superbly cut blazers, those Oxford bags and Cashmere sweaters moldering in a cupboard to suit his mother's peculiar fancy that her husband's room must remain exactly as he had left it. She had even refused to clean his hairbrush. Peculiar was the word for it. Justin could think of no other until she flew at him, a morning or two later, spitting fury, and tore from his back one of Toby's pullovers which he had pinched, in fact, several weeks ago. As she cradled it in her arms the word in her son's mind was "crazy."

He realized, without shock, that he did not like his mother. But, just the same, when he found the letter, he would not have given it to her — he was sure of that — if her "craziness" had not compelled him.

It was in the pocket of the camel hair overcoat he had always coveted, largely because his arrogant Uncle Benedict wore one with a swagger Justin had often tried to emulate. And although Toby had never swaggered, the coat had been a symbol, somehow, of Swanfield authority, a seal of worldly approval. Justin wanted it. Coming across it hanging on a hook in the now empty garage, realizing his mother had missed it because she could not as yet bear to come here and look at the space where Toby's car had been, he put it on, finding his father's driving gloves in one pocket — rather odd perhaps — and the letter in the other.

Toby had been wearing this coat, Justin remembered, when he came home from High Meadows the last time Justin had seen him. He had gone up to his room, the coat around his shoulders, and for it to be here, in the garage, meant that he had also been wearing it when he went out again. Perhaps, on that second occasion, the car had refused to start and Toby, taking off his coat to look under the bonnet, had simply forgotten and driven off without it. No one would ever know. And Justin, excited by his find, did not think it really mattered. Nor in his haste to conceal the coat from Eunice, would he have been likely to read the letter had not his fingers, locating the crumpled sheet of paper, in the depths of the pocket, mistaken it for a five-pound note. And then, from the first word, there was no stopping.

"Polly, my darling, I have loved you so long. As a brother I thought, or even a father — my Princess Polly, my best girl. I forced myself to believe that. But we know, how can we fail to know now how very far from the truth it has been. I would never have touched you — never — you know that — had you not turned to me in your distress, asking for love without knowing it, innocent as you have always been yet needing me, clinging to me as if you had been drowning. I rescued you and destroyed myself. I made love to you. Even writing the words brings it back to me. I made you clean of what had been done to you. Remember that and forget all my pleading of today. I was mad to hope you would consent to it. You have no cause to blame yourself. Polly — you lit up my life. My existence has been bearable, these five years past, only because of you. And now I have no wish to live in the dark. Polly, my darling —"

It was too much for Justin.

"Justin — ?"

Seeing the garage doors open — having found it necessary to watch her son like a hawk this last day or two — Eunice was waiting on the garden path.

"Justin — those are your father's things in there, *his* property — come out."

"Oh Mother — for God's sake."

He did not know what to do. It was as simple as that.

"Justin, stop poking and prying into what belongs to your father and *me*."

She saw the coat and flew at him again to strip it from him, tugging at the lapels, the sleeves, until she saw the letter in his hand. Toby's handwriting. Toby's words. *Her* Toby. How dare this little thief who had been her adored son take that from her? Frantic — when was she not frantic now? — she began to slap him across the face and head, looking demented again like the woman who would have badly scared him had she not been his mother.

It was too much.

He threw the letter at her and ran.

Miriam persuaded Polly for the first time to come downstairs for dinner, having made up her mind that all this skulking about behind locked bedroom doors must not continue. The scene at Toby's graveside had been quite bad enough and, since another prospective husband must — the sooner the better — be provided, it would not do to have it said that the loss of her first fiancé had turned Polly's mind. Therefore, she had persisted. Polly, realizing that she could not stay in bed forever, had finally consented to sit at the dinner table, pushing morsels of food around her plate with a fork. And the meal was just over, Benedict in his study, Miriam and Polly sitting in silence Miriam found distinctly unnerving in the drawing room, when Eunice flew through the door, having run all the way up the hill to murder her sister.

"Eunice dear — ?"

"Harlot," she shrieked.

Instantly, leaping to her feet, Polly understood.

"No —" she whispered. "No."

"You killed my husband."

"No — no — please —"

"Murderess."

"Oh no —"

"You seduced him and you killed him. He ran his car into that quarry because of you."

She had always hated Polly, or so she thought now. Always. And seeing Polly's terror, seeing how she shrank away, cringed and cowered like the whore, the vermin she was, she gloated, exulted. No weapon. Just her bare hands around Polly's throat. Just that. And Polly, who was taller and stronger and much younger, helpless to defend herself, doing nothing but whimper and shiver, because she knew she was guilty.

"Oh dear God —" Miriam, chalk-white, flew from the room calling out for Benedict who could not, for what seemed a long time to Miriam, do more than hold them apart.

And although she was not particularly devoted to either of her daughters the sight of Eunice foaming and raging and of Polly cowering in such abject terror, the sound, the smell of so much hatred and horror clawed holes in her heart. And what were they saying? These terrible accusations about Polly and Toby. How could it be true? Nothing so unspeakable *could* be true. She wouldn't have it. Yet Polly, instead of denying it, did nothing but shake and sob and plead with Benedict to keep Eunice away from her. While Eunice — had she gone mad? Would it mean doctors, an asylum — oh please not that. Closing her eyes, a great swimming dizziness in her head, she remembered pictures someone had forced her to look at in her youth of maniacs, chained and raving who had terrified her then just as her own daughter was terrifying her now. Or had Toby gone mad? Was that it? Had he made the letter up? Men had strange romantic fancies sometimes, at that age. She tried to intervene, to present them with her solution, something, at least, which one could tell the servants and the neighbors. But although she opened her mouth and moved her tongue no voice came. Or had she, perhaps, spoken and they had drowned her with their din? That had been happening lately — those noisy boys wanting their dinner. And now Eunice. She tried to speak again, rationally, calmly, her wisdom, she thought, far better than their truth — far safer.

"Children — do behave yourselves."

All that happened was that Polly, suddenly locating a spark of fire, began to pick up the sofa cushions — what ridiculous weapons to choose — and throw them at her sister, who was still held back by Benedict. But — oddly, strangely — they seemed so far away.

"Children —" And then, "Oh dear — I think I am unwell."

No one heard her. And it was, indeed, several moments before they noticed that she was not sitting quietly in her chair but had collapsed.

She was carried to bed, a doctor called.

"Look after her," Benedict snarled at Eunice.

"Go to your room and stay there," he rapped out at Polly.

They obeyed, Polly locking her door, her life at an end, she believed, whether Eunice killed her or not. And whatever happened to her now, she believed she deserved it. Nothing could be bad enough. She had gone to Toby as she would have gone to her father. And he had been so kind, so sweet, so familiar. She had liked him so much, trusted him, nestled against him so naturally, feeling so safe in a way she remembered feeling before, long ago, when she'd been very small. She had lost that feeling when her father died and now, meeting it again, how wonderful. "Toby, I do love you." She remembered whispering that to him and what had happened next had seemed no more than an extension of that so miraculously recovered sense of being with a man who would make everything all right, in whose hands she was so blissfully secure. His kisses, even when they became prolonged, intense, had not seemed

437

strange to her. He had been cherishing her not attacking her and even when he did what Roy Kington had done to her so shortly before, she had hardly felt it, hardly recognized it as the same. And it had been so brief, so soon over, that it had seemed scarcely to interrupt the nestling and stroking and "keeping her safe" of which she had been in such urgent need.

And he had died for it.

The next day he had asked her to go away with him and she had lost her nerve and her head. He had lost his life. Desperately she wished that Eunice would kill her. Kinder really, since she was not quite certain how to go about killing herself and it would be far better for everybody if she died. Yet, an hour later, when she crept furtively to the bathroom and came face to face with Eunice she pressed herself in terror against the wall and closed her eyes.

"So now you've killed mother," hissed Eunice.

"No." It was the only word Polly could say.

"Oh yes you have." Miriam was not dead, no longer in fact in any immediate danger, but the need, in Eunice, to kill had been suppressed now into a desire to maim.

"She's dead and you killed her. She said it was your fault before she died. And now you're alone with me Polly."

"Benedict?"

"Oh no." Eunice was staring and grinning. "He's gone off to make the arrangements."

It sounded horribly likely.

"So there's just me —"

Polly shrieked and pushing Eunice aside with the strength of raw desperation fled for what she believed to be her life, worthless to her though it seemed, along the corridor, down the stairs, and out — *out* — through the front door, down the drive, through the gates. Cast out. Anywhere. Away.

"Is Polly still in her room?" asked Benedict, suddenly remembering her an hour later.

"Yes," said Eunice, sufficiently restored to sanity to know that she was lying yet unable to stop herself.

"See that she stays there," he said.

The road from High Meadows to Faxby was downhill, a fitting direction perhaps, which she accomplished far too quickly, much too soon. Where could she go? The river perhaps? The railway track? But she knew, even then, her head still reeling with shock, that she could not physically harm herself. She would have to push herself in some other way. And it was in this mood that she encountered Arnold Crozier, his Rolls drawing up beside her, by no means surprisingly since she had wandered into the neighborhood of the Crown, his voice inviting her, like the spider she had always known him to be, to step inside.

She remembered little else that night, for she had eaten almost nothing for several days and the first sip of wine rose instantly to her head. He had watched her for a long time, had come to regard her rather as the original model on which his ever-changing series of young, fair-haired, long-limbed, scatterbrains was based. Polly was the blond among blonds, the flapper *par excellence*, the very spice his jaded palate needed. He had also considered her to be unattainable and now, seeing his chance, took it coolly and cleverly, aware that there was nothing to be gained in these matters by any undue consideration of scruples. And when, in the warmth of the Tangerine Suite, after a judiciously administered bottle of champagne, she became kittenish and coy, showing a great partiality for being petted and stroked, he placed her like a prize in the tangerine bed and made love to her in a way which even Polly, had she been sober, might have recognized as masterly.

Arnold Crozier, who had never been handsome, was nevertheless a man who not only enjoyed women but understood them, Polly's body, relaxed by alcohol, a jewel in his hands to be treasured and made to sparkle, a feast to be relished not greedily but with the delicacy of a *gourmet* who sips and savors, her pleasure to be carefully located from whatever sources it came and then released gradually through her limbs which were still virgin of pleasure, with a wizardry in which she had never believed and did not believe now. It was not happening. She was dreaming, most oddly, that she was in bed with Arnold Crozier and that something very strange was starting at the pit of her stomach and spreading all over her, something she'd dreamed about before once or twice, except that this time — Good Heavens — Good Lord — she had never got this far with it before. She had woken up, those other times, with a start and always missed the best of it. Not now though. And when, in the uncertain light of a rainy morning, she woke with Arnold Crozier still beside her, her head still swimming, and he made that incredible sensation come again, it seemed to her that she had found a fitting substitute for the railway track. The spider had caught her. And if what he was doing to her was repulsive —as it must be since it was Arnold who was doing it — it thrilled her as well. What better degradation?

She had told him she could not return to High Meadows. Where then? Normally such a declaration would have alarmed him, smacking as it did of involvement. But Polly was not only very much to his taste, she was also a Swanfield, a girl of good family, well-connected and rich. And he was beginning to tire of chance encounters, often costing more than they were worth, in hotels.

"Come with me," he said, and having been brought up to enjoy the authority of the older, powerful male, she got into his Rolls, wrapped in a velvet evening cloak his last blond had left behind, and was whisked away, first to buy clothes in Manchester and then to a boat-train, a boat, another Rolls and a hotel room in Rotterdam where Arnold had been going on business in any case.

Was she safe? She knew he had made a telephone call, or instructed someone else to make it, to High Meadows. And since no one had come after her, here she was, still rather stunned during the daytime, unable to get her thoughts together, falling asleep a great deal: still amazed every night when, her eyes closed, her head obligingly swimming with her bedtime champagne, he unfailingly made those wild sensations come, and come again.

"We could get married," he said. She burst into tears. How could she do that without a white dress, a dozen envious bridesmaids, an embroidered veil?

He shrugged his narrow shoulders.

"Think it over."

"Oh no," she said. "I really couldn't." An opinion she was obliged to reconsider, some three or four weeks later, when it became clear to her that she was expecting somebody's child.

22

MIRIAM had suffered a heart attack of adequate severity, brought on, she was in no doubt, by the shocking revelations of her daughters, her recovery, which was slow enough, further impeded by the mental collapse of Eunice, the moral collapse of Polly.

It had all been so terrible that even three months, four months later, she could not think of it without tears. And since she thought of little else, she spent a great deal of her time weeping. Benedict, of course, had done — she supposed — all that he could. But just the same, she could not help thinking he ought to have known that Polly was missing. True — *dreadfully* true — that Eunice had covered it up, pretending she'd spoken to Polly through her bedroom door when, in fact, she'd just chased her out of the house with threats of Heaven knew what. But Benedict — surely? — ought to have seen that Eunice had lost her reason, that it had all been too much for her, losing Toby and then finding out so brutally just *how* she'd lost him. Obviously she couldn't come to terms with that. What woman could? Because whether he'd set out to kill himself deliberately or whether he just hadn't seen that bend coming — either way — it didn't alter the fact that he'd been *leaving* her. Dreadful. And even more dreadful that Benedict had known nothing of Polly's flight, had thought her safe if not particularly sound upstairs in bed — if he'd given her a thought at all — until Arnold Crozier had telephoned the monstrous information that she was going away for a while with him.

And Benedict had let her go.

Naturally he said now that it had been because of Eunice who had chosen that moment to break down entirely, horribly, although her mother had been too ill to be aware of it. How could he leave two sick women, he'd said and four young boys, and — she supposed — whatever crisis was brewing at the mills, to go chasing off to the continent looking for Polly?

The damage would have been done by then, he'd told her coolly. "In fact, one assumes it had been done before he telephoned."

Yes, he had said that to *her*, Polly's mother, standing by her bedside looking down at her in his unfeeling fashion, making no allowance for her helplessness, the weakness of her condition. And here she was now, an invalid still, unable to leave her bed for more than an hour or two every day when, weather permitting, she would be carried into the garden to sit in a *chaise longue* and take the sun. Yes, here she was, with Eunice hanging around her like a stray dog, not bothering to wash her face or comb her hair by the look of her, staring all the time at absolutely nothing, no help to her mother and no company. And Nola, with all her grand ideas of service to humanity, being no help either, finding nothing to interest her in adultery and nervous breakdown, suicide or despair unless it took place in a back-to-back cottage or a lodging-house off Town Hall Square. And those boys, slamming doors and shouting and ruining the furniture she was sure of it, scratching the parquet and smoking — oh yes, they might deny it and Eunice did not care, but she *knew* they did — in bed.

Here she was. And there was Polly, sunning herself in Cannes the last anybody had heard.

Faxby did not quite know what to make of it. Naturally — as was only to be expected — as Miriam at least had been only too well aware — the events of that fateful night had not passed unnoticed by the servants. And just as naturally they had gossiped to other servants who had wasted no time in spreading the word, so that opinion among the "informed" classes of Faxby was divided among those who believed Polly had seduced Toby — the lucky dog!; those who believed it had been the other way round — asking for trouble with those short skirts in any case; those who preferred to think it had all been in *somebody's* sick mind — Eunice's or Toby's according to taste; and a fairly substantial number, female in the main, who thought Eunice a fool either not to have seen it coming or to have got so carried away by it when it did.

But, as all shades of opinion agreed, it was a bad business; Polly winning rather more sympathy than she might have done had not Arnold Crozier, although a noted lecher and a thoroughly dirty old man, also been a millionaire. And there were not a few, therefore, who found it easy to excuse her conduct on the grounds of her broken engagement to Roger Timms.

Not that anyone really knew what to make of that either. Everybody had been invited to the wedding. Most people had already purchased their wedding gifts, putting themselves in a position only slightly less inconvenient than those who had already sent them, since it would be awkward now to return them to Taylor & Timms whence most of them originally came. What to do for the best? Polly, it seemed, had got married abroad, privately, and having sent out no invitations had forfeited her right to gifts. Ought one to hang on to all this linen and china and *bric-à-brac*, perhaps, in case Edith Timms finally gave in to her son's insistence on making an honest woman of Miss Adela Adair and consented — as so far she had adamantly and hysterically refused — to attend their wedding?

Or might he too just go off somewhere, like Polly, and come back married? It rather looked like it.

What a tragic, tumbledown world.

It had never occurred to Edith Timms that a day might dawn when she would be unable to control her son. Yet, in the matter of Adela Adair, she knew herself defeated long before she could bring herself to admit it. No one had expected it, least of all Adela Adair herself. She was thirty-two and felt older, a woman of indifferent health, indifferent talents, indifferent looks too although, with a certain amount of touching up, her red hair looked well enough when she sat in candlelight at the piano, and she had become very skillful at powdering over her freckles. She was neither particularly ambitious nor particularly virtuous, accepting her limitations in both these directions and had seen nothing in Roger Timms but an easy source of apple brandy and Turkish cigarettes. Knowing what Polly was up to she had felt sorry for him and had also thought him a fool. And on the night when Polly had finally kept him waiting a little too long and he had offered Adela Adair a lift home, she had been expecting no more than that. Nor, once arrived at her flat, had she expected him to come inside, making an offer of cocoa and biscuits only because it seemed polite and she always liked to do the right thing. But he had settled down very comfortably at her fireside, her flat being shabby but colorful, very warm and clean, and after a while, because she was feeling lonely and because, more often than not, it was the usual outcome of cocoa and biscuits at her flat, she took him to bed.

Roger Timms was twenty-seven, powerfully built, highly sexed and still a virgin because his shyness, his complete lack of confidence in himself, prevented him from being otherwise. He had always been clumsy, "ham-fisted" his mother called it, never quick to understand how even relatively simple things should be done, much less this complicated and mysterious act of procreation. His mother had always laughed at his awkwardness. Polly had followed her example and the very extent of his adoration for her had made him even more tongue-tied and inclined to fall over his own feet than ever. That he would make a fool of himself on his wedding night he was painfully certain. The mere thought of it — and it preyed on his mind a great deal — causing him to break out in a cold sweat. He desired it and dreaded it. He was not sure how he would manage to get through it at all. Polly, of course, would laugh at him. Adela Adair, older, kinder, expecting far less from life than Polly, would never have dreamed of such a thing and although he was, indeed, every bit as flustered and inept as he had feared, giving her not the slightest enjoyment, she gave a very adequate imitation of it, taking the view that everybody has to learn sometime and the best way to teach him was by a little encouragement.

"That was marvelous, Roger." He couldn't believe it. She had made a man of him. And more than that she was kind to him, listened to his jokes and laughed at *them*, not him. He liked it. Very much. He had just never realized that women could be so *pleasant*, such thoroughly nice, ordinary people. And although he was not quick-witted it didn't take him long to understand that he could never experience this ease, this freedom from self-doubt, could never have this kind of fun, with Polly.

Events, thereafter, occurred rapidly enough to confuse sharper wits than Roger's. There was the diamond ring for instance, which Polly, when Kit telephoned her the next morning, declared hysterically she could never bear to touch again. "Give it to Roger and tell him to give it to somebody else." And when Kit obeyed her instructions, Roger chose to believe, because he wanted to believe, that she knew where he had spent the night and had given him his marching orders accordingly. Splendid. Having already decided not to marry her, he had not the least idea how to tell her so and had been much relieved. He went, therefore, to his mother to give her the glad tidings that he had chosen himself another bride.

"Nonsense, dear. Please don't be tiresome this morning. I have a headache."

So, more often than not, he thought, did Polly.

"Roger — really — what *is* all this?"

He was not clever. But he was stubborn and Edith had underestimated him. Moreover, she had never had the least conception of his fears of being sexually despised by Polly, and, therefore, could not gauge the extent of his gratitude to Adela Adair. His reasoning was totally straightforward. Why should he go round searching in other women for what he had already found in her, taking the now unnecessary risk that one of them might laugh at him? He had found his mate. It was as simple as that.

"Dear God," said Adela when it occurred to him to put her in the picture, "your poor mother. I can't do this to her, you know."

Taking her firmly by the arm, MacAllister led her to the other end of the bar. "Are you off your head?" he whispered. "He's Timms of Taylor & Timms. Never mind his mother. Just make the poor bastard happy."

So it was.

Polly returned to England to have her baby, Mrs. Arnold Crozier with an apricot-colored mink for summer, a blue one for winter, rings of good investment value on most of her fingers, even the diamond studs in her ears bigger than the solitaire she had returned to Roger, her husband's property including several department stores, it seemed, up and down the country, of a comparable size to Taylor & Timms. And she looked very lovely, very elegant, very pregnant, when she stepped out of the Crozier Rolls and into the Crown again, paying a short visit to Faxby with Arnold who had decisions to take about the future of the hotel.

"Hello Claire. Here we are again. What fun. I think you're expected to give me tea and keep me happy and cater to all my sudden cravings for terribly expensive, terribly hard to find things, while my husband — what a lark, eh! — and your — what do we call him? —"

"Employer," murmured Claire.

"All right. Be coy. Employer, although I've heard different and don't blame you one bit. But anyway, you're to entertain me while my husband and devastating old Hardie — not that he looks *old* to me anymore I can tell you — discuss real, important things. You know — how to make the money we spend. That *I* spend, at any rate."

Claire had last seen her as a desperate, terrified child kneeling in the mud by Toby's grave. Now she was brilliant and brittle, all flashing smiles and diamond sparkle, chattering, posing and watching herself pose and chatter, never still, never leaving the stage, never taking her eyes off herself, a rich man's young wife making sure everyone noticed how much she adored his money.

"Heavens — the dear old place hasn't changed a bit." But now, after these months of travelling with Arnold, she had grown accustomed to palaces, the grandest suite in every Grand Hotel, champagne in her bathtub if she'd ever had a fancy to bathe in it, which she hadn't. And clothes! Claire must come to stay with her soon — she'd send the Rolls — just to look at her clothes. Hats and coats and shoes mainly, in view of her present little encumbrance, but once she was thin again she knew exactly where she was heading. Paris. And she would have trunks and trunks and trunk loads of dresses to bring back with her. Of course Arnold wouldn't mind. He liked to see her spending money. Or, at least, he liked to see her so dressed up and so fancy that everybody noticed. It seemed to give him quite a thrill when people turned their heads to look at her. And he was very good about diamonds. Nanette, of course — bossy old Nanette, his brother's wife — seemed to think she should keep them in the bank. Good Lord — what a waste. No point in having them at all. She wore hers for breakfast. She even wore them in bed when she felt like it. Why not? She hadn't heard Arnold complain. And it made up for not having a proper wedding. Oh yes, they were legally married all right. She'd worn her apricot mink and a feathered hat and pinned a few orchids here and there. But — well — !

"Let's have a drink."

And gliding into the bar she held out both hands to MacAllister who, not having been asked to join the staff at Wansfell Howe, greeted her, as his employer's wife, with appropriate enthusiasm.

"What's it to be, Pol — Mrs. Crozier?"

"Polly will do. Gin and bitters. Claire?"

"I'm on duty."

"You're looking after me. Have one of those whiskey sours Roger used to sit and glower into."

She used his name without embarrassment.

"Has he married that woman?"

"I think so. She gave in her notice and left last week, at any rate. I suppose they've gone off somewhere quietly."

"Out of the way of Old Mother Timms. I don't blame them. At least he'll be happier with her than he'd ever have been with me."

What other memories haunted her? None it seemed.

"I have my own car, of course."

"Of course."

"And accounts absolutely everywhere — Harrods even. How about that?"

"I'm impressed."

And then, as MacAllister closed his grille and went off duty and they were about to leave themselves, she stood for a moment, the brittle, brilliant light going out of her, and walking to the end of the counter leaned suddenly and heavily against the last bar stool.

"This was where he used to sit — Toby, I mean."

"Yes, I know."

"Night after night. Hoping I'd come, and then watching me when I did. That's what he told me. Do you suppose it was true? Or just one of the things men say — ?"

A great wave of silence seemed to rush between them, such a weight of emotion remembered, wasted, misunderstood, that Claire's voice, cutting through it, sounded muffled, her words very slow.

"If he said it, Polly, then I think there's a good chance it would be true."

"Yes." She swallowed and, smiling, quickly blinked her eyes. "So do I. Let's go upstairs shall we to the infamous Tangerine Suite and have tea. Oh — and sandwiches, of course — smoked salmon — and cakes. Do we still have Amandine?"

"No. We have a little Swiss lady — about four feet nine — who makes perfect éclairs."

"Oh good. I'll have a dozen."

Sitting placidly in what had been the scene of her husband's fairly recent debaucheries, her slightly swollen ankles on a stool, she consumed éclairs and chocolate cake and currant buns with her usual appetite.

"I'm eating for two, you see."

"At the very least."

"Twins? Do you think so? How heavenly."

"Do you want a baby, Polly?"

"You wouldn't have thought so, would you?"

Claire shook her head.

"Neither would I. But one learns a lot about oneself. Being married to Arnold, of course, is an education all its own. I've *aged*, I think."

"Don't you mean you've grown up, Polly?"

"No. I know what I mean. Aged."

And leaning her head against the high-backed chair, her hair no longer the tousled mop of hoydenish curls but a sophisticated cap of silver, her eyes and her mouth beautifully painted, a fortune in diamonds on her fingers, her body curving softly around a child whose father she could not with any certainty put a name to, she smiled timidly at Claire and told her with many painful hesitations her version of the events through which Toby had died.

"I just wanted *somebody* to know how I felt, that's all. When I started to think again, which took quite a while, I blamed myself badly for not going away with him. But oh dear — what a life I'd have led him, as I was then. It would have done him no good. That's how I consoled myself. But just the same — did I kill him, Claire?"

"Polly, you were twenty. He was forty-five. He must have known you couldn't cope with it."

"Does that excuse me? And don't tell me he must have been pretty fed-up with Eunice in the first place to lose his head over me. I've thought of that. I suppose she's thought of it too. If all he had to live for was me, then he didn't have much, did he? Life really *had* worn him down, poor old thing."

"Yes."

"The trouble is, I miss him."

She began to cry, making no noise about it, just tears gathering on her eyelashes and then spilling one after the other down her cheeks, a sorrow which she allowed to flow free for a moment and then, with a few quick smiles and a cambric handkerchief, put an end to it.

"I shouldn't do that now, because of my baby. I love my baby — I can't tell you. I don't know what he looks like or who he is or whether he's a boy or a girl and I don't care — except, just perhaps, I might like him to be a girl."

"Why, Polly?"

"Oh —" She shrugged, smiling brightly, "One grows up thinking of babies as boys, I don't know why. Copies of their fathers. That's what I thought this one would be at first — which turns it all into too much of a guessing game, you must admit. And then I thought why not a girl, a copy of me, except *not* me. Not spoiled, I mean, and neglected both together, like me. I'll do a lot better than that for my daughter. And Arnold won't mind what I do. So far as he's concerned, a baby is just another toy for me to play with. And he's quite kind, really, you know."

"Yes."

"Claire — the thing is —"

"Yes. What do you want?"

What was it that Arnold couldn't give her?

"I'd quite like to see my mother. Do you think they'd throw me out if I turned up at High Meadows?"

"Oh Polly." She shook her head. "I honestly don't know."

With Toby gone she had no one to keep her informed on the state of play at High Meadows. She realized, not for the first time, that she missed him too. "I never hear from them Polly."

"Well, I'd have to be sure, you see. I couldn't risk Eunice trying to do me grievous bodily harm now, could I, because of the baby. And I don't want to upset mother and bring on another attack. But if she'd agree to see me and was really prepared for it — ? I won't be in Faxby again until after the baby and — well — one never knows. I just have

448

this superstitious feeling that if I don't see her now — Well. You know what I mean. You couldn't go up there could you and just ask — ?"

No. Claire could not. But Polly, who knew of no real reason against it, was not ready to leave it at that. While Arnold Crozier, whose policy it now was to please his "pretty Polly" in all things, expected everybody else to do likewise. It was quite natural that a girl in Polly's condition should want to see her mother. Arnold Crozier, in fact, would quite like to see Miriam himself, being strictly a man of peace when it came to family settlements and trust funds. Not that he stood in the slightest need of Polly's money. Far from it. Anyone could see that just by looking at her hands. But since the money was there, it offended his commercial instincts just to ignore it. Might it not be a sensible idea to settle it on Polly's first child? But, most of all, he didn't want his "pretty Polly" to be upset. In her condition, was it wise? Did Claire have some definite reason for her reluctance to visit High Meadows? Or was it simply — caprice? And one could not really afford to be capricious — my dear young lady — when dealing with *his* wife.

"I think you have to go," said Kit.

"No I don't. You can tell him to go to Hell."

"He has nothing to do with why I think you ought to go."

For a moment she was thoroughly dismayed.

"I've never been sure you knew, Kit."

"About Benedict Swanfield. Yes. I know. *Not* the best move you ever made."

"Call it battle fatigue — 'neurasthenia' since I was nursing officers."

"All right. Now go and face up to him. And while you're about it, ask him to release your capital to invest in Wansfell Howe."

Suddenly she was laughing, as thoroughly delighted as she had been downcast a moment before.

Although now, of course, she had no choice.

No time to waste either in brooding about it and no point in telephoning for an appointment since Miriam and Eunice were both permanently at home. Yet she telephoned, leaving a message for Benedict to warn him of her intention to call.

His car was in the drive and, parking John David's Talbot beside it, she felt herself to be liquefying almost with nerves. She had hoped he would not be there. Yet the hope itself was an act of self-betrayal. Was it also a breach of faith with Kit? Very likely. But she wasn't sure how much Kit would mind about that. He had not asked her to love him with passion, at a level where her mind could be uplifted or cast down, irretrievably shattered or made gloriously whole by his absence or his presence. Kit would not be comfortable with that kind of love. Was she?

What he asked, and what he gave, was a stimulating, free-wheeling companionship, enlivened by shared labors and plenty of them, spiced by imaginative, good-humored lovemaking and plenty of that too. Her shoulder to the wheel alongside his. *His* wheel perhaps, but always a bracing, invigorating experience to take her turn at steering it, as she had been doing these past few months, devoting every scrap of her spare time and energy to the fixtures and fittings of Wansfell Howe. Life with a good friend, the best friend one had, who happened also to be one's lover. That was Kit. And in the sense of enjoyment, straightforward pleasure, a sense of enterprise and a sense of fun, she had been happier, far happier, with him than with Benedict. Or with Paul. With anyone.

The butler, a new man, received her as a stranger, informing her with a deference his predecessor would never have accorded to "young Mrs. Jeremy" that "madam" would see her in the drawing room, after which Mr. Swanfield asked if she would spare him a few moments in his study.

She nodded, her smile going in and out like a flickering candle, aware already that the house was no longer the same. Not neglected precisely, polished and dusted as usual every morning, but uncared for, lived in only in patches, sick women in their sick rooms, Benedict behind his study door, separate meals on separate trays, uprooted children for whom the servants, growing idle in a household without supervision, would do the minimum. The plants on the hall table all dry and dead. High Meadows, Miriam's luxurious, carefully constructed nest, her life work, acquiring the stale air and odor of an impersonally maintained institution.

But Miriam herself, even in defeat, had retained too much cleverness to greet Claire with reproaches, as Dorothy might have done, knowing full well that an instant tirade of "So you've condescended to come and see me have you? High time. How is it you haven't come before?" would not produce the desired effect. Satisfying, perhaps, to one's understandably hurt feelings. But not wise. Therefore, she smiled and said in a small breathless voice which was now, indeed, all she could manage, "My dear — I am so *glad* to see you." She meant it. She had never felt so desperate in her life.

Illness had changed her. Claire had expected that. But it did not lessen the shock of finding Miriam so small and so old, just a child's frail body dressed up in a dowager's lace *peignoir*, sizes too large, the wedding ring of an eighteen-year-old bride slipping loose on a finger as brittle as a dried-out twig, a face emptied of its vivacity, drained of all its tea-rose softness and color, a mind which had concentrated all its artful scheming into the one frantic effort to get well enough and strong enough to scheme again.

"Pretty Mimi" no more.

Claire sat beside her and held her hand, aware, once again, of the changes in the room around her, Miriam's drawing room, the warmly beating heart of her house, in spiritual dust-covers now, the air chill with disuse, vases once vibrant with every season's flowers empty and slightly askew, ornaments not quite in their accustomed places, some of them no longer there at all, several pictures hanging at an awkward angle and left there by a maid whose job it was to dust, not to set the family portraits straight.

Claire, knowing how this must irritate Miriam, got up and straightened them.

"Thank you dear. How kind. I am quite helpless as you see."

But relatively serene until Eunice came into the room, or a caricature of her, Eunice who had never fitted easily into her clothes now looking as if they were pinned on her and more than likely to come apart at their seams, Eunice who had always been flustered bringing with her now such a seaweed trail of clinging, crawling anxiety — of frenzied search and frantic hurry, of turning out drawers, rooting through cupboards like a burrowing rabbit — that Claire's own nerves were at once affected by the strain.

So were Miriam's.

"*There* you are, mother."

Miriam shuddered and closed her eyes.

"Eunice — how are you?" Claire did not know what else to say.

"Extremely busy."

"Oh — good."

"Yes, there is so much to do."

And she began to wander around the room, moving ornaments a fraction this way or that, looking under the cushions, twitching the curtains, suddenly pouncing on a pile of newspapers she had in fact brought into the room herself and taking them to the window-seat where she proceeded to hold each one up to the light, checking the contents of one page against another with enormous concentration. What was she looking for? Reasons? A purpose? Forgiveness? And she would need a great deal of that.

No one had ever paid any special attention to Eunice but now she filled the room, overpowering it with the rustling of newsprint, the acrid weight of her sickness, a quicksand into which Claire's sound mind and Miriam's failing nerve were slowly absorbed, smothered, sucked in.

Miriam's hand descended on Claire's arm, her mouth approaching Claire's ear so that she was suddenly surrounded by Miriam's aging, medicated breath.

"She follows me everywhere," hissed Miriam, a prisoner whispering hoarse complaints behind her jailer's back. "And she follows Benedict too. She's always waiting in the hall to pounce on him, or else she's *hovering* outside my bedroom door — I can hear her there, breathing and creaking the boards, even when I've told Nurse not to let her in. Elvira Redfearn thinks she ought to go away somewhere for a while — *you* know. But then — what am I to do with those boys? It's too much for me, Claire. And they get on Benedict's nerves so much and he lets it show, which makes her cry — and cry — you wouldn't believe how much. My goodness. And Nola still bringing those odd people to the kitchen door, so that the servants are always leaving, or threatening to leave which is just as bad. And I can't interview staff anymore. Benedict managed about the butler, but it takes a mistress to choose maids, if you see what I mean — and I'm not up to it. The house is going to rack and ruin. I lie in bed listening to it happen. Is it any wonder that I'm not getting on as fast as I should?"

Noise erupted through the hall, heavily shod feet scarring the precious parquet, a sound of scuffling and giggling, a shout of warning, "Look out Simon" and then a sizable crash of china: a guilty silence.

Miriam closed her eyes again and shuddered.

"Eunice —" she said feebly.

But Eunice, her own mind intent on the perusal of last week's newspapers, paid no heed.

"Eunice — the boys."

What boys? She raised blank, lack-luster eyes. She had spent years of her life, the greater part of it, caring for them, planning for them, defending them. But it had been Justin who had handed her Toby's letter. Justin and Simon together who had made it clear to her that they expected their own lives to go happily on and hadn't seen the need — as she had — to give up their summer holiday. Even the little boys had been difficult about not going to Grange-over-Sands. She knew they were, all four of them, quite ready to forget Toby. In which case, why shouldn't she forget them?

Let Benedict handle them.

Let him handle Nola too who, just then, came tearing up the drive in her car, her arrival heralded by the coughing and sneezing of her engine and a great slamming of doors as she flew through the house, tweed-suited and purposeful. "Miriam," she shouted, appearing briefly in the doorway, "there's broken glass all over the hall. One of those little monsters again."

Eunice, who had just decided she did not like her sons, now burst into tears.

"Control yourself," said Nola who, compassion being a tool of her new trade, had none to spare. "Think it over carefully, Eunice, and you'll see, dear, that although you may be crying because you have lost your shoes — as it were — there are a great many, all around you, who have lost their feet."

Nola smiled briskly, her bearing erect, soldierly almost now that the stalwart Miss Pickles was due for retirement, leaving a place in All Saints' Passage which would have to be officially filled. Nola wanted that place and in her efforts to obtain it seemed to think it necessary — as Miss Drew had playfully pointed out — not only to apply for Miss Pickles' job but to *become* Miss Pickles.

"That's the spirit, Eunice."

Eunice continued to cry, rather more loudly, dropping her newspapers all over the window-seat and knocking over a plant pot.

"Would you tell Nurse," murmured Miriam, "that I would like to go back to my room."

Claire spent a mournful half-hour upstairs with Miriam as she was tucked into bed by a nurse who treated her like a child and, therefore, wished her simply to "eat up her supper," "take her nice medicine," "have a little sleep," "be good and *quiet*."

"I do believe we've tired ourselves out," said Nurse, smiling knowingly at Claire in a manner which told her that, in Nurse's opinion, she was entirely to blame for it.

"Just a moment," she said, indicating by her coolness that she would leave when she was ready. Although it did not take her long to ascertain that while Miriam herself would be overjoyed to see Polly again, it seemed hardly fair to Eunice. Hardly safe either, with Polly, regrettably, in *her* condition and Eunice, even more regrettably, in hers. Perhaps when she was better she could go herself to Bradford or Manchester or wherever it was that Polly was living and pay a visit. How terrible that she didn't even know her own daughter's address. Her favorite daughter too.

"I shall be better soon, you know." But it was a question, addressed with the shyness of a little girl to anyone who might be kind enough to answer.

"Of course we shall," said Nurse.

When Claire reached the hall again the floor was still dangerous with broken glass, the butler waiting not to direct its disposal but to remind her of her appointment with Benedict.

"This way, madam."

"Shouldn't somebody clear up that mess?"

"Certainly, madam."

He opened the study door, the barricade she thought between Benedict and the sick chaos prowling so insidiously outside, and ushered her in.

He was at his desk, a chair placed ready for her on the other side, an expanse of massive oak and gold-tooled red leather, of folders and official-looking documents, cut glass inkstands and heavy silver cigar boxes, keeping them well apart; the room around them, into which no one ever came without Benedict's express permission or at his command, remaining unchanged. An oasis. A stockade with the warring natives gathering all around it. How long before they broke down the door?

She shivered.

Noticing it, he gave her a brief smile, not asking the reason, looking self-contained as he always had, busy, a pen in his hand, the limit of his patience not far away. Rather older.

"I came with a message from Polly." Someone had to begin. Somewhere.

"Yes. Arnold Crozier wrote to me. I suppose I shall have to see him. How is Polly?"

Startled, she realized she had not expected him to ask.

"Sad and scared. And very guilty. But I think she'll be all right in the end. She is terribly pleased about the baby. And don't say she thinks it's just a doll to play with."

He put down his pen and looked at her.

"I don't think I was going to say that."

And the tug of his mind on hers, the reaching forward of his hands which never moved from the desk top but, nevertheless, *reached out*, the pull, the affinity, the gravitation was — unfair.

It should not be happening now. Not after so long. She didn't want to believe it. And didn't like it. Neither did he. Therefore, say what had to be said quickly. And go.

"I expect Crozier wants me to pay out her legacies in full."

"He said something about settling it on the baby."

"Yes. Understandable, when one takes into consideration that it may not be his."

"Can you afford to take so much out of the business?"

"One looks for ways and means. That's what I've just been doing. Moving figures from one column to another. Fortunately — like Arnold Crozier — I'm good at that."

"Are things difficult?"

"At the Mills? As well as can be expected. Better than some. Don't worry. The legacies are safe. Speaking of which it occurs to me you might be needing your own."

"Why should you think so?"

He smiled quickly, wryly.

"To invest in a lakeside hotel perhaps."

"Oh. You know about that?" she said, although there was no reason why he shouldn't.

"Elvira Redfearn knows about it, and draws certain conclusions. And since Elvira is always right —"

He opened a drawer, took out a document, and picked up his pen.

"This is the authorization to release your capital. I have only to sign it."

"Thank you."

He signed, handed the document to her, she looked at it for a moment and then put it down, neatly, on the desk.

"Would you invest it for me please, Benedict?"

"In what?"

"In Swanfield Mills."

He looked down quickly, so that she could see nothing of him but the dark, bent head, the rapid clenching of a lean, dark-textured hand.

And then he looked up at her.

"If I do that you could lose every penny."

"I don't seem to care."

"Your friend Hardie might."

She smiled at that. Very certain. "Kit doesn't need it. He can manage. He'll make a success of that hotel whatever happens."

And she knew she was very proud of that.

"He must be immensely gratified by your faith in him."

She smiled again.

"I don't suppose it bothers him much either way. He has faith in himself, you see. Enough for two."

"Lucky man. Please take your money, Claire and —"

"Go?"

"Yes."

"You sold the farm, didn't you?"

"I did."

"And everything — ?"

"It seemed best."

"And now?"

"What — *now*?"

"What do you do now — I mean — ?"

"Nothing Claire."

"Nothing at all?"

"I go to the Mill. I do my day's work."

"And then you come back here."

She couldn't bear it.

"Of course."

Night after night, sitting behind this desk, behind that door. No one should live like that. And who could live *with* him, who could penetrate his isolation if she did not? Who could repair the damage she had done him but herself!

"I see Elvira sometimes."

"No you don't. I heard her tell somebody she *never* sees you now. Benedict, it hasn't worked has it? You said you'd be as you were before, and you're not. Are you?"

"No."

"It's my fault."

"Yes. I'm afraid so."

"What can I do?"

Abruptly he swung his chair around so that he was sitting with his back to her, his voice coming to her like an echo from the far wall.

"I'm sorry, Claire. I made the attempt. I contacted old acquaintances and found the exercise pointless."

"And with Nola?"

"I failed — just that. Abysmally. And it should all have been so easy. God knows, it would have been a simple matter to turn Nola's head. She's always needed to devote herself to something or somebody, so why not me? She was ripe to fall at somebody's feet. When I took her to Italy I intended to make sure it was mine. I couldn't. It became a physical impossibility. And one cannot conceal reluctance of that sort from an experienced woman. That exercise turned out to be pointless too."

"And now?"

"Unless you come back to me, Claire, I don't think I shall see much point to anything again."

"Come back — how — ?" She heard her own voice faltering, her breath laboring with shock. She had never expected him to say this, had relied on him, she suddenly realized, not to. The blue chintz room. And nothing had altered. She loved him, she had harmed him, and there was still Nola, still Miriam who needed her now more than ever, still Christian and Conrad who did not care to acknowledge her at all, and to whom she could only be an intruder. And on the other side of the coin Kit — fresh air, smooth tranquil water. Life with a good friend who happened also to be one's lover.

"Come back and live with me, Claire — that's all."

"Here?" Dear God. How could she do that?

"I need you. I have no faith in myself now. Once — yes. But it's gone."

"I took it away?"

"I believe so. I lost control because of you. You weakened me somehow."

The ice had melted. She understood. She had endured vivid dreams in which she had seen it happen, gray water spilling out of him all over the dinner table while Miriam and Eunice and Polly went on with their chatter. And it had been her fault. If she had broken him, who else could mend him?

"I can't leave this house," he said. "You must see that. Not yet. Possibly not ever."

"Yes, I see."

"And I can't endure it, Claire — not alone. Really — I can't."

She saw that too.

"I need you, Claire."

Closing her eyes, fighting off a sudden vision of an uncomplicated, open-hearted sun glinting from a clear sky over Wansfell Water, she bowed her head.

"Yes, Benedict."

"So you'll come."

"I will." And it was spoken in the hushed, low, not altogether certain whisper of a marriage vow.

"Here — to High Meadows?"

"Yes."

"As my wife — giving up everything — and everybody. Except that you wouldn't be my wife — not to start with — possibly never at all."

"Yes, Benedict."

"When Claire?"

It had to be now. That clear, lakeland sky had misted over. The sun had gone in. And she would have to make her arrangements quickly and surely before it came out again.

"Today, Benedict."

He swung his chair back to face her.

"I believe you'd do it too."

"Of course — *What!*"

"That's all I needed," he said. "You're free."

He got up and took her by the shoulders, shaking her gently, his voice almost crooning to her like a lullaby.

"Claire — Claire — do you think I could do this to you? Of course I couldn't. It saddens me that you can think so poorly of me. I'll handle my own casualties my darling, not inflict them on you. I'm all right."

"No you're not."

"Yes I am. I indulged myself just now that's all. I asked you to do what I knew you'd find abhorrent, for my sake. I asked you to make a sacrifice. And you agreed to make it. Perhaps we both needed to know that you would. And that's *all*. I shall always know you loved me enough to do it. You'll always know that I loved you too much to let you. It's been said now — and done — and now it's over. We can give our minds to other things. You're free of me. I'm free of you. I needed that very badly. Didn't you?"

She did not believe him. Nor did she recognize in him, what she would have known at once, in another man, to be lightness of heart. In Benedict it had to be a cloak for something infinitely more complex. Something painful. Or sinister. Or dangerous.

"Benedict — you said you couldn't endure it."

"I was lying to you. I've done that before."

"You said you needed me."

"Well — yes. So does Hardie in his way. I in mine. But what *are* you, Claire? A prize for the one who needs you most? Is that how you see yourself?"

"Perhaps I do."

He nodded, briskly, a man suddenly and very definitely in full control of his situation and — as he'd always been — of himself.

"Very well. And shall I tell you, in my humble opinion, just who the person is, who needs you most of all?"

"All right."

"You, Claire."

And when she shook her head not in denial but in perplexity he rapped out, "Yes Claire. Not me. And not Hardie. Yourself. So go off and enjoy his hotel, or take your money and open one of your own in competition on the other side of the lake, if that seems best to you. Live for yourself now — for a while at any rate. Learn how to defend yourself. That's what I want from you. Go on — *away*."

She found herself back in John David's car and out on the main road without remembering how she got there, her head swimming not only with confusion but with a great wave of entirely physical fatigue. How much they had tired her out, all of them, worn her down, not so much by any demands they had made upon her but by the demands of her own compassion upon herself. And what had happened to Benedict? What had she done to bring about the change in him? Had it been the offer of her legacy to put back into the business? And then the offer of herself? Yes, she had given in to every one of his demands, made every concession, surrendered totally and quite irrevocably without so much as a murmur of protest. And why — it suddenly occurred to her — should that have wrought such a change in him when, had he been less restrained, more unscrupulous, he could have obtained the same result at any time these past eighteen months? He must know that. Realizing it herself she brought the car to an abrupt halt and spent a moment leaning against the wheel, her mind groping, sifting through words and impressions, nuances, every turn of every phrase that had been spoken, as obsessed as Eunice by the conviction that something — but what? where? — had been missed. He had talked of freedom. But *what* freedom? Fear struck her, nameless only because she refused to acknowledge it. No. Absolutely not. Yet she found herself reversing the car quite wildly in an ill-judged, awkward attempt to turn it round that landed her back wheels in the ditch. And, jumping out, she abandoned it there — John David's pride and joy — and ran back up the hill to High Meadows.

No one was there. No butler waiting, in supercilious inquiry, in the hall. No one anywhere. She had never seen a house so empty. Benedict! His desk, which had been covered with papers, was now completely bare, all those documents concerning the trust funds and legacies, Polly's money, Eunice's money, her money, signed and sealed and put neatly away in correct order so that everybody would know exactly what they were to have and how to obtain it. Everything dealt with, wound up, over and done with. He was free of that too.

Benedict! Running back into the hall, feeling the silence as thick and cold as insidiously piling snow, she shrieked his name to the full extent of her lungs and then, when he was suddenly *there* looking not at all as he ought to be looking at such a moment of high panic, not pained or anguished or bleeding to death, but just a little puzzled, slightly amused, she threw frantic arms around him, crushing herself against him not amorously at all and not caring in the least who saw it, but simply to check that his heart was beating, that he was whole and sound, still captive perhaps but undamaged.

"I thought —"

"What?" Incredibly he was laughing. "That I was going to shoot myself? Hardly. I once tried to shoot a grouse and I couldn't even manage that."

"Don't tease."

How amazing, when he had never teased before, that he should start now.

But her wild cries had attracted far more notice than she had bargained for and spinning round, weakened but totally single-minded in her relief, it was to see Eunice and Nola advancing side by side toward her, Simon considerably embarrassed and Justin elaborately bored at witnessing yet another of these middle-aged dramas, even Miriam's nurse peering over the banisters losing no opportunity of adding to the store

459

of anecdotes she carried as part of her stock-in-trade from one patient to another.

And Benedict was laughing.

"You can't do this," said Benedict's sister, wringing her hands in sorrow. "You can't be like this — the same as *them*."

"Oh Lord, so that's the way of it," said Benedict's wife, forgetting to be Miss Pickles and slipping back, refreshingly, to being Nola. "But I can't divorce you, you know. Sorry and all that, but the Probation Committee would never stand for it."

All Benedict's mistress saw was the family circle advancing toward him, ready to close in.

"Keep away from him," she shrieked, standing in front of him, arms outstretched, sheltering him.

"Shall we go into the study?" said Benedict, still laughing, and lifting her slightly off her feet, carried her across his threshold and set her down, with something of a thud, in a leather chair.

"Oh dear God," she said. "What have I done?"

"Rushed to defend me, I think. No one has ever done that before. I found it unnecessary, of course, but very sweet."

"Benedict will you stop laughing please. I can't bear it."

"Can't you. I'm sorry."

"I really thought you might have . . ."

A vision of Toby flooded her mind.

"No," he said. "I couldn't kill anything, Claire. I am, by nature — believe it or not — quite shy and not at all hard-hearted. Had I lived in the Middle Ages I would have gone into a monastery. Oh yes. Not for religious reasons. Just to avoid being a knight. That's what shy, good-hearted lads did, in those days. Much better than all that jousting and hunting and hanging one's enemies from the battlements. Yes, I'd have spent my time on a Scottish island, with a bracing sea view, illustrating learned chronicles or making wine. It would have suited me very well."

"What — just *what* — are you telling me now?"

"My father had no use for a shy boy and one learns, fast enough, how to appear aloof instead. My father had no use for a coward either."

"You're not that."

"Yes I am. I never liked being hurt and I *was* hurt rather badly in childhood. Not so much by what was done to me as by what no one had the time or the inclination to do. What I remember about that time is being cold — just that — nothing to do with lack of affection, just an absolutely biting physical chill. My father was very careful with his money before Miriam came, mean about heat and light, and High Meadows uses up a lot of that. Just one small fire in the kitchen, that's all he'd permit. Good enough, he reckoned, for the housekeeper — and me — since he went out every night to warm himself somewhere else. So that's what I remember, the housekeeper pulling her chair up to the fire, as you'd imagine, taking what warmth there was — punishing me because my father was neglecting her — and me, shivering and whining, trying to coax a kind word out of her and hating myself for it. The only solution was to learn to stand it, and that way, although it didn't make her like me, she stopped treating me with contempt."

"Did you want her to like you?"

"Of course. I don't remember her name or what she looked like. I was a child. She was the only other person in my life besides my father, who seemed totally remote. And terrified me in any case. Of course I wanted her to like me. She didn't. Christ — the poor woman had problems of her own. I see that now. Very likely she had nowhere to go and knew my father was getting sick of her. She may even have been in love with him. And since she can't have been very young she was probably desperate. All I saw at the time was that she didn't like me. And I may have drawn the conclusion that it was because, quite simply, I wasn't likable — in which case I'd better not try it again with somebody else. And all I really remember is that whenever I tried to get near the fire she gave me a clout and pushed me away. Occasionally I still dream about it. Nola — or her Miss Drew — would probably tell you that the pain and humiliation of those blows made me afraid of the very warmth I desired. Miriam, in her way, would say the same. I think they are quite right. I have avoided human contact all my life, beyond a certain level, because the pleasure of having it never seemed to compensate me for the fear of losing it. I think we ought to call that cowardice, don't you? And worse. I have drawn back from Nola a dozen times, in our early years, not because I was afraid of loving her but because I didn't want the bother of having her in love with me. When my father died I drew back from Polly, who *was* lovable, and who would have found a better father in me than in Toby or Arnold Crozier. I could have had a good friend in Eunice, if I'd had the guts to let myself care for her, and she'd have had me to lean on now — could have taken refuge in me, her brother, instead of this madness she's hiding herself in, if I'd ever been a brother to her. And what did I ever do for Toby but terrify him? If I'd been approachable — well, then I'd have been the obvious person to talk to, wouldn't I, man to man. And Toby's boys, of course, and mine. I intimidate them too, deliberately, because I have always found it — oh not easier — *safer*. Agreed — agreed — my father made it worse, setting me up as judge and jury — and jailer. But I make no excuses. It suited me. Claire — I have always known these things about myself. This is the first time I have ever felt either willing or able to change them."

"Why now?"

"God knows. Better not ask. Just pray it continues. I found myself smiling at your foolishness in thinking I could ever be so base as to impose all my cripples — including myself — upon you. I found myself moved by your generosity — very moved. Well — that has happened before, of course. But somehow, this time, it absolutely failed to scare me. Perhaps I'd stopped resisting. And if it was the resistance that caused the pain — Well — Who knows?"

He smiled at her.

"Poor Claire — have I confused you utterly?"

"Yes. You have rather."

"Very well. Then just answer me this —"

"Yes Benedict."

"Who needs you most Claire?"

She returned his smile.

"I do," she said.

23

CLAIRE installed her mother in the Tangerine Suite for Christmas that year, the Croziers being unlikely to need it with Polly so near her time, giving birth in fact to a daughter, Cassandra, on Christmas Day.

"Cassandra Crozier!" Dorothy clearly found the words clumsy on her tongue. "Cassy! Poor little mite."

Yet, when Claire finally had a moment to drive up to High Meadows with a basket of leftover Swiss pastries, the name, to Miriam, had a distinctly imperial flavor.

Queen Cassandra. She liked it. Although she was still somewhat puzzled by a letter from Polly, received this morning, in which her daughter had gone into raptures — my dear, positive raptures — about the whole sorry business of childbirth.

"Good Heavens." And Miriam, being delicately bred, gave a slight shudder. "She says she can hardly wait to get started again. How terribly — well, one could almost call it *primitive*. And what about her husband? He can hardly wish to father a tribe of children — one would have thought — at his age. Poor Arnold. One must hope he has not taken on rather more than he bargained for with Polly."

But Polly had sent her mother a wonderful lace shawl for Christmas, was always sending her little gifts of flowers and chocolates and perfume and sweet little notes on scented paper, pale pink with deckle edging — very smart.

Polly, in fact, was in the process of being forgiven; Eunice, since her departure for a "hotel" as Miriam insisted on calling it, on the south coast, in the process of no longer being thought of at all.

Naturally, she had had nothing to do with it herself. One could hardly expect *her*, Eunice's mother, to take the decision to — well, Claire must realize that it would have been far too painful, much too much to bear. And so Benedict had seen to it. And if it did seem so terribly expensive, and if Benedict himself had carried it rather far, writing letters to Eunice quite often she believed, and for ever going down to see her her — such a complicated journey — well, one must only hope, as Benedict insisted, that she would eventually get well.

Eunice had certainly been strange. And the boys completely out of hand. What a brilliant idea of Benedict's to get Justin into such a famous regiment where he could learn to do all those brave athletic things — polo and tinkering about with flying machines — which had so interested Toby. And the little boys into that very good school somewhere alongside the New Forest, so they could be near their mother. Now there was only Simon left at High Meadows who really was no trouble, particularly since Benedict had found dear, clever Mrs. Bishop to run the house. *Such* a treasure. So cheerful and so happy to be of service. Always putting herself out and taking trouble. Wonderful woman. And her daughter, Amy, always ready to sit and chat. A sweet-natured child, rather simple perhaps but *willing*. And so absolutely indefatigable when it came to reading aloud.

Yes, Benedict had put himself out, she couldn't deny it, to find Mrs. Bishop and Amy. And Nurse Evans, too, who was not stiff and starchy at all like that other creature — no, who *cared* what her name was? — but a pretty young slip of a thing with such pretty auburn curls and a most infectious laugh. Her husband would have been very pleased to see the trouble Benedict had taken, on her behalf, although what Aaron would have made of his son's move to Lawnswood Hill, the house they had been building for Polly, she dare not even imagine. Quite true of course. The house *had* just been standing there, all forlorn. Polly had never taken the slightest interest in it. All the Timms family ever wanted from it was their money's worth. And so Benedict, unable to get either Polly or Roger to decide what kind of a house they wanted, had built it to suit himself. And one had no option but to believe he had grown fond of it. Nearer to the Mills too, he'd said. Far more convenient for an early start and much quieter in the evenings when he brought work back with him. One had really no option but to believe that either. And she had quite definitely decided to take at its face value Nola's statement that her new professional responsibilities required her to spend five nights a week — or was it seven? — at the home of that insufferably prim and proper Miss Drew. They were embarking upon a course of study together, it seemed, attending lectures and writing dissertations on those terribly indelicate, in fact downright messy topics Nola was so keen on, how little girls went around wishing they had the — er — well — the biological equipment of little boys — you know what I mean, dear — and imagining they'd been maimed, or were unworthy or something, because they hadn't. Such nonsense. And really, with Amy Bishop and Nurse Evans both so young, it *was* a relief to be spared the worry of Nola suddenly enlivening the dinner table with those tales of little boys growing up to be *strange* — you know — because they hadn't been properly breast-fed, or impotent because they'd caught a glimpse of daddy at a rather private moment and were quite sure they could never compete.

Yes, it was all breasts and — er — biology — with Nola. Not dinnertable talk at all. Not at High Meadows, at any rate, although she couldn't answer for the conversation around the apparently genuine Queen Anne table at Miss Drew's. Not, of course, that there was the least cause for scandal. Faxby's Probation Committee could only appoint persons of good character to its service and the fact that Elvira Redfearn and Arthur Greenwood were both members of that committee indicated — surely — that any irregularity in Nola's character would have come swiftly to light.

Miriam certainly intended to think so.

"To think I used to be afraid of her," said Dorothy, reclining on the tangerine *chaise longue*, her most pressing anxiety of the moment being which of two dresses — one bought by herself at Taylor & Timms, the other a present from her daughter — to wear for dinner that night.

Dorothy was happy. She had her own home, no one to please but herself, she was younger than Miriam Swanfield, much healthier, and *her* daughter had not run off with a man — or was it two? — old enough to be her father. Therefore, Dorothy was happy and would be happier still on the day her daughter married Kit Hardie.

Amazing, really, when one thought how absolutely terrified Edward had been, and how he had terrified her, that Claire might "sink" as he had called it, to a servant. And the Swanfield's servant at that. Not that Dorothy herself could remember Hardie taking hats and coats or waiting at table at High Meadows. That had probably been in the days — before Claire and Jeremy — when Edward had not cared to risk, being "let down" by his wife in front of his important friends. But they had not really been his friends had they? How many of them had taken the trouble to come to his funeral? Only Eunice, who had ended up losing her never precisely powerful reason. And Toby, who, whatever anybody said, had been done to death by her and her sister between them. No wonder Mrs. Miriam Swanfield had had a heart attack and was living now in that great, lonely house with only a nurse and a paid housekeeper-companion, pretending, for all the world, how glad she was that Polly had married — in the very nick of time — her elderly millionaire; that Eunice was staying in a rather jolly little south coast hotel; that Benedict and his wife were really living together because they had attended the Chamber of Commerce Annual Dinner and the Lord Mayor's Banquet when everybody knew that he had taken up residence in that atrocious modern matchbox on Lawnswood Hill, with plain white walls, she'd heard, and black carpets and peculiar assortments of chrome and copper and steel that were light fittings, or that he was passing off as works of art. While Nola had taken to tweed suits and Russian cigarettes and female company.

Compared to all that it would be a pleasure to see *her* daughter married to a butler, particularly now that he was a hotelier in his own right, and had treated her like a duchess no less when she had gone up to Wansfell Water with Claire for his gala opening. She liked Kit. Not that she hadn't been anxious, in fact downright alarmed, when she'd found out that Claire had put money into Wansfell Howe. Not all she had, by any means, but quite enough to ensure a proposal of marriage. Particularly when one remembered how she had been running her blood to water for him ever since he'd taken on that old ruin and converted it — very nearly with his own hands and Claire's — into what looked and felt like a comfortable family home. Full every weekend, even at this dismal after-Christmas season, and doing very nicely Monday to Friday too.

Claire would do very well with him. And for that reason she'd chosen to ignore not only that he and Claire had certainly shared a bed on his opening night — she'd easily worked it out by simple arithmetic — but a remark she'd overheard her daughter make the next day. "You may not be husband material, Kit, but you're a good friend — and a wonderful lover." And giving Claire what Dorothy had thought a most affectionate little kiss on the tip of her nose and ruffling her hair, very playful and self-possessed, very much a man who had everything he wanted, he'd said "You always know where to find me."

Dorothy had not really understood that. Not at all, as a matter of fact. But then, this younger generation often puzzled her. And one ought not to forget that they had gone through the war, facing issues of life and death at an age when she had not been thought capable of choosing a new hat. Sometimes she envied them their independence. Sometimes she pitied them for the burden of choice it gave them. She had been told, in infancy once and for all, what was right and what was wrong. They had to see it for themselves, and decide.

And Claire had been steadier lately, much more purposeful, since Edward had died and she had made such short work of Richmal Lyall. Busy too, with Wansfell Howe to get ready and Arnold Crozier constantly dashing over from Bradford to make her tell him how things were going on at the Crown.

Steady and busy and clever. And most attractive, particularly in her long net dress covered with those shiny jet beads. Yes, Dorothy Lyall rather liked her daughter.

The Crown was busier than anyone had expected that night, gratifyingly so, thought Claire, particularly when it had already been reported to her twice that *Chez Aristide* was not more than half-full, Aristide himself in one of the smoldering tempers that usually meant they would be having Amandine back again for a week or two. Happily John David's successor, an almost equally neurasthenic Welshman, found and presented to her by Kit, had proved popular with civic appetites, his style of cooking rather more in keeping perhaps with the "plain fillet steak and dover sole" atmosphere Kit had seen coming. Although one had only to step into the cocktail bar to see that money, as yet, was by no means in short supply. Glancing through the door she nodded to MacAllister, checking that the jazz and the gin were still flowing, girls with long legs and cropped curls like Polly still dancing, flirting, hoping; neither Toby nor Arnold Crozier nor Roger Timms to be seen anymore, nor Roy Kington, a major now in the Black and Tans, she'd heard; nor Kit. And then she walked at leisure through the restaurant as she did every evening, pausing and giving each table her full attention, all the time in the world for each and every honored guest as Kit had taught her. "Is everything all right for you, sir? Lovely to see you Mrs. Redfearn. What a stunning dress Mrs. Timms. Did you enjoy the trifle, Mr. Greenwood — and can I tempt you to a little chocolate *mousse*."

The war was over. It had taken her a long time to realize it, to understand that what she did today could have a bearing on tomorrow, because for so long "tomorrow" had been a luxury, a prize one ought not to think too much about in case one did not win it. Now she had finally succeeded in believing that, in most cases, there was a good chance that it would follow, fairly naturally, upon today and must, therefore, be planned for or, at the very least, taken into some kind of consideration.

But when she had written to Euan to tell him so, he had not answered.

Her investment in Wansfell Howe was safe and sound. Her investment in Kit's friendship too. They had worked out a formula which suited them and she hoped it would never be necessary to explain it to Dorothy.

She went into her office — Kit's office — and sat down at the desk, a letter from him at the top of her pile, bills and account books beneath it and a long envelope full of Arnold Crozier's crabbed, illegible instructions.

Mr. Clarence came in and very pleasantly, knowing his feelings to be tender, she cleared up with him certain flaws in his arrangements for accepting advance bookings.

Mrs. Tarrant came in for authorization to replace certain items of damaged linen which Claire granted, thanking her at the same time for her kindness in keeping Dorothy company over all those plates of scones and pots of tea.

The new chef, John Michael, put his head around the door to say goodnight, hoping for applause which she gave in full measure.

She read her letters, replied at once to Arnold Crozier, adding an appropriate message for Polly, and then, lifting the telephone, catching the gleam of her lily bowl sitting under the lamplight as she did so, she asked the far-from-enthusiastic voice of the operator for the number of an atrocious modern matchbox on Lawnswood Hill.

This, too, was something Dorothy would find hard to understand.

"Swanfield here," he said.

"And here," she replied, hearing his low chuckle over the wire.

"Of course. Who else would ring at this advanced hour of the night."

"Am I disturbing you?"

"You always have."

"What are you doing, Benedict?" Almost — and then very clearly — she could see him.

"I'm being alone. And finding it rather pleasant. Would you care to come and be alone with me — when shall we say?"

"Tomorrow? Eight o'clock?"

"Fine."

"Are you all right?"

"Yes. Are you?"

She knew that he was busy and steady — happier.

"Tomorrow then. Goodnight."

MacAllister came in, furious and none too sober, complaining about the new pianist, Miss Sidonie, who gave herself more airs than Mrs. Roger Timms. She calmed him down, laughed at him until he was laughing at himself, sent him away feeling "understood."

She was busy and steady. She was recovering, learning how to grow. She was waiting, not *for* Benedict but *with* him. Waiting, quite patiently, as sure of herself as she had ever been and getting surer. Trusting him. Her lover who was her friend. With time, she rather thought, on their side, not Miriam's. Time, which would ripen his children to independence, hopefully to understanding. Time for Nola's feet, which were almost there, to reach the ground. Time, in itself neither an enemy nor a healer but which, quite simply, would pass. And in the meanwhile she was the Manageress of the Crown Hotel.

JAMES L. HAMNER PUBLIC LIBRARY
AMELIA COURT HOUSE

DATE DUE